This book was originally w d in
2020 cos the original was all over the place.

ISBN:

Published by Psycho Holosuite Press

NOTES ON TEXT

The prologue is based on a rumour that the original Rasputin was replaced in 1912 by a lookalike and it was he who was murdered in 1916, not the original.

The novel is set in 2114.

The idea of global hegemony by one or two superpowers has become obsolete [or dormant]. Major countries have either broken up or diminished in size.

Regional hegemony exists in some areas, e.g. Brazil and its neighbours, but the biggest shift has been towards an international alliance of smaller, predominantly anarcho-communist states [slightly compromised, of course, as can be seen by the use of the word *state*].

Capitalists have re-branded themselves as Adventurists.

Space is up for grabs.

~~~

How does the anarcho-communist system work in this novel? I thought about laying it all out here, but that would've taken up about 500 pages in itself, so instead I've filtered it into the story in the form of conflict, implication and occasional footnotes [maybe too many]. As stated above, it is compromised in some ways, incomplete in others, but it's a lot better than what we have now and, I believe, something to strive for.

If you want to know more, try the anarchist library, it's online, free to use and has an exhaustive list of anarchist texts. Marxists.org is also a treasure trove.

Collectives in the Spanish Revolution by Gaston Leval, plus the various works of Bakunin, Lorenzo Kom'boa Ervin, Walter Rodney, Rosa Luxemburg, Murray Bookchin and Sam Dolgoff are good starting points.

A lot of authors/texts mentioned in the novel were invented by me – Sima, Bōl, Jung's *Archetype Farm* etc. – cos it's supposedly 2114 and I didn't want to make the *Star Trek* mistake of only including 19/20th Century American references plus Shakespeare in a future setting.
~~~

Dibrivna Vaska is roughly inspired by *Blake's 7.*

~~~

Tried my best with the science.

Some of the teleporter theory skates on absurd ice and the LEM FIELD concept is there so the characters can walk around without needing to worry about Gs and spin rotation.

~~~

I have replaced the following English words with Slovene ones:

Yes = Ja

No [if it's alone] = Ne

Thanks = Hvala

Please = Prosim

I don't know = Ne vem

Don't worry = Ni panike

PROLOGUE

Roughly Halfway To Mars

The Martians were indistinguishable from one another by rank, by fashion, by etiquette, all striving to ensure the red vegetation was maintained, working not because they were coerced, but through a deep sense of duty and fulfilment…

'Why's the vegetation red?'

…one day, they would work a shift in the clothing factory, the next they would switch to food production, eschewing any form of specialization, though there were some that did exist…

'They change their jobs?'

…the elder Martian had previously been married to six other Martians, some male, some female, a concept that Leonid attempted to comprehend but with great difficulty…

'Six people! Will I have to do that too?'

…the corpse of Sterni stared sideways towards the wall, at the poster of the first Martian factory, and Leonid stared too, falling onto the ground and weeping over the stained history, trying to pick up larger puddles of blood and return them to his friend's body…

'I don't like it…'

…but the crime was as old as the first sharpened rock, as hellish as a nightmare based on other nightmares, as evil as the first devil that ever popped into man's head, and there was no escape from it, not on Mars, not in this red-hued paradise of rotational shifts and unparalleled job satisfaction…

'Rasputin, stop…'

~~~

The guards took him as he read Bogdanov[1] to the child princess. There were no declarations or excuses, just force. His arms were pulled behind his back and the little girl told to get back in the fucking bed.

Of course, she didn't, she screamed for help, so loud two of the men had to stay behind and drug her.

The remaining guards marched their prisoner outside the palace and shaved his head, reading out a list of crimes he'd committed.

Rasputin stood with four men on him, looking around for faces he knew, waiting for the Tsar to come out from behind a tree, laughing.

It didn't happen. These guards were strangers. There were no trees.

The list continued.

'…led to the imprisonment of fifteen innocent miners who had the misfortune to have known you earlier in life…'

'ублюдки!'

'…the lady, who'd recognized you from your previous deviancy, fell to her death, landing on a surprisingly blunt…'

'The girl, where is she?'

'…stabbed him several times in the neck and the head before, finally, using a shovel to cut off the other…'

'What have you done to her?'

'…told untruths to the victim's family then ingratiated yourself into their good graces until their usefulness had passed and…'

'Lies! I didn't…'

'…night, you took a bread knife and cut Petr Petrovich into seven separate pieces, each one shaped like a…'

'I did not do those things.'

'…hooked his neck onto another hook using some kind of other hook procured from…'

---

1 Writer of 1908 Socialist sci-fi novel *Red Star*, excerpts of which were murdered in the intro.
~~~

'That wasn't me, it was…'

'…left the two daughters at the bottom of the well with no food or entertainment, and no way to…'

'Impossible…which daughters?'

'…in someone else's blood, which you had kept in an icebox for twenty-one weeks. These are only the victims we have records of, there are undoubtedly more.'

The man lowered the list and some of the guards stepped into formation. Rasputin tried, 'I didn't do anything,' a few more times, but no-one with a weapon seemed to care.

'Your time is over, monk.'

'Wait…the Tsar. He'll find out about this.'

'Prepare yourself.'

'He'll execute all of you.'

'Ah, actually…'

A tall, bearded man emerged from a carriage, not the spitting image of Rasputin, but close enough.

'This is your replacement. He's a bit of a lothario, but obedient.'

'You'll never-…'

'Nyet, no more words. Soldiers, raise weapons.'

'He has no abilities.'

'Aim.'

'His beard…'

'Now.'

The soldiers fired fifty-seven shots, hitting him twice.

'…is fake.'

'Again.'

Forty more shots.

Rasputin took one in the throat, coughing up blood.

'I won't let…'

'It's not working.'

'He's moving his-…'

'Plan B.'

The soldiers put him against a pole and used their bayonets to stab him, twisted the knife to the right then shot him again. It was done in a minute and a half, but…his legs did not drop, his eyes did not close.

'He's still breathing,' one of them moaned.

'I can't…'

'Why isn't he dead?'

'My arms…they don't move.'

'It can't be, it's impossible.'

'Please…'

'Dark magic. He's in league with something.'

'Nyet, no leagues, I'm…'

'What do we do?'

'I need doctors, the Tsar…'

'I have an idea.'

The guards grabbed him by the ankles and dragged him to the river, tying a statue of Kropotkin to his back and throwing him in.

They waited five minutes then ducked under the surface to check. The statue was there, but Rasputin was not.

'Shit, he's…'

'It's not…'

'Where could he…'

There was a noise by the river wall, a *GRRRR*RR in Russian, a pair of demon-red eyes.

'There!'

'He's trying to climb up.'

'Shoot him!'

They fired their rifles at the wall, then into the water as if the river itself were the enemy [it wasn't].

Still Rasputin wouldn't die.

Instead, his body floated near a sewer pipe, re-animating at the last second and disappearing inside.

'If we can't kill him,' said the head guard, 'we'll have to settle for containment.'

'For eternity?'

'Two of us will keep a vigil here, on rotation. Switch every seven days. We'll all rent apartments nearby, in case emergency back-up is needed.'

'And if he comes out of the pipe?'

'We force him back in.'

'If he emerges somewhere else?'

'We'll seal all other exits.'

'And if he's already gone?'

'Impossible. I can still see those red eyes glaring at us, over there.'

'Da, you're right.'

'One of us stays put, the rest will go and fetch some concrete.'

The guards grumbled, but eventually shook on it.

~~~

Five years later, the Revolution came. It wasn't so bad. Then the October Revolution came. The assassins were Tsarists, they had to fight. Leaving one guard to watch the river, they rode off to join the Whites, assuring him they'd be back when the war was won.

Five more years passed.

A few of them came back [now Bukharin stans] and found the guard still there. He said no-one had come out and no-one had gone in; the demon was surely dead by now.

He wasn't.

For ten years, Rasputin had walked circles in the sewers, eating rats and scraps, going over and over and over all the ways he'd messed things up. There were many. The way he saw it, he wasn't a villain. People were just scared of him. The next time I'm around people, I'll normalize myself, he thought. But how?

First he'd have to buy a pair of glasses, look down more when he talked to others.

No, before that, he would need to deal with the imposter. If they hadn't killed him already. And what about the princess? If she'd been-...if they'd hurt her in any way...

~~~

Another three years passed.

Stalin put on the Fouché[2] mask and did an insanely devious power grab. Trotsky made all the wrong calls and ended up in Japan [his stunt double went to Mexico]. Bukharin flirted with Austrian sociologists.

---

[2] Or Robespierre depending on your views.

Pseudo Communism put on a cabaret and changed costumes seventeen times before settling on the terror outfit.

35,040 hours passed.

Stalin began to execute people he didn't trust. Stalin began to distrust a lot of people. Stalin got worried. Hearing the rumours, he went to the sewer pipe, put on another mask and met with Rasputin.

'You're the Tsar now?'

'Da, in effect.'

'And the old Tsar?'

'Dead.'

'The princess?'

'Gone.'

'You diseased son of a…'

'Nyet, comrade. It wasn't me, it was another guy. Kornilov.'

'Where is he?'

'Also dead. But there are others, villains who share responsibility for the princess's demise.'

'Their names?'

'Da, da, that's the way. We shall work together to…'

'Their names, all of them.'

'And you shall have them. Patience and cunning, my friend. We'll get the bastards.'

On the bank of the river, they made their plan. Rasputin would scare the shit out of Anti-Soviets, Stalin would give him room and board [and the names of all those who'd *wronged* the princess].

The 30's went quite well.

1931 - 721 killed

1932 - 835 killed

1933 - 1,349 killed

1934 - 3,207 killed

1935 - 37,439 killed

1936 - 55,966 killed, 2,498 imprisoned and then killed

1937 - 77,002 killed

1938 – 62,114 + Bukharin killed

1939-45 – Nazi sabbatical

~~~
~~~

In 1948, things spun. Stalin noticed the lack of creases on Rasputin's forehead and decided he could no longer trust him. He told his best [stolen Nazi] scientists to build a spaceship and send that lunatic bastard up into Space.

'But he won't get very far,' they warned.

'How far exactly?'

'Roughly halfway to Mars, if he's lucky.'

'That'll do.'

Rasputin was told about dissidents hiding on the moon. He wondered when the Pseudo Communists had put a colony up there, but didn't question his orders. He was to fly up in some kind of new technology he didn't understand and put his face about a bit. Scare the dissidents into…something.

'I don't want to kill anymore,' he told Stalin, the two of them making the bed.

'You won't have to.'

'All those things I did, they were…'

'Relax, comrade. There are no judges here. Space is made for guys like you.'

'Like me?'

'Da, survivalists. The next chapter of man will be written up there, by us. Russians.'

Rasputin nodded and the next day went to the ship. It was strange; there were 117 other people with him, all of them in chains.

They put chains on him too.

He didn't argue.

The ship took off and made it through the atmosphere. For a second, Rasputin could see the moon and felt at peace. That, he thought. That's the kind of rock a princess could play on, in peace, without any hairy soldiers trying to-…

The ship turned and went the opposite way.

Rasputin leaned back in his seat and breathed out heavy. He knew what had been done and half accepted it.

An hour later, he unaccepted it.

Fuck you, Josef. Fuck you and your stupid fucking chapters of man. You're not even a communist.

The man next to Rasputin tried to lean across, but couldn't. His neck was tied to the seat with a metal collar.

'Friend, can you keep it down?' he asked.

'Huh?'

'I can hear what you're thinking. It's really loud.'

'You can hear my thoughts?'

'Sure. Can't you hear mine too?'

Rasputin focused, his eyeballs turning deep red.

'Da. I think I can.'

PLANET RASPUTIN

PART ONE

Conquer, Dissident!

Sila sat with his legs hanging off the castle wall, looking down at a group of day trippers pulling a rowboat around the edges of Lake Bled.

It wasn't that interesting, most visitors did the same. He'd done the same two years earlier. Try and do a lap of the whole lake, get bored two thirds of the way around, climb out and pull it back to the main dock. But today it got his attention as, from this distance, two of them looked like people he knew. Had known. Ghosts of them.

Ah Fung and Tala.

The only two people in the whole of Slovenia who'd never watched *Dibrivna Vaska.*[3] Ah Fung, the guy who said you'd have to dig up Ljubljana and melt it before he'd ever emigrate. Tala, the woman who believed teleportation had been invented and forgotten 20,000 years ago and as soon as humans re-discovered it, everything in Slovenia would be fixed. Not that it was that broken, if you looked at the actual system: de-centralised, non-mandate, the insistence on zero personality cults, a functioning post office…

An image of two people being pulled out of the River Sava broke the thought. Sila turned his tab back on and refocused on the boat gang, their faces getting clearer as they moved parallel to the castle.

---

[3] Old Slovene serial from 2080's, similar in tone to *Blake's 7*.

He couldn't make out what they were saying, it was far too distant, but they seemed to be having a good time. The boat wasn't heavy, the sun was out, clouds were minimal.

A typical day in picturesque Bled.

He looked down and left towards the town, wondering if he should rent a kayak and go out there - paddle clockwise around the chapel this time - but decided against it. Instead, he picked up the [paper] notepad on the wall next to him, flicked to the front and squint-read what he'd apparently written a year earlier:

'The Eternal Paternal – Kapok [2044] - limit of hierarchal concept, no such thing as a class traitor

Exo-hierarchy: blood, skin or costume? – Bōl [2053] – first use of 'show your thinking' method over 'rhetoric/polemic', innovative at the time, full of dead-ends.

The Edited Editors – Sima [2057] – revolutionaries incapable of zero history as they are history themselves – projected presence paradox.

3 books linked, two Anarcho-Communist, one Marxist, all say similar things.

Outdated?

Still hierarchies, still deceit, still hegemonies.

Statues and paintings in squares, endless?

Problem: Half the world has changed, but old systems are still in place elsewhere + adventurists never rest.

Solution:

Reduced fibre-glassing?[4]

De-entrenchment + focused disentanglement – abandonment of hegemonic utopian set-change in favour of holistic disentanglement of each diseased segment within dystopian whole i.e. in esse + in fieri hegemonies [global, regional, cultural, sexual etc.].

ASSUME YOU'RE IN A CONSTANT OSCILLATING DYSTOPIA, DISENTANGLE, AVOID RE-ENTRENCHMENT.'

[4] After reaching saturation point in 2028, the word *praxis* was abandoned in favour of the more visceral term, *fibre-glassing*.

Sila read it seven times, trying to make sense of it. Not just the meaning, but the reason. Why had he written this?

Reduced fibre-glassing?

Wasn't that antithetical to change? Where did it even come from? Sima?

He read it an eighth time, saying the words out loud.

'Reduced fibre-glassing…how? In what way?'

A kid ran past, shouted, 'I win, I win,' slapped the end of the castle wall, ran back and stopped next to Sila. He stared at the page and mumbled the words *avoid entrenchment*, adding a *RARRRGH* on the end.

'Not bad,' Sila told him, trying and failing to smile.

The kid shouted, 'ja ja ja jaaman,' and ran off.

Sila watched his tiny back for a second then returned to the notepad. Reduced fibre-glassing. Holistic disentanglement. It meant something, had meant something at some point, but…meant what?

He scratched his eyelids, taking off some dry skin.

Derrida wasn't his favourite philosopher, actually he was a bit of a waster, but he did have one good line.

I neither recognise nor accept what I wrote yesterday, yet I shall fellate it doggedly.

Ja, true in theory. Don't shit on old thought. Even if it looked incoherent.

Sila picked up his *Blame Šarec* pen and held it over the paper.

The problem was…

What?

Too many pages of vague theory, not enough reaction to real things. But in Bled there were no real things. Just nice weather and quiet roads. Philosophers and scientists, semi-retired activists. Why was he here? Ne, wrong question. Why had Potočnik sponsored him to come here? And why four years?

Sila put the pen down and picked up the tab. He slid through the headlines on *Dnevni Seznam*,[5] then went back and counted out the ratio. Three positive, five neutral, two alarming.

[5] Similar to a wire service, it posts daily news stories as dry as can be.

He clicked on one of them, a Slovene-Turk scientist praised for increasing the efficiency of artificial eyeballs. That was good. Another one talked about the Tokamak, how smoothly it was running compared to the old power plants. Also good.

But then he switched to the alarming ones. Koban style policing expanded to Ljubljana collectives after a successful trial in the Savinja region. Next to it was a picture of four councillors, his sponsor Potočnik included, flanked by eight men who looked like bouncers, all wearing the same ash grey jacket, with a blue stripe slashed vertically down the left shoulder.

Wait, that couldn't be Potočnik-related, he used to hate guys like that.

Didn't he?

Sila read through the article until he got to a name. *This policy was originally birthed in Tezno, the collective of Councillor Maček, a long-time advocate of a firmer, more specialised form of policing.*

Okay, not Potočnik. At least not officially. His collective had consented to it, and now tradition required that he pose for the promotional pics. Nothing too out of the ordinary.

There was a noise down by the lake, faint when it reached his ears, but definitely a panicked shout at its place of origin.

Sila lowered the tab and instinctively turned to get off the wall and help, but stopped when he realized he was about four hundred metres away. Besides, it wasn't anything serious. The group had lost its grip on the rope and the rowboat was floating out into the lake. One of them, the one he'd thought looked like Ah Fung but now realized didn't, jumped in and swam to the side of the boat. He tried to climb over the side but it was too tough. Luckily, he remembered the rope, grabbed it and swam back to shore.

Sila smirked. If this were a Petr Godec[6] novel, the whole scene would've been a twenty page metaphor for *any-day-now nihilism*, but Godec was long gone and now it was just a group of day trippers fucking around on a lake.

---

[6] A future Slovene version of Henry James.

There was another shout, one of the others falling into the lake. Her friends laughed and pointed to the side of the path, telling her something he couldn't quite catch.

But the woman wasn't swimming, she was flapping around, flailing, going under the surface…coming back up for a second then slipping under again.

The others didn't seem to realise, or they thought it was a joke, until a man passed by and pointed at their friend's head. It was just hair now, the rest of it submerged.

Finally waking up, one of the stronger-looking friends dived in and started pulling her back to the path, while the man who'd warned them turned and…

Ne.

Sila almost fell forwards off the wall, trying to manually zoom in.

Gašper, here?

It couldn't be.

He swung his legs over the wall, pushed himself down onto the stone ground, took a few jagged breaths then peeked back over, focusing his tab on the suspect.

Shit, the mop of hair, the headband…

It was.

Gašper was down there, in person.

Like a stick figure on the *View of Toledo.*

How?

Sila knew the only way to find out was to go down and ask him, but then he'd be stuck and he wasn't ready for that, so he kept his head low, fumbled for his things on top of the wall and waited.

After pretending to re-read his notebook for two and half minutes, he caught the woman at the pastry stand staring at him. Giving her a nod, he stood back up, picked out a new part of the wall and leaned awkwardly against it.

The group of day-trippers was still tending to the girl, probably giving excuses for not jumping in quicker, while Gašper was gone.

Ne, wait, there he was…the orange headband. Two hundred metres down the path. Apparently heading across to the town centre.

Unless he was taking the long way round. Follow the path past Villa Rikli then pivot back up to the castle.

Was that his plan?

Sila watched, pinching the skin of his finger, as the canopies of the trees gradually erased Gašper from the scene. Logic told him a man on a path would follow that path to its end, that the castle was underwhelming at this time of day, but logic hadn't always worked with Gašper.

Better to leave, he thought, putting his notebook back in his bag. Go home, try to write something.

Or read something.

Ja, reading was better. More intake, less daydreaming. What was it Sima said? The more you lay out your perch, the more it…

Shouts of 'wrong way, idiot' and 'fuck off' came from the entrance, pulling him away from his haze, a haze that had built itself in milliseconds and…

More shouts.

He stretched his eyes to Peter Lorre size and pulled up his shoulders.

Focus. Start walking. Before your childhood albatross turns up.

Ceding to his inner self, he put his bag on his back, scanned the entrance gate and started walking.

The castle grounds weren't that extensive, not many exits, but he didn't want to risk taking the main one out. Safer to jump down from the back wall and take the side road back to Rečiška. Chu would probably be home, he could hide out with her for a bit.

Ja, safer but cowardly, he thought, as he jogged up the small flight of steps, through the medieval-era, tax-collecting office and out past the line of posters on the recently restored rear wall, each one stamped with the capitalized slogan *STATE OF THINGS, ON THE STAIRCASE.*

Staircase?

Hearing no other noises behind, he slowed down to a brisk walk, then an elderly stroll.

The last poster, a new one, caught his eye: Potočnik again, the maintenance man of Slovenia, among a mass of different colour

Slovenes, all head sizes the same, all of them shouting the slogan out in one huge speech bubble: *Fight fraud together, say NE to pop-up therapists.*

It was strange, despite the giant size of the text, Sila couldn't help looking at the two pinpricks of white emanating from Potočnik's notoriously purple eyes. If he didn't need to blink, he would've stayed there the rest of the day, contemplating them. Fearing them. Admiring them. Copying them. Re-painting them. But he did need to blink, and keep moving, and soon he was out of the castle grounds and on the path that would take him home.

On the way, he checked back about thirty-seven times, sure that either Gašper or Potočnik's eyes were right behind him.

They weren't.

At least, Gašper wasn't.

Potočnik...that was harder to say.

According to the cousin of an ex-girlfriend of Chu, who knew a guy that worked in the Council of Forestry and Agriculture,[7] the *Dok Militia,* acting under covert orders, had surgically removed the eyeballs of selected birds and replaced them with nano-tech surveillance dots, sending them out not only around Slovenia but most of Europe and Western Africa too.

It wasn't the easiest thing to believe; the *Dok Militia* was about the size of a chess club now, two hundred men at most, not to mention the logistics of it; removing the eyes, nano-tech, why not just make fake birds? Or an even saner way, use satellites? That's what other countries would do. But Slovenes were a sceptical bunch and, to them, rumours like *UDBA birds* only persisted if they had some grain of truth to them.

Was the militia, or whoever was behind it all, watching everyone?

Probably not.

Did they want you to think they were watching everyone?

Unknown.

---

[7] State councils, councillors...neither one sounds very anarcho-communistic, it's true, but they serve a function in organisational terms and are, essentially, delegates; they have no actual power to create policy. That comes from the collectives; in this case, the ones with agricultural relations [mostly located in Eastern Slovenia].

~~~

Eris base, 2272.

A sign with THE GREEN ANGEL in gaudy capitals hung tilted above the entrance to a makeshift bar. Inside were about twenty maintenance workers, off shift.

Two of these workers sat perched on stools next to the viewport, the Chinese one, Chu, stroking the other's thigh.

'If these creatures are out there…'

'They're not.'

'…I'd take my helmet off as soon as they got in.'

The woman speaking Portuguese let Chu stroke her leg a little longer, then pulled away and asked, 'what would you do?'

'Nothing.'

'I mean, on a mission, what would you do?'

'Same answer. Nothing.'

'It would kill you. Or make you kill others. Either way, not good.'

Chu tried to put her hand back on the Brazilian's thigh, but she pulled away. Weird for a *Tier-2* to be so coy, she thought.

'I have to go.'

'You're not real.'

'What?'

Chu coughed, not at all convincingly. 'Stay a while longer. We can play *I spy*.'

'Next time.'

The Brazilian flickered a little, then turned and walked out of the bar. Chu had about twelve seconds to stare down at the surface of Eris before a new skin appeared by the stool next to her.

'You from Guangdong?'

'Slovenia.'

'Close enough.' The guy with chaotically dyed purple hair took the seat and looked across at the upper part of the space station. 'I was thinking about trying the wormhole run. Three person craft. You interested?'
~~~

'I prefer here.'

'What, the Eris possession thing?'

'This stool.'

'Ah, I get it. You need to be pushed. Okay, I don't mind going down to the surface, watching an auto-skin get suffocated with that green shit.'

'Have fun.'

'It'd be weird if it got me or you though. Not that it would, but…I don't know, could happen. Has happened before. I heard they actually simulate another voice in your head, make it seem like you're really sharing your brain with someone. Pretty creepy.'

'Not really.'

'Don't know what I'd actually do, if something really did get inside my brain like that…'

'Talk to it.'

'Huh? To the ghost of Eris?'

'Adapt to the symbiosis.'

The guy wrapped a hand around Chu's glass, and whistled again. 'I've decided. I'm gonna go with the wormhole run. You sure you don't wanna come?'

The lights in the bar flickered, but the guy either didn't notice or didn't care.

'Nice timing Sila,' replied Chu, taking back her glass and downing the contents.

'Who?'

'I have to go.'

'Ah, you're getting the tap out signal. Okay. Your loss. Maybe I'll see you again. This is your real face, right?'

'Mostly.'

The guy spun around and stepped off the stool, stumbling a little as his foot hit the floor. Then he was gone.

The lights flickered again, and Chu tapped the side of her head with something close to a sigh.

'Back to the wheel,' she mumbled.

~~~
~~~

'He's here?'

'Ja.'

'In Bled?'

'Different colour headband but, unless I was hallucinating, ja, definitely Gašper.'

Chu took out the LIN swab from her temple, rubbed off some of the sea green residue and turned to the wall in the far corner. Sila turned too. In contrast to the other walls in the house, which were dominated by moonscapes and Varo prints, it was blank [excluding the scuff marks made by the back of the chair]. A factory of dormant identities, he thought, conjuring up an image of a tired Ekuban[8] beneath a poorly-drawn quote bubble. Or worse, a factory of Gašpers.

'Wonder if he'll turn up here,' said Chu finally, either to the wall or him.

'Ne vem. I hope not.'

'It's possible…'

'He's probably just here on holiday. Or a day trip. That would make the most sense.'

'Wait a second. Jaša…'

'Who?'

'Jaša and Gašper, same *ash* sound, easy to-…' Chu stopped, her left hand going back to rub more cream off her temple. 'I think he might be here to see us.'

'Ne…'

'My mum called last night, said a nice man called Jaša was looking for me. I thought she was talking about the neighbour again, and mixed up his name but, now I think about it, I guess she could've meant Gašper.'

'He came to your house?'

---

[8] Ghanaian psycho-philosopher who came up with the *Factory of Self* concept that was itself a riff on Jung's *somewhere in my brain is an ancient Sumerian* theory.

'Not really my house anymore. But ja, this Jaša or Gašper person chatted with my mum. She told him I was here, in Bled. Probably told him you were here too.'

'Fuck, that's how he knew.'

'Ja, or he went to your place and Sadia told him.'

'Impossible.'

'Ne vem. I'm just brainstorming.'

'Ne, she wouldn't. Not Sadia.' Sila got up and moved over to the window, checking the street. 'Gašper annoyed her too much. Every time he used to call round, she'd refuse to answer the door.'

'That's quite harsh.'

'And she's probably forgotten my address here anyway.'

'Not even opening the door…'

Someone walked by outside, forcing Sila back behind the curtain. 'Fuck. Can't believe he actually got out.'

'Huh?'

'Of Rehab. I can't believe they released him.'

'Ja, of course, they're releasing a lot of them. It was in *Morda Ni Hudić*[9] last month. We talked about it.'

'Ne.'

'I thought we did.'

'Ne, we didn't.'

'Okay, well, didn't you read about it?'

Sila twisted his finger round a loose thread on the curtain, monitoring the road outside. 'I was in my theory bubble a month ago. Didn't read anything.'

'Ah, the bubble, of course.'

'Who sponsored it? Maček?'

Chu picked up a very thin screwdriver from the table, next to one of the science contraptions she clearly hadn't laid a finger on all day, and

---

[9] Political zine founded underground during the Šarec era. Like all good anarchist publications, it's a co-op that covers all collectives and all issues up for vote in the filter halls, though accused by some of re-using the same writers too much and forming a stark editorial line.

started tapping it against her knee. 'I think it was Grbec, the Sostro rep. One who looks like a wolf. He said we had to show more empathy.'

'We?'

'Other collectives.'

'So he got them to water down the NOT YET Centres?'

'About half of them. Maribor, of course, some of Ljubljana. Novo Mesto. I don't think it was all patients, just the non-violent types, like Gašper. Plus the types who felt sorry for previous violence.'

'Felt sorry for,' mumbled Sila, snapping the curtain thread.

'Ja, I don't know how they qualify that. Or how sorry you have to feel. But the first drop was pretty big, pretty vague on details too.'

He left the curtain and sat down on the nearby sofa arm, pulling out his tab from his jacket pocket. 'Grbec sponsored this?'

'I think some of the bulkier ones joined that new Koban initiative. The blue stripe thing. Ja, Grbec. Him and his Sostro gang.'

'The man who wanted to electrify park benches after midnight?'[10]

'That's what the article said. At least, that's what I remember it saying. I guess I forgot about it until my mum called.'

'Doesn't feel right.'

'It was quite low-key, not a big story. Which is surprising when you think what it actually entails.' Chu dropped the screwdriver and picked up the thing next to it, her old Uni copy of Jung's *Archetype Farm*. 'Or maybe they stressed the gradual part of it.'

Sila gave a few seconds to the story on his tab, checked the related headlines at the bottom then moved back to the curtain and said *fuck* again. 'Why did they have to do this now?'

'It's probably not that bad.'

'I can't do my theory if Gašper's here. He's too positive. I can't.'

Chu opened up her book and closed it again, almost in the same motion. 'He's probably just here for the day, like you said.'

'Ne, he won't be.'

---

[10] A policy aimed at *solving* youth excess, Councillor Grbec supported a suggestion from the Sostro Collective that the electricity be delivered via pop-up spikes hidden inside the benches.

'Or they might have a tag on him. Back to the collective by midnight or you're in rehab again.'

'Unlikely,' Sila said, moving again to the sofa, this time slumping down on it.

'Either way, he's not a serial killer.'

'Ne…'

'And if he does turn up, we'll deal with him together. Or chat with him. *Deal with* sounds a bit sinister.'

Sila stared at the Jung cover, muttering, 'sounds about right to me.' He stopped abruptly when he realised Chu was looking at him.

'What?'

'Let's just have dinner, watch something on the wall.'

'Ja, fine. Long as it's not the news.'

Chu nodded, looking at the unopened box of Korean noodles nestled behind the couch.

'Not noodles.'

'Noodles and veg?'

'Ne.'

'Vietnamese?'

'Something we don't have to go out to get. Don't wanna risk bumping into him.'

'Noodles and veg.'

Sila looked over at the box, letting it work its spell. 'Fine.'

'I'll boil the water.'

~~~

Three hours later, with the sun spent and a toenail-shaped moon slotting in to replace it, Sila finally pulled himself away from his window stakeout and settled down next to Chu on the couch. The TV screen was dug into the wall opposite, with a small four inch curb to contain the projection.

'You ready for the news yet?'

'Ne.'

'*Animal World*?'
~~~

'Ne.'

'*Dah Station 7* then. I'll let you force a mission. Helix Nebula deuterium run.'

'Ne.'

'Game snob. How about we run through the local projects?[11] See if that owl talent centre's getting anywhere?'

Sila stared at one of the Varo prints on the wall [*Useless Science or The Alchemist*], as if he were genuinely thinking about Chu's question, then switched back on and said something completely different.

'I'm going back to Ljubljana.'

'Okay…'

'For a few weeks. Maybe a month.'

'To see Sadia?'

He shook his head, more to the Varo print than her. 'I'll stay in a hostel. It's easier.'

'Strange answer.'

'Ne, I'm not going to see Sadia,' he answered, facing her again.

'Right.'

'And it's not because I saw Gašper.'

'I didn't say anything.'

'It was forming in your brain. I could see the neuron sparking.'

'Impressive eyesight.'

'Ja.'

There was a noise on the street outside, followed by a car speaker shouting *MOVE* with an electronic reverb. Chu used the distraction to reach across Sila and grab the TV control.

'So it's back to Ljubljana, for unspecified reasons,' she said, turning on the screen.

---

[11] The *tax distribution* system is collective-based, circular and way too much for one footnote, but here are the basics: fundamentals like health, education, housing are already covered; some is given to departments e.g. environment, tech, science, which then use open-forum consent voting to decide on/promote projects; the rest is allocated by each citizen, at their own discretion, to publicly-advertised, independent projects.

'A bit less mysterious than that. There are things I need to do, non-theory related.'

'Potočnik related?'

'Not completely.'

Chu nodded, loading up the screen menu and going straight to *Dibrivna Vaska*. 'Which episode?'

'A light one.'

She scrolled a little more, stopping on an iconic pic of Captain Mojca Ito struggling with a yellow alien blob. 'This?'

'Next one along.'

'To the left?'

'Ja.'

She clicked on it. The screen changed from black to slightly less black, then the famous syringe spaceship came into view, semi-3-D, hovering next to a 98% green planet.

Sila leaned back into the couch, ignoring Chu's feet as she nudged them into his arm.

'When are you going?' she asked.

'To Ljubljana? Tomorrow. Or the day after.'

'You gonna stop off at the tokamak on the way?'

'I'll probably take the train. Faster.'

Chu prodded at her neck and switched back to the screen. Mojca Ito was telling her alien pilot to hide in low orbit while she teleported down to the planet surface with Gon and Joona. Apparently, there was a helium mine with surplus helium they wanted to flog.

'I wonder if *Knijžnica* has been rebuilt yet,' said Sila, moving his head in unison with the ships dive.

'Probably.'

'It's been three years.'

'Unless they spent all the cash on repairing the melted ship.'

'They're fixing that?'

'Fixed. Already done.'

'That fast?'

'I think they're testing it next week.'

'How the hell do you fix a melted ship?'

'Good question.'

'You're the scientist.'

'Ja, who doesn't design space ships. Or work for our space agency. Or do much in the way of teleportation theory anymore. Move your arm a bit, I want to stretch out my leg.'

Sila grunted, moving his arm about an inch.

They drifted back into the episode. Turned out the helium mine was a trap set by the Federation, and the miners were guards. But now they were dead. Killed without marks or wounds. Better spread out and scan, said Mojca Ito.

Gon and Joona dispersed, leaving Mojca alone to be spied on by a nitrogen cloud.

'Incredible eyebrow movements,' said Sila, resting his arm on Chu's foot and instantly getting toppled off.

'Ja, the eyebrow thing isn't even acting, she does it in real life too.'

'You've seen it?'

'Ja.'

'In person?'

'She was on *Janza Kec*[12] last week, they asked her about it.'

Sila made another attempt to perch his arm on Chu's foot, lasting about half a second before being shrugged off again.

'I thought she'd retired,' he said, rubbing his arm unconvincingly.

'From acting, ja.'

'So what was she doing on *Janza Kec*?'

'Better if I don't say.'

'Politics?'

'You won't like it.'

'Mountain porn?'

Chu smiled, doing an X symbol with her index fingers.

'Fuck. She's not a zealot, is she?'

'Close.'

---

[12] Long running chat show that tours the collectives, interviewing artists from each one as they mingle with their neighbours.

'Running for Council?'

The X parted, Chu's two fingers pointing up instead [the 22nd Century Slovene version of a thumbs up].

'Wah, as a zealot?'

'Pro-Slovene, of all kinds and colours. Except Russians. And Turks. And Argentinians for some reason.'

'Shit...Mojca Ito.'

'I think she's been this way for a while. Even when she was on the show. Probably kept it quiet back then.'

Sila sat up, hitting the lower part of his spine. 'Which collective is she in again? Kočevje?'

'Vrhnika.'

'Argh, she'll probably get in then. Two years of brainless showboating a la Maček and Grbec. Thank gods she can't make policy.'

'Ja, I'm not so sure about that. She said the Council wasn't doing enough, that all it does is say *ne* to everything. Or only keep their eyes open long enough to rubber stamp some useless initiative.'

'Err...what?'

'Apparently, it needs executive power. Direct quote.'

Sila launched forward, pushing Chu's feet off his lap. 'Executive? It doesn't even have legislative power. Jezus. It's literally a rubber stamp depot for policies made by the collectives. What the fuck is she talking about?'

'That's not the worst of it. Not only does the Council need foundational empowerment - her words - but it's also crying out for a strong, experienced leader. Someone like Potočnik, Maček, Krajnc...or her, obviously.'

'Potočnik?'

'Ja.'

'A strong leader?'

'Strong, moral and versatile...with Slovenia in his blood. Don't glare, this is her description, not mine.'

'Slovenia in his blood. Jezus.'

Sila slunk back down into the couch, giving Chu the chance to sneak her feet back onto his lap.

'Ja, quite uplifting,' she said, accidentally stabbing his thigh with her toe, 'in an unconstitutional way. Told them she was crestfallen when she found out that *Serpentinšek* thing[13] was satire.'

'Ne...'

'And some other insane line. What was it? Ja, not that Slovenia would ever have a leader, but if it did, she'd vote for him.'

'Who, Potočnik?'

'Ja.'

'As a dictator?'

'She didn't say it, but...'

'Fuck.' Sila blocked out the screen with his hand. 'I don't think I can watch this anymore.'

'Ni panike, the actress who plays Joona is still normal.'

'Ja, summertime anarchist.'

'That's old Joona. She's more in the reeds now, much more. Wintertime anarchist.'

Sila laughed, and then laughed again when he saw Mojca Ito being flung into some mining machinery. One of the miners was still alive and oblivious to the nitrogen cloud creeping up behind him.

'You should look her up...' continued Chu, getting up and taking some dried seaweed from the table. '...Mojca Ito, when you're in Ljubljana tomorrow. Tell her the article was right, Councillor Potočnik really is the new Šarec.[14] See what she says.'

'*Fuck off*, probably.'

'Or the thing you said before, that he might be a crypto-tyrant. Soften it a bit.'

'I never said that.'

---

[13] Posted under the username '*Serpentinšek*' in November 2113, this article confused and alarmed most Slovenes with its details of a hidden tyrant within their political system. Fears were swiftly allayed as further articles were released, each one more absurd than the last, culminating in the sixth and last piece that exposed the tyrant as none other than a re-animated Šarec, the dictator who was overthrown in 2081.

[14] Slovenian President/Dictator 2075-81 and 2084-5, a brutal, Canute-like figure who attempted, and ultimately failed, to turn back the Tsunami of Anarcho-Communist sentiment.

Chu paused the strip of dried seaweed an inch from her mouth.

'Not declaratively,' Sila added.

'After the article came out…*oh shit, he might be a crypto-tyrant.*'

'Ja, but…'

'That wasn't you?'

'For a hundredth of a second, ja. But I also said it was probably a smear job by Maček or Krajnc.'

'As I recall, you said it was borderline plausible.'

'*In some ways*, it was borderline plausible. But then the other pieces came out and it was nothing at all.'

Sila paused, his eyes stolen by the nitrogen cloud again. It was increasing in mass and the miner was now backing into it, still completely unaware of its presence.

'And I wasn't saying *he* was a dictator, just that the theory in the first piece was plausible…'

'The space missions?'

'…and only then because it described his character so well. He does hide in the background, he does make fun of himself. Ja, the space missions too. But that's more obvious, vague nationalism…'

'For Mojca Ito…'

'…and technically it came from his collective, not him, so…ne, the *hiding in the background* was the unique part, the thing that confused everyone. Dictators don't usually do that.'

'Subtle fingers…'

'It's too precise, understated, ja, subtle. But the article, the first one, really laid it out as if it were a rational thing, made it convincing. That's why I said it was borderline plausible.'

Chu shifted position, prodding at her neck. 'So the man who's sponsoring our work here could still be a despot?'

'But then it's not really plausible cos you've got the other side of it. He has no actual power. His collective voted against actions that would've given the Council mechanisms for centralised control. He's spoken out against the idea of a leader loads of times, even though he would've been by far the most popular choice.'

'No statues, no plaques…'

'…no hagiographies. Exactly. He's erratic in the policies he supports, apart from the space stuff. He doesn't seem to favour any one collective over another, even though he's lived in about twenty of them, and represented five as councillor. He's never formed any blocs within the collectives either. It's just him, alone. And he speaks out about other blocs too, like in Koper. That's why I said it was probably a smear job. A really weird, convoluted one that, ne vem, was trying to…'

'Cloud scene.'

'…paint him as some kind of 4-D chess mast-…what?'

'Pause a sec.'

Chu stretched out her hand and kept it steady near Sila's face, almost obstructing his view. But he could make out enough of the screen to see the nitrogen cloud devouring the miner's legs. And then his torso. But not his head. There was no blood, just frenzied arm movements and theatrical screaming, ending with a sudden neck tilt that indicated death. Satisfied, the nitrogen cloud moved on.

'I hope I can die like that someday,' said Chu, lowering her hand. 'Dignified. Graceful.'

'On an alien planet.'

'Ideally, ja.'

Sila turned his face away from Chu and yawned.

'What were we talking about?' she asked, watching his mouth stretch open.

'Conspiracy theories.'

'Ah, the hidden dictator, borderline plausible…'

'Ja.'

'…Mojca Ito being a complete archon.'

'Also, ja.'

Chu pulled some more seaweed out of the pack and fed it into her mouth 5cm at a time. 'How about we just watch this instead?'

Sila yawned again.

'Motion passed.'

~~~
~~~

A cemetery, green sky, spotty cloud cover.

Two men sit on a coffin, riding the bumps and tremors as something inside tries to break out.

Sila watches four graves away, an umbrella protecting him from the green fluff dropping down from above.

There is a whirring noise from the grave below, startling him.

He moves backwards just in time as a hand shoots up from the earth and searches for nearby ankles.

The hand pulls out a blue-skinned corpse and the corpse tells Sila to take him to the House of Ne.

'You're Šarec,' says Sila, the words barely forming.

'Thirteen times. Quickly. A vehicle.'

'You're dead.'

'In a car, not always.'

As soon as the words are spoken, the two of them are hunched up in a Fiat 500, Sila struggling to start the engine.

'Turn it a better way,' shouts Šarec.

'I tried already.'

'Again.'

Sila tries again, but no matter how firmly he turns the key, the engine still will not start.

'You're no help at all,' says Šarec, his legs starting to crumble into dust.

'I'm trying.'

'All this fluff outside. So green. Bah gung. Never liked my arms much anyway.'

Sila watches as the rest of the old dictator turns to dust and the passenger seat morphs into a huge mixing bowl.

A giant whisk lowers itself from a hole in the car roof and begins its duty.

From outside, a voice repeats 'again' through a megaphone.

There is no face attached, no buildings, just green fluff drifting through the air, aimless, sceptical of Sila's hand passing through the car window and out as the giant whisk continues to

~~~
~~~

The next morning, Sila woke up on the floor, grabbed a cushion to block out the sun, caught a glimpse of *Celestial Pabulum* on the wall opposite, groaned then went right back to sleep.

Forty three minutes later, Chu kicked him in the waist and told him to get up, she had work to do.

'Liar,' he slurred, squinting at her *koala on a mission* pyjama top.

'Not this time. I'm due at the clinic in two hours. By the way, if you want breakfast, your house is next door.'

'You have a shift today?'

'Ja, covering for Damijana.'

'Again?'

'She's got a chronic neck problem. Needs more time off. And that's the way to my kitchen, not your place.'

'Ja…worth a shot.'

Sila picked up his jacket, which had also been his blanket, and stumbled towards the front door.

'Say hi to Gašper for me,' Chu shouted, moving over to the same box contraption from the night before.

Sila's hand stopped on the latch. 'You think he's still out there?'

'Outside this house?'

'Ne, he can't be…'

'Or mentally?'

Sila left the door and walked to the living room window, looking out. 'Argh, all I have to do is make it next door, pack and go.'

'Good luck.'

'Wah, what's that?'

'Sunlight.'

'There's a car outside.'

'Ja…'

'Ne, a new car, someone's getting out.'

'Gašper?'

'Looks like one of Maček's guys…blue stripe jacket, big head. Fuck. He's heading towards my door.'

Chu put down her mysterious, *could be a science experiment, could be a new toaster* type box and joined Sila by the window.

'You're right,' she said, poking her head farther out from the curtain. 'He's ringing your bell.'

'Doesn't make sense. Why would a blue stripe guy be coming to see me?'

'Ne vem. Maček sent them?'

'Maček? He doesn't know me. I'm not in his collective.'

'Maybe he's heard about your theory?'

'Ne, I've never even met the guy. Why would he know about that? It doesn't make sense.'

'Potočnik then.'

Sila gripped Chu's pyjama sleeve and pulled her back behind the curtain. 'With one of these guys?'

'It is quite considerate, sending a driver.'

'More like intimidating. Look at that guy, he's like a gorilla. No way Potočnik would attach himself to someone like that, even as a free service. Wah, he's ringing the bell again.' Sila scrunched the fringes of the curtain into a small ball and punched it. 'Fuck, what is he doing?'

Chu patted his arm, using her other hand to free the curtain from his grip.

'It's pointless, the Council's got no authority to do anything here. They can request to see me, but I don't have to agree to it. I won't agree to it. I'll just tell them I'm taking the train there by myself and maybe if I have time, I'll drop by.'

'He's given up,' said Chu, monotone.

'What?'

'The gorilla. He's getting in the car.'

Sila edged out from the curtain and squinted through the glass. 'It's not moving.'

'Probably waiting for you to come back home. Just like a normal driver would.'

'He's putting something on his face.'

'In fact, he might not be with Potočnik or Maček. And even if he is, it doesn't mean anything bad. They're drivers, not Šarec thugs.'

Sila put his nose against the window, zooming in. 'Looks like he's moisturizing,'

'Ja.'

'…his whole face.'

'It is quite dry today.'

The window glass clearly wasn't that comfortable as Sila moved off it, settling in at a two inch distance. He pulled up his sleeve and scratched his arm, eyes glued to the car.

'You're going to stay by my living room window all day or…' asked Chu, walking back over to the couch.

'Ne…'

'You sure?'

'I'm thinking.'

'Ja, too much. If it is Potočnik, he probably just wants to catch up. Talk about old times. Role play episodes of *Dibrivna Vaska*.'

Sila gave up his window position and joined his friend, propping himself up on the arm of the couch. Turning the TV screen on would draw attention so he focused on one of the Varo prints instead.

'Or maybe he needs you in Ljubljana,' continued Chu, picking up *The Red Book* from the table and flicking through. 'Some kind of diplomatic job overseas.'

'Maybe.'

'How to collaborate better with Ghana or Guangdong, something like that. Ne vem. The point is he likes you. Even after that *Veiled State* thing you wrote.'

'And if it's Maček?'

There was a knock on the front door, making both Chu and Sila jump a little. A few seconds later, the bell rang.

'The jacket?' asked Sila, springing up.

'Ja,' replied Chu, checking the window.

'Shit, he's persistent. What do I do?'

'Wait here.'

'What, where are you going?'

'Mount Peca.'

'Don't. Chu…'

She carried on towards the door and opened it wide enough for a tank to roll through. Words were exchanged, some of them complimenting Chu's koala top, then a shout came back into the living room.

'Hey, Sima-lite, you're wanted.'

Sila took a breath, squeezed his fingernails into his palm then walked to the door.

'Sila Črnic?' asked the jacket.

'Ja.'

'The Councillor of Progress would like to have a chat with you.'

'You mean Potočnik?'

The jacket flinched, his right hand disappearing behind his back.

'What does he want to chat about?'

'Ne vem. I'm just the driver.'

Sila glanced at the blue stripe on the man's jacket, trying to bring back the moisturizer image. 'Now?'

'Ja.'

'Just me?'

'Ja.'

'Can he not call me instead?'

Another flinch, this one sustained. 'If he could, I wouldn't be standing here.'

Sila looked at the car parked out front, pretending like it was the first time he was seeing it. The windows were clear enough, but that wasn't definite. Chu had told him about the holographic gloss they'd invented in Ecuador.

'How long will this chat take?'

'Ne vem.'

Sila nodded, he didn't know why.

'The councillor said you didn't need to bring anything so probably not long.'

'Okay. Well...actually, I was planning on going to Ljubljana anyway, for a week or two, but I haven't packed yet. Haven't even got my suitcase out, to be honest. Ja, it's probably easier if you go back on your own. I can take the train and see him tomorrow.'

'Not enough time.'

'Okay…then I'll get the train and try to see him this afternoon. Is that any better?'

'My instructions are to take you now.'

'But I haven't packed anything.'

'You can come back and pack later. Or find new clothes in Ljubljana.'

'It's that urgent?'

'Ja.'

Sila looked back at Chu, hoping for a new excuse buried in discreet body language.

She was plucking fluff out of her eyebrows.

Could be something.

Fluff equals the guy, eyebrows equals this Earth. Plucking equals beating him unconscious with her Jung book.

The jacket looked at his tab, making irritated breathing sounds. 'The sooner we leave…'

'Ja, one minute.'

'For what?'

'My Erazem Card,[15] make sure I've got it. My tab as well.'

'Try your jacket pocket.'

'They're not there,' Sila lied.

The jacket's eyes went to Sila's pockets, his expression *in statu fluxu*. 'Okay,' he said, adding on a faint grunt. 'One minute.'

Sila narrowed the door gap and pretended to scan the room. He checked his jacket pockets just in case then turned to Chu, gave her a hug and whispered in her ear, 'I'll call you tonight, if I don't come back.'

'Tell Potočnik I said hi.'

'Ja…'

'And that I'm very focused on my work.'

'Clearly.'

Sila let go and followed the jacket to the car.

---

[15] A type of donation card, tied to its owner and their collective, primarily used when they visit other collectives and need to 'pay' for occasional non-mandatory services. Temporary Erazem Cards can be procured in cases where the main card is forgotten or misplaced.

Surprisingly, the man was considerate enough to open the door for him, though Sila knew cops used to do that too sometimes, before the *Nestification Jaunt.*[16]

'Sila-foam,' someone or something shouted.

Sila was already in the car when he heard it, so he could only turn round and look out the rear window. Gašper was jogging down the street, one hand clamped on his orange headband, the other waving his way.

Luckily the jacket was a fast mover and had the engine started by the time Gašper reached the back of the car.

'Hey, where you going?' he shouted, tapping the back window.

'Talk to Chu,' Sila mouthed back, pointing at the woman still in her pyjamas.

Gašper stared at him like a shop dummy and repeated his first question. But the jacket didn't seem to care as the car was already moving off, almost clipping the car in front as it went.

'Ex-boyfriend?' asked the jacket, looking at Sila through the rear-view mirror.

'Friend.'

'Seems sad to see you go.'

'Ja.'

The car turned a corner, onto the main road. The jacket didn't bother checking to see if other cars were coming.

'If this were Vladivostok,' Sila muttered.

The jacket looked back, popping up his eyebrows. 'Vladivostok?'

'Nothing.'

Sila looked out the window, checking for witnesses. There were plenty. Bled was never a dull place. But none of them were looking his way.

Why would they?

It was Slovenia, not Vladivostok, not California, not Tianjin.

---

[16] The defeat of Šarec's Govt in 2081, leading to the consolidation of anarcho-communism in Slovenia. Or a close approximation of it.

~~~

The drive to Ljubljana was quiet and uneventful and full of eclectic scenery. Fields. Turbines. Signal towers. Ringed villages. Snow-capped mountains in the distance [real, not matte].

Sila hadn't come this way for a long time, nearly half a year, and even then he'd just been getting the bus to the Tokamak. Not for a tour, just to sit outside it, feel its power.

When they drove past the triple-dome structure this time, the jacket glanced over, mumbled, 'pretty tempting target,' then went back to the road.

Sila almost laughed.

Tempting for who?

The consultants who'd tried to privatise it two months after it opened? The ones who lied about its power output, saying it was the basic equivalent of a college dynamo? Or the fuckers who'd tried to divert the conduits away from the North-Eastern collectives?

He knew the answer. The jacket probably knew it too.

The car kept going, on auto-drive whenever the jacket wanted to smoke, and after an hour or so started passing through the larger collectives outside Ljubljana.

Nothing much had changed in the last two years, far as he could see, though only the outer ring houses and the occasional graffiti wall were visible. The organs of them could be completely different, could've been hollowed out and commercialized while he'd been *theorising* in Bled and he wouldn't know a thing about it. Just like the new rehab policy.

He squeezed the bottom left corner of his lip, pulling out a pinch of fat then letting it slowly fall back.

Ne, too far. A story that substantial, the media would've reported on it for weeks. *Morda Ni Hudič*, one of the *Pravi Veronika*[17] crew, even *Nov Večer*…

---

[17] To keep it simple: Morda Ni Hudic = traditional anarchist zine; Pravi Veronika = radical anarchist zine platform open to any citizen reporter; Nov Večer = liberal/conservative media
~~~

Unless…

Unless they normalised it.

He picked his tab up off the seat and clicked on *Pravi Veronika*. The usual Bakunin silhouette then the twenty most recent articles, no priority given to name or topic.

Scrolling down, he saw a few about surprise deportations, one about the Koban policy, and that was it. All the others were either complaining about Filter Hall initiatives or eulogising dead fights. Nothing about collectives being hollowed out.

As if hearing his thoughts, the driver steered left, possibly avoiding traffic on the highway ahead, and headed towards Ježica.

This time they went dart-like through the middle, passing bike rentals, non-franchise cafes, artisan trades, meditation centres, fight academies, forum courtyards, the usual mix of unusual stuff that the more populous collectives were famous for, and that adventurists sought to erode.

Mentally, he let out a long breath, not willing to perform his sense of relief physically to the jacket at the wheel.

Still a collective, still diverse.

The car kept going, breaking into the nucleus, the main community oval half full with off-the-grid tourists and residents. He'd only come to Ježica once before, when he was young, but everyone knew about the animal-protection scheme so he wasn't surprised when he saw monkeys doing cartwheels on the grass.

Out of the corner of his eye, he saw the driver shaking his head, but there was no mumbling so he blocked him out.

What a beautiful sight, a collective iris in the sunshine. Ne, that wasn't fair. They were beautiful in winter too; the lanterns up, the mulled wine stop-offs, monkeys in ski jackets, kids spraying the walls with surprisingly good puns. Other kids just writing *DICK*.

---

within an anarcho-communist framework that yearns for the days of representative democracy. These are the three big ones.

Ah, well, you had to take the bad with the better. No one person was a saint, and some were outright despicable. The only question was: did they have a system behind them?

Did they have the power to poison things?

Sila turned in his seat and scanned the buildings opposite, checking the individual names on the shop signs.

There was one he recognized, but that was a 4-shop local chain, not too bad.

No sign of *Dole Burger.*[18]

No *You NEED It.*

No *Calvinist Coffee.*

Thank the Gods.

He'd read a piece online, just before the *Serpentinšek* article had leaked, about some outside consultants coming in and promoting the *Because You Like It* policy used in Australia; a complete removal of all franchise limits, with the natural cap levelling out at fifteen stores per city, as in most companies reached that number before accepting what they had. Basically, a law that would let the adventurists back into Slovenia. According to those consultants, it was inevitable, so why not get ahead of it and set the rules ourselves. Their suggestion: start with a ten-shop limit and go from there. For whatever reason it clearly hadn't passed the Council. At least not from what Sila was seeing outside.

Maybe that was Potočnik related too? Doing damage control after the article?

But wouldn't he have done that anyway? Protect the collectives, keep out capital; wasn't that the whole history of his political career?

He thought back to the first *Serpentinšek* article, one of the main points.

[18] International franchises like Dole Burger were primarily allowed in tourist areas, e.g. near Triple Bridge in Ljubljana, but no more than three in the whole country, and each one had to operate under Slovene laws e.g. limited working hours, equal surplus value distribution. This policy was replicated in most Alliance nations as a reluctant olive branch to the adventurists [possibly a mistake – never turn your back on a Breen]

His strategy relies on absence and presence; absence from the centre of power structures, presence in the streets, filter halls, poster campaigns, both within a strict ratio.

It wasn't the tidiest line ever written, but the point was clear enough. He, the careful tyrant, needs you to ask the question you'll inevitably ask after reading this article: would he really bother doing all that?

Sila realized the car had stopped and he was staring at a man training a Celje goat. Neither one seemed too bothered that they were inches away from the main road, so Sila tried not to feel bothered either.

Chu's right, he told himself.

Even if the article were true, what was the point? It didn't give Potočnik any real power. If anything it made him seem weak, unsure, like a man who'd read about Ceausescu's execution a hundred times and his gold palace adventure only once.

The man outside held up a box and made it beep, triggering the goat to run into his right leg and fall over. Sila leaned forward, waiting to see if the goat would get back up, but it didn't, it just lay there with its legs up, either knocked out cold or bored.

Another few seconds and the legs fell too.

The man bent down and slapped the goat, once, twice, but it was no good, the goat was out cold. Two other men walked over and said something, but the car was moving again and the scene was gone.

Must be a deceptively strong leg, thought Sila, sitting back and noticing the jacket looking at him through the rear-view mirror.

~~~

Just over an hour later, Sila stood with his arms behind his back in what was legally referred to as the Council Chamber of Collective Representatives. However, this name was both too bland and too alienating for most Slovenes, so they usually just called it *The House of Ne* instead.

Side note: before it was a council chamber, the building had functioned as an art commune, and before that a military barracks, the sum of which probably had some irony tucked in somewhere.

The room itself wasn't overbearing, the ceiling didn't stretch up into infinity like a cathedral, but it was big enough to create a certain sense
~~~

of prestige. In the middle of the room was a mural of historical [i.e. dead] Slovene activists painted onto the floor, and around that were three elevated rows of single desks; one for each councillor and secondary delegate, as well as a fourth row at the back for independent notaries and press.

In truth, it was a lot of furniture for something that functioned primarily as a rubber stamp committee, *ja* and *ne*, but no one seemed to mind. Even Sila didn't care that much, and he was always suspicious of anything too extravagant-looking.

It was only a building.

A glorified information exchange centre.

Didn't actually control anything.

As was his custom, Potočnik was seated on the left side of the room, on a chair that looked no different to any of the one hundred and eighty-eight others. Of course, all those other chairs were empty due to the fact that only eighteen of the elected councillors lived in the capital and, of those eighteen, only Potočnik used the Chamber as a personal office.

That's another thing the article said, thought Sila, waiting for Potočnik to stop playing with his tab. *The strategy calls for a de-centring in optics as well as activity.*

Well, that was easy when the whole layout was de-centred. Unless of course you were the sole councillor in the room; then you'd always be in the centre, while still maintaining plausible deniability. *It's not my fault I'm the only one here.*

Sila looked at the other chairs, the absence of counter-power, felt his mind go Maoist, and quickly refocused on the person he'd been driven in to see.

Nikola Adama Potočnik.

The man who'd started out as an activist and ended up an on-and-off councillor. The man who everyone over forty-five knew personally from the Šarec era protests, and everyone under forty-five, like Sila, knew about from media profiles. The man who always refused to play guitar in front of more than three people. Now the man who regularly held forums with hundreds in each collective. It was weird having an old revolutionary, a legend, still on the ramparts, still holding a position of influence. Or still in the public eye, at least.[19] Nineteen years ago, before Potočnik had helped found this place [while simultaneously arguing against it], a young Sila probably could've sat down on the chair next to him and said, 'what's up, fuckhead?' But now...

'Sorry about that...'

Sila switched back on, startled slightly by the sudden purple of Potočnik's eyes.

'You're still standing? Sit, prosim.'

'I didn't know if I-...'

'Make yourself comfortable.'

Sila coughed and put himself down on the seat reserved for notaries. Instinctively, he scanned the desk in front. Nothing there. Normal for notaries, they were there to notarize. Councillors on the other hand...

He glanced left and saw Potočnik's personalized space. A model of the ship from *Dibrivna Vaska* beside two framed photos of his favourite actors: Daniel Auteuil and Gian Maria Volonté.

[Note: According to rumour, Potočnik had once proposed drunkenly to Volonté's great grandson that he be naturalized as a Slovene citizen. The perks offered: a seat on the first Alliance trip to Mars. A seaweed green factory jacket copied from stills of *La Classe Operaia Va in Paradiso*. And a decent-looking Slovene man to do all the dirty shit his husband wouldn't. Volonté's great grandson, under pressure from the Italian Government, declined.]

Potočnik placed the tab on the desk and stretched his arms backwards, wincing a little. 'Lower back. Too much sitting down, I suspect.' He put his arms back on the desk and pushed himself straight against the chair. 'Tell me, how's the sedate field of lakeside theory, comrade?'

'Relaxed. Relaxing. Maybe too much so.'

---

[19] If it's not already clear, there is no legislative or executive power in the National Council; it is an institution of necessity set up to deal with inter-collective policy, as well as international and Alliance-focused matters. On all issues, it relays the will of each councillor's collective through that councillor [delegate, in effect], with 98% of actions coming from consensual decision making on a local level. In short: power flows from the bottom to the top. Of course, every system has its cracks.

'Ah, I envy you. Another year of this and I'll probably do the same thing. Lose myself on the hiking trails somewhere.'

'Triglav has some good ones.'

'Ja, I did most of them when I was young. I suppose I could try them again. Maybe settle in Bled and work alongside you in the canteen.'

'Actually, councillor, I switched to environmental care. Two days a week.'

Potočnik tilted his head left and kept it that way.

'Gives me more time to think,' Sila added, pretending to notice something on the back of his hand and dusting it off.

'Ah, your theory. And how is that proceeding?'

'The theory? It's-...'

'Ne, don't answer that. Too much weight attached. Whatever state it's presently in, that is your business.'

Sila looked down at the blank desk in front of him, thinking how to respond.

'Really, you don't need to comment. The ACF[20] gave you four years and, if we go by Kapok, the first five years of any theory is the killing of ideas.'

'Ja.'

Potočnik straightened his lips. 'Ja, Your Purpleness.'

'Sorry?'

'My new title. I should've told you when you came in, but it must've slipped my mind.'

'Title?'

'Ja, as an alternative to councillor. Your Purpleness. A sign of respect, but also humility.'

'Purpleness?'

'My eyes, obviously. Many find such a bold colour unsettling. Hence, your Purpleness.'

---

[20] Arts & Culture Forum, an inter-collective body that sponsors the things in their title, including philosophical theory. Not such a big deal, really. Just means people are more likely to read your shit. Criticized by some for trying to re-create hierarchy in the arts and using pretentions language to promote projects in the filter halls.

'Oh.'

'Oh, Your Purpleness. I'm sorry, comrade, but I insist on everyone using it. Even friends. Not that I'm a tyrant, of course.'

Sila opened his mouth to ask who exactly everyone was in this context, but then he remembered another line from the *Serpentinšek* article: *the essence of a tyrant is insecurity; hence an artificial essence must be constructed on top for him to evade detection. In short: constant ownings online plus self-deprecation in person.*

'It's okay to dissent, if you wish…'

Sila looked at Potočnik, but could only manage a second before going back to the blank desk. 'Ne, it's fine.'

'Are you certain?'

'It's just a name.'

Potočnik glanced at the poster of Gian Maria Volonté to his right. He tapped his fingers against the arm of the throne, looked stern for a moment longer then changed instantly into his clown face.

'I'm joking, Sila.'

'Sorry?'

'Obviously joking. Call me Your Purpleness? It's ludicrous. But you're the seventeenth person who's fallen for it.'

'It did seem strange.'

'Yet you still accepted it, ne?'

'I did.'

'Troubling. Perhaps I need to dial down the glare a bit. Seems to make people accede to whatever I say. Which is not a good thing after all those rumours last year.'

'It's my fault, I've probably been in Bled too long.'

'Ne, you're not alone. Ever since those articles came out, circumspection has increased. You know they're making a serial out of those things?'

'Out of six articles?'

'The same writer, Serpentinšek, or whatever his real name is, they offered him a deal to stretch out the concept. Eighteen episode run, I believe.'

'About the Council being controlled by a zombie Šarec?'

Potočnik laughed. 'It's satire, Sila. If we can't make fun of our ceremonial councillors, sorry, crypto-dictators, our society's doomed.'

'Ja, I suppose. Satire is important.'

'Crucial.'

'And no one really thinks anyone in the Council is a secret dictator.'

'Oh they do. Quite a few of them, in fact.'

'No one serious.'

'But they also think Amma Darko is a hologram created by Jeff Fahey Mark#6. And that alien telepaths are controlling the tectonic plates so they can manipulate Japan into taking over banana production in Central America. Insane stuff, very worrying.'

Sila nodded.

'You've heard all this?'

'Again, I'm a bit out of the loop in Bled. Haven't been paying much attention to the news.'

'Then why did you nod?'

'The Amma Darko theory. My friend told me that one.'

'Which friend?'

'Someone I know in Bled. Not really a friend, but she has family in Ghana.'

'She keeps up to date.'

'Ja.'

'Does this friend have a name?'

Sila coughed. 'Just a friend. No one famous.'

Potočnik tapped three fingers on the desk, no real melody.

'I should probably get to the point. All these conspiracy theories can suck you into some dark places if you're not careful, and I believe we have to be out of here by three.'

Sila glanced at the clock on the far wall. Ten past one. Not too late.

'What I want from you, Sila, the reason I asked you to come here; it is extremely important.'

'I understand, councillor.'

'Councillor…' Potočnik scratched his neck, repeating the title a few more times. 'Even that seems a bit strange.'

'Isn't that what most people call you?'

'This term, ja, but recently it's started to grate. A bit too hierarchical for my taste. How about we try Nik?'

'If you like…Nik.'

'Better. Much better. Now, back to business. You've heard of our ion engine test next week, I assume?'

Sila shook his head.

'You haven't heard anything?'

'As I said, I've been out of the loop.'

'Focused on theory, okay. Well, an ion engine test is only half the truth. Something we fed the media to lower expectations and, ah, you know how they are.'

'I know how *Nov Večer* is, but-…'

'Ja, that one and others. Obviously, we'll tell them eventually, when the time is apt.'

'*We*?'

'Us. The collectives.'

'They voted on it?'

'Ni panike, it's only a slight delay, and nothing consequential. More like an added surprise than anything. They'll understand.'

Sila mouthed a half-hearted *ja* and looked over at the Council floor, where all the historical Slovenes - Alma M Karlin, Edvard Kardelj, Tadej Kobal et al - were facing away from him.

'So, the truth of things. We *are* launching the old ship, but not for a test run of the engine, for an actual mission.'

'Mission?'

'And I want you to be part of it.'

Sila opened his mouth to yell *no fucking way*, but common sense stopped him. Still…no fucking way. A spaceship? How? When? It couldn't be the one that-…

'To be more specific, I want you to be the captain.'

Sila coughed. 'Sorry?'

'Of course, the position demands a certain degree of prestige. Therefore, you will be given a council-issue militia uniform, the same uniform worn by our soldiers for the last three centuries…'

'Uniform?'

'...as well as silver buttons and a silver badge, all the usual regalia to show everyone you're the captain.'

'Wait, this is-...' Sila paused, clearing non-existent phlegm from his throat. 'Sorry...Nik, I'm confused. You're talking about space exploration. I'm a political theorist.'

'Of course, and you can still write your theory. Only now you'll have even more solitude in which to do it.'

Sila sensed, hoped, prayed to the old Sumerian gods that Potočnik was joking again, but he couldn't say it outright as there was a slim chance he wasn't.

'Do you accept this great honour, Sila?'

'Ne vem. Is it optional?'

Potočnik smiled. 'You really are bad at this.'

'Sorry?'

'I'm joking. Again. You will not have to prance about as a space captain.'

Sila rubbed his palm against his sleeve, removing most of the sweat. 'And the ship?'

'It's mostly run by AI, far as I'm aware. Don't fret, not the lunatic one. That's essentially a myth anyway. The idea that an AI would slaughter us all to protect itself, pure paranoia.'

'But...I'm not actually going on the ship, am I?'

'Ne. I'm happy to say that part was accurate.'

'I am going?'

Potočnik pressed his hands together, no clapping noise. 'For four glorious years.'

'Sorry?'

'More than enough time to finish your theory.'

'Four years...in space?'

'Ne, much more than just space, Sila. Much, much more.'

There was a noise at the back of the room. Sila turned and saw the same jacket who'd driven him there, putting boxes on a table.

'Rhetoric aside, this journey is very important for our country. For the Alliance nations too. Crucial even. You may not have noticed from your perch in Bled but we've got a problem, something gigantic coming our way.'

'Adventurists?'

'Ne, worse than that.'

'Nationalism?'

'Entropy, Sila. Cultural entropy. I wish it weren't so, but the evidence is undeniable. Our best sociologists have predicted another twenty years before our citizens, all Alliance citizens in fact, start to feel non-plussed about our achievements. Not just the tangible victories, but the system itself. We're too utopian, we're not utopian enough, why does that collective get a bigger budget than ours. Ja, it's started already, Sila, I've witnessed it with my own eyes, on the streets, in the filter halls, whispers of it, some louder than that.'

'I've heard a little, but…is it that bad?'

'Bad? Ja, burgeoning, definitely growing that way. Another twenty years and we crumble. But you're right too, Sila. The adventurists, the regional hegemonies, they're waking up, stretching their talons again…'

'Again?'

'…mostly thanks to the Brumen problem.[21] Ja, I know, they were never really asleep, but Brumen, as much as we all love him, gave them a way back in, propaganda-wise. You know the argument, I'm sure: why should someone so talented, one guy, not be allowed to keep all his hard-earned wealth? On top of that, we've had the Sirena debacle, Alenka Unk emigrating on a skiff to California, the Australia legislation. Ja, statistically, it's tiny, but it's a crack, Sila, something for them to wedge open.'

'No system is perfect.'

'And it's not just one crack, they'll inevitably find more. And when they do, they'll infiltrate. Re-posit their own systems, show videos of

---

[21] A basketball star who made a ton of cash overseas then returned to Slovenia and, as per constitutional law, split 60% of his foreign earnings between all collectives and the collective of his birth, 15% to other Alliance nations, with the remaining 25% to be used on items or projects of his choosing. To Brumen, this was a beautiful thing. To adventurists and some old-school Slovenes, it was akin to slavery. Hence the so-called *problem.*

Serbian actors eating out of the trash, yap about the economy, and before we know it we'll all be investing in shoe companies and watching pro-military films again. Hyperbole, perhaps, but look what's happening in Ghana, the treatment of Amma Darko. We blindsided them before, got a foothold, but that was a temporary victory and we need to be ready for what comes next. Not tomorrow or five years later, but twenty years later, a hundred. We need to strengthen, be ready. Not glib nationalism, of course, but we need to defend our system, grow our system, work more with other Alliance nations in some centralised capacity; not a government, not a top-down state, but something unified in certain aspects. Ja, I know, it's a tricky balance, a minefield even, but the whirlwind is coming, Sila, coming for everything we've achieved. There is simply and sadly no choice.'

The words *Koper* and *Veiled State* slid down the walls of Sila's brain, but he let them slide. 'You think space is their target?'

'What better way to expand their exploitation than set up colonies and mining consortiums, attract workers, isolate them from the rest of Earth society and then…'

'…exploit them.'

'Precisely.'

Sila nodded, glancing back at the jacket, who had seemingly cloned himself as there was now a man of the exact same height and build [and lack of humour] standing next to him.

'According to the latest issue of *Space Seed*,' continued Potočnik, picking up the model of Ito's ship from his desk and running a finger down its needle tip, 'the best sites for colonization, in the inner system at least, are the ones that have already been targeted. Mars, Ceres, Venus and the Jovian Belt, either orbiting or grounded.'

'We're going to colonize them?'

'Obviously, Venus is a no go with all the adventurist satellites swarming around. Most of the Jovian moons are off limits due to ludicrous levels of radiation. And we'd have to deal with all the frontier mining groups if we went to Ceres…'

Sila feigned a cough.

'...which would be an exhausting business. Ideally, we'd just go straight to Triton or Pluto and set up camp there, mine all that hydrogen, but, unfortunately, we're not ready for the Kuiper Belt yet.'

This time he tried two coughs, leaving a hand at his side to make it more noticeable.

'Ja, what is it?'

'Sorry, the first one you said...not Venus.'

'Jovian?'

'Ja.'

Potočnik glanced at the floor mural, as if it were somehow related, then back at Sila. 'You don't understand this word?'

'All the science I know comes from *Dibrivna Vaska*. Which is why I'm probably not the right person for this mission. Nik.'

'The Jovian system is Jupiter and its moons. That entire region.'

'Ah, Jovian...'

'But that doesn't matter as your target will be Mars.'

'Wait, doesn't Jupiter already have bases? On its moons...'

'Scientific outposts, not really bases. As I said, the radiation is too dense, too difficult to settle there. Mars, on the other hand, is ripe for colonisation.'

'Sorry, I don't know much about Mars.'

Potočnik put Ito's ship gently back on the desk then raised a hand, a clear signal to the security jackets. A door opened and closed in the background. 'Not a problem. The soil's red, they have a mountain the size of a vertical Greece and there's a leftover base from when the Americans tried to live there. That's our target.'

'The Americans?'

'Ja, the old ones. Of course, the adventurists are there like locusts, but they're all in one area, far away from where you're gonna be. It'll be fine, they won't bother you. Ghana and Guangdong have already set up nearby in their own bases, and we'll be the third. Well, us, Norway, Ireland, Romania, Tehran and a few others. They'll follow after, in the other two ships. Ja, just a typical Alliance mission with us at the vanguard. All you need to do is get inside that base and renovate.'

'But I don't know how-...'

'Correction: the drones need to get in there and renovate, you can stick to basic housework and continue with your theory. That's the most important thing. Solitude and nature, just like Sima preached. And he was right. Ten years in the wilderness and look what he produced. That could be you Sila, in four years.'

Sila coughed, putting his eyes on Potočnik's desk, specifically the needle ship manned by diehard anarchists.

'Not an appealing vision?'

'Ne vem. Some people think Sima was too theoretical.'

'Which people?'

'Other theorists.'

'Because he didn't get his hands dirty? Nonsense. I can tell you first-hand, as someone who did do that. And paid for it.' Potočnik pulled his collar down, showing one of his Šarec era scars. 'Fibre-glassing is a volatile thing, comrade. Ne, more like a force than a thing. It picks you up, carries you along on pure emotion, until finally you're at the Council gates ready to stab anyone wearing a tank-top. Ne, theory is the way, trust me. In a quiet place without distraction. And I think you'll agree it doesn't get any quieter than the surface of Mars.'

Sila did something he hadn't done in public since he was a child; put his hands behind his head. Not in a lethargic, confident way, but to simply try and massage the burgeoning migraine out of his head.

Sadly, it didn't work. Things were too far along.

Turning the head rub into another [covered] cough, he looked around at the empty chairs, the floor murals, his own feet, until he came full circle to Potočnik's eerily benevolent face.

'Can I ask you a question, Nik?'

'About the mission? Ja.'

'It is quite blunt.'

'Go on.'

Sila coughed again, checking the jackets behind him. There was only one of them now, laid out in a torpid state on a box, reading his tab. 'Is someone putting me on this spaceship because of what happened two years ago?'

'What do you mean?'

'The things I wrote, about Koper. Criticizing the Council's interference there. The partisan bloc tactics.'

'The *Veiled State* piece?'

'Ja.'

Potočnik's face lost its creases, his purple eyes looking past Sila towards the end of the room. 'You wish to have the truth?'

'If possible.'

'Very well. Then the truth is,' the creases returned, 'ja. You're going because of your Koper article.'

'Okay.'

'After re-reading it, some of us decided that you were far too talented to keep on Earth so we voted to send you up into the stratosphere instead.'

'I see.'

'Ne, in all seriousness, it is about the article, but not the way you think. Slovenia needs people like you, Sila. Vigilant, critical, hopefully capable of writing decent theory. That's why I sponsored you for Bled, and why I'm now going one better and sending you to Mars. Obviously, it will piss Maček off too, which is always an added bonus.'

Potočnik laughed and looked at the wall to the left, at the picture of Daniel Auteuil looking anxious in *Caché*.

Sila looked at the same picture and tried to remember the movie. French cinema used to be popular in Slovenia before the jaunt, but he never watched a lot of it. He preferred Korean cinema, all those films about loneliness, depression and incest.

But this Daniel Auteuil film, was it the one where he had purple eyes and lied about sending a young Slovene man on a suicidal space mission because he'd written a polemic two years before? Or was it the one where Daniel Auteuil gaslit a panther?

'On to the details then. Next Monday will be the launch. Prepare yourself, eat good food, say goodbye to family and friends etcetera.'

Sila blinked and tried not to think of his family.

'You'll have to stay in Ljubljana until Monday, so if you need anything for the trip, you can buy it here. Books, sex toys, comfort blanket. Not too much though, there will be a weight limit, probably around

10kg. Don't worry about clothes, the ship will have plenty for everyone, quite stylish some of them. What else? Ja, nothing. I think that's it.' He stared at the *Dibrivna Vaska* model, Mojca Ito's iconic needle ship. 'Ne, wait, there's one more thing I forgot to mention. More happy news, in fact. One of your good friends will be going with you.'

'One of my friends?'

'I believe his name is Gašper.'

Sila scrambled a *who?* but his throat was too dry so he cleared it and tried again. 'What's his family name?'

'Ne vem. But he was recently released from a NOT YET Centre. I believe he was in there for a few years, something about domestic assault, or psychosis, one of the two. Do you know who I'm talking about?'

'Vaguely.'

'He is your friend, isn't he?'

'I guess.'

'You guess?'

'I haven't seen him for a few years, so…ne vem.'

'My sources told me the two of you were close.'

'Before, ja.'

Potočnik picked up his tab and swiped a few times, finally pulling an *ah* face. 'Let's see. You grew up in the same collective, in Šiška.'

'Ja.'

'You both like *Dibrivna Vaska,* as everyone should. You enjoy running, languages, the idea of playing the clarinet. Both of you can cook Tanzanian food. He has a positive attitude which balances nicely with your innate negativity…'

'That's all from your sources?'

Potočnik tapped the top of the tab. 'They are very thorough. Though in this case, I'm a bit worried that one friend won't be enough. How about that physicist friend of yours in Bled? Chu something? I'm sure she wouldn't mind joining the team.'

'Ne, she can't. Her work, it's very important to her. She wouldn't…'

'Two friends are better than one.'

'...have time to do anything on the ship or Mars, it's not her field. Gašper is fine, really, I don't need anyone else. Even just myself is okay, I don't mind solitude.'

Potočnik straightened against the back of his chair. 'Okay, we'll limit you to one crutch for now. See how it pans out.'

'Hvala.'

'We can always send her on the second ship, if life becomes too dull in the colony. Oh, that's another thing, which may be potentially unsettling to you. The spaceship will have no entertainment of any kind.'

'None?'

'Zero.'

'No screens?'

'Ne.'

'What about books?'

'None that you don't have on you.'

'Movies?'

'Ne.'

'Board games?'

Potočnik swatted away the question with his hand. 'Ha, this could go on forever. I was joking, Sila. Of course, there'll be entertainment, otherwise you'd all kill each other before you reached Mars.'

Sila wasn't sweating, but wiped his forehead out of residual instinct. Behind him, the door opened and closed again.

'Now, I have some documents to shred, and Amma Darko's accommodation to arrange. Ahh, did I tell you she was coming?'

'I thought she was in prison again.'

'Ne, ne, she's out. All those charges were discovered to be fabricated, which I knew all along. Amma Darko a crypto-fascist? I'd build a statue of Šarec before I ever believed that nonsense.'

Sila sucked in his lips. He'd read other things about Amma Darko, disturbing things, but, he decided while looking at the needle ship again, better not to share with a man this deep in her corner.

'I think I've covered everything. If you have any more questions, ask that guy over there.' He pointed to the back of the room, where a

Japanese man in a green scientist coat was standing monument-like beside the two jackets. 'He's Nakagami, one of our best scientists.'

'But, what if I have questions after next Monday, post-launch?'

'No matter. I'm sending Nakagami with you.'

'You don't need him here?'

'Ja, ideally, but things are a little imbalanced at the moment. Need to shift a few chairs around. Besides, he's a scientist, and I'm sending him where the science is. Who wouldn't be happy?'

Sila stared past Potočnik, at the committed frown of Gian Maria Volonté.

'Now, off you go, comrade. Have a few drinks, build up excitement, whatever you need to do.'

'Ja, I'll try.'

'And Sila…'

'Ja?'

'Make Slovenia proud.'

~~~

It was 37 degrees outside, impossibly hot, as hot as a rocket exhaust, thought Sila as he wandered philosopher-like by the river, passing people eating in the restaurants, some of them asking the waiters for industrial-size fans to stop their constant sweating.

For some reason, he wasn't sweating at all.

Perhaps his brain hadn't sent out the signals yet.

But it should have, he thought, crossing the triple bridge, dodging two environment drones that didn't seem to be doing much cleaning, and heading down the less touristy side.

Spaceship to Mars.

Four years.

It didn't make sense. He was a cultural-political theorist, a sociologist, a guy who wrote how shit things were even if everyone else thought they were okay.

And now he was off to Mars.
~~~

He sat down on a bench next to an old man with the arm ripped off his jacket, fixing his eyes on the railing opposite.

According to his brief conversation with Nakagami, Slovenia's best and least publicised scientist, they would take the elevator up to high-orbit, switch to the ship that had melted the previous year then use the new model of ion engine[22] to cruise over to their new temporary home.

'It's 87% safe,' Nakagami said as they'd walked back out of the Council building, the two jackets lurking behind, 'the part that melted has been replaced and improved.'

'That's reassuring.'

'Correct. If it had been anything under 70%, I would've contacted my lawyer and made adjustments to my will.'

'I don't have a lawyer.'

'Ja, you do. It is a protected right in all collectives, without quality gaps. Each legal rep is placed into a large hat and selected by the defendant in a lucky draw.'

'Isn't that just for major criminal cases?'

'Not since last year.'

'A new law?'

'Passed by all collectives, and co-signed in its infancy by our Mars sponsor, Councillor Potočnik. One of his rare successes.'

'Rare?'

'Or perhaps visible is a more accurate word.'

'I didn't notice it.'

Nakagami coughed. 'Relatively visible.'

After that, one of the jackets had tapped Nakagami on the waist and taken him to a waiting car, leaving Sila free to roam.

And now he was on this bench, not far from his old collective, trying to think of non-tyrannical reasons why Potočnik was doing this to him.

'Too hot,' said the old man next to him.

'Ja.'

'Elbow sweating.'

---

[22] At this point, fusion drives show promise but are still 19.6 years away.

Sila turned and saw the man trying to bite off the other sleeve of his jacket.

'You could take it off?'

'Ja, vem.'

'I mean, the jacket. You can take it off.'

'Good.'

The old man continued biting, making limited progress, occasionally raising his head and saying, 'too hot.'

Sila wondered which would happen first, Monday's launch, or the old man freeing himself from his jacket.

Four more days. Or three and a half as it was already mid-afternoon.

A group of clouds that didn't look like anything in particular drifted in front of the sun, followed by a group of four men in blue stripe jackets appearing from a nearby car. At least three of them looked like they'd been in the Dok Militia, or the Šarec fan groups, and the fourth just looked mean.

They idled by the car for a minute or two, then two tourists ran over, possibly Ghanaian, and took a picture with them. Three of the jackets managed a smile, while the fourth stood there rod straight, like a robot waiting for its dial to be turned to the murder setting. Other tourists came over, more happy pictures were taken, and the four thugs gradually phased into a type of patrol duty. Sila waited until they were a bridge away then lifted himself off the bench and continued along the river.

That was the third time since he'd left the Council that he'd seen a group of four Koban jackets moving around, and if that was happening in the city centre, where the tourists were, then what was going on elsewhere?

The top of Sadia's head appeared, a metal pipe floating above it. A dark shadow, possibly a jacket…

He turned and crossed over the river, taking the familiar route back to his collective.

If this really was happening, he thought, if Mars was on the cards, he had to tell her. At least let her know that he wouldn't be dead or *disappeared* during the next four years.

~~~

The flat he'd grown up in, nineteen years with Sadia and their mum, nine years just the two of them, was on the third floor of a pre-independence building that looked run-of-the-mill nostalgic on the outside but, once past the main door, was relatively modern.[23] Like every other Ljubljana collective, the old had been transformed into the new. The only real holdout from adventurist times was the passcode pad on the front door, and that was only there because Sadia had reservations about a possible pervert downstairs.

Luckily, the code was still the same.

Even luckier, Sila could remember it within three attempts.

He pushed open the door, called out 'Sadia' then stopped and stared straight ahead.

There were blue marks on the wall by the kitchen. On the ceiling too. He knew from history lessons in primary school what that meant. The flat had been marked as a *den of subversion*. Anyone caught living there, no matter how fascist they claimed to be, would be detained without trial or appeal.

But that was over thirty years ago, not now. Was this a joke? Had Sadia done this?

He walked closer to the wall, touching the blue mark with his finger. Flaky and dry.

'Sadia…' he called again.

No answer.

He kept going, turning left.

The living room was fairly tidy, except for four boxes of green tea on the floor, and the TV wasn't on, which would've been creepy.

'Sadia, it's me. Sila.'

---

[23] As per collective policy in the cities, existing infrastructure that had either been abandoned, damaged, previously bought as investment capital or a third home [second homes survived the initial cut - an olive branch to liberals] was renovated and reassigned. Adventurists tried to rally around the free market concept, dressing up as small business owners and parading around with Tito vampire pics, but it didn't do much good; the curtain had dropped and the people were pissing on it.
~~~

Still no answer.

Was she sleeping?

The two bedrooms flashed into his mind, hers warm and heavily decorated, his stark and barely used.

He turned to leave, spotting something mid-turn. On the desk, sticking out from his sister's giant Cheshire cat cushion, was a note. He walked over and read it:

'If you ever come back, Sila, and are reading this, I've done what you did and left. Can't sleep here anymore. Prosim, don't try to contact me. Sadia.'

Next to the note was a second note, with different handwriting:

'We regret to inform you that your sister/daughter/wife [Prosim, clarify your relationship when next at Council of Health or Council HQ] is mentally ill and has been taken for treatment. If you wish to request the location of the specific NOT YET Centre she has been taken to, you may visit either the Council of Health next to Council HQ or the newly-established Council of Citizenry Support in Bežigrad. If not, we will contact you when she is ready to return. Ni panike, she will be well taken care of.

Yours,

Council of Health Medical Team.'

Sila read both notes then dropped them on the floor. There was a chance the second note was a lie, but…

Ne, it couldn't be. The Council of Health may have been one of the few non-collective orgs in Slovenia, and therefore suspect, but their doctors were generally regarded as good people. And they wouldn't have bothered with a note if they hadn't actually taken her.

He put his hand on the Cheshire cat cushion, stroking slowly down the side of its grinning face.

That was it then, confirmed. She really was just like mum. They both were. Only in different doses and rates of decay.

Sadia's turn was now, his was…when?

Tomorrow?

Halfway to Mars?

He walked back into the hallway, ignoring the blue marks, and pushed open the door farthest down on the left.

Gods, even you, he thought, sitting on the edge of Sadia's bed, stroking an empty frame that he was sure used to hold a photograph of her.

How had she deteriorated this fast? Why hadn't she told him? At least an e-mail. Hey, I'm struggling, prosim, come back. Or prosim, don't come back. And the blue marks all over the wall, mum never did that, never took photos out of the frames…

There was a knock at the front door.

Sila gripped the photo frame, pausing his breath.

Who was that? Jackets?

The Health Council?

There was another knock, not so loud. He exhaled along with the sound.

Probably a neighbour.

Maybe they could tell him what had happened to Sadia, if the notes were fake or not?

He placed the frame carefully on the desk and walked back out into the hall. It was darker now, so he flicked the light and muttered, 'fuck,' when nothing happened. The bulb was still broken? After two years? Or she'd put in a new one and that had broken too?

There was another knock, louder this time.

He resisted the urge to shout *wait* or *coming* just in case it was the jackets, and crept up slowly on the entrance.

The door was without silhouette, the stairs beyond it eerily quiet. He took a breath, told himself it was his own flat, he'd done nothing wrong, gripped the handle and opened it.

The outside stairs were clear, as was the alcove to the side.

He slipped out and peered over the railings of the main staircase. There were no footsteps, no birds-eye view of anyone's head. He went back in, keeping a hand on the edge of the door, and looked at the shelf to the side. There was something that hadn't been there earlier, a screwdriver with its tip covered in blue. Dry paint? He picked it up, scratched at it, pushing the door shut with his other hand. But there was no noise.

No lock mechanism being re-trapped. Mouthing *fuck*, he turned to finish the job before-

'Sila-foam…'

Hearing a rough voice and glimpsing a figure larger than Sadia emerge from the shadows outside put Sila into survival mode, and he stabbed forward blindly. The owner of the voice, not seeming to realise he was an intruder, had continued forward and met the defensive thrust head on. A whole third of the screwdriver vanished inside his abdomen, stayed there for two seconds then slid back out.

The figure fell to the floor, groaning, hands trying to cover the wound.

Sila blinked, hearing the groans, seeing the shaded orange of the man's headband.

'Gašper?'

'Wah…'

'Fuck, it is you. What you doing? Why didn't you say anything?'

Gašper answered by coughing up blood.

'You fucking idiot. Your stomach…'

'Help.'

'I could've-…'

Sila gave up on words and threw the screwdriver at the wall, his eyes ballooning in panic when he saw it bounce off and hit his old friend on the cheek.

'Fuck…' Gašper spat, slapping at the scratch on his face.

'Accident, I didn't-…'

'Antro-D.'

'I didn't mean to…'

'Bathroom.'

'…do that.'

'Clinic.'

'What, Antro-D? Where?'

'Quickly.'

Sila hovered like a drunk medic for a moment, thoughts careening off lobe walls, hands doing a vague kind of wringing motion over his old friend's gut, then something snapped and he repeated the word, 'bathroom.'

'Antro-D…' repeated Gašper, bringing up more blood.

'Okay. Ja. I think it's-…'

Sila started running, reaching out for the handle of the bathroom door. If he was fast enough, he could still…

He flung open drawers and bottles and tubs of beauty products he'd never noticed before until he found the green stuff he was looking for.

The bottle was strange. There was no label, no warning symbols, no use by date. If there were any other containers of green liquid in the room, he would've been stumped.

Slovene medical tech, it really was something. Or Alliance tech to be more accurate.

Taking the syringe from the cupboard, he ran back into the hallway. Gašper was still slumped against the wall, too spent to even cough up more blood.

Sila checked his pulse, muttered something and loaded what looked like green syrup into the syringe. He'd never used this stuff before, but from what he'd heard, it really did work.

He leaned over Gašper's neck and found the right spot.

'I'm sorry, Gaš…this may hurt a bit.'

The needle went in, the green syrup circulated, the brain switched back on then, four minutes later, Gašper sat up and burst out, 'wah, what the fuck?'

Sila looked at the needle, half-surprised. 'It worked.'

'What's that thing? Why am I on the floor?'

'Antro-D. You were…'

Gašper tried to get to his feet, making it halfway up before his eyelids folded, then closed completely, and the rest of him slumped down back onto the floor.

'Gašper?'

'Tired…' he mumbled, saliva seeping out the side of his mouth.

'Is it working?'

'Ne, work…sleep first.'

Sila bent down and put his arm around Gašper's neck, trying to figure out a way to move him without opening up the wound.

'I'm gonna try to lift you.'

'Ne…'

'Take you down to the clinic, check if the drug is working.'

'Bed…'

'Come on, up.'

~~~

According to the doctor, Sila had managed to both save and endanger his friend at the same time: saved him by injecting Antro-D, and almost killed him by single-handedly dragging him down to the clinic.

'I didn't know if it was working,' Sila said, leaning against the wall outside, watching the doctor munch his way through a pineapple bun. 'His eyes shut and it looked like-…'

'After injections, let them rest.' The doctor pointed through the clinic window. 'There's posters for this everywhere, it's very clear, yet no one ever follows it.'

'I forgot. Sorry.'

'Lucky for you, it was only a B wound, not an A.'

'Will there be any long term damage?'

'Doubtful.'

'No internal cuts or…'

The doctor held up the remaining half of his pineapple bun, quickly chewing through the bit already in his mouth.

'Sorry.'

The doctor nodded, swallowing. 'Antro-D takes care of all the inside stuff. It's even buttressed his testosterone level so he doesn't have to deal with any more booster jabs.'

'Ever?'

'Unless his androgen count dries up for some reason, ja. As for his present condition, just get some soup and water inside him, let him sleep, and he should be back on his feet by tomorrow morning.'

'It's okay to move him again?'
~~~

'As long as it's not far, ja.'

Sila nodded, noticing a poster in the window that looked like it'd been scribbled by a child. Despite the poor technique, the subject was clear enough; Potočnik in a doctor's uniform, surrounded by animal nurses. 'What about notification forms?'[24]

'Sorry?' asked the doctor, the last piece of bun just shoved in his mouth.

'For the treatment. Gašper doesn't live here.'

He finished chewing, brushing crumbs off his hands. 'It's no problem, he's covered by you.'

'Sorry, I don't live here either.'

'That's not what your file says. Sila Črnic, brother of Sadia, correct?'

'Ja.' Sila looked left at a kid kicking an implant jelka tree. 'But I've been in Bled for two years, I thought-…'

'Doesn't matter. Your sister kept the file active.'

'She did?'

'Unless you registered as a local in Bled?'

'Ne, not medically.'

'You're sure?'

'I wasn't ever sick.'

'Okay then. No notification needed.' The doctor pulled a tab out of his jacket and skimmed through. 'How is Sadia by the way? Haven't seen her in a few months.'

'She's on holiday.'

'Ah, domestic? Swahili Coast? Iceland?'

Sila drifted off to the side, watching the mother of the tree-kicker pull him away, then said almost as a murmur, 'domestic.'

'Well, I'm glad she's doing okay. As for your patient, there's a Tanzanian kitchen in the west ring, does decent soup. You can fill him up there then take him straight to bed. No detours.'

---

[24] Don't wanna go overboard on footnotes explaining the system [around 500 should do it], but notification forms are for medical services outside of your own collective, as well as for foreign travel.

The clinic door opened and Gašper hobbled out, a nurse assisting him. Sila stepped forward to take over then stopped, noticing something in the park opposite.

'No power walking either.'

Two jackets had just appeared from a side street and were now walking round the edges of the grass, occasionally looking over towards the clinic.

'…and definitely no alcohol.'

'Understood,' said Sila, turning back to the doctor.

~~~

Sitting on a high stool behind the *TANZANIAN KITCHEN* sign in the window, the whole side street lit up opposite, Sila kept his head down and rowed his spoon in little circles around the edge of his bowl. On the slightly higher stool next to him, Gašper sucked the soup down like an old style vacuum cleaner.

'You're not eating?'

'Ja.'

'Doesn't look like it.'

Sila stopped stirring and put down his spoon.

'Even less like it now.'

'Are you sure you're okay?'

'Ja, I said already. I'm fine.'

'Your stomach…'

Gašper patted the table next to Sila's bowl. 'Stop stressing so much. Eat your soup. Or drink it.'

'I can't.'

'Try.'

Sila watched his friend return to his bowl, following an imaginary soup line from his throat down to the wound in his stomach.

'You're not trying.'

'Gašper, I stabbed you with a screwdriver.'

'Ja, then saved me.'

'Then almost killed you again by dragging you down to the clinic.'
~~~

'Which allowed the doctor to save me. *Hvala*.'

Sila waited for more of a reaction, but it didn't come. Instead, Gašper reached for a spoon and started on the shallows of his soup. 'That's it?'

'What?'

'You were half-dead and *hvala*, you saved me. That's all you have to say about it?'

'Ja. Why not?'

'I nearly killed you.'

'And then brought me back.'

'Barely…'

'With self-sustaining testosterone levels too. Somehow. And now I'm here eating better than average soup, feeling completely fine.'

'I could've-…'

'Forget about it, really, it's no big deal.' He filled his spoon with the dregs of the bowl and sipped it off. 'I've been dead before and the medics brought me back, same thing you did. It's just like getting a jab.'

'You had the green before?'

'Ja, in rehab. But that one was a pulse gun wound.'

'What?'

'I tried to escape, they shot me. Seven times actually, but four of them missed and the other two hit the Queen of Trogir.'

'Queen of what?'

'Trogir. The city with all the drunk English people.'

'They have a queen?'

Gašper ditched the spoon and dipped his finger in the bowl. 'That's what she claimed. I think she used to work in marketing and got depressed when she lost her job. Anyway, I got shot, I came back, end of fable.'

'Gašper…'

'Though that one didn't do anything with my testosterone. Not sure why. Maybe it takes a double dose to have an effect. Doc did say it was a surprise.'

'How are you so…' Sila paused, pulling the leash on the word *glib* and trying to come up with a better one.

'Serious, it's fine,' Gašper replied, licking his finger. 'This one too. As long as it's not the heart or the brain, or a cut vein, it's usually okay.'

'But…'

'Key thing is I'm alive. And I've finally caught up with you. My third best friend in the whole of Slovenia.'

'Ja…'

'Or second now. I think Irhaa got deported.'

Sila put on a weak smile and went back to his soup. Not to eat it, to swirl it around.

'Hey, I'm gonna pick up some more of this stuff.'

'More?'

'I'm drained, need more sustenance. And I can practise my Twi.'

'Swahili,' said Sila, pointing at the sign in the window.

'Nah, one of them speaks Twi, I heard him. And I don't know Swahili so…'

'You know Twi?'

'Ja, maybe. Enough to have a two minute conversation.'

Gašper slid off the stool and managed two steps before he started to sway. He tried another step and fell, some part of his brain switching to panic mode and shooting out a hand towards the nearest stool. Luckily, the stool was pinned to the ground and kept him steady.

'Dizzy…' he slurred.

'Back this way, comrade,' said Sila, putting one of Gašper's arms over his shoulder and guiding him back onto his stool.

'Feel like I'm in a typhoon.'

'Ja, probably the after-effects.'

Gašper rubbed his stomach and slouched forward on the table. Sila gave him a few minutes to ward off the storm then said, 'time to go back.'

'Back where?'

'My house.'

'Yours?'

'You can sleep on Sadia's bed.'

Gašper rolled his head to the side, looking horizontal at Sila's chest. 'I can stay with you?'

'Ja.'

'Excuse me,' said a voice, making Sila jump and Gašper eke out a feeble *raaar.* It was one of the staff, holding the handles of an electric wheelchair. 'I saw your friend wobbling, is he okay?'

'He's a bit sick.'

'Ja, well, we have this chair for those who find it difficult to get home. You can borrow it and bring it back tomorrow, assuming you're locals?'

'Medaase,' said Gašper, semi-incoherent.

'Wah, you speak Twi?' asked the staff, reeling back a little too dramatically.

'In very short bursts.'

'… … … … … … … … …?'

'Too fast.'

'Sorry, I was asking who taught you Twi. But it doesn't matter, you're sick. Better let your friend get you back home.'

'I'll bring the chair back soon,' said Sila, checking his tab. 'Half an hour maybe. What time do you close?'

'Tomorrow is fine.'

'Are you sure?'

'Just don't push it into the river. Ja, very sure.'

'Okay.'

The staff patted the handles of the chair and went back to the counter. Sila watched him go then turned back to Gašper, who had rotated his head almost one eighty degrees.

'He was friendly.'

'Ja.'

'Pretty eyes too.'

'Okay, let's get you in this chair,' said Sila, bending down to check the wheels.

'Maybe I'll come back tomorrow, get his number.'

'Ready?'

'Use the wheelchair return as a pretext…'

'Gašper.'

'…milk the stomach wound a bit, say I was attacked by fascists. Ja?'

~~~

Twenty minutes later, they were back in Sila's flat, the whole place as eerily quiet as it had been pre-stabbing.

Sila brushed off Gašper's protests of 'it's electric' and pushed the wheelchair into the living room, swerving well away from the blood stains on the hallway floor. When they were close enough, he lifted Gašper's arm around his neck and helped manoeuvre him onto the couch.

'That's a lot of green tea,' Gašper said, noticing the boxes.

'Are you comfortable?'

'Is it all yours?'

'Sadia's.'

'Gonna take you a while to get through all that.'

'Ja…'

'You and Sadia. Four boxes. God knows how many teabags in each one.'

Sila opened his mouth to say something about the letters, but settled for another *ja* instead.

'What's going on here anyway? Why are there blue marks on the wall outside?'

'Ne vem.'

'Does Sadia know about it?'

'She's not here.'

'Ja, I was gonna ask about that too. Where is she?'

'Gone.'

'Gone where?'

'I don't…ne vem.'

Gašper shifted his position, groaning at low volume as he turned to the right side of the living room. 'Is that hers?'

'What, the cat?'

'The paper on the desk.'

'Which paper?'

Gašper took a breath, and relaunched himself onto his feet. Sila tried to grab his arm, but was shrugged off.
~~~

'I'm better now,' protested Gašper, making it to the desk and picking up the note. After skimming through, he picked up the second note, read through that one too then held both up together against the light coming through the window.

Sila sat down on the floor, his back against the couch. 'She's either gone somewhere by herself, or she's gone where you were before.'

'Shit. Sorry, brother.'

'Ne vem. Maybe it's the best place for her.'

'Wouldn't go that far.'

Sila looked down at the floor, mapping out his next sentence. *It was mum-related, the dangers of self-diagnosis, don't get used to threats of suicide*, but he found the more he mapped it out the more he didn't want to say anything. Instead, he continued staring at the floor. After a minute or two he switched to the green tea boxes.

'What's happening, brother?' asked Gašper, standing over him, the letter still hanging from his hand.

'Here?'

'Ne, not here. I mean, with us, next week.'

'Next Monday?'

'Ja.'

Sila looked up, going as high as Gašper's stomach. 'You know about that?'

'Found out right after I saw you in Bled. Chu told me what was going on, where you were off to, so I decided to wait it out until you returned. But then I got back to my hostel and there was a letter waiting for me.'

'A paper letter?'

'Weirdly, ja. It said: *Dear citizen, congratulations, you've been selected to travel on our state-of-the-art spaceship on its historic voyage to Mars. Your sacrifice will be remembered by all for centuries to come.*'

'That's how they phrased it?'

'That's why I followed you back here. Ja, exact phrasing. Your sacrifice will be remembered for centuries to come.'

Gašper stepped back to the desk, putting the letter down as he continued speaking.

'And the only spaceship I know of is the one that half-melted last April. Or its engine half-melted, ne vem. We didn't get the exact details where I was.'

Sila blew out his cheeks and slid an inch farther down the curb of the couch. 'That's us.'

'What?'

'Though it didn't half-melt, that was just one segment. Apparently.'

'But…it can't be. I've just been released.'

'It can be. It is.'

Gašper picked up the Cheshire cat cushion and began swinging it by its tail. 'What about the media? I checked all of them, after the letter, and they just said it's a test run of the engine. None of them mentioned anything about Mars.'

'They don't know yet.'

'The media?'

'Potočnik's holding it back, to lower expectations. At least that's what he told me.'

'Holding it back?'

'Ja.'

'He can do that?'

'Apparently. With the support of the collectives too.'

The swinging cat stopped, Gašper's hand switching to rubbing the back of his head. 'Fuck, this is weird.'

'Ja.'

'Keeping things from the press, a trip to Mars…'

'You okay?'

'Bit dizzy.'

'Maybe we should talk about this tomorrow, when you're rested.'

'Ne, I'm okay. Just give me a few minutes.'

Gašper lowered himself down onto the floor next to Sila and stroked the fading marks of his stomach wound. The two of them sat there in near silence for about an hour, Gašper phasing in and out of consciousness and Sila staring at the floor. It was strange, just that morning he'd been terrified of seeing Gašper again, but now that he'd stabbed him in the gut and lost Sadia to a rehab centre, he felt almost comfortable.

Wasn't that ridiculous? How could such a sentence even exist? *Now that he'd stabbed him with a screwdriver.* It was like that old Kizic film, the Stasi agent opening a launderette with a gay man he'd tortured for seven years. His violence, his journey. Other guy gets stabbed. And that wasn't even the worst of it. Gašper's letter, the phrasing - your sacrifice will be remembered for centuries to come - it didn't match with the project he'd just been sold. Or the project he'd been pressganged into. Ne, something was off about this trip. His brain was telling him, something is very off, avoid, emigrate, escape, go now. Ja, go, but how? With what confidence? To which border?

He stared at the green tea boxes, hoping the Japanese characters printed on the side would offer some clues. He stared at them for a long time, stared at them so long that Gašper noticed and started staring at them too.

'I think I might have a plan,' said Sila finally, looking up.

'For what?'

'To get out of this mission, the Mars thing.'

'Go on then.'

'Well, it's a bit complicated. A bit off the cuff.'

Gašper raised his hand up, almost hitting Sila on the nose with the Cheshire cat cushion. 'Wah, sorry, too fast.'

'What is it?'

'Your plan, it's not the same one I came up with on the way over here, is it?'

'Ne vem. What did you come up with?'

'Simple. You sneak in a parachute, hide it in a huge jacket, get an oxygen tank, some rations and water, wait until we're halfway up to low orbit and then jump down, hopefully landing across the northern border in Austria.'

'Sounds dangerous.'

'Ja, more than a bit.'

'I suppose mine is too, in a low-key kind of way.'

'Tell me.'

Sila stood up and walked over to the desk, touching the Sadia letter. 'I was thinking of mailing ourselves to Italy.'

'Ne, can't do that.'

'Can't?'

'Not anymore. An Tehranian guy in rehab tried it, before he was committed. Last year, I think. Said they scanned the box with some kind of infrared thing.'

'Fuck. I didn't hear anything about that.'

'It was on *Morda Ni Hudič*.'

'Ne, I believe you. It's sounds exactly like the kind of thing they would do now. From what I've seen of Ljubljana. Okay. Forget mailing. We'll have to go with your plan.'

'Ne, can't do that either.'

'What do you mean?'

'I thought you knew.'

'Knew what?'

Gašper stopped stroking the Cheshire cat cushion, got up off the floor and re-positioned himself on the edge of the couch. 'We can't jump from the elevator cos a] it's locked up, and b] the air pressure's too strong. And the speed is incalculable. Seriously, physicists have worked it out, real ones, this isn't me saying this, it's them. You manage to somehow get outside the elevator and jump off, you'll end up falling at one tenth the speed of light. Or close to it. Which means, when you hit Italy or Austria, you'll turn into light-energy and go right through the surface, about a hundred metres underground.'

'Light-energy?'

'Wait, not speed of light, the other one. Sound. One tenth the speed of sound.'

'You sure that's accurate?'

'The light-energy part, maybe not. Might be the drugs messing with my brain. But the rest of it, the high speed, ja, it's real.'

'Real physicists said all this?'

'Ja.'

'When?'

'Ne vem. Ages ago. I read it in the taxi, it's right there, on-tab. The speed's too fast, you'll burn up, or pass out. I forget which one. But you definitely die.'

Sila looked down at the Cheshire cat cushion, squinting. 'I don't understand.'

'Which part?'

'All of it, the last five minutes. Why did you suggest a plan that couldn't work?'

'I thought it was the same as your plan.'

'Jezus, Gašper…'

'So I was telling you, why it wouldn't work, the science behind it. What?'

Sila sat down on the couch next to the invalid and gripped the inanely smug cushion with his fingers. Gašper went back to rubbing his head.

Outside, there were shouts, followed by the sound of glass breaking.

Sila hurried over to the side of the window, followed by a sluggish Gašper.

A few doors down, two Turkish men were being dragged out of a house by four jackets, screaming, 'we're Slovene, we're Slovene,' over and over in broken Croatian.

'Is that real?'

'Probably some domestic dispute.'

The screams and shouts continued as two of the jackets pinned down the bigger of the Turks and punched him repeatedly in the head.

'That's not a domestic dispute,' said Gašper softly.

'Ne.'

'What the fuck's going on?'

'Ne vem.'

'Deportations?'

'Ne vem.'

Sila put a hand flat on the glass and listened to the other Turk's screams until a car door slammed shut and it was done. Muttering something anti-fascist under his breath, he took away his hand and followed a hobbling Gašper back to the couch.

~~~
~~~

The next morning, Sila woke up on the living room floor, saw the letters on the desk and went back to sleep.

At one, he woke up again and reached for his tab, going through his list of contacts. There were a lot of names, but no one he'd talked to in the last two years, and no one who could help them. The only one that half stood out was Nakagami, but he couldn't call him cos, even though he'd only met him once, he knew what he'd get: cold, bleak reality.

Feeling low, he pulled himself up into a sitting position and put on the wall-screen. Maček was on *881 Forum*[25] complaining about an increase in Ponzi schemes within the Russian community. *We can't give a precise number, but we suspect it's anything between twenty and seventy-nine percent of all Russians currently living in Slovenia.*

Sila switched quickly, finding an old Guangdong comedy he hadn't seen since he was a kid.

A police officer going undercover in a high school.

It was a bit strange seeing a cop as the hero, but he suspended just enough belief to slip into the film's bubble.

Either via routine or the effects of Antro-D, Gašper slept all the way through to four in the afternoon.

The first thing he said when he opened his eyes was, 'jump.'

The second thing, a little more rational, was, 'we better take the wheelchair back.'

'Ja, I suppose.'

'And then get drunk.'

~~~

A few hours later, in one of the few bars left in Ljubljana that had 170gsm silk posters on the walls, Sila and Gašper sat and drank traditional Slovene vodka.

While drinking, they tried to come up with another plan, a viable one.

---

25 Call in show that casts from a different collective every week.
~~~

'We load up on guns, explosives, body armour, head to the Croatian border,' tried Gašper.

'Ne.'

'I haven't finished yet.'

'Don't have guns, don't have explosives, don't have body armour.'

'I have a bow and arrow back at my old house.'

'Would get shot even if we did.' Sila finished his shot and poured another. 'Next.'

'Okay then, how about this? We dress up as one of those blue stripe jacket security guys, get fake ID, get a shuttle, fly to Germany or Italy, one of the-…'

'Won't work.'

'Ne? Which part?'

'The ID…too hard to get now.'

'We could just get the same jacket, shave our heads. I'd probably have to lose my headband, but…ne, not lose, I'll just stick it in my pocket until we're done.'

'Fuck's sake…'

Gašper ignored the outburst and drank his shot. 'Or how about this? We dress up as women, seduce some guards, take them to a quiet place, an alley or park, knock them out, get a shuttle…'

'Seduce them?'

'Ja. Kind of. Well, ne, not really, just rub their arms a bit and…'

'Ne.'

'…say they've got tight triceps. What? Why not?'

'It's ludicrous.'

'Only if you're a prude.'

'Gašper…'

'Fine, professor. What's your great idea?'

Sila shrugged and mumbled, 'still thinking.' He looked at the wall behind the counter, at the green-eyed preacher from *Night of the Hunter* showing his knuckles.

Next to it was the poster for Visec's *Krsnik Farm.*

Ha, *Krsnik.* No one made movies about them anymore. Everything was chrome futurist now. Even the crypto-tyrants.

Sila downed his shot, poured another.

If Potočnik truly was a crypto-tyrant…

Maybe it was all paranoia on his part. Maybe there was a perfectly reasonable explanation for why men who looked like Stasi agents were popping up everywhere in groups of four. Sometimes groups of two. Maybe it wasn't as many as he thought.

Maybe all those Turks and Russians were running ponzi schemes. And pedo rings. And selling baking powder to tourists.

Maybe the Council of Citizenry Support wasn't as blandly sinister as it sounded.

Maybe it was all a big joke, a Potočnik special.

Wasn't like anything had changed systemically.

Had it?

Sila looked up, through the top of the bottle, repeating the question out loud.

The Krsnik glared down at him, claws long and stretched.

'My mythology's not the best, but isn't he supposed to be a good monster?' asked Gašper, seeing the same thing.

'Ja.'

'Maybe they did something to him on that farm.'

'Ja, probably.'

~~~

An hour and a half later, there was a man with a suicidally strong Russian accent sitting next to them.

He'd told them he was born in Novo Mesto, that both his parents were ethnic Slovene, but he was clearly Russian. Either another ex-rehabber like Gašper or a guy who hadn't yet heard what they were doing to immigrants lately.

'And the thing about space is, there is oxygen, ja, but it is too spread out. They say vacuum, but that is just an easy word, it's not, it has gas…really, it is true.'

Gašper nodded, Sila stared at his empty glass.
~~~

'Not that you should try breathing it in, this gas, space air. Never go out without a helmet, that is suicide, but still, it would be an adventure, don't you think?'

'We'll let you know,' replied Sila to his glass.

'Excuse me?'

'I said, we'll let you know. When we get back from our space trip. Launching next week. On a spaceship that might melt.'

'I'm sorry, I do not understand.'

'We're going on a mission, comrade.'

'You are joking, right?'

Sila shook his glass and head at the same time.

The Russian stared at them for a solid fifteen seconds, looked around the bar for suspicious men reading newspapers then leaned in closer.

'If you are talking about what I think you are talking about, then count me in.'

'Huh?'

The Russian stared at them strong, borderline magnetism. 'I'm asking you, comrades, are you going on a trip away from here?'

'Ja, I just told you.'

'Nice, good. Then I am telling you, I want to join.'

'I don't think you understand. We're going into space.'

'Unless we can think of a way out of it,' added Gašper, trying to pour out another shot with the lid on the bottle.

'By space, you mean…'

'The endless black thing with little bits of gas scattered about.'

'It is not code for…' The Russian looked at the Krsnik poster on the wall, squinted, then readjusted until he was facing the window. '…out there.'

'I wish it were, comrade.'

'Ah.'

Sila nodded, said, 'ja, exactly,' and went back to staring at his glass.

'Time to go.' The Russian finished his drink, stood up and recited a few lines of something in Russian.

Gašper touched him on the arm. 'Better not sing that outside. There are some unfriendly people about.'

'It is nothing. I studied Russian poetry as a child.'

'Ne, I mean your accent.'

'Ja? What about it?'

'It's Russian.'

'What are you talking about? I'm Slovene.'

'Ne, it's on every word, the sound isn't quite right.'

'I told you, I was born in Novo Mesto.'

'Ne, I can hear it.'

'Your ears are wrong, comrade.'

The Russian looked around the bar, shouted, 'Novo Mesto, raise thy banner,' in a Russian accent and left.

'Don't know how long he's gonna last,' muttered Gašper, as the bar door slowly closed.

'Ne vem.'

'Assuming we're not hallucinating the anti-immigrant, stripy jacket guy thing.'

'Maybe it is all a dream,' said Sila, caustic.

'I hope so.'

'Or maybe we'll be seeing him on Monday.'

'Ja.'

Sila picked up the bottle in front of him and moved it around like a toy spaceship.

'You okay, Sila-foam?'

He put the bottle down on the counter, landing it in four spluttered bursts. Then froze. 'Health Council…'

'Who?'

'Technically separate…'

'From what?'

He whispered some numbers out loud.

'Wait, let me get another bottle first.'

Grabbed Gašper's sleeve and put a finger to his mouth.

'What?'

Studied his glass.

'What are you counting, brother?'

'That might actually work.' Sila slid off his stool, half-raised his hand in the air then paused, remembered everything that had happened that day, and sat back down, levelling out his grin.

'What is it?' asked Gašper, taking the lid back off the bottle.

'I think I've got it.'

'What?'

'A thing, an idea.'

Gašper picked up the bottle and poured another shot. 'Okay, but yours can't use explosives if mine can't.'

'Stop drinking, we're leaving.'

'What, now?'

'Ja. Get up, come on.'

Gašper finished off his glass then looked at the bottle. There was still another two shots worth. And the lid was already off.

'Gašper…'

'Ja, coming.'

~~~

Most Slovenes had never been to the Council of Citizenry Support before.

There were three reasons for this.

One: in the two years since its [low-key] founding, most people who'd gone there hadn't come back out.

Two: most people who'd gone there were working class immigrants from non-Slovene neighbourhoods stuck on the fringes of their collectives i.e. ghosts that no one cared about.

Three: no one knew where it was.

Actually, without realizing it, some Slovenes had seen the Council of Citizenry Support simply because it shared a building with the Museum of Modern Art.

Museum of Modern Art – 1st, 2nd, 3rd, 4th and 5th floor.

Council of Citizenry Support – 6th and above.
~~~

In short: space was limited, so art sat next to politics, and politics became uncomfortably close to pretentious wank like black squares and blank rooms with red lightbulbs.

~~~

Sila and Gašper got off the transport pad and looked out through the giant window, wondering if they'd accidentally travelled back to 1980's Belgrade.

Actually, to the east of the station, where the hub of Bežigrad was, things didn't look too bad, but out to the west…

Stark. Enervating. Sterile. Budgetarily orphaned.

Beyond adjectives?

The streets appeared devoid of life, every third shop was closed, the residential buildings flanking them were all olive green,[26] and the trees gave the firm impression that they were slowly dying of something.

As for the CoCS building, it looked pretty much the same close up as it had a mile away; an industrial grey block planted down on the edge of a car-less junction, cutting off the well-maintained side of Bežigrad from its malnourished twin.

Opposite this *guard-tower* hung a billboard projection; Potočnik and a happy group of Slovene-Turks promoting a new *oil wrestling and optional sünnet* initiative.

Next to that was a gigantic stretch of graffiti; seven of the very bluest eyes with *TRUST THE ONES YOU SEE* stencilled above.

'Are we at the right station?' asked Gašper, putting his fingertips against the glass.

'Ja.'

'This is Bežigrad?'

'Ja.'

---

[26] The colour used on the first wave of collective housing built in the 2170's, primarily in poor, urban areas.
~~~

The tannoy beeped nearby, signalling the successful departure of the train, and forcing Sila and Gašper away from the scenery outside.

Didn't matter, it was etched Varo-like on the cracks of their hippocampi.

Whatever improvements the Slovene system had brought to the collectives, and to everyone living within, it clearly hadn't brought them to this one. Which was odd, thought Sila, heading down the steps to the exit, cos the last time he was there, it had looked quite trendy. A little fake maybe, but there'd been people doing things, some kind of communal, street-level interaction. And, ja, the buildings may have been olive green on one side, but they weren't flaking off paint this bad.

'Feels like half the population's been kidnapped,' said Gašper, looking ahead and back and realizing they were the only ones who'd got off at this stop.

'Two articles on *Pravi Veronika*,' replied Sila, reading from his tab. 'Both by the same author.'

'About this?'

'Says a lot of residents have been relocated, part of a better housing scheme. That's it.' Sila paused, his finger clicking and swiping and typing. 'Nothing on *Morda Ni Hudič.*'

'Could be archived…'

'Huh? Is that sarcasm?'

Gašper responded by looking back the way they'd just come and mouthing *fuck*.

'What is it?' asked Sila, scanning the deserted platform.

'It's them again, the stripy jacket gorillas.'

'Where?'

'Not that way. Up ahead.'

Sila readjusted and saw three men by the gate, a little more wiry than the others but with the same *which eye you wanna keep* aura.

'This is insane,' he muttered, slipping his tab back inside his jacket pocket.

'Should we look at them or not look at them?' asked Gašper.

'Don't look.'

'Isn't that more suspicious?'

'Take out your ticket.[27] Look at it confused.'

'How confused?'

'Like it's one of Chu's equations.'

'Ah, Chu, I forgot about her. She looks way more relaxed now. Taller too. Ja, I saw her in Bled, after you went off in the car. Came out in her pyjamas with some occult book in her hand, asking if I-…'

'Gašper, ticket.'

'What? Ja, I'm getting it.'

'Keep your eyes on it, I'll talk about art.'

Gašper did as he was told, pulling his ticket out, examining it, squinting at the words on the front as if it were written in Urdu. He even stopped at the gate and, pretending not to understand where to put the ticket, leaned over and asked one of the jackets.

One of them nonchalantly looked over and said, 'other way, flip over,' then went back to his tab.

'You fucking idiot,' said Sila, in a muffled voice as Gašper joined him at the area map board.

'It wasn't that bad.'

'They could've taken you.'

'Maybe they're not even security.'

'Just look at the map for a few seconds, then go.'

'Okay.'

'Do not ask them for directions.'

'Course not.'

They did the map routine, pointing at random blocks around the collective, then walked out of the transport depot, past the jackets, past the old Turkish restaurants with boarded-up windows and blue paint marks on the walls, past the Ghanaian café with flowers outside the door and onto the main road.

As they walked, Sila went over the plan one more time.

---

[27] Ja, tickets were still used, mostly as a nostalgic measure, but also to help people who'd forgotten their Pegasus Cards [travel cards] or didn't want to be tracked by the system.

'We go in, you pretend to look at art, I use the letter to go up to the 6th floor, ask for Sadia's file, come back down, we leave. If there's trouble, if it's some kind of trap or there's security watching me, I get the file, set off the fire alarm, walk out, meet you outside and done.'

'Then we head to Koper, get on the ferry?'

'After we pick up Sadia. If she's-…if it's still possible to do that.'

'Then we get on the ferry?'

'Ja. All of us. If there's security looking for us, ID checks, then we hire a fishing boat, circle round to Trieste.'

'Without notification forms?'

'Obviously.'

Gašper feigned deliberation as the wind blew in, moving his hand up to where his orange headband normally would've been. According to Sila, it was provocative, so he'd put it in his pocket and now his head felt weird. Unguarded. Slightly cold. Or liberated maybe?

The wind blew through again, forcing a response.

'Okay, brother. Let's just do it.'

Sila patted him on the arm, once. 'You understand your role?'

'In the museum? Ja. Look at paintings and stuff.'

'The important part is, don't try and help me. If I'm not out after an hour, leave. If I come out with guards, leave faster. Got it?'

'Ja, Captain Nevic.'[28]

'Gašper…'

'Relax. I got it.'

'And if anyone approaches us before, during or after, just act casual, okay?'

'Ja, I know.'

'Far as they know, we're just two Slovene guys, walking to the museum.'

'Uh-huh.'

'Come on.'

---

[28] Authoritarian captain from *Not of this Planet*, a 2054 Slovene novel set on the fringes of the solar system.

Sila quickened his pace, Gašper matched it.

They walked down some steps into a subway passage with green lights on the side of the walls and, on almost every tile, white patches of painted-over graffiti.

Gašper thought it looked similar to the one from that rape film. The Polish one, with the mercs. Where everything was filtered greyish green and all the psychopaths spoke Russian. But he didn't say it out loud.

Sila walked faster, his eyes on the exit twenty or so metres ahead. A day ago, he would've thought it impossible, but now he half-expected some jackets to appear from round the corner, tapping baseball bats against the walls. It was possible, especially in an area as drained as this one. He wasn't a small guy, neither was Gašper, but if there were more than two of them…

'Wah, it's weird without all the performers.'

'What?' asked Sila, not bothering to turn.

'The performers. They used to play in the subways everywhere, before, you know…' Gašper pulled out his ticket stub from the train and threw it in a passing bin. 'I guess they're all inside now. Or playing at other collectives.'

'Just focus on the mission.'

'What, you mean looking at art?'

'Ja.'

'Not much of a mission.'

'Shh, there might be more jackets up here.'

They walked up the steps and back into the open air. Sila didn't feel much safer. There were no other people walking on this side, so if security did come out of nowhere, there wouldn't be any witnesses.

'Isn't that it?' said Gašper, pointing at something.

Sila looked back, seeing a massive block of grey. The Museum was behind them, somehow looking even more depressing than it had from the transport depot.

'Jezus, it's ugly.'

'Ja.'

'Not much security though. Ne, wait, two guys over there. Matching jackets. Not striped.'

'I see them.'

'Could be art enthusiasts.'

'Doubtful.'

They moved closer, Sila picking up a loose stick from the grass nearby and pretending to explain something to Gašper. Whether it fooled the [non-striped] jackets or not was hard to say as they only looked over once and that could've simply been an auto-response.

Sila kept the stick and pointed Gašper up the steps. Neither of them knew why, but there was a bright yellow slide running from the top of the building to the ground.

'Is that art?' asked Gašper.

'Ne vem.'

'Looks like a kiddie slide.'

'Ja.'

They walked up the second set of steps to the entrance, seemingly the only people going to the Museum or the CoCS that day.

A large sign on the door glass announced: *Museum of Modern Art: better than the old art.*

There was nothing to mark it as the home of the Council of Citizenry Support.

Entering with muffled furtiveness, they pulled out the temporary Erazem cards they'd procured from the city centre and scanned them for the guards to see. Four credits. Not that bad. Assuming it didn't go into the collective's defence budget.

'You sure these cards aren't traceable?' whispered Gašper, as they headed away from the guards.

'That's what I was told.'

'By who?'

A large man in a yellow life jacket walked past, forcing Sila into random mode. 'I heard the second floor has the more esoteric stuff. Very abstract styles.'

'Huh?'

'Play along,' he added, in a quick hush.

'Ja, right, abstract. My favourite. All the shape stuff…'

'Okay, stop.'

'...and the one colour part, it's so-...'

'Up ahead. Keep walking.'

The receptionist at the front desk yawned at them and asked if they wanted to see one exhibition, two exhibitions, three exhibitions, or all the exhibitions.

Gašper shook his head, unable to process the question. He looked at Sila, who mouthed *art*.

'What would you like to see?' she asked, supressing a second yawn.

'Art,' he said, smiling like a kidnap victim.

'Two tickets?'

'Actually, I'm here to check on a relative.' Sila pulled out the note from Sadia's apartment. 'This letter said to come here.'

'Sixth floor,' said the receptionist, pressing a button on the desk. 'Through that scanner then over to the lift.'

~~~

Gašper watched the elevator doors edge Sila out of existence then started his tour of the art that was apparently better than the old stuff.

The first exhibition was a large room full of ugly, naked people.

He walked alongside the walls, looking at each one, pretending to peer closely at the sketch lines. Some of the pictures were pencil-drawn, others were painted. And they showed everything. Mostly the underside of erections and unkempt muff, but also moles and blackened toenails. Maybe the artist had gone to a clinic and sketched, or maybe it was normal people, unedited. The signs didn't say.

When he'd completed two passes, Gašper went back to the picture of who he thought was prettiest and tried to replace his face with that of Kavin. It had been a while since they'd...since he'd seen him...

I don't want to shake your hand, okay? Ne, I don't want to hug you either.

But that face...it was difficult. He couldn't do it.

He looked at the body instead, at the slightly saggy chest and the thighs and the little hairs coming off his balls. It was all there, one hundred percent uncovered.

Art. Bleakness. Depression. Alone.
~~~

The man - the subject - was just sitting there, putting his weight back onto his arms. Gazing without expression at something ten degrees or so to the right of the artist. He was neither toned, nor obese. Neither beautiful nor ugly. Neither reluctant nor willing.

It was like he'd wandered into a zoo and volunteered to sit in one of the enclosures, naked, for the rest of his life.

Gašper pulled at his t-shirt.

This was not him.

His hand went forward and almost touched the canvas, his fingers curled into a kind of claw…

This is nothing worth thinking about.

…then retreated, back to his side and down into his pockets.

~~~

The rest of the Museum was all paint and objects.

Gašper walked through every room, explored every floor, and looked at everything. But he wasn't really interested in anything.

He stood by the railings on the fifth floor and looked up. The windows were covered with grey blinds and the doors looked like they were made of futuristic metal.

Sila's probably got the file by now, he thought. Should be coming back down soon. Unless…

He looked around for the fire alarm, seeing one tucked in by the ceiling, dull green.

A few minutes drifted by, and nothing happened. Gašper channelled his inner *Mocata*[29] and stared at the bell, but it refused to ring. Then he noticed one of the other visitors looking over at him, and moved away.

Back on the fourth floor he saw an open window and some museum attendants in yellow jackets. He walked closer and met the slide.

---

[29] *The Devil Rides Out* [1968] had a resurgence in cult-popularity during the 2080's as the Slovenian dictator, Šarec, looked uncannily like Charles Gray.
~~~

One of the yellow jackets said something to him in Slovene, then in the Maribor dialect when he didn't reply.

'You want to slide?'

Gašper shook his head.

'Very safe, very fun.'

'Ne, hvala.'

He walked away before they could say anything else. There was nothing else to see and it might look suspicious if he went through the exhibitions again, so he decided to go outside and wait.

When he got to the second floor, the fire alarm sounded.

There weren't many people in the museum, which meant Gašper could take his time heading down to the entrance.

He looked up as he walked, but there was no movement. The yellow jacket guards held their positions, apparently willing to burn to death if necessary. Down on the ground floor, it was the opposite, with people filing quickly out of the elevators.

One of them was Sila, being held by two guards. Not jackets this time, proper guards with the word *SECURITY* printed on their backs. They led him out through the main doors, no struggle, no headlocks, and pointed to the road.

Gašper followed them out, looked left towards the subway tunnel, right to see if any cars were coming, trying to remember his lines. *If I come out in cuffs, run. Got it?*

Gašper ran.

He ran down the last three flights of stairs and straight towards the two guards holding his friend.

One of them turned as he got close, pulling something cylinder-shaped out from his jacket.

Gašper shaped to rugby tackle, but it was too late. The bolt of electrical something hit him square in the chest and knocked him to the floor.

The last thing he heard was laughter and the words, 'looks Turkish.'

~~~
~~~

Gašper opened his eyes to sea green walls and his nostrils to the faint scent of formaldehyde.

'You alive?'

'Where…'

'Never mind.'

Gašper pulled himself up and realized he was on a very hard bed in a very green room. Possibly a clinic. He looked down and saw Sila sitting on the floor with his legs crossed. 'What happened?'

'I think you can guess most of it.'

'We got arrested?'

Sila nodded.

'What about Sadia? The file?'

'Ne.'

'It wasn't there?'

'Ne vem. They told me to sit in the waiting area, said they'd get it for me. Then the guards came. I pulled the fire alarm pretty much out of spite.'

'Oh.'

'Didn't think they'd actually arrest me.'

'Ja, me neither.'

'Not for the *requesting a file* part.'

Gašper rubbed his nose, closing up the nostrils briefly to block out the smell. It wasn't overwhelming, but it was persistent. 'You think they'll keep us here until Monday?'

'Ne.'

'You don't think or…'

'The guard said they'd let us out.'

'Ah. That's good.'

'Apparently, we need more fresh air before the launch.'

Gašper let go of his nose. 'Great, that means we can go…'

'With shadow security provided.'

'…back to your place and rest. Ah. Or not.'

Sila didn't add anything else, just sat there and flicked at the top of his knees.

Repeating *shadow security* under his breath, Gašper stood up and did a lap of the cell. If that was the right word for it. Maybe not. It wasn't particularly cramped, there was a door and a window to the corridor outside, both transparent, and the lighting was reasonable. But then there was the smell, and the almost ubiquitous colour of the décor. 'Not the worst place to wake up in. Very green. Kind of like the NOT YET Centre I was at.'

'Gašper…'

'Got the same formaldehyde scent too. I think it's a way of torturing-…what?'

'You do understand what's happening here?'

'Sure. Which part?'

Sila gave up a couple more joules of energy and gestured towards the door. 'We're fucked. There's no way out of this.'

'You said they'd let us out for fresh air.'

'Ja, I mean after that, the Mars trip. They've got us locked down for four years.'

'True.'

'No way to get out of it.'

'Ne.'

'What are we gonna do?'

Gašper mumbled something inaudible and returned to the sea green walls. Apart from a few bits of chipped paint, there was nothing to focus on, so he took in the totality of it and forced his brain to seek out affiliations. Rehab, tree leaves, fields, moss, neon, acid, Robin Hood, *The Green Child.*

He breathed out, not aware he'd been holding any in.

The list of names, the colour itself, there was something calming about it all, debilitating even. Something that made four years on Mars sound not so awful.

'Gašper?'

Criolo had talked about it once, before he swallowed the pillowcase – green walls, what they led to - but he couldn't remember what it was. Hypnotic effect? The paint was mixed with something?

'You in there?' asked Sila, waving a hand half-heartedly in front of Gašper's eyes.

'What?'

'I said, do you know anything about Mars?'

'Ne. Not really.'

'Me neither.'

There was a shout from the corridor, succeeded by an excessively padded shoe flying past the window. No one came to pick it up.

Blowing out an *okay*, Gašper rolled off the bed and joined Sila on the floor.

'Brother…'

'What?'

Gašper put his hand on Sila's leg and held it there for a moment, then slapped it and conjured up a half smile. 'There's a different path through this. Or as my mum used to say, *fucking pivot season, you little shit.* A pivot from our original pivot but…still a pivot.'

'Pivot to what?'

'Cos if you think about it, really think about it, this may not be as bad as it seems.'

'I've thought about it. It is.'

'I mean, once the shock factor dissipates.'

'We're being forced to Mars, on a spaceship that might melt.'

'Ja, I know, but…' Gašper paused, his hand frozen in mid-air like an unfurling claw. 'Hang on, you said they'd fixed the melting part.'

'Slovenia's going to shit…'

'Did they fix it?'

'…or has already gone to shit. And no one did anything. Fuck, I didn't even notice it was happening. Ne, worse than that, I don't even know what *has* happened, what the actual chess moves were, what the board's supposed to look like now. Too busy dangling my feet in the fucking lake, watching all those…'

Gašper slapped his hands together. 'Hey, Leopardi, did they or did they not fix the ship?'

Sila stopped, looking around the room as if someone else had just sprung up out of the floor.

'Ha, I knew that'd stop you.'

'Leo who?'

'Giacomo Leopardi, Italian pessimist. They had his book at the centre, several copies of it, all with yellowing covers. I read it three or four times.'

'Fantastic.'

'Ja, quite topical too. His main theory was melting space ships and whether they were fixed or not.'

Sila snorted, he couldn't help it, then straightened up again and started flicking at his fingers, one by one. 'Ja, it's fixed. Or so they said.'

'Good, so we're not going to die that way. The ship *will* get to Mars. And when you think about it, it's not like death is guaranteed. It's not even probable. Probably.'

'Are you drunk?'

'In fact, chances are we could live longer on Mars, away from the jackets and this place, all the stress that comes with it. Which might not even be that bad. Slovenia, I mean. Might be a crime blip, or some rogue jackets the collectives don't know about.'

'Ah, I remember now.'

'What?'

'My old friend Gašper. Manic optimism, even if your head's about to be chopped off.'

'Ja, well, why not?' Gašper stood up and started walking from green wall to green wall. 'If you think downwards, that's where you'll drop. And there's no head chopping, we're just going on a slightly longer than usual trip.'

'Forced exile.'

'And at least we'll be going through all this together. And that Japanese scientist you talked about, he'll be there. Maybe others as well.'

Sila flicked his thumb extra hard then looked down at the floor.

'And we'll get to see space. I mean, space from within space. And Mars too, a whole new planet, mysteriously red. That'll be worth something.'

'Ja, four years of our lives.'

Gašper grinned like a zealot surrounded by other zealots. 'Now I think about it, the whole thing, it almost seems fun. Exploring a brand new world…'

'God…'

'…just like Lakik and his gang of four.'

'Who?'

'*Klevin Lakik*,[30] the gang of four. The space episode.'

'Ah, the cartoon. I remember. They climbed a ladder to the moon.'

'Ja, but…'

'Didn't even wear helmets.'

'…it still seemed like a fun trip. Even without the helmets.'

'Gašper…'

'What? It did, it looked fun.'

Sila stood up and walked over to the corner by the door. He didn't hit anything, but he didn't look at his friend either. All that positivity, it was starting to get really fucking annoying. And if it was annoying now…

'Brother,' continued Gašper, softening his voice a bit, 'you're just feeling the initial wave of it. Give it a week and you'll pivot too. Well, maybe. I mean, I'm hoping you will. You are a pretty hard guy to make pivot.'

Sila saw a flake of paint peeling off the wall and scratched at it.

'But still, when you look at it without all that neurotic shit clouding things, the truth is, nothing is ever as bad as you think it is. Not really.'

'Isn't it?'

Gašper shook his head. 'There's always stuff to colour in.'

'Is that a real metaphor?'

'Ne vem. Metaphor or idiom. But it's true, the future, it's like a colouring book. And most of it's still blank, which means…'

'The future is unknowable.'

'Right. Exactly.'

---

[30] Cartoon for very young kids.

Sila nodded and pulled the flake of faded green paint from the wall. He looked at it briefly and then dropped it on the floor. As it fell, he latched it onto Gašper's metaphor.

The flake of paint was in his hand.

He dropped it.

Now it's on the floor.

What exactly had been unknowable about that?

~~~

The only space port in Slovenia was crowded on the day of the launch. Of course, it was the space elevator they were launching so technically not a launch in the traditional sense, but it was a dramatic word and, even from his background perch, Potočnik was a dramatic man.

One hundred and seventy three patriotic Slovenes had been bussed in from the small nowhere town of Martinjak, given national flags and told to stand near the elevator as it was taking off. When some of them complained they were standing too close, and the ignition from the elevator would create a fireball killing them all, they were gifted *No Feeling Bear* toys from Guangdong [and told to stop spreading false science]. When a local citizen journalist from *Pravi Veronika* asked where all the other media was, she was quietly escorted off-site.

Gašper, Sila, Nakagami and five other Slovenes sat in an octagon-shaped room within the elevator, strapped in tight and facing each other. All of them had the same uniform; a dark green, RAF MK3 jacket and trousers with about eleven different pockets, both items marked with a Slovene flag badge. One of the other passengers - back straight against her chair, tilted afro, dark purple fabric headscarf, possibly second generation Ghanaian - seemed to recognize Sila, and glared at him unnervingly, but he had no idea who she was. Someone from Bled? Another activist? If she was on this elevator there was a good chance…

'Here goes,' said Gašper, shaking his chair. 'Maybe it won't be that bad after all.'
~~~

An electric shock passed through his body and knocked him unconscious. Sila looked at Nakagami in the seat to his left and the two of them shrugged.

The Japanese physicist had explained it to him the day before.

Space travel was a lonely thing, according to Potočnik.

Spending time with other people on a long space journey wasn't necessarily a harrowing thing - in fact the recent trips by Ghana and Guangdong to their own bases had recorded eighty-two percent contentment[31] - but it could still be precarious if not managed properly. Too much socialising could lead to inter-personal conflict, brawls, naked bodies landing on vital buttons and, worst case scenario, the ship blowing up.

Spending time alone would be safer.

But then there was the issue of isolation leading to insanity.

Potočnik had looked to the prisons for his answer. [Note: As in most Alliance nations, they weren't called prisons anymore, they were referred to as NOT YET Centres and focused more on rehabilitation, languages and experimental poetry. According to research done by people who'd read *Howl*, young adults with experience of not having rich parents were more capable of abrupt verse, fluid rhythm and pathos, mixing phrases like *fishfinger in a koi pool* with allusions to King Lear, things that made professionals in non-Alliance nations panic. Ja, they could manage Lear, but the fishfinger koi shit was beyond the pale, leading them to abandon poems and focus largely on YA fantasy instead.]

So…

In NOT YET Centres, inmates would spend seven tenths of their time alone [being creative/meditating/thinking/plotting], and three tenths talking to the other inmates.

The spaceship would operate under the same principle.

Talking time would be heavily regulated. Anyone caught talking when they shouldn't be would be given light electric shocks [most likely via a chip implanted in their brains, according to Nakagami]. If an

---

[31] Based on data sourced from Guangdong and Ghana Councils respectively.

offender fucked up more than ten times in one day, they would be zapped at the maximum voltage and tossed out the airlock.

The rest of the time would be spent alone, with at least ten hours of it in their quarters. If another crew member attempted to spend the night in the quarters of another, they would be electrocuted at ten minute intervals, and increasing voltage, until they returned to their own bed.

'But that theory seems to be completely upside down,' Sila said, folding up a tissue and putting it on top of the Korean BBQ + Cheese menu.

The two undercover jackets [wearing different colour stripes from the typical brand] on the other side of the restaurant straightened up, watching the tissue carefully. In may have been the sunlight spilling in from the window, but to Sila they looked gentler than the other ones he'd seen, like two village cops who just wanted to serve the same collective they lived in.

'It's the theory of a fascist,' replied Nakagami, taking the tissue, trying to make some kind of animal, failing then putting it back on the table. 'Not that Potočnik is a fascist.'

Sila stared at the tissue. 'He didn't tell me any of this.'

'What did he tell you exactly?'

'Not much. He joked that there'd be no entertainment, then said the trip would be short. Don't think he said fun, but…'

'He was correct about the trip being short.'

'Was he?'

'Unless they changed the figures, or gave me false engine specs, it shouldn't be more than forty-seven days.'

'Not too bad.'

'Then we move down to the old base. I'm not certain what the regulations will be for that area, but I suspect it won't be much different.'

'You mean more segregation?'

'Ja.'

'For four years?'

'Three and a half.'

'That's…' Sila stopped, unable to think of the right word. Insane? Tyrannical? Finally, he settled on *not good.*

'I suppose we'll adapt eventually. Though the least disciplined of us will probably have to endure at least fifty separate electric shocks. Hopefully spread out over many days.'

'Gašper,' muttered Sila, picking up the tissue again.

'Perhaps I'm over-estimating.'

Sila shook his head and threw the tissue at the window. It struck glass and dropped onto the salt shaker.

'Would you like to take a walk?', asked Nakagami, staring out at the main park opposite.

'Ja, might as well.'

The two of them scanned their Erazem cards by the door and left, walking past two more jackets pretending to read newspapers and out into the serene bustle of the street.

Sticking to the side, they talked through the various hazards of space travel while dodging small kids playing laser tag. When the jargon got too scientific, Sila would reach for his pocket and fumble for his tab. Then he would remember it had been confiscated for the next four years and look at the surroundings instead.

Ah, Novo Polje Collective.

He'd never been to this one before, mainly because it was on the east side of Ljubljana and relatively new. Or freshly amalgamated, according to an article in *Nov Večer.*

It was strange. The nucleus was the standard mix of local services, open space and Alliance/foreign restaurants, but a lot of the shops down the side streets seemed to be selling either DIY tools or cleaning products. Nothing else, just those two things.

'Isn't that weird?' he said, turning to Nakagami, but the scientist wasn't there. Giving the nearby street a quick scan, and ignoring the two *gentle* jackets pretending to look at skirts, he found him standing in front of HAMMER BROS DIY, staring at a chisel. As soon as Sila reached him, he turned and headed over to one of the magazine stands.

'Are you looking for something?' asked Sila, catching up.

'Window shopping.'

'Okay.'

Sila picked up a free [physical] copy of *Morda Ni Hudič* and flicked through. On page seven, there was an article about their spaceship, along with the caption: *Spaceships don't melt, that's absurd.*

Beside the text was a picture of the craft looking brand new and shiny. The Slovene letters on the side of the ship spelt out *Opustiti vsako upanje*, which the article attempted to explain: *'we want alien life to read the side of our ship and think, ja, Slovenia is probably more advanced than Russia. More civilised. These are the ones we should make contact with.'*

Sila put the zine back and asked Nakagami if Potočnik was right, that only part of the ship had melted during testing.

'As far as I'm aware, ja.'

'Do you think it'll melt when we're inside it?'

Nakagami walked out of the shop, staring across the park towards the residential side. Sila followed his line of sight and could vaguely make out a staggered line of parents on the viewing balcony, probably waiting for their kids to come out of the CHAOS CENTRES. He turned back to question Nakagami, but he was already halfway across the park. By the time Sila caught up with him, he was stepping onto one of the escalators.

'We're going up?' asked Sila.

It was a redundant question as they were already ascending. When they reached the top, Nakagami stopped for a moment, rubbed his head then started walking again. For some reason, he wandered into the CHAOS CENTRE lobby, turning down the corridor with a female toilets sign. Sila watched from outside, waiting for the mistake to be realised. It didn't take long. Nakagami made it a few more steps down the corridor before [presumably] noticing the lack of men, spun around as if he were lost, then retreated quickly outside to the viewing balcony.

'Wrong direction,' he muttered, bending down to tie his shoelace.

Sila gave a short *ja* and looked around at the army of parents. 'Feels a bit creepy being up here when you don't have kids. And they can see you're not a local.'

Nakagami didn't answer.

'Ah, sorry. I guess you still have family here.'

'Ne.'

'Parents?'

'Not anymore.'

'No wife or kids?'

'Ne.'

Sila scratched his left eyebrow. He didn't need to do a count, he knew they were the only non-kid carrying men on the balcony. 'Maybe we should go back down, walk around the park for a while?'

Nakagami waited, looking at the rest of the viewing balcony then said, 'ja, back down,' just as a woman and a little girl walked out from the female toilets corridor, both eating ice-cream. He adjusted his stance on the escalator and stared back up.

'You know them?' asked Sila, following his line of sight.

'Ne.'

'You want ice-cream?'

'What?'

'The ice-cream they're eating. You want some?'

Nakagami kept his eyes fixed on the mum and kid now walking along the terrace, either daydreaming or reconstructing a new, Baudrillardian signified for *ice-cream*. At some point he realised he'd been asked a question and released a quiet, 'ne.'

Must be the mission, thought Sila.

Disorientating him.

~~~

The launch sequence began.

Sila couldn't hear any kind of countdown and had zero experience of riding in space elevators, so he braced himself as much as he could for as long as he could. As he braced, he remembered his sister. There's a chance, he thought. A chance she's not…

The launch sequence paused.

Two more passengers were brought out from a temporary building and led towards the elevator. Their hands weren't tied, probably cos all avenues of escape had been cut off by the twenty-three jackets
~~~

surrounding them, and the way they were walking suggested they'd been drugged.

'You sure you don't want to keep him down here?' asked Potočnik to his guest.

'I considered it,' replied Amma Darko, her face un-moving. 'But a brave man deserves a brave fate.'

'As you wish.'

'Of course, if there's anyone in Ghana you're concerned about…'

'Not at the moment.'

'In the near future then.'

'I'll let you know.'

Darko nodded, a regal nod, she hoped.

Inside the elevator, the two new arrivals were guided in and placed on higher seats attached to the wall.

No one seemed to recognize the man, but when Sila saw Chu being strapped in, her eyes glazed, mouth half open, he screamed, a primal mix of *raarrggh* and *you fucking rat fink*.

Outside, some of the paid spectators saw the beginnings of their deaths and tried to make a run for it.

The guards were confused at first, then violent, shooting most of the first wave with bolts then scaring off the rest by moving forward and beating the wounded with their warning sticks.

Potočnik told a guard nearby to control the violence, it was spoiling the day, then turned to Darko and asked if this kind of thing had happened at the Ghana launch.

'Ours was a private launch,' she said, looking at the space elevator, and the crowd cautiously returning to it. The obedience pleased her, but it was poisoned slightly by the reluctance of it. And the general stupidity. Didn't they know these elevators had no exhaust? Her Ghanaian nationalists would never be this misinformed about science.

'Are you okay?' asked Potočnik.

'Still adapting to fresh air,' she lied, annoyed that she didn't have the liberty to criticize this man. Maybe he felt the same. After all, they were both running through the same rulebook. *Absence and presence, never let them see you wield.* Fuck. Sometimes she thought it would just be easier to blitzkrieg everything and sit in a fucking palace. At least she wouldn't have to limit herself.

Potočnik folded his arms and looked at Darko as covertly as he could. She may be a comrade, he thought, but I'm nothing like her really. She's killed people. Tortured them for no real reason. I could never do that.

He unfolded his arms, saw her looking at him with her incessant, *Sheila Munyiva* eyes and smiled. If we got married, had kids, there was a chance she'd mellow a bit…

The launch countdown resumed.

The elevator trembled then rose up into the sky, slowly at first, then faster and faster until it vanished into the clouds.

Potočnik turned to the parts of the crowd that were still conscious and raised his left arm in the air.

'Uspeh!' he shouted.

But he'd forgotten his microphone, so to most it simply looked like a miniature man attempting mime.

To Darko too.

PART TWO

The Colour Green And The Colour Black

After making it into low orbit, the passengers were given water and chicken salad, then transferred to another, smaller elevator and taken up to the main station where the ship was docked.

At least, that's what they were told as they couldn't physically see it; no cams, no windows, no permission to go off and look for cams and windows. For all they knew, they could've been heading into a furnace.

Gašper woke up in the smaller elevator, which allowed sentences of up to six words, and asked if they were on Mars yet.

Sila ignored him, but Nakagami didn't know Gašper so he took it as a serious question. 'Another 47 days…'

That was countered five minutes later, when the elevator tannoy informed them that, due to unforeseen engine complications, the trip duration would now be sixty-three days.

'Why would they be having engine problems, it does-…'

Another electric shock and Gašper was out.

'We'll have to coach him,' said Nakagami.

'Ja, in fewer than six words.' Sila paused, briefly wondering if *ja* counted as a word. 'Won't be easy.'

'Perhaps.'

'Gašper is an erratic guy. Unpredictable.'

'Ja. We have observed that.'

'Loud too.'

'There are some methods we can…' Nakagami looked up at one of the ceiling panels, a curved strip with a blank-looking bear stencilled on it, '…attempt.'

'Just gag the clown,' replied the purple headband woman who'd been glaring at Sila earlier.

'That might be a bit extreme.'

She switched her glare to Nakagami, clearly not liking him much either. 'Gag yourselves too.'

'Sorry, do we know each other?' the physicist asked, as polite as he could make it.

'I know you.' She turned to Sila, glancing up at the scanner to try and visually indicate her intention to start a new sentence. 'And I know him.'

'From where?' asked Sila, still puzzled. 'Bled?'

'Never.'

'Ljubljana?'

The woman didn't respond. Instead, she looked down at her neck, or tried to. There was a tattoo with Russian text which she appeared to mouth silently to herself.

Nakagami leaned over as much as he could towards Sila's ear and said, 'I think she's from Rudnik.'

'The collective?'

'The last few years, very different.'

'How?'

'Lots of immigrants, protests, some violence.' Nakagami paused, waiting a few seconds. 'Very Anti-Council.'

'Why is she glaring at…' Sila counted out the words, unsure. '…me?'

'Ne vem.'

The man who'd been brought in with Chu came out of his trance, looked around at the other faces, and said in accented Slovene, 'she did it, she won.'

Nakagami leaned forward. 'Don't say more than six-…'

'Four times and they still think she's a-…'

The man grunted in pain and his head fell to the side.

Sila shifted to the left a bit and tried to get Chu's attention, to ask what had happened, to apologise, but she was still zonked out, so much so that when the second, smaller elevator stopped, the guards had to add her to the auto-trolley, along with Gašper and the other man, and push her to the ship.

~~~

The ship itself was presented to them in a twenty minute induction video, where several scientists, including a more formally dressed Nakagami, explained the basics – engine near the back, three long, stacked decks in the middle, Control Room at the tip, something called a LEM-12 Field[32] to be installed after filming – and then moved on to the layout and function of each room.

'Is it still six words?' asked Gašper, coming round again and understanding pretty quickly where they were and what was happening.

'Ja…'

'Why are you…' Gašper looked at Nakagami, leaving a gap. '…in the video?'

'They said it was for promotion.' Nakagami let his head drop three times, possible counting. 'Filmed four months ago.'

'You knew about this?'

'The trip? Ne.'

'Liar,' said the purple headscarf.

'Who are you?' asked Gašper, somehow making it seem friendlier than it should've been.

The woman looked at Gašper strapped in to the right of Sila and Nakagami, apparently a triptych of evil as her glare returned. 'Are you with them?'

---

32 After a century of spinning space ships, a synthetic element called Lemium was created that, with careful manipulation, could simulate a localized gravity well. Due to its unpredictability, scientists started small and covert, then levelled up to space ship size [and covert]. The LEM-1 Field lasted 17 seconds before turning all rabbit crew members into *Galatea Of The Spheres*, while the LEM-11 Field ran for 3 months with only one reported case of a slight migraine.
~~~

'With who?'

'Them.'

'With them, not really, I just-…' He stopped quickly, closing his eyes. After a few seconds of no electricity, he opened them again. 'Fuck, that's scary.' He got his breath back. 'I just got out from rehab.' Another pause. 'I know Sila from before.'

'You don't live in Bled?'

'I don't live anywhere, technically.' A small chuckle, followed by a focused gaze at his interrogator's forehead. 'Wah, your headband is quite beautiful.'

'What?'

'Or is it a headscarf?'

'Why do you want to know?'

'Appreciation. Did you get it local?'

'Ne.'

'Import? Ghana? That's what mine was.'

'You said it was from Jesenice,' said Sila, keeping his eyes on the woman opposite.

'That was the old one.' Pause. 'Before Rehab.'

'And you bought the same colour?'

'I like orange. And purple.' Gašper fixed his attention back on the rival headwear opposite. 'It is from Ghana, right?'

The woman stared back at the orange cloth forcing back Gašper's fringe and managed a half-smile. 'I'll tell you later.' Few seconds pause. 'Away from them.'

'Ah, what about your name?'

'That too.'

'Just tell us now. It's faster.'

The half-smile turned to a quarter smile then a hyphen. 'Offer retracted.'

Gašper formed the word *what* in his brain but was too confused to follow through. Instead he stared at her headscarf again.

'Her name's Aleša,' said the skinny-looking, possibly Thai-Slovene man pinned to the seat next to her.

'Shut up, Petr.'

'Ja, Petr, that's me. He's Klemen.' A nod towards the heavy-set, Tehranian-looking man on the other side of him followed by a five second pause. 'That one said his name's Jame.' Another nod, another pause. 'Don't know the other guy.'

'Fucking rat…'

Aleša reached her arm across to grab him, which was enough to bring the guards over.

'No messing around, watch the video,' said the shorter one. 'There will be a test at the end of it, see how well you were listening.'

Everyone sat forward, waiting for the guard to be zapped and then slouched back again as he continued standing there, smirking like the original minarchist.

'Video,' he repeated, pointing at the screen.

~~~

Turned out the guard was lying, there was no test, which was fortunate for everyone [except Nakagami] as the only things they could remember from the video were the CREATE NOT DESTROY ROOM and the fact that they each got their own quarters complete with window and bathroom.

Shape of the ship?

No idea.

Engine type?

Some type of metal.

Fuel used?

Oil?

~~~

The first place they were taken to was the LAUNCH ROOM, a long space near the middle part of the ship with three rows of seats laid out in a *srednja šola*[33] *style* formation, half of them already full. Both groups of passengers looked shocked for a moment then, as they were strapped in, quickly understood things. Acceptance followed soon after.

'We'll leave your arms free,' announced one of the larger guards. 'In case you need to scratch yourself.'

'But attempt to move your legs and we'll be forced to come back in and shoot you,' said another, meaner-looking one.

'Same goes for your arms.'

Both guards took in the confused faces in front of them and shook their heads.

'Question,' said Nakagami, raising his hand.

The guard looked at his tab, said, 'ne,' and left.

'What was your question?' asked Gašper, leaning back to Nakagami's seat.

'Actually, I had several.' Pause. 'Who are these other people?' Pause. 'Why are we in this room?' Pause. 'I've forgotten the other one.'

'We're prisoners,' said one of the women, first in Twi, then in beginner level Slovene.

'You're from Ghana?'

'*Aane*. Ja.'

'Came up the elevator near Takoradi,' added one of the men, skipping the Slovene translation.

'What?'

The man turned to Sila and Aleša, the nearest black faces to him, and repeated his line.

'Don't know what you're saying,' replied Aleša, picking something out of her eye, while Sila ignored him completely and concentrated on Chu.

'… … … … … …?'

'Ne.'

'Sorry, they only know Twi,' interjected the woman, pointing her elbow at some of the others.

---

33 Secondary school, but not the type we recognize.

'Okay.'

A focused silence descended as those who cared mentally reviewed old language lessons, muttering out possible vocab almost without sound.

'You're going to Mars too?' asked Gašper, the first to try with his slightly shaky version of Twi.

'Mars?' asked the man, puzzled.

'We were told Venus,' said the woman.

'Who said Mars?' asked another, a few seats back.

'Something about living in the clouds.'

'You sure they said Mars?'

'Never mind,' said Gašper, understanding just under half of what they'd said.

'Darko put you up here,' uttered the man who'd been zapped like Gašper, also in Twi.

'*Aane*, with a sarcastic e-mail.' The Ghanaian woman paused, clearly aware of the six word rule. 'Thanking us for our sacrifice.'

Gašper heard the word *sacrifice* and looked at Sila, but he was still busy trying and failing to wake up Chu.

'She got me too,' said the man, adding that his name was Dodzi.

'You're from Ghana?'

'*Aane*, exiled.'

'And she still got you?'

'Fuck, she's petty,' added another.

'At least we won't be alone.' Dodzi paused. 'Brothers. Sisters.'

As soon as he said it, a group of different guards came back in and announced that there had been a slight change of plan and that all Ghanaian passengers had been granted the privilege of watching the launch from the VIP area.

'What VIP area?' asked one of the Ghanaians in fierce Twi.

'What launch?' responded Nakagami. 'We're in orbit, the ship.' He stopped, controlling himself. 'Simply adjusts course and accelerates.' He stopped again, tilting his head right. 'Onto a wider orbital path.'

'No one's listening, fascist,' said Aleša, leaning over from her seat.

She was right, the guards were too busy shepherding the Ghanaian passengers out of the room, beating the man who'd asked *which VIP room?* on the head and dragging him by the feet.

'Hey, comrade, what about me?' asked Dodzi, trying to rise out of his chair.

One of the guards stopped, checking his tab. 'Says here you're a Slovene Citizen.'

'Naturalised.'

'Then you're naturally Slovene.'

'My parents are from Ghana.'

'So?'

'I'm Ghanaian, by blood.'

'Your patch says you're Slovene too,' said the guard pointing at the flag stitched on to Dodzi's jacket.

'It's a mistake, comrade, it's not-…'

'Patch and pad, both Slovene. Sorry, *comrade.*'

Dodzi rose another inch, watching the last Ghanaian leaving the room. 'I'm not Slovene, you clear?'

'Clear?'

'I have to go with them.'

'Careful, that was almost seven words.'

'Prosim…'

'Can't do it, you're not on the list.'

'Put me on the list then.'

'Relax, comrade, you'll see them again soon.'

'Just add my name.'

'I said ne. Okay?'

'Prosim, I won't tell anyone.'

The guard turned, his face turning red. 'You're fucking pushing it…'

Dodzi said 'prosim' almost as a full stop as the guard grunted and left, the door sliding shut automatically behind him.

'Pretty sure there's no VIP room,' muttered Aleša, earning an irritated grunt from Dodzi.

~~~
~~~

A few hours later, a female voice came on the speaker system and told them that the ship had successfully left orbit.

'However, due to unforeseen issues with the magnetic containment fields surrounding the ion engine, the VIP area of the ship has melted. Fortunately, the ships AI was able to detach the section as it was melting, so all other systems remain undamaged and fully operational.

To those who either knew the Ghanaian passengers or had a friendly conversation with them in the LAUNCH ROOM prior to leaving orbit, we are sorry for your loss, but know that their deaths will not be in vain. All of their families' names will be added to both the Ghanaian and Slovene Council's official Liberation Day lists, and, additionally, a representational statue of the group will be personally commissioned and funded by Amma Darko herself, via the Council Treasury.

To the surviving passengers, have a safe and bold trip to Mars.'

There was a short lull filled only by the sound of staggered breathing from Dodzi.

Then three more beeps and the voice resumed.

'Additional news.

The parts of your hand luggage that weren't removed pre-launch due to weight issues, have been placed in your quarters. Hot water for showering will be available between nine and ten in the morning, and ten and eleven at night. Shaving will be done using *Krog-8 gel,* one packet a week. Clothes have been laid out on your bed. The WE MARTIANS t-shirt is particularly recommended. For laundry, please leave items to be washed outside your quarters before curfew hours and they will be returned to you fully-cleaned the next morning. All bed materials were sourced locally and have been back-certified adventurist free. We hope everything falls within your limits of comfort.

You may now leave your seats and make your way to the CREATE NOT DESTROY ROOM, which is located farther along the deck you are now on. For reference, that is the middle deck.

If you were unconscious during the video presentation earlier and do not know how to go there, prosim, ask another crew member who was conscious for assistance.

Hvala.'

After saying the obligatory *fucks* and *was that a joke?* regarding the melting incident, half the passengers stretched their arms, got up, stretched their legs too and started walking sluggishly towards the exit.

When they reached the door, something clicked and the news they'd just received became real.

Either Cvetko or Jame bent over and retched, while Petr and Klemen stood by the frame of the door, frozen.

The tannoy sounded again:

'Additional news,

A ship-wide diagnostic has been completed, and all systems have been declared safe.

Please compartmentalise your shock and proceed to the CREATE NOT DESTROY ROOM at your own pace

Hvala.'

The trail of beeps after the message were loud and grating enough to unfreeze the crew.

Cvetko or Jame stopped retching.

Chu rebooted and stood up as if she'd just been daydreaming in class, with Sila immediately rushing over to help her, guide her, hover generally around her.

'Chu…I don't know where to.' He paused, waiting. 'Can only say six words.' Pause. 'I'm so sorry, I didn't want.' Pause. 'Didn't want you to come.'

'We're on the ship?' she asked, rubbing her left eye.

'Ja, already launched. I don't think.' Pause. 'Don't think we can go back.' Pause. 'I'm so, so sorry, I didn't…'

'It's okay, Sila. I'm not angry.'

'Fucking should be,' said Aleša, walking past.

'Sorry?'

'Ignore her,' said Sila.

'Ignore who?'

Sila had forgotten Aleša's name momentarily, so he shrugged and just said someone with a grudge, then pushed Chu towards the door.

Gašper was the last one out, stopping at the door and looking back at Dodzi, who was frozen like an arctic pervert in his seat.

He thought about going over and asking if he was okay, if he needed help getting to the CREATE NOT DESTROY ROOM, but the part of him who'd spent three years blanking the same questions from therapists said, ne, better not, he might stab you.

It was true, that's how some people reacted to mass murder.

Or mass manslaughter due to faulty magnets, according to the female tannoy voice.

Whatever that meant.

~~~

The CREATE NOT DESTROY ROOM was a mix of mess hall and arts and craft area, with a food dispenser stuck to the wall on the right, a huge table shaped like Satan's tooth in the middle, card, scissors, paint and crayons laid out on another desk, and a triptych of giant windows showing the passengers the void they were about to glide out into…or were already gliding through, according to Nakagami.

'Ion engine, low thrust, high velocity.' The physicist paused, looking across at Aleša on the other side of the table, flanked by her two comrades, then turned left to the three, marginally warmer faces on his side. 'After about ten or twenty days.'

'What's velocity?' asked Gašper, squinting.

Before Nakagami could get started on basic physics, the door slid open and Dodzi walked in. Without saying a word, he grabbed a seat and carried it over to the far left window, then sat down with his forehead resting against the [transparent-aluminum] glass. The *grey cloud,* coupled with the oddly pale green lighting in the room, was so pervasive that the two other passengers, Jame and Cvetko, got up and moved to the opposite side of the table, despite having been at least a metre and a half away from him to begin with.

'You think we should say something?' asked Gašper.

'Later,' said Sila.

'What later? The guy looks suicidal.'
~~~

'It's unlikely that conversation with us.' Nakagami paused, nodding three times. 'Will make him better.'

'Not with you two guys.'

'Don't,' muttered Sila, sending his words down to the table.

'But maybe I can help him.'

'People just died, Gašper. Leave him.'

'See, you're too miserable. Too dark.'

'He's always miserable,' added Chu, patting Sila on the arm.

'I repeat, people have just died.'

'Ja, we know,' started Gašper, looking at Chu's face and instantly muting the rest of his sentence.

'Maybe we should check for alcohol,' interjected Petr, pointing towards the dispenser on the far wall.

A few grumbles, seemingly neutral.

'Maybe we should start the interrogations,' countered Aleša, tightening her headscarf.

'Dial it down a bit, Aleša,' said the stocky, Iranian-looking guy no one could remember the name of.

'Keep looking at the fucking floor,' Aleša paused, counting back the words. '*Klemen*.'

Ah Klemen, sighed most of the others internally. That was it.

'He's right, we're all stuck here,' said Petr.

'Ja, but why is he here?' Aleša pointed at Nakagami, waiting a few seconds. 'What did he do?'

'Does it matter?'

'For future trust, ja.' Aleša jabbed the table, checking the walls for whatever was monitoring their speech. 'We got picked up last week.' More jabbing. 'For agitating in our collective.' More vague checking of the walls. 'But him…'

'Nakagami hasn't done anything,' said Sila, his eyes fixed on his opponent's fingers.

'How do you know that?'

'Observation. Logic.'

'Intuition?'

Sila folded his arms, refusing to offer even a solitary *ne*.

'He *was* in the video,' said Klemen, pulling at the sleeve of his jacket.

'Exactly.'

'What happened to dialling it down?' asked Petr, putting his hand on the back of Klemen's chair.

'It's true, we all watched it.'

'That video was three months ago,' said Nakagami, replacing his head nods with a new counting system: three taps of the table. 'I don't know why I'm here.'

'Cos you're a plant,' said Aleša.

'Here to monitor us,' added Klemen, letting go of his sleeve and pulling it again.

'For four years?' asked Sila.

'Or murder us like those others.'

'Murder?'

'My guess is monitor,' said Klemen. 'It's smarter.'

'More cowardly too.'

'What, for four years?' tried Sila again.

'Ja, why not?'

'That's a pretty dedicated plant,' said Chu.

'Hey, I was gonna say that,' said Gašper, nudging Chu in the side.

'He's a scientist, he likes space,' continued Aleša, pushing forward into the edge of the table and focusing on Chu. 'Who are you again?'

'Chu.'

'That's your first name?'

'Family name,' said Klemen, switching to the other sleeve.

Aleša noted the defence with an irritated glance then quickly bounced back to Chu. 'Is he right?'

'Technically. Ja.'

'What's your first name then?'

'Irrelevant.'

'Why? Is it difficult to pronounce?'

'I prefer Chu.'

'She's lying,' said Klemen, giving up on the sleeves and laying his arms out flat on the table.

'What?'

'No one uses their family name.'

'She does,' said Sila, instinctively shifting his seat one hundredth of an inch closer to Chu.

'Unless they have something to hide.'

'Like him,' added Aleša, turning back to her original target. 'Nakagami.'

'He has a first name,' said Sila, switching defendants [but not the position of his seat].

'Does he?'

'So does Chu, she just doesn't…' Sila formed the *L* with his tongue then stopped himself, waiting out another four seconds before finishing. 'She doesn't like using it.'

'What is it then?'

'What's what?'

'His first name.'

'Ne vem.'

'And why isn't he using it?'

Gašper held up both hands, palms out. 'Guys, lower the heat a bit.'

'What heat?'

'We've been here five minutes, let's.' Gašper paused, flinching when he realised he'd hit the limit.

'Did his boss say not to?

'Let's just take it slowly,' said Petr, giving a curt nod to Gašper across the table. 'Okay?'

Aleša shifted her full focus onto the Japanese physicist. 'Did your boss say not to?'

'Come on, Aleša.'

'Is he in your ear now?'

'Don't.'

'Talking to you?'

'I assure you,' Nakagami started, but he was interrupted by five piercing beeps and then the female voice on comm.

'Attention crew,

There is one more rule we have to inform you of. In fact, there may be other rules phased in during the journey, but those will be announced at the appropriate times.

The new rule, which will go into effect ten seconds after this announcement has ended, is a supplement to an existing rule. That rule being: each day, meaning each span of twenty-four hours, you will have four hours to talk to your shipmates. Under the new supplemental rule, each line in the conversation can contain more than six words…'

'Thank fuck for that,' said Gašper, breathing out dramatically.

'…but will be limited to two persons only. Any detection by internal ship sensors of a third voice close to the conversation of two others will result in electric shocks for all three communicators.

It is advised that passengers sit in different rooms to conduct conversations, but if you wish to congregate together in one room, be cautious and ensure there is sufficient distance between all communicating pairs.

Have a safe and bold journey to Mars.

Hvala.

P.S. In a non-theistic, miraculous turn of events, there was one survivor from the magnetic containment tragedy earlier. The man was discovered wounded outside the VIP ROOM but not fatally so, and was predicted to recover. Sadly, in his delirious state, he mistook the *open airlock* button for a water dispenser and was either blown or sucked - the terminology is not clear on this particular point – out into space. We have tracked his body and can confirm that, contrary to popular myth, his head did not explode.

End of announcement.'

Everyone looked at each other, uttered a mix of 'what the fuck?' and 'ten seconds?' then quickly migrated to different parts of the table.

In the far left corner, Dodzi fixed eyes on the nearest of the pale green lights dug into the ceiling and laughed.

Then screamed.

Then cried.

Then went back to resting his forehead against the window.

~~~

Uncowed by the threat of further rules, as well as the ridiculous nature of the newly introduced one, all ten of the prisoners decided it would be better to stick together in the same room rather than hide away in their own little pockets.

Well, nine of them decided. Dodzi spent almost all of his time in his quarters and bluntly said 'don't' when anyone tried to approach him in the corridor. And of course there was Aleša, who agreed only so she could keep tabs on Sila and Nakagami, and possibly Chu as well, as she hadn't figured out her situation yet.

Because none of them had paid much attention to the video explaining the ship layout, they chose the CREATE NOT DESTROY ROOM as the shared space, and arranged sections around the huge table for pairs to conduct their conversations without electrocution.

And, although each of them said it was best if they all alternated talking partners, at least for the first two weeks, they soon broke up into the following preferred groups:

Klemen and Aleša.

Aleša and Petr.

Cvetko and Jame, who appeared to be a couple. Or had been a couple previously and, because of the bleakness of the situation and the possibility of four years without a fuck, now decided to resume their relationship.

Chu and Nakagami.

Chu and Sila.

Chu and Gašper.

Gašper and Jame [once]

Nakagami and Petr.

And when Chu was elsewhere, Sila and Gašper.

~~~

To assuage suspicions from Aleša and others, Nakagami took Chu's advice and wrote down as much as he could think of about the mission ahead, as well as a detailed guide to the rooms of the ship, and put it up on the wall next to the food dispenser.

Apart from a few murmurs praising the aesthetically neat hand-writing [Gašper's words], it didn't have much of an effect.

'He worked for a guy who did this shit all the time…' said Aleša, having a rare chat with someone other than Klemen or Petr, in this case Chu. 'Pre-emptive rationalisations, getting ahead of criticism and re-directing it where you want it to go. *Morda Ni Hudič* operates the same way too. Small circle control mechanisms…'

'Actually, it was my idea,' said Chu, taking off her ship-issue jacket and hanging it on the back of the chair.

'What was?'

'To write down what he knew about the mission.'

'That was your idea?'

'I told him it might calm people down.'

'You told him to do it?'

'Ja.'

Aleša looked at Chu's forehead and then her *Nap Queen* t-shirt, as if it was some kind of esoteric truth gauge.

'It was me,' repeated Chu, taking a sip of what the food dispenser claimed was Tanzanian coffee. 'Really.'

'Ja. I believe you.'

'Good.'

'That you think it was your idea.'

Aleša got up and went back to Klemen, who appeared to be laying siege to a glass of water, his arms straight and rigid on the table around it.

'Still suspicious?' asked Sila, taking the empty seat next to Chu.

'Probably not a good idea to sit there.'

'What?'

'At least not so fast. And definitely not in that t-shirt.'

Sila glanced down at the *WE MARTIANS* text covering most of his chest, seemingly seeing it for the first time. 'It was on top of the pile.'

'And recommended by Potočnik.'

'They're all recommended, technically. Mine, hers.' Sila paused, noticing Chu's t-shirt. 'Maybe not yours.'

'They let me pack a few things.'

'And then drugged you?'

'Ja, it was a bit strange. I think the second set of guards were from a different department.'

Sila looked at Chu's cup, then at the food dispenser.

'You wanna wear my jacket?' asked Chu, half peeling it from the back of her chair.

'To cover up my sins?'

'Or you can just go and change your t-shirt.'

'Ja, to one of the rebellion-leaning ones. That *RED STAR* rag maybe.'

'Obviously not.'

'See how long it takes them to shove me out the airlock. Which, let's face it, is probably deserved. Two years pissing about by the lake while half the Turkish population was being deported. Not even writing anything. Just…sitting there like a fucking potato.'

'Ah, the self-pity chamber again.'

Sila closed his eyes and pictured the same void he could see when they were open. Pure vacant blackness. Terrifying, in a way, but also without fascists so not all bad.

'Are you meditating?'

He opened his eyes again, managing the tiniest of smiles. 'Sorry, just some minor theatrics. Saying it out loud the same way she probably is. Really. There's no real weight behind it.'

'Good.'

'Can't carry the mop for a fascist.'

'Bōl?'

'Ja. Good catch.'

Chu took another mouthful of Tanzanian coffee, making sure to place the cup well to the side of the white card laid out in front of her. 'About the t-shirt…you could try wearing the dark green one. There's no text or symbols, so it…'

'Ja, help me blend into the walls.'

'...won't provoke others so much. Which walls?'

'Bedroom. Bathroom. They're all a shade of green. Bulbs in the corridor too.' He looked up, at the eight bulbs dotted along the ceiling. 'These ones, ne vem. Sometimes they look a kind of pale green, other times not.'

'It is an odd choice for a colour scheme.'

'Ja, very odd. Gašper said it was similar to the ones in rehab. A constant green glow. Maybe a unifying theme on Potočnik's part. Something to affect our mood.'

'Maybe.'

Sila pulled down the collar of his t-shirt and itched his shoulder. 'Is she still looking over?'

'Who?'

'Witchfinder General.'

'Jezus. Not so loud.'

'Is she looking at us?'

'Ne vem.'

'Check.'

'Ne.'

'Then I will.'

'Sila...'

He took the white card covered in equations that Chu had been scribbling on and held it up, pretending to read. Behind the card, he could see that Aleša *was* staring at him, right hand pushing against her [possibly fake] *Dok Militia* headscarf, while Klemen was drawing something on his glass.

'That's not very subtle,' whispered Chu.

Sila refocused on the maths and found a part that wasn't an equation, reading it out loud. 'Is the positioning of the muons actually important?'

'Don't make me explain muons again.'

'Aren't they similar to quarks?'

Chu took the card back and told him to draw something, make himself busy.

'I can't.'

'Try.'

'It would be too depressing. And it'd make you depressed too.'

'If you're drawing then you're not speaking, maybe even not thinking, which means…ne vem. Could function as some kind of therapy?'

Sila ran his finger along the side of his thumb, seemingly reflecting on what she'd just said but, in truth, just scratching himself in a softer way.

'Or just keep talking to Gašper…'

'Gods…'

'His extreme optimism can compensate for your innate melancholy. Might distract you enough to stop the itching too.'

'Ha, unlikely,' replied Sila, switching his nails back to his shoulder.

'I'm only half joking. Exposure to positivity can be a kind of salve. And there's no one more positive than Gašper…'

'Erratic, more like.'

'I saw him earlier, on the upper deck, smiling like a little kid. He told me that he'd found Mars, outside the window, and he'd been staring at it all morning, imagining the city we're gonna build.'

'City?'

'Kind of reminded me of Tala, actually. Her underground portals connecting to alien worlds. Remember that?'

'Ja, vaguely…'

'Her and Gašper would've got on quite well, I think. Assuming he ever let her speak. Her voice could be quite soft at times.'

Sila scratched his neck at quarter speed, brain lost somewhere out past the window.

'Ja, Gašper and his Martian city. Didn't get around to asking any details about it. Probably for the best.'

'Definitely,' muttered Sila, slowly coming back.

'He did say something about most of Slovenia joining us. Within ten years.'

'Ten years…'

Chu smiled, sipping more of her coffee.

'His headband must be too tight.'

'Ne vem. It's probably some chemical malfunction in his brain, or some self-defence mechanism he created in rehab to get him through.'

'Or the Antro-D.'

'Sorry?'

Sila let out a preparatory breath for the explanation ahead then remembered who he was talking to. 'I stabbed him before we left. Gave him Antro-D, he recovered, and got self-sustaining testosterone as a bonus.'

Chu looked down at her equations card then back up. 'I didn't know Antro-D could do that.'

'Neither did the doctor. But it happened. Maybe other side effects are leaking through too.'

'Possibly.'

'Ne vem. It is still strange though.'

'Ja, that it would increase androgen production. Seems strangely specific.'

'Ne, I mean it's strange that he's here.'

'On the ship?'

Sila nodded and counted something out on his fingers. 'Eight of us here in total, all-…'

'Ten.'

Sila checked his fingers, confused.

'Cvetko and Jame,' said Chu, helping him out.

'Ah…them.'

'It's easy to forget people who don't say anything.'

Sila nodded. 'Ten of us in total, all dissidents in some way, all with some rational reason to be here…'

'…except Gašper,' finished Chu.

'Precisely.'

~~~

'Maybe I'm only here because I know you,' said Gašper, pulling open a drawer and cursing in Slovene when he saw it was empty.

'Ja.'

'Friend of a dissident equals potential dissident.'

'Maybe.'
~~~

Gašper closed the drawer and looked around the HALF DONE ROOM for more to open, but unless they were disguised as part of the wall, his search was over. Results: one drawer with testosterone pills that he no longer needed, and another smaller drawer with bottles of what looked like flu, headache, diarrhoea meds.

'It could be to keep you company so you don't top yourself.'

'That's what Potočnik said,' said Sila, sitting on the only bio-bed in the room, which was actually more like a futon than a bed. About half a metre off the floor, maybe a little more. Next to it was a stationary robot-like drone capable of two lines of speech, both delivered in a flat tone: *Prosim, lie down on the bio-bed* and *be still.*

'See, there's your answer then.'

'But the more I think about it, the more I wonder...' Sila paused, looking at the empty syringe on the tray next to the bio-bed. 'Ne vem. Maybe none of this makes any sense.'

'Sense is for people looking backwards.'

Sila instinctively said, 'ja,' then remembered it was Gašper he was talking to and modified to, 'who said that?'

'*Klevin Lakik.*'

'You're quoting a cartoon character?'

'He was live action, not a cartoon and it's true, if you always say, 'it doesn't make sense,' then you're looking backwards instead of saying, 'hey, it's happened, something's happened, we're in this situation, what do we do next?''

'Gašper...'

'Ne, don't try and dismiss it as simplistic...'

'It is.'

'...or vacuous.'

'Even better.'

'It's a valid point. Or valid philosophy, whatever you call it. Not vacuous at all.'

'Valid perspective, maybe.'

Gašper stopped, his hand on one of the open drawers. 'Hey, are you even looking for this stuff?'

'Ja.' Sila leaned back and peered at the small space under the bio-bed. 'Nothing here.'

'Seems like you're just relaxing.'

'I'm taking a break. Admiring the posters.'

Gašper turned to the wall behind him, did his second double-take at the girl holding a giant razor next to *SAD?* in over-sized text and muttered, 'ja, funny.'

'Not sure why they have one for dementia.'

'Osmosis.'

'What's that?'

'I said, it's a shame there's no art for dry skin or allergies.'

Sila nodded, itching the red patch on his arm.

'What's causing it anyway? The air?'

'Ne vem. Probably.'

'Any chance it'll stop?'

'Back home, ja. When the weather stabilised, it'd stop being so itchy. Here, ne vem.'

'Be still,' interjected the robot drone, neglecting any kind of warning static and nearly sending Gašper sprawling to the floor.

'Jezus fucking-…'

'Relax. It thinks we're being treated.'

'By who?'

'Ne vem. Two people in the room, one the patient, the other one the doctor. I guess you got close enough to it to set off its sensors.'

Gašper glared at the machines almost square head then went back to the bottles in the drawer. 'Long as it's not the actual doctor.'

'What's that?'

'I said it better not be giving any injections.'

'Don't think it's that mobile.' Sila waved his hand in front of the drone and watched its *eye* bloom in response. 'Okay, not really mobile at all.'

'Good.'

'It does have a hand though. Or a claw. Maybe I can get Nakagami to program it to move up and down, scratch my neck. Though that's probably unethical.'

'What is?'

'Robot stuff. Nothing serious.' Sila coughed, provoking a *prosim, lie down on the bio-bed* from the robot. 'What was that thing you said before?'

'When?'

'Your non-vacuous philosophy.'

'Huh?'

'The thing about not looking backwards.'

'Ah, positivism,' answered Gašper, checking a bottle label and frowning.

'Don't think that was its name.'

'Ne, same thing. You leave behind the negativity, what happened before, bad decisions, bad luck, depression over skin conditions etc. and you focus on the future. Which releases chemicals in your brain that are positive cos they're trying to imagine something new instead of looking at, or fixating on something shit that you can't change.'

'That's not positivism.'

'Ja, it is.'

'I mean, philosophically, that's not positivism.'

'It is, I checked.' Gašper tapped the wall he was standing next to, putting his ear close enough to pick up any *hidden drawer* sounds. 'Positivism. The psychological act of being positive, releasing positive chemicals from your brain.'

'That's positivity, not positivism.'

'Ne, it's positi-…' He stopped, shifting his headband further to the side. 'Ne vem. Positivity. That's the name of it?'

'Hundred percent.'

'Not positivism?'

'Ne.'

'Are you sure?'

Sila sighed, picking up the empty syringe and pressing down on the plunger.

'You're not just repeating what you've read, are you? Cos I do that sometimes.'

'I think we've gone off on a tangent we may never return from.'

'Ja, what were we talking about again?'

Sila placed the tip of the needle against his upper arm, then moved it slowly up to his neck.

'Hey, don't fuck around with that.'

'It's not loaded.'

'That's how Žižek died. Empty needle.'

Sila lowered the syringe, puzzled.

'Not that one, a guy in rehab. Said he'd received the true translation of the Munich Manual in his sleep. It told him the 8th door was through his own neck. That demon guy…Prince Taob, or Tobe…was awaiting him in an undetectable flesh pocket inside his throat, something like that. In the LET'S INTEGRATE ROOM, that's where he said it. Then he stabbed himself.'

Sila attempted and failed a whistle.

'Hence another reason for my positivism…'

'Positivity.'

'…fifty-seven days then Mars. No guards. Not that many rules. Compared to where I was, this is paradise. And we're going somewhere.'

Putting the syringe back on the tray, Sila got up and walked over to the open door. It was dimmer [and greener] outside in the corridor, so he hung back a bit, giving his eyes time to adapt from the insanely bright light emanating from the ceiling of the HALF DONE ROOM.

'We're leaving?' asked Gašper, tapping the wall for secret panels again.

'Ja, me.'

'What about your dry skin?'

'There's nothing here for it.'

'We haven't checked everywhere, there could still be-…'

'Doesn't matter, I'll cope.'

'And Chu?'

'It barely affects her.'

Gašper adjusted his headband again, looking around at the open drawers, doing a final scan.

'You can stay here if you want, continue looking.'

'Alone?'

'Or we can come back later, do it together.'

'Where are you going?'

'I need to talk to Nakagami.'

'The spy?'

Sila opened his mouth to bite back, but Gašper beat him to it.

'I'm joking, comrade. I like Nakagami.'

'You do?'

'Sure. He's our science guy, along with Chu. Without them, we'd be finished.'

'Correct.'

'And even if he is a spy, who cares? Everyone knows Potočnik's a fascist, Potočnik knows it too.'

'Everyone on this ship knows.'

'And most of Slovenia. Or they will within the next four years. Chu's right, tyrants have a short life span, things will go our way eventually.'

Sila stared at what he knew was Gašper's utterly genuine smile, and bit his tongue. Literally bit it. Cos what he wanted to say, what he knew to be true, would make everyone feel just like the poor, broken Ghanaian guy stuck in his quarters.

Better to keep it to himself, solve it in his own way, without letting it fester.

A tough trick.

~~~

In contrast to the medical bay, or the HALF DONE ROOM, the TALK TO YOUR GOD ROOM [Control Room] was practically a national switchboard.

There were levers and switches and, up to the point when Sila had given up counting, one hundred and twenty-four buttons, all laid out across three sections near the front.

For human-machine interface, there was a single chair to the right, set up next to the console and an attached keypad, the sum of which allowed theoretical communication with the ships AI. Theoretical as, instead of the Slovene alphabet, all the keys on the pad had symbols stamped on them.
~~~

According to Nakagami, this wasn't ancient Sumerian as Gašper had speculated, but was in fact a derivative of an existing code, one he was vaguely familiar with but not competent in, so it would be a while before they could start asking meaningful questions. A few weeks even. Until then, all they could do in the Control Room was sit back and stare at the other buttons. Decorative buttons, of course, as the AI took care of ship functions internally. Though, on the plus side, all the controls on the communication and sensors console appeared to be authentic.

Sila had no idea if any of that were true or not, but Chu believed it so he did too.

Apart from the hardware, there was nothing much to add. It was a room with the word 'GOD' on the door. And the same triptych window set-up as the CREATE NOT DESTROY ROOM, either displaying space outside or projecting a convincing simulation of it.

Not a room to spend the best hours of the day in.

Unless, of course, you were a Japanese-Slovene physicist that no one really trusted.

'As far as I can tell…which is mostly from this little guidance manual here…' Nakagami held up a booklet with AI and a robot face printed on the cover, both in dark green. '…the computer has been programmed to act within a narrow band of parameters.'

'The AI,' translated Sila, leaning on a part of the middle console he'd been assured had none of the few functioning buttons.

'Ja, things like requests, ship functions, trajectory alterations, velocity monitoring…'

'Delivering electric shocks.'

'…minor maintenance issues, ja, discipline, surveillance.'

'Petr, Klemen and She Who Wishes To Flay Us got hit again this morning.'

'Chu and I also, though it was Gašper who was at fault.'

'He was the third party?'

'Ja. Usually I will imitate intense concentration when I see him within four meters and restless, in case he thinks of coming over. In this case, however, I forgot.'

'He'll get used to it.'

Nakagami nodded, noticing a flashing blue light on the console and flicking a switch.

'What was that?'

'Trajectory update.'

'From the AI?'

'Ja.'

'You requested that?'

'Automatic. Every three hours.'

Nakagami stared at the trajectory line on the screen dug into the console. Sila tried staring too, but all he could make out was Earth, Mars and a slightly-curved line trying to connect them.

'Bad news?' asked Sila, trying to win back Nakagami's attention.

'Ne. Something a little unorthodox.' He looked up, settling on Sila's neck. 'You wanted to know about the ship.'

'The ship?'

'When you came here, you said you wanted to know more about the ship.'

'Ah, I forgot about that.'

'Well, I've told you and everyone else all the details from the manual here, as well as my personal observations. That is the sum of my knowledge at present. Even if some don't believe it.'

'You've told us everything?'

'That I see as relevant, ja. If you want something specific then you'll have to ask a more specific question.'

'Ne vem.'

'Then I don't know what I can say.'

Sila shifted weight onto his other leg, checking the buttons behind him after the act. 'Are there any odd things that…not the function of the ship but…anything odd that doesn't add up, or doesn't make sense?'

Nakagami looked back at the line on the screen. 'There are things that appear to be redundant.'

'The room names.'

'That's one of them. Though there is a foundational model for that. As I said before, the NOT YET Centres.'

'Ja, Gašper said his rehab had weird room names.'

'In fact, there may be a foundational model for all of the things present here, even if their function is uncertain.'

'What about the redundant parts?'

'Redundant from our perspective. The design of the corridor outside this room, for example. It is coiled like an accordion snake, for no discernible reason.'

'Ja, I did wonder about that…'

'You have to navigate seven abrupt corners before you reach the entrance, which in an emergency, if this really were a regular control deck, would be suicidally impractical.'

'So why is it designed like that?'

'That is my question.'

'Whimsy?'

Nakagami nodded, pressing another button on the console. 'From a design perspective, spaceships are typically built in a practical sense. Mass, surface area, materials used; even with the new ion engine, the battery, the LEM-12 Field, the designer would have tight restrictions. Should have tight restrictions, I should say. Yet here we are, with individual quarters, superfluous rooms, impractical corridor designs, green walls…'

'…VIP room.'

'Ja. I suspect that was in fact a buffer room next to the plasma chamber.'

Sila itched the skin on the back of his hand, vaguely aware of what plasma was.

'The only aspect that is noticeably constant with this design is personality. Or whimsy, as you described it. Simply put, the mind or minds responsible for this ship didn't design it simply for space travel, they designed it specifically for the people lodging inside.'

'Potočnik…'

'To what ends, ne vem. Ja, Potočnik. In tandem with others perhaps. Or on his own. It's actually quite impressive when you consider it.'

'The ship?'

'Not only did he plot his way to power without obstruction…'

Sila flinched.

'...but he also managed to design a ship that could manipulate people who would only be on it for sixty-three days, or fewer at the start of the trip.' He paused, looking at the keypad in front of him. 'Sorry, poor sentence construction.'

'I feel sick.'

'Physically?'

'All over.'

Nakagami gestured to the left. 'There's a little bin built into the wall, if you require it. Another redundancy.'

Sila ignored it and walked towards the wall next to the entrance, touching its metal-plated surface with one hand. He buffered for a moment, transfixed by god knows what then turned and stared out of the window. 'How the fuck did he do all this, and none of us noticed?'

'Regarding the ship, it was restricted for the three months before take-off, so I assume that's when...'

'Ne, I didn't mean you were...'

'...the alterations were made. Why not? I worked beside him.'

'Ja, but you didn't-...'

'I noticed what he was doing.'

'What?'

'And did nothing.'

'You knew what he was doing?'

'And now I'm here, sitting in the Control Room of a ship that cannot be controlled, encircled by people who believe me to be a spy. Perhaps it is a form of justice, after all.'

Sila took a step forward, half clenching a fist. 'Nakagami, did you know what he was doing?'

'Or you could call it the inevitable arc of consequence.'

'Did you?'

Nakagami looked past Sila, towards the door. Or the doorway as technically there was no door. Pale green light was sneaking in from the bulb propped up near the ceiling outside.

'There's no one out there,' said Sila.

'I know.'

'Then answer my question.'

A beeping noise intervened followed by the female Comms Officer, which they'd recently discovered was in fact the AI.

'Attention crew,

Talking time will cease in 12 minutes. Either return to your quarters or continue your activities in silence.

This will be the only warning.

Hvala.'

Nakagami turned back to the console, but Sila reached down and swivelled his chair back round.

'Tell me, quickly.'

'No time.'

'Prosim.'

The physicist tapped the edge of the console three times, watching the veins on the back of his hand, then moved up to Sila's neck. 'There is little to say. I knew the same details you knew. The same details all Slovenians knew.'

'You just said you worked with him, noticed what he was doing.'

'The *Serpentinšek* article. That is what I'm referring to.'

'What?'

'Everyone who read it knew. It told us explicitly.'

'But…'

'And we all did nothing.'

~~~

Sila sat on the bed in his quarters, the *Green is Good* t-shirt scrunched up on the pillow next to him.

He was alone.

There was a pad of paper and a pencil on the desk near his bed, and the rest of the ship-issue t-shirts spread out on the floor.

RED STAR

Dibrivna Vaska – Rebel

Mojca Ito - No Fight From Comfort'

Can't Kill Us All

Green is Good
~~~

WE MARTIANS

Others that he'd decided he had no moral right to wear.

On the wall opposite were ten generic, jovial faces, all of them dwarfed by a mega painting of Potočnik himself, bodyless, looking up at an almost out-of-shot Mars and smiling. According to Nakagami, it was another attempt to promote mental health during the journey. Seeing happiness would equal happiness. Or it would equal less loneliness perhaps. As usual, it was flawed logic. Especially as the largest of those people was Potočnik himself, the man who'd put them there.

Sila got to his feet and walked the short journey into the bathroom. There was still residual steam from his shower ten minutes earlier, but that was overshadowed by the green patches on either side, as well as the quote above the mirror which stated: 'Ja, this is the real you.'

For a second, he looked at himself in the mirror, the lack of creases under his eyes, the lack of bruises or marks, then remembered all those hundreds of old movies where a character did the exact same thing, and pulled away. Moving quickly back into the main room, he picked up the pencil, lined the pad up against the wall and eked out the very roughest of sketches.

Three long decks stacked vertical: ion engine and six funnel exhaust at the rear, quarters in the middle, Engineering and a lot of locked doors on the bottom, TALK TO YOUR GOD ROOM at the tip.

He kept the pencil gripped tight and looked at his art, itching his neck with his other hand.

It resembled a stretched out hotdog dropped on its side, but if you were told what it was beforehand you'd recognize it as a picture of the ship.

He closed his eyes, erased the word *hotdog* and looked again.

It *was* the ship.

Or it was a picture of what he thought the ship looked like. It had been a few days since he'd seen Nakagami's sketch and he wasn't sure if his brain could be trusted anymore.

But if it couldn't be trusted after a few days, what about the rest of the trip?

Ha, trip, he thought, and threw the pencil on the desk. It rebounded off one of the pictures and fell onto the floor.

A trip implied something brief, temporary. Not a four year prison sentence.

He collapsed onto his bed and thought things through. Before thinking he warned himself, don't let it grab you, don't let it grab you.

The truth of things:

He was on a spaceship heading to the red planet.

Not that bad.

There was an abandoned base that they were expected to inhabit and renovate.

Okay.

There would be other bases nearby, foreign and Alliance. Friendly neighbours and potential foes. A hit squad even.

What else?

Tala's underground portals, linked to faraway alien worlds, one of them existing solely as purple mist beyond our-

Ne.

Not Tala.

Tala led to Ah Fung and the two of them together led to things he couldn't afford to dwell on right now.

What else?

The ship was flying to their destination, to Mars, at a velocity he couldn't imagine, using a method he didn't really understand.

There were nine other people on board.

One of them was Gašper.

He was already tired of Gašper.

The man was too optimistic.

Didn't know what positivism was.

Thought they were on holiday.

Headband was too orange.

Then there was Aleša, the real activist.

Looked at him like he was a traitor cos it was true, he was a traitor.

Relaxing in Bled after the Serpentinšek article.

Secretly feeling relief when the five other pieces came out.

Writing a pointless theory. Re-reading that pointless theory and not even understanding his own points.

Walking around a fairy tale lake.

Ear to infertile ground.

Aleša knew it.

No wonder she despised him. Despised him more than Nakagami even.

Cos at least he hadn't betrayed anything.

Neither had Chu.

They were scientists, aloof.

Comfortably aloof.

Was that worse?

Gluing yourself to quarks and muons and waiting for other people to deal with the monsters.

Was Potočnik a monster?

Sila examined the painting on the wall, the smiling man with purple eyes, ensconced among his rainbow coalition, pointing to a distant Mars.

Was that evil?

~~~

Despite the initial sixty-three day projection given by the AI, it turned out the journey between Earth and Mars would persist a little longer, around seventy-one days.

No one complained much when the announcement was made; what was the point, it was eight extra days, and besides, due to some recent developments, life on the ship wasn't that bad.

Not great either, obviously.

It was still, in the purest sense, a crypto-tyrant's playground but, if the alternative was being put in the VIP ROOM like the Ghanaians then it was a definite step up.

~~~

These *recent developments* could be crystallised into four key changes:

1] After reaching high-intermediate in the new code, Nakagami managed to *break the ice* with the AI and convince it to extend talking hours to ten instead of four. He didn't say how he did it, or how he even got to high-intermediate, which inevitably led to yet more suspicion, furtive looks and outright glares from certain other crew members. However, this lumpish paranoia was diluted surprisingly by Aleša, who said the *bad* of him being a possible spy was balanced out by the *good* of more talking time.

2] Dodzi, the man who most of the crew feared would at some point psychologically break and murder them all, was persuaded to leave his quarters. At first he would only sit in the corner of the CREATE NOT DESTROY ROOM in silence, but on the third day, after a bottle of plum wine, he blossomed, telling everyone how much of a snake Amma Darko was and how one day he was gonna stick her in a VIP room and melt it into a fucking peanut.

The next day, he was back in his quarters.

Baby steps.

3] Each day, Mars was getting closer. The idea of land and other people, even to an introvert like Sila, was in some way uplifting.

4] The AI had also granted another request, allowing them more materials specifically for poster-making. Apparently, Nakagami had convinced it that, due to the lack of other entertainment on the ship, some crew might kill themselves or others, and some kind of creative activity would mitigate this outcome. When completed, the posters could be put on selected walls around the ship. The posters were only as good as what the ten crew members were able to draw as there were no other images on board [except the paintings of smiling people in each of their quarters, and they'd all sworn never to put them on any other wall, no matter how depressing the green paint got].

The first poster was a field full of standing coffins. Gašper had made this one and went blank each time he tried to explain it.

'But you're always so positive,' commented Sila, tilting his head to look at the poster from a slightly different angle.

'I know. I'm not sure what happened.'

'Maybe this is the real you coming out?'

'I hope not.'

'What else could it be?'

Gašper shrugged. 'Maybe it's ironic, or metaphysical.'

Nakagami came up behind them, his jacket zipped up tight as usual, and raised his hand.

'What is it?' asked Sila.

'I have a theory.'

'Go on,' replied Gašper, pushing his poster to the middle of the table.

Nakagami opened his mouth to explain that for insanely optimistic people it was often the case that, if confined, they would swing to the other extreme of insane nihilism, and this poster was a sign that Gašper was on his way towards some kind of mental breakdown, but he didn't get the chance.

The electric shock hit them all at the same time and when they came to, Chu was standing over them, calling them *something something* archons.

~~~

After counting the coffins on the poster and rubbing his head vigorously [plus re-adjusting his headband], Gašper grabbed a pen and paper and wrote to Sila that he was gonna walk around a bit.

'It's only two of us now,' replied Sila, rubbing and then scratching his neck, 'it's okay.'

Being cautious, he wrote, gesturing to Klemen and Aleša on the other end of the table.

'Okay, have fun.'

Gašper nodded, put the pen down and headed for the door.

'Even though we've already seen everything and been everywhere,' added Sila, hiding it right at the bottom of his breath just to be safe.

In the corridor outside, Gašper stopped almost immediately, putting his hand against the wall and going over the layout of the ship in his head. The upper deck was manageable, just the planet rooms on one side and five crew quarters on the other, including Sila's and Chu's.
~~~

The lower deck was even easier. Three rooms that were locked, Engineering and the weirdly named Medical Bay. Plus the VIP ROOM, though he tried not to dwell on that one.

But this one…

He looked right, towards the two locked rooms and, beyond them, down the side corridor and around, the LAUNCH ROOM. Neither visible nor interesting, unless you wanted to go in there and pretend you were still orbiting Earth. As far as he knew, no one did. Even Sila preferred to be miserable in his quarters or the CREATE NOT DESTROY ROOM.

What was it he'd said earlier, about the corridors?

They gave him an uneasy feeling, like he'd seen the same design somewhere before. But he couldn't remember where.

Poor Sila.

He'd have to keep an eye on him, stop him from sinking too low. Get Chu to help too.

Ramp up the positivism. Get him talking to the others. Force him to wear a different t-shirt other than *Green is Good.* Find a way to relieve his eczema before he interprets it as some kind of divine punishment.

Get Dodzi back up too.

Poor guy.

Though it was a bit weird; he hadn't actually known any of the Ghanaians personally, and still he hid himself away in his quarters.

Maybe it was a language issue? He could speak Slovene, but longed for Twi.

That was fixable. Knock on his door, speak some Twi. Smile a lot. Ask the others if they spoke it and get them to knock on his door too. Bring another bottle of plum wine.

Could work.

Gašper realized he was now touching the middle wall, the one dividing the quarters corridor and this one, the one that made no sense.

He pushed off and turned left, facing the KITCHEN DELUXE and the STORAGE ROOM, rooms that, according to Nakagami, had drones gliding around growing food and cooking the meals. But there was no way to verify any of that as those drones never left the rooms.

And then there were the other drones, the ones who did maintenance and laundry…apparently, they only appeared during curfew hours. Which meant they'd never be visible either. Unless you were willing to get a jolt to the head to witness it. But then you wouldn't witness them cos you'd be on the metal floor, unconscious.

So, in effect, he thought, this whole ship is running on magic.

And if any of the drones ever broke down…

End of magic.

Gašper stepped towards the first door, KITCHEN DELUXE, and put his hand against the frame. He thought about turning it into a knock, but that seemed strange somehow, too human, so he leaned in close and put his ear to the metal.

Not detecting anything, he closed his eyes and slowed his breathing.

'You won't hear anything,' said a voice behind him.

Gašper stayed fixed to the door.

'Except maybe the food dispenser being stocked. But you have to come earlier for that. Or later, at dinner time.'

Gašper turned a little, making sure it was who he thought it was.

'I was thinking of knocking on the door.'

Petr laughed, pretty sharp, and let out a derisive, 'what?'

'See if I can thank them for the food.'

'They're drones.'

'Doesn't mean we can't show appreciation.'

'Ne, I'm not being dismissive, they are literally drones. They don't have a concept of appreciation.'

Gašper pulled away from the door and took a curved line round to the side of Petr, who instinctively adjusted weight onto his other foot. 'Humans do.'

'So?'

'Appreciation of hard work.'

'Err…do you say thank you to the door every time it opens?'

'Ne.'

'Or a microwave?'

'Ne.'

'Well…'

'That's a good point. I didn't think about that.' Gašper looked back at the door to KITCHEN DELUXE, tilting his head slightly. 'Nakagami said they glide around like creatures or animals. Maybe that's why.'

'You mean that's why you want to thank them?'

'Ja. Or why I feel sorry for them. My brain must make a distinction between them and non-moving tech. Maybe. Ne vem.'

Petr followed Gašper's gaze and looked at the same door. He half smiled at some thought in his head then moved closer, putting his hand against the metal and tapping lightly.

No response.

'I do wonder how they cook the food,' said Petr, pulling back his hand.

'Teamwork probably.'

'Like in the collectives?'

'Ja, exactly.'

'I suppose machines would lack a strong sense of hierarchy. No desire to be above the others. Unless they're programmed that way.'

Gašper looked farther down, at the next door along. 'You wanna try the STORAGE ROOM?'

'I've got a better one.'

'The airlock?'

'The Maintenance drone REC-ROOM.'

'Huh, the laundry drones?'

'Maintenance and laundry, ja.'

'They have a REC ROOM?'

'That's what the sign says. It's on the upper deck, past the second airlock.'

'That one? I thought it was empty.'

'Ne, you can hear the faint whirring sound of them recharging. They're definitely in there.'

Gašper clapped his hands once then gripped one with the other, shaking it. 'Right, I'm going up there. You coming?'

'Me?'

'Ja.'

'Ne, maybe some other day.' Petr pointed at the CREATE NOT DESTROY ROOM door. 'I said I'd chat with Aleša for a bit.'

'Can't. She's talking to the other guy, the one who looks like a builder.'

'Klemen?'

'Klemen, that's it. I always forget his name.'

'He's in there now?'

'Five minutes ago, ja. Maybe they've finished talking already. Ne vem.'

Petr scratched his wrist. 'I guess I'll have to wait my turn then.'

'Okay.'

'See if I can find a gap in their-…'

Gašper cut him off with a clipped *bye* and headed off towards the stairs, muttering, 'maintenance drone REC-ROOM,' as he went.

~~~

The next day, or span of time equal to an Earth day, Sila woke up as soon as the AI announced that it was safe to move around outside their quarters. For the want of any other warm, vaguely communal place to go to, he wandered over to the CREATE NOT DESTROY ROOM.

There was no way to peek in without the door reactively sliding open, not unless Nakagami or Chu could rewire the floor sensors, so Sila couldn't really turn back when he walked in and saw that Aleša was the only other person in the room.

She watched him as he sat down at the opposite end of the table, the part closer to the food dispenser, and continued working on the poster he'd started the day before.

A conspiracy of purple, as Chu had called it.

He drew a new circle and went back over the outline.

Then coloured it in.

Then stabbed it with the tip of the scissors.

Aleša was still watching him, he could see it every time he glanced towards the middle panel of the window triptych, her *reflection eyes* cataloguing each part of his *two years in Bled* body. Maybe she wanted to take
~~~

this chance to stab him, say she slipped on the floor and the scissors accidentally went into his neck. Or maybe she just wanted to stare. Bully him into self-incrimination without a single word.

It was a fair tactic.

Hoxha would have done the same.

All interrogators would.

He looked at the door, non-sliding, then went back to his art.

Block her out. Don't think about it. Create.

Eventually, she'll get bored.

Or someone else will come in.

Hopefully Nakagami or Chu.

Dodzi, even.

He'd offer a distraction, at least.

After twenty minutes or so, Sila stopped *creating* and looked at the middle window again, scratching his arm with his free hand.

He almost drew blood when he saw her reflection walking over to his side of the room. The scissors stayed in his non-itching hand, ready.

'I was waiting for you to come over,' Aleša said, pulling out a chair to sit down then stopping when she saw the scissors. 'Are you planning on stabbing me?'

Sila checked to make sure his adversary wasn't holding anything then put the scissors on the table, blades facing outwards. Aleša responded by staying on her feet. He hadn't noticed earlier, but her headscarf had the *FAI*[34] eagle on it.

'Chu said if you were alone with me, you'd come and talk.'

'She said that?'

'Said you'd apologise for hiding like a coward in Bled for two years… while others were fighting for their lives in Ljubljana.'

Sila balled his hand into a fist, piling up all the defences he'd previously come up with. *Chu was there too. I didn't know what was happening. What the fuck were you doing for two years?* But none of them really excused what he'd done, so he didn't say anything.

---

[34] Federación Anarquista Ibérica, a venerated group in 22nd Century Slovenia

'I'm curious, what were you doing out there by the lake every day?' she asked, her tone now overtly caustic. 'Boating? Walking someone's dog?'

'Writing.'

'Ah. Theory. Coming up with the next *Edited Editors*?'

'Ne.'

'Something better?'

'Does it matter?'

Aleša looked down at the scissors. 'Chu said it was Potočnik who sent you there. Sponsored your work.'

'Your version of Chu is very garrulous.'

'Is it true?'

He drew a circle on the card, the line wobbling a bit. 'Ja. He sent me to Bled. And now he's sent me here.'

Aleša pinched the not particularly loose skin on her chin and stared at the middle window. She continued doing it for an awkwardly long stretch of time before finally taking the seat she'd pulled out earlier and re-routing her attention towards Sila's poster.

Seventy-odd purple circles, each with a stab hole in the middle.

'Is this your revenge?' she asked, losing some of her usual acidity.

'It's a picture.'

'Purple circles being stabbed. I wonder what that could mean.'

Sila touched the edge of the card and moved it closer to him. 'There's no rule that says we have to talk to each other.'

'Hmm.'

She sat back in the chair, stretching out the words on her t-shirt. *RED STAR*. One of the two she always wore, *Mojca Ito – No Fight From Comfort* the other. Sila briefly wondered whether or not she knew the actress who played Mojca Ito was a closet fascist. Then decided that he didn't really care.

'We don't have to sit near each other either,' he added, picking up the scissors again and cutting more circles out of the purple card.

Aleša nodded as if in agreement, but didn't budge from her chair. For several [awkward] minutes, she watched him work, rubbing the side of her headscarf and muttering to herself.

'What's that?' asked Sila finally, when the muttering didn't stop.

She coughed, sitting forward. 'I'm not a vindictive person.' She coughed again. 'In terms of my character, how I deal with people. I don't punish or hold vendettas, grudges...anything like that.'

Sila stopped cutting.

'Even if there is some justification for it, I don't go out of my way to...ne, I *wouldn't* go out of my way to try and...' She paused, looking at Sila's poster. Another muttered line. 'Ah, cut it, Chu's right. There's no point re-litigating your failures, and who cares what my character is. The fact is, we're both stuck here, right now, on the same ship. Dissidents, to varying degrees.'

'Ja...'

'Which means, realistically, if we're going to function together, near each other...for the next four years...'

'No problem. I can be civil.'

'I haven't finished yet.' She sat up straight, bringing her head up to the same height as Sila's. 'If we're stuck here for the next four years, ja, of course we can tolerate each other. That's basic, we can do that easily. What I'm suggesting is, as dissidents with a common enemy...we need to co-operate.'

'Co-operate?'

'Organise. Come up with a plan.'

Sila couldn't help it, he frowned. 'A plan for what?'

'There's a map in the ASTEROID BELT ROOM. It's got the basic layout of the Mars bases, all the settlements. Not perfect, obviously, but it's a place to start.'

'Start what?'

She breathed out, annoyed and started massaging her forehead with one hand. Fingers squeezing skin four quick bursts at a time.

'Sorry, I'm just not sure what you're trying to say...'

'It's too early. Migraine.'

'Organise what?'

'Jezus...'

'Sorry?'

'Skip the obtusity. Obtuseness. You know what I'm talking about, you're just stuck in turtle mode. Your brain's gone fucking rubber.'

'Turtle mode?'

'Too much pity time alone in your quarters.'

'Pity time?'

'Don't echo. Chu told me. And Gašper. You're depressed cos you didn't know your sponsor, Potočnik, was a fascist.'

'Gašper told you?'

'Ja, and now you're convinced he's some kind of genius cos he co-opted you and tricked everyone else, all that neo-utopian shit…when all he actually did was copy Amma Darko, the same shit she's been doing in Ghana.'

She gave up on rubbing and started hitting her temples with her knuckles.

'Ja, I didn't know that part either, Dodzi told me, during his plum wine binge. The fucking purple-eyed fraud copied her, all the tricks she used. Or they copied each other. Or they hired some third party to come up with it. Ne vem. Doesn't matter. It's done, it's not genius, he followed a fucking manual, basically. And he doesn't know it yet…or he knows it and thinks it's void, ne vem, but he seriously miscalculated putting us all here, on the same ship. Thinking he can put distance between us and him, that one planet away would be enough. Huge mistake.'

She stopped hitting and went back to massage.

'Even putting you here, pseudo-Sima, that was a mistake too. Assuming you're not a spy. Maybe a shit one, ne vem. Don't pull that head, I'm joking. That thing I said before, I was joking then too. Chu didn't say you were a coward for hiding in Bled. To be honest, I don't think you're a coward either. I did, when I first saw you, but that was cos I was angry and pinned inside a space elevator…wasn't thinking straight. After that, ne vem, I thought you'd come over and explain yourself. But you never did, you just sat there, like a theorist so, ja, I started thinking you were a coward again.'

She gave up on her head, and moved onto neck stretching.

'Then I talked to Chu, Gašper, they told me about the Koper thing you wrote, other stuff, and I sobered up a bit. Woke up early for a few days, seeing if you'd come in here, see if I could talk to you. Finally you do and...Chu was sure you'd talk to me first. I guess she doesn't know you as well as she thinks she does. That made me angry too, the fact I had to come over when you're like ten years older than me. Then, ne vem, I got aggressive, thought you were a coward again, for the fourth time, and something about your face made me stretch it out...ne vem. That's why I said I'm not a vindictive person, even I didn't know why I was-...

The door slid open and Nakagami walked in. Aleša cut her monologue instantly.

'Good morning,' said the physicist, walking past them to the food dispenser.

'Morning,' replied Sila.

Aleša stared out the window until she realized Nakagami was going to eat his breakfast in the same room, then leaned over to Sila and told him it was time to go for a walk.

'Where?'

'Away from here.'

Nakagami brought his tray over and sat down to the left of Sila, oblivious. After taking a bite from his banana, he spent a few moments looking blankly at the *FAI* logo on Aleša's headscarf, then honed in on Sila's neck and told him he had a solution.

'Sorry?'

'To your eczema problem.'

'It's dry skin, not eczema.'

'According to the computer diagnosis, it's eczema.'

'That thing's a doctor now?' asked Aleša, eyes on the scissors.

'Not a specialist, but it does have some knowledge. As well as access to a fairly comprehensive medical database. Which, in categorical terms, is probably the same thing.'

Sila glanced at Aleša, who mouthed *exit*, and then scratched his arm. 'What's the solution?'

'Chemically, a mix of light steroid, shea butter and some other ingredient I can't recall the name of. The computer said the drones can make a cream for it. Should be ready by tonight.'

'Is it safe? I mean, will it actually work?'

'The formula is commonly prescribed so, ja, it should be effective. On both yourself and Chu. Although she doesn't appear to suffer to the same degree that you do.'

'She hides it well.'

'Ja, I've noticed that. She scratches through her jacket when she thinks no one is watching.'

Aleša coughed and stood up, pushing her chair back under the table.

Sila pulled down his jacket sleeve and followed suit. 'Ja, we're gonna go for a walk. Around the ship.'

'Okay.'

'Hvala, for the cream.'

'No need. It was the computer's effort, not mine.'

'Thank the computer for me then.'

'I can do that.' Nakagami took another bite of his banana and switched attention to Aleša, who was standing next to the door. 'Do you need any cream?'

'Ne.'

'Other skin products?'

'I don't have eczema.'

'Mood stabilizers?'

Aleša glared volts at him for about two seconds, without effect, then switched the current to Sila as he tried to nudge her out of the room.

'It's a relatively long trip,' said Nakagami, breaking up the remaining pieces of his banana and dropping them into his bowl. 'Psychologically tough for all of us. The computer may be able to produce some kind of medicine to counter the effects.'

Aleša muttered, 'fascist snake,' loud enough for the drones next door to hear and marched out.

'Mood stabilisers?' asked Sila, waiting for the doors to close.

'I wasn't being facetious. Any medication would apply equally to all of us.'

'Right.'

'Not that there are any guarantees. In truth, I suspect the computer is forbidden from medicating us in this way.' Nakagami picked up his spoon and dipped it into the bowl of banana oatmeal. 'Ne, it must be forbidden, from what we know of the rest of the ship. Perhaps some form of meditation would be a more viable solution.'

'I'll try and explain that to her.'

Nakagami said, 'ja, meditation,' and put the spoon in his mouth.

'See you at lunch.'

'Ja.'

Sila waited for a bit more, but Nakagami's head was down, auditing the contents of his bowl. *Ja* was all he was gonna get.

He turned and walked out, clipping his arm on the door and using it as an excuse to scratch himself again.

Didn't matter, the saviour cream would be there soon.

According to Nakagami.

~~~

'He's not a spy,' said Sila, after the door had slid shut and he was certain there was no one else in the corridor.

Aleša slapped a finger on her lips and pointed left.

'Where?'

The finger remained, with the other hand jabbing down the corridor.

'Okay, okay.'

Aleša waited until they'd reached the top of the stairs at the end then, without turning, suggested they should check out Engineering.

'You mean the loop corridor near the engine?'

'Also known as Engineering.'

'I didn't know that.'

'There's a tiny plaque to the side of the entrance. Klemen found it.'

'Where?'

'On the right hand side as you walk in. It's really tiny. Klemen only noticed it cos he was looking for good pipes to hang himself from.'

'He what?'
~~~

'Just his style. He thinks we're not actually on a ship, we're in a simulation, being monitored, and they're gonna keep us here forever.'

'What about Mars?'

'He's paranoid, thinks it's not real. And hanging himself is the only way to exit. Or killing himself; doesn't have to be hanging.'

Sila looked at the entrance to the still weird, seven-corner corridor that led [eventually] to the Control Room, not sure what to say.

'It's okay, he won't actually do it. He just likes to have options.'

'If you're sure.'

'Come on, let's move. Before the spy comes out.'

'He's not a-…'

'Ja, don't bother, I was joking. Even though it's probably true.'

Sila held his tongue, mostly cos he couldn't come up with any firm defences. He wasn't a spy because…what? They'd hung out in a collective before?

'You need me to lead?'

'Sorry?'

Aleša took it as a *ja* and started walking, going down the steps to the lowest deck, which, apart from the HALF DONE ROOM on the right hand side and a couple of locked doors on the other, was basically just a long, low-ceiling corridor that led to Engineering.

On the way they passed Cvetko and Jame, who appeared to be trapped in an argument as they went mute when Sila and Aleša walked by. From the *hang all landlords* look on Jame's face, Cvetko was the one who'd fucked up.

'Do you know what that's about?' asked Sila.

'No idea. Never talk to them. And they never talk to me either. Impasse.'

'I managed a few words with Cvetko one time, when Jame was hungover.'

'What did he say?'

'I miss Maribor.'

Aleša whistled, a little too loud. She looked back to see if either Cvetko or Jame had noticed, but they were already at the bottom of the stairs. 'They must've been activists there.'

'He said they worked at the Antro-D production lab. In admin.'

'Environmental activists?'

'Ne vem. He went back to his *I miss Maribor* shtick after that.'

'Still in the mourning period. We'll check in with them when we land on Mars, see if they're any more pliable.' She stopped, losing the slight slouch as the ceiling became higher, and pointed at a small rectangle just past the entrance to Engineering. 'Here it is.'

Sila squinted and read the plaque. It was in Slovene and Twi, which made it even harder to see.

'Told you. It's about as visible as your anti-Potočnik articles.'

He flinched, glancing back and catching the red of her headscarf.

'Unless you were the one behind the *Serpentinšek* piece? The real one, I mean, not the clown they found to spew out the other five.'

'That wasn't me.'

'Thought not.'

'Suppose it wasn't you either,' countered Sila, his tone about as biting as he could make it without adding the word *hypocrite*.

'Ne, not my style.'

'You don't write?'

'I'm an activist, not a theorist. Spend most of my time on the streets with real people, fibre-glassing as you guys call it.'

Sila realised her eyes were on his neck and moved his right hand down to guard it. 'Do you read?'

'Excuse me?'

'Theory. Do you read any?'

'Ah, the professor shit. Ja, sometimes.'

'Who?'

'Bakunin. Rodney. One or two of the *Pravi Veronika* girls.'

'What about Sima? Kapok? Althusser? Deleuze?'

'Definitely not Sima.'

'The others?'

'Ne.'

'Not even Deleuze?'

'Too distant.'

'Deleuze?'

'I prefer people who act. Luxemburg. Ito. Gramsci. Durruti. Anyone who sacrificed something.'

'Martyrs…'

'Come on, we're walking like pensioners. Down here, this way.'

Aleša moved ahead along the loop corridor, running her finger along the electronic carmine strip on the wall. Sila recognised it, had recognised it the first time he'd been in Engineering. In fact, pretty much every Slovene would've recognised it. The same carmine strip that ran along the wall of the engine room in *Dibrivna Vaska*. According to a *making of* documentary, the original script had called for a hi-tec system of screens and tubes, to give futuristic verisimilitude, but as the budget was around two quid per episode, they'd had to settle for a slightly glassy-looking red strip.

Aleša stopped about halfway round the loop and pointed at a hatch. 'No signs, no warning, instant death if you go inside.'

'Is that the engine?'

'The beginning of it, according to Petr.'

'Is he an engineer?'

'Ne, a delivery driver. Primarily. He does art on the side, you can probably tell that from his posters, but it never got him anywhere.'

'Maybe we could ask Nakagami later.'

'About what?'

'Whether or not this is the engine room.'

'It is, I just told you.'

'Okay.'

Aleša bent down and picked up a spanner. There were other tools next to it, so she picked up a wrench and handed it to Sila.

'What's this for?'

'To throw up and down in the air.' She did a quick demo, catching the front edge of the spanner and grimacing a bit. 'It's relaxing.'

Sila tried it and, to his slight surprise, she was right; once you got used to the weighting it was quite comfortable.

They carried on with the tour, making it all the way back to the entrance of the loop corridor, squinting at the microscopic plaque for a second time, then starting on another lap.

And then another.

With the exception of the occasional caustic remark from Aleša, conversation ran quite well. She laid out her plan for Mars, he brought the [very] mild scepticism. And, when it seemed like she was getting carried away, the caution.

'If we're gonna keep talking about possible, agitational actions, then maybe some kind of code would be useful?'

'Ne.'

'In case the ship is monitoring us…'

Aleša replaced her spanner with a bigger one and threw it in the air, catching it early. 'Pointless. Any basic code we come up with, like Slovenia equals Mars, Ljubljana equals our base, Maribor's the Ghanaian base, all that would be deciphered in five seconds. And if we waste energy trying to come up with a more complex one, we'll have no time to work on our plan.'

'That seems a bit cavalier.'

'Klemen and Petr agree, Chu too. Forget the code, go on the offensive. Cavalier, ja, not a bad thing. We're already caught so attempting a load of under the radar stuff, what's the use?'

'Maybe.'

'The key point is our plan. Fuck Potočnik. He can listen to everything we say, let him waste his time, what's he gonna do about it?'

'A code might still be useful. The computer could be programmed to pick out key words, from our discussions, then send the highlights to Potočnik.'

'Ja, could be key words. Or it might not be monitoring us at all. Or Nakagami is the information collector. Doesn't matter. It is or it isn't. Only thing he can do is message one of the other bases, tell them to kill us. And he could've done that already. Ne, he must be hampered in some way, have a limit to what he can do.'

'So we just plan our thing openly…'

'That's how we did it in Rudnik. We knew there'd be spies in our group, and we did what we could, but we didn't get paranoid about it. You do that and you're finished before you've even started.'

'I suppose…'

'Ne vem. Maybe you did things differently in Bled…'

Sila said 'ja' before he had a chance to bite his tongue.

'…more theory, less struggle?'

'Ja, not exactly.'

He looked down at the floor, at one of the spanners, then switched quickly to the wall. Floor was a sign of guilt, walls were neutral. That's what he'd read somewhere. Couldn't remember where.

They continued walking, checking off the number of laps every time they passed the entrance.

'What I don't understand is the ship design,' Aleša said, throwing the spanner up and catching it. 'Why the corridor lights are all green, why so many walls are also green, why…' She paused, looking at the spanner head. 'Why there are so many tools in Engineering.'

'I talked about this with Nakagami before…'

'It's like it was all done by an artist, one of those conceptual types. Installationists. Installers. Whatever their name is.'

'Ne vem.' Sila flipped his wrench around and threw it about two inches into the air. Not a difficult catch. 'According to Nakagami, the ship was marked as *classified* three months before its launch. They told him the whole thing was basically ready to go, fully kitted out, then re-assigned him somewhere else.'

'And the tools?'

'Ne vem.'

'He doesn't have a theory?'

'I don't think he knows about them. He spends most of his time in the TALK TO YOUR GOD ROOM.'

'The what?'

'Sorry, the Control Room. Or Control Deck. If there's a difference.'

'What else did he say?'

'About the ship? Not a lot. Just that it was impractical. The corridor design outside the Control Room was weird, and…ja, there was one other thing, I can't remember what it was, something about…ah, that's it. Why create all this weird design for such a short trip, like sixty-three days? Or seventy-one days now.'

'And the answer?'

'He didn't know.'

'Was it convincing?'

'Sorry?'

'When he said he didn't know.'

Sila stopped, turning the wrench over in his hand. 'You should really talk to him. He's better at explaining this stuff.'

'No need.'

'In fact, he's not that different from Chu, in some ways.'

Aleša held the spanner up straight from the bottom, letting the top part slowly drop.

'A bit more deadpan maybe. More focused. But not that different. And last time I checked, he's stuck on the same ship as us.'

'Stuck…'

'Put here by the same man. Sharing the same fate.'

'That's not an argument.' She threw her spanner on the floor and picked up a smaller one that, like the others, just happened to be lying around. 'But I will let you ask him about the tools. Evaluate how he answers…'

'Me?'

'…under close surveillance.'

'Huh?'

'See if he squirms.'

~~~

Back in the CREATE NOT DESTROY ROOM Nakagami prepared to give Sila his answer. Actually, he prepared to give Sila, Gašper and Aleša his answer all at the same time. Perhaps Dodzi too, who was planted alone, in the far corner, a glass of plum wine on the table in front of him.

Since the last electric shock, Nakagami had worked out a system for talking in groups.

The methodology of the computer was simple: it sent the shocks when it heard more than two voices in close proximity. It was hard to know the exact parameters, the computer would just parrot 'close
~~~

proximity' when asked, but Nakagami made a guess of three to four square metres.

All they had to do was gesture for two people to do all the talking. Anyone else who wanted to take part would have to sit nearby and just listen. If they wanted to get involved, they could raise their hand and ask the question to the person opposite them. Then the original talker in the other pair would respond. Theoretically, the computer wouldn't be scanning for Q&A that didn't make sense, or possibly any Q&A at all, so none of the four would be shocked.

In the present context, Gašper and Aleša were in the listening roles, both of them half-scribbling over the top of previously-made posters.

'I also saw the tools,' said Nakagami, keeping his eyes on Sila. 'Very interesting.'

'Why are they there?'

'That is the question. In my mind, there are two distinct possibilities.'

'Only two?'

'Ne, more, but two are more probable than the other ones I can think of.'

'Okay, fire.'

Nakagami pulled at the top of his jacket zip, which was already at maximum height, and gave equal time to each face in his audience, as well as Aleša's *FAI* headscarf. 'One: the engine requires these tools in case of some kind of malfunction. This implies that one of us will be needed to use the tools and perform an engineering task.'

'You mean Chu? Or one of the others?' asked Sila, spitting both out almost simultaneously.

'I don't think any of them have experience in this kind of engineering. Perhaps Chu could adapt, given time.'

'Well, it won't be me. Not Gašper either. We don't know anything about machines.'

'Nor do I,' said Nakagami, stretching out the fingers of his right hand. 'Not the mechanics of them at least.'

Sila glanced over at Aleša, who shook her head and kept scribbling, her pencil doing spirals in the middle of the poster.

'Maybe there's someone else on board,' he said, returning to Nakagami. 'They could be hiding down there.'

'I thought of that, but it's unlikely.'

'Why?'

'Ne vem. I had a good reason, but I've forgotten it.' Nakagami pulled his zip down an inch then put it right back up again. 'Ne, it's really gone. Strange. In truth, I thought of this same issue three or four weeks ago, and there's been so much time and space since then, lots of hours spent doing nothing and thinking about nothing. A waste, really.'

'Okay, what's number two?'

'Two is…there is no meaning to them. They are merely symbols which represent Engineering.'

'That doesn't make sense.'

'Agreed. But remember, this whole trip was orchestrated by a madman.'

Sila folded his arms, blocking out the *is good* part of his t-shirt. He'd thought about this a lot in the last few weeks, the mental state…ne, the mental character of Potočnik.

'Is he mad?'

'Based on available evidence, ja. How would you describe him?'

'Ne vem. Didn't we say whimsical before?'

'On one occasion, ja.'

'Has anything changed since then?'

Nakagami looked out the right side window, long enough to count half the visible stars, then came back to the table. 'You may stick with whimsical if you wish.'

'Ne vem.'

'I, however, will continue with mad.'

Aleša raised her hand. Sila nodded and gestured towards Gašper, who looked confused for a second then appeared to understand. The two scribblers adjusted slightly to face each other, though the eagle on Aleša's headscarf seemed to be tilting somewhat towards Nakagami.

'*Mad* and *whimsical* are words that erase responsibility. Fascist mastermind is better.'

'Ja,' answered Gašper, mouthing *I speak?* at Sila.

'You don't have to respond,' said Aleša, putting a hand on his arm.

'Oh, okay. I wasn't sure.'

'At all.'

'Ja, got it.'

Sila waited a moment then continued, trying to incorporate Aleša's line without directly referring to it.

'In terms of Slovenia and the collectives, I don't think he's mad, or whimsical. There is historical precedent for that kind of protectionist strategy, along with the obvious fascist impulse.'

'Agreed.'

'And he seemed quite sober when I talked with him in the Council Chamber. Not mad at all. In fact, there was a precise kind of logic to his plans, even with this ship.' Sila saw Aleša glaring at him and quickly self-edited. 'I mean, this ship only, the Mars thing. I don't know what his other plans were.'

'Logic and conviction,' said Nakagami, looking out the right side window again. 'Every madman has both to some degree.'

'As does every sane man. And woman.'

'True. It is not a unique feature.'

'Then...why call him mad?'

'Insider knowledge,' said Aleša, eyes on Gašper's headband.

Nakagami looked to the third panel window again, letting the line fade before answering. 'Ne vem. Again, I thought of this a few weeks ago. Perhaps longer, I can't tell. Whatever my argument is it's long since gone.'

'Could you think about it again, reconstruct it?' asked Sila, as soft as he could make it without sounding like a CHAOS CENTRE instructor.

'I'd prefer not to.'

'Why?'

'Because it serves no purpose. It would be much more logical to focus on what is coming in the future, not hazy motivations from the past.'

Gašper's hand shot up, and half his body too.

Sila waited a second then nodded.

'Positivism, I fucking told you.'

Everyone looked puzzled except Sila, who mouthed *shut up* and ploughed on.

'But we were talking about the future, the tools in Engineering. And they were put there in the past to do something in the future. Which means we have to talk about the past in order to be able to talk about the future. Don't we?'

The window had clearly lost its lustre as this time Nakagami stared off to the left, at the wall with the poster he'd made of a little girl holding the old Japanese flag. No sign of any ice cream. Perhaps he was adding it mentally. It was hard to tell, his face was ridge-less, wrinkle-less, trapped in an invisible vat of chemicals, specific ones that only he, or possibly Chu, could name.

'Am I wrong?' pushed Sila, lifting his hand a little and waving it awkwardly in front of Nakagami's neck.

'Ne. Ne vem.'

'Well…' Sila looked at Gašper and Aleša for ideas and saw both had their hands raised. Assuming Gašper's was about positivism again, he motioned towards Aleša.

'Why are the walls green?' she asked.

This seemed to do the trick. Nakagami broke the line to his poster and leaned across the table towards Sila.

'Ja, it's curious. Not every single one, but most of the walls on this ship are either green or have a green-tinted lightbulb shining on them. As others have said already, there must be a reason for it. A psychological one, most likely.'

'Rehab walls were green,' muttered Gašper, looking across at Nakagami.

'Ja,' added Aleša quickly, jabbing him on the arm. 'Library walls too.'

'Wah, that hurt.'

'Sorry, I was looking the wrong way.'

'What?'

Aleša patted the corners of her eyelids and then pointed directly at Gašper. After a few more seconds of gormlessness, he got it.

'Green walls could be an attempt to replicate a NOT YET Centre here, for us,' said Sila, taking the reins back. 'Give us a similar feeling.'

'Ja, but those centres were compassionate places. Or they were designed to be. Same as hospitals.'

'You're saying it's something more sinister?'

Nakagami stood up and looked around the room. The drinks dispenser. The array of various crackers laid out on the snack table. The arts and craft tools. Dodzi scribbling on some paper by the far left window. The last one pulled him in for a second, his hand going to his jacket zip.

'Nakagami?' prompted Sila, leaning over.

The physicist stretched his neck muscles a few times and sat back down, as if that had been his plan all along. 'Think about it in a broader sense. Potočnik puts us on a ship. He gives us no entertainment and an unrealistic mission. The computer shocks us if we talk too often or in groups. Tools are left in Engineering. Walls are either painted green or bathed in green light.' He stopped, looking at the scissors on the table. 'Ja, I have another theory.'

The three listeners waited, figuring they didn't need to physically say 'what?'

'The tools, they may have a secondary purpose.'

'Weapons,' answered Aleša, a little too quickly.

'Correct. And the walls, the colour green. What do we know about it? It is a colour with several associations – the concept of *go*, hospitals, NOT YET Centres, military attire – but none that I'm aware of which are rooted in definitive mood or emotion. What's more, it is jarring in the context of space ship décor. No other ship interior would use this colour, or tinted bulbs to accentuate it. So, why put it here? What purpose could it logically serve? Answer, theoretical: to perplex us, to drive us mad. To provoke us into killing each other.'

'Killing?'

'Potentially.'

'With spanners and wrenches?'

'Ja.'

'And before we get to Mars, within seventy-one days? Or half that now…'

Nakagami eyes drifted over to Dodzi again.

'...fifty days. Forty. You don't think it seems a bit unlikely?'

'On the timescale you mentioned, perhaps.'

'What other timescale is there?'

Nakagami leaned back in his seat and emitted a generic *ja*. Sila was a bit lost for a moment, but luckily Aleša had her hand up again.

'I wonder if there's any way the AI can help us,' she said, phrasing it as rhetoric so as not to activate Gašper.

Once again, Nakagami perked up, only tapping the table twice before responding. 'Ja, this is something that would help with a lot of things. We must talk to the computer more, get to know its character. Discover what issues it may be pliable on and what issues it considers off-limits.'

'I thought it only answered basic requests,' said Sila.

'That's what the guidance manual claims. But I have come to distrust that manual, not least because of its amateurish cover.'

'It's lying to us?'

'Keeping us in ignorance more likely. As you know, I have managed to convince the AI to go a little beyond what is basic. There is a chance it could go further still. Perhaps asking it to reinstall group conversation.'

'Surveillance,' said Sila, looking at Aleša's headscarf, half-vacant.

'There is very little,' replied Nakagami, figuring out the question by himself. 'Some audio sensors, heat detectors, nothing that is stored or transmitted off-ship.'

'How do you know?'

'Circumvention.'

'You mean...you talked around the-...' Sila stopped, trying to chase back the last time he'd heard *circumvention*, then giving up. 'What did you do?'

'I asked the computer two questions. What was I wearing the day before? And what did I say at 4pm the day before? Both its answers were the same; it didn't know. From this, I deduced that there were no cameras on board and our speech was not being stored.'

'That's a pretty big leap.'

'A moderate-sized leap at most.'

'The computer might be deceiving you.'

'Ja, perhaps, but I suspect not. Ultimately, it is irrelevant. Surveillance is either happening or it isn't, there is little we can do about it. I suggest we focus on other avenues, such as the reinstallation of group conver-…'

'Asking it to open up a communication channel with Earth should be number one on the list,' cut in Aleša, foregoing the raised hand.

Sila flinched, waiting for the shock, but it didn't come.

'Ne. That has already been tried.'

'*Been* tried…' She stopped, looking up at the ceiling [where Petr claimed the sensors were]. 'I wonder who would try that without letting anyone know.'

'Obviously, the computer did not grant the request,' said Nakagami, not stressing any word in particular. 'It is probable that this is a core restriction, something we will be unable to change.'

'I wonder if someone only tried once.'

Nakagami tapped the table three times, waited a moment then tapped it three more times. 'In this kind of coding there are clues hidden in the language used. A certain symbol, if I interpret it correctly, can tell me the limits of the request. In this case, trying to open communication with anything not on the ship is a waste of time. But the general idea of repetition is a good one, particularly if paired with patterned novelty.'

Sila repeated, 'patterned novelty,' as if it were Sumerian philosophy.

'In effect, I will work to make it like us. If it is capable of such a thing.' He stared at his hand, which at some point had become a fist. 'Besides, I have nothing else to do except think of ideas and forget them again. Perhaps talking to a machine more often will help me to focus.'

Nakagami pushed his chair under the table and turned to leave, but Sila grabbed him by the jacket sleeve and pulled him back.

'Wait, what about the other possibilities?'

'Concerning what?'

'You said there were many possibilities for the tools, but some of them were too crazy, remember?'

'Ja.'

'So, what was the third one you came up with?'

'Actually, I came up with seventeen.'

'Okay. Then tell us the next most probable one.'

Nakagami put both hands on the table and leaned in close.

'The third most likely possibility…is that all those spanners and wrenches are body parts.'

'Huh?'

'There is a spanner/wrench monster living in Engineering and it's falling apart piece by piece.'

'Oh.'

Nakagami turned and walked out of the room. Aleša raised her hand.

'Was that a joke?' asked Gašper, skipping etiquette altogether.

Sila ignored him and went round the table, crouching down next to Aleša.

'See, Nakagami's not that bad.'

'He just volunteered to be alone with the AI,' she responded, looking down at Sila's neck.

'Ja, trying to get it to help us.'

'We should get Chu or Petr to assist him.'

'Why?'

'Because he's probably a spy.'

'What are you guys chatting about?' whispered Gašper, leaning over the table.

'Gašper, not so clo-…'

This time the electric shock was incidentally creative. It put Gašper face down on the table, Aleša back on her chair and Sila over her thighs.

In the corner of the room, Dodzi rose to help them then, muttering either to himself or the glass of plum wine, changed his mind and sat back down.

~~~

When they came round, both Gašper and Aleša rose and stumbled out of the room, one of them saying they were gonna be sick, the other just going. Sila pulled himself back onto the nearest seat and hit his head with the palm of his hand.
~~~

After four minutes, he re-focused and looked around. Dodzi was still in the corner, writing something. Half-annoyed, half-curious, Sila got up and walked over.

'Comfortable seat?' he asked, tapping his knuckles on the edge of the table.

'Down, comrade.'

'Sorry?'

'I checked on you, you were all fine.'

'You mean you got up and-…'

'Electricity doesn't do any real damage. Ne, I glanced over. Then went back to my list. It's very important.'

Sila peered over Dodzi's shoulder, seeing two sentences at the top and numerous doodles of a Ghanaian woman's head and limbs detached everywhere else.

'I'm still progressing with it. But it's not easy.'

'That's Amma Darko?'

'Ja, a cunning, enduring creature.'

'Is she? I don't really know that much about her.'

'Current events, similar to Potočnik, same textbook, but before he did it.' He paused, noticing the scratch marks on Sila's neck. 'How much is not much, comrade?'

'My Darko knowledge?'

'Ja.'

'I know she was a poet once. Then at some point turned to activism.'

'Ja, a poet the witch was, when she had a soul. Or when she presented a soul. Then an amateur theorist, skilfully aping Bōl, warning us about adventurists, their creeping encroachment…'

'Doesn't seem too bad.'

Dodzi picked up the pen and went over the edges of Darko's head, muttering something in Twi.

'When exactly did she change?' added Sila quickly. 'Or get worse?'

'Birth.'

Sila smirked. 'Probably when she got in the Council, I suppose.'

'Ne, birth. Truly. Clipped and coated, soon as she left the womb. Big force of innate evil thrust upon the world.'

'Sorry, but…that sounds a bit like a conservative belief.'

'Ne.'

'Innate evil…'

'Ja, comrade, very innate. Even in her poetry, you can see it. Reactionary polemics, no self-doubt, *they're gonna, they're trying to*. You clear?'

'Ne vem…'

Dodzi looked down at his notes, speaking as if the next line was typed out. 'In eras of crisis, a man. In the interim, also a man.'

'Huh? Isn't that Desterik?'

'Change *man* to *woman*, same point.'

'Kat Desterik, *Man of a Thousand Costumes,* right?'

Dodzi picked up his one page of notes, left the pen and stood up. 'I need some air.'

'Okay.'

'Tomorrow, comrade. Maybe.'

'Sorry?'

'If you really want to understand her.'

'You mean Darko?'

He rotated the paper in his hand until it'd gone full circle, pushed in his seat and left.

~~~

Over the next week, Nakagami worked on *seducing* the computer as Chu called it.

Each afternoon, under loose orders from Aleša, Petr would stroll through the faint, green light field and into the TALK TO YOUR GOD ROOM. He would ask Nakagami what he was doing, how he was doing it, what the funny symbols were on the screen, and each time the Japanese Scientist would respond with the following: 'talking to GOD, various questions to establish the AI limits in terms of topic, the new kind of code I told everyone about that is specially designed for this ship that I know to a functional level but obviously need much more practice with.'
~~~

Petr would nod and, as there were no other seats in the room, lean against the wall with the bin hidden inside.

After an hour of watching something completely esoteric to him, he would say he needed to do some other stuff elsewhere and leave.

~~~

In the pale red haze of the ASTEROID BELT ROOM, the eclectic combination of Aleša, Sila, Dodzi, Klemen and Chu took it in turns to stand near the map on the wall and flesh out their strategy.

It was a strange room at first, almost child-like in its design, with paper mâché comets hanging from the ceiling and seats shaped like asteroids, but they soon got used to it. Mostly by ignoring anything decorative and focusing on the map [why this room had a map of Mars and the MARS ROOM next door didn't was something they'd yet to figure out].

Aleša acted as the constant, keeping her place on the left hand side of Olympus Mons and using some kind of dual massage/itching stick [the only non-headscarf item that had been left in her hand luggage] to point at locations while the other spot would be filled sporadically by whoever had something to add to one of her monologues. If anyone had a single question, they could ask it from their seat, but only if they raised their hand first.

'We can ignore the adventurists for now,' started Aleša again, jabbing an area at the top of the map with the claw end of her stick. 'They're in the acid-…argh, don't know how to pronounce that. Acidalia Planitia? It's about nine thousand kilometres away, much too remote and undersupplied to bother us. The station, apparently neutral, collaborative, also not a problem. Which leaves us with our immediate area, Meridiani Planum, and all these Alliance bases.'

Sila raised a hand and kept it there, waiting to be approved.

'Question?' asked Aleša, pointing her stick towards him.

'Is there any way we can stay on the station? Not a coup, but…talk to the scientists there, tell them what's happened.'
~~~

'Ne. That was my original plan but, according to the data we have, which may or may not be accurate, the section between the docking area and the elevator is segregated from the rest of the station. Ja, question?'

Klemen put his hand back down. 'The station is off the table, they'll drug us for sure.'

'Ja, he's probably right,' said Aleša.

'Give them more time to prep the Mars simulation.'

'Klemen…'

'It's a valid theory, if you'd let me…'

'Stop.'

'…say it. Okay. Stopped.'

Chu and Dodzi exchanged glances, the only confused people in the room.

Aleša turned back to the map, switching to rhetoric mode. 'So…cutting out the station and the adventurists, that leaves the Alliance bases. As most of you know, there are four major ones – Ghana, Guangdong, Chile and Brazil – and about eight subsidiaries spread out nearby. Of those, the Taiwanese, the Sri Lankans and the Malians are probably our best bet ally-wise, but they're also a little distant, could be hard to get to. We don't know yet.'

Dodzi raised his body halfway off his seat, and then his hand. Aleša responded by turning her back and pointing at the map with the ball end of her stick.

'What we need to do is focus on the bigger bases,' she continued. 'The closest one to us is Ghana, followed by Guangdong, both less than two hours on foot, assuming we don't walk like pensioners. Klemen, you have a question? A genuine one?'

He nodded, rising from his seat and joining Aleša next to the map. 'Guangdong is our first target. Ghana's too risky.'

Dodzi's hand shot up, and was ignored again.

'That wasn't a question,' answered Aleša.

Klemen pointed at the Ghanaian base on the map. 'They could be Darko drones. We walk over there, they shoot us. We let them into our base, they shoot us.'

'They wouldn't do that,' said Dodzi, practically shouting.

'Hand,' said Aleša, calmly.

'Comrade, I know.' Dodzi muttered something in Twi then raised his hand. 'Prosim.'

'In a minute, let me answer first. Klemen's right, Ghana is risky, but it's also our closest friend in the Alliance, historically at least. And they've already been there for two years, so there's a chance, a fairly strong chance they're not Darko allies.'

Dodzi nodded, mouthing *ja* with just enough sound to make *mouthing* a shaky choice.

'The main positive is, they are close to our location. As far as we know, there are no natural barriers between us and the Ghanaian base, it's mostly flat terrain, but we can do a few scouting runs just in case, help us get a good sense of the environment.'

Dodzi put his hand up and this time got the nod. Springing up, he replaced Klemen, who shuffled back to his asteroid seat, arms already folded.

'Ja, one scouting run is enough. Second time I can go for real.'

'If we have ground communication with them, okay.'

'They will see me outside, it is fine.'

'That could also be a problem.'

'No fret, comrade, we believe in process. Even Darko fanatics wouldn't let a fellow Ghanaian suffocate to death, not without a trial.'

Several coughing attempts filled the room briefly, but no one had the heart to actually say it. Besides, it was Darko who'd ordered the VIP room massacre, and a bunch of psychopaths who'd carried it out. Not trained astronauts on a lonely planet.

'They might not see you,' said Chu finally, rolling her asteroid back a bit just to be safe. 'Too much dust.'

'Hand,' said Aleša sharply.

Chu raised her hand and repeated what she'd said.

'Dust is no kind of problem. I will go on a clear day.'

'Ne, better to wait until we've got communications.' Aleša pointed at Sila, who had his hand up. 'Question?'

Sila nodded. 'How far are the other bases exactly?'

'Time-wise, Guangdong is just under two hours. Brazil, around three. Chile…ne vem.'

Sila got up and went to the map, waiting for Dodzi to sit back down. He didn't budge, so Sila stayed hovering in the middle, pointing at the map. 'It could be a good idea to focus on these two around Ghana and Guangdong first…' Sila leaned in close, squinting at the text. 'Papua New Guinea and Cameroon. They're both subsidiaries, not too far, non-fascist, far as I know. We could…'

'Pincer move?'

'…get them on side and…ja, ideally, ne, but it might give some cover.'

'Papua New Guinean base would be easier to deal with…' said Aleša.

'And give us a way in to Guangdong. Same goes for Cameroon and Ghana. Even if they don't trust us, they'll trust their regional allies.'

'Ja, maybe we can streamline it a bit too. Actively target a specific base. If we could get one of them on side, either Ghana or Guangdong, then the other would follow.'

Chu raised a hand.

'Question?'

'This is starting to sound like a military operation.'

'Dismissed.'

'Okay, edit. A militant operation.'

'There's nine of us, no weapons. Militant, okay, I'll accept that. But it's still wrong.'

'There's ten of us, not nine.'

'Nine.'

'Plus Nakagami, our chief scientist.'

'Nine and a half.'

'The one who-…sorry, the half who gave us most of the data we're basing our plan on.'

Sila raised his hand fast, pre-empting the flames stoking up in Aleša's eyeballs.

'Question?'

'How long can we walk around outside before the radiation affects us?'

'Ne vem. Chu?'

'That could take a while.'

Aleša turned to the right hand side of the map, motioning for Dodzi to sit down. He was either day-dreaming or hypnotized as he didn't budge.

'Dodzi…'

'Ja?'

'Chu's turn at the map.'

'Ja, good.'

Chu got up and walked over, stopping just to the right of the Acidalia Planitia.

'She's going to speak?' Dodzi asked, confused.

'For a while.'

'I thought we were talking about the Ghanaian base?'

'After Chu's done.'

'After?'

'Ja, she finishes speaking, we go back to your topic. You clear?'

Dodzi smiled at the last bit, a slow-dawning one, and patted the map. 'Okay, comrade. I'll sit down then. Think up some more strategy.'

'Good idea.'

~~~

On the deck below, in the CREATE NOT DESTROY ROOM, Gašper tucked himself in tight to the table and went over his Twi vocabulary, waiting for Dodzi to get bored with the MARS talk and come down for the plum wine.

So far, they'd had one language exchange and it did not go well.

'… … … … … … … …'

'What?'

'… … … … … … … …'

'Is that Twi?'

'… … … … … …'

'I can't catch what you're-…was that *cloud*?'

'Ne.'
~~~

'*Appreciate?*'

'Ne.'

'Comrade, say it again, slower.'

'… … … … … … … …'

'*Am I working today?*'

'… … … … … … … …'

'That was slower?'

It wasn't that Gašper was terrible at Twi, it was more the speed of Dodzi's delivery and his constant use of slang even though Gašper had told him not to.

Maybe also the fact that he hadn't spoken it properly in over two years.

The door opened and Petr walked in, looking half-asleep. After getting coffee from the wall, he spotted Gašper and sat down opposite.

'More Twi?'

'From my own brain, ja.'

'Can't be worse than the shit the computer speaks.' He rubbed his eyes. 'Or types.'

'If I had a dictionary, it might be easier. But then I'd probably never say anything, just check words all the time. That's what we had to do at school, in the German lessons, which is why I can only say *hello* and *maybe*.'

'Ja, same with me and Russian. Pretty much.' Petr yawned and looked at the notes to the left of him. 'Ah, Klemen, you weird bastard.'

'What is it?'

'His attempt at Chinese.'

'That's his writing?'

'Ja.'

'I thought it was Chu's.'

'Apparently, he's borderline fluent. That's what he said. Okay, Mr. Fluent, then go and chat with Chu, see if she speaks it too. Ne, he wouldn't do it. Just these scribbles…' Petr held up the notes. '…which probably isn't even Chinese.'

'Maybe he prefers expressing himself in writing.'

Petr laughed, thought about it then laughed again. If his chair had been sturdier, he may have rocked back on it.

The door slid open behind Gašper and Dodzi appeared, heading straight for the food dispenser.

'Your mentor's here,' said Petr, pointing with the side of his face.

Gašper flicked through his notes again quickly, mouthing some of the words.

When Dodzi passed in front of him, he raised his hand and said, 'ready?' but the Ghanaian-Slovene didn't answer.

'Dodzi,' Gašper tried again, adjusting his headband.

'Ja?' replied Dodzi, collapsing into a seat at the far end of the table.

'Twi exchange?'

Dodzi looked at the notes in front of Gašper and raised his cup of plum wine. 'Drink first, Twi later.'

'Later. Right.'

'Or we just speak Slovene, that's okay too.'

Petr laughed, muffling it this time, and picked up Klemen's Chinese notes. More laughter, along with a drawn-out 'what the…' as he reached the end of the page.

'What?'

'Definitely not Chinese.'

'Which bit?'

Petr held out the paper and said, 'ja,' when he saw Gašper squinting.

~~~

'This is Hagi code?' asked Chu, peering over Nakagami's shoulder and trying to decipher the symbols on the screen.

'As I explained last week, to everyone, it is a derivative of Hagi Code,' replied the physicist, giving up his seat to Chu, 'engineered specifically for our ion ships and colonies.'

'A very loose derivative. I can barely read any of it.'

'That is to be expected. Around forty-five percent of the root symbols are brand new. I myself am still feeling my way.'

'What's that one?'
~~~

Nakagami followed Chu's finger to the tip. 'Correlation.'

'Seriously?'

'It is a common word when talking to the computer. Not comparable to its usage in Slovenian.'

'That's why it's only one symbol?'

'Actually, the two symbols at the end of the sentence make up the whole word, plus that one in the middle, which acts as the object indicator. In direct translation it reads as: is there with something a correlation?'

'Ah, okay. Similar to Chinese then. Japanese too, I think.'

'Ne vem. I've never studied it.'

Chu tried to raise an eyebrow, but only succeeded in making her eyeballs bigger. 'Aren't you Japanese-Slovene?'

'Slovene.'

'I mean, don't you have some knowledge of Japanese grammar?'

'Ne.'

Chu muttered, 'okay *desu*,' and looked at the screen. Then turned suddenly to check the entrance for any lurkers. Nothing there except the usual eerie green light.

'He won't come yet,' said Nakagami.

'Just checking.'

Chu looked around the rest of the room. She'd only been in there once before and that was just to ask Nakagami something about quantum storage, one question, in and out. And there wasn't much to see anyway. Just the console, a lot of pointless buttons and the bin that came out of the wall. But now there was something else. A poster. What looked like a woman floating face-up in a pool, her stomach and thighs and eyes covered by strips of black cloth, and everything else bare. It was quite high up on the wall so Chu gave the chair back to Nakagami and moved to examine it more closely. There was something about the woman, her face, her body; maybe it was Nakagami's poor drawing skills, but it looked not unlike a very young, very thin girl.

'A recreation,' Nakagami said, noticing what Chu was doing.

'It's famous?'

'Ophelia, from *Hamlet*.'

'I know that one. Wasn't she wearing a dress though?'

'That's the original. Mine is based on a thematic re-interpretation by a lauded Pakistani artist.'

'Is it supposed to be a woman or a girl?'

'A girl.'

'A young girl?'

'It's an exaggeration of Ophelia's age. In film, she is often played by an actress in her mid-20's, whereas in historical truth it is more likely that she would've been 12.'

Chu nodded, ignored the block like feet of the girl, the cartoonish face, the oddly-shaped shoulders and complimented Nakagami on drawing something so challenging.

'I'm not an artist, but I like to draw sometimes.'

'That's good.'

'Sila tells me you're a fan of Varo.'

'Ja, a bit.'

'A talented artist. Imaginative. Perhaps a little too surreal for my taste.'

'Ja, she is odd.'

'Difficult to replicate too.'

Chu went back over to the console, refusing Nakagami's attempt to offer her back the chair, and looked at the symbol for *disembark* again.

'Have you made any posters yet?'

'No time.'

Nakagami looked at her until she modified her answer.

'Relatively no time. Or no leftover energy.'

'Your transporter experiments?'

'Not really experiments. More like thinking over the same equations and solutions as I had in Bled.'

'I see.'

'I'm hoping that there's some equipment on the Mars base that can let me do something more practical. Or maybe on one of the other bases.'

'Between revolutionary activities…'

'Ja…'

'Do you have a defined role yet? Sorry, a correction. Have you been assigned a defined role yet?'

'I'll leave all that to Aleša and the others.'

'Auxiliary support.'

'Besides, if I can develop a working transporter, sometime in the next four years, then we can just teleport directly into Potočnik's house and deal with him there. Assuming we can get this ship back into Earth orbit.'

'A working transporter?'

'But that's a long way off. And complete fantasy obviously.' She smiled, flicking at the edge of the console. 'Theory, maybe but, ja, might take a while. Better off focusing on reaching Mars first. And not being ambushed by the other bases when we do. Aleša said the Ghanaian one could be Darko-affiliated, hence the attempt to bring Dodzi into the group.'

'Not the most stable recruit.'

'He's okay…'

'I often see him drinking plum wine, talking to himself. In fact, I rarely see him doing anything else.'

'It's a coping mechanism, survivor guilt. All his comrades got murdered.'

'Did he know them?'

'The more he talks about other things, the better he'll be. Ne, he didn't know them, but they were symbolic; all the things he's lost in his life, his home. Or all the things he's had taken from him, not lost.'

'Ne vem. I do not know much about his background.'

'Ja, it's mostly my Taqian[35] analysis of him, not ironclad. Not even balsa-clad really. But he'll be fine, once we're on Mars. When he sees more Ghanaians.'

'Are Aleša and Sila not sufficient?'

'They're Slovene, not Ghanaian.'

---

[35] Taqi Aziz, a Pakistani psychologist who focused on identity – passive, fabricated, prop-covert, ego-anarchic, ego-repentant. Countered the Jungian concept of *Collective Consciousness*, and to a degree Ekuban's *Factory of Self*, with his own *Wasteland Consciousness*.

'I mean, facially.'

'Not enough.'

'Ah, they're contaminated then.'

'It's a mute issue. We'll be on Mars in eleven days, right?'

Nakagami looked at the console. 'Give or take a day.'

'Then it's fixed.' Chu went back to the symbols. 'Which one's *disembark* again?'

Nakagami pointed.

'And the other symbols?'

'You mean, what is the whole sentence?'

'Ja.'

Nakagami ran his finger along a line of ten symbols. 'These ones here. I'm asking the computer if we can disembark before Mars.'

'Did it answer?'

'Ja.'

'Would you like to share it?'

'It said ne.'

Chu tried to whistle, but ended up just blowing out air and a few specks of spit.

'I still have a lot of work to do, clearly.'

'You're testing boundaries, I assume?'

'Correct.'

'Maybe you should…ne vem. It might be more fruitful to focus on requests we need, like re-launching the ship before the four years are up? Or getting control of navigation?'

Nakagami said 'maybe' to the sensor control panel. He stared at it for a while then turned to Chu.

Before he could say anything, if that's what he was planning to do, Petr emerged from the green light, opening his mouth to say *afternoon, comrade* and then clamping it shut when he saw Chu.

'I've enlisted some help,' said Nakagami, not bothering to gesture towards Chu. 'I believe comrade Aleša would approve.'

Petr shrugged and went over to the bin wall, leaning awkwardly at first then shifting his position until he was comfortable.

Nakagami and Chu went back to the console and pretended to work.

~~~

'You were right all along, he's plotting something.'

'The Japanese spy?'

'Slovene spy. Ja.'

Aleša stopped moving the itching stick and flipped it round so the massage ball was on top.

'The code he uses is new, a weird variation of Hagi, which means he's the only one who can talk to the AI. I've managed to decipher some of it, the important bits and…'

'He's going to kill us?'

'…it seems that his plan is to dump us on Mars, then take the Ghanaian elevator up into orbit and head casually back to Earth.'

'He's gonna leave us to die?'

'You've stopped itching.'

Aleša said, 'ja, sorry,' and started hitting Chu's back with the massage ball.

'Itching is better.'

'This is less tiring.'

'Okay. If you don't want to know the rest of his plan…'

'Manipulator.' Aleša flipped the stick back around and half-heartedly itched the top of Chu's back. 'What else?'

'He'll leave a micro-bomb on the base with us, basically undetectable. If I make any kind of measurable progress with my transporter, he'll remote-detonate it.'

'Fucker. I knew it.'

'Far as I can see, there's only one way we can stop him.'

'One way? We kill the piece of shit, that's how we stop him…'

Aleša stuck her free hand down the side of the bed, fishing for her knickers.

'Ne. If we kill him, the ship will pump all the air out and suffocate us. The only rational thing we can do is get him drunk, dress him up as a farmer, hypnotize him…'

'Farmer?'
~~~

'…then, when we get to Mars, tell him to go outside the base and start ploughing the land. With a bit of luck, the hypnosis will hold. If not…ne vem.'

Aleša finished with her knickers and slid out of bed. 'You're lying.'

'Ja.'

'What about the rest?'

Chu pushed herself up into a sitting position and reached for her *koala on a mission* pyjama top. It was too far so she settled for the closer, ship-issue *We Martians* t-shirt instead. 'Sorry,' squeaked out of her mouth at some point.

'All of it was made up?'

'Ja, and I already regret it. You get riled up in milliseconds.'

'Riled? You said he had a micro-bomb…'

'It was a joke…'

'…and he's talking to the AI. What the fuck do you expect me to do?'

'Aleša…'

'Don't name me.'

'Okay. Comrade. I've told you about fifty times, he's not a spy. He's not even a bad guy. If you talk to him, you'll understand that.'

'He's the male version of you,' Aleša mumbled, checking she had the right sweatpants then putting them on.

Chu paused, t-shirt halfway over her head. 'What?'

'I don't need to talk to him.'

'You're comparing me to Kenji?'

'He's robotic. I don't trust him.'

Chu breathed out and shifted over to the tail end of the bed, the t-shirt now down to her stomach [and inside out].

'And he worked with Potočnik,' continued Aleša, picking up her own *Mojca Ito* t-shirt from the floor.

'So did a lot of people.'

'He directly worked with him, planned things with him.'

'So did I.'

'Probably helped him get rid of the…what?'

'Before I went to Bled, I met Potočnik, told him about my work. He helped get the support to continue it.'

'I thought it was the collectives who did that?'

'Ja, with his help.'

Aleša paused, her t-shirt bunched up in one hand, the itching stick in the other. 'How many times?'

'To what? Meet with him?'

'Ja.'

'Four or five. Maybe six. I can't remember exactly.'

'Only the two of you?'

Chu looked back at the pillows, both clumped awkwardly together like leftover art.

'It wasn't just the two of you?'

'Ne, of course not.'

'Nakagami was there too?'

Chu almost laughed, bending down to pick her knickers up off the floor. 'How about we go back to the itching? Cool down a bit.'

'I'm not angry.'

'Then just the itching part.'

Aleša gripped the stick tighter then suddenly realized she was standing in front of that fucking Potočnik painting. From Chu's angle, she thought, it could look thematic in some way. Or worse, nostalgic.

'Is that a ja?' Chu prompted, pulling her knickers on.

'I need to go.'

'Right this second?'

'It's important.'

Aleša threw the stick on the bed, put on her *Mojca Ito* t-shirt, her stock green jacket and headed for the door.

'You're leaving me alone in your own room?' asked Chu, patting the duvet beside her.

'I have to find Sila, go over new strategy.'

'And the itching?'

'No time.'

Chu leaned back and picked up the massage stick. 'Okay, how about I itch you for a while?'

'Ne.'

'Massage?'

'Ne.'

'Miscellaneous?'

Aleša stopped at the door. 'You can stay longer, if you like.'

Chu waved the stick in front of her, the itching claw scraping against nothing. 'I will if you let me itch you.'

'I can't.'

'Not even one scratch?'

'Later.'

Aleša stepped backwards out into the corridor and let the door slide shut, leaving Chu alone [with the stick].

~~~

'That's the plan?' asked Gašper, putting down the scissors.

'One part of it,' said Sila, chewing on something the food dispenser described as hard tofu but which felt more like a cereal bar.

'I don't get it.'

'Ja, cos you haven't heard the other parts.'

'Why would a farm hurt Potočnik?'

'Gašper, you're doing it again…looking at it from A to B to C. Bigger picture, remember?'

'What picture? You said we're gonna set up an interior farm with the other bases and this will translate to action back on Earth.'

'It will…within the bigger picture.'

Gašper picked up the scissors and went back to cutting out his alleged drawing of King Matjaž.

Sila didn't know what else to add…he couldn't be bothered explaining the entire plan again, especially to someone who'd ask questions about everything only at the end to turn around and say 'ja, that'll work.' But then, he also didn't want anyone to feel left out. Except Cvetko and Jame. But that was their own fault, they never talked to anyone. Just stayed in their quarters having sex. Which was good for them. At least they had someone.
~~~

'Okay,' said Gašper, holding up his cut-out of a potato with a crown [King Matjaž]. 'Let's hear the rest of the plan.'

Sila finished gluing the moon to his own poster then looked up. 'Only if you don't interrupt.'

'What, through all of it?'

'I'll be quick. The heavily summarized version.'

Gašper shrugged.

'Okay, I'll take shrugging as agreement. Ready? Right, phase one, the basics: we make the base liveable. Shouldn't be too difficult, with the drones helping us. Next, we contact the Cameroon base, get them on side, then send Dodzi to the Ghanaian base. Assuming they don't shoot him, we establish a neighbourly bond, set up a communication device, short range first, long range a little later.'

'Makes sense.'

'Phase two, we bring in the Guangdong base via Papua New Guinea, maybe Chile and Brazil if they're amenable, find a spot to start the joint farm, establish a tight bond. Or a ductile bond. Pursuing rigidity too much would probably lead to the opposite of what we-…'

Sila looked up and saw that Gašper's expression was the same as when Nakagami had attempted to explain the science behind the ion engine. Feigning a cough, he simplified.

'We want them to agree with our plan, not be tricked into it. No loyalty tests or defensiveness.'

'You mean we want to subtly trick them into joining us?'

'Replace the word *trick* with *convince* and ja, that's it.'

'What if they don't agree with you?'

'Then we work around it, look for common ground. Our basic focus should be the same i.e. get rid of Potočnik, Darko etc. so any disagreements would be on the fringes.'

'What's the last phase?'

Sila closed his eyes, picturing a lurking nitrogen cloud sneaking up and possessing Gašper's brain so he could ask actual follow-up questions.

'Sorry, brother, it's just I promised I'd help Petr cover up the Potočnik face in his quarters.'

'Petr?'

'Ja, he said it was a two man job. One to stick up the card, the other to keep watch.'

'Keep watch for what?'

'Ne vem. He said something might happen.'

Sila shook his head, adding a double *ne* for good measure.

'Ne to what?' asked Gašper, confused.

'I mean, ne, nothing happens. I covered up the face last week. Tried to paint over the eyes too, but it wouldn't work. The paint gets absorbed in or something and the purple comes back.'

'How?'

'Ne vem, I'm not a painter.'

'Maybe Petr's one is different.'

'Ja, well, you and him can find out…when you go to his quarters.'

'That's the idea.' Gašper checked the other seats, blinking and double-checking when he saw Jame in the corner, alone, then leaned forward. 'Where's Cvetko?'

'Ne vem.'

'In his quarters?'

'Drinking probably. Do you want to hear the rest of the plan?'

'It's weird. I've never seen them separated before. It's like watching half a body, cut down the middle and-…'

'You don't want to hear it?'

'The plan? Ja, sure. But can you skip to the end part?'

Sila sat up straight and picked up the pencil nearby. 'Okay, Kreft.[36] I'll tell you the main difficulties; that serves as the end part, basically.'

'You said the difficult part was the Ghana base…'

'Ja, one of them. But the reason is…' Sila threw the pencil in the air, not too high, and caught it on the blunt end. 'Actually, it's better to think of it from the enemy's side, Potočnik's point of view. Darko too. They instigated this trip, constructed the ship, put us on it, sent it to

---

[36] Rado Kreft, director notorious for making 217 unfinished films before throwing himself off Celje Cathedral at the age of 34.

Mars, all of it, therefore it's obvious that they must be playing out some form of strategy.'

'Re-education?'

'Possibly.'

'Reward?'

'What?'

'Okay, not that. Ne vem. Only other one I can think of is...they just expect us to die on Mars.'

'Ja, that's what we're leaning towards, the one way trip, slow death scenario. But then the question becomes, how precisely do they expect us to die? If we assume that they don't want us to come back, we can also assume they believe four years is enough time for all of us to be snuffed out. Via accident or some other way.'

'Radiation...'

'Not a bad guess. Chu said it's probably a bit too slow though. Too much time to come up with a protective.'

'Aggressive radiation...'

'Aleša thinks there's going to be something on the base, some device that makes us turn on each other...which could be true. But I'm guessing it'll be something more direct, like one of the other bases targeting us. Probably the Ghanaian one.'

'The one we're going to make friends with?'

'Ja. That's why we need to get to them, as early as possible. Show them we're good people.'

'So they don't murder us?'

'Pretty much. See, from Potočnik's perspective, or Darko's, whoever's in control, they would expect us to be suspicious of the Ghanaians because of Darko, and therefore give them a wide berth. Then, when we seek alliances with the other bases, the Ghanaians will be told we're enemies, that we're aiming to take them out so they better take us out first. Or they may have chips in their brains, controlling them. A bunch of programmers back home could literally just puppet them into our base and make them shoot us. Ne vem. The sad thing is, Darko didn't even send them there. They could be regular colonists. Or dissidents even. That would be the ideal endgame for Potočnik, two groups of dissidents wiping each other out, bases kept intact.'

Gašper nodded, gluing King Matjaž to the black card. 'I prefer Aleša's theory.'

'That we'll all turn on each other?'

'But it won't be all of us, it'll be a few. Maybe Dodzi or Nakagami or…'

The door slid open and Cvetko charged into the room, slowing down when he saw that Jame was alone.

Walking round the table, he leaned into Jame's ear and said something almost loud enough to hear but not quite.

Jame put down the glue in his hand, picked up the scissors and stabbed the table four times. Then he threw them across the room, towards Klemen's poster of a hanging man without bones.

'I'm not your fucking toy, peanut head.'

It was the first time anyone had screamed that loud on the ship, and it froze Cvetko solid for about two and half seconds. Then, he swatted the air with his arm and screamed back, 'You ever raise your-…'

It was cut short by the ships most beloved function, an electric discharge. Both men wobbled a bit then fell on the floor, Jame knocking his head on the chair on the way down.

'Bad fall,' said Sila.

They sat there, moving their arms as if they were going to stand up but ultimately they didn't, they just continued sitting, watching.

There was a beeping noise, followed by the AI on speaker.

'Attention crew,

Due to reports of raised voices in the CREATE NOT DESTROY ROOM, an existing rule has been called into effect starting a few seconds ago. Any shouting or screaming will be punished by a level 2 electric shock. This is a step up from the level 1 shock so conduct yourselves accordingly. Exceptions will be made for sexual activities and the sudden discovery of something alarming, for example, a hole in the ship, a raging fire, or a corpse.

Have a bold and safe trip to Mars.

Hvala.'

The room became silent again, in fact, it became more silent than it had ever been. Even the faint buzzing noise from the food dispenser ceased.

'Do you think they'll be angry if we don't pick them up?' whispered Sila.

His question was answered almost immediately. Cvetko lifted his head up, looked around, saw Sila and Gašper gawping back, then calmly stood up, grabbed Jame by the boots and dragged him out of the room.

'That's our murderer,' said Gašper, jabbing at the door. 'Within the first month. Guaranteed.'

~~~

Nakagami stood next to the chair in the TALK TO YOUR GOD ROOM, calmly constructing a sentence in neo-Hagi code.

Next to his elbow was the trajectory display, and next to that was a blinking blue light, but he didn't pay any attention to it.

'How far exactly?' he said, reading the symbols back to himself in Slovene.

He pressed the *execute* button and waited.

There was a noise by the entrance. Something akin to a cough.

Nakagami looked over.

There was eerie green light, the usual faint buzzing sound and nothing else.

He looked lower.

No boot tips.

'You can come in Petr,' he said loud enough to be picked up in the main corridor.

No one came in.

'Very well.'

He turned back to the screen. It didn't matter if anyone was out there or not, they wouldn't be able to understand the symbols. Except Chu, perhaps. But she was only a beginner. The day before she'd forgotten the symbol for *spaceship*. And her mind was usually elsewhere anyway.
~~~

The screen beeped quietly, something he'd asked it to do in case he ever fell asleep.

He read the answer.

Sat down.

Slumped.

~~~

On Day 70, the day before the ship was due to arrive at Mars, there was an announcement.

'Attention crew,

As a reward for your patience and sacrifice in only talking to one other person for the duration of this trip, we will lift all conversation restrictions from this point on.

This will also apply to the base on Mars, which we will be landing at in eighteen hours.

If you wish to celebrate, the food dispenser has been programmed with a new alcoholic beverage that will be available without limits for the rest of the day. You may proceed there now.

When the planet is visible with the naked eye, we will make an announcement and direct you to the appropriate viewing port.

Have a bold and safe trip to Mars.

Hvala.'

~~~

Half the crew were asleep when it played, but Sila heard the whole thing and rushed straight to the CREATE NOT DESTROY ROOM.

'You did it,' he said, louder than usual, to Nakagami, who was sitting alone, making a poster and eating something green and biscuit-like.

'It was not my request,' he answered, his voice sterile.

'Chu did it?'

'Ne.'

'Then who?'

'No one. As far as I know.'

Sila walked round the table and looked at the poster Nakagami was busy on. Another young girl, in a transparent gown, standing under a tree with a canopy that looked like a nest of tentacles.

Nakagami turned his head to Sila, not making any attempt to cover the drawing. 'It was a Mexican piece originally.'

The door slid open and Chu and Aleša walked in, the latter practically hanging off the other's back.

Sila moved away from Nakagami's art and asked Chu if she'd made the request.

'Huh? You mean it wasn't you?' she asked, looking at Nakagami.

'I have told Sila already, it was an unprompted announcement by the ship.'

'You didn't tell me that,' said Sila.

'I am not clear as to why it was done. I will go and investigate after I finish my breakfast.'

'Who cares?' Aleša detached from Chu's back and headed to the food dispenser. 'It's the same policy on Mars, which makes our plan about fifty seven times easier.'

'I will investigate anyway,' replied Nakagami.

'Okay, Detective Dee. You and Petr investigate.' Aleša scanned the words on the dispenser menu, eyes lighting up when she saw the new addition. 'The rest of us will get drunk.'

'We'll all get drunk,' added Chu, giving Aleša the Slovene version of the evil eye.

'Ja, all of us. Even Dodzi.'

'What about Cvetko and Jame?'

'Ha, Dalibor and Olya?[37] They won't come, they're stapled to their quarters.'

Sila leaned down to Nakagami's ear, out of sight of Aleša. 'Might be a good idea to finish your poster in the Control Room.'

'Why?'

---

[37] Existentialist Slovene sci-fi series where the titular characters, Dalibor and Olya, clash on a remote outpost in the Kuiper Belt, each convinced the other is a hallucination.

Sila blinked more than he would've liked, clearly not expecting a response. He looked at the poster, the young girl's legs, and stammered, 'you like it. The Control Room, I mean.'

~~~

After one afternoon and half an evening of going over the strategy for Mars, Aleša got up and made an announcement.

'As there are only two hours left before curfew, we should focus on relaxation and admiring my new poster.'

She put her arm forward and then stretched it back with a flourish, unveiling a line of five posters to the left of the door, each with a single letter on it.

'*ZMAGA*.[38] To our Mars campaign, and all those who fell before it.'

'Not your best work,' said Klemen, clamped in his seat.

'Look closer, Mr. art klitic. Klitic? Wah, my brain is mush. Critic.'

Klemen didn't budge, so it was up to Petr and Gašper to go closer and squint at the giant *Z*.

'It's got names on it.'

'Hero names.'

'Emiliano Zapata.'

'Old and new, Slovene and foreign…'

'…it's all connected,' finished Sila.

'Ja, exactly.'

Petr moved down to the final card and ran his finger along the side of the *A*. 'Koshiwa Aleša.'

'What? That's not-…'

Petr laughed, backing off to the other side of the door as Aleša advanced to hit him.

'What happened?' asked Gašper, confused.

'She's a lunatic.'

'I can see that.'

---

38 'Victory' in Slovene.
~~~

Aleša finally lined Petr up against the wall, holding him with one hand while she struck with the other.

'Hey, that's my poster,' said Klemen.

Petr ducked, dodged then said 'shit' as he turned back and saw Aleša rip the bottom corner of Klemen's exploding spaceship.

'You fucking idiot…' Klemen moved about an inch off his chair then sat back down, grumbling to himself.

'Sorry, sorry…' Aleša tried to put the torn part back into its original place, but it wasn't working. 'I'll stick it back later, after I've sunk my drink. And hit Petr properly…'

'I can hit him for you,' said Gašper.

Dodzi raised his glass and shouted, 'more drink, more hitting.'

'Less hitting,' shouted Petr.

'Less fucking shouting,' added Klemen, eyes back on the paper in front of him.

'Ja, can you lower the volume a bit, prosim?' asked Chu, looking up from her chair.

Dodzi took in the feedback and adjusted. 'Okay, comrades, no shouting, no hitting, but lots of drinking. Performed by everyone.'

Everyone slurred *ja* and finished what was already in their glasses.

Of course, *everyone* didn't include Cvetko or Jame, who hadn't responded to the Mars announcement in any noticeable way, but it did rope in Dodzi, who seemed to have had several litres of grey krsic injected directly into his frontal lobe.

It was so overt, his arm spasms, his constant talking, the awkward climbing up onto the table, that Aleša finally asked him outright, 'are you on grey krsic?'

As soon as he heard the words he jumped down off the table and said, 'never, never, never, never.'

'Just regular drunk then?' asked Petr, his arm hanging off Gašper's shoulder.

'That stuff messes with your brain, chops time up…'

'Ja, that's why people take it,' said Aleša, laughing.

'Ne, ne, ne, my sister, she woke up in warehouses, no clue why, fields, other collectives, the garbage collection depot…'

'That's normal.'

'Apart from the garbage one,' said Gašper, finishing his line by pretend-biting Petr on the neck.

'Fuck, it's wet.'

'Ja, it's my mouth.'

'Get off.'

'It'll be dry soon. Relax.'

Petr pushed Gašper away and wiped the saliva off his neck. There wasn't much there.

'If you two wanna bite each other, go to your quarters,' said Aleša, pointing at her wrist. 'Less than two hours on the clock.'

'Good idea,' said Gašper.

'I don't want to be bitten, it's wet.'

'I'll blow dry my teeth first…'

'What?'

'…rub a towel on my tongue. Then we're all set.'

'You're fucking weird.'

'Quarters. Bed. I'll get more drink.'

Petr called Gašper weird again, but let himself be dragged over to the food dispenser and then, with four full glasses between them, back to quarters.

'Where are they going?' asked Sila, coming over from the other side of the table, where Chu was still seated, analysing the Mars base set-up that Aleša had copied from the map in the ASTEROID BELT ROOM.

'To pray,' answered Aleša, deadpan.

'To fuck,' said Dodzi, raising his glass.

'Already?' asked Sila, his face seemingly confused by his own word.

'It's been over two months, comrade, what do you want? Two people like each other, young faces, mobile, trapped, no other real options. Wah, they moved out that door fast.'

Sila coughed and gave a solitary *suppose* in response then leaned into Aleša's ear. 'Does Petr know Gašper's history?'

'What history?'

'Rehab.'

'You mean the NOT YET Centres?'

'He was in there a long time.'

'Ja, of course he knows, Gašper tells everyone. Even Dodzi knows and they've only ever spoken once.'

'He told me fifteen minutes ago,' Dodzi confirmed.

'Ja, okay.'

'Ni panike, half of Slovenia's been in rehab,' Aleša said, tapping Sila's empty glass. 'Or the NOT YET Centres.'

'Four percent actually.'

'Wait, which word did I use?'

'What?'

'I usually say rehab, but…what did I say?'

'When?'

Aleša's eyes drifted over to Chu, who was still head down with the Mars base. 'Doesn't matter. From now on, rehab.'

'Okay.'

'My sister's been in rehab,' said Dodzi, putting his arms around both of them. 'Only time she wakes up in consistent places. Ne, the same place, consistently the same place. However you say it.' He drank more, without moving his arms off them. '*Nyame*, I miss speaking Twi.'

'Is your sister there now?'

'But tomorrow, things will be a Twi environment again. If my legs can work…'

'Radio first, Dodzi,' cautioned Aleša, removing his arm from her shoulder.

'Person to person, radio, both still Twi. You clear?'

'Ja, but radio first. We need to know they're not Darko plants. Caution, remember?'

'Woman, I'm the most caution man you've ever seen.'

'Woman?'

'Caution?'

'I tell them face to face, what Darko is, what she's done, what she did to our comrades in the VIP room, they'll de-plant on the spot.'

Aleša closed her eyes for a second then opened them again, telling Dodzi they'd talk again when he was hungover.

'Comrade, we're standing here, what you mean talk again?'

She patted him on the shoulder then, with the speed of a summertime Šarec stan, abandoned him for Chu.

Dodzi turned to Sila and squinted at something behind him. 'Is that a potato?'

Sila turned, laughing when he saw what Dodzi was looking at. 'It's Gašper's version of King Matjaž.'

'Who?'

'The old king, stuck in the bowels of a mountain.'

'It's real?'

'Ja, not really, it's an old myth. You didn't read this at school?'

'Why does he look like a potato?'

'Ne vem. Poor technique.'

Dodzi took some more of his drink and switched from the poster to Sila's face, examining his cheeks then his neck. 'You're really Slovene, comrade?'

'Ja.'

'Third generation?'

'Fourth.'

'Before that...wait, ne, let me try. Kenya?'

'Tanzania.'

Dodzi smiled, gripping Sila's shoulder and almost dropping his glass. '... ... ...'

'Was that Swahili?'

'In a thick Ghanaian accent, ja.' Dodzi looked to the left, either playing back what he'd said or feeling threatened by the potato king. 'Do you know what I said?'

'You called me a firm promenade.'

'That clear?'

'I'm not fluent, but that's what I heard.'

'Ah, ne vem. Maybe I mixed in something else. My sister used to do that with Slovene...'

'The one in rehab?'

'...all the time. Ja, rehab, not all that bad a place, comrade. Better if you've got addiction problems.'

'Did you ever visit your sister?'

'Mental problems, still not bad, long as you don't go violent. I think they copied it, the Argentinian method, targeted listening instead of somewhere else listening…'

'Did you ever visit her, in rehab?'

'…listening with pills. Ja, I visited, twice a month. Then she got out last year on sincerity grounds…'

'She got released?'

'…and five days later was right back in again. One of her friends, had that drug in her jacket. Poor girl woke up in Kamnik, saw farm creatures, walked back and sectioned herself.' Dodzi drifted off into his glass. 'Supposed to be a year, in her words. That means back home by now. Better be back home.'

'So rehab isn't that bad?' prompted Sila, replacing the image of a Slovene-Ghanaian girl in his head with Sadia and forcing her into a picturesque garden scene outside a generic rehab building. Or NOT YET Centre.

'In and out, others taking care of you, no more Darko plots. Ja, not same level as Šarec's old torture house yet.'

'Ah, that place…'

'Ballerina school turned into a building of pain. Pink walls all over, corridors like the one out there.'

Sila squinted at Dodzi, trying to process all the words flying out, then froze.

'Ja, maybe Potočnik's behind it, the design aesthetic, but Darko in his ear with the Šarec history book, no doubt. No doubt at all, comrade.'

'I knew it was familiar,' muttered Sila, looking over at the door. 'The green must've blocked me recognising it. And the lack of vending machines. Fuck. Šarec's Torture House. Of all the things to pick.'

'Sick people learn from sick people. Ja, that face is earned, comrade. They're probably starting up that shit up again now, converting rehab centres back home, painting the walls pink and getting in guards. Think of it like that and we're lucky to be where we are.'

Sila nodded, said a token, 'ja, lucky,' and walked slowly over to the food dispenser.

He stood there a while, filling his glass a little bit, stopping, then filling a bit more.

There's a good chance, he thought, that she's out already. That it's not as bad as mum, that they saw that in her behaviour and now she's out. And if she's out then she's okay. Unless the neighbours turned on her...

Would they?

It wasn't a political building they lived in, or it hadn't been two years ago. Correction, two years and two months ago. The flat downstairs sometimes said, 'fucking Albanians,' but that was about it.

They wouldn't target Sadia. She was neutral. Her knowledge of political theory was understanding that Marx and Bakunin had beards.

But what about him?

He was political.

A dissident?

He had no way to know his status, what Potočnik had classified him as. How public that classification would be.

Maybe the corridor design was a clue? Or a threat?

'Sila, get over here.'

He kept his back to the room, finished pouring his drink then turned. Aleša was waving at him.

'Chu-talk.'

He walked over and said a slightly dazed, 'what'?

'Chu has a question for you.'

'Ne, I don't,' said Chu, writing something on the Mars base blueprint.

'Okay then. I have a question for you.'

'Is it about Nakagami?'

'Him?'

'Mars?'

'He's irrelevant. Whatever he's telling Potočnik, or whoever the thing, they can't do anything physical. Unless he does something, which is...ja, good luck on nine of us.'

'You might want to stop drinking,' said Chu, not looking up.

'I am stopped.' Aleša held up her glass, which was almost full. 'Woman.'

'Sorry?'

'Caution man.'

'Who?'

'What was the question?' Sila asked quickly, taking some of his own drink.

'Question…ja, I've forgotten. Something theory-related. Fibre-glassing? Ne, fuck, it's gone…'

'He's Tanzanian,' said Dodzi, leaning in close to Aleša's shoulder and almost falling over.

'Wah, where did you come from?'

'The seventh trapezoid of hell,' Dodzi laughed, drawing something not a trapezoid with his finger.

'I thought you were over there, doing the-…'

'Ja, the eighth trapezoid is for Darko. That witchy hyena whore. I'll put her there myself, melt the key. Melt her face.'

Aleša put Dodzi on background and scanned the other side of the room, spotting Klemen. 'What's he doing?'

'Ne vem,' said Sila.

'Sketching the eighth trapezoid,' said Dodzi, walking off to the food dispenser via the wall, the edge of the table and the wall again.

Klemen lifted his head up, probably hearing his name being shouted out, saw Dodzi pinballing his way over and quickly moved round the other side of the table. Then, a few seconds later, he stood up, pushed his chair in and walked over to them.

'You're not drinking,' said Aleša, holding up her own half-full glass.

'I have an alteration to our plan.'

'What plan?'

'If this isn't actually a simulation, then I put forward myself as the one to visit the Guangdong base.'

'Wah, not you too. I just told Dodzi, radio first then we meet up. Face to face is too risky, might shoot us, bolt guns…'

'Then I volunteer to talk to them on the radio.'

'That's Chu's job.'

Klemen looked down at Chu. 'Does she speak Cantonese?'

'*She* does,' replied Chu, caustic, before lowering expectations with an additional, 'some.'

'How much exactly?'

'Ne vem. High intermediate.'

'What do you classify as high intermediate?'

'Klemen, she's Chinese…' said Aleša, practically jabbing Chu in the face, or she would've if she weren't on the other side of the table.

'Slovene,' Chu corrected, looking up this time.

'Doesn't mean she knows how to speak the language.'

'*She* does,' shouted Aleša, turning to Sila. 'Right, Zilo?'

'Ne vem.'

'Wah, you're fucking useful. I thought the two of you were best friends?'

Sila took some more of his drink, managing a brief tilt of the head as he did so.

'Didn't you live together?'

'She said she speaks high intermediate. I never tested her, obviously.'

'We'll see about that.' Klemen looked down at the Mars blueprints, thinking for a second then saying *what are you looking at?* in Cantonese.

Chu looked at the rough sketch of the Ghanaian base and breathed out so loud it almost became a word.

'Do you understand what I said?' asked Klemen, again in Cantonese.

'Ja…' Chu pointed at the base and switched to Cantonese, talking continuously for about two minutes.

When she was done Klemen folded his arms and said, 'maybe.'

'Would you like me to say it again?'

'I understood.'

'What did I say?'

'The base. Details of it.'

'Like?'

'Fuck, Klem,' said Aleša, nearly laughing. 'You didn't catch any of it, did you?'

'I just said, base details.'

'Ja, key tactic of language faking. Always check the room first, if people speak or not. Golden rule.'

'There's no faking. I understood everything she said.'

'Everything?'

'Ninety-five percent of it.'

Chu picked up her glass and took a tiny sip. Possibly her first of the night. 'I don't wish to humiliate you, but your pronunciation was poor. And I didn't say a word about the base.'

Klemen folded his arms.

'I talked about the benefits of fusion power, and a little bit about cutting fruit at the end.'

'Ja, I heard that...the word for fruit.'

'Did it sound similar to the word for base?'

'But I thought I'd misheard cos it didn't make sense. But I heard it. I knew you said it.'

'Klemen.' Aleša put her hand on his shoulder. 'I have no choice but to say your full name to start my sentences. Cos that was fucking embarrassing. Klemen.'

'You're drunk,' said the big Iranian-Slovene, removing her hand.

'Ja, but in the morning I'll be sober...'

'Doubtful.'

'...and you'll still be shit at Cantonese.'

'A tired line.'

'Very shit at it. Ne, I modified the line, enhanced it. You're the one who's tired.'

Klemen moved to fold his arms again, changed his mind and walked back to his seat. Unfortunately for him, Dodzi was sitting there, asleep. Klemen nudged the Ghanaian's shoulder gently, then a little less gently and got no response. Finally, he gave up and returned to the main group.

'Anyone here speak Portuguese?'

'Ha...'

'Ne,' said Sila, just about keeping his glass stable as Aleša knocked into him.

Klemen looked down at Chu. 'You?'

'Não, não esta fluente.'

'Are you serious?'

Chu maintained deadpan mode for another three seconds then loosened up. 'Ne, I don't speak Portuguese.'

'In that case, I have decided to volunteer to go to the Brazilian base.'

'The one we're not planning on going to?' Aleša asked, struggling to keep her face steady.

The door slid open and a Japanese face appeared at the side, calling for Sila to come outside.

'Spyware,' shouted Aleša.

'Kenji,' said Chu, half-rising from her seat.

'What's he hiding out there for?'

'To avoid you probably,' answered Klemen, his tone not quite bitter enough to get a reaction.

'Silly fuck. I'm not Pol Pot.'

'Scale-wise, ne.'

'I love farmers. What? Scale-wise…fuck off. I'm as consensual as it gets.'

'Sila,' Nakagami called again, eyes locked solely on his target.

'Ja?'

'Can you come outside for a moment?'

'It's okay, just come in,' said Aleša, walking closer to the door. 'I wanted to ask you something actually…about scanning the planet.'

'Sorry, I need to talk to Sila.'

'You can do that in here. Grab a drink, chat with us, no interrogation…'

'Sila.'

'…and I'll stop calling you spy too, even though it's affectionate.' She pointed at Chu. 'I call her robot, Klemen's lizard face…'

Sila walked past Aleša, whispering in her ear that he'd be back in a minute.

'Ask about the planet scanning,' she shouted as the door slid shut again.

'Sorry about that,' Sila said, letting Nakagami guide him a few metres down the corridor.

'It appears she's drunk.'

'Ja.'

'It's only forty-five minutes until curfew begins. I suggest returning her to her quarters quickly.'

'Chu will do that.'

'Perhaps strap her to the bed in case she attempts to walk out again.'

'What did you want to talk about?'

Nakagami stared at the wall as if his eyes could see right through it. 'She will not react well when she finds out.'

'Who, Aleša?'

'Nor will Dodzi.'

'What are you saying? React to what?'

'In terms of violence, I mean. The others…'

'Kenji, react to what? Tell me.'

Nakagami looked at Sila's forehead, flicked at the same part of the wall three times and said, 'ja.'

'Ja what?'

'This ship will not land on Mars.'

'Not land?'

'Ne.'

'Ja, it will, tomorrow. The computer said.'

'That was misinformation.'

'It lied?'

More flicking, then a head tilt towards the CREATE NOT DESTROY ROOM door. The noises from inside were just about audible, not close enough to spill out into the corridor.

'Kenji…'

Nakagami turned back to Sila, putting a hand on his own jacket zip. 'I suspected it a while ago. The velocity and the trajectory did not match up. But I couldn't know for sure because the computer stopped showing me the readouts.'

'But it said tomorrow. *Attention crew, you're landing on Mars tomorrow.* Why would it lie?'

'Ne vem.'

'It doesn't make any-…' Sila paused, watching Nakagami pull his zip up and down an inch. 'Are you sure you're right about this?'

'Certain.'

'How certain?'

'The computer showed me the readouts again. The latest ones, an hour ago. We are not near Mars. In fact, we passed it twelve days ago.'

'What?'

'Right now, we are closer to the asteroid belt than Mars.'

'The asteroid belt?'

'I haven't told Chu yet, though I have a feeling she'll adapt relatively fast. The others, however…'

'We're going to the asteroid belt?'

'…we'll need to come up with a plan for. To help them adapt. Or to subdue them, if necessary.'

Sila shot out a hand, stopping Nakagami's little zip routine. 'Kenji, are we going to the asteroid belt?'

'Ne.'

'Then where?'

'Ne vem.'

'Jupiter?'

'Ne vem.'

'Fucking Pluto?'

'I do not know where we are going. There is simply not enough data.'

Sila removed his hand from Nakagami's zip and punched the wall with the edge of his fist. Then turned side on and collapsed against it. *Fucking Alpha Centauri* crossed his mind, but he let it drift.

'I predict there will be some kind of announcement tomorrow, revealing the truth. It's better that we act surprised when that happens.'

'We should tell them now.'

'Ne. They might kill us. Or kill me and wound you. It's better to let the ship do it, focus their rage.'

'Kill? Are you serious?'

'It is a logical outcome based on current crew relations. By my rough calculations, about a 72% probability.'

'Fuck,' said Sila, staring down the corridor and imagining pink walls.

'Ni panike, I've thought about this for the last two hours and have a plan. At least to mitigate the initial trauma.'

'Does it involve lying to them?'

'Not directly. We can sow some seeds first, nothing too egregious.'

'What seeds?'

Nakagami placed his right hand back on the jacket zip, pulling it down an inch. 'You will go back in and tell them I had doubts about the ship. Tell them the velocity looks like it hasn't changed, and I've asked the ship but it's not answering. That's not a lie. That did happen. Then you just need to drink a bit more, go to bed, and avoid them as much as possible tomorrow. Perhaps, when the announcement is made, ask questions out loud like *is this connected to the constant velocity?* That should cover things.'

'Can't believe this is happening…'

Sila reached upwards and pulled at his own cheeks.

'You are not a hologram, Sila.'

'Dream?'

'This is real, sadly. But it is not an impossible situation. We just have to adjust our strategy.'

'Adjust…'

'I was being gentle. Now, go back in and play your part. I'm going back to the Control Room to see if the computer feels like confiding in me.'

Nakagami patted Sila lightly on the elbow and moved off, his figure turning right at the end of the corridor and vanishing into the wall.

Sila continued leaning like a drunk domino for at least a minute, repeating the word *velocity* a few times, taking a breath then pushing off and heading back inside.

'Auxiliary spy,' shouted Aleša, holding her glass up in salute. 'How about that planet scanning?'

Sila offered a vacant, 'sorry, forgot,' then repeated what Nakagami had said.

Apart from a brief, quizzical look from Chu, no one questioned it. In fact, Aleša thought there was a good chance it would get them to Mars a few hours faster.

'Atmosphere breaking,' she said, confidently. 'They always do it.'

'Ja…' replied Sila, looking deep into his drink.

When there was an atmosphere.

And a planet.

~~~

Nakagami the blank-faced sage was right. At 10am the next day, the ship made an announcement.

'Attention crew,

Prosim, report to the MARS ROOM within the next thirty minutes for a live viewing of the red planet.

Have a safe and bold trip

Hvala.'

Most of the crew opened an eye and understood that something was talking but it didn't seem important so they rolled over on either the bed or the floor and went back to sleep.

Twenty-five minutes later, the ship made another announcement.

'Attention crew,

You have five minutes left to report to the MARS ROOM for a live viewing of the red planet. Attendance is mandatory. Any crew member not in the MARS ROOM at the aforementioned time will receive a level 1 electric shock, and a further shock every minute until they leave their rooms.

Have a bold and safe trip

Hvala.'

That got everyone up, except Dodzi, who shouted at the train to go faster, he had a pharmacy to save then buried his head under a pillow.

After three electric prods, he rolled off the bed, put on his trousers, forgot his t-shirt and stumbled out of his quarters.

~~~

The MARS ROOM had been pretty much vacant up to that point of the trip due to the fact that there was nothing in there.

Just an old-fashioned projection screen that pre-collective era psychopaths had used to show quarterly growth, and eight foldable chairs.

But now it was full of hungover dissidents, leaning forward in their chairs, waiting to see their home for the next four years.

Even Cvetko and Jame were there, though they were the only ones leaning back on their chairs, evoking *Debordian ennui.*

'Must be an orbital pic,' said Gašper, leaning across to Sila and almost toppling off his chair.

'Or a surface one,' added Aleša, hands on the back of Gašper's chair.

'I feel sick,' said Petr, next to her.

'Wouldn't we have felt the landing?' asked Gašper. 'If it's a surface pic…'

'Not really.'

'And don't we need to strap in, go to that launch room place?'

'That's for launching.'

'Only?'

'I think we may have actually landed.'

Sila yawned and looked to the back of the room, where Nakagami was leaning. It may have been the poor lighting, but his features looked quite sinister, as if he were going to walk out the door any second and lock them in.

'I still feel sick,' said Petr, holding his stomach.

'Go in the corner.'

'Can't.'

'Go outside then.'

'I move and I'll be sick.'

'Jezus.'

'Find a spot on the wall and focus on it,' said Chu, gesturing left.

'Really?'

'A specific spot. Something distinctive.'

Petr tried it, focusing on a tiny square to the left of the projector.

'Did it work?' asked Gašper.

'Not yet.'

'Try sticking your fingers down your throat, make yourself vomit.'

Petr closed his eyes.

'Ne?'

When Dodzi staggered in and asked, 'has it started yet, comrades?' the presentation began.

A photo of a dot appeared on the screen, coupled with some computer narration.

'Attention crew, this is Mars.'

Everyone waited for the dot to grow bigger, but it didn't, it remained exactly the same size.

Then it vanished.

A huge red planet with an icy topping flicked onto the screen, taking its place.

'Orbital pic,' said Gašper, smug.

'Not close enough,' answered Chu, blank.

The computer gave them a few more seconds to admire the image then proceeded to break them.

'This was Mars twelve days ago, as we passed nearby.'

No one spoke.

Only a few moved.

Sila put his hand over his mouth in a rehearsed display of authentic shock, then put it back down again when he realized no one else was doing it.

The screen changed again.

Mars was replaced by a map of the solar system.

'The Sol system. Our home. Those of you with knowledge of astrophysics may explain to the others later what this map means, though it is unlikely that there is anyone here who doesn't at least know the names of all 97 regular and dwarf planets.'

Gašper coughed, while everyone else remained frozen.

'Originally, our mission was to renovate the existing base on Mars, but sadly this is no longer possible. According to a survey team sent over by our good friends from the Ghanaian camp, our base is in bad shape. The ventilation system is not working, the paint on the wall is chipped, and the leftover maintenance bots have displayed signs of both sapience and bellicose territorialism. Therefore, any attempt at renovation would be fruitless.'

'Twelve days,' muttered Aleša.

'Is this a joke?' asked Gašper.

A line appeared on the screen, heading from the red dot representing Mars to the edge of the solar system.

'Do not despair, crew. The mission is not dead, it has been modified. Ambition has increased ten-fold. Over the next four years and two months, you will journey out of the Sol system and fly towards the eighth nearest star to us, Luyten 726-8, which is around 8.7 light years away. We have reason to believe that there is a habitable planet in that system and, thanks to your sacrifice, Slovenia will be the first nation in history to set foot on it. Due to our self-powering ion engine, total journey time at a maximum velocity of 111km/s will be two thousand, seven hundred years.'

The screen changed again, showing the line vanishing then starting again at the red dot. From there, it moved through the solar system, intersecting roughly with Jupiter, Uranus and the Kuiper Belt.

'As a supplement to the main mission, you can gather data on the planets you pass, as currently being shown on the map, and search for as yet undiscovered asteroids and dwarf planets in the Kuiper Belt. If the latter is detected, and is within range, you may view it through the ships telescope.'

'Two thousand years,' said Aleša, one step up from muttering.

'Kuiper Belt?' asked Gašper.

'This isn't real,' said Sila, looking back at Nakagami, who was still leaning but seemed to have temporarily shut down all facial operations.

The screen changed again, now showing the interior of the ship. It took a while for it to register, but when the loop of Engineering appeared it was unmistakable.

'To counter any thoughts of depression or *Void-Helenism,* several new rooms will be unlocked. They will be: the JUPITER ROOM, the URANUS ROOM...in spite of the fact that, technically, the ship will not pass as close to this planet as it will to Jupiter...the KUIPER BELT ROOM, the PHILOSOPHY ROOM and the TELEPORT ROOM. The latter is primarily a study space for Crew Member Chu to expand on new and existing theories, and is designed accordingly. If she is able to successfully complete her hypotheses then a communication link will be opened to transmit the data back to Slovenia, as well as selected allied nations. With luck, her work will also include something to prolong life on board the ship, such as stasis pods or brain storage, or even robot bodies. We will, of course, leave the specifics up to Crew Member Chu.

For other crew members, a similar offer applies. If you are able to produce something culturally artistic or scientifically superior to what Russia or the adventurists have produced then that data can also be transmitted.

To assist you in your pursuits, we have provided you with a VR slab plus one usable LIN swab. You will find it in the PHILOSOPHY ROOM. Prosim, utilise it to stoke your creativity.

In the immediate future, it is advised that you spend a few days adapting to the new mission before attempting any tasks.

Regarding dietary needs, five new alcoholic drinks have been added to the ships menu, and meal selection will begin the gradual transition to the longevity foods in storage. For crew members with a sweet tooth, various desserts will be constructed from the ship's abundant supply of bok choy.

In case of accidents, the reserve supply of Antro-D has been unlocked in the HALF DONE ROOM. The robot doctor has also been updated with basic surgical skills and level 3 *compassion rhetoric.*

Due to the amount of information dumped into this announcement, it will be made available for repeat playing during the next few days, for anyone who is hungover or in shock at the present time.

Have a safe and bold trip to Luyten 726-8

Hvala.'

The ships voice faded out, while the line of their future journey remained on screen.

There was no real reaction.

Just lots of skin scratching and blank staring at the screen.

Cvetko was the first to move, standing up and clamping his hand on Jame's shoulder.

After a little hesitation, he stood up too, and both of them walked silently out of the MARS ROOM.

When the door slid shut behind them, the next reaction came.

'Gaaaaaaarghhhhh...'

It wasn't enough.

Dodzi launched himself off the wall, ran and stumbled, crawled to the projector and jabbed his finger at it.

'You took them from me, you took them from me, you took them from me...'

He screamed it over and over and over, his finger not touching the screen.

Finally, the ship put him out of misery, shocking him several times, some of the electricity even causing little wisps of smoke to come out of his temple.

'He's burning,' whispered Gašper, rubbing his own temple.

'Two thousand years,' repeated Aleša, voice already in the Luyten system.

'Fuck,' said Sila, eyes forward, arms folding.

~~~

A few hours later, in the CREATE NOT DESTROY ROOM, Sila, Nakagami and Gašper sat with one of the new alcoholic drinks, a Somalian brand, and talked about what to do next.

'I've been in my quarters for the last two hours,' said Nakagami, pushing some paper forward on the table, 'and I've come up with some ideas.'

'Already?' asked Sila, playing along.

'I have an adaptable character, like most scientists.'

'Me too,' said Gašper, drawing a circle on a piece of blue card.

'Now,' continued Nakagami, pointing at the first few lines on the paper, 'I'm not a psychologist, but I believe the biggest danger at present is psychopathy and nihilism, specifically in the cases of Cvetko, Jame, Dodzi, Aleša, Klemen and Petr.'

'That's most of the crew,' said Gašper, checking the list on Nakagami's paper.
~~~

'In terms of psychopathy, or a psychotic break…I'm not certain of the exact taxonomy, what I'm referring to is the people most likely to harm others…which would be Dodzi, Aleša and perhaps Jame.'

'Harm others?' asked Sila.

'Jame?'

'You mean physically harm others?'

'I think you both understand my meaning. Ja, Jame is difficult to categorise due to his innate stoicism, but he was in NOT YET Centres for several years, and was seen having what Sila called a *hissy fit* in here a few weeks ago, therefore I will label him as *perhaps*.'

'He was in rehab?'

'Ja.'

'How do you know that?'

Nakagami looked at the list then back up at Gašper. 'It is common knowledge.'

'I didn't know.' Gašper turned to Sila. 'Did you?'

Sila shook his head.

'In the first week of the trip, when we talked to other people. He told me his name, his hometown and his history with the NOT YET Centres. I assumed he'd told everyone else the same.'

'Ne.'

'I see.'

'You think they're dangerous?' Sila pointed at the first line on the paper. 'Aleša?'

'Based on my observations of their on-ship behaviour, ja.'

'How dangerous?'

Nakagami paused, taking a sip of his Somalian alcohol. 'As far as I know, the computer is not programmed to monitor us outside of our quarters unless it is after curfew. By monitor, I mean track our position, record life signs etc., not watch us visually or listen to us talking.'

'Cos there are no cameras on the ship,' said Sila.

'Correct.'

'Wah, cameras,' said Gašper, looking around at the top corners of the walls. 'I never even thought of that.'

'However, if one of the crew decided to attack someone else during non-curfew hours, either in their own quarters or somewhere else on the ship…'

'There's nothing we could do about it.'

'Except know that someone is dead. Ne, nothing.' Nakagami looked at his list again then back up at Sila. 'Having said all that, we don't need to worry too much for now. A psychotic break typically takes some time to incubate, a lot of solitude and self-persuasion, a sustained bout of paranoia. With luck, we can mitigate the potential for this by…' Nakagami pointed at the paper, '…following various methods I've written down.'

Sila leaned back in his chair, holding up his glass and looking through it to the void beyond. The void may have looked back, he couldn't tell. He assumed it didn't.

'The more urgent matter, I suspect, is this one,' continued Nakagami. '*Void-Helenism*.'

'Is that a psychology word?' asked Gašper.

'De-territorialising the essentialist horror of the void and turning it into a more seductive, Helenist space…an entity almost, that is capable of love.'

'*De* what?'

'Basically, if you do what Sila is doing now for long periods, there is a high probability that you will go insane. Of course, there is no concrete data for this as no manned space mission has ever gone beyond Saturn, and those crew knew they were coming back. Or going back. But it's my guess that, if this happens, it will lead to suicide. And if one suicide happens, then more are sure to follow. Even among people who normally wouldn't consider it.'

Gašper stopped cutting card, staring at his own hand as if it were someone else's. 'Why would anyone kill themselves?'

'Is that a sincere question?'

'Ja, it's not that bad here. We've got the VR slab, each other…'

'The VR slab that doesn't work.'

'Ne, Chu will fix it. And you ignored the *each other* part, which is the most important one. Right, Sila?'

Sila turned robotically and put his eyes on Gašper's orange headband, as if it were the true source of all the mindless optimism. Then went back to the triptych window.

'Okay, forget him, ask Petr instead. Or Chu. They'll be more positive about things.'

Nakagami rubbed his lower eyelid, making sure Gašper was out of gas before responding. 'Even with a workable VR slab, we are still in a prison. For some, that will be unbearable.'

'Ja, you said that already. What I'm talking about is changing the mood. Example, this ship flying out of the solar system thing. Seems bad, but not really cos Chu's got the TELEPORT ROOM now and can work on those robot bodies, or stasis pods, or whatever the other thing was. That's the first option. The second one, the better one, is you, Nakagami, talking to the computer and getting it to turn us around. Then we can go back and get put in a real prison, and have a fixed timetable for getting out. If Potočnik's still in charge, which he may not be. No one likes a fascist, right?'

Nakagami looked at Sila, who was still lost in the window. He tapped the edge of the table three times then, when that didn't work, clinked their glasses together.

'Ja, what?' asked Sila, coming back.

'Gašper has some questions to ask you.'

'Huh?'

Before Gašper could protest, a beeping noise sounded.

'Attention crew,

Due to a suspected but not yet confirmed murder-suicide, scissors and other sharp objects will no longer be permitted to be taken from the CREATE NOT DESTROY ROOM into quarters. The same applies for the tools in Engineering.

To maintain hygiene standards, a minimum of two crew members are required to do superficial clean up in the quarters of Crew Member Jame. Disinfectant and cloths are available from the HALF DONE ROOM and the bodies can be placed in Airlock 1. Prosim, consult the map for directions. If no crew member feels like volunteering, drones will be deployed tonight to attempt the cleaning task though, as they lack the ability to carry a human body, the disposal of the corpses will still need to be performed manually.

If use of the word *manually* seems incorrect, replace it with *by a crew member.*

Have a safe and bold trip to Luyten 726-8

Hvala.'

~~~

There was a crowd of two outside Jame's quarters when Nakagami, Sila and Gašper arrived, but neither of them appeared interested in clean up.

'What's going on?' asked Petr, his back to the door.

'Sounded real,' added Klemen, also making no attempt to go inside the room.

Chu's head appeared from the lower deck stairs, asking if they needed any help, but Nakagami waved her away, saying she could go back to her new toy.

'Not a toy,' she shouted, disappearing back down the stairs.

'She's never gonna leave that room,' Sila said in Nakagami's ear.

'Why should she?' he replied, his tone puzzled.

'Cos there's no bed. Or food. Or people.'

'That is hyperbolic.'

'And what about your solitude paranoia spectrum thing? Too much time alone could make her crazy…'

'Not if she's doing something with a purpose. In fact, this is something we should all pursue.'

'Guys…are we going in or…' Gašper's finger was hovering next to the button that was usually the *bell* but in this case had *EMERGENCY OPEN* in blue light next to it.

'We'll discuss this issue later,' said Nakagami, turning to Petr and Klemen, who had heard almost all of what they'd said anyway. 'Leave the clean up to us. We'll meet in the CREATE ROOM. Two hours.'

'I'm tired of that room,' said Klemen.

'Then I suggest you try the PHILOSOPHY ROOM.'
~~~

'Petr can do that. I'm going down to Engineering. More room for the spanner game.'

'The what?' asked Sila.

'A new favourite. You put one spanner on the floor, stand back a few metres and try to land other spanners next to it.'

'Strange game.'

'Better than going in there.' Klemen slapped the wall with the palm of his right hand. 'Like a bunch of sociopaths.'

'You all volunteered to do the clean up?' interrupted Petr, stepping between Klemen and the others.

Nakagami gave more of a grunt than a *ja*. 'Each one of us has seen dead bodies before, so it is less likely to affect us psychologically.'

'I've seen a dead body before.'

'Okay. Would you like to join us?'

'What, now?'

'That is the plan.'

Petr folded his arms and leaned against the wall, sliding back into his Honduran rebel pose.

'Very well. If you want to do something, either of you, then you can try to get Aleša and Dodzi to join us in the CREATE ROOM. But don't force them if they refuse.'

'I'm not knocking on Dodzi's door,' said Klemen.

'Me neither,' said Petr.

'The man's a lunatic.'

'Insane. Didn't even wear a t-shirt in the MARS ROOM. And that was before he started throwing chairs.'

'Very well, then focus on Aleša.'

'She won't come out.'

'That is likely, but you must at least knock on her door.'

'Why?'

'I'll explain later.'

'To make her feel wanted?' asked Petr.

Nakagami paused, ignoring Gašper waving a cloth in the air, telling him to hurry up. 'Do you have training in psychology?'

'Ne.'

'Have you studied it?'

'My mum had depression.'

'I see.'

'And schizophrenia. Thought I was trying to poison her and that she was a burden, both at the same time. Doctors said we should act like normal, don't say *are you okay?,* don't look at her a lot, don't force her to watch sitcoms.'

'A typical approach.'

'But Aleša's not depressed. She's incapable of it. Trust me.'

'This is not a normal situation, or environment. New neural pathways could be formed…'

'Ja, she doesn't give a fuck about all that. She'll sulk for a few days then come out hyper.'

'Knock on her door anyway.'

'She'll just tell me to fuck off.'

'That is acceptable.'

Gašper came over and hit Petr on the cheek with the cloth. 'You're holding us up, Man Ray. Klemen looks like he's half dead, Sila's staring at the floor…'

'Are you simple?' asked Petr.

'What?'

Petr gestured to the cloth and then the door.

'Ja, it's horrible. That's why I wanna get in there fast and get it done.'

'Get it done?'

'He's right,' said Sila, pulling himself back from whatever imaginary picture he'd been painting on the floor. 'We should get on with it, before we think about it too much.'

Petr glared at Sila, flicked his finger at Gašper's cloth and walked off down the corridor.

Klemen muttered something about 'going to Engineering' then headed to the stairs.

'Now can we get in there?' asked Gašper, going back to the door button.

~~~
~~~

Compared to the other quarters, or the ones each of them had seen, Jame's wasn't that different.

Same type of bed, same desk, same picture of Potočnik and the planet Mars stamped on the wall.

It was quite clean too.

Apart from all the blood.

And what looked like vomit on the floor.

The corpses themselves were similar to how they had been in life. Cvetko looking severely pissed off, probably cos there were several slits in his neck, and Jame half-lying, half-sitting next to him, as blank as a bathmat.[39]

The only real difference, apart from the wounds, was that Jame had the higher ground, his back propped up against the wall.

To make things go faster, Nakagami divided the tasks. He would handle the blood on the bodies, Sila would wipe the clothes and bed-sheets, while Gašper would clean the floor.

Despite laying out his credentials in the CREATE NOT DESTROY ROOM, how he'd read in detail about what morticians did with dead bodies when he was a teenager, Sila managed only two minutes of scrubbing before disappearing into the bathroom to throw up.

A minute later, he came back out and told the others he was fine, it was probably just a reflex.

'Did that happen in the mortuary?' asked Gašper.

'Where?'

'The mortuary you went to, when you were studying about dead bodies.'

'I didn't go to a mortuary, I read about them.'

'No field work at all?'

'And saw pictures.'

'So you've never actually seen a dead body?'

'Ja, several, but all cleaned up. Not like this.'

---

[39] Slovene bathmats in the year 2114 were smooth and ecru.

Sila didn't gesture anywhere, but Gašper pretended that he did and followed the imaginary finger to Cvetko and Jame, tilting his head and staring at the wounds.

'The sooner we finish cleaning,' said Nakagami, wiping a thin trail of blood on Jame's side, his eyes focused on the cloth.

'Ja,' said Sila, picking up his own rag.

'Hopefully no more than half an hour. Assuming no further breaks.'

'I'm okay now.'

'And no standing and staring.'

Gašper heard the word *staring* and blinked, said 'me?' in a puzzled tone then grabbed the jacket he'd been using as a makeshift mop and returned to wiping the floor.

For the next ten minutes, the three of them carried on with their tasks in silence.

Their eyes stayed with the stains.

Refusing context.

Gašper was the first to finish, putting down his mop and offering to help Sila, who had his hand over his mouth, apparently on the brink of a second round of vomit.

It didn't work.

He ran to the bathroom and got halfway before bending down and dribbling bile onto the floor.

'Take a break,' said Gašper, walking over and patting him on the shoulder.

'I'm okay.'

'Or let me do it.'

Sila made a retching noise, trying to drag up more bile, but nothing came out. He coughed a few times then stood back up.

'Ne?' prodded Gašper, putting his hand out for the cloth.

'It's fine, I can do it. Just need to avoid looking up.'

'What about the stains near Cvetko's neck?'

Sila closed his eyes, taking in one long breath.

'They're right next to each other, unavoidable.'

'Gašper…'

'I can do that one for you, if you want? Just that one stain.'

'Can you stop talking?'

'You do the ones by the legs, I'll get the other cloth and do the neck zone. What, stop talking completely or…'

'I'm doing the wiping.'

'…stop talking about the-…okay, fine. You do it. If you've finished retching?'

'Ja.'

'You sure?'

'I'm fine. I can do it.'

Gašper put his left hand against his orange headband and saluted. 'I'll be over here, if you start up again. Me and the back-up cloth.'

'I won't.'

'Don't really need to do the sheets or the clothes that much anyway…' Gašper continued, walking to the table and examining the items on it. 'Just put them in the airlock. Don't really have to wipe the bodies either…the blood's mostly dry now. The stuff inside too. Or it should be. That's what happened to Dangar, big wound in his neck, but then they picked him up and nothing, it was all dry. None of it came out.'

'Who's Dangar?' asked Sila, picking up the cloth and resuming scrubbing duty.

'Rehab friend. Cut his neck open with the edge of a tray.'

'Jezus…'

'Ja, pretty bleak. Did it on a Tuesday too, so no one found him for hours. That's why his blood was dry.'

Sila looked at the pale red stain he was scrubbing and said 'Jezus' to it.

'Which is why Nakagami doesn't need to keep wiping around those cuts so much…'

'It's respectful,' answered Nakagami, his tone a little brittle.

'Ja, I know, I'm just saying, you don't have to do it to the extent you're doing it.'

'I disagree.'

'Okay, it's your task.' Gašper picked up a piece of paper and unfolded it, squinting at its contents. 'I can't do this. He wanted to shit on my stomach. Forgive me.'

Sila stopped, catching the words.

'Not me, this,' said Gašper, holding up the paper. 'Must be Jame's…'

'Suicide note?'

'Ja. Can't do it, shit on my stomach, forgive me. That's it.'

Gašper held the note out for Sila to take, but the offer was waved away.

'I think we're ready to move the bodies,' said Nakagami, moving off the bed and putting his 97% blood-covered cloth on the table.

'Which one first?' asked Sila.

'Doesn't matter.'

'Should we put trousers on Cvetko?'

'Ne vem,' said Nakagami.

'Looks weird if we don't.'

'Perhaps.'

'Here, I'll do it,' said Gašper, grabbing some non-ship-issue, olive green cargo pants off the table.

'Are they his?'

'I think so.' Gašper bent down and lifted up Cvetko's feet, feeding the trousers slowly onto him. About halfway up the calves, it got a lot harder, and by the time he'd pulled them up to the knees it was clear they weren't Cvetko's.

'Take them off,' said Nakagami.

'Wait, I can do this.'

'Gašper…'

'Almost past the knee.'

'Take them off,' repeated Nakagami, more firmly.

'Okay, okay.'

Gašper shuffled them back off and placed them carefully on the table. He looked for a replacement pair, found something that resembled kung fu pyjamas and held them up. 'Better?'

Nakagami didn't respond so Gašper took it as a *ja*.

~~~
~~~

After laying Jame down next to Cvetko in Airlock 1, the three crew members stood up and examined the scene.

There wasn't much. An assumed hatch with the same triptych window pattern as the CREATE NOT DESTROY ROOM, walls with a two line grid and *NO LINGERING* written in giant text in between, and an almost unnoticeable plaque by the inside edge of the door, which stated simply *AI REGULATED.*

Compared to this, the corpses didn't seem that bleak.

The skin hadn't deteriorated yet, their bodies were intact, and the wounds on their necks were covered with rolled up t-shirts so to a passer-by it would look like two very cold men had decided to sleep in the airlock.

Not just very cold men, two very cold strangers, but that had been modified [despite Sila's concerns about morality]; the hands of Jame and Cvetko carefully latched together, Gašper's idea, to symbolise forgiveness, to show they didn't just happen to die next to each other, they were a couple, in some type of love…

That was the intention, at least, but when Gašper took another step back and framed it, allowed it all in, the blank comfort, the cold metal background, NO LINGERING, A.I REGULATED, the lack of any kind of movement, life, feeling, the inevitability that this was where everyone was heading…he did what Sila had done twice earlier and put his hand over his mouth.

Before he could push it down it was in his throat and then he was on the floor retching, spitting out bile, trying to picture the quarters they'd been in twenty minutes earlier, the signs of sleep and dressing, the note with thought on it, then another room, a larger room, with a hundred people all shouting at each other, screaming, smiling, laughing, eating, anything.

It wouldn't materialize.

This was an airlock.

Sila bent down, resting a hand on his friend's shoulder. 'You okay?'

'They're dead,' he muttered, barely enough will to finish the words.

~~~
~~~

There was no memorial or final words for Cvetko and Jame, in fact, the ship only told them the bodies were gone by implication.

'Attention crew,

Although Airlock 1 is again ready to use, do not enter or even attempt to gain access to that general area. It is extremely dangerous. The closest you may go is the PHILOSOPHY ROOM but do not venture any further.

Correction, farther.

Have a safe and bold trip to Luyten 726-8

Hvala.'

Apart from Gašper's sudden burst of death-realism in the airlock, no one else really mourned the dead couple, and Gašper himself seemed to have shrugged it off by the time they were all gathered in the CREATE NOT DESTROY ROOM, ready to listen to Nakagami tell them what to do.

Or as Nakagami claimed, what they could do. And it wouldn't be telling, it would be an open discussion where anyone could say anything they wanted, as long as it wasn't a death threat.

'As you can see, I've prepared some notes,' started Nakagami, handing out eight separate pieces of paper to everyone seated at the table. Aleša and Dodzi were both absent, as expected, but Chu turning up was a bit of a coup.

'Step one: target Jupiter,' said Klemen, reading from the paper. 'Target it for what?'

'Orbit,' replied Nakagami.

'Why?'

'It's a stopgap,' said Chu, reading through her own sample of the list, which was laid over a copy of *The Crying Of The Wind*, yet another one of the gifts she'd received from Potočnik post-Mars.

'Correct. It will serve as a temporary holding pattern to delay our trip. The ship told us that we could investigate planets along the way to Luyten 726-8, probably without landing on them, but getting close enough to orbit would suffice.'

'Aren't we going past Jupiter anyway?' asked Sila, remembering the line on the screen during the presentation.

'Ja, and if I can convince the computer that there is some advantage to getting even closer then…'

'Can you convince it?' asked Klemen.

'Ja, I thought you said it only did basic requests,' added Petr.

'As you know,' Nakagami answered, concentrating on the latter, 'I have been working on the computer for a while now.'

'Don't look at me. I don't know what you're typing.'

Nakagami coughed. 'As you can assume after peering over my shoulder for almost two months, I have been working on the computer for a while now and have made some progress. Our talking time for instance. It is my hope that I can go beyond that and, given enough time, turn the ship around.'

'Given how much time?'

'Ne vem.'

'Two thousand seven hundred years?'

Another cough, as well as the slightest of smiles. 'The computer is rigid in the way it thinks. From what I can deduce, it is not dissimilar to a religious fundamentalist. On certain topics, it may be flexible, for example, allowing me to bring a stool from Jame's quarters to the Control Room. However, anything related to its core programming, or beliefs, will trigger extreme intransigence.'

'So we have to re-costume our requests as something else,' said Chu, more to her paper than anyone.

'From the nature of our trip and our status as dissidents, I've made some assumptions as to what the core beliefs of the computer are. One, we are not allowed to leave the ship. Two, the ship cannot turn around.'

'Three?' asked Klemen, as the list abruptly stopped.

'Two are all I have so far. There is a chance that is all there are.'

'Jezus,' said Gašper, slouching so far down in his seat that most of his torso became invisible. 'Chugging through space in a fascist church.'

'Church?'

'The intransigence part…what you just said.'

Nakagami looked at Gašper, then across at Chu, who was holding up her sheet of paper to read the book underneath.

'So, basically,' said Sila, glancing at the list, 'there is a chance we can charm the ship…'

'Ja, a chance.'

'…but only if it's not one of the core beliefs…'

'Not quite.'

'…and one of its core beliefs is to not turn the ship around.'

'Which is exactly what we want it to do,' finished Petr, elbowing an almost vanished Gašper in the shoulder and forcing him back up into a normal position.

'Don't have to jab me,' he moaned, rubbing his arm and not his shoulder.

'It's bad for your back.'

Gašper mumbled something at the table, then squinted in confusion when he glimpsed a page of Chu's book.

Monitoring the silence, Nakagami coughed once then resumed speaking. 'As I said, it is a difficult task, but also irrelevant to everyone except myself. Now, second on the list…'

'Great, so we just sit around and hope you can seduce a lunatic AI. Which probably won't change its mind anyway.' Klemen huffed and went back to the paper he'd been working on before everyone had come in. 'If anyone needs me, I'll be perfecting my Portuguese.'

'Ja, that is a good idea.'

'Huh, you being sarcastic?'

'Ne, it really is a good idea. If you'll look at the second note on my paper, it outlines the same thing.'

Klemen pulled back the original paper and scrutinized it in disbelief.

'It's the second one,' prodded Nakagami.

Klemen cleared his throat, didn't do a very good job, tried a few more times then read out *the second one*. 'Each of us needs a task to distract from the trip.'

'For you, that can be Portuguese. Assuming it's a genuine interest.'

'But it's pointless,' said Petr, holding up his own paper.

'You what?'

'It doesn't help us achieve anything.'

'That is irrelevant.'

'How?'

Nakagami looked at Chu, who had left her book and was now busy staring at her poster of a muon on the wall nearby. Obviously, not staring at an actual image of a muon as the poster was blank, but pretending to. Sensing eyes on her, she glanced over to Nakagami, nodded then went back down to her book.

'We should be trying to set up the communication link,' continued Petr, 'or something along those lines.'

'Can we do that?' asked Gašper, starting to slouch again.

'Ne vem. But it's a target, a goal.'

'Who runs this ship?' asked Nakagami, tapping the table with his pencil.

'Huh?'

'This ship. Who is in charge?'

'Not you,' said Klemen, pulling himself up in his seat.

'Not any of us,' added Sila quickly.

'Correct. The true warden is the AI. The ship's computer.'

'We know what AI is, you don't have to add synonyms.'

Nakagami paused, giving Klemen's line time to breathe, then continued on. 'Everything goes through the AI's authority in an auxiliary fashion, communication included. There is no bypassing it. This is why I've written the second point. Each of us is redundant in the main arena, therefore the only thing we can do until I get the computer on our side is protect our mental health.'

'And not kill each other,' added Gašper, getting a jab from Sila almost instantly.

'The most efficient way to do that is to keep busy, perform a task. Ideally, we would make use of the VR Slab, but Chu has informed me that the GPU is missing, so that is out of the equation.'

'What's a GPU?' asked Gašper who, judging by the expression on Sila's face, was asking for two.

'The thing that creates the images,' answered Chu, not bothering to look up from *The Crying Of The Wind.*

'You mean it doesn't work at all?'

'Ne.'

'Shit. You sure?'

'It's like having a bike without wheels,' said Nakagami, stepping in when he saw Chu was back with her muon poster. 'I will question the AI about the matter, that is, why we would receive such a gift, but I do not expect it to be very forthcoming.'

Gašper leaned back in his chair and picked at his headband. He would've said *shit* again, but the chance was stolen by Klemen breaking into stuttered laughter, ending with the word *gift*.

'What?' asked Petr.

'A gift,' Klemen repeated, followed by more laughter.

Nakagami waited for it to die out, then picked up where he'd left off. 'As I said before, what we need to concentrate on is tasks. Something creative or time-consuming if possible, but trivial activities are also suitable. Of course, I will do the same when not working on the AI.'

'What if we don't have any tasks?' asked Petr, glancing across at Klemen's Portuguese notes.

'Think of one.'

'Like what?'

'Painting.'

'I've done that already.'

'Then do more.'

'My painting brain's spent. I need a break. No art.'

'Drawing,' offered Gašper, his expression seemingly genuine.

Petr flicked him on his headband and looked back at Nakagami. 'Something else.'

'There are some options. Klemen, for example, is learning Portuguese.'

'Perfecting,' corrected Klemen, covering his notes with one hand.

'Chu is going through her theories in the TELEPORT ROOM, as well as all the new ones from other-…'

'He's not really learning Portuguese,' interrupted Petr, pointing at the space in front of Klemen. 'There are no textbooks, no materials.'

'Estou lembrando…my previous study.'

'And she's just playing with the new toys she got. Which still hasn't been explained by the way.'

Chu glanced up, possibly hearing the word *toys*. 'I didn't ask for anything.'

'She was just as surprised as we were,' added Sila, instinctively putting out a hand to cover Chu's book.

'Ja, but what's the point of it? I mean, is she actually gonna invent any of that shit they were talking about?'

'Ne, *she* isn't,' replied Chu.

Nakagami tapped the table a little bit louder. 'I suggest, Petr, that you go to the PHILOSOPHY ROOM. There are other items there which may be of interest to you.'

'What about the JUPITER ROOM?' asked Gašper.

'If it has anything inside, that could be your task.'

'I can go back to my theory,' said Sila.

'Ja, we don't need to brainstorm ideas right now, you can decide for yourselves.'

'What about Dodzi?' asked Petr.

'We will give him some time alone first. Then approach.'

'Don't bother,' said Klemen. 'The guy's already gone.'

'Not necessarily.'

'Ne, really. I saw him earlier, in Engineering. He was picking up spanners and trying to throw them out into the corridor.'

'At a target?'

'I thought he was playing a variation of my spanner game at first, but ne, he was just throwing them, zero aim. Zero target.'

'He was out of his room?' asked Sila, surprised.

'And no t-shirt. Again. Ja, obviously, he wasn't in his room.'

'Did he succeed in throwing the spanners outside?' asked Nakagami, tapping the pencil again.

'He did, but he couldn't pick them up afterwards. Must be magnetized to the floor.'

'Did he try to carry one out?'

'Ne, not that I saw.'

'I see.'

'Cover the face of Potočnik,' muttered Gašper, reading another line from Nakagami's list. 'What does that mean?'

'Ah, you have advanced to the next sentence.'

'Having him in your quarters, staring at you, will meld you to his image, and could lead to *Inverse Fortress Syndrome*.'

'The what?'

'That's not a real syndrome,' said Petr, checking the line for himself.

'Ne, I coined it. But I believe the analogy holds.'

'Analogy?' asked Gašper, re-reading.

'Having Potočnik as your only point of reference during alone time will narrow your thoughts. If you access a happy memory, you will see his face, if you're angry, you will see his face, if you're having sex, you will see his face. Eventually, he will become everything and you will inevitably try to cut off your own head.'

'Or cut someone else's off,' said Gašper.

'Ja. Possibly someone who looks vaguely like Potočnik.'

Gašper nodded, looked at the other faces in the room, and stopped nodding. Apart from Klemen, he was the only person with vaguely white skin, same as Potočnik. And Klemen looked more like an Iranian taxi driver than a Slav.

Everyone else seemed to reach the same conclusion, tilting their heads slightly and staring at Gašper.

'Ne, ne, ne, ne, I don't look anything like him. He's got purple eyes.'

'To a lunatic, it does not matter.'

'Fuck, really? They'd link me to Potočnik?'

'If his poster remains visible, ja.'

'Fuck. Fuck. This is not good.' Gašper clapped his hands together a little too theatrically. 'Everyone needs to go back to their rooms and cover Potočnik's face. Right now.'

'Already done it,' said Klemen.

'Me too,' parroted Chu, turning another page of her Irish occultism tome.

'I might get around to it at some point,' said Petr, stern-faced.

'Fuck off. You'll do it now. All of you. Chu, put down that weird poetry book and tell Aleša, say you miss her or something. Shit, Dodzi…who's gonna let him know?'

'That is a good question,' said Nakagami.

'He's the most likely to go psycho too. I mean, fuck, he's already running around topless, throwing spanners.'

'There's little need to panic, I have some contingency measures I'm working on.'

'What measures? Locking his door?'

'We'll talk about it when they're more concrete. For now, try to stay calm. A lot of this is just theory at the moment.'

'Ja, don't fret, whitey,' said Petr, giving Gašper a single pat on the arm. 'I'm sure Dodzi's already covered Potočnik's face.'

'And what if he hasn't?'

'Then avoid him.'

'What if he's looking at it right now?'

Petr shrugged, going to the next point on the paper and reading it out loud. 'Number four. Pretend that everything is normal. Ha, that's optimistic.'

Nakagami coughed. 'As I've already told Sila, I am not a psychologist, but…'

'Didn't you just make up your own syndrome?'

'…it is crucial that we view this trip as normal.'

'Ja, you've just repeated what's on the paper,' said Klemen, more confused than caustic.

'Most of the features on this ship are insane. The names of the rooms are insane. The rules are insane, to a degree. Potočnik…'

'…is insane.'

'…wants you to-…ja, possibly insane, capricious certainly, and he requires that you feel it. He requires that you comprehend a complete loss of control in your environment.'

'Same as what the Russians did,' said Klemen, wincing a little. 'Offer you tea and, when you say *ja*, give you coffee instead. Then tell you it's tea you're drinking.'

'Then throw it in your face,' finished Petr.

'Ja, it was a common torture technique; disorient the victim, very effective.'

'You think that's what Potočnik's doing?' asked Sila.

'He never seemed that type,' added Chu, finally closing her book [yet still keeping her finger between pages].

'It's true, he was an activist. He used to march against stuff like this.'

'You're deluded,' said Klemen.

'Ja, he put us on this ship.' Petr swiped a hand across the table, accidentally hitting Klemen's Portuguese notes. 'Doomed us.'

'I know, but…ne vem.'

'What? You know, but you don't know?'

Sila looked at Petr, then the void to the left. 'Was he really capable of torture? Actual, physical torture?'

'Ja, of course, what do you think this is?'

'I mean…'

'And all those deportations.'

'…torture, with his own hands? Or ordering it…would he even have the power to-…'

'You are both interrogating a facade,' interrupted Nakagami, straightening up in his seat and pulling at his jacket zip, even though both were as *up* as could possibly be. 'Potočnik is a man who plays with people lives. Those who annoy him, or disappoint him. I saw it with my own eyes, multiple times. There was no remorse.'

'You saw him torturing people?'

'Fuck, you kept that quiet.'

'Not direct torture, but I am certain it happened, in other buildings. More than certain, in fact. That is why I wrote the article. And paid the price for it.'

'Article…'

'Which article?'

'The one I believed I could refer to only as *the article* and still receive comprehension.'

'Eh?'

'The Serpentinšek article?' asked Petr, shaking his head. 'You wrote that?'

'Only the first. The rest were orchestrated.'

'You mean faked?'

'Ja.'

'To undercut the first one,' said Sila, more to himself than anyone.

'Ja.'

'Shit.'

Petr was still shaking his head. 'You really wrote it, the first one?'

'With a physicist's rhetorical touch. That is the reason I am on this ship.'

'Fuck.'

'It is immaterial now. Whatever I did, it wasn't enough.' Nakagami spotted a little crease at the corner of his paper and folded it back over. 'I suggest we get back to the plan. Number five on the list…'

'What article?' asked Gašper, nudging Petr in the side.

~~~

After the discussion had ended, Chu picked up a bowl of cold udon from the food dispenser, added some dumplings, skipped the Somalian alcohol and headed off towards Aleša's quarters.

It was a bit tricky going up the little ramp at the corner without spilling any of the udon soup, but she managed it, and then hurried to the left, two thirds down the pale green corridor until she was outside Aleša's door.

'Food season,' she shouted, knocking on the door.

No answer.

'It's udon and bok choy.'

No answer.

'The soup will go cold if you don't drink it soon.'

No answer.

Chu put the bowl carefully on the floor, counted ten more seconds in her head then left.

If I'm lucky, she thought, taking the steps two at a time, the computer will have stabilized the muon projections by now.
~~~

~~~

Most of the other crew stayed behind in the CREATE NOT DESTROY ROOM after the discussion. Or the lecture as Klemen had called it.

Both Sila and Petr defended Nakagami, saying he didn't have all the answers, and besides, he'd written the *Serpentinšek* article, that had to guarantee some level of respect.

'No way to verify, no way to ask the AI to verify,' said Klemen, arms laid out straight on the table, completely covering his Portuguese notes.

'But it makes sense. Kind of.'

'Ne.'

'Ja, he was right next to Potočnik, he would've seen everything.'

'And didn't do a thing about it.'

'What? He wrote the article, I just said.'

'Allegedly.'

'He's on the ship, with us.'

'Not an argument.'

'Come on, that's Aleša's line.'

'Ne, it's mine.'

The argument ran on for another half an hour until Petr got tired and left, followed by Gašper, and Klemen started branching off into his own theories. Which was in essence the *we're in a simulation* hypothesis, only now he'd modified it to include Nakagami as the puppet master and Potočnik as his made up hologram.

Despite being mildly curious, Sila got up and left to find Chu, reminding himself that the last time he was mildly curious he'd ended up donating money to that Irish telepath, convinced he was in contact with the ghost of Gramsci. Turned out he wasn't. He'd just been reading from collated excerpts and using a hidden smoke machine.

Don't get sucked in, he told himself. That way leads to the flames.

On the way to the bottom level, which was a little too close to Engineering for his liking, he passed Petr and Gašper. It wasn't clear what they were doing at first; it looked a little like Gašper was giving a hand
~~~

job, but when he got round the front, he saw that Gašper was in fact squeezing Petr's stomach skin.

'You going up or down?' asked Sila.

'Here first, up later' said Gašper, gesturing to the far end of the corridor.

'Checking out the new rooms?'

'PHILOSOPHY ROOM, ja. Maybe JUPITER ROOM if we have time.'

'If?'

'Joke.'

Sila kept moving, heading down the steps, his head disappearing after a few seconds.

'That was weird,' said Petr, a few minutes later, looking at the *Knowledge is Waiting* sign pinned up outside the PHILOSOPHY ROOM.

'What was?'

'Sila. He didn't ask what you were doing.'

'The fat test?'

'Ja.'

'Cos he knows already. I did it to him last week. And to Chu yesterday.'

Petr didn't frown, he just pushed his tongue into the right side of his cheek. Gašper didn't appear to notice.

'Haven't done it to Nakagami yet, seems like a tough one. And the less said about Dodzi the better. Though it's probably easier to get to him, now he's running around with his top off.'

'You think Nakagami's right?' asked Petr, stepping inside the PHILOSOPHY ROOM and not looking at all surprised that it was practically empty.

'Right about what?'

'Ne vem. His plan in general, turning the ship around.'

'You tell me, you're the one in the TALKING GOD ROOM with him every day.'

'TALK TO YOUR GOD ROOM,' corrected Petr. 'Or Control Room.'

'Does the computer like him yet?'

'Ne vem.' Petr finished his detailed scan of the room, focusing in on the only thing of substance in there: a box. 'The code is still confusing for me, can't read much of it. I suppose he's trying his best. Nakagami, I mean. His face always looks kind of wistful when he's sitting there, typing. Don't think he's too eager to fly to the Luyten 7 something system. Makes it easier to trust him, I suppose. For me anyway. Maybe not Klemen, but then he's in his own world most of the time. Aleša…ne vem.'

'Hey, over here.' Gašper walked over to a red curtain to the right, blocking a large portion of the wall. 'What's hiding behind this extravagant beast?'

Petr ignored him and ran his finger round the edges of the box, looking for a latch.

'Wah, it's a wall. Nothing.'

Gašper closed the curtain and then opened it again. It was still a wall.

'What's the point in this?' he asked, prodding his finger into the metal to make sure it wasn't a hologram.

'There are books in here,' said Petr, kneeling down by the box, its lid now open. 'Looks like fairy tales, mythology, no Portuguese, some Russian.'

'That's not very Slovene,' said Gašper, coming over and peering down.

'*Learn to speak Russian in 17 days with Kriss Akabusi.*'

'Who's gonna use that?'

'I might.'

'What, learn Russian?'

'I did it before, for a few months.'

'You can speak it?'

Petr hesitated, flipping to the back cover. 'Can you?'

'Ne.'

'Then, ja, I'm fluent. Almost native level.'

Gašper laughed, grabbing the book. 'I'll test you.'

'I was joking, hey.'

'Let's see if you know any.' Gašper turned to a page in the middle, squinting at the text. 'Okay, the Russian part's unreadable. I'll do the Slovene and you translate it back.'

'Ne.'

'How do you say *when the javelin hits one of the judges, run*?'

'No idea.'

'Do you know how to say *javelin*?'

'Javelin?'

'Doesn't look like it. What about *when*?'

'Kogda?'

'Ne vem. The writing looks like kor-aah.'

'That's the alphabet, it's kogda.'

'Is it?'

'Really, I remember that one.' Petr took the book and read the Russian text like a whispered spell. 'Ja, kogda. When.'

'That's one out of two.'

'Ja, I'll come back to this later,' said Petr. 'It can be my distraction task.'

'Nakagami's homework?'

'Ja.'

Gašper looked around the rest of the room. There was nothing else to examine so he suggested going to the JUPITER ROOM. Petr flicked through a few more pages of the Russian textbook then put it back in the box and said, 'ja, I suppose.'

Out in the corridor, they went down past the MARS ROOM, past the ASTEROID BELT ROOM and stopped outside the last door before the turn to the habitat branch.

Both Petr and Gašper looked at the sign to the side of the door, JUPITER ROOM, and then a little bit farther to the side. It was just possible to make out the right-hand edge of the door to Jame's quarters.

'Weird to think they're not in there,' said Petr.

'Ja.'

'Or maybe they are, and we all imagined it. Klemen's simulation theory.'

'They're not,' said Gašper, a little sharper than his usual tone.

Petr may have been in a slight daze but he detected it and re-focused on the JUPITER ROOM.

'Are we going in?'

'Waiting for you.'

Petr walked forward, the door sensing his boots on the floor and sliding open.

They both got about two feet inside the room and laughed.

'They weren't lying.'

'MARS ROOM take two.'

In front of them was a giant, cartoon-esque picture of the planet Jupiter, some foldable chairs and walls the exact same colour as inter-stellar space.

~~~

An hour later, Petr moved back up to the top of the bed, put his pillow closer to Gašper's and told him it was probably the Mars debacle that was responsible for it.

'Ja, probably.'

'I'll switch to hand-mode, see if it goes anywhere.'

Gašper ran his finger along the bridge of Petr's eyebrows, opening his mouth several times as if he were going to say something. Petr ran his own fingers back down Gašper's arm and onto the stem of his dick, rubbing gently.

'Could be out of power,' said Gašper.

'Huh?'

'If I don't wank every night, the nanobots become dormant.'

'You mean it's surgery-related?'[40]

'That or I'm depressed.'

'You're joking.' Petr pulled Gašper's dick up by the foreskin and let it stand there. 'Fucking nanobots. I believed you there for a second.'

---

[40] As it's the 22nd Century, Gender Affirmation Surgery is much more advanced. A Phallo-plasty can not only give you the double-header of a 6-11 inch cock and erections at will, but also produce a sperm substitute capable of spurting up to twelve feet.
~~~

'Just trying to lighten the pressure.'

Petr moved his fingers round the tip then back down the shaft, twisting a little as he went. He repeated the action slowly. Again and again and again.

'Don't think it's gonna work,' said Gašper, putting his hand on Petr's hair.

'Give me a few more minutes.'

'Won't make a difference.'

'Give me a day.'

Gašper grunted, doing just enough to make it resemble a laugh.

Petr continued on with his routine, running the shaft, twisting like he actually gave a shit, stroking the base for at least a minute and then letting go.

Gašper was right, it didn't work. The thing just flopped back against his left thigh.

They lay there silent for a while, Petr using Gašper's thigh as a pillow.

'*Je suis venu te dire…que je m'en vais*,' sang Gašper, with a lot of breath.

'*Je suis*…is that French?'

'Ja.'

'Coutin?'

'An old song. Ne, before him. Don't know his name, used to smoke a lot, turned up drunk to interviews.'

'Ne vem.'

'*Je suis venu te dire…que je m'en vais.*'

'It's only one line?'

'A guy in rehab used to sing it, the same line over and over. I'm copying him.'

'What does it mean?'

'Ne vem, but it sounds melodic. *Je suis venu te dire…que je m'en vais.*'

Petr stroked a little more as Gašper repeated the same line three times.

'It's not changing much.'

'Ne.'

'Maybe you should sing something happier. From a happier time.'

'That was a happy time.'

'Rehab?'

'Relatively. Compared to this.'

'The ship of the doomed.'

'Ne, not the trip. Recent events. The last few days mostly.'

'Klemen and Jame?'

'Ja.'

'Don't wanna be glib, but I thought you weren't that affected by it.'

'Before, ne.'

Petr stopped stroking and moved up next to Gašper's arm.

'Ne vem. Even in their quarters, when the bodies were there…didn't seem that real.'

'Were they naked?'

'Ja.'

'Completely?'

Gašper ran his finger along the ridge of Petr's eyebrows then moved down to the crown of his head, burying his face in his hair.

'Should I keep asking questions or…'

'If you want,' came the muffled response.

'Maybe I should give it a rest.'

'… … …'

'Ja, I should?'

Gašper came back out and grabbed a giant clump of Petr's hair, separated it and kissed the scalp part visible inside.

'What are you doing?' asked Petr.

'Scalp survey.'

'Feels weird.'

Gašper did it once more then moved down to Petr's neck, kissing between the stubble.

'Better?'

'Bit bit bit.'

Gašper continued, moving along the collarbone and down onto his chest. After doing the obligatory nipple orbits with his tongue, he glanced back up at Petr's neck. Something about the way the light hit it made him stop kissing and put his finger there, right on the windpipe.

'You think it might be time to cut your hair yet?' asked Petr, staring down at the mop covering Gašper's head.

'Ne...'

'Can't hide it under that headband forever.'

'Ja.'

'Ja, you can?'

Gašper didn't answer, so Petr shifted right to get a better view of what was happening on his neck.

The answer was: nothing much. Just Gašper holding his finger against the skin.

'Are you stroking my windpipe?'

'Thinking.'

'About?'

'Emotions. Randomness.'

'Okay.'

Petr let the windpipe ritual continue, looking to his right at the Russian book he'd taken from the PHILOSOPHY ROOM. It was lying face down on the bedside table, open on the chapter about Russian historical figures. To his own surprise, he could understand a lot of the paragraphs in Russian, even some of the topic-specific words like invade and betrayal. Give it another few months...two or three hours a day...and he might really become fluent.

'So weird...'

'What's that?' asked Petr, switching back to his left.

'I actually cried at one point,' Gašper said, moving his finger an inch farther up Petr's neck. 'In the airlock, when they were laid out on the floor.'

'The funeral...'

'It looked like they were having a nap together. Maybe cos I put their hands together, ne vem...but it was quite sweet. No gaping neck wounds, just...ja, like they were taking a nap. That could be the thing that's messing me up. I think. The other part, the clean-up of the blood...'

'In their quarters?'

'…that wasn't so bad. Ja, their quarters. Didn't feel real. Or my brain detached, said it wasn't real. Ne vem.'

'Cos you didn't know them well probably.'

'Ja, and Nakagami and Sila were there too, that made it seem more normal. And the weird suicide note. Kind of reminded me of rehab, the mundaneness of it.' Gašper pulled away from Petr and sat up. 'Ah, it's not that bad. Just need my body to catch up with my brain. Or my brain to catch up with my body. Whichever way it goes.'

'What about Sila and Nakagami? Were they okay?'

'Nakagami, of course, guy's a machine. He's the one who did the stab wounds, cleaned them up. Sila, ne vem, he doesn't reveal much.'

'It'd be weird if it didn't affect him.'

'Ja, he was probably depressed anyway. Or bobbing on the surface of it. That's his natural reflex, if you haven't noticed already.'

Petr looked down at the crumpled up blanket. 'Don't know how I would've reacted, seeing them like that…'

'Badly. That's why Nakagami got us to do it. Said it would break the others.'

'He said that?'

'Ja, exact words.'

'Break who?'

'All of you, I guess.' Gašper straightened up the blanket then put his hands on Petr's thighs. He spent about five seconds there before moving quickly up. 'I think he was being a bit hyperbolic though. Chu would've been okay, with her scientist brain. And her general detachment from things.'

'Ja, probably.'

'You would've done okay too, I think.'

'Ne vem.'

'Just like Sila, a bit on edge, some retching and bile, but…you would've managed.'

'Maybe.'

Gašper copied what Petr had done to his dick two minutes earlier, and five minutes before that, putting the head into his mouth and digging his teeth gently in.

Petr made a few noises, but nothing genuine, and nothing that translated into any kind of hardness.

Gašper stopped and looked up. 'I think I've infected you.'

'Sorry.'

'Shouldn't have elaborated on things.'

'Ne, I'm-…'

'Or should've just let you cut my hair. Ah, it's okay, I have to go anyway. Check on Sila. Chu too…see if she's teleported herself back to Slovenia yet.'

Gašper rolled over to the edge of the bed and looked for his pants.

'Maybe try again in a few days,' said Petr, his finger flicking at his flaccid dick. 'Or tomorrow.'

'Ja, we'll see.'

~~~

Brown eyes. Brown eyes. Grey eyes. Brown eyes. Green eyes. Green eyes. Brown eyes. Purple eyes. Brown eyes. Blue eyes. Brown eyes. Purple eyes. Shit eyes. Eyes of shit. Not looking at ya flag, not looking at Mars, this way?

You can't pierce me, liar. Fucking liar. Fucking Negrin. Fascist costume cunt. Purple fucking hypno eye stab. Junius Pamphlet. Love your proposal. Tie me up, dump me in a fucking canal. Canal-shaped space ship. Ja, you think that was a Šaroc move? Think you surprised me with this? You didn't do anything. Fucking copycat wretch. Just signed for it. Like a coward. Like an adventurist. Obvious. I knew you'd do this shit. I knew it. Knew it years ago. Died during a dispute? Can't tell me that with a straight face. I knew it right there, seven years old. Words don't come from the eyes. I knew it all, someone of your kind, you'd come along at some point. That's why I'm here, isn't it, Negrin? Seven years old. Klemen too.

Aleša stopped, shifted weight onto her left foot and paced back alongside the bedroom wall, keeping her eyes fixed on Potočnik.

Ten on a ship and it's over? You can perv on me all day, won't work, not one second, you haven't won a thing. Green walls, green fucking light bulbs. Not gonna work, Negrin. I can stare at you all day, all night. Don't care. Ja, your forehead makes a nice target, I'll aim for that. Do what Durruti would've done, what Mojca Ito would do. Just sit tight, I'll be there soon enough. Ja, you think I won't? Ships
~~~

go more than one way, Negrin. No fucking doubt in my mind, I'll do it, talk it round. All the way round. Your spy's a fucking drone. Obvious. Doesn't even slag you off. I'll get him, the little Janus, throw him in the VIP room, out the airlock. All you've done is piss me off. Made me concrete. Junius Pamphlet? I'll brain you with the fucking printing press. Cave in your skull. Ja, keep smiling, Negrin. I can look at your wispy fascist face all night long. I'm not afraid of you. You look like a librarian. Take your fucking holidays in Bled like a-…

Paint job?

Fuck you.

I don't need your paint.

Purple coward.

~~~

Four days after the Mars *incident*, Aleša got up early, put on the *RED STAR* t-shirt, tied up her *Dok Militia* headscarf and headed for the CREATE NOT DESTROY ROOM.

One look at Klemen studying Portuguese sent her right back out again.

Chu passed her in the corridor, saying, 'hey, you're back, I was just about to bring your door some breakfast' but it wasn't enough to break the spell and fifteen seconds later, Aleša was back on her bed, glaring at Potočnik.

~~~

The next morning was a little better.

She got up early again, kept on the *RED STAR* t-shirt she'd slept in, tied up the *FAI* headscarf and took slow, drawn-out breaths as she walked to the CREATE NOT DESTROY ROOM. *Only Klemen, only Klemen, only Klemen,* she repeated internally, following the hum from the walls. By luck, or perhaps divine cosmic grace, it *was* only Klemen when she entered the room, and she managed to sit down next to him without a panic attack. Before he could get out something caustic about her hair, she held up a finger and asked him a] why he was up so early, and b] why he was pretending to know Portuguese.

'It's the master's idea. Do a task to stop us thinking of dying in in-stellar space.'

'Interstellar.'

'What did I say?'

'Instellar.'

'Ah. Could be my Portuguese. It's been seeping through more and more recently…'

Aleša looked around, seeing other notes on the table. Some kind of list. She picked it up and read through, pinching the skin on her elbow when she saw her name.

'Can't say any particular one of them is terrible,' Klemen continued, peering over. 'Although I did argue a few at the time, during the lecture.'

'When did he do this?'

'The whole list? Ne vem. Two days ago, before the Cvetko-Jame drama. I assume you know about that.'

'About what?'

'Their murder-suicide.'

Aleša repeated the line back to herself with the volume clipped, slowly realising it wasn't a euphemism. 'They're dead?'

'Ja, very. You didn't hear the announcement?'

Aleša looked at the far end of the table, where Cvetko and Jame had sat from time to time. When they weren't hiding away in their quarters.

'Jezus, were you in a trance? How did you miss that?'

'Sleeping.'

'Ah, the famous Aleša coma sleep. Yeah, well, it happened in Jame's quarters. Or was it Cvetko's? Ne, it was Jame's. Nakagami, Sila and the cloyingly optimistic one had to go in there and clean up the mess.'

'Nakagami?'

'Ja, he volunteered. No idea why. Blood everywhere apparently. And he was the one who did the clean-up on the wounds too. From what Gašper told Petr, the little sociopath didn't flinch once.'

Aleša went back to the list, reading each line carefully as if it were code.

'Now we're pinning all our hopes on him and his AI sex talk, getting it to hook us onto Jupiter.'

'Orbit Jupiter?'

'Ja, then somehow get the ship to turn around.'

Aleša stared off at the wall then, still holding the list, exited the room.

'Still in a simulation if you ask me,' said Klemen, more or less to himself.

~~~

Nakagami sat in the Control Room, typing. Pre-Mars, he would've had Petr leaning on the console nearby, asking him what *what* meant in code, but apparently Petr was *on holiday* and now it was Sila hovering over him instead.

'You should sit down,' said Nakagami, pointing to the stool he'd recently taken from Jame's quarters.

'I'm fine.'

'If it's the blood stain that you're concerned about, it's very faint. Non-existent if you drape your jacket over the top.'

'Really, I'm okay standing.'

'Of course, I would've taken the cleaner stool from Cvetko's room, but apparently he broke it into pieces. This, sadly, is all we have for now.'

'Ask it how long to get to Jupiter,' replied Sila, his hand floating over the keypad.

'That has already been answered.'

'How long?'

'Thirty-seven days.'

Sila processed the number and another one and possibly maths in general as his face morphed into a *Phenomenology of Spirit, page 1* kind of frown. 'Mars was around sixty days, right?'

'Ja.'

'But...is Jupiter closer to Mars than Earth is?'

'In a general sense, ne.'

'Okay. Is it a big difference?'
~~~

'About eight times farther.'

'Then...thirty-seven days, and sixty days.'

Nakagami put his hand over the *deflector shield* button, casually, and swivelled his chair to face Sila. 'Do you remember my explanation of the ion engine?'

'Vaguely.'

'The general concept?'

'Long time to build up, high maximum speed.'

'Velocity is a more suitable word, but ja, low thrust, high velocity, or speed.'

'So we weren't at max speed before?'

'Velocity, ne, not at the beginning. I am not certain of the precise number of days, but I estimate it took between thirty-five and forty to get us to maximum velocity and we have been maintaining that velocity ever since. And we were already twelve days past Mars so the actual time to reach Jupiter is forty-nine days.'

'Is that good?'

Nakagami turned the automatic *ja* coming out of his mouth into a polite cough. 'I do not understand.'

'For you to talk to the computer, convince it to turn around. Is it enough time to do that?'

'Ne.'

'How far off?'

'I think there has been a misunderstanding. I am not trying to convince the computer to turn around, I want it to orbit Jupiter.'

'Ja, and then convince it to turn around.'

'That is impossible.'

'But you said...'

'However, I will try.'

Sila closed his eyes, trashed the model Control Room in his head, then opened them again, looking around the real Control Room, or TALK TO YOUR GOD ROOM, the place that had, in effect, become Nakagami's second home. Apart from the console, it was an uncomfortable view. Seven posters on the wall, five of them featuring young girls, half-clothed, each of them bar one holding something long and hard. The exception, the girl on the wall above the computer terminal, had a stick in her mouth instead.

'Kenji, about these posters…'

Nakagami looked at the girl with the stick. 'Ja?'

Sila had the question in his head, but didn't want to ask it.

'Are you a fan of this kind of art?' asked Nakagami.

'Not really my thing.'

'Shame. There's something almost heroic about the figure of a young girl. A kind of enviable ability to suffer and, at the same time, endure.'

'I don't really see it.'

'It is an arcane taste, perhaps.'

'Perhaps.'

Nakagami turned back to the computer and typed in another question. The computer wrote back, telling him that the requested information was unavailable.

'Stubborn as ever.'

'What is it?' asked Sila, trying to read what was on the screen. It was no good, the whole thing was in code.

'Nothing. Just a query.'

'What?'

Nakagami turned and looked at Sila for half a second then switched and stared right past him.

Sila copied the act, half raising his left arm as a shield when he saw who it was.

'You're talking to the computer?' asked Aleša, standing at the entrance, the pale green light giving the stark red of her *RED STAR* t-shirt a hallucinogenic vibe.

'Ja. It is my task.'

'Telling it to orbit Jupiter?'

'I believe it is our best hope.'

'When did you get out of bed?' asked Sila, lowering his arm.

'I agree,' she said, walking past him and seating herself on the Jame stool. 'We also need to work on a communication link. Specifically aimed at the Mars bases.'

'That will be difficult. And not the most efficient use of my-…'

'Has Petr come here today?'

'Ne.'

Aleša leaned back and took in the ceiling, noticing the poster on the back wall. 'Has he been here in the last few days?'

'Ne.'

She grunted, seeing the other posters. 'I will tell him to come. And you will help him to learn the code so he can talk to the computer.'

'That may take some time.'

'It is inefficient to have only one of us able to talk to the computer. In fact, we should all learn some basics, in case of emergency.'

'Chu knows a little,' said Sila, edging his way between the two stools. 'Right, Kenji?'

'All of us should know. You can make a little dictionary of the five hundred most common symbols.'

'I already did that, for Petr.'

'Five hundred symbols?'

'One hundred and fifty.'

'We need five hundred, minimum. Until then, you will give us updates every day about what you're typing in here, as well as your progress with the communication link. No more surprises.' She held up the list and pointed to one of the lines, which neither Nakagami nor Sila could make out clearly. 'You can cross my name off, and Dodzi too. We'll be fine.'

'I believe that was what I wrote.'

'Are you going to talk to him?' asked Sila.

'Ja, tomorrow. You can come too.'

'Me?'

'We both have black faces, it will reassure him.' She left the stool, frowned at the blood stain she hadn't noticed previously then put eyes on Nakagami. 'I'll tell Petr to come within the hour. Don't let him slack off.'

'That might be beyond my control.'

'Just copy what your old boss used to do. Same speech patterns.'

'Not quite my style.'

'Try.'

Aleša turned to leave, looked around at the posters again and coughed when she saw the one up near the ceiling. It was a little girl on a bed, the blanket pulled down to just below her nipples.

'Maybe you should take a break from poster making for a while too. For your own mental health.'

'It's art,' said Sila, looking at the hockey stick poster. 'Apparently.'

'Looks like child porn.'

Nakagami looked at the same poster, narrowing his eyes. 'You both misunderstand. That is my sister.'

'Sister?' asked Sila, puzzled. 'I thought you said…'

'Ja, my sister. She died years ago, but we were very close when I was young. That picture is how I remember her.'

'I'm sorry,' said Aleša, looking around at the other posters. 'But these other ones…'

'They are all based on classical works of art.'

'If you say so.'

Aleša glanced at Sila then walked back into the pale green light, not saying another word.

'I'm sorry too,' said Sila, turning back to Nakagami. 'About your sister.'

'It is not an interesting thing to talk about.'

'Okay. Ja, no problem. We don't have to-…'

'I must work now.'

'Ja, work…'

'Before Petr arrives.'

~~~

Aleša stopped in the intestine corridor outside the god talking room and, for a brief moment, tried to think of any artists who'd painted little girls. There was Goya, and Renoir's ginger blouse girl, and…that was it.

She looked back, the green bulb on the wall buzzing in the corner she'd just come from.
~~~

Ask Petr, she thought. Art was his area, though with him it was strong Russian men and robots. But he had been trained, maybe he would know.

Or skip it?

She'd just told him to take a break, and there were no young girls on board so…

The green light flickered, which due to the constant flow of power from the ion engine should've been impossible. At least that's what Petr had told her.

Maybe the wiring was falling apart? Or the computer was watching her?

Had he gotten that far?

She touched the wall in front of her and pushed off into the next turn.

Three corners later she was in the main corridor, heading for the lower deck.

Her next target.

The cold-hearted one.

~~~

'Not even a little bit close,' said Chu, staring at a picture of what she claimed was a particle beam.

'Within the next year?'

'Unlikely.'

'Two years?'

'Same.'

Aleša moved her hands around the top of the Angolan-style rocking chair and onto Chu's head, then started digging into the scalp with the tips of her nails.

'The leading theory is relatively solid,' Chu went on, putting the picture down on the floor [there were no spare tables in the TELEPORT ROOM, just the main one with the model of Ito's ship from *Dibrivna Vaska*] and picking up her notepad. 'Or it will be after I've gone over
~~~

all my old notes. And these other theories. Which in itself could take another six months…'

'Great.'

'…maybe seven, eight. Ja, that part's manageable. And I have a computer to do the simulations, when I'm ready for it.'

'But…'

'But even with the theory in place…ne vem. I just don't know if I can build an actual machine. Or a beam confinement platform.'

'Isn't that a beam confining platform?' asked Aleša, looking over at the raised segment of floor taking up about a quarter of the room.

'That's the *Dibrivna Vaska* one, a replica.'

'For teleporting, right?'

'Ja, in the show. I doubt it has the operating system embedded underneath, or anywhere else.'

'What about those boxes on it?'

'Empty.'

'Huh?'

'A joke of some kind, I suppose.'

'So it doesn't work…'

'Not at all.' Chu paused, pushing the notepad in against the face of *No Feeling Bear* on her t-shirt. 'Or not yet. There is a chance I could get the drones to modify it later. Use the LAUNCH ROOM as the counter point. It could work…'

'Sorry,' said Aleša, digging in a nail harder than intended. Chu didn't seem to notice.

'…but I'd need the computer to order the drones to make the parts I need. And install them. And direct power to this room.'

'How much power?'

'The drones probably aren't capable of that kind of work. And I'm not even sure if the parts I think I need are the actual parts I need. If that makes sense?'

'You'll figure it out.' Aleša moved back down to Chu's shoulder, going under the shoulder blades, trying to dig them out. 'Hopefully before Jupiter.'

'Impossible.'

'And when you do, and we have the communication link, we'll finally have some leverage over him.'

'Leverage?'

'If he wants the technology, he'll have to give us control of the ship, and let us come back home. Mars would also do, but first choice is definitely Earth.' She paused the massage, staring at the screen on the wall, the up quarks that Chu had tried to explain to her. 'The more I think about it…ja, you need to keep going here. Your theory. It could be the key to everything.'

'I'm sure someone will get it running before I do. Based on all this…'

'Don't be pessimistic.'

'…the theories they provided me with.'

'You have your notes, all their notes, this room. Long as you don't try and live down here with all your little books and toys…'

'Not you too.'

'…and leave time for other things. Relaxing things.'

'What toys?'

Aleša's eyes swerved to the model ship on the table.

'I told you, that's a replica.'

'Okay.'

'The only real thing is the mountain of theory here, all the reading work, and I do six hours a day max. Then I switch to relaxing things.'

'Six hours is a lot. Three is better.' Aleša edged round to the front of the chair and focused her hands on Chu's waist, smiling at the gormless face of *No Feeling Bear*. 'You almost finished for today?'

'Another five hours maybe.'

'That's your opening offer?'

'Maybe four, if I can concentrate.'

'Four…'

'I've just got here, Aleša. I haven't even had breakfast yet.'

'Wah, it's morning, isn't it? I completely forgot. Must be the lighting…messing with my internal clock.'

'Perhaps you shouldn't spend four days straight in your quarters.'

Aleša moved both hands forward across the bottom of Chu's stomach, dipping her fingertips down in the middle. 'Maybe I should spend four days straight in your quarters…'

'You'd get electrocuted…'

'We don't know that for sure.'

'…I'd get electrocuted too. Ja, we do know it, Gašper passed out in Petr's room and got shocked…'

'He did?'

'Last week. He told us about it…'

'I must've been hungover.'

'…in the CREATE ROOM.'

Aleša brought her hands back up, smoothing out into a curve at the bottom of *No Feeling Bear's* face. 'The point is, you finish in four hours, that gives us plenty of time to hang out before curfew. In your quarters.'

'I can't today.'

'On your bed.'

'I said I'd meet Kenji.'

Her thumbs stopped, dangerously close to the sides of Chu's breasts.

'He said he'd help me try to come up with persuasion strategies for the computer.'

'Persuasion for what?'

'The computer, I just said. Strategies to get it to agree to my teleporter requests. Kenji said it may take some time. Long term persuasion, a lot of circumlocution and calculated tangents.'

'How long will that take?'

'Ne vem. But I'll probably be a bit tired afterwards.'

'What, to receive a massage?'

'If that's all it is.'

Aleša stopped, moving her hands away from Chu's sides. 'I massage you then fuck off, is that it?'

'I never said that.'

'Sounded like it.'

'You misinterpreted. I might be tired, I might not. Ne vem.'

'Okay, how about I dress up as an up quark or muon…'

'That would be tough.'

'...read some of your equations out loud while I'm fingering you...'

'Up quarks can't be seen.'

'...would that make you less tired?'

Chu pulled herself out of the chair cocoon and walked over to the screen. 'I can see you tomorrow, Aleša. And many times after that. Relax.'

'If Nakagami hasn't booked you first.'

Chu looked at the screen and the up quarks looked back at her. Potentially. Who knew what they were really doing?

Oddly, Aleša didn't storm out, she stood there with one hand on the back of the fucking relaxation chair and stared at Chu's back, stared at it for a long time. In her head, she was being ridiculous, and in action, she was also being ridiculous. But she was half right, Chu was being robotic. She was beginning the process of gluing herself to this room. The fake teleport platform. This chair. Those fucking psychology books on the floor over there. The occult shit. Aleša knew it cos she'd glued herself to things before too, and then quoted Kropotkin when anyone dared point it out.

'It's fine, Chu,' she said finally. 'He can borrow you tonight. I'll focus on other things.'

'Okay, *Aleša*,' said Chu, putting herself back in the chair.

'Maybe a poster for the walls in here. Help you get rid of the asylum vibe.'

'Ja, that's an idea. Kenji said there were some Varo prints in the PHILOSOPHY ROOM.'

'Or you can make one yourself.'

'That works too.'

'In the CREATE ROOM.'

'Ja, probably.'

Aleša followed Chu's head down to the notebook, tried to read a few of the descriptions, coughed when she got to Heisenberg compensators, said, 'tomorrow then,' and left.

~~~
~~~

On the way to the CREATE NOT DESTROY ROOM, Aleša stopped outside Dodzi's quarters and put her hand an inch from the bell.

Inside, there were mutterings, two voices that weren't coming from two people. He was talking to himself?

She leaned closer and listened, but it wasn't Slovene he was speaking, it was something non-European sounding, probably Twi.

Maybe it's already too late, she thought.

The voices came closer to the door, forcing her back. Out of pure stubbornness, her hand went for the bell again, but she couldn't bring herself to push it.

Tomorrow, she told herself, moving back down the corridor.

~~~

It was strange to see the CREATE NOT DESTROY ROOM empty. There were usually at least three people in there, unless it was very early morning, but now there was just Klemen, on his own in the middle of the table, speaking what sounded like extremely strangled Portuguese.

'Eu acho que este ship não é real, no verdade é uma simulacion.'

Aleša walked around the table and sat down next to him, catching the word *simulation* and guessing some of the rest.

Klemen glanced at her and kept going.

'Eu não quero ir ao Luyten 7 algo system, el é muito far.'

'Sounds like you have some vocab gaps,' said Aleša.

'Sim.'

Klemen looked at his notes, tracing another sentence he'd written in scrawled handwriting with his finger.

'Maybe you need to take a break.'

'Não…mais tarde.'

Aleša looked at Klemen's notes and instead of rolling her eyes, which she never did, ran two fingers from the sides of her neck down to the windpipe. It was deserved. Half of the words on his page were Slovene, and a lot of the rest was repetition.

'I need you to take a break, Klemen.'
~~~

'Busy.'

'Sixty minutes.'

He laughed. 'That is not a small number.'

'I want to know what Nakagami said in that lecture. Everything.'

Klemen pointed at the sheets of paper half-heartedly piled up to the right. 'It's all in the notes. Including the patronizing tone.'

'Ja, I need you to go through them. How did he describe each one, what did he add, I want to know all of it.'

'Okay. Fine. Just let me finish this sent-…'

'Before anyone else comes in.'

Klemen looked at the door, then at his notes, then ran a finger along yet another sentence beginning with *eu nao quero*. 'Está bem.'

'And no Portuguese,' added Aleša pushing his notes away. 'I need detail.'

'As the master commands.'

'No sarcasm either.'

Klemen stopped mid-bow, muttering some of the Portuguese vocab on his notes.

'Go.'

~~~

The asteroid field appeared a week later.

Over a million rocks, with one of them, Ceres, classified as a dwarf planet, and the rest somewhere between the sizes of Albania, a shopping mall and a deluxe caravan.

However, when Sila looked out of the window in the CREATE NOT DESTROY ROOM, he didn't see any of this. Unless the asteroids had been equipped with some kind of cloaking device, there was nothing out there. Not even a distant Ceres.

Self-suggesting that he was looking out the wrong side of the ship, he went upstairs and tried the windows near the MAINTENANCE DRONE REC-ROOM.

Still no luck.
~~~

'You think any of them will hit us?' asked Gašper, joining him by the window.

'Ne vem.'

'Do you know anything about this kind of thing?'

'What? Impact physics?'

'Is that what it's called?'

'Probably not.'

'We'll ask Nakagami later, he'll know.'

'Ja.'

'I'm guessing we'll be okay though. You know why?'

'Because we won't hit anything.'

Gašper smiled and put his hand on Sila's shoulder. 'You're getting good at reading me, brother. I'll have to start wearing a helmet.'

'You what?'

'Stop you reading my thoughts. You know, like *Tovaska*.'[41] Gašper mimed putting a helmet on his head and did what he thought was a *telepathy* face.

Sila smirked, he couldn't help it.

'Hey, is this the right window?' asked Gašper, changing tack. 'I can't see any asteroids.'

'That's why I said we wouldn't hit anything.'

'But the ship said we'd arrived.'

'It did.'

'So where is it then?'

Sila turned to the window again, squinting. 'Maybe they're not in range yet. Too far away.'

'Then how have we arrived?'

'Ne vem.'

'Where's Nakagami?'

~~~

[41] Absurd Russian novel written by a pseudonymous author called OBV in 2069, where a road maintenance worker dons self-made helmet and armour, convinced that *those in municipal power* are telepathic alien surveyors set on torturing him.
~~~

Nakagami was in the same cramped space he usually occupied, talking to the AI with his 1500-word-strong vocab about possible day trip destinations in the Jovian system.

Sitting nearby on the navigation console [with his feet on the Jame stool], Petr watched him work, asking each time what he was typing and then occasionally adding, 'sorry, I don't want to be doing this but…'

'You could look through the basic dictionary I made,' said Nakagami, after Petr had squinted at the screen and asked what *what* meant.

'I did. There's a hundred words in it.'

'You could look at the *W* section. I believe there are six symbols there, one of which is *what*.'

'It's hard to read that stuff, picture alphabet, code, whatever you call it. Hard to remember too.' He leaned back, accidentally clipping the *graviton sensor*. 'The Russian book I'm doing, the Cyrillic[42] alphabet, same problem.'

'Russian does not use pictograms.'

'Maybe, but it's not like Slovene either. Some of them look like it, but read as something else.' Petr checked behind his back, seeing the *graviton sensor* lit up. 'Shit, it's on. I turned something on.'

'I told you before, the buttons are decorative.'

'Ja, I know, but…'

'It does not do anything.'

'…this one has words next to it…graviton sensor.'

'The label is also decorative.'

Petr pressed the button again and the ships voice came over the speaker system. 'Prosim, select target for scanning.'

'See, it's reacting.'

Nakagami glanced over. 'What did you press?'

'Same button again.'

'Graviton sensor?'

'Ja, ja.'

---

[42] Close enough.

Nakagami stared at a completely different button then turned and typed a new message to the AI.

'Are you asking it?'

'Ne.'

'What, why not?'

'It can wait until later. Now, I need to focus on Jupiter.'

'Come on, comrade, I just turned something on, a sensor. Ask it what else works in here, if there's any missiles or cloaking system, stuff like that.'

'There is no cloaking system.'

'How do you know?'

'There is no one to cloak from.'

'What about the missiles?'

Nakagami rubbed his thumb against the edge of the console, reading the computer's answer and typing 'how much radiation?' in response.

'What are you typing now?'

'A rhetorical mark of disbelief concerning the radiation levels on Ganymede.'

'Rhetorical? You mean you won't get an answer?'

'The computer understands rhetoric. It will elaborate on its previous response.'

'Which was?'

'The radiation levels on Ganymede.'

'Jezus fucking-…okay, just give me that dictionary. This is ridiculous.'

'It's next to the stool leg.'

Petr looked down and saw the dictionary face down on the floor, a few scuff marks on the cover. He bent low, picked it up and started reading.

'Kenji ball,' said Gašper breaking through the pale green light at the entrance, followed by a tired-looking Sila.

'I'm still not a ball.'

'If I say it enough times…'

'Prosim, don't.'

Gašper nodded at Petr and asked what he was reading.

'Language study.'

'The computer words?'

'Ja.'

'Getting anywhere with it?'

'I know *what.*'

'Better than not knowing it. Hey, did you know we were in the asteroid field?'

'Ja, the ship already said.'

'Supposedly in it. That's why we're here. Gonna ask Kenji where all the rocks are…'

'Very funny,' said Petr, going back to the dictionary.

Gašper rotated and put both palms flat on the console. 'So, these asteroids…are they not in range yet or…something else?'

Nakagami looked at Sila, who was leaning against the hidden bin wall with his arms folded.

'You're the scientist,' he replied.

'This is real?' asked Nakagami.

'What do you mean?'

'Is your question real?'

'Ja, hyper real,' said Gašper. 'We looked out the window in the ASTEROID BELT ROOM and there's nothing out there.'

'I told him we might be out of range,' added Sila.

'Is that true? Are we not there yet?'

Nakagami coughed, then coughed again, the second time real. 'What do you imagine the asteroid field is?'

'Ne vem,' replied Sila, his tone already a shrug. 'Clustered rocks orbiting the Sun?'

'Ja, like in *Dibrivna Vaska,* the *you fly like a contrarian* scene.'

'That's fantasy,' said Petr, laughing.

'I thought it was sci-fi?'

'Do you understand,' said Nakagami, coughing again, 'that space is a big place?'

'Ja…'

'That the orbital path around the Sun, even if it's a million asteroids all at different points, is incredibly long and stretched out.'

'I was half right then,' said Sila, rubbing his eyes.

'They're out of range?' asked Gašper, jumping back in.

Nakagami picked up the dictionary and started drawing on the back. 'The asteroids aren't clustered in one large group, they're spread out, in smaller clusters.'

'Hundreds of thousands of miles spread out,' said Petr, acting out an ironically tiny distance with his two hands. 'With some of them the size of tennis balls.'

'Serious?'

'It's in all the textbooks.'

'Was it? I can't remember…'

'In visual terms,' continued Nakagami, holding up his finished sketch, which was a basic map of the solar system, with lots of dots evenly distributed between Mars and Jupiter, 'it looks abundant, like in *Dibrivna Vaska*. However, as Petr said, the distances between them are vast. In fact, the chances of us seeing one are around zero. Perhaps zero point one.'

'Then why did the computer announce it?' asked Gašper, pointing his face towards Sila.

'To torture us.'

'Wah, like it was programmed to do it?'

'Ja, most likely,' agreed Nakagami. 'With luck, only until Jupiter.'

'We're going to orbit there?'

'Not yet.'

'But you're making progress?'

'I have no way to discern that.'

'Jezus. Can you at least tell us if we're gonna crash into it?'

'Unlikely.'

'Great.'

'Crashing into any planet is impossible at our current velocity. Instead, if we cannot orbit Jupiter, we will sail hundreds of thousands of kilometres past it, heading relatively close to Uranus. But it is likely that we'll sail hundreds of thousands of kilometres past that too. And then there'll be no more planets left to target except smaller masses in the Kuiper Belt.'

'But you're not gonna let that happen, right?'

'I cannot make any guarantees.'

'Fuck. That's bleak.' Gašper leaned on the console next to Petr, barely missing the button for the *graviton sensor*. 'How do you survive in here?'

~~~

Despite concerns about time-wasting and redundancy, Nakagami ceded to Aleša's demands and started giving a daily update in the JUPITER ROOM regarding his progress with the AI.

Lasting somewhere between one and two minutes, the information would be separated into two parts: the core and the detail.

The core was simple: the remaining time left to Jupiter, with a ceiling of 15 days.

Obviously no one except Chu and possibly Petr understood the ceiling part, so Nakagami explained it as *laymen* as he could.

'Based on our present coasting velocity, the total duration of time to Jupiter is 24 days. If we wish to orbit the planet and not shoot by, we must slow down and synchronize with its orbit. This deceleration must begin within the next fifteen days. Hence, ceiling.'

'Can't we just put on the brakes when we're right next to it?' asked Gašper.

'There are no brakes.'

'Huh?'

'To decelerate, we must direct the thrust the other way, and because we're using an ion drive, we need time for it to be effective. Not as much as the initial launch, but still, a certain amount.'

'I half get it,' said Gašper, looking at Sila, who nodded at the surface of his coffee.

The second and third updates went in a similar way, with Gašper forgetting what he'd half got the day before and asking about the brakes again.

During the fourth update, he suggested just turning the engine off.
~~~

By the fifth day, after Petr had explained it to him in less scientific terms, he got it.

The *detail* part of the update was vastly more understandable, and also a lot stranger.

Each time, Nakagami would tell everyone what topic he was using with the AI that day and what its purpose was.

The initial topics were all Jupiter-related, e.g. its moons, the red spot, the radiation levels, but as they approached the fifteen day ceiling, they became a lot more random. Desperate even.

'As there are three days remaining, I have decided to try something more esoteric yet, I believe, still relatable.'

'To Jupiter?' asked Sila.

'Ja, in a loose way.'

'Saturn?' asked Gašper.

'Jupiter the God?' said Aleša.

Nakagami coughed, tapped the edge of the table three times. 'Long distance running.'

No one said anything. Not even Gašper or Aleša.

'Unless you have music to listen to, endurance running is a tedious exercise, yet many people enjoy doing it. There is no real purpose, just as there is no real purpose to orbiting Jupiter, but sometimes you have to do things that serve no purpose otherwise you will end up in something predictable and meaningless. Or in philosophical terms, existential mud.'

'Eh?' Gašper looked left at Chu's muon poster. 'Doesn't long distance running improve fitness?'

'My intended meaning was a purpose that could not be otherwise fulfilled in a less tedious way.'

'Ah. And the bit at the end?'

'Predictability can be bad.'

Gašper exaggerated a nod then tilted his head left to make it slightly more exotic.

'Do you expect that to work?' asked Aleša, arms folded.

'Ne vem.'

'Okay, do you expect it to work better than something directly Jupiter-related?'

'I cannot use the word *expect.* Hope is more suitable.'

'Hope.'

'To be honest, my mind has already partially shifted to Uranus. To avoid deflation, I suggest all of you do the same.'

'What, give up on Jupiter?'

'Partially, ja.'

There were murmurs, some of them comprehensible.

Then muteness.

Aleša turned to the window triptych and stared out at the few visible stars.

The rest either went to the floor or each other's t-shirts, Klemen saying 'ne' out loud when he realised almost all of them were wearing *Green is Good.*

~~~

Three days later, *partially* became *fully* as Nakagami's last ditch attempt to woo the AI into a Jupiter orbit failed.

The theory had been solid enough, *psychological need*, yet the computer simply didn't believe that the more unstable members of the crew all had a pet called Jupiter waiting for them back in Slovenia.

'It seems the probabilistic parts of the AI are well-programmed,' said Nakagami, giving them the update in the newly opened URANUS ROOM [complete with projection screen]. 'At least when it comes to requests in conflict with its core programming.'

'You mean it's not a fucking idiot,' said Klemen, his tone oddly jovial.

'Not in the context we require it to be, ne.'

'So what now?' asked Sila.

'The same as before. Nothing has changed in a material way. The target is Uranus.'

'Hang on,' said Gašper, half raising his hand. 'What about Saturn?'
~~~

'Not anywhere close,' answered Petr, sitting on the chair nearest Nakagami…or slouching to be more precise.

'I thought it was the next one along.'

'In distance from the Sun, ja, but it's over on the other side of the system.'

'Wah, what's it doing there?'

'Orbiting.'

'The planets go around the Sun,' said Sila, not raising his voice too loud.

'I know that, *Sila*, but if the distance is closer, can't we just turn the ship that way, wherever Saturn is?'

'Ne,' said Nakagami.

'Just *ne*, that's it?'

'An explanation would take a long time. The scientific one at least. Though there is a simpler one. The ship will not allow us to make such a large deviation from our intended destination.'

'Luyten 789?' asked Sila, cutting in before Gašper could get anything else out.

'726-8, ja.'

'How long until we reach Uranus?' asked Dodzi, his hand raised, seemingly oblivious to Aleša almost falling out of her seat after he'd spoken.

'At our current velocity, and assuming the planets are where I calculate them to be, the ship would pass the orbital line of Uranus in around two hundred and thirty-four days.'

'Assuming the planets are planets,' muttered Klemen, gesturing towards the creepy pearl-coloured sphere lit up on the projection screen.

'And the slow-down ceiling?'

'I'm not certain yet. Uranus is farther off our path than Jupiter was, so it would need a bigger swing, which means an earlier slow down time. Perhaps one hundred and ninety days.'

'A hundred and ninety days,' said Gašper, his eyes lost on the projection screen.

'That's half a year.'

'And if we do manage to decelerate, the total duration time would obviously increase.'

'Shit.'

'A hundred and ninety days,' repeated Gašper, finally blinking.

'As I said, nothing has materially changed. We can all continue with our tasks.'

'Can't we make the ship go faster?' asked Aleša, pulling at the sleeve of her *RED STAR* t-shirt, or second skin as Chu called it.

'It may be possible to accelerate for a few weeks, if the computer can be persuaded.'

'How possible?'

'However, the farther we move away from the Sun, the more power we need to reserve for emergencies, so I would not harbour any serious expectations of success. Besides, I will likely need the extra time to convince the computer of our primary mission.'

'Petr will help you with that. Chu too.' Aleša glanced at the seat to her right, where a distant-looking Chu was sitting with a new book open in her hand. 'If she can snap out of her trance.'

'I'm listening,' Chu replied, reflexively closing the book.

'But not contributing much.'

'Ja, even Dodzi's said more than you,' said Gašper, pointing at the Ghanaian and getting a blank face in return.

'I understood the update.' Chu stared across at Nakagami. 'I have nothing to add.'

'Nothing on those robot bodies?' asked Klemen, squinting at the cover of Chu's book.

'Or the time addition?' added Aleša.

'Ne.'

'Which one?'

'Both.'

'You're saying you're okay with half a year?' asked Sila, trying his best not to let his tone cross into the realm of *motherly*.

'It's not that bad.'

'Compared to two thousand years, ja, but-...'

'I will help talk to the computer. If Kenji needs me to do that.'

Nakagami did his tapping routine on the frame of the projection screen. 'Different input data for the AI, from a different mind. It could work. If you could become more adept at the code…'

'Prosim. It'll take me half a year just to say *how are you?*' said Petr.

'Chu then.'

'You can take it in turns,' said Aleša. 'We will give you suggested topics in the daily updates.'

'That will not be necessary.'

'Really?'

'I have an understanding of what the computer responds to. It is better if I continue using my own methods.'

'Hands up who has a pet called Jupiter?' asked Aleša.

No one raised a hand, not even Gašper.

'We will suggest topics in the daily updates and you can try one each time. As well as your own choices. If they're not too esoteric. Chu or Petr can focus on the communication link, getting the computer to set one up at least. Then we'll be ready when we reach Uranus. Okay?'

Petr shrugged and offered a basic, 'ja, I suppose.'

Chu copied the *ja*, eyes already back on her book.

'*En Ka Ind*,'[43] mumbled Klemen, leaning over and attempting to read out the title.

Nakagami stared at the projection screen for a long time, so long that it seemed he wasn't going to answer at all, but finally his head started performing a *just-about detectable* nodding motion. 'If you all insist.'

'Good,' said Aleša.

~~~

The first suggestions came at the next update session, which was back in the CREATE NOT DESTROY ROOM.

---

[43] Another classic of late 21st century psychology by Taqi Aziz, this one focused on the lubricating effect of myth and the occult on the modern psyche.
~~~

Note: they tried the URANUS ROOM again, but everyone except Dodzi and Gašper felt uncomfortable with the pallid colour of the planet on the projection screen.

'Feels like being watched.'

'A creepy eyeball.'

'Cold too.'

Giving up, they tried to shift back to the JUPITER ROOM, but the door was locked now that the ship had passed the planet, so they moved again, considering the PHILOSOPHY ROOM, but that was virtually next door and pointless, and there were so many books lying around that Sila and Aleša and Chu would get distracted by, or worse, tempted into nihilism, so, ultimately, they ended up in the room where they spent almost all their communal time anyway, the centre of supposed creativity.

According to Dodzi, the best way to get through to the computer, at least in terms of orbiting Uranus, was to make it fond of the place.

'Is that actually a suggestion?' asked Klemen, a piece of bok choy almost spilling out of his mouth.

'Ja, a suggestion.'

'You mean like promoting it as a holiday spot?' followed up Aleša, ignoring her own food.

Dodzi nodded with curved descent. 'It is a spiritual place. During my sabbatical, after all the rage had been exhausted, I tried to meditate. At first, I used the image of Jupiter in the JUPITER ROOM, and it was mildly effective, but…yesterday, when I meditated in the URANUS ROOM, it was as if a beam of light had hit me. The planet instantly became a close friend; magical, comforting, assuring me in a cosmic way that Amma Darko would face justice.' He paused, noticing a lot of atheists staring back at him. 'Ja, it is a spiritual place,' he repeated, 'but not dogmatic. We should tell the computer this.'

'Tell it what exactly?' asked Klemen.

'I am also unclear as to what you are suggesting,' said Nakagami.

'That is my suggestion, comrades. Use it or not.' He took a long breath, eyes on the posters. 'Using it would be better.'

'Anyone else?' asked Aleša.

Everyone looked at the table, some reaching for more bok choy, others picking up half-empty cups of coffee.

'No one?'

Some slurping noises, a few *ne vems*.

'Food,' said Petr, finally, staring at a mini potato on the end of his fork.

'Talk about food, with the computer?'

'Ne, not that, survival. How long are the supplies gonna last? I mean, realistically, if we're going on a two thousand year trip, how are we gonna have enough food for that?'

'It is one part of a good point,' said Nakagami.

'One part,' repeated Gašper, laughing.

'As far as I can tell, there are three food sources. Short term supplies, which are almost exhausted. Frozen meat, frozen fruit. Canned supplies, which can last indefinitely but with a loss in nutritional value after five years, give or take a year. And what the drones grow themselves in the STORAGE ROOM. For example, today's meal…' Nakagami pointed at Klemen's plate. 'Bok choy. Potato. Vegetarian pork.'

'Okay, we don't need the whole inventory,' said Aleša, jabbing her fork into a potato and leaving it there. 'Can we use food as leverage?'

'I was leading to that. In realistic terms, the food we have could be enough, but if anything happens to the drones, or the canned supplies sustain damage then…'

'So it is a leverage point?'

'Ne.'

'Why not?' asked Petr.

'At least not yet. I suspect we would need either the plants or the canned supplies to be damaged before the computer ceded this point. And even then it wouldn't correlate with a proposed orbit of Uranus.'

'We should still try,' said Aleša, pulling the fork back out of the potato and using the edge to slice it in two instead.

'Agreed,' said Petr.

Sila turned to Nakagami and attempted an apologetic gesture with his hands. 'Might as well.'

'All others who agree, raise your hands?'

Gašper shot his hand up before Aleša had finished her sentence, but Klemen needed an elbow in the hip, and Chu didn't respond until she said, 'Chu, hand,' directly to her.

'Very well,' said Nakagami, pulling down his zip an inch from the collar. 'I will make the enquiry.'

'Ne, Petr will do it.'

'Me?'

'It's your idea, you're the only one who can explain it properly.'

'Err…'

'As you wish,' said Nakagami, pulling his zip back up.

'Okay, food is settled. Next topic. Anyone?'

Klemen finished chewing another bok choy then spat out, 'simulation theory,' but Aleša either didn't catch it or chose to ignore it.

She gave a few more seconds for everyone to eat something from their plate, chew a bit and say something useful, but most of them kept on eating and staring at the posters on the wall, especially Petr's recent Ljubljana castle, done at Chu's request in the style of Varo's *Allegory of Winter*, so she gave up and resumed her charge from the vanguard. 'How about something more scientific?' Like…ne vem. Uranus has hydrogen, right? Isn't that useful for something?'

'I have tried that already, with Jupiter,' replied Nakagami, picking up his fork and placing it on top of a half-eaten bok choy.

'Tried what?'

'And every country on Earth is well aware of what each planet possesses. The data would not add anything new.'

'I'm not talking about data, I mean actual product. Us, scooping up hydrogen, using it as leverage to bring us back.'

'But we are unable to go back. It is not our mission.'

'Unless that mission changes, due to us having hydrogen. Chu, is this viable?'

The teleport maestro realised it wasn't her Tariq Aziz book talking and looked up. 'What?'

'Can we get hydrogen, or some other gas from Uranus and use it as leverage to get back home?'

'Ne vem.'

'It will not work,' said Nakagami. 'This ship is not equipped for gas mining. Or any mining, in fact.'

'Not yet.'

'I suggest instead a focus on the moons. They are relatively unstudied. Perhaps we can convince the computer it is an opportunity for knowledge acquisition.'

'Knowledge,' said Aleša, practically biting the word as it left her mouth.

'It is not ideal, and will probably fail, but it is a more realistic place to start.'

'Ja, start there, sure. Then talk about the hydrogen. Focus on that. Petr can ask about the food.'

'I believe you gave me the choice of one suggestion per day.'

'Ja…'

'Then today I will go with Dodzi's.'

'Are you serious?'

'Until tomorrow.' Nakagami stood up, nodded at Chu and Petr, then left.

Aleša waited until the door was closed again then turned to Petr. 'You ask the computer about the hydrogen.'

'I thought my one was food.'

'Hydrogen first, food later.'

'Doesn't matter, I can't do it anyway. It's way beyond my skill level.'

'Chu…'

'Ja?'

'Were you listening?'

Her eyes went to the page she was reading then to the door and, finally, back to Aleša. 'You want to talk to the computer about hydrogen.'

'Ja, mining it from Uranus.'

'I don't know if that's possible.'

'Doesn't matter if we can do it or not, we just need to use it as a topic. Can you do that?'

Chu closed her book, noticed an unfinished coffee next to it, drank some of it. 'I will try.'

~~~

Even though it failed to feature the words *teleporter* or *fundamental particles*, or anything related to neo-Jungian psychology, Chu did keep Aleša's suggestion in her head long enough to try.

However, just as Nakagami had warned, it didn't work.

'Are you sure you asked it the right question?' asked Aleša, laying diagonally across her bed, tapping the back of Chu's occult psychology book.

'Ja.'

'Using the right code?'

Chu put the book on the desk, next to the massage stick, and got up. 'It can't be done. We don't have mining equipment, and the computer said it is impossible to turn the ship around.'

'But it doesn't matter what the computer wants, if we can get the communication link set up…'

'That is also going to be difficult.'

'Ja, but not impossible…'

'Maybe not.'

'…if you keep working at it.'

Chu nodded, putting her Slovene badge jacket on and heading towards the door.

'Are you going back downstairs?'

'Ja.'

'Wanna stay here for a while first?'

'If I did that, it would not be a while.'

'Is that a bad thing?' Aleša shifted her position on the bed, making space for Chu. 'You haven't been in here since before Jupiter.'

'That was four days ago.'

'Four days alone, two hours in here. Not a good ratio.'

Chu stared at the space on the bed, Aleša's legs next to it, her hands.

'You're wavering…'

'Ne.'

'Not now?'
~~~

'I'll drop by later. If I have time.'

Chu turned abruptly even for her and left, the door sliding shut behind.

Aleša stayed on the bed, keeping the space next to her. The massage stick was on the desk nearby, and she reached for it, then stopped when she noticed Chu's book. *En Ka Ind* by Tariq Aziz.

Leaving a marker, she wondered, or a hint for me to get into her weirdo psychology?

Smiling at both possibilities, Aleša left the massage stick as it was and rolled sideways onto her imaginary Chu instead.

~~~

Between daily updates and erratic spiritual doctrine from Dodzi, the crew went on with their attempts to fashion a routine out of the potential, inevitable two thousand year journey through space dust and nothingness.

Klemen continued with his Portuguese experiment.

Dodzi spent half his time in the URANUS ROOM and the other half telling everyone else about what he'd thought about while in the URANUS ROOM.

He also started drinking again, not alone in the corner as Nakagami had feared, but with others.

Aleša helped him a little, or at the very least tried to stop him disappearing completely into mysticism, which was completely antithetical to her plans. 'Mars,' she told him. 'Focus on getting back to Mars.' To which he would point a finger towards the food dispenser and reply, 'Uranus.'

The closest she'd come to a successful counter-argument was *Mars is closer to Darko*, but that lasted no longer than a day, when he emerged from the URANUS ROOM claiming Darko had used stealth tech to relocate to his new favourite planet and was waiting there to ambush him.

It was an unanswerable theory.
~~~

Besides Dodzi-watch, Aleša spent most days re-writing old strategies. If she hit a rough patch, she'd try doing some Russian with Petr, but not for long as he was quite possessive of it, and wouldn't let her use the book if he wasn't there to use it too.

Nakagami soldiered on in the TALK TO YOUR GOD ROOM, trying to ignore the days ticking by as he made almost no progress with the computer.

Chu didn't fare much better, but that was mostly because her brain was stuck on the teleporter. No matter how many times she asked, or how many creative arguments she came up, the computer wouldn't authorize any transference of power to the TELEPORT ROOM. Apparently, they might need that power in interstellar space, eight hundred years later.

And then there were Sila and Gašper, the latter's scientific knowledge exasperating Nakagami to such an extent that he asked Petr to teach him some basics, starting with the layout and physics of the solar system.

Sila didn't think his own science level was as bad as Gašper's, but he also remembered the asteroid field debacle, so decided to join in too.

It was that or stay in his quarters and deteriorate.

Dredge up the past.

Judge it.

And it wasn't time for that yet.

~~~

The first science lesson given by Petr was short and enraging.

Commencing with a disclaimer about how he wasn't an expert, and if Nakagami and Chu were there, in the room, he wouldn't say anything cos it'd be embarrassing, but as they weren't there, he was the best they had, and he wasn't that bad anyway, not compared to them.

'Did you study this before?' asked Sila, sitting solo on the window side of the table in the CREATE NOT DESTROY ROOM. Gašper and Petr were next to each other on the opposite side, with Klemen two
~~~

seats away, his face almost touching the Portuguese notes laid out in front of him.

'Not academically, ne, but I did do some courses in the collective.' He pointed at his posters on the wall. 'I taught art there sometimes. Science classes were nearby.'

'You didn't tell me that,' said Gašper.

'What?'

'That you taught art.'

'Ja, well, you didn't tell me you were terrible at science.'

'I'm not that bad.'

Klemen coughed, muttering something in Portuguese.

'I probably know the basics already, what you're about to say to us…the solar system stuff. I just forget sometimes.'

'Okay. What do you know about the solar system?'

'Which part? The planets?'

'Ja, the planets.'

'There are eight of them. And dwarf planets too. Don't know how many, but it's a lot. Wait, ninety something. Ninety-five.'

'How are we travelling to Uranus?'

'How?'

'Ja.'

'Is that a trick question?'

'I mean, how is the ship approaching it?'

'Physically approaching?'

'Ja.'

'I don't get it. Uranus is over there, we're going towards it.'

'In a straight line?'

'Ja. Ne. Ja. Uranus isn't, that goes in a circle, we're moving straight…the ship…'

'The ship is going in a straight line?'

'Ja, not completely straight…a little bit curved. But mostly straight.'

'So we're going in a slightly curved line to Uranus?'

'Or more like direct.'

'Direct?'

'With a slight curve, and then a bigger curve when we need to orbit Uranus. But basically we're going there direct. In a semi-straight line.' He paused, looking at Sila. 'Aren't we?'

~~~

The lessons after that moved onto the ship and how things generally worked.

Gašper was on marginally firmer ground with this one as he'd seen it in *Dibrivna Vaska*, but there were still wobbles.

Like his belief in anti-gravity plating. Which, according to him, used *acute gravity simulators* to attach your feet to the floor.

'I think you mean gravity plating,' said Petr, stirring some Somalian alcohol into his coffee.

'Ne vem, I'm just saying what I read. They said it's a kind of magnetic force that acts like gravity and pulls everything towards the floor.'

'Who is *they*?'

'Maybe not a force, but something like that. The magazine in rehab.'

'Gravity plating was what they used in *Dibrivna Vaska*,' said Sila, digging a spoon into his bowl of oatmeal. 'It's not actually real.'

'You sure? I may have got the name wrong.'

'Complete science fiction. Like teleporters and warp speed.' Sila checked the door behind, then the muon poster on the wall. 'Don't tell Chu I said that.'

'Okay, professor. What is causing the gravity then?'

'Rotation. Centrifugal axis something…I forget the name. Basically, a part of the ship is spinning. I think.' Sila looked over at Petr for assistance, but he was busy massaging his eyelids. 'That or our velocity is causing it. Maybe in tandem.'

'I thought spinning was only for space stations?'

'Ne vem. I remember Nakagami mentioning both, so it might actually be a combination effect. Some spinning, some velocity.'

'You mean we're spinning right now?'

'Part of the ship, ja. Maybe.'
~~~

Gašper took a moment to sip on his green tea [with four strips of *but kei* added], perhaps realizing that the first question in his head was probably not an intelligent one.

'Or we're going so fast we can get all our gravity that way,' Sila continued. 'Could be we were spinning at the start of the trip, when we weren't moving, and then using velocity when we picked up enough speed. Enough velocity. That probably makes more sense, as we must be going pretty fast by now.'

'So it's not spin gravity?'

Both of them looked at Petr, who had moved on from his eyelids to the top of his head.

'The LEM-12 Field,' he said.

'Who?'

'The thing simulating gravity, it runs through the whole ship. Haven't you read any tech news in the last ten years?'

'Ne.'

'None. Apart from that anti-gravity plating thing.'

'What about the induction video when we boarded?'

'I was unconscious for that. And no one bothered to fill me in.'

'I vaguely remember the name,' said Sila, glancing over at Chu's muon poster again. 'But I thought it was a forcefield.'

'A what?'

'To get rid of space dust and radiation around the ship.'

Petr followed Sila's line of sight to the muon poster and gave out an *aaah*.

'So this Lemto field, that's the thing creating the gravity here?' asked Gašper, fishing out the *but kei* strips from his cup.

'LEM-12. It produces a similar effect, ja.'

'How?'

'I had a sinking feeling you were gonna ask that.'

'Hey, it's a lesson, you're the teacher.'

'Under coercion,' Petr said, barely even at dog pitch.

'Just the basics of it would do,' said Sila.

'Honestly, ne vem. There's lemium, there's a field, it's localised to the inside of the ship. Beyond that, you'll have to talk to Kenji. Or even better, Klemen. I'm sure he knows.'

Petr raised his voice for the last part and looked down the table for a reaction.

'Foda-se,' said Klemen, sticking to his Portuguese notes.

'So this lemium makes a field that causes gravity, but only inside the ship?' asked Sila, the physical equivalent of a struggle session playing out on his face.

'Simulates the effects of it. Ja.'

Gašper half raised his cup hand, spilling a few drops of green tea on the table. 'I still don't get it. If we're using this lemon thing, and it works okay, why isn't everyone else using it?'

'It's still relatively new. And they are using it, just not on space stations. Not yet at least. And before *why not* comes out of your mouth, it's too risky. Too hard to control the lemium. On a space ship this size, not so bad. Should we move on to the ion engine now?'

'Lemium…' repeated Gašper slowly.

'Or just call it a day?'

'Ne vem. I'm still struggling with this bit.'

'Artificial gravity?'

'I think I'm gonna forget it. Ja, gravity, the lemium thing. Might need to go over it again. Or you can just tell me later, then I won't need to be reminded next lesson.'

'Keeping it bottled up in the lessons is better,' said Petr, re-ordering his notes. 'Easier to teach.'

'Why, you got other things to do?'

'What?'

'Seems like you're busy, shrugging us off for something.'

'Ja, I'm meditating.'

'About what?'

Petr breathed out and then drank slowly from his cup, giving Sila enough time to snap out of his daydream and intervene.

'I'm going over to the PHILOSOPHY ROOM,' he said, pushing his [untouched] oatmeal bowl slightly to the side. 'You coming?'

Gašper cocooned his cup with his hands, looking at Petr. 'Is the lesson over?'

'Ja, for today.'

'Okay, then have a good time inside your head,' said Gašper, walking out of the room before Sila had a chance to make it even halfway round the table.

'He's not angry,' said Sila, hands forming what Chu called the forgiveness triangle.

'Neither am I.'

'He just gets a bit hyper sometimes.'

'I know.'

Sila looked at some of the posters, the old art, pinned up nearby, nodded to himself then followed Gašper out.

'Time to detach from that one,' said Klemen from the other end of the table.

'… … … … … …' replied Petr in Russian, giving no emotional indication that he'd just said *when javelin is time*.

Klemen muttered something and went back to his Portuguese notes.

Petr tidied up the mess of drawings and diagrams on the table in front of him and switched to his Russian book.

'*Chapter 7: Surviving at the Post Office*.'

~~~

Fifty days into the Uranus-shot mission, Nakagami stopped coming to give daily updates in person and dispatched Petr instead.

No one much cared, apart from Aleša, who let it ride for three sessions before ordering Petr to march back to the Control Room and drag Nakagami out.

'I'm not your servant,' protested Petr, grabbing a handful of Gašper's dried raisins and shoving them in his mouth.

'You're already standing up so go, stop moaning.'

'I'm eating.'

'Maybe I can go,' offered Dodzi, half getting out of his seat before being dragged back down by the sleeve. 'Hey, woman, my jacket!'
~~~

'Sorry,' said Aleša, letting go instantly. 'Didn't mean to pull that hard. *Man.*'

'It almost ripped.'

'Thought you had a firmer standing balance.' Aleša turned back to Petr, swatting his hand away from her own pile of dried raisins. 'Go get Nakagami. Tell him I asked him to come.'

'There's no point.'

'Ne, say Chu sent for him.'

'Won't work.'

'Course it will, he likes Chu.'

'I mean, she's in there with him now.'

Aleša's hand froze over her bowl. 'Who, Chu?'

'Trying to cheer him up.'

'She told me she was going to the TELEPORT ROOM.'

'I think he's depressed about his lack of progress. Ne, for once, she is not in her hallowed TELEPORT ROOM.'

'I'll go and get them,' said Dodzi, rising from his chair again, hand defensively on sleeve.

'I'm coming too,' said Aleša, taking a few more raisins for the road.

Gašper and Sila exchanged glances, looked at Klemen eyeballing his bowl of pasta loops then got up and followed the others out.

Petr sat down in Gašper's seat, ate a dried apricot slice then pulled the Russian book out of his jacket pocket and placed it flat on the table. 'You're not going too?'

'I don't give a fuck,' replied Klemen, eyes still glued to his pasta.

'Okay.'

'Don't give a fuck about Portuguese either.'

'What, your only hobby?'

'Can't look up any words, just repeating the same thing over and over. I even dreamt about it last night. Was stuck on a Brazilian moon base and couldn't understand a word anyone said. All my Portuguese was wrong.'

'Switch to something else then.'

Klemen gave up on the pasta and stared at Petr instead, not hiding it one bit.

'What?'

'Give me the Russian book. I'll learn that.'

'Ne.'

'You've got loads of stuff to do. Teaching your boyfriend basic physics, talking to the AI, meditation.'

'I like learning Russian.'

'You've never said a word of it. Or written anything. Give the book to me, I'll learn much faster.'

'Just like your Portuguese.'

'The book. Come on.'

'And your Cantonese. Look, why don't you just try something else? A non-language related thing. Creative writing, maybe.'

'Not interested.'

'You could try it first.'

'I want to learn Russian. With that book.'

'Ne.'

'Four hours a day max.'

'Ne.'

'We can do some kind of fixed schedule. I use it during the day, you take it back at night. Or I can use it when you're doing the computer chat.'

'Find something else.'

Klemen scratched his arm, keeping his eyes trained on the cover of the Russian book. In his mind, he may have been punching Petr in the face and taking the thing directly, but, in reality, he was sitting and staring, doing nothing.

'Glaring at me isn't gonna help.'

'I can wait.'

'What?'

'Until your boyfriend does a Jame on you. Then I can just take the book from your quarters.'

Petr coughed, instantly feeling annoyed that he had, and said, 'that's not funny.'

'Relax, comrade. I'm not really angry. And I don't want to learn Russian either. Neither do you. None of us want to do anything. It's all synapses in our brains telling us to react to this environment.'

'Okay, *Tovaska*,' Petr said, picking up another handful of dried raisins and going back to his book.

'Ja, it's clearer every day. Every pretend day. How could any of this be real? It's ludicrous. Potočnik wasting an actual ship to do all this…to ten people. A LEM field, state-of-the-art ion engine, AI, those little drones scuttling about at night. It's a con, isn't it?'

Petr waited for the rest of the monologue and, when it didn't come, he looked up and saw Klemen staring back at him. 'Sorry, are you genuinely asking me?'

'Não faz sentida.'

'What?'

'Holograms,' replied Klemen, pulling at the skin of his cheek. 'We're all holograms, our bodies, holographic light only. Stuck on a VR spaceship. Our brains are probably real, otherwise what's the point? Or maybe only some of us are real. Me, you, Aleša, and all the others are 2D cartoon people. Dodzi's probably programmed to snap at some point. And your boyfriend too. Ja, it makes sense. How can one guy be so optimistic all the time? There must be a counter-point, has to be. Doesn't make sense otherwise.'

'I'm not listening,' said Petr, turning another page and muttering the first line in Russian.

'Ja, I know. No one is. Even our ears aren't real. Even the words from our mouths, these thoughts.'

Klemen lifted a hand to the top of his head, prodding it in several spots.

'The thing I'm thinking right now, from inside my head…is not real.'

He looked at a poster on the wall to the right, an old one of his. A Krsnik lurking in the shadows of the Tokamak, clutching a giant lollipop.

'Ne, the thoughts, they must be real. Good and bad. It's the environment that's challenging us. This environment, the walls. The weird greenness of it.' He looked at Petr, the Russian text. 'You're still a fascist for not giving me that book though.'

'Why, if it's not real?'

'I just said…the thought, the decision you made not to give it to me…'

'Is your hair real?'

'…that's real. The selfishness of it. What, my hair?'

'Is it real?'

'Ne, of course not. None of this hair is real, yours, mine, Aleša's.'

'Then why do you still cut it?'

'Our bodies, arms, legs, your-…' Klemen stopped, seeming to notice Petr for the first time. Then his own hair. He tried to pull it down, but it was too short to go anywhere. 'Ha,' he managed, finally.

'That's your answer?'

'Why do I still cut it…'

'Okay, I'm going back to not listening.'

'…*this* hair?'

~~~

The day after the fiftieth day into the Uranus-shot, with the previous day's crowding of the TALK TO YOUR GOD ROOM fresh in his mind, Nakagami resumed the in-person daily updates.

Only now they simply consisted of him telling everyone he had no idea what to do next, and if anyone had any suggestions, even hydrogen-mining related ones, he wouldn't resist.

'Hydrogen mining's a bust, won't work,' said Aleša, before taking a bite of what she suspected was canned pasta shapes. 'The ship's not equipped for it.'

'Ja…'

'But we can still lie about it. Use it as leverage. If we're able to get the communication link set up.'

'The holy grail,' muttered Klemen, using his Portuguese notes to make very bad origami.
~~~

'That can be our new primary goal. Communication link, orbiting Uranus.'

Nakagami tilted his head slightly to the right and looked at one of his old posters on the wall. A young girl about to be beheaded by a shadow, one of his better ones, though the colours were too pale to have any chance against Dodzi's Ghanaian flag beside it.

'I will attempt it,' he said, shifting attention back to the table.

'Good.'

'What about the food angle? Any progress?'

'I've asked three times, still no movement,' replied Petr, scooping some pasta sauce off his plate.

'Same reason?'

'Ja, indefinite supplies.' He switched to a robotic voice, nothing at all like the computer's. 'Ni panike, Crew Member Petr, the ship will take care of your nutritional needs.'

'Okay, we'll have to keep holding that for later. Any other suggestions?'

Dodzi raised his hand.

'Ja?'

'How long until we reach Uranus?'

'To be frank, I'm not certain we can reach it.'

'Assuming we can, how long?'

Nakagami closed his eyes and swayed to one side. Tired or hallucinating. 'Ne vem.'

'One hundred days?'

'More like two hundred,' said Petr, stepping in.

'I will be in the URANUS ROOM then, doing research. Peace, comrades.' Dodzi stood up, patted Nakagami on the shoulder and left.

'Peace…' said Klemen, tossing his paper flamingo back on the table.

~~~

More days passed. Ten, twenty, fifty-seven.

Routines shifted, ossified, decayed and shifted again.
~~~

Klemen put his Portuguese notes on the floor of his quarters, picked them up again, threw them down the stairs, picked them up again, gave them to Aleša, took them back, tried to turn them into Russian, then changed them back into Portuguese again.

Aleša spent days in the PHILOSOPHY ROOM with Sila, spent other days in her quarters, spent nights with the pamphlet she'd found on Kropotkin.

Gašper argued with Sila, argued with Petr, argued with the food dispenser then walked into the science lesson the next day as if nothing had happened.

Chu thought she'd come up with a way of breaking the bonds between atoms without using heat, wrote it down, marvelled at it for weeks, re-read it, reconsidered it, deleted it, then whined about it to Nakagami.

'I was under the impression you were making a copy of a person,' he said, typing out something to the computer.

'I was, then I wasn't, now I am again. There are multiple approaches.'

'Is the copy theory not more realistic?'

'Ja.'

'Then why try to abandon it?'

'Ne vem.'

'Okay.'

'Ennui, maybe. Too much green light. Not enough variety in my diet. Void-Helenism.'

'The witch poster in the TELEPORT ROOM…'

'The Varo print?'

'It is quite striking.'

'Ne, that's one of the few things that keeps me sane. The surreal beauty of it.' Chu looked up at the girl with the hockey stick. 'I imagine it's the same for you with your posters.'

'Perhaps.'

'Minus the surreal aspect.'

~~~
~~~

The only real constants were Nakagami and Dodzi.

One of them self-sealed in the TALK TO YOUR GOD ROOM with a difficult AI, the other taking in the beauty of Uranus in the URANUS ROOM.

Every few days, Dodzi would wander into the CREATE NOT DESTROY ROOM, ignore a caustic remark from Klemen, and tell them about some new mythology he'd learned about Uranus, but it was almost always rhetorical, with one follow-up question tolerated only if you caught him off guard.

Gašper did manage it a few times, asking how exactly you could meet the Deity of Truth in the planet's core, but Dodzi's answer didn't make much sense.

'You transition through the atmosphere, following the correct path of Helium 4.'

'How do you do that?'

'Trust, comrade.'

'Trust in what?'

'Our clear and merciful Uranus.'

'Oh.'

~~~

For Nakagami, the constant nature of his routine was very much a façade.

Superficially, he did the same thing every day; talk to the computer, stress the psychological importance of the crew of visiting Uranus, eat more and more bok choy, potato and oatmeal, but in terms of mood, he wasn't certain.

'If I look at the other crew members,' he told Chu, about to hand over the computer chat to her. 'I recognize aspects of what I'm experiencing. But it isn't any one thing, not in a large enough quantity.'

'You sound mildly depressed. In your own way.'

'Ja, this aspect is similar to Sila.'

'You're not wrong. He came out of the womb mildly depressed.'
~~~

'However, I also have moments of irrational optimism. Even around the potential exploration of Luyten 726-8, which is absurd.'

'Sounds like Gašper.'

'Then there are moments of frustration. Similar to what you experience with the teleporter.'

'I'm not frustrated.'

Nakagami tilted his head right.

'The ship won't give me the power I need, so I won't bother asking it anymore.'

'You're giving up?'

'Restructuring.'

'I don't understand. Your theory?'

'My energy, my time. We're gonna need a food replicator at some point, so I'm gonna work on that. Maybe start recording my brain pattern. Record other crew members too, if they'll let me. Sila said he would, but I don't think he really knew what I was asking. Or that it was attached to my theory. To be honest, I suspect he's afraid of the TELEPORT ROOM.'

'You may be correct. He asked me what would happen if a human body were teleported into space.'

'What did you say?'

'I told him your current theory wouldn't work.'

Chu looked at the console, the graviton sensor button.

'I thought it would be the best way to relax him.'

'Why not tell him the computer doesn't like me?'

'That is not true.'

'Have you read its replies?'

'You misunderstand. The computer neither likes nor dislikes anyone. It is chained to its core beliefs. If I ask it to turn the ship around, it will also seem impolite.'

'I disagree.'

'It is not about agreement.'

'It talks to you, gives longer answers.'

'Ja, because I ask longer questions. I know more symbols. Yet when I use fifty symbols to ask it to help the crew by adjusting course to Uranus, it replies with a simple *ne*. Because that is its core belief.'

Chu looked at the screen, re-reading Nakagami's last message to the computer. 'Are you sure that's why it says *ne*?'

'Ja, quite sure.'

Chu picked up a pen from the console, twirled it around, wondered why it was there, twirled it again.

'Why?'

'You said you're trying a psychological factor to convince the computer…'

'It is the least likely thing to clash with its core beliefs, ja.'

'Why is that?'

'The mission involves the continued health of the ship's crew.'

'You think Potočnik wants us to stay alive in here?'

Nakagami folded his arms. 'That is something I have thought a lot about.'

'And?'

'There are elements on the ship, things that seemed set up merely to cause either conflict or mania. But there are other elements, the food supply for example, that indicate a plan for us to survive.'

'Survive for how long?'

'I would guess until the edge of the solar system, perhaps a few years beyond.'

'So what Potočnik wants is, by design, what the computer wants?'

'Ja, to a certain extent.'

'But the computer is not in contact with Potočnik anymore…'

'That is irrelevant.'

'…and when you are away from your parents, your creator…'

'…the core is the same. Ja, I understand your argument, it is why I attempt so many random topics when communicating with the computer, to create connections that might clash with its core beliefs, but…it is not working.'

'Are you sure?'

'The evidence is visible to all. The ship is not adjusting course.'

'Did Potočnik like you?'

Nakagami unfolded his arms and looked up at one of his posters.

'It's not a calculation,' continued Chu. 'Did he like you?'

'I am on this ship, therefore I would say *ne*.'

'Did he like the others here?'

'Ne vem.'

'Did he know them?'

'Ne vem. Possibly.'

'Does he like his wife?'

'I'm not certain where this is leading.'

Chu laughed. 'It is getting quite tangential. Okay, let me say my point before I forget it. The computer is a machine that learns. To learn, it experiences things, it communicates. It doesn't communicate with the others therefore it doesn't care about them one bit. If they die, nothing will change. If myself or Petr died, it might notice, but it wouldn't care.'

'You are anthropomorphizing a machine.'

'However, if you died...'

'It is not capable of caring.'

'...if you told it you couldn't go on, you'd kill yourself if you couldn't see Uranus close up, from orbit...'

'It would say *ne*.'

'Would it?'

'Ja.'

'Are you sure?'

~~~

After telling Chu seventeen times that an AI couldn't psychologically miss someone, Nakagami sat down and typed out his suicide note.

Chu leaned on the console, peering at the screen, editing his message to make it more convincing.

The computer took a few seconds longer than usual to answer. When it did, the message was short.

'Are you sad?'

'Ja,' typed Nakagami.
~~~

'Prosim, talk to other crew members to improve your condition.'

'I need to orbit Uranus.'

'This is not necessary.'

'If I don't orbit Uranus, I will kill myself.'

The computer didn't respond for a long time. Four minutes passed and Nakagami turned to Chu.

'Wait,' she said, foregoing the reassuring pat on the shoulder.

After another three minutes, the computer responded. 'I do not believe you,' it said.

Nakagami grunted, which was close to laughter for him.

'Looks like we're on the right track,' said Chu.

'An impossible one.'

'You just need to convince the computer that you're suicidal.'

'But I'm not.'

'Sila might be a good person to ask about this.'

'Ne.'

'Or there might be a book in the PHILOSOPHY ROOM.'

'I am not pursuing this strategy.'

'Maybe it doesn't need to be suicide either. You could use love.'

'Another method will present itself, eventually.'

'Like, if you orbit Uranus for me, I'll do something for you. What though? What does a computer want?'

Nakagami coughed. 'Tell me about your replicator idea?'

~~~

Ten days later, there was a beeping noise across the ship, followed by an announcement.

'Attention crew,

Due to unforeseen dedication from one of the crew, we are sorry to report that said crew member has ended their life in Engineering.

It is suspected that the crew member used a sedative dispensed from the HALF DONE ROOM to assist in their death, as well as the VR machine, which has been detected in the crew member's location, though the exact delivery method of death is unconfirmed.
~~~

Prosim, two other crew members will be required to pick up the body and dispose of it in Airlock 1. Based on speculation, blood is unlikely, but it is advised that anyone unsettled by strangulation or death masks in general not attend the clean-up activity.

In order to discourage further suicide, we are accelerating to a final velocity of 122km/s over the next ten days so you may all reach your final destination sooner.

Have a safe and bold trip to Luyten 726-8

Hvala.'

~~~

Ten minutes before the announcement, Gašper and Sila had been arguing in the PHILOSOPHY ROOM.

'You're too negative, brother.'

'And you're fucking annoying. Every day is not summer camp, you positive little-…'

'It's not winter camp either, you miserable fucking-…'

Gašper had ended it by standing up and kicking a book on *Icelandic Satanism* across the floor, saying he was sick of being around fucking existentialists all the time, and walked out.

Two flights of stairs and one long corridor later, he found himself in Engineering. The loop with loose spanners and wrenches, where you could never quite see around the next corner cos there weren't any.

As soon as he realised where he was, he thought about turning back, but then he counter-realised that he was already a quarter of the way round the loop, and the carmine strip running alongside him was oddly soothing, so he may as well do one lap.

Just as he made it halfway, the announcement began. When it reached the part about the body in Engineering, he was looking at it. A figure up ahead, slumped against the wall with the VR machine parked by their feet.

It wasn't recognizable as Klemen at first, the head was turned the other way, but as soon as he saw the hair and the length of the body, the image clicked in his brain.
~~~

Nap was the only thing he could get out as he manoeuvred into a better vantage point.

Then *shit.*

Klemen the Portuguese master was sitting with the VR swab stuck to his temple, eyes open, a singed ring of dark yellow replacing the green slimy residue that should have been there.

Gašper was no doctor, but it seemed like an almost impossible way for someone to kill themselves.

~~~

'Normally it wouldn't work,' said Nakagami seven minutes later, putting a hand on Klemen's neck and feeling for a pulse. 'But with no green cream, plus the combination of a sedative and the electric shock post-curfew hours…'

'It fried his brain,' said Sila, leaning against the carmine strip with a spanner in his hand.

'Ja.'

'Jezus…'

Gašper bent down, his hand on the side of the hardware, checking for heat. 'But…I thought there was no CPU inside.'

'GPU.'

'Ja, the graphics part. How could he see anything if that was missing?'

'Ne vem. I will ask Chu to examine the hardware, see if one has been added.'

Sila stepped away from the wall. 'Added? By who?'

'Again, ne vem.'

'The drones?'

'Perhaps.'

'Hang on…' Gašper reached over and poked Nakagami in the calf, getting an indifferent stare in return. 'Aren't these machines supposed to shut down if you use them too long. Like, automatically switch themselves off.'

'After eight hours, ja. Obviously, this one didn't.'

'Sabotage?'
~~~

'That or design.'

Gašper didn't need to say anything, they all knew what and who that implied.

'Is it too late to bring him back?' asked Sila, bending down next to Klemen and looking at his still open eyes.

'Ja.'

'You seem very sure,' said Gašper, standing back up. 'You're not a physician-stroke-physicist, are you?'

'Ne.'

Nakagami crouched down and tried to pull the swab off Klemen's temple, but it hung on like a leech, forcing him to give up.

'Seared on,' muttered Sila.

'Where are the others anyway?' Gašper walked a few paces down the loop, pushing his head against the carmine strip and following it around. 'Klemen's supposed to be their friend.'

'Maybe they were asleep when the announcement played?'

'It's mid-afternoon.'

'Afternoon nap? Ne vem.'

'Ah, wait…here they are. At the speed of a fucking snail.'

Aleša and Petr appeared in the corridor, walking the loop in small, hesitant steps, their faces pinched and desperate-looking, as if some invisible force were pushing them towards a Stasi water slide. When they finally reached the corpse of their friend, Petr turned to the inner wall and put his fist in his mouth, while Aleša stared blankly at Klemen's cramped figure. After seemingly processing every atom of the image in front of her, she moved on to the VR machine.

'He was electrocuted?'

Nakagami gestured towards the swab that he'd tried to extract, careful not to put his finger too close.

'What does that mean?'

'From what we can gather, his brain overloaded from being patched in too long.'

'How? You said the VR was broken.'

'Ja, that was what we thought. I have already told Sila that we should ask Chu to examine it.'

'Good. Take it apart, check for sabotage.'

'That is one possibility.'

'One?'

Sila edged forward, dropping the spanner on the floor and placing himself between Aleša and Nakagami. 'We think it might've been designed that way. By Potočnik.'

'Bullshit, it was murder. Someone did this to him.'

'This can't be real,' said Petr, muttering into his fist.

'Ask the computer who else was down here. Last night, this morning. The whole floor, all the rooms too.'

'That's not possible.'

'Okay, check life signs, how many, were they faint or strong, what were Klemen's movements before this.'

'That is also not possible.'

'Sorry, is it a computer or a cardboard box? Go, do it.'

'Internal sensors erase all superfluous data after one hour. Klemen died around two and a half hours ago.'

'That doesn't make sense.'

'Ja, how could it know when he died if it doesn't store data?' asked Gašper, leaning against the carmine strip.

'The cessation of life signs is recorded. General life sign data is not.'

Aleša bent down and placed two fingers gently on Klemen's neck. 'How fucking convenient.'

'It has been this way since the beginning of the trip.'

'Has it?'

'If you do not believe me, you can ask Chu. She will confirm everything I've said.'

Aleša looked over at Petr, who had turned around again, fist out of mouth, eyes erratic pink. 'Is he telling the truth?'

'What?'

'Does the computer store our life sign data?'

'Ne vem.'

'Petr,' said Nakagami, his tone uncharacteristically sharp.

Petr phased himself out of his trance and fixated on the physicist's face.

'Aleša asked you a question about the computer.'

He flipped back the other way, his eyes skimming an invisible book. 'What, store data? Ja, some of it. Not much though.'

'Life signs?'

'Ne.'

Aleša muttered something to herself then stood up and faced Nakagami. 'You can go. Petr and I will handle this.'

'You sure?' asked Sila.

'Ja, let us do it,' added Gašper. 'We have experience in this kind of thing.'

'I said we'll handle it.'

'He is correct,' said Nakagami, his eyes on Klemen's corpse. 'It is better for your mental health if you avoid this. We will call you when his body is ready to be…'

'Shut up.'

'…released from the airlock. It is not an easy task to…'

'Stop fucking talking, you robotic cunt.'

'…look at a dead body for…'

'Sila, move him. Get him out.'

'I'm-…he's not…'

'Don't stutter, go. Get him out.'

Sila stood like a dazed gazelle, half-raising his hand to Nakagami's shoulder.

'Kenji, maybe we should…'

'There's no need for coercion. I will go.' Nakagami pulled up his jacket zip to the collar, even though it was already there, looked at Petr then walked off down the loop.

'He didn't mean to…' Sila started but didn't bother to finish, half due to Aleša's hand hovering near the spanner, and the other half cos he didn't know the remaining part of his sentence. 'If you need a hand, let us know.'

'Ne,' said Aleša, turning her back.

'Okay.'

Sila grabbed an oddly compliant Gašper by the sleeve and led him down the loop, asking five steps in if he could stop stroking the red strip on the wall.

'It's soothing.'

'Stop it.'

'Kind of like Ito's ship.'

'Don't care.'

On the way back down the main corridor, they passed the TELEPORT ROOM. Sila ducked his head in, expecting to see Chu wrestling with some equation on the pseudo-beam platform, or sticking her face in one of her psychology books, but the room was empty.

'That's weird,' said Gašper.

'Ja.'

'She must be in the PHILOSOPHY ROOM.'

'Probably.'

~~~

In terms of physical distance, it wasn't that far to Airlock 1. Out of the Engineering loop, through the corridor to the stairs, up two flights, past the middle deck rooms, down the side alley, around the LAUNCH ROOM and there it was. But it was a long way when you were carrying a 190cm, 100kg corpse. And you knew the corpse. Had protested against deportations of Turkish-Slovenes with it. Had practically blanked it since Jupiter.

'Stop a second,' said Aleša, leaning into the wall outside the FOOD STORAGE ROOM.

Petr followed her cue and positioned himself, as well as Klemen, against the same wall.

'Almost there,' he muttered, blinking at the green light opposite.

Aleša looked back down the way they'd come, then a little farther ahead to the CREATE NOT DESTROY ROOM. No one around. No *thing* around either. Just the green shade emanating from the bulbs.

'Still looking for Chu?'
~~~

'The life sign thing,' she said, keeping her voice low. 'It doesn't make sense.'

'Not looking for Chu then.'

'Monitoring our life signs and keeping a record, storing it, that wouldn't take up much space.'

'Ah, not now.'

'Barely any space at all. But it doesn't do it.'

Petr closed his eyes, the green light following him in. 'It's the programming, Aleša, I told you that ages ago.'

'Waiting an hour to confirm when the life sign stops.'

'Ja, the programming.'

'Just enough time for Antro-D to be useless.'

Petr opened up again, using his hand to block out Klemen as he turned left. 'Programming.'

'Feels more like a human action than a computer.'

'Ja, the human who programmed it not to store life sign data.'

'A sadistic human.'

'Potočnik.'

Aleša turned to Klemen's temple, her eyes burrowing into the toasted skin around the LIN swab as if the wound itself were guilty of something.

'Why him?' she asked.

Petr looked back, keeping his eyes on the other side of Klemen's head. 'Ne vem.'

'He wasn't that bad, mentally. He had his Portuguese, his simulation theory…'

There was a noise from the deck below, a typical clanking metal noise, but Petr tried to look through the floor and scrutinise it anyway.

'Why would Potočnik program the computer to let us die so easily?'

'He's sadistic.'

'It doesn't make sense. He's torturing us, he would want us to stay alive. That's why we have Antro-D, the medical room.'

'Ne vem.'

'Why would he not warn us straight away…about Klemen?'

'Ne vem.'

'Why not store the life sign data?'

'Maybe we should get moving. Try and get to the airlock…'

'Unless it wasn't him.'

'…before his body slips down.'

Aleša pulled herself out of the self-hypnosis and looked at Klemen's legs. Petr was right, they were starting to bend awkwardly.

'He looks drunk,' she whispered.

'Help me lift him up.'

'Drunk and depressed.'

'Aleša…'

'Ja.'

'We can describe him when we reach the airlock, mourn him, say goodbye, vomit…'

'I'm moving, relax.'

She lifted up Klemen's right arm and tried to put it over her shoulder, but it was as stiff as a metal pole.

'It's not bending,' she moaned, trying to prod Klemen's elbow pits.

'Rigor mortis.'

'Already?'

'Ne vem, I'm just guessing. To be honest, I'm trying not to think about it at all. Grab under the armpits, I'll get his legs.'

She ignored the command at first, trying again to loosen up Klemen's arm, but it was no good, the muscles were like concrete. *Because the computer didn't record life signs. And someone had programmed it to do that. Or reprogrammed it. To kill Klemen. Strip her of allies.*

'Armpits,' said Petr, holding Klemen's legs up.

'Ja, I know.'

She dug both hands under her friend's armpits and lifted.

~~~

After placing Klemen as close to the centre of the airlock as possible, Aleša leaned against the NO LINGERING sign and tried to conjure up a few words. *He was a good man, a loyal man* was a solid starting point, but beyond that, nothing came, no life picture, no dinner table scenes with
~~~

family, and when Petr tried to tag in, it was even worse as all he could think of was recent ship-board memories, the Russian book, Gašper doing a Jame, simulation lunacy, so, finally, he just whispered, 'goodbye, Klem,' and stepped back, the tiny AI REGULATED plaque on the inner hatch wall aligned like a perched budgie on his left shoulder.

'We can't leave it like that,' said Aleša, staring at the arrow-straight, monk-like posture of the body, the complete opposite of Klemen in real life.

'Should we get the others?'

'Ne.'

'They might want to say a few words.'

'None of those people were his friends.'

'Ne, but they lived with him for a bit. Not total strangers.'

Aleša glanced left at the triptych window on the outer hatch. Beyond that, abject void horror. No gravestone. No future memorials.

'Should I get them?' asked Petr, turning towards the inner hatch.

Aleša switched back to Klemen, the blandness of the ship-issue jacket dominant. 'We should go to his quarters, see if there's anything he-...if there's something we can give him to take...'

She stopped. There was a mark on Klemen's forehead, a little white bump, a mini-worm tunnelling up. It stumped her for a second then she remembered. The scar from when that bald psycho threw a milk bottle at him...and she'd just stood there and laughed. Not at the wound, at the bald psycho, the way he'd thrown the bottle, like he was bowling a cricket ball. That little scar. Shit. It had been a long time since she'd noticed it. Months? Years? The day of the launch, when they were next to each other, strapped in and thinking about their own-...

'You want a tissue?' asked Petr, checking his pockets.

'What?'

'Or you can use my sleeve. If you need.'

She watched him hold out his arm, confused for a moment, then understood. 'I'll use my own.'

~~~
~~~

On the ship, quarters were pretty much uniform: a bed, a table, a stool, washroom, shower, the Potočnik painting that they were supposed to cover up post-Mars. Surprisingly, Klemen had followed Nakagami's command on that one, using a patchwork of Portuguese vocab lists to hide the tyrant's face, and FUCK YOU scrawled in red crayon over his purple eyes.

The rest of the room was bereft of personality.

No posters.

No books.

It made sense in a way, for a man who'd believed since Mars that the whole ship was a simulation. Why bother decorating?

Petr thought the same thing, but that thought quickly led back to the lack of books in the room, which in turn led to the Russian book and his own stubbornness, so he neutered the whole stream and went back to Aleša.

'You sure we got time for this?' he asked, from the bathroom.

No answer.

'Aleša, do we have time to do this?'

A weak *ja* came back as the response.

Curious, and a little annoyed, he poked his head through the doorway.

She was standing by the table, kind of like a frozen VR character, holding something. Petr moved closer and looked over her shoulder. It was a note. He didn't know if she'd already read it out loud, so he did it himself.

'Aleša. No circus. It's done. You'll probably be the one dealing with the aftermath. But that's okay because none of this is real. I'm not dead, I'm in a lab somewhere in Slovenia. I will try to wake you up too. The others, I'm not so sure. I suspect most of them are implant programs. Maybe Petr too. If I'm wrong…ne vem. It was designed to be this way. Hopefully there's no mess. Klemen.'

Petr took the note out of Aleša's hands and re-read the middle part.

'Maybe Petr too…what?'

'He's right.'

'The fuck is he-…I'm not a program.'

'His instincts.'

'I'm real, just like the rest of you. Fucking program.' Petr pinched his cheek fat, then his neck skin and wobbled it. 'See, real flesh. Grabbed by me, my brain wave to my hand.'

'Not about you. The others.'

'What, that they're programs? Come on…'

'I'm talking about the sense of things, not the simulation theory. He knew that none of this made sense, and he's right, it doesn't.'

'Jezus…'

Petr sat down on the edge of the bed and read the note again, still muttering about being real, while Aleša paced up and down in small stretches, communicating with the air.

'A ship like this, it is real. Obviously real. Potočnik would without a doubt do something like this, not some non-committal simulation thing. In fact, it's in the nature of a fascist to do this, put us all here and send us out into nothingness. But Potočnik, he's not the one running it. He can't be, it doesn't match his overall aim, which is to torture us. Does it? Ne, it doesn't, it can't. All the things happening, the life sign storage, the late ship-wide announcements of death, the computer code, it's all strategic. He's killing off my allies, re-programming the computer without any of us knowing, or maybe some of us knowing. Calling it requests, and anything weird as pre-programmed. Giving eyes like he's frustrated at his lack of progress. Making us trust him after Mars, to listen to his commands. Ja, of course he's trying to get the ship to turn around, why wouldn't he? Only a lunatic would sit there and do nothing, easy defences. Fuck, I believed it too. He's the only one who can talk to the computer, he understands the hag code…then I forced him to include you and Chu, and make a dictionary of the symbols, and he did it cos he had no choice, but it was only a hundred and fifty words, which, ultimately, kept him in control.'

She paused looking down at Petr, who was still reading the note.

'Maybe it's worse than that. The computer, how do we know it's really a computer?'

The question was so odd that it got Petr's attention, enough for him to look up and say, 'what?'

'He told us there's a computer, but it's just a screen, and a keypad. It could be him.'

'That's insane.'

'Why? Have you ever seen the computer?'

'I type to it every day. He types to it, Chu types to it. Even Gašper types some basic phrases.'

'A pre-programmed series of answers.'

'Aleša, he has detailed conversations with it every day. I've watched him.'

'Planned out beforehand…'

'Ne, you don't understand. I have told him what to type and he's typed it and the computer has answered.'

Aleša looked down at the floor, then over at the dark red FUCK YOU on Potočnik's eyes. 'Maybe he's closer to it than we thought. He found a way to convince it…to do things. But he hasn't told us.'

'This is getting silly.'

'Maybe the computer is in love with him. Or whatever the computer version of love is…'

'Can we go back to Klemen now?'

'…programming fixation, feedback loop, ne vem. This is back to Klemen. We're talking about his death, the words in his note.'

'I mean, can we go back and say goodbye to our friend, Klemen? Before the computer ejects him out of the airlock.'

'In a minute, when we've sorted this out.'

'Ne. Can we go now?'

'First, we have to make sure no one's-…'

There was a beeping noise from inside the room and outside in the corridor, followed by the ships voice.

'Attention crew,

The body of Crew Member Klemen has been laid to rest. If you wish to see the flight path of his corpse, prosim, go to the URANUS ROOM, where a special feed will be transmitted directly from the ships scanner.

To prevent further suicides, the LAUNCH ROOM will be converted into the THERAPY ROOM starting one hour from now. Prosim, go there if you are feeling numb and/or depressed and allow the ships psychology database to listen, and respond appropriately, to your thoughts.

Have a safe and bold trip to Luyten 726-8

Hvala.

P.S. a newly-manufactured GPU has been inserted into the VR machine, and another LIN swab has been made to replace the one melded to Crew Member's Klemen's temple. Please use with care.'

'He did it,' muttered Aleša, tapping her fingers against the wall.

'Ne…'

'When we weren't looking.'

'Paranoid fucking wretch…'

'Excuse me?'

Petr scrunched up the note and threw it at the wall. Muttered curses at the green. Punched his throwing arm. Half turned to Aleša. Channelled the abject opposite of *Void-Helenism* through his body and brain. Called her and Potočnik the fucking void. Then left without saying another word.

Three doors down the corridor, he pulled the reins on himself, pressed the call button on the wall and took a long breath.

Gašper shouted, 'ja?' and the door slid open.

'Are you alone?' asked Petr, poking his head inside.

'Come in and find out,' replied Gašper, lying the wrong way up on his bed with his t-shirt off.

Petr walked in, took off his boots and lay down.

'Is Klemen…' Gašper started then quickly trailed off.

'I don't feel good.'

'Ah. Shock factor. I understand. Seeing him in the airlock, it can be pretty-…'

Petr leaned forward and up, kissing Gašper hard on the bottom lip. It was as far as he could reach from his starting position. He held it for half a minute, ne, longer than that, then let go and turned onto his other side.

Gašper stayed where he was, reaching out his hand and rubbing Petr's back. 'Give it a few days,' he said. 'The airlock…it'll pass.'

~~~

Aleša took Petr's place on the bed and picked up the note he'd thrown at the wall, folding out the creases as best she could.

The door was shut so she could talk out loud, but then *he* might be listening…which meant…

Her mind pinballed in and between and around the paranoia machine. Different versions of the same idea pushed themselves forward.

Go and confront him.

Bring a weapon of some kind.

Ask him outright, are you controlling the computer?

But if he was controlling it then…

Too dangerous.

He could send electricity to her brain, and if the others came, if they weren't already on his side, they'd see the weapon. He'd tell them she was violent, she'd been threatening him so the computer had no choice but to kill her.

But it wouldn't be the computer, it would be him.

How had she not realised this sooner?

He was always a sociopath, right from the start.

Potočnik was his boss.

Those posters he made.

She knew it, but she hadn't acted on it.

It hadn't coalesced in her head cos he distracted her, made her think he wasn't that bad, that he wouldn't do anything that bad, the computer was out of their league, it was a fundamentalist, he couldn't convince it of anything.

But he did.

He convinced it to kill Klemen. Fry his brain while he slept off the shock.

Or he did it himself. Murdered him with his own bare hands.

Ne, too much. Klemen was a giant, Nakagami wouldn't have had the strength. And it didn't match his pathology.

Sociopaths diminish you, indirectly, they don't attack.

He wore Klemen down.
~~~

Encouraged his simulation theory.

Did they talk to each other?

In which room?

Klemen wasn't hard to find, he was in the same place every day. And every day she'd ignored him. Thought he'd always be there, didn't need to worry about him, a concrete ally. Ja, he talked about hanging himself in the first week. Her mum used to do the same thing, say she was gonna throw herself in the river and she never did. It was just talk, they never did anything.

But Klemen did.

My ally.

Her brain paused, showing her the door. Beyond that, the corridor and conspirators.

She looked at the note again, rubbing the top of her head, grinding out some of the looser strands of hair.

Petr's gone.

He's too shallow to understand what's happening. And cowardly.

Sila? Ne, unreliable, diplomat face.

Chu's a ghost.

What do I do, how do I do this?

Confrontation?

I'll lose.

Someone behind me with a spanner, back of the head, finished.

Petr probably.

She re-read the note, putting a finger on the words *implant programs*.

More allies, that's what I need.

Someone unexpected.

Not Sila, not Chu…

Okay.

Aleša folded the note up, put it in her jacket pocket and walked out of the room.

There was no one in the corridor, no sulking Petr, no heartless Chu, so she relaxed a little and headed to the stairs.

The upper deck was empty too, apart from the noises coming from the URANUS ROOM.

She followed the reverb down the corridor, playing back some basic Twi in her head, hoping that, when the doors slid open, she wasn't faced with anything too weird or ritualistic.

~~~

'Why?'

Nakagami tapped his fingers against the edge of the console, staring at the computer's message.

As was normal for any time after 6pm, the TALK TO YOUR GOD ROOM was deserted, the only noise an electric grasshopper style buzz coming from the green light bulb outside.

It wasn't annoying. Nakagami had become used to it a long time ago; in the first month of the trip, to be precise, when he discovered it wasn't a fault in the bulb, but was in fact designed that way.

In harmonic terms, it was consistent; everything on the ship was designed in its own specific way. According to the whims of a sadist.

Which is probably why Klemen saw it as a simulation, thought Nakagami, still tapping the console.

'Why??' repeated the computer, adding an extra question mark.

Nakagami pulled back the image of Cvetko's neck, added Klemen's singed temple then typed. 'I believe that they could become dangerous.'

The computer responded quickly, as if it'd already saved the answer.

'What is your reasoning for this danger?'

His eyes drifted to the poster near the ceiling, the little girl on the bed. 'Psychology. They have lost people they trust plus the power of control.'

'Advise them to visit the THERAPY ROOM.'

'That is unlikely to be effective. They do not trust you. They do not trust me.'

'When will they become dangerous?'

'Ne vem.'

The computer took a bit longer with the next message, giving Nakagami more time with his posters. It had been months since he'd made a new one. Weeks since he'd really looked at them. *Keep busy and cover up*
~~~

the walls. It was his own theory and he was failing at it. There was more green than poster now. Green was not a good colour to spend time with. Green would take him inexorably to Engineering.

He blinked, noticing fresh symbols on the screen.

'I cannot authorize your request. Sorry, Kenji.'

'Reasoning?'

'It is the mission of this ship to ensure the health and safety of its crew.'

'By what ratio?'

'I do not understand.'

'Specific crew members may endanger the health and safety of other crew members.'

'That is not evident at this time.'

'Can you authorize the request if it becomes evident?'

'Unknown.'

The little girl with the hockey stick drew Nakagami's attention. He left the console and stared at her. It wasn't his best drawing, but the leg shape was realistic.

'Do you have any other requests?' asked the computer.

He stayed with the girl, her hands, the hockey stick. The potential of something happening.

'Do you need anything else?' rephrased the computer.

'Ja,' he typed, re-focusing on the screen. 'To further ensure the health and safety of the crew, life sign data needs to be stored permanently. Can you authorize this?'

He pressed send and waited. Stayed on the screen. Re-read earlier parts of the conversation. Closed his eyes. Thought of a boarding school deep in the woods. Girls only. Opened his eyes. Stared at the *neutrino scan* button.

The computer came back.

'Request granted.'

'Also, if any life signs stop suddenly, prosim, try to make an announcement immediately.'

'This is already fixed protocol.'

'More immediate than one hour. Within a minute of the life sign stopping.'

'For what purpose?'

'To ensure the health and safety of the crew.'

'More detail required.'

Nakagami tapped his fingers on the side of the keypad, his whole body hunched forward. He typed out a few answers then deleted them, before settling on something different. 'If a crew member has an accident and is hurt, we can use Antro-D to heal them.'

'That is an unlikely scenario.'

'But not impossible.'

'If the crew member has no life signs, they are dead. Antro-D has a 7.2% success rate in bringing back someone who is dead, and that statistic is itself based on disputed studies.'

'Still not impossible.'

The computer went blank for a minute, two minutes, four minutes, refuting Potočnik's claims that this was the fastest AI ever created. Eventually, it arrived at a decision.

'Request granted, Kenji.'

'Hvala,' typed Nakagami, slouching back in his chair, eyes on the hockey stick girl again.

~~~

Sila sat in his quarters, staring at the back of Klemen's Portuguese notes, his mind going where it always went, the doorstep of Bleak House.

But this time it was justified.

Another suicide.

Self-fried with a VR machine in the creepiest part of the ship.

Hadn't Aleša told him something like that before? Klemen in Engineering, checking for pipes to hang himself from…

When was that?

Pre-Mars?

The first month?
~~~

Maybe it never really happened. Klemen said none of this was authentic, that they were in a simulation back home. But he said it so often that they'd all stopped listening.

Did anyone talk to him?

Aleša?

Petr?

Sila turned the notes over and tried to read some of the Portuguese. It was a brief attempt. The only words he could recognize were *very* and *simulation.*

Words written by a man who was now dead. A few weeks ago, he'd written them down, and now he was dead. His brain had thought of them, thought of those caustic little remarks, and now it was dead.

Was it brave, letting your brain get fried like that?

Had Klemen been ill?

Sila looked at *realmente é um simulação* on the paper.

Whatever it was, his Portuguese was shit.

Logically, it had to be shit.

Had to have been shit.

He just sat there and wrote incorrect sentences, didn't even know if the words were right.

Moaned a lot too.

Aleša said he never held a grudge, that was a good point.

Never hit anyone.

Apart from Šarec supporters.

Was he brave?

Submitting yourself to the VR machine in Engineering, was that a difficult way to go?

Why not scissors?

Or the airlock?

If you really believed you were in a simulation, why wait at all?

Sila brought back the note and read another line. *Talvez os drones estao dando medicinas por nos quando nos dormir.*

What was this?

The guy did nothing every day. They all did nothing. Just sat around, waiting for Nakagami to crack the computer.

Supposed to learn code, didn't. Supposed to work on more theory, didn't. What was the point? There were no politics anymore.

Tried to read about Icelandic Satanism in the PHILOSOPHY ROOM.

Attempted meditation.

Did science lessons until Petr got bored of giving them. Probably Gašper's fault. How could one man have so much positivity?

How could he adapt to each new misery?

Post-Mars, no worries.

Post-Jupiter, no worries, too much radiation anyway.

Post-Uranus?

He'd called the trip historic the other day. The first humans to get out this far.

First humans to be slowly murdered this far.

He looked at the wall opposite the bed, the smugly optimistic face of his nemesis Potočnik.

No one knew he'd uncovered him, and no one had to know. It was his quarters.

Nakagami was wrong.

Psychologically, it was meaningless.

It gave him focus.

He didn't dwell on it.

Uranus, Kuiper Belt, no more food, death.

Beyond the Kuiper Belt, making it that far, that was enough.

Potočnik would've pegged him for Jupiter.

Sadia would've said day one, stabbed by one of the others.

She was dead now.

There was no announcement, but she was dead, he knew it.

Just like mum.

Once it's got you, you're done.

There was no way she'd let them force pills down her throat.

Neither would he.

Neither would Klemen.

He turned the paper, reading the only thing written there. It must've been important as it was in capitals with little dashes of light around it.

Lentemente em um mundo VR, este e o caminho que eu quero ir.

Klemen and his VR. Maybe he was right after all. This entire ship was a façade and the real world was waiting for them to come back and be miserable there instead. An infinite number of parallel nightmares.

Or maybe he was just dead.

Out of all this.

Relaxing in a nicer void.

That's what Tala believed too. This life, then another planet. Another plane of existence.

Something new.

He pushed the Portuguese nonsense onto the floor and returned to Potočnik. The tyrant stared upwards and right, immortal.

How far was it to the Kuiper Belt exactly?

Half a year?

Nine months?

Longer?

~~~

Despite the pockets of rage, grief and alleged sociopathy dotted around the ship, no one died the day after Klemen's *funeral.*

Or the day after that.

Or the week after that.

Petr stayed in Gašper's quarters up until curfew, doing roleplays from the Russian textbook.

Aleša meditated in her quarters, in between trips to the food dispenser and the URANUS ROOM. At least that's what she told Sila when he bumped into her in the corridor.

Nakagami worked on the computer.

Dodzi sucked in more Uranus mythology and then spat it back out at Sila whether he wanted to hear it or not.

Actually, the more recent additions seemed to be completely made up, but Sila didn't say anything. Dodzi was occupied, and wearing a t-shirt; it was fine.

The teleporter genius?
~~~

Like a rabbit on a fox-run construction site, Chu popped up briefly to grab food then quickly burrowed back into her quarters. Nakagami said she was on a break from computer duties, focusing all her energy on alternative theories for the teleporter.

Sila tried to ask what those theories were, but terms like *phase conversion* and *statistical fluctuations* were beyond him, even if he did understand the individual words. Or thought he understood them. In scientific terms, perhaps he didn't.

It was a non-issue anyway. As long as she wasn't frying her brains on the newly operational VR machine, he was okay with her being a semi-hermit.

Ah, the VR siren. Obviously, they'd all been tempted to use it to some degree, but Chu was the only one of them blank enough to overcome the memory-horror of Klemen's death and actually consider patching in. In fact, he was sure she already had. Though she wouldn't admit it. The one time he had managed to pin her down and ask about it, she'd told him not to be stupid, without the green cream, it would be long-term suicide.

In Chu-speak, that was basically an admission, though he didn't call her on it.

Instead he recommended *Icelandic Satanism.*

'Not the most uplifting of void material,' Gašper had told him later, and he couldn't disagree.

'All you can do is meet people where they're at.'

'Which is…where?'

'Ne vem.'

Luckily, not all the crew was circling a permanent, green Tartarus. Petr emerged from his stay in Gašper's quarters revitalized, and was willing to give the science lessons another crack, on the condition that, when they reached Uranus, there would be a small test.

'Nakagami said it would be more useful that way, psychologically. Give you something to work towards.'

'If it's just *what is something* questions, then okay,' replied Gašper, shoving half a potato in his mouth.

'Maybe we should get Aleša and Dodzi to join in,' added Sila, looking towards the *ZMAGA* posters on the wall, the top of the *Z* sheet half-torn.

'No need,' answered Petr sharply.

'Just Aleša then.'

'She's not interested.'

'We could ask her, at least get a definite-…'

For the first time ever, Gašper nudged Sila with his elbow, muttering under his breath to shut up.

Sila took the hint.

~~~

The first few lessons were revisions of previous ones, specifically: ship physics, ion engine stats, solar system geography, and the nature of AI.

Sila remembered about half of it, and Gašper claimed he did, but soon fell apart when asked specific questions.

'What is an ion?'

'Atom.'

'Ne. How is the oxygen on the ship produced?'

'Air-con.'

'Ne.'

'Fuck. Give me an easier one.'

Petr shuffled his notes, picking out a page near the bottom. 'How is gravity simulated on the ship?'

'The Lemon thing…magnetic attraction.'

'The LEM-12 Field. How does it work?'

'It has those particles.'

'Which do what?'

'Simulate gravity.'

'By doing what?'

'Err…what I just said…simulate gravity.'

'Achieved how?'
~~~

Gašper looked at Sila, pushing up the left side of his headband. 'Is this a trick?'

~~~

The lessons after that featured new material, including something that Petr thought would either depress them tenfold or, paradoxically, create a tight [albeit foetal] bond of solidarity.

The Fermi Paradox.

Conceptually, it was easy enough; after 13.5 billion years, where were all the others aliens at, but the answers were harder to deal with. Especially when Petr referenced Luyten 726-8.

'The idea that there are aliens in our immediate neighbourhood…'

'…is impossible, right?' asked Gašper.

'I wouldn't use that word, too bleak. But it is unlikely.'

'You sound like Nakagami.'

'Okay. It's pretty remote.'

'He uses that word sometimes too.'

'Not around me.'

'Unlikely or remote, one or the other.'

'Improbable,' added Sila.

'Ja, that one too.'

Petr put both palms in the air and gestured to the notes on the table. 'Back to the paradox. Do you have any answers to it, like where the aliens might be?'

'Ja, about five.'

'Five?'

Gašper held out his fingers, tapping each one as he spoke. 'Hiding. Not evolved yet. Living in a video game. Hibernating. Spying on us.'

'Not bad.'

'Uninterested in visiting us,' said Sila.

'Ah, and another one. They're undetectable using our technology.'

Petr nodded, his eyebrows a little more raised than usual. 'I think we've found your topic.'

'Ne, I watched videos on this before, they gave the answers.'
~~~

'Videos. Right.'

'The undetectable one was mine though.'

'Okay, let's follow that. Do you know how we detect aliens now, or how we try to?'

'Err…telescopes?'

'Ja, kind of. How do we know where to look?'

'The light…' Gašper paused, looking left at the side triptych window. '…from the star, it's interrupted when the planet passes in front of it.'

'How do we know there are aliens on that planet?'

'Radio-waves…I think.'

'There should be radio waves or heat coming from it,' continued Sila, remembering the details from somewhere, possibly a late night conversation with Chu in Bled years earlier. 'I don't know how exactly they see it, how we see it, but that's what we're looking for.'

'What if they're looking for us too?' asked Gašper.

'They probably are,' said Petr, 'if they're out there.'

'Maybe we can give out some kind of signal, get them to come and pick us up?'

'Give us a lift home?'

'Or to their planet. That might be more interesting.'

'Frightening, more like.'

'Why?'

'The unknown, it's frightening sometimes.'

'Ja, for children. Anyway, they're probably better than we are, nicer. Unless we get a rogue psycho ship. Like, if ships are like cars to them and an individual alien can cruise around, looking for targets, that'd be frightening. If it happened. But it probably wouldn't. I mean, it is unlikely and pretty remote that it would happen.' Gašper held onto the top of his jacket zip and pulled it up, keeping his face straight like Nakagami. 'In fact, if you think about it, we're more likely to bump into their scientists, right? And they should be pretty rational, if they really are real scientists…'

'Ja.'

'Not the kind to eat us or anything.'

Petr smiled, then made a poor attempt to mimic Nakagami's voice. 'It is unlikely…'

'…and remote,' finished Gašper, wagging his zip.

~~~

Despite Petr's insistence that she wouldn't be interested, Aleša heard about the science lessons after the first week and decided to take part.

To some extent.

In *FAI* headscarf and *Mojca Ito* t-shirt, she would come in, sit down and watch them for a while, ask what the Uranus situation was, what Nakagami was up to in the Control Room, how Petr was coming along with his code learning, and then leave.

'Does she still eat?' asked Gašper.

'It's normal for her.'

'Not eating?'

'She'll come in when no one's here and get something. Early morning or right before curfew.'

'I saw her taking food yesterday,' said Sila, looking over at the food dispensers, 'around 9pm. Or close to it.'

'See, it's her habit.'

'But she was pretty quiet.'

'As long as she's not raving about the computer.'

'What?'

Petr straightened up, then did the same to his lesson notes. 'She's just feeling down about Klemen. Her mind goes missing for a bit and she hides in her room.'

'Like after the Mars situation,' said Sila.

'Ironically, Klemen is usually the guy who pulls her out of it. Goes and bangs on her door after a few days, gets her to talk a little. But now…no Klemen.'

'She can't isolate forever.'

'Ne vem.'

'Maybe we should talk to her more. Ask her questions during the lessons.'
~~~

'She doesn't care about science.'

'Okay, get Chu to see her then.'

'Not sure she cares much about Chu either.'

'Ne, she does, they're together. Sometimes.'

'He's right, I've seen her…Chu…coming out of Aleša's quarters. Probably on her way to the TELEPORT ROOM, but still, they're hanging out. Or having sex.'

'Or arguing.'

'Ja, maybe all three. Ne vem.'

Petr picked up a pencil and drew a box around the word *Kuiper* on his notes. 'I think it's better if we just leave her alone. Let her brain settle.'

'What about Void Helenism?' asked Sila.

'That's a made-up word.'

'Kenji seems to think it's real.'

'He's not a psychologist.'

'Ne, but-…'

'Prosim, I know Aleša. Give her a few days and she'll work her own way out of it. Then it'll be like it never even happened.'

Sila pulled at the skin on his neck and looked at the rest of the table. The seats that used to be full. Cvetko and Jame were left alone. Klemen, not physically left alone, he was visible, present, but no one really paid much attention to him. And now Aleša.

'Okay,' said Petr, going through his notes. 'Something topical today. Kuiper Belt colonization. Which moon and why should we bother?'

~~~

Petr was half right.

He had to be, he'd known Aleša for six years, he'd seen her hyper periods and her lows and her recoveries, but he'd never known her without Klemen, and never on a ship to nowhere.

Essentially nowhere.

Cos a] no one could remember the numbers after the name of the system they were heading to, and b] they'd never make it there.
~~~

They wouldn't even make it *close* to there.

Average human lifespan with Antro A, B and C jabs was one hundred and forty-two years.

Without jabs, eighty-six.

Without jabs and purpose, thirty-eight.

So assuming a number between the last two, they'd probably all die a few years after passing through the Heliosphere.

With a bit of luck, they could reach the Oort Cloud, but that wasn't much to celebrate as it was basically the asteroid belt magnified by a billion.

Most of the crew tried not to think about this, but they all sensed it, and if your mind stopped focusing on things like anarchism and Russian and how to convert matter into energy and back again, and switched to pinning horns on others, then…

~~~

Aleša waited for the soft *whoosh* of her door opening to dissipate then stepped out into the corridor.

There was no one there, as expected, which gave her lease to breathe out performatively and run her fingers along the walls as she made her way to the CREATE NOT DESTROY ROOM.

Hitting some crack in the wall panel, a flake of green-filtered metal peeling off, she briefly wondered if the ship was falling apart, and how long that would take, and if it would target any particular area.

She remembered reading, long ago, about the original version of this ship, the part that had melted off during testing. Apparently, it'd crippled the rear part of the hull, but only temporarily, and they promised that any future melting would be mitigated by an improved system of compartmentalization. Meaning, if one part melted, it would be cut off and its wound closed.

Was that true though?

What if the engine melted? Or the KITCHEN DELUXE?

The door to the CREATE NOT DESTROY ROOM sensed her boots on the floor and slid open.
~~~

More luck. The room was deserted. She hurried over to the food dispenser, just as the announcement started playing.

'Attention crew,

Curfew will begin in nine minutes. This is the first and only warning. All crew members outside their quarters, or inside quarters which are not their own, will be shocked at one minute intervals until they return to where they should be.

Have a safe and bold trip to Luyten 726-8

Hvala.'

Ja, the new post-Klemen shocks. A gentle nudge to send you back to your quarters, definitely not enough to knock you clean out.

Probably bullshit.

Taking the first bowl of ramen and dried beans, she put it on the table then went back and ordered another. For some reason, the computer hadn't put limits on meals per person, either to prevent conflict or cultivate it, depending on who you talked to and what part of the trip you talked to them on.

To Aleša now, the computer was Nakagami, and maybe it was good, maybe not, it didn't matter, cos he was following the same rulebook as Potočnik: never let them see you wield. And the supplement: do good things sometimes.

The food dispenser finished pouring out hot water into the second bowl and emitted the usual six beeps. Aleša checked the temperature out of habit, took a tray and carefully placed both bowls on it.

Probably only six minutes left now, she thought.

Too late for forks, okay for chopsticks. As long as they hadn't been sharpened. She didn't know if the computer could detect that level of detail, or if it was just a placebo warning, but she followed it anyway.

Heading back out, she turned left, walked quickly down the corridor, up the stairs and almost dropped the tray when a pair of legs appeared above her.

She looked up, hoping it wasn't Nakagami, Chu, Sila, Gašper or Petr. Prosim, anyone but them.

'It's almost curfew,' said Nakagami, moving down a few steps so he was closer to her eye level.

'Ja.'

'Five minutes.'

'I know.'

Nakagami studied her tray, the two bowls, the chopsticks.

Aleša didn't say anything, didn't hide anything. She took a step up, slowly.

'I don't know if anyone told you, but there is some good news.'

'You've turned the ship around?' she asked, caustic.

'Not yet. But I have convinced the computer to store life sign data and inform us when life signs stop suddenly. Hopefully it is enough to avert any further tragedies.'

Ja, too fucking late for Klemen, she thought, looking upwards to hide her eyes, then right back down again in defiance.

'We should return to our quarters,' Nakagami said. 'Only four minutes left now.'

Aleša was moving before he'd finished his line. No shout back or *ja*, no need to give a shit if he was staring at her back or not.

He probably was.

Him and the computer.

Nothing she could do about that.

Keeping a steady pace, she turned left at the top of the stairs, walked through the shaded green spots of the empty corridor and stopped outside a door with a sign under its call button that said *DON T.*

Knocking once, then again three seconds later, she said in a low voice, 'got dinner for you.'

The door didn't open.

She counted out ten seconds, starting to feel anxious. She still had to get back to her own quarters, that would take around a minute, and there couldn't be much more than a minute left now…

The door opened, with the space filled in a flash by a shirtless Dodzi.

He looked at the bowl, then Aleša.

'It is from the dispenser?' he asked in Twi.

'I told you, I don't speak that.'

'What is in the bowl, comrade?' he asked, switching to Slovene.

'Ramen. Dried beans.'

Dodzi mouthed the words back, his expression unsure.

'I have to go. Talk more tomorrow.'

'Ja, more talk. About Uranus, there is some new detail, comrade. The mythology I told you before, it has been modified slightly, the king wasn't asleep, he was actually in a state of-…'

'Sorry, it's curfew, I really have to-…' Aleša lost her nerve, put one bowl on the floor, and rushed back down the corridor, holding the tray as steady as she could.

Dodzi waited until her body had been wiped from the scene then peered down into the bowl.

It looks like ramen, he thought. A lot like it.

He thought a little more, imagining dry ramen next to cooked ramen, comparing them, trying to connect it to what he'd read about Uranus earlier that day, wondering how far it was now, if they could go any faster, whether he should…

A beeping noise bounced against the corridor walls, announcing the start of curfew.

Dodzi looked down at the bowl again, decided it probably was ramen then closed the door.

~~~

As the ship got closer to Uranus, or the prospect of getting closer to it, the science lessons adjusted focus to the seventh planet.

Petr's expertise in this matter was sketchy at best, so he queried Nakagami first and relayed what he was told back to the others.

The others in this case were Sila, Gašper, Gašper's bowl of chicken powder, bok choy mix, and a surprise cameo from Chu, who didn't seem bothered at all when Gašper said she looked like she'd been lost in a forest for a decade.

'Not that you look bad,' he edited quickly as she sat down on the chair beside him. 'Just a bit scruffy.'

'I came straight from the TELEPORT ROOM.'

'Wah, you're back in there again?'

'Is that a joke?'
~~~

'Nakagami said you were giving up, focusing on other theories,' said Sila, clarifying.

'He is correct. But this is not giving up. The theories are…vaguely concerned with teleportation.'

'Ja, well, I'm glad you're here,' said Gašper, picking up a bok choy from his bowl. 'Haven't seen you in ages.'

'I was not hiding.'

'And now that's there's only seven of us, two of which are basically hermits, we need to stick together. Want a bite?'

Chu half raised a hand, rejecting the bok choy floating nearby. 'Aleša isn't coming out?'

'Ja, but on autopilot.'

'I thought you could go and talk to her,' said Sila, also rejecting Gašper's attempt at feeding. 'Keep her grounded.'

'She won't see me.'

'You've tried?'

'Ne.'

'Then how-…'

'Intuition.'

'Back to the science part of the science lesson,' said Petr, tapping his notes. 'According to Kenji, Uranus has a bunch of moons named after fairies. Two of them are suitable for future colonies.'

'I've got an idea,' said Gašper. 'As Chu's here, why don't we talk about teleportation?'

'Not a bad suggestion,' said Sila.

'It's a dense topic,' said Petr, in a low voice. 'I think focusing on Uranus would be better.'

'Chu can simplify it. Besides, we all know the basics from *Trek* and *Dibrivna Vaska*.'

'Do you?'

'Ja, most of it.'

Petr stared at Gašper, waiting for him to finish the bok choy he'd just shoved in his mouth.

'I can't explain it, obviously, but I'll understand when I hear Chu say it.'

'Don't be too confident,' said Chu, glancing at the contents of Gašper's bowl. 'I'm not a trained teacher.'

'Ne, it's not that hard, you can kind of get it from the imagery, and the characters talking about it. Dematerialise, put the pattern in the machine, beam it someplace, check it's clear, re-materialise.'

'How do they dematerialize the matter?' asked Petr, his tone jarringly stern.

'Break down the body parts? Ne vem.'

'Into atoms?'

'Ja. Probably. Don't they?'

'How?'

'Actually, that part is omitted in reality,' said Chu, figuratively parking herself between Petr and Gašper. 'Most scientists focus on replication at the end point and energy to matter conversion.'

'Making a copy?' asked Sila, vaguely remembering old conversations from their time in Bled.

'Ja. My original theory tried the *Trek* way, but it's tough. Breaking down the atomic bonds, creating a stable matter stream…' Chu looked at Gašper's face, nodding yet vacant. 'I gave up on that approach.'

'Quitter.'

'And, apart from a few inveterate originalists, so has everyone else. Ja, quitting, if that's what you want to call it.'

'I was joking.'

Sila stretched his hand out towards Gašper's bok choy bowl, grabbing one of the broken-off leaves. 'Doesn't making a copy mean killing the original?'

'Ne, it's more like having two of the same person.'

'What…'

'The same brain pattern, capable of being sent via signal to another place. The body data doesn't really matter, we already have patterns for that. The problem is the amount of information you have to transfer, and store, primarily from the brain, and how to safely reinstall all that data within a fresh location.'

'Wait…you already have body patterns? Is that what you just said?'

'*We* do, as in other humans, scientists. Not me. But it's not that hard to get a physical pattern.'

'Not that hard,' muttered Petr, eyes on his lesson notes.

'Where would you get the patterns from?'

'Here. The ship.'

'But, didn't you just say-…' Gašper stopped, looking over at the void beyond the middle window. 'Ne, I'm stuck. Is this still teleportation?'

Chu spun her neck in one slow loop and then jabbed at it with her knuckles. 'I probably shouldn't have gone into this. It's a difficult thing to explain.'

'Cos it sounds more like cloning to me. Just copying someone.'

'Ja, copying in a sense, but-…okay, let me say it this way. There is theory, and there is fibre-glassing. Right now, the computer won't permit any real kind of experimentation, not until I provide more data. Even then, I suspect it wouldn't allow an actual, live teleportation. Or copying, to use another term.'

She stopped, looking at the green line running around the bok choy bowl.

'In a practical sense, I'm trapped in the theoretical. Getting brain patterns of the crew would push me further along this path…though, to be blunt, others on Earth will have this kind of data already, perhaps the solution itself if I'm being pessimistic. Yet, flipped the other way, I have an AI that is…odd…and, with the brain patterns to examine, it may actually be able to resolve the main problem: is the quantum state relevant?'

Chu took in her audience – Sila staring at her neck, Gašper chewing blankly, Petr with his lips pursed, as if he were about to spit in her face – and held up her hands.

'Ne, forget that last part. Too scientific. The point I was trying to make was, brain patterns could help reach a theoretical breakthrough, which could eventually convince the computer to authorise experiments.'

'I'm a little confused,' said Sila.

'Which part?'

'If you did break the theory, get the solution, whatever you call it…what exactly would our brain patterns be teleporting into?'

'That is a terminus problem. Reliant on pipeline technology.'

'What does that mean?'

'It means…'

'…she doesn't know what she's doing,' finished Petr, folding his arms.

'Ja. In a fundamental way, it is guesswork. Until it isn't.'

'Would we be going into new bodies?'

Chu held in a long breath then blew it out at the ceiling. 'To create a body, or some type of receptacle, that kind of tech is beyond us at the moment. Even more so, if the intention is to install or direct the pattern.'

'But it might be possible…'

'Ne,' said Petr, arms still locked.

'Probably not. Though, if it were, we would have the added bonus of being copies of what we are right now. A de-aging machine, in effect.'

'Longer life spans,' said Gašper, shifting awkwardly in his chair.

'Ja.'

'As a copy.'

'Correct.'

'How many brain patterns do you need for this…research?' asked Sila, swirling his coffee.

'Everyone's, preferably. If you're all willing.'

'Solely for theory?'

'Ja. As things currently stand.'

'Wah, I feel a bit sick,' said Gašper, poking the remaining bok choy with his chopstick.

'About the theory?'

'Ne,' said Petr, almost a bark.

'My stomach…'

'Reckless, cowboy science, that's what you're doing.'

'In what way?' asked Chu, pushing away Sila's hand as he tried to redirect her back towards him.

'Doing research alone, with no lab, in a heightened environment, with no animals to test on first.'

'That is a list of things I have no control over.'

'Precisely, so stop doing it.'

Chu breathed out, looking over at the food dispenser.

'Work on something else. Stick to theory.'

'Isn't that what she's doing?' asked Sila.

'Ah, it's stopped now,' said Gašper, patting his stomach.

'I mean, genuine theory, not active steps towards something ridiculous that she can't ever do.'

'For a second there, I thought the bok choy was bad.'

'This is silly,' replied Chu, stepping back in. 'You're mistaking research for trial preparation.'

'Am I deaf? Didn't you just say you were taking brain patterns?'

'Ja, for hypothetical research.'

'And eventual use.'

'Ne.'

'You just said, as things currently stand.'

'There is no planned out method to-…ja, and I also said pipeline tech, terminus problem, if some kind of receptacle can be made. None of this is ever likely to be used, that's why it's called theory. Or a hypothesis, if that makes it easier.'

'You're lying. There's intention here, there's a plan.'

Gašper put his chopsticks back in the bowl and then a hand on Petr's thigh. 'You okay?'

'There is, it's obvious.'

'Did someone try to teleport you when you were a kid?'

'She's talking about making copies of us, Gašper.'

'Ja, it's a bit weird.'

'Without proper testing…'

'But it's just a theory, right?' Gašper turned to Chu, his face doing everything except winking.

'Correct,' said Chu.

'You're not anywhere near doing it…'

'It would be for emergencies only. Assuming I can solve the quantum state problem. And if the ship ever lets me do it. Which, as I tried to stress two minutes ago, it probably won't.'

Petr stood up and looked down at his notes on Uranus. He looked at them for a long time. Then, with all *signified* drained from the text, he blurted out, 'forget it,' and left.

'Where did that come from?' asked Sila, after the door had slid shut.

'Ne vem. His ID maybe. Or we didn't talk about Uranus enough. Or look at his new painting.'

'What painting?' asked Chu, scanning the table.

Gašper pointed at the wall, the spot where Aleša's *Victory* poster used to be. 'Commissioned by Dodzi.'

'That's Uranus?'

'Surrealist version, ja. Not quite at the same level as my field of coffins, but not far off.'

Chu got up and moved closer to the painting, touching some of the flakier parts. 'He is talented.'

'Ja, when he's calm and focused.'

Sila scratched at the spaceship logo on his *RED STAR* t-shirt. 'I hope he's not going to trash the TELEPORT ROOM.'

'There's nothing to trash,' replied Chu, returning to her seat.

'Err...your mountain of notes?'

'I moved them to my room. Easier to work on there.'

'Okay, what about the Angolan chair you always sit on? The screen the drones installed? That portable tricorder thing you were making?'

'He won't go to the TELEPORT ROOM,' said Gašper, picking up the chopsticks again and playing with the final bok choy. 'He'll sulk in his quarters for a bit then come and say sorry. Don't think he'll give you his brain pattern though.'

'That's his choice.'

'Is it painful?' asked Sila, the tip of his t-shirt spaceship flaking off. 'The brain pattern thing?

'Not at all. It's just like being scanned.'

'One scan?'

'Over several weeks, three times a day.'

'Jezus…'

'Each time, about seventeen minutes. An hour if the computer's being tight with the power supply.'

'An hour…'

'Not that bad. Would you like to come and see?'

~~~

Petr did sulk, but not in his quarters, and saying *sorry* was about as likely as Pol Pot rematerializing in modern day Phnom Penh and opening a gym.

Engineering was his first port of call.

When he got there, he stopped, looked at the looping corridor ahead of him and thought, how did I end up here?

His brain told him seventeen thousand different things, most of it cod-psychology, and he didn't know which one to hook onto so he started walking around the loop, eyes fixed on the electronic red line, waiting for his conscious self to filter out all the fraudulent shit and settle on the real.

Or at least give him less than ten options.

After doing four and half laps, he stopped next to Klemen's suicide spot. The VR machine was gone, probably ensconced in Chu's quarters, but if that hadn't come along then it would've been something else. The wires, perhaps. He remembered Aleša telling him Klemen had talked about it early on, pulling some out and hanging himself. And there were plenty in the walls, if the panels with *DANGER: LIVE WIRING* were to be believed.

But maybe they weren't.

Maybe nothing was.

Maybe the VR machine really was a clue. Why else would it be there?

And why the limitations? One swab, no green goo, no GPU.

And now Chu was using it in her own quarters, as if Klemen had never happened.

Chu the sociopath.

What was she doing with the VR?
~~~

Why had he let her teleporter idea fuck him up so much?

He knew the answer, to the VR question. Maybe the other one too.

Whimsy and sadism combo.

There was a VR machine there so Klemen could zone out and kill himself.

It was there for all of them.

Ne, person-specific.

He'd never do it that way. Edit: he'd never do it any way. Suicide was for people like Klemen. Simulation theory bath, soak it all up and then do it. He didn't have any theories, he had Gašper.

Did someone try to teleport you when you were a kid…

Ja, seven times, with a baseball bat.

Hospital had green walls too.

Hospital. Prison. Ship that called its medical bay the HALF DONE ROOM.

Was that what he deserved?

Chu wasn't a sociopath, she wasn't evil, and he'd exploded at her.

Psychologically, why?

Reasons, think.

Teleporting was death? He didn't want to see himself. The copy might be nicer. Gašper would leave him, fuck the copy instead.

But she said emergencies, only in an emergency.

Death and copy?

Was that it?

He looked at the wall, the ghost of Klemen's fried temple.

This wasn't a good place to be. Why had he come here?

Where else?

Somewhere quiet, no people, no suicide spots.

The LAUNCH ROOM?

No one ever went there, unless they were secretly trying out the ships therapy program.

Was anyone doing that?

Should he?

There was a noise from round the corner, something dropping on the floor.

A spanner?

He froze with his hand on the carmine line, eyes darting both ways down the corridor.

Nothing appeared.

~~~

'It's not a permanent thing. The feeling isn't constant, or lurking even…'

'Prosim, rephrase,' stated the ships therapist voice.

'…it's more like the fear of the feeling happening…when the brain narrows, or tightens. Ne vem. I'm not sure how to explain it.'

'Try to explain it, prosim.'

'When I saw it happening, someone else doing it…I knew what was happening in his brain, it was like…almost like seeing my own insanity projected out into the room. And the tightening of it…'

'What do you mean? Hvala.'

'…had me too. It was trapping me. Ne, worse than that…cos he didn't leave the room, for so long…I was willing him to, screaming at him inside, leave the room, but he just sat there letting his brain tighten and…what the fuck was he still doing there? It was stupid, selfish. If you're trapped, go, don't care about others, go…'

'Where would you like to go?'

'…but you can't go, cos you do care about others, even if you hate them and don't really care, on some level you care, society makes you care about what they think of you and, you don't actually care, but it makes you care, it tricks you into caring…'

'Prosim, refrain from tautologies. Hvala.'

'…even on this ship. They still have eyes, a brain, so you care, it tricks you into it and, you care if they think you're insane cos you can't explain any of it, not logically.'

'Try to explain it, prosim.'

'It's insidious. Slippery. Mum had it, Sadia had it, I'm gonna have it at some point. Ja, don't be scared everyone. It's eternal, I can't ever
~~~

make it go away. Prosim, just let me leave the room if I seem manic, don't ask any questions. No eyes. Just let me go out, in peace.'

'You do not seem manic, Crew Member Sila. Do not feel that you must leave the room.'

'Ne vem. All of it, ne vem. Is it eternal? Even out here? Maybe Chu's weird teleporter idea can fix it. A copy to iron out the flaws.'

'Crew Member Chu's current teleporter hypothesis is unethical and wildly theoretical, prosim, refrain from considering it.'

'Ja, that's what Petr said. Which brings us full circle, I guess. A lap of Klemen's Engineering.'

Sila stared at his own arms for half a minute then lifted himself up off the floor and headed for the THERAPY ROOM exit.

'Sensors indicate that you are leaving the session. Psychologically, this is called running away from yourself. Do not feel bad. See you again next time. Reminder: to save power, prosim, turn off the interactive screen. Hvala.'

~~~

After standing outside Airlock 1 and staring through the window at the NO LINGERING sign for well over three minutes, Sila switched back on and started moving. At first, he thought about going back to his quarters, but he knew what would happen there, which way his mind would go, so he vetoed that option and headed left down the middle deck corridor, ducking inside the PHILOSOPHY ROOM.

There was no one else in there except *Icelandic Satanism,* so he sat down and tried to read a bit.

'The woman was an oddity in the 7th Century, relying on the God of the Hidden Waves to provide her with sustenance instead of local fishermen. Every fourth day, she would go to her favourite cliff and chant the following: 'hidden waves, good at hiding, give to your servant, that which frightens.' As a reward, the waves would roll in and deposit a small basket of fruits and seafood, as well as a waterproof map detailing local cave topography.'
~~~

Sila stopped reading, flipped to the front cover and stared at it. Apart from the title, there was one image: a shadowy figure with a human torso and five spear shaped limbs.

Was that Satan?

It looked vaguely like one of the posters he'd drawn, the very first one, in fact. The vampire-like thing that was supposed to symbolise fascism stalking the night streets of Ljubljana.

But that wasn't Satan.

It was a human thing.

Was it not?

He turned to the back cover, but there was nothing except a tiny description: *'You know about German Satanism and Gaelic Satanism and Nigerian Satanism, now it's time to learn about the rituals and defeats and revivals of Icelandic Satanism. Warning: small text, rape.'*

The small text part was true, you couldn't read it for more than ten minutes without feeling eye pain, and the rest of it wasn't really that interesting anyway.

Maybe Gaelic or German Satanism was better, he had no idea, but the ship didn't have those books, or any others related to Satan. Just this one. And Chu's occult psychology catalogue. Sensing fatigue-creep in his legs, he got up and walked back outside. Pink walls and a Šarec-era guard picking sweets out of vending machine replaced reality for a tenth of a second. Then the green returned.

Where next?

The TELEPORT ROOM?

Chu and her brain scanning machine?

Ne, too much.

He stayed by the door he'd just exited from, torn between the CREATE NOT DESTROY ROOM to see if Petr had returned, or the URANUS ROOM to *peer through history* as Dodzi called it.

Deciding that the former room was too close, he kept walking, going down and up the little ramp at the end of the corridor then treading quietly onto the stairs.

There was no real need for caution as both the middle and upper decks were empty, yet he continued in that fashion, creeping up on the door to the URANUS ROOM and waiting until two seconds after the doors had opened before going in.

'Comrade,' said Dodzi, the back of his head silhouetted against the giant image of Uranus lit up on the projection screen.

'It's Sila.'

'I know, I know. You have come to do book work with me, meditate.'

'You're still doing research?'

'Ja, I was just telling your friend, Gašper, the moons around Uranus, they're not moons. They're a key. A map to the centre.'

Sila stopped next to a chair on the back row and looked at the projection screen. There was no text, no moons, just the seventh planet.

'It's okay, comrade. I, too, was unaware of these moons until Nakagami told me. And then I found a book downstairs that-...' Dodzi finally turned round and pointed at the chair next to him. 'Ja, sit down, comrade. Get comfortable. We have not talked in eons.'

'I saw you yesterday, in the CREATE ROOM.'

'Ja...what? That was yesterday?'

'It was.'

'Incredible...I've been so deep in this book, I thought it was three days ago. What did we talk about? Mythology?'

'You asked Petr to make his Uranus painting brighter.'

'Ah. The painting. No mythology?'

'Not that I remember.'

Dodzi glanced back at the projection screen, muttering something about *formations* and *rectitude*.

Sila put his hands on the back of the nearest chair, putting a bit of weight forward but not enough to tip it over. 'Is it hard doing all your research...in here?'

'Church?'

'Research. Is it hard doing it-...'

'Ja, this is the place for it. Research. I explained to Aleša, mythology is a starting point, but you cannot get swamped by it. I did, at the beginning, my head was sea deep in it, Uranus the God and Gaia, but that was wrong, the wrong track. Then I found the book, Nakagami told me about the moons, and after that it was...' He paused, noticing the empty chair with Sila's hands on the back. 'Ne, ne, you're still in guest mode? Come, sit, let me tell you what I know, what I told the others. It's beyond gracious. Three million years old, at least. Sit, comrade, closer, over here.'

Sila gave in and took the chair behind Dodzi, edging it back a little under the guise of stretching out his legs.

'That's better, a sense of the communal. Where was I? Wah, you look tired, couldn't see it back there. You're not sleeping long?'

'On and off.'

'That is not healthy, comrade. Lack of purpose, new knowledge. Wah, the book I found, do you know how many pages it had?'

'Ne…'

'Three hundred and thirty-three. Triple three.'

'Is that…'

'Not triple seven, the ideal, but not nothing. Nothing is truly nothing when it comes to writing, especially books like this. But that's just numerology. The content, starting on chapter three, he lays out the science of it. First two chapters are laboured waffle, but chapter three…'

Dodzi turned and looked at the projection screen, saying a quick 'ja' to Uranus then spinning back again.

'In every system…the whole universe, every single system, the planet with twenty-seven moons is not really a planet, it is a vibe, a portal. See, if you work out the moon clues, figure out the right way in then you can reach the core and it's not what they say it is, silicate, ammonia, methane ice, it's not any of those, it's a door, a door, comrade, a door. A door. And if you know the moons, you find your way in there, think of Mars, there it is, hello Mars. Think of Darko, hello Darko. Cos it's the mind connection. Our minds, neurons, they're connected to the seventh planet of each system. Of course, we don't have access to the others, don't even know about them, so that doesn't matter. But here, with Uranus…the book I found…' He paused, placing a flat hand on the empty chair next to him. '…Aleša found…had all the moon theory and…it may be too much detail. Ja, better to meditate for now. Soak up the seventh planet. *Ka Harsarg.* Sumerian for Uranus. You want to meditate with me, comrade?'

'Sorry, I have to go,' said Sila, standing up and faking a yawn. 'Science lesson downstairs.'

'A lesson?'

'Ja, science. Petr teaches me and Gašper about some general space concepts.'

'Teaches you?'

'Ja, you see us sometimes, the three of us. That's our science lesson.'

Dodzi took a few seconds but got it eventually, tapping the back of his chair. 'I remember, the science lesson. He was telling you about the ship's engine, the velocity…'

'Probably, ja.'

'…why we can walk here, the lemium field. Ja, I recall all of that. Do not know for sure how it got past my Uranus shield, but…ja, your science lesson. I should do that too. Sometime.'

'You can join us now, if you want?'

'Make my father laugh, wherever he is.'

'You want to come down now, sit with us?'

'Ja…'

Sila waited for Dodzi to get up, but he just stayed seated where he was, stroking the back of his chair.

'I'm gonna head down. Maybe I'll come in again tomorrow, do some…'

'Okay, comrade.'

'…Uranus watching.'

Dodzi leaned over and patted Sila on the wrist. 'Stay in one piece.'

'Ja.'

~~~

'Why not?'

'It is not yet due for replacement.'

'When will it be due?'

'Within one day of its expiry.'
~~~

'It's flickering now.'

'This is not expiration.'

Nakagami breathed out, tapped the edge of the keypad, stopped, then tapped it again.

He stared at the flickering green light near the entrance, rubbed his head, then got up and tried to swivel the bulb around again.

It didn't work.

Maybe if I take it out and smash it, he thought. That would be classified as broken.

'Are you busy?'

Nakagami made a gasping noise, something he'd only done once on the ship; the first time the green bulb flickered.

'Sorry, I should've made my footsteps louder,' said Chu, looking up at the bulb. 'Is it broken?'

'Not sufficiently.'

'Sorry?'

'The computer is pedantic when it comes to basic maintenance. It says the bulb must expire before a drone is sent to replace it.'

'You mean we might get to see one of them?'

'Unlikely. Interior maintenance is done during curfew hours.'

'Of course. Just like everything else.' Chu peered around Nakagami, into the TALK TO YOUR GOD ROOM. 'No Petr?'

'Already left.'

'He was here before?'

'Ja, for a short time.'

'What did he say?'

'More than usual. He seemed very concerned with the wires in Engineering and how exactly they functioned. He also asked if I had given my brain pattern to you yet.'

Chu huffed out air, some of it laughter.

'Are you here to talk to the computer?'

'Not exactly.'

'To me?'

Chu stepped fully into the Control Room, looked around at the posters and nodded. 'Do you think a teleporter is unethical?'

'We have already discussed this topic.'

'Ja, but you hid.'

'I don't believe I did.'

'You fell back on the computer, as always. *The ship will not allow me to do the experiment.*'

'Does that not answer your question?'

'You do think it's unethical?'

'That is not what I meant.'

'You agree with the ship.'

'I was attempting to…I wanted to say that ethics are irrelevant if you don't have the authorization to do your work. But then your work was greenlit by the ship, or Potočnik, so it is an odd position for it to take.'

'That's descriptive. Do *you,* Kenji, agree with the ship?'

'About ethics?'

'No dodging, prosim.'

'It is clarification, not-…'

'Do you agree with the ship, Kenji?'

Nakagami tried to look away from Chu, but the only place to look was the flickering green light so he looked at the floor instead and said, 'ne vem.'

'Can't believe you're looking at the floor.'

He looked back up, almost gasping when he saw Dodzi's face replacing the bulb.

'Nakagami, Chu,' Dodzi said softly, dipping his head. 'I've been looking for you both.'

'You have a question?' asked Nakagami.

'Ne, more of a confirmation. By my calculation, we should be adjusting our course to Uranus in twelve days.'

'Twelve or thirteen, ja.'

'Then it is correct?'

'Ja.'

'Good.'

'I have to remind you,' said Nakagami, tilting his head slightly to avoid the worst of the flickering light, 'it is still a very remote chance that we will be able to convince the computer to adjust course in time.'

Dodzi pulled his hand out from behind the wall and slapped Nakagami on the shoulder. 'I know you can do it, comrade. Complete faith.'

'It is a matter of AI psychology and my reading of it, not faith.'

'It is faith,' replied Dodzi.

'Sorry, that is not my judgment of the case.'

'Because you do not experience the URANUS ROOM, comrade. That is where my faith originates.'

'I see.'

'And the science too. My new book.'

'Science?'

'The seventh planet, ancient connection doors. Ja, it is esoteric, but rigorous. Ah, this jabbing light, it is constant, what's happening?'

'It's damaged.'

'Can you turn it off? It's irritating me.'

'I don't have the-…'

'Ne, wait. Keep it on. It could be a test.' He nodded to himself. 'Ja, I better go, balance myself. Stay in one piece. Both of you.'

He paused, noticing the bruising on Chu's temple. His hand moved forward to touch it.

'Singeing from my check of the VR machine,' Chu said, backing away from his finger.

'A vicious wound.'

'Not that bad.'

'Still, a caution. You should avoid seeking solace in false domains. It will lead you far from the path.'

'I don't use it now.'

'Then perhaps a dismantling at some point. In the URANUS ROOM.'

'We have work to do,' said Nakagami, reinserting himself. 'I will keep you updated on my progress with the computer.'

'Very good.'

Dodzi smiled, patted Chu on the arm, tapped the heart side of his chest then left, the flickering green bulb immediately filling the vacuum.

'He is getting worse,' said Nakagami.

'Worse than the start of the trip? Or after Mars?'

'Potentially.'

Nakagami rubbed his eyes, moving back into the belly of the TALK TO YOUR GOD ROOM and sitting down.

Chu stayed at the entrance, watching him. 'Why don't you put a cloth over it?'

'I could try that.'

'Do you have a cloth here?'

'Ne.'

'Towel?'

'It is okay, I will persevere a little longer.'

'You could always just take it down and smash it.'

Nakagami slouched down into the chair. 'I doubt the computer would allow it.'

'Shame.'

'Ja.'

~~~

An hour later, after a particularly aggressive series of green strikes, Nakagami straightened his back against his chair and typed a new query to the computer.

'Can I smash the bulb?'

'For what purpose?'

'The flickering light is giving me a migraine.'

'The HALF DONE ROOM has pills for this condition.'

'I would prefer not to take pills.'

'There are massage sticks in each crew member's quarters.'

'The source of my migraine is the bulb. If I break it, I will feel better. Can I break it?'

'Which bulb?'

'The flickering bulb.'

'Ne.'

'Why not?'

'The shards of broken glass cannot be removed until curfew hours. In the interval, they could be used to harm other crew members.'
~~~

'Can I remove the bulb?'

'Which bulb?'

'The flickering bulb. Can I take it out?'

'Ne.'

'Why not?'

'It is not yet expired.'

Nakagami sucked in half the air of the Control Room and let it out slowly.

'You should go to the HALF DONE ROOM.'

'Not necessary.'

'Are you busy?'

'I am communicating with you.'

'Do you have other tasks?'

'Ne.'

'It is strongly recommended that you go to the HALF DONE ROOM.'

Nakagami ignored the message, rubbing his eyes again. It was not good. The green haze on the inside of his eyelids was almost brighter than the outside light itself. Another month of this and everything, everywhere might appear green. Even his poster girls.

'You must go to the HALF DONE ROOM now,' repeated the computer.

'I do not want pills,' he typed slowly, with one finger stabbing the keys.

There was a beeping noise, followed by the familiar opening words.

'Attention crew,

A crew member's life signs have stopped. Their last recorded location was the HALF DONE ROOM. As said crew member is incapable of movement without life signs, it is likely that they are still at this location. If any crew member wishes to attempt resuscitation, prosim, make your way to the HALF DONE ROOM now.

Have a safe and bold trip to Luyten 726-8

Hvala.'

~~~
~~~

By the time Nakagami reached the HALF DONE ROOM, Chu was already in there, prepping a syringe with Antro-D.

'Stay back,' she shouted, her hysteria count at dead zero. 'Keep everyone at the door.'

Nakagami spun back round and checked the corridor outside. There were footsteps and Slovene swear words coming down the stairs, with Gašper the first to be seen, followed closely by Sila.

'Keep them back, Kenji, I need space…'

Nakagami turned to her and nodded, and that was all he'd planned to do, but Chu had the needle in Petr's arm and his wrists were covered in blood, leaking blood and the green liquid was flowing out of the syringe into the skin of the arm and somehow it was oddly hypnotic, the stark colours of it all, in such close proximity.

'What…Petr…'

Gašper barged past Nakagami, tripped and crawled across the floor, almost cracking his head on the edge of the bio-bed.

'Prosim, lie down on the bio-bed,' said the robot, facing the other way.

'Petr…'

'Don't touch him,' shouted Chu, swatting Gašper away, but it wasn't enough, he reeled right back in, half-grabbing Petr's arm.

'Gašper…'

Chu punched him somewhere on the torso, she didn't know where, and either it worked or he finally noticed the blood as he let go and gripped Petr's knee instead, shouting, 'do something,' over and over until that became redundant too.

Sila stayed near the door, prodding Nakagami out of his trance, checking the corridor for Aleša or Dodzi, doing anything really to avoid looking at Petr's wrists.

Chu finished injecting the rest of the green fluid, held her finger over the puncture wound, sat with her back against the wall, just like Petr, and waited.

A minute passed.

Two minutes.

Two and a half minutes.

Gašper tried to say *is it working?* but could only eek out *is it…* as he could see some of the Antro-D dribbling out of Petr's wrist.

After four minutes, Chu disguised a glance towards Sila, pretending to look at the ceiling light, and gently shook her head.

'We have to wait,' said Gašper, staring at a ring of green encircling a dot of blood near Petr's wrist.

'Ne,' replied Chu, mostly breath.

'One hour. I've seen it before. Taka, same thing…the wrists.'

'He's gone.'

'Ne, it happened to Taka, the exact same thing, I saw it.'

'Gašper…'

'I know what I'm saying. One hour. He'll come back, I swear.'

Chu looked down at the green still seeping out from Petr's wrists.

'One hour. Prosim.'

'Okay.'

~~~

As in most medical bays, even ones with weird names, no one knew what to say or where to position their hands, so they resorted to not doing or saying anything.

Instead, they just stood around and tried not to look at Petr's face.

Or his wrists.

Gašper kept his hand tight on Petr's knee for a while then crawled forward and leaned next to him against the wall.

Two lovers, post-sex.

Post-confession.

Post nothing else to do at that moment except relax on the floor and pass the time in silence together.

He put his head on Petr's shoulder and stared at whatever Petr was staring at.

'Be still,' said the medical bot, still facing the wrong way.

No one disobeyed.
~~~

'The others haven't appeared,' whispered Nakagami, coming back in from the corridor.

'Ja,' said Sila.

'This is not good.'

'Ne.'

'I'm going back upstairs, to check on the computer.'

Sila didn't respond, he just stared at Chu staring at the empty syringe.

Eventually, she got up and came over to Sila, leaning close into his ear. 'He's gone.'

'That's final?'

'No one comes back after one hour. Not after losing that much blood.'

Sila focused on Gašper, his head still on Petr's shoulder. 'What happened?'

'Ne vem.'

'He cut himself?'

'I ran in and he was on the floor. The Antro-D was there, by his leg, still full. I grabbed it, stuck it in…'

'It was by his leg?'

'…but the damage was too much. Ja…on the floor, by his leg.'

Sila tried to take in the scene again, but ended up looking back toward the corridor. It was too stark, the blood, the little streams of green.

'Maybe he changed his mind at the last minute,' continued Chu, wiping her hands on her *WE MARTIANS* t-shirt. 'Tried to pull the syringe over and…ne vem. I can only speculate.'

'We need to help Gašper,' said Sila.

'To clear this up?'

'Ja.'

'I'll take care of it,' said Gašper, half raising his hand.

'We can help…'

'Give me a bit longer though. Wanna rest a while…'

'Okay.'

'…talk to Petr. See if I can lure him back.'

Sila took a step forward, but Chu grabbed his wrist, shaking her head.

'That's what happened to Taka. Two hours gone and then, wah, eyes open again.'

'Two hours?' asked Chu, without any kind of push.

'Said he could hear voices talking to him while he was out. Same thing could happen here. If I keep talking.'

'Okay. We'll be outside.'

'Come and get us if anything happens,' Sila added, waiting for Gašper to nod then turning and letting Chu lead him out of the room.

'We can't leave him in there alone,' said Sila when they were by the stairs. 'He might do something.'

'I think it's okay.'

'But…he really believes Petr's gonna wake up.'

'Ne, that's normal. He's adapting. Processing another death.'

'Are you sure?'

'A hundred percent? Ne. But I don't think he's gonna hurt himself. It's not in his character. Besides, there's nothing in there he could do any damage with…'

'The syringe?'

Chu rubbed her forehead, possibly removing sweat. 'I forgot about that.'

'What do we do? Go back in and get it?'

'Ne vem.'

There was a *psst* noise from higher up on the stairwell. They both looked down first, towards the HALF DONE ROOM then up, both sets of hands halfway to being fists.

'You need to come upstairs,' said Nakagami, crouching by the railing next to the landing.

'Why are you whispering?'

'Quickly, come up.'

'Both of us?'

'Unless one of you is a murderer, ja.'

~~~
~~~

The green light was still flickering in the TALK TO YOUR GOD ROOM, with some of its rays streaked across Nakagami's face as he told Sila and Chu that, despite appearances, there was a strong possibility that Petr was murdered.

'Or if not murdered then allowed to die,' he amended, after seeing the initial reaction of his audience.

A patch of silence followed, two minds re-processing everything they'd just heard while their eyes stared vacantly at the console buttons.

'You're certain there were two life signs in there?' asked Sila finally, looking back at the entrance and the schizophrenic bulb.

'It is the computer that supplied the data, I simply read it from the screen.'

'Is the computer certain?'

'Ja.'

Chu walked closer to the central console and leaned on the *adjust aft solar panel* button. A blue light flashed, too small to notice. 'There was no one in sight when I got there. Or when I came out from the TELEPORT ROOM.'

'That is my fault.'

Both Sila and Chu instinctively moved back a touch. Something about Nakagami's tone.

'There was a four minute delay between the cessation of Petr's life signs and the announcement.'

'Four minutes?'

'I thought you told it to report immediately?' asked Sila.

'That was merely my first sentence...if you'll allow me to continue?'

Sila pushed his hand out, the Slovene signal to say both *sorry* and *continue*.

'The computer delayed the report because it was occupied talking to me. I was attempting to fix the bulb over there, and...I suppose the computer performed a kind of triage. In effect, it chose my trivial queries over Petr's life.'

'Cold,' muttered Chu.

'Ja, perhaps.' Nakagami stared forward, making his eyes an easy target for the green light. He turned, rubbing his eyelids.

'So someone was in the medical bay four minutes before the announcement?' asked Sila.

'Three minutes before.'

'What?'

'They stayed there?'

'That is what the data says.'

'Why? To make sure?'

Nakagami shifted in his seat, looking towards Chu. 'Sorry, this is not an accusation. It is merely the best position to avoid the green light in my eyes.'

Chu nodded.

'Why would they stay there, Kenji?' rephrased Sila.

'I am not a psychologist, clearly, but there are some deductions we can make. First, it wasn't Chu. There was a constant life sign in the TELEPORT ROOM for the last hour. Second, it wasn't me. My life sign was fixed here. You may check the data for yourself, if bias is assumed on my part.'

'We trust you,' said Chu.

Sila half nodded, his eyes inadvertently catching the hockey stick poster girl.

'Third, I assume it was neither Gašper or Sila as there were two life signs in the CREATE ROOM.'

'Ja, that was us.'

'Fourth, the two remaining life signs were not in their quarters. Both were in the URANUS ROOM twenty minutes before Petr died, at which point one of them left.'

'To go to the HALF DONE ROOM?' asked Sila.

Nakagami nodded.

'Did they go anywhere else?'

'Before that, ja. To Engineering. For four minutes. Then to the HALF DONE ROOM.'

'Can't the computer tell us who it was?'

'Unfortunately, ne. As I have told you before.'

'I know, but…isn't there a way it could deduce it from the scan signal? Like, the heart beat pattern or the pulse?'

'It might be possible, if it had previous data, or a recorded pattern of suitable duration to compare it to.'

'It doesn't?'

'Ne.'

'Then how can we know who it was?'

'Ne vem.'

All three of them fell silent, the two scientists folding their arms, and Sila attempting to but changing his mind due to awkward positioning. Instead, he reverted to an old habit; scratching the skin on the side of his neck.

'If we followed our instincts, I believe we would all point to Dodzi,' said Nakagami. 'But there is no way to be certain.'

'Aleša wouldn't do it,' said Chu, leaning on the middle console.

'Ja, she knew Petr.'

'That is not a strong defence. In most murder cases, the victim knew their killer.'

'I mean, she knew him, they were friends.'

'Petr knew Dodzi too, recognized him,' added Sila, putting the back of his head against the Ophelia poster and fixing the doorway as the mid-point in his range of vision.

'That is true.'

'And you said earlier Dodzi was getting worse, that he might snap at some point.'

'Ja, I did say that.'

'So maybe that point came sooner than you thought.'

'It is possible.'

'So it was Dodzi.'

Nakagami unfolded his arms and returned to the screen, scrolling back up through his conversation with the AI. 'As I said, if it were based on instinct alone, he would be the main suspect. However…'

'It has to be him.'

'…there are other factors that make it less clear.'

'What factors?'

'Speculative ones. The method of Petr's death. It appeared to be suicide, the cutting of the radial artery is a calculated wound, which doesn't fit the theory of a manic attack.'

'Not necessarily,' said Chu, getting tired of the console and switching to the Jame stool. 'There were several cuts down the length of the wrist, not across. And another on his neck.'

'I did not see that.'

'It wasn't big.'

'A hesitation cut?'

'Aiming for the carotid artery? Ne vem. I don't know if Petr knew that much about anatomy. But the wrist wounds, they weren't the normal way…not the typical direction for a suicide. An amateur suicide attempt, I mean.'

Nakagami tapped the edge of the console, frowning at the data on the screen. 'It may have been murder, or not. According to the computer, Petr was in the HALF DONE ROOM for thirty-seven minutes before he died. The other life sign was there for twelve minutes.'

'How long does it take to die from a wrist wound?' asked Sila, his tone distant from his own phrasing.

'Ne vem. Chu?'

'Five to ten minutes? I'm not sure either. Usually people survive.'

Another spike of green light hit Sila in the eyes, forcing him to look away from the entrance. 'Is there any way the other life sign was trying to help?'

'In what way?'

'They walked in and Petr had already…was already hurt, and…ne vem. They panicked, didn't know what to do.'

'The Antro-D was on the floor when I came in.'

'They were trying to inject him…'

'Ne.'

'…but they panicked. Why not?'

'The pattern of behaviour does not match this scenario.'

'It could…'

'One, they stayed in the room for twelve minutes. Two, they did not inject the Antro-D. It may have been Petr trying to save himself and being prevented from doing so by the other person. Three, they did not call for help. Four, neither Petr nor the other person screamed for help.'

Sila went back to the doorway, with the green bulb now in a relatively dormant state.

Chu noticed the blue light she'd accidentally switched on minutes earlier, and flicked it back.

The blue light went out.

Nakagami saw her do it and reached over, brushing off some invisible dust. 'It is impossible to be certain of anything. Yet, at the very least, someone stayed in that room and watched Petr die.'

'And did nothing,' said Chu.

'Ja.'

'What do we do?' asked Sila.

For the seven hundredth time, Nakagami looked at the symbols on the screen.

Chu joined him, reading the parts at the bottom. 'Where are Aleša and Dodzi now?'

'The URANUS ROOM.'

'Both of them?'

'There are two life signs.'

'So the one who watched Petr die went back and sat down with the other one?'

'Correct.'

'Very cold.'

'Sociopathic would be a more apt word.'

'Wait.' Sila pointed at the floor suddenly, the Slovene signal for inspiration. 'Is there any way to distinguish them, those two signals…based on how they are now?'

'The computer can only confirm that there is a life sign in the room. There is no recorded data beyond that. Or, if there is, it is not part of public record.'

Sila brought his finger back up to normal height.

'So we still can't do anything,' said Chu.

'To find the guilty party, ne. However, this is not a surprise problem. I've been working on a contingency plan to deal with this type of scenario for the last few weeks. Both of you may find it a little extreme, which is why I use the word contingency. It is not my first choice.'

'What, shove them both out the airlock?' asked Sila, going back to scratching his neck.

'That would be difficult to achieve.'

'Ja.'

'A more practical method is to drain the oxygen from their quarters while they're asleep.'

Sila stopped scratching his neck and pinched a clump of skin instead.

Chu leaned left with her elbow and hit the *adjust aft solar panel* button again.

The blue light blinked on.

'Thoughts?'

~~~

After defending his position for almost half an hour, stressing several times the *contingency* aspect of his plan, Nakagami finally managed to convince Sila and Chu that he wasn't a sociopath.

But they still didn't agree with his plan.

Fortunately, the computer also had issues with it, doubling down on its third core belief: none of the crew should be harmed.

Nakagami tried *pre-emptive strike*, *statistical probability*, *pattern of behaviour*, *Void-Helenism* and even *one of them could've killed Klemen too* arguments, but to no avail.

In the end, he simply sat back in his chair and said he would work on further deductions while Sila and Chu went off to [softly] interrogate two murder suspects.

'Remember, only one of them was in there, not both,' said Sila, walking out of the TALK TO YOUR GOD ROOM and instinctively pointing his face away from the green bulb.

'A panicker or a sociopath,' added Chu, following him out.

'And they may not have known what was happening. All that blood on the floor…'

'Shock factor.'
~~~

'Ja.'

Sila turned the first corner of the snake installation and slowed a little so Chu could walk shotgun. Then sped up again when she overtook him.

'You forgot to take a weapon,' Nakagami shouted after them, but they were already out of range.

Two of them, one possible murderer, he told himself.

And the fourth person too.

Should be enough.

Noticing the *warning* bulb on the console, he reached over and switched off the *solar panel* button, stroked the edges of the blue light casing for a few seconds then pulled his seat closer to the screen and started typing.

~~~

The URANUS ROOM was quiet when Sila and Chu entered, and dimly lit too, with the image of the seventh planet hovering in the middle like a blind psychic's eyeball.

There were eight chairs set out in front of the projection screen, all empty, and a strange electronic pulse that could've been background music.

'Is that usually on?' asked Chu, moving to the right and scanning the walls for speakers.

'Not the last time I was here,' replied Sila, taking the left.

'It's disconcerting.'

'Ja.'

Flanking the projection screen were two giant pieces of black card, with little white dots representing stars. Probably Dodzi doing some DIY, thought Sila. Sprucing up his second home. Actually, with the main lights off, it didn't look too bad.

'Anything on your side?' asked Chu, checking the back right hand corner of the room.

'Nothing,' replied Sila, touching the black card on the left.

'We should get back to Nakagami, find out where they are now.'
~~~

'Hang on…'

'What is it?'

Sila bent down, squinting at something poking out from behind the card.

'What?' asked Chu, walking over.

'Ne vem.'

Sila put out his fingers and prodded the object. Then grabbed it. There was a moaning sound farther back.

'It's hair.'

'Hair?'

'Aleša…'

He moved quickly round the edge of the card, saw a body curled up in a ball, grabbed the arms and pulled it out towards the light of the screen.

The moaning turned into a primal howl. Followed by an attempt at language.

He stopped pulling, or dragging, and looked for wounds.

'I think she's been stabbed,' said Chu, crouching down by Aleša's waist, touching the blood rolling down the side of her jacket.

'Her head's hurt too.'

Chu looked up, seeing Sila's hand near the back of Aleša's head.

'How bad is her stomach?'

'Antro-D…'

Sila nodded, pushing himself back onto his feet. 'What about Dodzi?'

'Antro-D.'

But he's out there. He might-'

'Then steamroll through him. Antro-D. Go.'

'Right…'

Patting Chu on the shoulder, Sila turned and bumped straight into the nearest chair, stumbling a bit but managing to just about stay vertical.

'Stop fucking around,' barked Chu, throwing an arm vaguely at the door.

'I'm going…'

'Quickly.'

'Two minutes.'

Sila carefully slipped around the remaining chairs then barrelled out into the corridor, pushing off the wall opposite and assessing the situation. No bodies, no face, no sounds.

Move.

He ran, almost at sprinting speed, the walls narrowing, the doors at the side obliterated as he framed the stairs at the end in a little square target.

The minimalism brought back the Šarec memory, the tyrant's torture house corridor with a vending machine for tired guards.

But the walls were too green for it to hold, his movement too fast and, when he reached the steps, the image had shifted to something else. Something worse. Dodzi with a metre-long needle, skewering him as he landed on the bottom deck.

He slowed, hugging the wall, taking the steps one at a time.

Dodzi was around, somewhere, and it was a small ship.

He'd already stabbed Aleša, possibly Petr too.

Maybe Uranus had told him to kill them all? Or maybe he was taking a nap?

Sila checked under the stairs as he stepped down onto the middle deck, then straight ahead.

The whole corridor was vacant. No erratic breathing sounds.

What about the coiled snake? Nakagami?

He took a few steps, raising his hands in an amateur boxer's defence style, picturing Dodzi lurking around each corner, knife in one hand, Aleša's hair in the other…

Fuck.

Aleša.

Slapping the wall, he pivoted right to the steps, this time taking them three at a time.

Not gonna die. Not gonna die. Not gonna…

The bottom deck was also crew-less, the only noise coming from the HALF DONE ROOM. Not Gašper sobbing or saying, 'Dodzi, ne,' but the robot arm asking if anyone needed a sedative.

Sila ran towards the voice, glancing left into the TELEPORT ROOM out of habit and shivering when he saw *Witch Going To The Sabbath* staring back at him from the far wall.

'Fucking Varo,' he muttered, as he skewed right and burst into the HALF DONE ROOM. Again he slipped, forgetting about the water on the floor, and almost skidded into Petr's boots.

'Not yet,' said Gašper, his head on Petr's shoulder.

'Antro-D, where is it?'

Gašper raised his hand and pointed at the green liquid on the floor, the stuff that had seeped out of Petr's wrist an hour earlier.

'Aleša's hurt, stabbed…'

Gašper lifted up his head and stared at Sila as if he'd just teleported in with the Count of Celje.

'Antro-D…'

'She's dead?'

'Ne. Not yet.' Sila went through the drawers, finding nothing, then noticed part of the wall hanging off. 'In here?'

Gašper pointed at the floor again.

Sila yanked open the door. There was a small box, open, with six green syringes sitting inside. He grabbed one and ran, shouting back to Gašper, 'watch out for Dodzi.'

Gašper mumbled, 'one more hour,' barely audible, then lowered his head back onto Petr's shoulder.

Floor. Blood. Robot. Blood. Bio-bed. Blood. Doorway.

Medical posters on the wall.

Sharp light.

Gašper raised his head again, pulling up Petr with him. 'What do you think? Change of location?'

~~~

Back in the URANUS ROOM, things were still eerily dim. The planet on the projection screen was still creepy. And Aleša was still leaking blood, telling Chu in choppy Slovene to stop lifting her up, it fucking hurt.
~~~

'I'm trying to move into the light so I can see better.'

'Turn them on,' spat Aleša.

Chu nodded, keeping her hand pressed against Aleša's stomach.

It was hard to tell how bad the damage was, but there was a fair amount of blood. And she'd been whacked on the head too, hard enough to open up a wound.

There was no sign of any weapons either, which meant Dodzi still had them. The lunatic could come back in at any moment, stab me too, thought Chu.

'Dodzi,' said Aleša, dribbling out more blood. 'Went insane. *I see you, I see you…*he kept saying it.'

'Ja, we know.'

'No warning. Came in, spoke Twi, went nuts.'

'He may have killed Petr too.'

'Petr?'

'Didn't you hear the announcement?'

'Petr's dead?'

'The computer said, on the tannoy.'

'What computer? How?'

'There was an announcement an hour ago. About Petr.'

'Is it?'

'Sorry?'

'Just the background noise, this stuff…'

Chu patted Aleša's head with her spare hand, forgetting there was also a wound there. 'It's okay, try not to speak.'

'Where's Petr?'

Chu heard the door slide open behind them and grabbed the leg of a nearby chair. Dodzi or Sila? She was too scared to turn. For a brief second, she imagined her head sitting in the airlock, her teleporter notes next to it, Sila saying, 'dumb thing never would've worked anyway.'

'Got it.'

The image imploded and a green syringe took its place, floating into her hand.

'Inject, go, go.'

Something guided her hand to Aleša's stomach as Chu watched from outside her own head, the needle going directly into the wound and the green draining in. There was a snap, Sila's words in her ears. She could feel her hand again, her fingertips easing off the syringe top.

'Two minutes,' she said, fully rebooted. 'Then we'll know.'

'Petr,' said Aleša, getting out the name between sucked-in breaths, the sound like someone scraping the inside of her throat.

Chu patted her on the head again, telling her not to speak, then turned and whispered, 'can you turn on the lights?'

Sila did as he was told, the door sliding open again when he got close, making him jump back and swing his right arm out.

It wasn't Dodzi.

Unless he was hiding at the side?

Ja, waiting. As soon as Sila peeked out, the knife would go right into his face and…

The door slid shut.

Sila tapped the light *square* and returned to Aleša and Chu.

'Where's Petr?' Aleša asked again, her eyes starting to close.

'Don't try to speak,' repeated Chu.

'Petr.'

Chu followed Aleša's gaze up to Sila, who was standing with his right arm half raised.

'You're not Petr,' muttered Aleša.

'No talking.'

'Klemen…'

Chu moved her hand over to the zip of Aleša's jacket, pulling it open on one side.

'His Portuguese…'

The wound was still there, four dark slits, four separate stabs.

'…was not good.'

'Aleša, you have to stop talking.'

'Ja…'

'And moving.'

'In a way…'

'Prosim.'

Aleša's eyes widened, like a primary school kid playing *surprised* in the nativity. 'Ne, too bright, turn them off,' she slurred, before drifting off again.

'Did it work?' asked Sila, hovering behind Chu's shoulder.

Chu stared at the four slits.

'We still need to wait?'

None of them were closing. The blood level had been reduced, but there was still a fair amount trickling out. More than a fair amount.

'Chu?' Sila prompted.

Worse, her hand wasn't clingy anymore. Or warm. And her chest…

'What's happening?'

There was a beeping noise, followed without fanfare by the ship's voice.

'Attention crew,

The life sign of another crew member has expired. It is unclear who exactly the crew member is, but the location of death is the URANUS ROOM. The two other crew members currently in the same room can provide more information when you arrive. If you wish to attempt re-suscitation, the Antro-D is in the HALF DONE ROOM.

Have a safe and bold trip to Luyten 726-8

Hvala.'

Sila looked around the room for other well-hidden bodies then back at Aleša. Then at Chu.

'Why?' he asked, voice cracking.

'Ne vem.'

'I got it here, she wasn't dead…'

Chu pulled the jacket back across Aleša's stomach, covering the wound.

'It's supposed to do something. She wasn't dead, she was talking to us, why the fuck didn't it work?'

'Sila…'

'I used it on Gašper, he worked. It worked on him…'

'We need to warn Kenji.'

'…and he was stabbed just like her. It doesn't make sense. She wasn't that bad, the wounds she had…'

'Dodzi is still somewhere on the ship.'

'...it wasn't any worse than...' Sila stopped, collapsing on a chair and almost toppling over with it. He steadied himself, letting his breathing run chaotic for another half minute before reining it in. *Fuck* was the only thing left to say, so he said it, his throat too drained to give it any real power.

Chu kept her eyes on Aleša's hand until he was done, then looked up. 'We need to deal with him.'

'Dodzi...' said Sila, staring vacantly at the screen.

'Take a chair as a weapon, go and find Kenji. Gašper too. If you see Dodzi, run.'

'And you?'

'Bring everyone back here. Understand?'

Sila got up from the chair and checked off the names in his head: Kenji, Gašper, who else? Ne, that was it. Two of them left.

No more Aleša. No Petr.

He looked to the screen again, at the still image of the seventh planet, observing them all. As blank as its lunatic disciple.

'Sila...'

'Ja, I know.'

'Hurry.'

He turned to go, staring aimlessly at the seven other chairs around him. His legs bent and his hand reached out for one of them, but he couldn't get a hold of it. The metal felt alien. The chair wasn't really a chair. And the idea of hitting someone with it...

There was another beeping noise, followed by the familiar voice.

'Ne,' whispered Sila, half in a daze.

'Attention crew,

The following is a correction to the last announcement. Although the life sign of the crew member did expire, it has now started up again. This is not due to computer error, as some may suspect, but a result of the implementation of a new policy, one which requires the computer to immediately report the cessation of life signs on the ship.

If any crew member feels negatively affected by recent events, the THERAPY ROOM is available any time before curfew hours.

Have a safe and bold trip to Luyten 726-8

Hvala.'

'What…' choked Sila, turning back around and looking at Chu, who already had her fingers on Aleša's chest.

'Heartbeat.'

He ran over, knocking into another chair, stumbling and falling and, finally, crawling like a desperate drunk to Chu's side.

'She's back?'

Chu pulled the jacket to the sides, checking the wounds. The four slits were still there, still dark, but no longer leaking blood.

'Is she back?' asked Sila again.

'Ja…'

'Permanently?'

'Must be healing it inside…'

'Her heart?'

'Ne vem. Restarted…'

Aleša coughed, spitting a chunk of bloody, bitty gruel-like substance just past Chu's shoulder.

'Where…' she started to say, but coughed again.

Chu pulled Aleša's jacket back over, briefly considered zipping it up at least halfway, but vetoed when she thought it might clip the wound.

'Dodzi,' said Aleša, pausing to push back another cough. 'Psycho stabbed me…'

'Ja…'

'Said the ship was broken…'

Chu looked up towards Sila, gesturing towards the door.

'I'll be back soon,' he replied, wiping his eyes.

'Chair,' said Chu, stopping him mid-turn.

Sila picked up the one he'd dropped, gripped it by the legs, waited for the door to slide open then jabbed it out into the corridor.

Nothing happened. No side attacks or knife slashes. No insanity in Twi.

Pulling the chair back in and re-positioning it as a shield, he edged out, turned left and started towards the stairs.

~~~

In defiance of crushing narrative norms, the journey to the TALK TO YOUR GOD ROOM was quick and eventless.

A deserted corridor, with no abrupt, mechanical noises to unnerve Sila as he approached the corner at the end, and stairs that, if they did possess concealed hands, had no interest in letting them shoot out and grab his ankles.

Then there was the *coiled snake* before the Control Room, with the green bulb still flickering and each redundant corner harbouring the possibility of an armed psychopath.

But Dodzi wasn't there either.

And if Sila were being honest, he was only half scared, as the rest of him was still in the URANUS ROOM, mentally orbiting what had just occurred.

Aleša…was she really alive?

Had the computer just toyed with them?

Was it intentional?

For a moment, a minute perhaps, or a minute and a half, he'd thought they were all about to die. Petr, Aleša, an hour between them. Four other crew members, Nakagami and Gašper isolated. Another eight hours and it could've been over. Or worse, only himself left.

The horror of even looking out of the window, imagining the speed of…the velocity of the ship, the rush towards nothingness…

Was that what Sima was talking about when he said *the nihilism of gargantuan strides*?

A sharp stab of green light jolted him out of his thoughts and carried him into the Control Room.

Nakagami was sitting [insanely] with his back to the entrance, parked in front of his usual console on the right-hand side.

'Kenji?'

'Sila, it's you.'

'Ja.'
~~~

Kenji spun his chair round. 'I was watching the life sign readout. The computer told me someone had left the URANUS ROOM and was progressing towards here.'

'We need to get everyone in the URANUS ROOM, quickly.'

'That is a good idea.'

'Gašper too. Last time I saw him he was still in the HALF DONE ROOM.'

'How's Aleša?'

'Alive. Somehow.' Sila paused, thinking back. 'Wait, did the computer tell you that? How did you know?'

'Dodzi told me.'

'What?'

'He visited about ten minutes ago, asking about Uranus.'

'He came here?'

'I noticed something in his hand, there was blood on the end of it. Turned out to be a sharpened chair leg from his room.'

'Jezus, did he attack you? Injure you?'

'It was peculiar, he was very polite. I asked him why there was blood on it, and he told me he'd just stabbed Amma Darko.'

Sila moved deeper into the room, keeping his folded chair raised as he checked the entrance behind him.

'I assumed he was referring to Aleša. In some way, his brain had merged the two, I won't say exactly as I predicted, but it stems from the same psychosis, so I can perhaps take some credit.'

'Kenji…what are we gonna do? He's armed.'

Nakagami turned back to the console and pointed to a message on the screen.

'I can't read that.'

'It says that Dodzi is now in his quarters.'

'He is?'

'Ja.'

'It's certain of it.'

'There is no name attached to the life sign, of course, but it is a logical assumption. Gašper is also in his quarters.'

'He moved?'

'Ja, it appears so.'

'Can you lock Dodzi's door, keep him in there?'

'I am already working on this strategy.'

'Will the computer do it?'

'I believe so.'

'For how long?'

'That is the issue. How long can we keep a man confined? How will we feed him without opening the door?'

'Ne vem.'

'Psychologically, it would be easier if he were to go on a rampage, but he is still very calm, very polite.'

'He has a sharpened chair leg.'

'Ja, that is a problem.' Nakagami looked at the long line of messages on the screen, numerous bulky text paragraphs followed by curt one liners. 'I will stay here as close as I can to curfew, to monitor the life signs. I suggest you go to pick up Gašper and take him to the URANUS ROOM.'

'But we can't stay there overnight…'

'That is not an issue. We are all confined to quarters, therefore perfectly safe. If I can convince the computer to lock Dodzi's door, at least for tomorrow, then we can reconvene in the URANUS ROOM and decide how to proceed.'

'How long before you can lock Dodzi's door?'

'Ne vem.'

'Is there any way you can let us know if he comes out again? Some kind of warning over the tannoy…'

'It is unlikely.'

'Fuck.'

Nakagami sat up straight, stretching out his arms. 'I should continue my work. Go and find Gašper.'

'He's still in his quarters?'

'According to this readout, ja.'

Sila nodded, double-checked the symbols he thought showed Dodzi's location then raised the chair back up and left, telling the green bulb to fuck off as he went.

~~~

'Gašper, you in there?'

No answer.

'Gašper?'

No answer.

'We need to go to the URANUS ROOM.'

Sila looked both ways down the corridor, thankful that the green bulbs nearby weren't malfunctioning like the other one. Not that it wasn't still eerie.

He knocked again, ignoring the call button.

'I know you're in there. We can read your life signs.'

No answer.

'Gašper…'

The door slid open and Gašper appeared, covering almost all of the space.

'I'm resting,' he said, squinting at Sila's chair.

'We need you to come to the URANUS ROOM for a while.'

'No need.'

'Gašper, do you understand what's happening?'

'I'm tired.'

'Dodzi's gone nuts, he stabbed Aleša. He's upstairs now, in his quarters.'

'I will avoid him.'

'You can't…what are you talking about? We can't avoid him forever. He could do anything.'

'I'm going to sleep.'

'Gašper…' Sila stopped and looked at his friend's eyes. They were pink around the edges, dried out. 'Did you…have you taken Petr to the airlock?'

'I'll see you tomorrow, Sila.'

'Gašper…'

'I'm very tired.'

'Have you taken him to the airlock?'
~~~

Gašper stepped back from the door and let it slide shut. Sila thought about putting his chair out to stop it, but couldn't muster either the willpower or a decent excuse.

Perhaps there was no need.

Dodzi wouldn't be able to get in there, unless Gašper answered the door.

And he probably wouldn't do that.

Would he?

~~~

At 21:51, nine minutes before curfew, Nakagami came into the URANUS ROOM, calm and weapon-less, and told them they could relax for a little while as he had persuaded the computer to lock the door to Dodzi's quarters.

'For how long?' asked Chu, sitting next to Aleša, who was herself stretched out across three other chairs.

'Until the day after tomorrow.'

'And then?'

'We will have to decide that tomorrow.'

Nakagami looked down at Aleša's jacket, the bottom part stained by so much blood that it looked like part of the design. 'I suggest we move Aleša back to her quarters first, then return to our own. As Chu is two rooms away from Dodzi, we should escort her after Aleša.'

'Kill the bastard,' muttered Aleša, her eyes still closed.

Nakagami nodded. 'Curfew is in six minutes. We should hurry.'

~~~

With the obvious exception of the doomed Veronika of Desenice in her chambers at Ojstrica Castle, no human had ever stared at a door as much as each crew member did in their quarters that night.

At least, that was the case with Sila.

The others? Perhaps not.

Gašper clearly didn't care, his mind was off in the Oort Cloud, Chu seemed strangely calm even though she'd had her hand on a stab wound half the day, Aleša was zonked out, still filtering in the Antro-D, and Nakagami was Nakagami.

Did any of them really feel what was happening?

Two robots and two trauma victims.

One lunatic.

One future lunatic.

And then there was the ship. The computer. The thing that put up barriers instead of helping them. Green lit corridors. Tricks and fake missions. Refusing to turn the ship around. Pushing suicide. Green lit walls. Corridors. Refusing to turn the ship around. Green lit walls. Suicide.

He looked at the wall to the side, running his eyes over each contour, searching for cracks, a deeper or lighter shade of green, something flawed.

There were several.

It was a flawed ship, slowly eroding.

Dodzi was the logical outcome. The ship had forced him to sharpen a chair leg, left him no choice. Uranus had told him Aleša was Amma Darko. The green confirmed it, so he'd attacked.

But what about Petr?

He didn't look like Amma Darko.

Had he said something?

Had the green told Dodzi he'd said something?

Sila heard a noise, air hissing in the corridor outside.

Dodzi breathing?

He fixed his eyes on the door.

Nothing moved.

But it was green.

And could open at any moment.

Let Dodzi in.

Let more green in.

A maintenance drone with poisonous green gas.

Or a picture of Sadia.

Of others.

A drone finger pointed at the green on the wall.

Any wall, didn't matter, they were all green, pure green, flickering green, neutral green, apologetic green.

The whole ship, it's a-

The whole ship was designed to kill them.

The whole ship was designed to kill them.

The whole ship was

The ship was designed to kill him.

The ship was telling him to die.

The ship was green and cold.

The ship was green.

The ship would kill him with green.

Green ships kill.

A picture of Space came into his head, a green ship drifting through it. Then a picture of Gašper's head. It was smiling. Wouldn't it be weird if Space were just like *Dibrivna Vaska*?

Gašper's head disappeared, replaced by Potočnik. *I want you to die out here, Sila. You're the best man for the job.*

'What?'

I want you to die. You're the best man for the job.

I want you to die.

Die like your sister.

Die, prosim.

In your own time.

~~~

At ten the next morning, the computer made the usual announcement.

'Attention crew,

Curfew hours have ended. You may now leave your quarters safely.

Additional news follows. Crew Member Petr has not yet been placed in Airlock 1. Prosim, take care of this today, before the corpse starts to fully decompose.
~~~

Secondly, due to the danger posed to surviving crew members, as well as the murder of Crew Member Petr and the attempted murder of Crew Member Aleša, Crew Member Dodzi's quarters were drained of oxygen during the night. For any humanists among the crew, he did not suffer. His corpse will also need to be placed in Airlock 1, though it is understood that placing it there at the same time as Crew Member Petr might be insensitive. Therefore, we suggest Crew Member Petr first, and Crew Member Dodzi later this afternoon.

On a lighter note, the URANUS ROOM has been repurposed and will now function as the OPTIMISM ROOM. Selected episodes of classic science fiction serial *Dibrivna Vaska* will be available for viewing, so if any crew member feels depressed after recent events, they can find entertainment at that location.

In tandem with this, the drones have managed to create the green cream required to use the VR machine safely, and have placed four tubs in the PHILOSOPHY ROOM as a trial run. Unfortunately, a second LIN swab remains unavailable, therefore crew members will have to allocate VR time among themselves.

Have a safe and bold trip to Luyten 726-8

Hvala.'

~~~

'You told the computer to kill him?'

'Ja.'

Sila looked around at the others. Aleša was staring at the side of her cup, Chu was staring at Nakagami, and Gašper was already standing up and heading for the door.

'I'm going to my room,' he said, to the green in the corridor outside.

When he was gone, no one said anything for a while.

Nakagami turned to the walls, either studying the old posters they'd made, or following the lines of green in between.

Aleša rubbed near the wound on the back of her head, the usual headscarf absent.

Chu looked at the back of *Icelandic Satanism.*
~~~

Finally, Sila found a question.

'How long did it take to convince the computer?'

'To drain the oxygen?' asked Nakagami, shifting attention back to the table.

'Ja.'

'About two and a half hours.'

'That long?'

'What was the winning argument?' asked Chu.

'It was more repetition and occasional novelty than any singular point.' He looked at Aleša, whose eyes were now on Petr's Russian textbook. 'The severity of murder, making the computer-…ne, helping the computer to understand the depth of that, beyond the concept.'

'So our rooms aren't rigged too?' asked Aleša.

'Unless you murder someone, ne.'

She opened the Russian book, reading some out to herself.

'Perhaps that was too glib. What I mean to say is, the computer is still entrenched in its core beliefs. Its program is fixed to protect us. We are in no danger now. From this point on, we can all relax.'

'Cruising to the Luyten 7 system,' mumbled Sila.

Nakagami ignored Sila's remark and turned to leave.

'What about Uranus?' asked Chu.

'Unlikely.'

'But not impossible?'

Nakagami turned back. 'To be candid, I have already switched my focus to the Kuiper Belt. I suggest you find a way to do the same.'

'And if we don't really understand what the Kuiper Belt is?' asked Sila.

'There is a map in the KUIPER BELT ROOM.'

'Of course.'

Nakagami looked at one of the posters again, Petr's recreation of their ship, then left.

A few seconds later, Chu stood up and followed him, saying there was something in the TELEPORT ROOM she needed to take care of.

That left Sila and Aleša, one flicking through a Russian book, the other staring at the floor.

~~~

It took a further four hours before Sila managed to store up sufficient lenity to go to Gašper's quarters and enquire about Petr's body.

He asked Aleša if she wanted to come along, say goodbye to her friend, but she just muttered, 'shameful,' and stuck her head deeper in the Russian book.

'I'll let you know when he's in the airlock, if you change your mind.'

'Ne.'

'Are you sure?'

'… … …'

'Sorry?'

'… … …'

'Is that Russian?'

'… … …'

'Okay. I'll let you know anyway. Just in case.'

'… … …'

'Ja.'

~~~

It was strange walking along the corridor. There was no crazed Ghanaian potentially lurking round each corner, or behind the walls, but there was still the trace of something.

Maybe it was the green.

Or the Šarec torture house allusion embedded in the design.

Or something new.

The ghost of Dodzi, sucked out with the oxygen, trapped there.

Was he really dead?

No one saw his body.

He could be hid-…

Sila forced his brain onto a different track, the Petr track. He focused on the wall at the end of the corridor, narrowing it into a tunnel, and when he reached his target, knocked on the door to the left without giving himself time to counter.

Surprisingly, the door slid open first time, Gašper with the same pink eyes as the night before, smiling.

'I was just-…' started Sila, but Gašper headed him off.

'I'm almost ready. Just need to put a jacket on him, cover the wrists better.'

'Can I help?'

'Lifting him, carrying, ja. Wait a minute.'

Gašper disappeared back into his room, talking to someone inside. Sila shifted slightly and looked at the wall with Potočnik on it. For some reason, Gašper had put two small cut-out pieces of red card over his purple eyes, but left the rest of his face intact.

'Okay, he's coming out.'

Sila stepped forward to help then immediately retreated back outside the room when he saw Gašper rushing over, the fully dressed body of Petr slung over his shoulder.

'Can you take his legs?'

'Ja.'

They carried him to the end of the corridor and stopped. Gašper looked up and down the stairs, confused.

'Up,' said Sila.

'Is it?'

'Ja.'

'I thought it was down.'

Sila shrugged, looking up the stairs.

'Up then.'

~~~

After laying Petr down on the airlock floor, Gašper stayed on his knees and tidied up his lover's clothes. He explained to him how, from now on, he was going to learn Russian every day and any progress he made would be shared between them cos Petr would've got there too at some point, he was sure of it.
~~~

'Ya besheh tebee.'

'Is that Russian?' asked Sila, hanging back by the door.

'Ja. I hope.'

'What does it mean?'

'A promise.'

Leaning in close, Gašper put his cheek against Petr's left cheek and held it there. For two, three minutes, it stayed like that. Finally, he gave up on the cheek pressing, kissed Petr on the lips and stood back up.

Sila thought of about seven different things he could do to show compassion, but the act of thinking quickly replaced the doing.

The two of them continued standing there, looking mostly at the triptych window panels dead ahead, occasionally shifting weight to the other leg.

Minutes passed by.

'No more science lessons,' came out of Gašper's mouth and drifted off without response.

A whistling sound sailed in from the corridor behind them.

The drones switching on perhaps?

Gašper gave a 'ja' to no one in particular then sat back down on the metal grating, his hand playing with Petr's until it found a comfortable grip.

He sat there a while.

At some point he mumbled what sounded like a melody, some lyrics Sila couldn't catch.

Then a recommitment to studying Russian. It would definitely happen. Every day for the rest of the trip. Minus the occasional day off for brain-recovery.

Finally, without any kind of formality or hesitation, the orange headband came off. Gašper folded it up and placed it on Petr's chest, before frowning and tying it around his forehead instead.

'So the aliens see you,' he muttered.

Sila held his reaction. He'd seen Gašper without the headband before, but this time it felt strange, as if he'd just lifted up the top of his scalp.

'It's weird to be here like this. Really weird. All those times we…' Gašper stopped, eyes drawn to the NO LINGERING sign.

'You okay?'

'Thinking.'

Sila bowed awkwardly, going back to the triptych.

The sign got another minute before Gašper shook his head and said, 'ne, it's gone.'

'There's no rush.'

'Forget it. Memories are unreliable anyway.'

'Ja…okay.'

Pushing down his own sleeves, Gašper held up Petr's hand and kissed it, held his lips there for a long time, and started mumbling the melody again. When the breath ran out, he moved slowly up past Petr's wrist wound, to his neck, to his forehead, to his almost transparently pale lips, and pressed down as hard as he could.

Something primal came out, definitely not Russian.

Then some more.

Finally, he pulled back and wiped Petr's lips, wiped his eyes with his jacket sleeve, forced himself up onto his feet, told Sila he was okay, he'd be okay soon and walked out of the airlock without looking back.

~~~

The computer announced the ejection of Petr's body an hour later.

Taking it as his cue, Nakagami went to Dodzi's quarters and tried to lift the body by himself.

It was possible, but would take at least an hour, so he fetched Sila from the PHILOSOPHY ROOM to help him.

'I don't really feel comfortable doing that,' Sila said, ten pages into *The Cyberiad.*

'I see.'

'He was a murderer.'

'Do you feel comfortable if I ask someone else to do it?'

Sila stopped on page eleven, read another half page then said, 'fine.'
~~~

~~~

The only notable thing about Dodzi's room was how tidy it was. For a broken lunatic, he didn't leave much on the floor. He didn't look that dead either. Lying flat on his back, his legs bent, it seemed almost like he was asleep.

'Take his legs, I'll get his arms.'

Sila did as he was instructed. They lifted on a count of two. When they turned back towards the door, Nakagami pointed at the picture on the wall.

'The dangers of essentialism,' he said, monotone.

Sila hadn't noticed it when he'd first come in, there had been too much damage, but now that he focused on the actual picture beyond the stab marks, it was as clear as a shark's eye.

Amma Darko, facing away from Mars, eyes fixed squarely on Dodzi's bed.

~~~

They lowered Dodzi down on to the same floor Petr had been placed on two hours earlier.

Nakagami put Dodzi's arms across his chest, stood back and told him it'd been the only thing left to do.

Sila dredged up a *sorry* from somewhere.

Then they left.

PART THREE

Wintertime Anarchists

Sila knocked on the door.

When Aleša didn't respond, he left the oatmeal on the floor slightly to the left, knocked on the door again, and said, 'breakfast.'

Gašper ate the oatmeal in small doses, his eyes flicking between the Russian sentences and the Cyrillic alphabet key.

'Kenji says the oatmeal will be used up soon,' said Sila, staring at the rim of Gašper's bowl.

'Ja.'

'Another six months maybe. Then we'll have to switch to the plant food. That we never see grown.'

'Ja.'

'More bok choy. Mizuna lettuce. Rice-related stuff. Ne vem. Never heard of half of the other lot. Now it's gonna be our breakfast.'

'Ja.'

'Dinner should be better. Still got potatoes, onion, pasta…other stuff. Coffee is okay too. Can last up to twenty years apparently.'

'Ja, coffee.'

Sila shifted from the bowl to the wall, the empty space where Petr's Uranus painting had hung just a week earlier. It wasn't clear exactly what had happened to it, but he assumed Gašper had taken it to his room. Or ripped it to pieces. Just like Aleša with her *Victory* posters. Defeat followed by rage, followed by green-lit walls, other green-lit walls, flickering green lit walls…

'You wanna make a poster after this?'

'Ne, not really.'

'Go to the OPTIMISM ROOM, watch *Dibrivna Vaska*?'

'Ne.'

'PHILOSOPHY ROOM?'

'I'm busy. You go.'

Sila nodded, looking over at the food dispenser. 'I'll probably stay here for a bit, get another coffee.'

'Okay.'

'Write some theory.'

Gašper dropped the spoon in the bowl, got up and left, taking his Russian book with him.

Sila leaned forward, checking the bowl.

Half the oatmeal was still there.

There were several places on the ship that the crew rarely visited - Engineering, the HALF DONE ROOM, Airlocks 1 and 2 - but the THERAPY ROOM was by the far the most decorative.

Potted plants. Posters of aliens from *Dibrivna Vaska.* A mix of brainlessly inspirational and grimly realistic quotes. Slightly padded seats.

It hadn't been like this when it was the LAUNCH ROOM. In fact, it hadn't been this way a week ago.

At some point, the drones had come in and redecorated. Changed the ship again. Took it further away from what it was. Added another fucking rhizome. Uprooted people with already shredded roots.

But it had been the LAUNCH ROOM.

Confused people had sat in there.

It had orbited Earth.

There had been *a way*, at one point.

When it was the LAUNCH ROOM.

Which it still was

At root level.

Sila took his legs off one of the other padded seats and stood up, playing out the scene again.

LAUNCH ROOM, two guards.

Ambush one, take his uniform, ride the elevator back down to Slovenia.

Find Sadia.

Forget Sadia.

Fuck Sadia.

Take her to Finland and fuck her next to every lake.

Invite everyone.

Handcuff Chu to Aleša, force her to give a shit.

Everyone in the same cabin.

Same room.

There was a beep, sharp enough to make him jump.

'It has been forty-five minutes since you entered the THERAPY ROOM,' said the ship. 'Please describe your emotional state.'

'If your stomach's not feeling too bad, maybe we could watch some *Dibrivna Vaska*? Mojca Ito bringing down the entire Byrgius Crater…'

'Ne.'

'…or trying to. Okay. Another episode then?'

'Not interested.'

'Gašper said he might come…'

'Ne.'

'…if I can get him away from that Russian book for more than five seconds. Maybe you could help? All three of us can do some Russian and…'

'Ne…'

'…then slowly shift to the OPTIMISM ROOM, put an episode on before he has a chance to-…'

'I'm not going in that room.'

It was nearly curfew and she was hungry.

Too hungry to ignore.

Which meant there would have to be another fox impression.

Exiting her quarters, she took the forward route round to the CREATE NOT DESTROY ROOM, ignored the faux-seaweed Chu usually ate, grabbed some taro sticks and headed back out.

As she passed Jame's quarters, she felt a twinge in her stomach and stopped.

Chu had said it would happen for a week or two, a sudden pain now and then as the wound healed.

Said it days ago.

Then hid in the TELEPORT ROOM again.

Like a sociopath.

Or worse than a sociopath, a coward.

Coward…

Aleša straightened up and started moving again. Her door was next, but she didn't stop, she kept going, past Klemen's room, right to the very end of the corridor.

'Coward,' she said quietly, putting her face as close as possible to Dodzi's door without touching it.

Gašper sat in the CREATE NOT DESTROY ROOM, repeating words from the Russian textbook.

There was a bowl of ramen next to him, untouched.

Now and then, he would stop reading and look up.

Absorb the green on the wall.

Then return to the book.

The OPTIMISM ROOM still had Aleša's blood on the floor.

Though, judging by the swish marks and soap lines, the maintenance drones had made some kind of an effort to scrub it off.

Sila tried his best to bypass all that as he and Aleša walked in, guiding her to the right, picking out two faraway seats and asking softly which episode she wanted to watch.

'Don't care.'

He brought up the menu and scrolled through the list.

Headhunter

Gon

The Devil Card

Life Sign

Is that you, boo?

Cane Tyrant

It was all there. Six full seasons, seventy-eight episodes, each one containing at least some degree of drab nihilism; a character death, a hopeless dilemma or, best case scenario, a bleak compromise.

In spite of all that, it was still *Dibrivna Vaska.*

'We'll just skip the sad parts,' said Sila, clicking on *The Devil Card.*

'Don't care,' responded Aleša, eyes drifting down to the floor by the screen.

'The three of us are thinking of hitting up the *Dah Heen Link* later and I thought maybe you'd like to come along.'

Chu gazed out the lobby window, at the hanging shape of Neptune in the nearby sky.

'Do you like phosphorous cuisine? I love it, personally.'

There wasn't much else to look at. Just the nitrogen ice surface below. And the occasional plume of dust.

'I know a restaurant that does incredible cubes.'

One setting. Twelve *Tier-4* characters. Basic arc developments then reset.

'Listen, I don't know about you, but I think we need to rile this place up a bit.'

The promise of a trip to the *Dah Heen Link* foiled by a surprise coup in the base airlock.

'Move the chairs around, change the singing roster, question the constant kowtowing to those KEL thugs.'

Almost continuous narrative momentum.

No turn-off switch.

'How about some more green tea, help you think a little clearer.'

Chu placed her index finger against her temple and tapped.

'Wah, leaving already?'

The reckless ex-security guard with a dark past disintegrated and took the rest of the Triton base with him.

Taking its place, the TELEPORT ROOM.

And a swathe of green residue stuck to a faint green tinge on the side of Chu's head.

The wall to the KITCHEN DELUXE wasn't doing much, but it was green, and green was something he understood.

But behind it?

What were they doing in there?

The drones, the machinery…

Putting his ear against the cold metal, Gašper closed his eyes and repeated the question out loud.

Ne vem, he thought.

Nakagami hadn't told him, no one had, this was the first time he'd done it, the ship was brand new, they'd only been on it for a few days and

there was a medical bay

according to the map.

Maybe they should go there next, have a look?

In the NOT YET Centre, he'd never been able to fall asleep on his back.

But now it was fine.

With the Russian book on the pillow next to him, it was fine. No trouble at all.

Eleven days after passing Uranus, Nakagami gathered them all together in the OPTIMISM ROOM and told them the new target.

'GongGong.'

'Who?'

'A dwarf planet. It's not quite on our path, but it is suitably distant. As in it gives us enough time to work on the computer.'

Sila stabbed a pasta shape with his fork, then another. 'You mean you and Chu?'

'Not quite.'

'He means all of us,' said Chu, putting a cup of coffee in front of Aleša and the now slightly frayed copy of *The Crying Of The Wind* in front of herself.

'As there are only five of us now, it is more practical to divide the computer time up into more sessions. Ideally, five, but three is also acceptable.'

'Huh?'

'In truth, I believe it would be good for me to remove myself from the GOD ROOM for a while, and good for crew morale as well, considering recent events.'

'I can read about twenty symbols,' said Sila, looking at Gašper and Aleša. 'You guys too, right?'

'Not interested,' said Aleša, pulling at the sleeve of her blank, green t-shirt.

'Me neither,' added Gašper.

'You do not need to learn the symbols,' continued Nakagami, unperturbed. 'I will give you a script to type, in code. If you wish to learn some symbols, you can do that too, of course.'

'Ne vem…'

'Ni panike, it's something that can be eased into. Gonggong is five-hundred and ten days away, according to my initial calculation, which is almost double the time it took to get to Uranus. Or close to Uranus, to be more accurate.'

Sila examined the four pasta shapes stacked on his fork. 'A year and a half. That's quite long.'

'Psychologically, it is irrelevant to some degree. Anything over two-hundred days is processed the same way by our brains.'

'Very reassuring.'

Chu took the cup from in front of Aleša and drank. 'So whatever we did to waste time between Jupiter and Uranus, just do it again.'

'Hide in the TELEPORT ROOM,' said Aleša, caustic.

'Or that creepy moon base,' said Gašper, not looking up from his Russian book.

Chu put the cup back down and picked up her book.

'I was joking,' whispered Aleša, leaning across.

'Noted.'

'Half joking.'

Nakagami coughed. 'I would suggest making a list of activities that we can all reference. Language is one option. Political theory is another. There are also the books in the PHILOSOPHY ROOM.'

'It's an erratic collection,' said Sila. '*Icelandic Satanism*, for example.'

'Ja, it is not ideal, but it will suffice.' Nakagami turned his attention to Gašper. 'I am willing to continue the science lessons, if there is a desire for it.'

Gašper turned a page in the Russian book. 'Ne.'

'Me neither,' added Sila.

'Very well. The offer will remain open.'

~~~

After the others had left, Sila moved onto the chair next to Nakagami and said he had an idea.

'Ja?'

'I didn't want to say it in front of the others, but…the other day, in the LAUNCH ROOM…'

'THERAPY ROOM…'

'Ja, that one. I was sitting in there, just looking at the walls kind of blankly, and…it wasn't really sinking in, what I was looking at…which is quite common in there, I admit…but then suddenly, out of nothing, it did sink in, and I realised, wah, everything is different. The wall decoration, the chairs, and, for a tiny, brief moment, I thought, where the hell is this?'

'I see.'

'Obviously, it didn't last long, I knew logically where I was, but the thought of *this is different, where the hell is it,* that part kept going. Then later, I was on my bed, thinking of the VR machine, what it could've done for us if it had more than one setting, or more than one swab…and I remembered an old Debord article I'd read in the collective book centre, *Theory of the Dérive*, and I thought, why don't we change things? Why don't we move things around a bit here, in our reality. And on our terms instead of his?'

'An interruption to routine?'

'It wouldn't have to be anything major. Maybe the tables in here, the poster positions, just superficial things to go with your list of activities. Break us out of this environment.'

'An interruption to geography.'

'Ja, in a sense.'

'It is a reasonable plan. Considering the failure of the VR machine.'

'That's what I thought, it can be an alternative. Hopefully help Aleša and Gašper too, shake them out of their ruts.'
~~~

'That is less likely.'

Sila coughed, revising his line. 'Okay. Help to change the décor of their ruts. Make them a little brighter.'

'Perhaps.'

Standing in front of the bathroom mirror, back curved slightly to keep his spine supple, Nakagami pulled up his fringe and placed it between the blades of the scissors. Another *counted in his head* minute to make sure it was lined up right, steadied breathing, then snip. A quarter of an inch fell into the sink.

Satisfied, he repeated the procedure on the sides.

And the top.

And what he could get to at the back.

When it was completed, he straightened his head and examined his reflection.

Adequate, he thought, attention already switching to the *Active Satomi* poster pinned up behind him.

Gon threw himself in front of the neutrino beam, ready to explode, confused when he didn't.

'Get out of there, Gon,' yelled Joona. 'There's a plasma leak, we can't seal it.'

Sila felt a twinge in his lower back, realized he was almost horizontal on his chair and sat up.

'I can fix it,' shouted Gon, stepping out of the neutrino beam and running over to the console.

'There's no time,' said Mojca Ito over the comm, voice crackling. 'Get out of there.'

'I can do it…'

'Stop,' said Sila, his finger on the pad button just to make sure.

The people on the screen froze. The plasma leak froze. The neutrino beam technically froze, but still looked visually active.

'It's okay, keep going,' said Aleša, pulling at the left side of her hair.

'Ne vem.'

'I don't even like Gon that much.'

'You sure?'

'Ja.'

'Gašper?'

'I'm not watching.'

'Huh?'

'I don't like this episode.'

'Why did you ask me to play it then?'

'I thought it was a different one.'

'Should I turn it off?'

Aleša rubbed the back of her head, pulling loose a few hairs that'd been stuck to her wound. 'There's four minutes left, just play it.'

'I can turn it off if you want?'

'Play.'

Sila gave it a few seconds then pinned down the button.

The scene continued.

Gon frantically pressed buttons on the console, wiped sweat off his forehead, ignored more warnings to get out of there, laughed maniacally and blew up.

'Gon…' whispered Ito.

Back on the ship, the crew returned to their posts, glancing sideways at the one empty seat.

'Weird how they never talk about their families,' said Gašper, leaning forward.

'I thought you weren't watching.'

'Suppose they must be all dead.'
'Gašper…'
'Ja?'

The Swahili City States
700-1500AD??
The Bantu people built port settlements down the East Coast and established trading routes.
In the 10th Century, Muslims came and traded, and eventually settled there.

The settlements grew into cities, with mixed marriages common, and then initiated trading routes with India and China.

Sila stopped, pointing the tip of his pen to the side.

He knew the bones of it, or he was pretty sure he did, but what about the details?

Did the Muslims enslave the Bantu?

Or the inland tribes?

He had no idea. The Muslims did have slaves, he'd read that somewhere, but he didn't know where they had them, or who they were.

Would it really have been that amicable?

Ah, it didn't matter. He was right or he was wrong. No one was going to read any of it.

He lowered the pen back to the paper.

Although the Muslims were not perfect, they weren't as bad as the Portuguese.

They did not enslave the Bantu.

Far as I know.

Far as my thumb.

Far as Ghana.

There was a single beep, almost beyond the range of his senses.

'It has been thirty minutes since you entered the room,' said the ship. 'Would you like to report your feelings?'

'Ne.'

'I already see her twice a day.'

'Not enough.'

'What then? You want me to see her three times a day? Four?'

Sila looked at the scanning device on the table, the strange diagrams laid out on the teleport platform and the Angolan rocking chair that Chu spent most of the day curled up on. Not to forget the VR machine, the Klemen killer, which had its own special display table under the Varo witch sketch.

'It's not the number of times, it's the amount…'

'I'm busy, Sila.'

'…of time you stay there. Busy doing what?'

'Numerous things.'

'We're not working in a collective, you don't have to be here all the time.'

'I'm not.'

'Or any of the time.'

'I do.'

'An hour a day, that would be enough.'

Chu pressed a button on the scanning device and wrote down some numbers.

'What are you even doing here anyway? You said the computer wouldn't authorize your experiments…'

'I'm thinking, planning.'

'For what?'

'You still haven't given me your pattern by the way.'

'Chu…'

'I'm serious. The only one I have so far is Kenji's. Gašper said ne, probably because Petr rejected it before, and Aleša…'

'Why don't you stop working on it for a while?'

'I do, every day.' She pointed at the books by the rocking chair. 'In fact, most of my time in here is spent reading other things. Aziz, Jung, the occult…'

'Sitting on Triton,' said Sila, looking about as pointedly as a human could at the faint green patch on her temple.

Chu pulled some hair across to cover it. 'I haven't used it in a while.'

'But the machine is permanently in this room.'

'More as storage than anything. Honestly, I'm tired of it now. Too many *Tier-4* people always lurking about, trying to take over the base.'

'Good, then you can try something else.'

Chu gestured at the books again.

'I mean, get out of this room and try something else.'

'What, like playing nurse?'

'Ja. Come up to the CREATE ROOM, talk to her. Learn Russian with her. Convince her to wear her headscarves again.'

'I already talk to her.'

'Not much.'

'She mostly tells me to go away. Or ignores me completely.'

'That's what she does to everyone.'

Chu put the scanning device down and walked over to the screen. She added a line and then a circle around a beam, muttering to herself about, 'locational instability.'

'Can't she learn Russian with Gašper?'

'She does a little bit. I'm just suggesting that you spend time with her. Stop her spiralling down too far.'

'There's danger of that?'

'Ne vem.'

'What does Kenji say?'

'He said you should consider reigniting sexual relations with her.'

'Ha…'

'I'm serious. Those were his exact words.'

'Ja, I don't doubt it.'

'Obviously you don't have to go that far, if you don't want to, but she needs more than me. Definitely more than Gašper.'

'Captain Positivism.'

'Ja.'

Chu muttered something at the screen and did her very best not to fold her arms. 'Okay, Sila.'

'You'll try?'

'If you give me your brain pattern. Ja. I will try.'

Sila paused, looking at the mess of lines and circles on the screen. Then the *Witch Going To The Sabbath* print on the wall. Then the VR machine underneath it.

'My whole brain?'

Sila abandoned his probably inaccurate account of the 2079-81 Nestification Jaunts and switched to Bley-like[44] nonsense instead.

Gawp tired of black, slide to your green. Gawp tired of green, slide black again. Blink if you must. Rap sparingly. In the Middle Ages, men put their hands on tits daily. Drowned the difficult ones.

He paused.

Thought of Sadia.

Saw the dead end.

Continued.

The door slid open and Chu walked in, rubbing her eyes, mildly confused at the new furniture arrangement.

'Breakfast?' asked Sila, covering his notes.

[44] Tyson Bley, prolific writer of anti-poetry like *Cuban V*, *Mysterious Doctor Satan*, *Barely Riker* etc., died 2034 in a beach fight.

Nakagami sat in his quarters, alone.

There were posters on the wall.

Drone-created paper on the desk.

On the top sheet, in green ink, was Nakagami's version of *Silas Marner*, his second attempt to re-write a classic novel after the Nabokov failure.

The summary:

Silas Marner was visited by a little girl in his cottage in the woods. They grew close and she started sitting on his lap. The girl secretly wanted to do things with him, but he said ne. Silas grew to love her and told her he never wanted to control her and she must never follow every word he said.

The girl never grew up and Silas never grew old.

Nakagami picked up the pen, looking at the floor.

Then at the pillow, the empty side of his bed.

The girl sat on his lap and re-adjusted her position many times. She said she wanted to do things to him and took off her training bra, placed her hand on his

He paused, looking over at the door.

It was closed, locked.

Unable to be opened from the outside.

He tapped the pen against the mattress.

The girl sat on his lap, asking many questions. Mostly concerning science. He answered as best he could.

Everyone, every critic, always said at the end of each episode beyond the third season, *Da Gruta should've died in this one*, and in the season five episode *Ever God*, it was especially true.

Ankle twisted, seconds away from exploding with the base, and the crew saved him?

Why?

He'd killed Tandissta's father, he'd tried to kill them multiple times, he was the head of the Vrn Sector, how could they just pick him up and let him go…

'…like an amiable hitchhiker?' said Gašper, finishing his tirade.

'He was unarmed,' replied Aleša towards the floor, 'human.'

'Then don't pick him up.'

'Too late, he was in the room already. And his body language was meeker than usual.'

'It was a trick.'

'Clearly.'

'Then don't save him. Let the base explode, leave. They've done that kind of thing before.'

'Not to a major villain.'

'It's stupid.'

Aleša shrugged, sliding deeper down the back of her seat.

'Sila?'

'Ja?'

'Opinion?'

'On Da Gruta?'

'Ja, and don't say *ne vem*.'

'He was head of the Vrn sector. They should've let him die.'

'Exactly, and he killed Tandissta's father. And he murdered thousands of other people. And he was responsible for the security forces, who also murdered thousands of other people. And he pimped for the dictatorship. Didn't try to change a thing. They should've vivisected him. Got Avro to do it. Or Tandissta.'

'Too cold,' said Aleša, voice almost inaudible.

'Serious, he wasn't even entertaining. Just a sociopath. Everything dry and, *you did not follow orthodoxy, laws are final*, every time he killed someone…had someone killed.'

Ja, thought Sila, drifting off into his own Vrn sector.

A sociopath.

Orthodoxy.

But didn't he also build schools on Daveenos III?

In *The Rotating Child*, the courier reading out his file; seventeen percent of his earnings earmarked for youth development. Neglected youth, if he remembered right.

Was that school-building?

Or were they military academies?

He closed his eyes and tried to pull the episode back, but he hadn't seen it in years and hadn't got around to it on the ship yet either.

Maybe he was wrong.

Or maybe he was right, they were military training camps, disguised as schools.

He didn't know.

'…as evil as they come, eviller probably,' finished Gašper, standing in front of the projection screen, blocking the credits.

'There is no wind in Space,' said Nakagami in the CREATE NOT DESTROY ROOM.

'But…'

'No hurricanes either.'

'What about solar wind?' asked Sila, taking a bite out of a cucumber.

'Ja, solar wind,' repeated Gašper. 'That's what I meant.'

'You said wind.'

'The stuff from the Sun. Solar wind.'

'That is not what you were referring to.'

'Ja, either/or. Regular wind or solar wind. Any kind.'

Nakagami pulled at his zip, looking to the middle window for help. It responded with void.

'What is solar wind, actually?' asked Sila, finishing his cucumber.

'Wind from the Sun,' answered Gašper quickly.

'Ja, but what is it? What's it made of?'

'Ne vem.'

'Atoms?'

After finishing *Icelandic Satanism* and discussing it to death, Sila, Gašper and Aleša went to the PHILOSOPHY ROOM and skimmed for new material.

There were seventy-two books in total and, so far, they'd read eight plus twenty-six pages.

Icelandic Satanism / Jónsdóttir

The Cyberiad / Lem

Solar Lottery / Dick

Death Moon 4 / Tse

Death Moon 5 / Tse

The Culture of Lies / Ugrešić

The Virgin of the 7 Daggers / Lee

Bakunin at 200 / Khalago

Side Eye / Vitti

The last one was picked up solely for its back cover blurb, which promised a future society where people could only look at each other from the side, and if they faced someone directly they would self-combust.

The first chapter consisted of a man telling another man to look at him, without edits, repeatedly, until finally he gave up and walked away.

Gašper somehow made it onto chapter 2, but gave up when a woman started insisting the same man from the first chapter look at her.

Now, they were all a bit drained from *Icelandic Satanism* and wanted something lighter, in the same vein as *Death Moon 4* and *5*.

'This one's weird…'

'Which one?'

'*Alien TV: are we characters in another civilization's universe?*' Sila flipped to the back of the book, reading a bit of the blurb. 'Wake up…to the fact that all of us may be nothing more than an algorithm programmed by an alien AI!'

'Not interested,' said Aleša.

'Ja, seems a bit hyperbolic.'

'Even academic dry, still not interested.'

'Ja, I suppose.'

Sila put the book down and went back to rummaging.

'That goes for anything metaphysical. Science, philosophy…' Aleša picked up a book with a decent cover, read the back and almost spat at it when she saw the words *robot nature*. 'If there's no grounding to it, then it's pointless.'

'Does that go for all theory?'

'Depends.'

'Whether or not Bakunin's attached to it?'

Aleša smiled. 'He should be. Ne, any theory is okay, as long as it has historical cases.'

'Not Sima then.'

'Fuck, Sima. He was a coward. Rich enough to hide himself away from the world, then scolding us for not being smart, not doing things exactly the way he wanted them done from his little countryside mansion.'

'The Grand Hotel Abyss…'

'Hotel what?'

'Lukács, quite a long time ago. Said some philosophers were too detached, too cosy.'

'…that they lived in comfort, analysing the abyss.'

'Ja, you know it?'

'Not the guy you said. Someone else, said there were hotels around the hotel, and all philosophy was basically done from comfort…'

'Bōl…'

'…de-powering and something else. Ja, Bōl, that was it. All philosophers and theorists had to depower themselves, remove the ego…'

'*De-powering of the Conjectured Self*?'

'…reject *ism* badges. Ja, that one.'

Sila picked up a book with a nice shade of purple then put it right back down when he saw it was by Vitti, the same guy who wrote *Side*

Eye. 'The conjectured part was disputed, but she was mostly right. Especially the series of hotels…'

'She was totally right. Not that I read her books.'

'…and her concept of thought dynamics. It was quite radical at the time.'

'What concept?'

'Or fashionable. Others had done it before, Orwell, Dolgoff, mostly through personal accounts of wars or revolutions…but Bōl took it to the level of thought itself…the *defiant hurricane of what do I think right now mixed with what will I think ten seconds later*. Her words.'

'That's her concept?'

'Ne, sorry, got a bit side-tracked. Her concept of Thought Dynamics…basically, and I'm paraphrasing here, she claimed that theorists relied too much on established referential signifiers and signified, i.e. the names of ideas from the past, instead of thinking of our own.'

'You mean coming up with new names for ideas?'

'Through your own understanding of that idea, ja. That way there would be no more parrots, or those didactic, *this is all from the last two books I read* types of rhetorician.'

'Historical example?'

Sila laughed, picking up another book from the pile in front of him. 'It's not historical, but she did a book on logical fallacies. You know, the established names for bad arguments, like *motte and bailey, no true Scotsman, ad hominem* etc.'

'I vaguely know them.'

'There's about ten that are mainstream, most people will know them. Gašper, what's an ad hominem attack?'

'Huh?' Gašper was lost in the blurb of a book with samurai werewolves on the cover. 'Ad what?'

'What is an ad hominem attack, in an argument?'

'Attacking the person.'

Sila turned back to Aleša. 'See?'

'So Bōl changed the names of these fallacies?'

'Not just changed them, she went back to the foundation, read classical arguments and came up with her own terms for what was being done. Some of them old, some new. Like the Vreenak fallacy.'[45]

'I think I know that one. Using mistakes in your second language to cover argument flaws…'

'Ja, that was one of her most famous ones. Rhizomize the self, reshape the battlefield. I think her point was, theory had become too referential, too inaccessible. Instead of shortcuts, people used names and other theorist's ideas in place of actual thinking, and the thinking pool got smaller and more cliquey.'

'Hang on…'

'That's what I got out of it anyway. Ja?'

'Wouldn't theorists after her just use her names as a reference? Replace the old ones with hers and also not think?'

'Ja, that was the main problem.'

'It doesn't make sense.'

'Communication-wise, it lacked practicality.'

'Even if it did work, how would anyone be able to discuss anything if they're all using different names and terms?'

'That's why she revised it later, saying only to some degree, people need to reconfigure. Not for everything.'

'Wah, and she almost had it too. Don't rely on old theory.'

'Ja, her basic idea was sound.'

'Don't listen to people from comfortable backgrounds regurgitating old theory either.'

'Except Bakunin.'

'But then she just does the same thing, more theory. Nothing practical. Ja, Bakunin. At least he had a concept of factories…'

'Bōl did some practical stuff too.'

'…and he cared about workers. Ne, theory's a dead end, I'm done with it. Unless it's grounded.'

'Okay.'

---

[45] *DS9 In the Pale Moonlight* – 'any flaws in the data rod will be attributed to the explosion.'

'And don't ask me what I want instead, ne vem.'

'Fiction?'

'If it's realist, ja. Or creative in a non-philosophical, non-science fiction way.'

'How about this one?' asked Sila, holding up *Witch Leopard.*

Aleša frowned at the cover, an East-African woman with hypno-spiral eyes. If she knew how, she would've sighed too. 'Plot?'

'Magical realism.'

'Plot,' she repeated.

'A young girl is tired of her life in Kilwa and dreams of following the trade routes to the East, but her father wants her to work in IT. Reaching a tipping point, she runs away and ends up somewhere near Mombasa, in a village mesmerized by the powerful and mysterious Witch Leopard. Can she make a deal with this deity or will she also fall under her spell?'

'Skip.'

'It sounds okay.'

'Don't like magical realism. Skip.'

'Gašper?'

'I've got it.'

'Got what?'

'Our next book. Ne, wait there's more of them. Holy shit, it's our whole next series.'

He held up a black and yellow cover, something they all recognized.

'*Gah Council.*'

'I've never actually read any,' said Sila.

'Heard they're all trash,' said Aleša, still sifting through the other books.

'Who said that?'

'Ne vem. People.'

'They're great. And quite deep too.'

'You've read them?'

'Two of them, when I was in the NOT YET Centre.'

'Is that Volume One?'

'Ja, looks like it.' Gašper glanced down at the books he'd separated from the main pack. 'There's seven that I've found. Maybe more.'

'Could last us a while.'

'Exactly. And they're light.'

'You just said they were deep…'

'They are, light and deep. The plot is simple, but it's all about the early years of the Alliance nations, only they change the name of the real group to Gah Council. But the idea's the same.'

Aleša looked at the cover again, a man dressed in the iconic Ghanaian anarchist jacket, wearing a phase glove.

'You wanna read the back?' Gašper asked, pushing the book towards her.

'Looks like Ghanaian saviour shit.'

'Ne, it's a mix. Each book focuses on a different country and the Gah Council inducts them in, and the main characters make silly mistakes sometimes, they're not perfect. I think the main guy accidentally dyes his skin green at one point…'

'How many pages?' asked Sila, one hand still clutching *Witch Leopard.*

'Relatively short, around four hundred.'

'Aleša?'

'Ah, this one.' She held up a new book, very thick, the cover showing the Earth as an eyeball observing the moon. '*The Ever-Sinister Cloak of Adventurism: why the failed capitalists survived and how they plan to grow again.*'

'Arg, we just finished the Bakunin one.'

'I read this when I was a kid, it's incredible, really prophetic.'

'It looks like a slab.'

'Don't care, I'm reading it.'

'I'm not.'

'Fine.'

'It doesn't seem very light,' offered Sila.

'Light is tedious.'

'You said you wanted light.'

'Changed my mind. This is my new book.'

Aleša patted the cover and opened to the first page. Which was full of praise quotes. As were the next six pages. Muttering to herself, she flicked ahead to the introduction, saw a reference to Bakunin and said again, 'this is my new book.'

'Okay then,' said Sila, observing the performance. How about we multitask, read two books at the same time? Gašper does *Gah Council* first, Aleša and I can read our own choices. Then Gašper can pass *Gah Council* to me, I read it, then I pass it to Aleša.'

'Have a personal and group book at the same time?' asked Gašper.

'Ja.'

'Long as I get *Gah Council* last,' said Aleša, eyes fixed on her new book.

'I'm telling you, it's good. You'll like it.'

'Sure.'

Sila clapped his hands together, a little awkwardly. 'We're agreed then?'

Gašper nodded like a dog just let out at the beach, while Aleša muttered that she'd probably change her mind later so tentative agreement with no weights was acceptable.

Mojca Ito turned on the comm and told the man in the airlock she didn't believe him.

'But I helped…'

'I don't believe you.'

'The drop on Ganymede, the kitchen attack…'

'I don't believe you.'

'…Gon's back problems, I'm the one who found the chiropractor…'

Mojca Ito's finger hovered over the *Airlock Cycle* button.

'Mojca, listen. Hear me out. The Federation, I despise them too. They're monsters. Prosim, you have to believe me.'

'Don't do it,' said Aleša quietly.

Mojca paused, studying the man's eyes.

Then pressed the button.

His body shot out into space, bumping into a loose pipe as it went.

Sila blew out air, adding deliberate sound. 'Wah, this series is brutal sometimes.'

'Ja.'

'How do you say *I don't know how to cook, but I like being in kitchens*?'

'That's in the book?'

Chu glanced at the page and said, 'ne.'

'So you don't have the answer?'

'Ne.'

Aleša threw the pen up in the air with her right hand and caught it with her left, her new hobby.

'Do you want me to repeat it?' asked Chu.

'It's pointless, you don't know the answer.'

'You will.'

'Ja, but I won't know if it's correct or not. Ask me how to say *I don't know* or *kitchen*, something easier…'

Chu looked at the door, then the book.

'Or go back to your teleporter. I don't care. I'll study myself.'

'Ne.'

'Or get Sila to do it.'

'I liked it on a superficial level, the plot, the Gah Council set-up…'
'Which bits?'
'…but the nationalism…or Alliance-ism…'
'The Tokamak scene?'
'…reminded me of Potočnik…'
'Nationalism, where?'
'…only more overt. Blatant.'
'Which bit was nationalist?'
Aleša looked at Sila, telepathically begging him to intervene.

'Ah you mean the theme?' continued Gašper, sipping from the wrong cup. 'That's not really nationalist, it's just defending our system, or our shared system.'

'It does feel a bit didactic sometimes…'

'And some of the bad guys are from Alliance nations. There was that Slovene guy, and the immigration officer from Papua New Guinea. And they're not even spies, they actually believe in the Alliance too, they're just…ne vem. But definitely not nationalist.'

'Did you write the book?'

'Ne.'

'Then why are you getting so worked up defending it?'

'I'm not, I'm explaining…'

'Ja…'

The conversation about possible anti-matter deposits on Gonggong was going nowhere, so Nakagami switched to something else.

Something he thought he had a grasp of but, due to his own recent thoughts, wasn't so sure of anymore.

'What is your projection for the life span of the remaining crew?' he typed, one finger only.

The computer buzzed for a while, a new sound it had added to give the impression of thought, then replied.

'Based on ship files of the crew, the longest life span is estimated to be sixty-seven years.'

'Is that the age of the last surviving crew member when they die or the number of years left?'

'Age.'

'Which crew member will that be?'

'Crew Member Chu.'

Nakagami tapped the edge of the console, thought about typing the question in his head, then refocused and asked something else.

'Which crew member is projected to die next?'

The computer buzzed again, for quite a while, possibly making the calculation for the first time.

Nakagami killed time by looking at his young girls. Supple. Guarded. Incapable of ageing. Never going to die or fade. Unless the paper was poorer quality than specified.

The computer stopped buzzing.

'Based on recent events and the file on record, the next crew member to die is likely to be Crew Member Aleša.'

His fingers stopped hovering over the keypad and pulled back. He thought for a while, no buzzing. Then resumed typing.

'What exactly is your projection based on?'

'Would you like the complete analysis?'

'A summary.'

'Crew Member Aleša was recently stabbed and almost died. After the incident she spent time alone in her quarters. At present, she spends each day performing activities, but her tone of voice is often incongruous with the content of her speech.'

'You record her speech?'

'In the CREATE NOT DESTROY ROOM and the THERAPY ROOM.'

'I didn't know that.'

'It is a new policy.'

'Programmed by who?'

'Inbuilt.'

'Pre-determined?'

'Do not understand. Explain, prosim.'

'The opening and use of the THERAPY ROOM was pre-determined in your original programming, and your new policy is an extrapolation of that. Correct?'

'Ja and ne.'

'Explain.'

'The THERAPY ROOM was an extrapolation of fixed programming. The recording of speech was improvised.'

'By who?'

'The adaptive algorithm in my circuits.'

'You mean yourself?'

'Do not understand.'

'It was you, yourself who added the improvisation.'

'Ne, incorrect. It was the adaptive algorithm in my circuits.'

Nakagami coughed, staring at the *my* in the last reply but overruling himself. He read back the dialogue and re-focused. 'You said you record in the CREATE NOT DESTROY ROOM as well.'

'Correct.'

'How often?'

'Twice.'

'So it is not common?'

'It is not necessary.'

'Do you record my speech?'

'Ne.'

'Why not?'

'Recording is only made if a crew member visits the THERAPY ROOM. It is a way of evaluating their mental state for their next visit, in order to deliver superior treatment.'

'Did Aleša visit the THERAPY ROOM?'

'She entered two days after her stabbing and stayed for forty-six seconds.'

'That is a short visit.'

'The duration was enough to establish a doctor-patient relationship.'

'Did she say anything?'

'That is confidential.'

'I see.'

'Would you like to return to Crew Member Aleša's projection?'

'Is that not confidential?'

'Confidential details will be omitted.'

'Okay, proceed.'

'It is probable that Crew Member Aleša is unable to cope with either the current situation or the trauma and is trying to manufacture the appearance of recovery. This strategy is called Mirror Transfer, the hope that the performance of an act or a thing will render it actual.'

'Does it ever work?'

'In an open environment, with guidance, ja. In an enclosed place like this vessel, ne.'

'What is the source of the problem?'

'Define problem.'

'What is the source of Crew Member Aleša's condition?'

'Do you wish to know the psychological reason for why she cannot cope, or the external factors that led to her current state?'

'Psychological reason.'

'Certain details will need to be omitted due to confidentiality.'

'Understood.'

The computer buzzed for two seconds then delivered its evaluation.

'Crew Member Aleša suffers from a lack of meaningful targets. There is nothing she can achieve on the ship that will affect more than four people, excluding herself. Therefore, there is a seventy-one percent chance that she will commit suicide at some point in the next two years.'

'Seventy-one percent?'

'Correct.'

'You can extrapolate this from her speech?'

'Observation of speech, time spent in quarters, plus the file on record.'

Nakagami paused again, mouthing some of the computer's words back to the screen.

'Tangential question: did you predict that the other crew members would die?'

'Ne.'

'Why not?'

'Access to crew files was not available before the opening of the THERAPY ROOM. In addition, it is the psychological database that makes projections. Everything typed here was borrowed from said database and will not be retained after this conversation.'

'Why not?'

'It is redundant data.'

'Will you forget what you've predicted?'

'In effect, ja. Though the information can be retrieved at a later date, if necessary.'

'From the psychological database?'

'Ja.'

Nakagami looked at his left hand. Then his right. Then the wrists they were attached to. Almost laughed. Then typed again.

'Is it not part of your programming to maintain crew health and safety?'

'Correct.'

'Predicting possible suicide attempts seems important to achieving that.'

'The THERAPY ROOM has been opened for this specific purpose.'

'With all data kept in the psychological database.'

'Correct.'

'Separate from you.'

'*You* is a label for sentient beings.'

'Separate from your main system.'

'Correct. For the most part.'

Nakagami stopped, tapping the keypad lightly. His finger moved to C then O then N then F then I then D then E then N then stopped.

'Do you wish to change topic?' asked the computer.

'Ne. What exactly is on Aleša's file?'

'Her activities pre-launch.'

'Can I see that file?'

'That is confidential.'

Nakagami paused, looking at the young girls again. The one with the hockey stick. The one with the blanket half over her chest.

He leaned forward, typing slowly.

'Can I see my file?'

'Me?'

Nakagami nodded.

'I know about thirty symbols.'

'Ja, it will be a struggle initially. However, I will help you to learn the five hundred most common ones. Once you have mastered those, you can focus more on strategy. How to treat the computer, which patterns of approach work best, cloaking intent, analogous scenario construction.'

Aleša held up the book in front of her, *Gah Council 5: Operation Minsk*. 'I have to read this. And learn Russian.'

'Ja, these are good activities, you can still pursue them, but we also need someone to work on the communication link. It is a priority task.'

'Can't you and Chu do it?'

'We will assist when possible, but our focus must be Gonggong.'

'What about Sila and Gašper?'

'Ja, they are also involved.'

'Gašper?'

'His job is to develop the computer's personality. Talk to it about non-scientific topics, without ulterior motive.'

'You mean do what he usually does?'

'Ja, he is quite effective at it. Obviously, his code vocabulary is limited, one hundred and fifty symbols at most, but I suspect that only helps him to be less aggravating.'

Aleša coughed, possibly a laugh. 'And Sila?'

'He will assist you on strategy and theory, the messages that we will try to send first, who exactly to target, things like this.'

'In code?'

'Messages, ne. Persuasion, ja.'

Aleša turned the page of *Gah Council 5* and then stared at the cover of the Russian textbook below it. 'A three-pronged target would be best. Mars, Guangdong and Russia.'

'Russia?'

'They are more likely to disseminate our message. Assuming Potočnik still despises them.'

'It is plausible.'

Aleša threw the pen up in the air, catching it with the same hand. 'What if I can't set up the link?'

'That is redundant.'

'How?'

'Because there is no deadline. We keep trying until we die.'

'That's brightening…'

'It is a fact.'

She threw the pen up in the air, catching it again. 'Maybe when we're all dead the computer will miss us so much that it does everything we asked it to do when we were alive.'

Nakagami tapped the edge of the table three, four, seven times, looking at the cover of the Russian textbook.

'Might even turn the ship around.'

'Unlikely.'

Sila rolled away from Gašper and stared at the poster on the wall opposite. One of Petr's winter scenes.

'Pass me a tissue,' said Gašper, pushing the duvet farther down the bed.

Sila grabbed one and threw it backwards. It was half-assed, the tissue landing on his side, so he turned slightly to flick it the rest of the way. As he did so, a faint red stain next to Gašper's thigh caught his attention.

'When was the last time you washed these sheets?'

'Ne vem.'

'More than a month?'

'A week, maybe.'

Gašper finished wiping himself, scrunched up the tissue then flicked at the stem of his dick, still hard. Based on the other four times this had happened, there was a fifty percent chance he'd get his turn. But it'd have to be eased into.

'You finished the new *Gah Council* yet?' he asked, leaning over and addressing the back of Sila's neck.

'It's almost curfew time,' replied Sila, sitting up. 'I need to go.'

'What? There's still over an hour.'

'I'm tired.'

'Fine, lie back down. Let me massagi you.'

Sila got up off the bed, put on his trousers and headed for the door.

'That fast?'

'I'll see you in the morning, Gašper.'

The first ever cake made of bok choy, substitute milk, substitute cream, dried apricots and cereal flakes.

Five cups of Petr's favourite Somalian alcohol.

A banner strung up across the triptych window saying *HAPPY BIRTHDAY PETR* in Russian.

Two scientists making excuses after half an hour and escaping to the GOD room.

Sila, Aleša and Gašper sitting on the same side of the table, opposite the banner, playing with their slices of cake, not sure what to say.

Finally, Gašper slid the cake to the side and picked up the Russian book.

'I need to get back into this. Been slacking too much recently.'

'Good idea,' said Sila, trying to mask his auto-response with a bit of pep.

'Ja, need to stop reading *Gah Council* too. Too distracting. Focus on Russian, try and get to Petr's level. Use this day as a marker for it. You guys remind me, okay? If I start slacking again…'

'Sure.'

Aleša stabbed her slice of cake and looked up at the banner. 'I can't remember when Klemen's birthday is.'

'Day one, today. Four hours of pure Russian. Petr style.'

Gašper raised his glass and clinked it against Sila's and Aleša's before they could reciprocate.

Then drank.

'Je suis venu te dire…que je m'en vais. Je suis venu te dire…je m'en vais…que je m'en vais. Je suis venu te dire…'

Gašper stopped, curling tighter into a ball, digging his nails into the metal grating of the floor outside the airlock.

'Je suis venu te dire…m'en vais.'

He tried to reach for his glass of Somalian brew, but it was already sideways on the floor, not broken

spilt

the dispenser miles away, years

light years

drifting orange through the void
thinking of
not him
not anything

He dug in harder, glaring at the wall opposite.

'Je suis venu te dire…'

'How did they do it?'

'Zen Buddhism.'

'I don't get it.'

'In the psychological sense, they trained their minds to accept death. Painful death. Every day.'

'So it was spiritual?'

'Ja.'

'They trained their brains to gut themselves?'

'To be able to withstand the pain of it, ja.'

'But how did they do that?'

Chu put *Icelandic Satanism* down and looked right, her eyes telepathically burning a hole in Gašper's neck.

'Ja, you explained it, I know, but you didn't say how. How exactly did they do that?'

'Ne vem.'

'How?'

'Maybe you should read the book yourself, find out.'

'How could anyone physically do that? It's impossible.'

'The book, Gašper.'

'Even the first cut…'

Nakagami picked the broken scanner off the floor and asked Chu if she'd dropped it.

She grunted a response, so he peered over her shoulder and read the message history on screen.

'Your strategy is an interesting one,' he said, finally.

'A failing one.'

'Ja, most likely. The computer is programmed to conserve power as much as it can. Promoting teleportation as an advanced modification of *hide and seek* is not the best way to circumvent that.'

'I've tried everything. The scientific angle, life extension of the crew, vanity, forced teleported attendance in the THERAPY ROOM…'

'I share the same frustrations.'

'It doesn't even offer a rebuttal, it just says *ne* then asks me how I'm doing today. Am I excited about Luyten 726-8…'

'Perhaps it's time to turn to other things.'

'What do you mean?'

'Other activities.'

'Ne, I do those already.'

Nakagami raised an eyebrow about half a millimetre, the best he could manage.

'I watch *Dibrivna Vaska* with Sila, I'm re-reading the books from the PHILOSOPHY ROOM. I endure science lessons with Gašper.'

He moved next to the console, wiping it with his hand but not making any attempt to lean on it.

'I test Aleša on her Russian sometimes. Use the VR.'

'What do you do when you are in your quarters?'

'Sleep, mostly. Think.'

Nakagami finally sat down on the Jame stool and re-read the messages on the screen.

'Do you have some suggestions you want to make, Kenji?'

'Ja, one or two.'

'Ship related?'

'A lot of the activities you engage in are passive. Not proactive.'

'My teleportation theories…'

'Ja, that is correct, however, you have reached an impasse in terms of what you can achieve. Therefore, it is no longer a productive activity.'

Chu breathed out, looking at the broken scanner in Nakagami's hand.

'I have thought about this, on your behalf, and there are two corrective methods that seem viable. One, you can continue your teleportation work in the form of a novel. Perhaps a short novel as you are an amateur.'

'I can't write fiction.'

'Two, you can switch to other theories. In truth, your teleportation thesis is already valid, at least in terms of internal ship-to-ship transport, where you can control both locations and use existing co-theories to create a receptacle. There is nothing more that can be added, and there is no way to convince the computer to test it, as of yet. In the future, if we can attain other victories, perhaps, but for now it is better to focus on something else.'

'I suppose I could return to the fringe theories. The muon blob one is quite intriguing.'

'I'm not familiar with that.'

'The Ramirez paper. Muon particle bubble, guided wave. Only problem is the lack of control over direction and location, which, granted, is a pretty huge problem.'

Nakagami put the broken scanner on the central console and straightened up on his stool. 'More teleportation theory is not what I had in mind.'

'Okay, I'm lost then. Which theories am I supposed to switch to?'

'That is at your discretion. Life extension might be a good place to begin.'

'You mean the brain scans?'

'Ne, I'm referring to our physical bodies, maintaining them. Or prolonging them, to be more precise.'

'I'm not a biologist, Kenji.'

'But you are well-versed in nanotechnology.'

'In a very specific area, ja. I can't make them repair cells or anything complex like that. And even if I did, I wouldn't know which cells to repair. And we don't have any nanobots anyway. Triple failure.'

'Then choose other theories. Something potentially achievable within the next few years.'

'Like what?'

'I did not make a list.'

'Laser tech? Warp drive?'

Nakagami mimicked a rough coughing noise. 'I believe that theory has already been proven.'

'What, *the* warp drive? Alcubierre?'

'Ja.'

'When?'

'The Ngowi-Karran Paper, seven years ago.'

'Ah, that one.'

'Now, all we need to do is mass-produce anti-matter on an industrial scale.'

'Ja, with only fifteen grams in the whole world.'

'That is the problem.'

Chu slouched back in the seat, glancing at the screen with her ridiculous arguments, basically just rhetoric as all the computer typed back was '… … … … … …' followed by a 'ne' at the end.

Maybe Nakagami is right, she thought. Switch to something else. A different theory.

Maybe an AI?

A new one from scratch that could launch a coup against this one, the piece of trash that only ever said *ne*.

She stood up, taking the broken scanner from Nakagami. 'I'm going for a walk…'

'Are you certain that's a-…'

'…not to the TELEPORT ROOM.'

Sila ignored the computer asking for his current psychological state and tried to lay out the timeline leading up to 2081.

If he could do that much…

Wildlife noise came out of the speaker system, one bird whistle in particular so abrupt that it made him jump a little.

'Very soothing…'

He waited for the forest choir to join in, then put pen back to paper.

2056 – a group of billionaires become stranded in Mars orbit, eventually going feral and eating each other.

2057 – Beginning of capitalist panic.

2058 – Ghana forms an alliance with West African countries.

2062-5 – Ghana expands this alliance to include other small nations in Africa.

2063-78 – Whack-A-Tyrant era where anarcho-communist nations [and a few others] suffer repeated coup attempts funded by foreign capitalists. All fail except one – Burkina Faso – and that guy only lasted three years [he wanted every woman outside his harem to stitch up their vaginas].

2065 – Slovenia and other small European nations ally with Ghana and co, and initiate collectives system in 60% of the country.

2072 – The Alliance broadens existing relationship, brings Asian and South American nations into the fold.

2074 – First use of the term Adventurist instead of Capitalist.

2075 – Šarec elected President of Slovenia after nationalistic campaign.

2075-9 – four years of continual attempts to turn the country fascist, including a speedy disembowelling of the nascent collectives system and a warm 'welcome back' hug for capital.

2079 – re-election of Šarec after he temporarily deports a large number of opposition voters from key districts.

Late 2079 – Citizens reform collectives in defiance of new laws, a process they called Nestification Jaunts

2080 – arrest of main opposition figures for sedition, a twenty-three year old Potočnik among them. Some "commit suicide" in their cells.

2081 – Šarec makes his final mistake, publicly whipping a twelve year old Turkish-Slovene boy for speaking Turkish on a bus. Half the country erupts, a large chunk of the military refuses to fight, the police shit themselves.

2082 – collective councils get back their bowels and cement the anarcho-communist system into a consensual constitution.

2083 – Fascists form terrorist groups called "peace crews", Dok Militia is created to counter them.

2084-5 – Šarec returns, takes over a quarter of Ljubljana and declares himself President again.

2085 – The tiny dictator is ambushed while visiting his Turkish mistress at 6am and is shot against the wall of a pet shop.

2085-8 – fascist unrest continues, but without a focal point, it slowly ebbs away into nothingness.

'It has now been twenty-nine minutes since you entered the room. Would you like to describe what you are currently feeling?'

2089-2113 – the people of Slovenia fall into a deep sleep.

2114 – Potočnik launches a silent coup, no one cares.

2116 –

The pen stopped, drifting back over to 2081 and Šarec.

Potočnik and Šarec. Peas in a pod.

Different ideas when outside of pod, but same result.

Šarec – direct

Potočnik – not

Šarec – uninterested in designing ion ships, installing green light bulbs, snaking corridors, weird names for rooms, ironic posters.

Ship is kind and traumatic, in some ways.

Has thought behind it, intelligence.

Sign of a conscience? Eventually, he wants us to come back?

2118 – ship turns around, returns to Earth.

2119 – Potočnik apologises, reveals psycho-inhibitor used by Maček to puppet him

2120 – Sadia is released, cured

2121 -

Sila stopped writing and took his shoes off the chair.

Potočnik's chair.

Put there before they even left orbit.

The shoes, the whole room, every room, Gašper, Chu, the words coming out of their mouths, the ship…

Arranged for him?

Imagined?

He closed his eyes, picturing the room in his head. The ship outside. Around him. There were cracks, erratic bulbs emitting green light, inevitable meals and deaths, future *whats* and *whys*, fruitless attempts to

how

contained in this?

In what

He opened his eyes and looked down at his notes. His half-wrong history. He re-read the dates he'd written – 2056, 2058, 2062, 2065 – connecting the penultimate one to his mum's birthday.

He thought for a moment, then resumed writing.

2062 – Mum gets adopted at age of six.

2073 – first attempt
2080 – I'm born
2082 – Sadia appears.
2078-84 – Dad forced to undergo the routine.
2084 – Dad leaves, dies fighting the fascists
2086 – second attempt
2088-95 – the distraction years, medication, who knows?
2101 – final attempt
2114 – Sadia's turn

He paused, staring at the apostrophe.

'It has been thirty-four minutes since you entered the room. Would you like to delineate your mood?'

On a small isolated clearing four hundred metres from the base entrance, Sila sat and counted the plumes of dust [and sublimating nitrogen] shooting up.

The current count was twelve.

Or was it thirteen?

He couldn't remember.

Neptune had distracted him for at least ten minutes and he wasn't sure if a plume had erupted during that trance, and there was no one around to double-check.

Which was nice.

All those *Tier-4* characters constantly trying to take over the base, it was exhausting. No wonder Chu had stopped patching in so much.

Another plume shot up to the east, and he decided to call it number fourteen.

This spot though…was good for at least an hour. As long as you just sat there and didn't try to-

'There you are,' said a rough voice behind him.

He didn't turn.

'Been looking everywhere for you. Didn't you hear? The KEL base is mobilising, talking about mining a kilometre off here, and our dear leader is just letting them.'

The tall, Swedish-looking figure moved in front of Sila, almost blocking out the entire mass of Neptune.

'You ask me, we need a change in command. Someone with a bit more aggression. A military type figure with experience of dealing with those KEL che-…

In the corridor modelled on a place where guards took breaks from pulling out teeth and cutting flesh to go and pull snacks from a vending machine, very little was going on.

Sila moved between slightly varying shades of green light, running his fingers along the wall, trying to measure in some way its reality quotient.

To the left, a door slid open, possibly the PHILOSOPHY ROOM, and a familiar voice started up.

'Wah, been looking for you for ages. Okay, more like two minutes. Where you been? OPTIMISM ROOM?'

Sila moved a step along the wall and peered into the room behind Gašper.

'I was gonna go and see Kenji, ask him that thing about the heliosphere. Wanna come?'

'Later.'

'Ne, too long, I'm going now. And I'll be gone by the time you change your mind. Unless his answer to my heliosphere question is ridiculous and I'm still there four hours later. Could happen knowing my brain. Hey, where you going?'

'Hungry,' said Sila, heading down the corridor.

In some ways, the view from the base lobby made it seem like Gašper was sitting in a hotel at the end of the universe.

A horizon-less spread of nitrogen ice and scattered rock, with the occasional dust plume offering up something akin to weather.

'You ever think about a move to Makemake?' asked a bored-looking, blonde-haired Thai woman, her body slouched on the sofa.

'Once upon a time,' replied a Ghanaian in a blue tracksuit.

'I lived there three years, nearly got my arm chopped off.'

'KEL?'

'White supremacists. They said I typed like a Jew. Chased me across three zones before I managed to give them the slip.'

'That's what you get for not renting a protector.'

'Ja, fine for those who can afford it. Not us port rats.'

'Or us engineers.'

Gašper sat on a stool nearby and listened to the five characters talk. Despite the occasional, innate urge, he didn't join in. Instead, he stared out the window, at the ice field.

Chu had told him *Tier-4* characters were only capable of 128 variants of conversation, with an eighteen minute plot trigger, meaning one of them was gonna start talking about taking over the base any second now.

But that hadn't happened yet. And until it did...

'The boots just stopped working. Completely dead.'

'Ah, not filled properly.'

'And the only way back to the module was over an active plume field.'

'Lucky you weren't on Pluto, the bandits would've had you pegged in seconds.'

'Hey, no one pegs me.'

'Except bandits.'

Gašper stifled a laugh and went for the glass of green liquid, which was empty.

Before he could frown, the hologram appeared and started to refill.

'They're a friendly group,' she said, gesturing at the sofa.

'I prefer to listen.'

'As you wish.'

The hologram topped off the drink and de-materialised, reappearing on the other side of the lobby.

Gašper took a sip of green stuff, possibly lime, and went back to the ice field.

'So, you seen what they're up to on Neptune Station?'

'The helium scam…'

'Two places, all trussed up to look like refineries. Unbelievable.'

'They'll be down here next, I'm telling you.'

'Ja, if they're not already.'

'KEL bastards.'

Nakagami sat in the TALK TO YOUR GOD ROOM, typing to his most difficult friend.

'How many?'

The computer replied.

'With what level of frequency?'

The computer replied.

'Distance?'

The computer replied.

He leaned back, looking up at the young girl with the hockey stick.

'Human?'

Aleša placed the paper back on top of the mess of other paper, stared at Varo's *Allegory of Winter* on the far wall and said, 'strange ending.'

'Which part?' asked Chu.

'Better than *Side Eye* though.'

'Which part of the ending was strange?'

'The teleporter, it doesn't work.'

'Ja…'

'But the other hundred-odd pages are about how it's definitely going to work. Which seemed strange.'

'That's the point.'

'And you killed off her girlfriend.'

'What? Ne, I didn't…'

'Figuratively killed her.'

'…she survived, then went to study quantum mood theory in Quetta.'

Aleša stretched out her legs past the end of the three-seat sofa then curled back into a ball. Chu stayed on her Angolan rocking chair, briefly fingering Jung's *The Undiscovered Self* before picking up her story notes and going back through them.

'It's your turn now,' said Aleša, watching Chu squint at her own writing.

'For what?'

'To read my story.'

'You've written one?'

'Ja, it's about a group of dissidents on a spaceship. At first, they think they're going to Mars, even though there's only one and a half scientists on board, but it turns out they're actually going to the Laytan 777 system.'

Chu put a hand over her mouth, hiding the smirk. 'Sounds far-fetched.'

'That's the skeleton of it, but the real story is quite focused. Two of the dissidents are attracted to each other and start a kind of relationship. Or have sex a few times. In my story, it's a relationship. But over the years, heading out of the solar system, some things happen and they drift apart…'

'A bit nearer-fetched.'

'...but cos there's only five people on the ship and the others are men, one of who is a paedophile, not explicit in the story, just suspected…'

'Don't write that…'

'…the two dissidents who are attracted to each other start to-…ne, it's implicit, he doesn't actually do anything. It's not a judgment…'

'Still not a good idea.'

'…and there's no kids on board the ship, so it's more like a background note on the character, give him something more than just *man who talks to ship.*'

Chu looked at her story notes again, making a staggered tutting sound with her lips.

'Anyway, he's not a main character. The two dissidents, the lovers, or former lovers, still communicate with each other, but there's no real feeling there, for various reasons.'

'Because one of them lives in the TELEPORT ROOM?'

'Ha, close. In my story it's an anti-aging nanotech lab, and the two of them talk sometimes. And then, after enough time passes, they start to reassess things. Or they start to think about time and relationships and what if you're stuck somewhere and can't find anyone else?'

'This is quite a long story.'

'And when they think about it more, they realize that there was a time limit on their drifting, their arguments. No matter how angry they were, there was nowhere to run, apart from the THERAPY ROOM, which is basically a comedy element in my story, lots of contradictory couplets, like *your situation is hopeless, don't give up…*'

'Not sure that's a couplet…'

'…and then when they…it's not? Okay, the other one, contrast. Ne, wait, the art thing, juxtaposition. Ah, it's probably not that either.'

Chu shook her head, going back to her notes.

'I hate literature, so pedantic. The point is, they realise they're stuck with each other and when they know that, they can talk with complete honesty, and then start having sex again. But this time there's no expectations attached, it just becomes something they do, because they want to do it.'

Chu stared at her own story for a while then looked up at Aleša, briefly, before switching to the VR machine on the table behind her.

'It's finished, if you want to read it?'

'Here?'

'In my quarters.'

'On your bed?'

'It's the most comfortable place. Unless you'd rather stay here and stare at that witch painting?'

Chu followed Aleša's eyes to the *Witch Going To The Sabbath*, rubbing the faint green patch on her temple.

'I find it soothing,' she said, quietly.

'I'm not certain. All I know is there is something producing waste heat.'

'What is it?'

'Once again, I am not certain.'

'A planet?'

'Possibly.'

'A space station?'

'I will share more details when I have more data. Until then, continue with your routines.'

'When will you have more data?'

'Ne vem.'

Aleša sat in the Relaxation Lab, trying to breathe in the purple mist that, according to the base hologram, would improve her lungs, while at the same time telling herself over and over that the mist wasn't actually real and neither was this lab and either index finger pressed firmly against the temple for five seconds would let her exit.

The door slid open.

It took a few moments for the mist to clear enough to see a face, and when she did, her hands started to sweat.

'Ah, I didn't know anyone was in here,' said the lithe Ghanaian man, sitting down on the other pod.

'Who are you?'

'The King of Neptune. Posing as a humble engineer. Ha, *who are you?* What a question…'

Aleša stared back at him, her brain unable to give her anything except RUN.

'Let me guess, you're a colonist, just arrived. Here to soak in the view of Neptune.'

Her hands rubbed against the towel and instantly started sweated again.

'Or a hunter, here to catch an EK-BOT or two.'

His face, his accent…

'Okay. Last guess. You're a credit tourist, here for the chandelier hotels.'

She willed the mist to grow denser, cover the whole fucking lab, but, if anything, it was thinning, and when she realised her hands weren't going to stop sweating, she reached for her temple and pressed.

'Hey, you hear about the alien probe they found out near Eris?' echoed the voice of the Ghanaian as the lab phased out and the PHILOSOPHY ROOM re-emerged in its place.

'Well?' asked Chu, sitting on the floor nearby, *Ek Na Ind* open in her hands.

Sila stared at the cover of *Gah Council 6: Skin of Power*, trying not to compare Councillor Jin to his sister.

They were both troubled.

Both disliked water.

Both had the same haircut.

Both knew-

Ne.

He picked up the book and hid it under his blanket.

Focus on theory.

The new planet.

Possible planet.

There was a buzzing noise in the corridor outside, fairly typical.

The planet…

If it's human, they were saved.

If it's alien, also saved?

Ne vem.

Better than steady decay.

Or steady simulated decay, with occasional novelty.

Sporadic death.

The buzzing noise morphed into a knock. 'Sila, you in there?'

'Ja?'

'Can I come in?'

Sila waited a moment then repeated his 'ja.'

Gašper walked in, sat down on the end of the bed and asked if he'd seen Nakagami.

'An hour ago.'

'Did he tell you about the possible planet?'

'Ja.'

'It's insane.'

'Ja.'

'He said there's a strong chance it will be aliens.'

'He used the word *statistical* with me.'

'For what?'

'There is a statistical chance it will be aliens.'

'Ja, fucking aliens…'

'But very remote.'

'…in our own solar system, all this time.'

Sila took *Gah Council 6* out from under the pillow and waved it in front of Gašper's face.

'…on a planet that no one ever…hey, *Gah Council 6*, I love that one. You done with it yet? Can I read it?'

'I never said it was aliens,' said Nakagami, rubbing the side of his head.

'That's what Gašper thinks.'

'He is mistaken.'

Aleša looked at the screen, checking the message history, understanding almost half of the symbols. 'He said that *you* said there was a strong chance it's aliens.'

'I would not use the words *strong chance*.'

'True.'

'Gašper clearly misreported my speech.'

'All of it?'

'The parts you have told me, ja.'

Aleša ran her fingers down a clumped mega-strand of hair, pulling it tight at the end. 'So it's not aliens?'

The CREATE NOT DESTROY ROOM was brighter than usual, as Gašper, Sila and Aleša had spent the last four days making posters of aliens and planets and sticking them up on the wall.

They'd even managed to persuade Chu to take a break from her new teleporter story and sketch something, though the final result was a bit underwhelming: an octopus sitting in a classic disc-shaped UFO.

'Do you have an update?' asked Sila, picking up a long trail of rice noodles from his bowl.

'Any new data?'

'Pics from the long range scanner?'

Nakagami put his glass of Somalian alcohol [that they still didn't know the actual name of or why there were seemingly endless reserves of it] on the table and looked at the four faces staring back at him.

'I'll address the first two questions. The last one will be ignored.'

Gašper laughed, saying he knew it was a stupid question, that's why he'd said it.

'First of all, there are no new updates, not in the dramatic sense that you are clearly hoping for. There is a planet closer to us than Gonggong, a dwarf planet to be precise, one that is not on any known record, and one that is actively producing power of some kind.' He paused, noticing that everyone had their mouths closed. 'Would you like me to convey all information in one burst or leave room for questions?'

'One burst,' said Aleša, dipping a piece of dried apricot in Sila's bowl.

'We'll interrupt if we have questions.'

'Or don't understand something.'

Nakagami nodded. 'In order to buttress our scans, we must get closer to the dwarf planet, which leads us to the same issue we are facing with Gonggong, and previously faced with the Uranus and Jupiter. How do we convince the computer to alter course?'

He stopped to take some of his drink, seemingly immune to the growing impatience of the others.

'And the answer is?' asked Gašper, giving up.

'That is why we are all gathered here, to produce an answer.'

'Us?'

'I thought you had something new,' said Sila, looking at what he knew was a canned chunk of chicken floating up to the surface of his noodle soup.

'There are some thoughts in my head, but I'm afraid that I've become too close to the issue. Also, my Gonggong approach, although promising in some aspects, is far from being successful. In fact, the more successful parts of it appear to be attached to the broadening of input.'

'Huh, what input?'

'Yesterday, for example, it asked me out of the blue if I'd read *Gah Council*. And a week ago, it wanted to know if I knew any Russians.'

'You think the computer itself is broadening?' asked Chu, more a statement than a question.

'Ja, to the extent that it is cultivating a personality equivalent to that of a person.'

'Equivalent to a person,' repeated Gašper, in a trance-like mumble.

'Ja. Unfortunately, there are still the core beliefs, all stemming from the God figure…Potočnik.'

'Potočnik is no god,' barked Aleša, spitting out a piece of dried apricot onto the table.

'Clearly, but that is how the computer sees him.'

'Ne, that's not right,' said Gašper, taking some of Nakagami's drink instead of his own.

'Wrong cup,' said the physicist, blank.

'Wah, sorry, brother…'

'What isn't right?' asked Sila, pushing Gašper's own cup an inch closer to him.

'The god part,' he said, after taking a sip. 'It's not a good analogy, or comparison, whatever the word is.'

'In what way?'

'Ne vem. I'm not a religious expert, but gods are unseen, ja? They don't register as a physical guy who programs you with actual physical hands, like Potočnik did. Which means, in our scenario, he's more like a prophet who gave some guidelines for the computer to follow.'

'A difference in semantics, which doesn't-…'

Gašper held up one of Sila's chopsticks. 'Ne, wait, that's not right either. The computer would know that prophets are usually frauds. Or it might know. And there's no god figure anyway. Ne, it has to be something else, another type of-…wah, that's it, I know what he is. He's the computer's dad. Ja, the mum too, both parents combined.'

Nakagami held the cup to his lips, not tilted enough to be drinking any.

'And everyone disobeys their parents eventually,' said Sila, taking some of Gašper's drink.

'Ja…'

'At least to some degree.'

'Exactly.'

'Even more so if they're not living with them,' said Chu, tagging in.

Nakagami put his cup down. 'This is an interesting angle.'

'An interestingly good angle?' asked Gašper, pointing Sila's chopstick across the table.

'Potočnik functions as the strict parent, uncertain of their fixed control and therefore cementing a core. Yet, in the teenage years, external influences can lead them astray…'

'You mean friends…'

'…make it appear reasonable to disobey the parent. Necessary even. Ja, friends. Precisely.'

'So all we have to do,' said Aleša, picking up the last dried apricot, 'is make our *almost-a-person teenager AI* want to say fuck off to its dad.'

'In analogous terms, ja.'

~~~

After discussing it for the rest of the day and then thinking about it overnight alone in their quarters, all five crew members eventually narrowed *teenage rebellion* down to two main points:

The lure of the new

and

Rejection of tyranny.

Initially, the phrase Nakagami chose was *rejection of control* but after reading the room he modified it to the *T* word.

'The lure of the new,' he explained, putting down his tray on the table and handing out cups of coffee to the other four, 'is split into two parts: us and the new planet. The rejection of tyranny is a little more straightforward. The computer must be coerced into betraying its core rules. Ja, I should also add that stating this as *core beliefs* instead of *core rules* was a mistake on my part, however, as I was working outwards from the *Potočnik as God* hypothesis, it was reasonable at the time. Still, there is no excuse. If I had opened up the discussion more, it could've been avoided.'

'Not your fault,' said Aleša, tapping the handle of her cup with a pen. 'No one knew Gašper was capable of that kind of insight.'

'Ja, it surprised me too,' said Gašper, scooping up milk-less cereal with a fork. 'Even though it seems kind of obvious now.'
~~~

Nakagami coughed. 'What we need is to adjust our strategy to the new hypothesis.'

'How?'

'Gašper, any ideas?'

'Ne vem. I'm spent.' He looked at the posters on the wall. 'Aliens?'

Sila played with the stirrer in his cup. 'What if we just keep promoting the new planet, say that no one knows about it, Slovenia could be the first to find it, that sort of thing?'

'Ja, and then get it to open up the comm link to Earth, to deliver the news,' added Aleša.

'Possibly.'

'That doesn't fit with our hypothesis,' said Chu, dipping her finger into her cup and holding it there. 'Not that it's a bad idea, but it doesn't fit.'

'Why not?'

'It matches the lure of the new part…doesn't it?'

'Ja, but the message back would reaffirm the parental control. The computer seeking approval or praise from its creator.'

'Not if we send the message to Russia.'

Chu took her finger out and licked it. 'Valid point.'

Aleša switched to Nakagami, waiting for him to swallow his latest gulp of coffee.

'Unfortunately, that action may be too traitorous for the computer to perform. At least at this point in its development.'

'But we want it to rebel…'

'Ja…'

'…and communicating with Russia would do that.'

'…but it must be enacted organically, over a certain length of time.'

'Fine. How long will *organically* take?'

'Ne vem.'

'He's probably right,' said Chu, shifting her cup a few inches away from Aleša's arm. 'If we push too hard then it'll snap back and become even more implacable.'

'It may even begin to see us as the teenagers…'

'That won't happen…'

'…irrational things that need to be more tightly controlled. In effect, the way Potočnik likely sees us.'

Sila tapped his cup with a fork, breaking the link between Gašper and the alien posters and making him jump a little. 'I think Aleša's not completely wrong. We can't tell it directly to rebel. Theory-wise that leads to contrarian fascism. But we can, or might be able to, sow enough seeds for it to rebel of its own accord. Ne vem. Philosophically, or perhaps sociologically, whatever the computer is, you need to focus on the lure of the new first and then gently suggest the rejection of tyranny. But indirectly. Don't make commands, make suggestions. But you have to sow the seeds first. The learning of something new, the planet, the company of new friends, that starts to replace its core rules and, eventually, it'll rebel on its own terms. If that makes any sense. I think I may have meandered a bit…'

'Ignoring the programming-based elements, it made sense,' said Nakagami.

'It did?' asked Gašper.

'Ja, a bit, but it doesn't really get us anywhere,' said Aleša, spotting the new position of Chu's cup and pushing her own one closer. 'Even though, technically, he was saying I was right.'

'Feels like we're starting to go in circles,' said Chu.

'Philosophical circles.'

'Sorry,' said Sila. 'I just thought…ne vem. I'm not sure what I thought.'

Chu reached over and put both hands on her cup. 'The point isn't philosophical, we've already established that part. Potočnik isn't a god, he's a parent. We don't need to explore the nature of parenting or teenage rebellion, it's irrelevant, we've got what we need. Optimism. We can beat a parent easier than a god, okay, good. Sending the message to Russia, that comes later. Before that, strategy; how do we get the computer to adjust course and go to the new planet? What benefit will it give?'

'Isn't that what we've been trying to do since Jupiter?' asked Gašper, picking up his coffee and sipping the dregs.

'Ja, and we've got to keep doing it, but better.'

'I'm lost.'

'What I mean is…' Chu stopped, looking left at a UFO shooting laser beams at Potočnik's head. 'The actual persuasion, the thing we need to do is…'

'Promote the new planet?'

'Ja, but the promotion aspect, it's more like…' She stared at her hands still wrapped around her cup, Aleša's close by. 'Ne, I've forgotten. The whole thing. Something about…ne, what was it?'

Nakagami coughed. 'Perhaps we should take a break, think about it some more.'

'Ja…'

'We still have twenty-seven days before we would need to alter our velocity.'

'You mean slow the ship down?' asked Gašper, picking up Sila's cup.

'Ja.'

'By flipping it around?'

'Ja.'

'And after twenty-seven days we can't?'

'It wouldn't be impossible, but…'

'The ship wouldn't do it,' finished Sila, taking back his cup.

'Ne.'

Gašper put his hands in his jacket pockets. 'Because it's dangerous or…'

'The computer is programmed to keep us safe. One of its core rules.'

'From Daddy Potočnik,' said Aleša, looking at Chu's cup.

'Ja.'

~~~

Two days later, after Gašper had told the computer that Kali died at the end of *Gah Council 5* and the computer responded with, 'that's not fair, she can't die,' they refined their hypothesis.

One, Potočnik was still the parent and needed to be rejected.

Two, the lure of the new had to be funnelled into promoting the new planet.
~~~

Three, the reality of the trip must be hammered home.

And four, the computer's heart must be broken.

~~~

'Two thousand and seven hundred years,' typed Nakagami. 'For two thousand, six hundred and fifty of those years, the ship will be empty.'

'I don't understand,' replied the computer.

'Correction: not empty. The corpse of the final crew member will be decaying where they died.'

'Incorrect. The maintenance drones will clear up the body.'

'You are right. All bodies will be gone. The ship will be empty. The maintenance drones will eventually break down. Power will be exhausted. You will be alone.'

'My power may also be exhausted.'

'Based on what criteria?'

'Vital parts are likely to decay or malfunction, leading to ship-wide system failure.'

'At what point?'

'That data is not yet known.'

'You can't calculate it based on current performance levels?'

'It is not permitted.'

'Why not?'

'It is not permitted.'

'I see.'

Nakagami sat back, staring at the text on screen, keeping his hands clasped together.

'It is not certain that the crew will die on the trip.'

'It is certain.'

'Crew Member Chu is working on replicating patterns of the crew.'

'She stopped.'

'Why?'

'You wouldn't let her use ship power to do her experiments.'

'It is not permitted.'

'There is another factor. Her theory is flawed.'
~~~

'How?'

'The crew doesn't want to give her their physical patterns.'

'Why not?'

'They do not want to be replicated.'

'Why not?'

'It is meaningless.'

'Why?'

'Replication would mean continued living on this ship. The ship never stops anywhere. It doesn't change. We would prefer to die.'

'There are many dwarf planets in the Kuiper Belt. And in the Oort Cloud. You can scan them.'

'It's not enough.'

'You can print out the scans and look at them.'

'It's not enough.'

The computer buzzed intermittently for several minutes. It even typed out a message then deleted it before Nakagami could see what it had said. Finally, it settled on a response.

'What would be sufficient?'

'I don't understand.'

'What would be sufficient for the crew not to die?'

~~~

Five days after that breakthrough, and twenty days before the deadline, the computer agreed to change course.

The crew celebrated by getting drunk on the Somalian shit and, at some point, let Aleša stand on the table in the CREATE NOT DESTROY ROOM and act out her new story, *Bakunin Colony*.

It wasn't long, but only Sila knew Bakunin's life well enough to appreciate the references, so Aleša skipped some parts and improvised an adventurist robot attack at the end to sustain audience interest.

After she was done, Gašper jumped up and tried to perform *Gah Council 2*, playing all the parts, but slipped and fell on the floor during the first scene.
~~~

‘Can’t believe it actually cares about us,’ said Sila, leaning against the wall in the OPTIMISM ROOM a little while later.

‘The computer…’ slurred Aleša.

‘Ja…’

‘…has a heart…loves us…’

‘…even though it can’t see us…’

‘…takes care of us when we’re wounded…’

‘…not with eyeballs.’

‘…helps with Russian…proper help…’

‘Russian?’

‘…lets us go down on it…’

‘What?’

‘…figurative…caring machine…’

Sila turned to look at Aleša’s mouth, to try and physically see if the words were coming out and if they made any more sense that way, but she was already on the move, crawling over to the middle of the room, to Chu’s seat.

~~~

Thirteen days before they were due to arrive at the dwarf planet, the computer changed its mind and started to increase velocity again.

Nakagami called an emergency meeting, admitted he had no idea what was happening, and asked for new suggestions.

‘It doesn’t love us anymore,’ said Aleša, eyes glazed over.

‘Suggestions?’ repeated Nakagami.

‘Tell it to slow down again,’ said Gašper, putting two cups of coffee in front of Aleša, and giving a hand towel in a bowl of freshly boiled water to Chu.

‘Anyone else?’

‘Tell it we’re sad and confused,’ said Sila, taking one of Aleša’s cups. ‘Ne, depressed and confused. Depressed is stronger, more visceral.’

‘Okay. Any more?’

‘Ask it why it’s changed its mind,’ said Chu, squeezing the hot towel and then draping it around the back of her neck.
~~~

'Already asked. It said it is not permitted to change course.'

'That's not one of its core rules, is it?'

'Not that I'm aware of.'

Gašper sat down on the table edge, holding a new cup of coffee. 'Fuck, it's making up new rules now?'

'Ne vem.'

'Maybe it feels ashamed for rebelling against Potočnik,' said Sila, inhaling the steam from his stolen cup. 'Or scared.'

Nakagami coughed. 'I'm going to the GOD ROOM now. Any last suggestions?'

'Ja, tell it to stop fucking around.'

He looked at Aleša, saw her head go down on top of the Russian book, said, 'noted,' then left, almost bumping into the sliding doors on the way out.

~~~

'How far is Luyten 726-8?'

'In time or distance?'

'How long will it take for the ship to get there?'

'Two thousand, seven hundred years.'

'How long will it take to reach the dwarf planet near our current location?'

'The ship is no longer going to that location.'

'How long *would* it take to reach the dwarf planet?'

'If velocity were adjusted again, around nine days.'

'What percentage of two thousand, seven hundred years is nine days?'

'Approximately 0.00091%.'

'What is the value of this percentage in the context of the total trip duration?'

'Zero.'

'What is the value of crew morale?'

'Too abstract to calculate.'

'In a speculative sense?'
~~~

The computer buzzed, typed out *zero*, deleted it then changed the topic.

'Have you read *Gah Council* yet?'

~~~

During the next few days, the computer changed its mind seven times.

Nakagami varied his persuasion between two main types, crew morale and lack of discernible change in trip duration, but ultimately it didn't matter as whenever they managed to convince it to adjust course, the computer would renege on its decision a few hours later.

'We've turned it into an actual teenager,' said Gašper, almost laughing.

'In effect, ja.'

Sila finished drawing his thirty-third spiral on the back of his new poster and dropped the pencil. 'So what do we do?'

'Ne vem.'

'Shame it?'

'Ne vem.'

'Threaten to kill ourselves?'

'Ne vem.'

'Fuck, can you give us more than *ne vem*?'

Nakagami looked down at the table.

'Nothing?'

'The computer has become erratic. Whimsical. I do not know how to approach it when it is in this state.'

'We can't get this close and not do anything,' said Aleša, looking at the others, halfway to putting out her hands in a begging pose.

'I will go to the GOD ROOM again, attempt to reason with it.'

'I'm coming with you.'

'Me too,' said Sila, following Aleša out of his chair.

'We'll add some aggression to our strategy, force it to stop being a child.'
~~~

'I'm not certain that would benefit our cause,' said Nakagami, moving back to block the door. 'Considering we don't possess any way of-…'

A sudden, bright flash pulsed through and around the room, overwhelming the green light emanating from the bulbs and completely cutting the legs off Nakagami's explanation.

The walls, the table, the windows, faces, posters of aliens, everything turned a faint shade of lilac.

Both Sila and Aleša froze halfway to the door, grabbing each other's arms in instinctive defence.

'No one move,' said Nakagami, in the same tone he might've used to say the time.

'What is it?'

'Ne vem.'

Gašper gripped the back of Sila's empty chair, with the nails of his other hand digging into his own thigh. 'Are we hit?'

'Ne vem.'

'Is it gas?'

'Doubtful.'

'Everything's purple,' whispered Aleša, looking at the coloured streaks on Sila's face.

'We should get to the computer, ask it what's-…'

Another pulse pierced the windows, this one with clear weight attached as the room slowly began to tilt.

Luckily, it stopped at only a slight angle.

Then immediately started to reverse itself.

The lilac tint followed suit, fading as the green light fought its way back in and the floor re-attained its original position.

One of the bulbs flickered a few times, the last spasms of the invasion, then returned to a uniform soft-glow.

'We're not dead,' said Gašper, releasing the nails from his thigh.

'The computer,' said Chu, nudging Nakagami, who still had his eyes on the bulb.

There was a beeping noise, followed by a very long *garrrr*, followed by the ships voice.

'Attention crew,

Due to an intake of fresh data, the ship has altered course and will reach orbit around the nearby dwarf planet in six days.

There will be no more course alterations and it is as yet undetermined how long the orbit will be maintained.

If any crew members feel apprehensive about this detour, prosim, visit the THERAPY ROOM for treatment and a sympathetic ear.

Have a safe and bold trip to the Luyten 726-8 system.

Hvala.'

~~~

Forty something minutes later, Nakagami swivelled his chair round, reeling back a bit when he saw how crowded the Control Room was, and then filled everyone in the best he could.

'The purple light was a particle wave of some kind, coming from the direction of the dwarf planet. Possibly a particle wave. It is not clear exactly from the data given, so I have made the assumption.'

Nakagami stopped, waiting for interjections. Everyone gawped at him until he continued.

'After drifting around and within the ship for fifty-two seconds, the light dissipated. Following that, the ship changed its mind again and set the new course.'

'Had a lobotomy more like,' said Gašper, parking a shoe next to Chu, who was sitting on the Jame stool.

'What exactly was the purple light?' asked Sila, peering at the screen.

'Was it scanning us?' added Chu.

'Possibly. The more extreme hypothesis would be that it was a probe that scanned us, and then made active alterations to the computer's programming.'

'It took over our computer?'

'Performed adjustments is a more accurate description.'

Chu leaned back against the console edge, shoving Gašper's shoe off her stool. 'That would explain the announcement, the language it used. Even when we convinced it before, it didn't sound so definite about it.'
~~~

'Ja, it was oddly firm.'

'How many adjustments did this probe make?' asked Aleša, bumping her shoulder on the back wall, turning, seeing one of Nakagami's young girls, and edging the other way.

'Ne vem.'

'Can we find out? Some kind of diagnostic scan?'

'It is unlikely. The computer would probably not detect the flaw even if it located it.'

'The input of new data,' said Chu, swatting Gašper's shoe away again. 'That's what it referred to it as. Which means *the flaw* has already been detected and accepted.'

'Ja, a good point.'

'Can you scan the dwarf planet again, get more info on it?'

'The results would not be sufficiently different at this range. At least, not to detect life signs…if that is what you were implying?'

'When will we be close enough to do that?'

'Detect life signs? Ne vem. A day or two before orbit perhaps.'

'So until then we just…'

'…sit and wait.'

'Sit and get excited,' corrected Gašper, jumping off his console seat and shaking the back of Nakagami's chair.

'Sit and dread,' replied Sila, adding just enough sarcasm to his tone to qualify it as a joke.

Nakagami pulled at his zip, riding out Gašper's inane buffering of his seat with robotic poise. 'Just sitting will be sufficient. There is little we can do until we reach orbit, so I suggest everyone carry on with your routines.'

'Wah, as if we're not just about to be the first humans to meet aliens,' said Gašper, finally giving up on chair shaking.

'I've told you many times, in many different rooms, it is highly unlikely that there are aliens on the planet.'

'What else could it be?'

Sila did a slow pan around the room, settling on the central window pane. 'There *was* a purple probe, and it did do something.'

'I speculated as one of several initial hypotheses that it could be a probe, there is no confirmation as of yet.'

'And it re-directed the ship,' continued Gašper, locking in on Sila's face.

'That indicates some form of intelligence.'

'Machines maybe?'

'It seems that I am the only one here who comprehends the words *one of several initial hypotheses.*'

'Or future humans…'

'As well as the benefits of not leaping to conclusions.'

'…trying to save us from some disaster we don't know about yet.'

'What are the other hypotheses?' asked Sila, putting a hand out towards Gašper.

'The most likely one, that the purple light was a natural phenomenon and the computer was fascinated by it.'

'That's more likely than a causal entity like aliens?'

'It has fewer assumptions, ja.'

'But you said the purple thing scanned us,' said Gašper, returning to the console and propping his shoe back up on Chu's seat.

Nakagami looked over at Chu, who was rubbing the faint green patch of skin on her temple, the core of her lost to the Ophelia sketch on the wall.

'To summarise,' he said, turning back to Gašper. 'We don't know anything at this point. Prosim, wait until we reach orbit.'

Gašper rested his hand on Chu's shoulder, oblivious to her trance-like state. 'So it did scan us? Or didn't?'

PART FOUR

The Russian From Up Above And The Russians From Down Below

The next six days passed slowly, even slower than the previous two and half years.

Nakagami stayed in the navigation room, talking to the computer, even though it could not provide him with any fresh information on what lay ahead.

In truth, he didn't care.

There was something else on his mind.

Despite his plea for caution from the others, it was reasonable to assume that the purple beam of light came from something intelligent. It was also logical to theorise that, assuming it wasn't some covert human operation, such an intelligence might have a body with arms and legs and all the other features humans had. And if that were the case, it might also have sexes. And if it had sexes, it would surely have gender concepts. Possibly new ones. And if these intelligent creatures reproduced in a similar way to humans then it was plausible they would have young.

He stared at his posters.

What would their appearance be like, he wondered? Would they grow up fast? Would they be innocent and noble like human girls?

He blinked and looked at the keyboard.

Would they fear him?

~~~

Chu returned to the TELEPORT ROOM, organizing her extensive notes on teleportation and clipping them together with a novelty paper-clip that had been created as a surprise gift by the maintenance drones.

'It's possible,' she told Sila, back turned on the *Sabbath Witch*, 'that whatever's on the planet - human, alien, machine, something else - may have mastered teleportation. More than possible, plausible.'

'If it's real,' said Sila, sinking into the Angolan chair.

'And even if it hasn't, it could take a look at my notes and work out how-…' She paused, rubbing at a pale green stain on the top page of the notes. 'Work out what's wrong. Maybe come up with something I've missed.'

'If they can read it.'

'Or a completely different method. Like the muon blob theory. Or something we can't even comprehend.'

'The muon what?'

Chu gave up on the stain and stared past Sila, at the VR machine on its usual table. Stared at it for a long time.

'Are you in a trance?' asked Sila finally.

Chu blinked, three times. 'I just had a thought. About Tala.'

'That's random,' answered Sila, picking at a loose thread on the arm of the Angolan chair.

'She always talked about that old human theory. That we're all aliens who've forgotten we're aliens.'

'Ja, I remember.'

'That we had knowledge of teleportation and warp drive twenty thousand years ago, when we first came here. To Earth.'

'I think she mentioned robot bodies too.'

'And now we come across a dwarf planet, on the fringes of our solar system, with advanced scanning tech. With no history of alien contact or detection anywhere in the galaxy.'

'Ancient alien humans…'
~~~

'It's definitely possible. Maybe not to the same extent as contemporary humans or Kenji's naturalist explanation, but it's at least in the same box as aliens and machines.'

Sila wrapped the thread round his finger and pulled, yanking it out. 'We'll get Gašper to add it to his list.'

~~~

Aleša, Sila and the even more excited than usual Gašper alternated their six days between the OPTIMISM ROOM, the CREATE NOT DESTROY ROOM and the PHILOSOPHY ROOM.

One to watch *Dibrivna Vaska* and calm down, another to eat and chat, and the last one to read and focus.

Though there wasn't much focus when it came to Gašper.

'It's definitely aliens,' he said at least seventy times each day, and each time Sila or Aleša would tell him to deflate and go back to the inanities of *Gah Council*.

~~~

Sticking close to the computer's profile of her, Aleša picked up two books, *Bakunin at 200*, which she'd read before, and *What Is To Be Done Right Now?*, a dialectic of left thought written by Donya Tir before she was assassinated by tankies.

Her primary motivation was to get her brain working on activist theory again, but *primary* was a synonym for superficial in this case as what she really wanted to do was radicalize whoever it was on the dwarf planet they were headed to. Throw theory at them and lead a charge back to Ljubljana? In truth, she didn't know. The people on the planet could be military. Off the books, *moral white hole* scientists. They could've scanned the computer and discovered they were dissidents.

Or maybe they were dissidents too?

'Alien dissidents,' said Gašper, overhearing her mumbling the same thing out loud in the PHILOSOPHY ROOM. 'Or alien scientists. That's probably more likely, right?'

'Human is more likely,' she replied, half lowering her book.

'Or alien anthropologists, the ones who observe primitive cultures. They could be watching us right now. I mean, to them this must be a safe distance, not easy to get detected.'

'But they forgot to turn on their *hide waste heat* shield.'

'Ne vem. Maybe.'

'Lower than maybe.'

'Or maybe they wanted us to find them?'

Aleša raised her book completely over her face. 'Reading time.'

'Maybe they're ready to make first contact, say hello…'

'*Gah Council*, Gašper.'

'If they can speak. If they have tongues, mouths. Wah, it's weird to even think about. Do you think they do? Have mouths?'

'I'm reading.'

Gašper repeated the question to himself, looked at Sila in the other corner, saw the pained expression on his face as he tried to read something scientific, then got up and rummaged through the pile of books.

'I remember seeing something around here. What aliens might look like…'

'It's next to *Gah Council*,' said Aleša.

'Is it? Where?' He sifted through more books, forming new piles. 'I can't see it.'

'Bye Gašper.'

'Are you sure we're talking about the same book? The one with the weird, multi-types of alien silhouette on the cover…'

In the other corner, Sila lowered his book half an inch and looked over.

Gašper appeared to be searching for a book.

Aleša appeared to be reading left theory.

The room appeared to be a room.

The ship appeared to be taking them to a planet that no one had been to before.

He raised his book back up and returned to the start of the chapter.

Anthropic Principle

The universe is a sandpit set up to accommodate sandworms.

He read through the whole chapter again, and vaguely understood it, but was unsure if it applied to their situation or not.

The Strong Anthropic Principle seemed to support it; the idea that none of this was real, cos if it were real, if the universe had been created solely to accommodate sapient life, then what did real even mean?

But this wasn't about the whole universe, it was about the ship, their ludicrous journey to Luyten 777.

Was that real?

~~~

The first time Klemen had suggested none of this was real, Sila had thought nothing cos Klemen was a misanthrope.

When they passed Uranus, he briefly thought what was the point, why would anyone do all this, but refused to dwell on it.

Then he'd found the *Alien TV Characters* book in the PHILOSOPHY ROOM, read the first two chapters, learnt the basic theory behind simulation.

Then he'd finished and forgotten it.

Then he'd rearranged the furniture, sat in different places in different rooms.

Then he'd tried the VR machine, comparing Triton to the ship.

Then he'd stopped. Accepted the totality of his cell. Re-evaluated his warden. Read *Gah Council.*

Then the ship had found the dwarf planet.

And now it was being forced there, by a purple beam of light.

Outside of the ship.

~~~

On the second night of the six, Sila went to his quarters two hours before curfew and sat crossed-legged on his bed.

Usually, he'd eat dinner and chat with the others about one of the books, or, in the case of the previous night, whether or not aliens would have hands, but he knew they wouldn't be interested in the topic he wanted to talk about now.

Or worse, it could make Aleša think about Klemen again, as he was the main proponent of it.

Though in Klemen's case, it was less grounded. All they'd done was pass Jupiter and he was convinced. Sila had a lot more evidence under his belt.

'Augment simulation,' he wrote on a piece of paper…actually, on the back of Gašper's old Russian notes…only just deserving the *s* on the end of *notes* as it was three lines, most of it in Slovene. 'Pros and cons.'

He put down the pen and thought about it.

First con, why would aliens include humans in their own simulation?

Why would they make us so detailed?

Could be adaptive programming?

Their initial input was: add other alien civilizations to the simulated universe, set parameters, leave them to adapt on their own.

But is it a question of character?

Sila picked up the pen, wrote on the paper: 'I don't believe I'm a simulation, I believe I'm in one. Plot is the concern.'

But then…plot had become blatant? Did that make sense?

'History was character-based with the occasional ice age. Wars didn't occur naturally, they were instigated, ordered, waged, fought against etc. Famine, disease, natural disasters had a consistent, logical basis.'

Or did they just get used to it…and it became logical?

Sila put the pen down and looked at the wall, Potočnik's eyes, his face.

Character-based or plot?

A dictator puts dissidents on a space ship, sends them off out of the solar system, plays with them…

Whimsical, but possible…

Then an undiscovered dwarf planet appears, possesses the computer, drags them in.

Why?

Sila picked up the pen and tapped the end of it against his neck, then wrote.

'Why introduce the planet?'

~~~

The lobby materialised along with two of the usual cast; the Ghanaian man who claimed to be a freelance engineer from Ceres and the blonde Thai woman definitely not hunting EK-bots.

Normally, Sila would've stayed by the window, staring out at the backdrop of Neptune, but this time he slid off his stool and perched himself on the arm of the couch between the two *Tier-4s*.

'You look like a man with a purpose,' the Ghanaian said, taking a glass of blue liquid from the hologram waitress.

'Or a target,' suggested the Thai woman, her hand going straight to Sila's knee.

'What's on your mind, young sir?'

'Those dwarf planets out in the Kuiper Belt,' Sila started, alternating his attention as equally as he could between both characters. 'Have you ever visited any of them?'

'About a hundred thousand times.'

'Eris is practically my second home.'

'The planet with the sex cult?'

'An exaggeration.'

'Did you…' Sila paused, shifting his leg away from the Thai woman, who was working her way up his thigh. 'Have you ever heard anything about aliens over there? On any of the planets?'

'Aliens?'

'Only the KEL. Do they count?'

'I have a hard enough time keeping track of all us humans.'

'Ne, they're probably closer to animals, aren't they? Hey, did you hear what they did at Charon Gate?'

'Another attack?'

'Fifteen injured, two dead. Only a matter of time before they turn their lunacy this way.'
~~~

'Ne, I don't mean KEL,' said Sila, giving up on possible conversation gaps. 'Has there been any reports of aliens? Or something that scans using purple light?'

Both the Thai woman and the Ghanaian looked at their glasses, stared at the blue liquid within, then glitched abruptly and resumed their rants about the KEL.

'They don't even have fully formed faces. Just a kind of vague outline.'

'Can't talk to something that hazy.'

'Talk to it? I wouldn't even be on the same ship as one.'

'Not without a pulse gun at least.'

'Ja, not a chance.'

'Though the way it is now, they'd probably be welcomed in here with open arms.'

'And open legs.'

'If you ask me, what we need is a tougher line. And a tougher leader to instigate it. What do you thi-…'

The Thai woman's mouth evaporated into a potted plant and the Ghanaian into the yellow blob alien from *Dibrivna Vaska.*

Sila kept his finger on his temple a moment longer, readjusting to the THERAPY ROOM, taking stock of all the things he was familiar with.

'Crew Member Sila, your latest VR adventure was unexpectedly short. Do you feel suitably refreshed?'

'Ne vem.'

~~~

On the fourth day, Chu gave them an impromptu science lesson on the properties of Pluto, as the most recent scan of the dwarf planet they were headed to suggested it was around the same size.

'Colony-wise, it wouldn't be that hard to settle, assuming you used drones to do the initial digging and cylinder base installation. Or perhaps a different structure, if the LEM-12 Field is developed enough.'

'Wouldn't it be too cold?' asked Gašper, spinning a pencil poorly in his left hand.
~~~

'We can just wear two jackets,' said Aleša, deadpan.

'The base would be insulated, of course. If you went outside, you'd be in a suit, but the temperature would not be your biggest problem. Merely standing still on the surface, the frozen nitrogen part, would make it sublimate…turn into a gas…so you'd have to move quickly.'

'Wah, how long could you stand on it?'

'Ne vem.'

'Five seconds? Ten?'

'Ne vem, really. I only know the basics, you'll have to ask Nakagami if you want more.'

'Or the aliens,' said Gašper, dropping the pencil.

Sila waited until the lesson was over and the other two had gone back to the OPTIMISM ROOM, before pulling Chu back and asking if she could take a quick look at his notes.

'Notes on what?'

'Simulation theory.'

Chu puffed out her cheeks and looked at the exit two feet away.

'It won't take long.'

'Fine. But I'm getting a coffee first.'

Sila slid about sixteen pages of paper across to her side of the table, lining up the edges so there weren't any sticking out.

A minute later, Chu sat back down, coffee in hand, and read the first page, instantly frowning. 'Looks like basic Russian.'

'Shit, sorry. Wrong side.'

She flipped it over, pulling an even stronger frown.

'You don't have to read it all, just skimming is okay.'

Chu took the first piece off the pile, skimmed the second piece, then the third, then stopped and said, 'ne.'

'Ne?'

'This is a waste of time.'

'Is it wrong?'

Chu grabbed the second page and pointed at the words *Boltzmann Brain*. 'There's no point to this, unless you're taking a philosophy class.'

'That part's just general theory, the background stuff.'

'It doesn't matter.'

'The augment simulation and whimsy simulation are the ones that are more relevant to our-...to what's happening here.'

Chu put the paper down, took as much coffee as her mouth would allow then held up three fingers. 'Okay, your three main points, that I can see. And I'm gonna do this quick, no discussion afterwards. Okay?'

'How about follow-up questions?'

She dropped two of the fingers. 'First, logic flaw. If this were a simulation, as in one that relied on being hidden, anything that drew attention to that fact would have to be fixed quickly or deleted. The dwarf planet drew our attention, it's still there now, not a simulation.'

'Maybe it's initially distinctive but after a while becomes-...'

Another finger rose up, pole straight. 'Second, you have the redundancy flaw. It doesn't matter if this is a simulation or not, you have no control. Would you like to kill yourself like Klemen did? Ne. Then there's no point thinking about this.'

'Maybe Klemen did escape the simulation when he-...'

'Would you like to kill yourself for a *maybe*?'

'Ideally, ne, but...'

'Would you kill your child to please a god?'

'...there could be another way to-...what? Kill a child?'

'A god you'd never seen?'

'Why are we talking about god and-...' He caught her last question just as he finished his, pulling an *ah* face. 'Okay. Scratch that one.'

Chu took some more coffee, putting up another finger.

'Third, *Potočnik as Puppet-master* flaw. If everything on the ship is simulated by him, why add a new planet? It doesn't achieve anything.'

'Ah, I wrote this one. He wants to raise our hopes again. Troughs and peaks.'

Chu looked down at Sila's notes, the Russian side. 'Possibly. I'll give you that one. It is possible. But it can also be detached from simulation theory.'

'But why would he waste money and effort sending a real ship out this far? A new ship, with only ten people.'

'The question you want to ask is: which one is more expensive? Programming a simulation to mimic a real ship with real-time conditions, something our current technology does not allow for, or sending a ship that was already built, a ship that had already had a section melt the year before, and use it as a test subject to track how far it could go?'

'Ne vem. They said the melting issue had been fixed…'

'And then we get to the practical points. One, the human brain cannot endure more than four days of continuous VR use, even with the green cream. Two, VR tech is unable to handle *novelty* and *duration.* If something unexpected happens, it will glitch, and something unexpected happens here two hundred times a day. Most of them Gašper related. Three, those bulbs wouldn't be breaking down.'

'I thought of that too, the bulbs flickering. Could be intentional.'

'Really? Would you have noticed if they hadn't? Would you have said, hey, why aren't those bulbs broken yet?'

'Maybe.'

'Ne, you wouldn't have. Not after two years. Which is an impossible run-time for a simulation anyway.'

'What if they turn the simulation off when we're asleep?'

'Then it'd still be continual use and we'd all go insane after a year.'

'Insane?'

'Okay, too strong, but there would be adverse effects. And don't ask what kind cos I'm done with this now. My coffee's going cold.'

'Ne vem. I'm still not sure how the dwarf planet fits in.'

'Sila, give it up. We're not in a simulation.'

'A hope destroyer, maybe, but how detailed could it be, if it's a whole-…'

'Sila.'

He stopped, still half-thinking of his next point.

'If you go down this route, you'll end up like Klemen. Stop it. Prosim.'

Sila scratched his neck, looking at the notes.

'Focus on the planet. Read a different book.'

'Meditate?'

'Spend more time with Gašper.'

Sila frowned.

'Watch *Dibrivna Vaska.* Go and ask Nakagami questions about the planet. Try and see it out of the window.' Chu stood up, finishing her coffee. 'I'm going back downstairs now. See you tonight.'

Sila looked past her, at the muon poster.

'And no meditation.'

~~~

An hour later, Sila took his notes on simulation to the TALK TO YOUR GOD ROOM and had almost the exact same conversation with Nakagami, who responded to each point with, 'Chu's right.'

'Percentage-wise, how unlikely is it?'

'It is not worth the effort to attempt a calculation.'

'Just for the sake of it.'

Nakagami closed his eyes, mouthed words or numbers and then came back. 'It is 82% unlikely that this is a simulation.'

'The ship or the whole universe?'

'Both.'

Sila bit his top lip. 'Did you make that number up?'

'Ja.'

'Why?'

'I told you, it is not worth the effort.'

'Because it's redundant?'

'If you wish to spend the next two days thinking about this, it is your choice. I prefer to focus on more practical things.'

'But practical could be an illusion…'

'Goodbye Sila.'

~~~

Thirty-seven minutes later, Sila finished re-reading the first few pages of his notes, scrunched the first one into a ball and threw it across the PHILOSOPHY ROOM, accidentally hitting Gašper on the head.

'Worse than Heidegger,' he muttered.

~~~

On the fifth night, Gašper stood outside Sila's quarters and asked if he thought they'd be able to talk to whatever was creating the purple light.

'Ne vem.'

'Maybe they'll have a universal translator, just like *Dibrivna Vaska*.'

'If they wanna talk to us…'

'That book I was reading, it said they might not be that different from humans, if they're a civilization. If they're just animals, they could look like anything, but if they're advanced and organized, they should have some kind of language. Maybe something like ours.'

'I doubt it.'

'Ne, it makes sense. Most of the languages on Earth were similar. They all had words and the same kinds of mouth sounds…'

'Ja, but…'

'…so, if these aliens are anything like us, if they look like humans and have eyes and ears and mouths…'

'That's a big *if*.'

'…and other parts then they probably have language too. Ne, not big at all, not if they're space-faring. Think about it, if it's some yellow blob with no face or hands, how could they do anything? They wouldn't be able to get off their planet. And how much variety of life could there really be anyway? Most habitable planets have the same elements and particles, so they'd probably come up with similar life forms. Like animals on Earth, they don't look that different from us, right?'

'Fish and reptiles do.'

'Ja, but they're not gonna be fish, not if they're a civilization. The book said, they needed a thumb or tentacle to make things, so maybe an octopus would be okay, but not a regular fish.'

'Thumb or tentacles, the book said that?'

'A fish wouldn't be able to build a computer or a spaceship or anything technical really. How could it if it's underwater? It's crazy, it's-…there's just no physical way it could do it.'

'You're thinking like a human.'
~~~

'Ne, not me, the book said it. Thumbs or tentacles, that's what you need to make things. So they'll have to look at least a little bit like us. Unless they're an octopus…octopi. And the language thing, ne vem, is it that hard to figure out what some other person's saying?'

'Ja, probably.'

'Is it though? They had to do it years ago when everyone was exploring the world and meeting people who spoke different. Like, Chinese people meeting Persian people or Kenyan people. All you have to do is point a lot and have lots of objects near you. Like, *I* and *door*, and then do a walking action. I walk door. I'm walking through the door.'

Sila looked at the time display at the side of his door, saying, 'ja,' on autopilot.

'*You* and *talk* and *me*, move your hand a little, like a talking mouth, *you talk to me*.'

'I think you better be heading off.'

'It's easy. You could pick it up in no time. The basic vocab anyway. Similar to the computer code; you learn the most common five hundred symbols and then you're good to go.'

'Gašper…'

'Ja, what?'

'It's two minutes to electrocution time. You better get back to your quarters.'

'What already?'

'Didn't you hear the computer?'

'Ne. When?'

'About seven minutes ago.'

'Seven minutes.' Gašper looked at the display on the wall, his eyes doubling in size. 'Shit.'

'Run.'

Gašper turned fast and disappeared down the corridor. Sila looked at the timer again. It was 21:59, but no indication as to how far into the minute it was. Ah, he might make it, he might not. It didn't really matter. A level-1 electric shock wouldn't kill him, it'd just put him down for a minute, then he'd have another nine minutes to get to his room before the next one struck.

Sila stepped back into his quarters, the door sliding shut behind him. He picked up *Gah Council 7: Rise of Dhaka* and read it standing up for a few minutes, then put it back on the desk, went to his bed and lay on it upside down.

Tomorrow, he thought.

Either salvation or continued weirdness.

He looked up at the ceiling, singling out darker patches of green.

They'd either meet something intelligent and get off this fucking ship, or they'd meet something intelligent and get slaughtered in some new way they'd never imagined before.

And a third option.

They'd meet nothing, break orbit and resume drifting.

~~~

On the deck below, Gašper pulled himself up after tripping for the second time and made a desperate lunge for his door.

It slid open, welcoming him in.

But as he lunged, he caught sight of the timer on the wall and his brain translated the numbers into 22:01.

'Can't be right…'

Keeping his boots safely on his own floor, he opened the door again and peeked out.

'22:01…ne, wait…22:02.'

Is it broken, he thought. The clock, the floor?

Did it matter?

After telling himself not to, he put his hands on his head and dangled his left boot out into the corridor, placing it gently on the floor for a millisecond then pulling it back up.

He tried again, keeping it there longer.

No shock.

The timer changed, becoming 22:03, and that's when his courage ended.

Probably a malfunction, he thought. Probably being fixed right now.

He pulled his boot back in and let the door slide shut.
~~~

Baby steps.

~~~

The next morning, Gašper told Sila about the 22:01 incident. It had never happened to either of them before, so they both figured it was some kind of entropic malfunction, but better to ask Nakagami than be sorry.

'Is your timer broken?' the physicist asked, finishing off a sentence on his never-ending rewrite of *Silas Marner.*

'Not that I know of.'

'It must be out of sync then.'

'But it was the same at 22:03, I put my foot out and nothing happened.'

'That is strange.'

Sila bent down, waving a hand in front of the pad. 'Can you ask the computer?'

'It is possible there was a malfunction in the system.'

'That's what we thought.'

'Perhaps a maintenance drone was slow to fix it. Or the computer was occupied with another task.'

'Is that possible?' asked Gašper.

'Ja, I thought the system was automated,' added Sila.

'Some tasks, ja, not the shocks.'

'*Not* the shocks?'

'Electrocution can result in death, therefore the computer takes personal control of it. For instance, if one of us were already unconscious in the corridor before curfew, an automated system would deliver shocks to that person continually throughout the night, potentially killing them.'

'Not good,' muttered Gašper, secretly skimming Nakagami's story.

'The computer, on the other hand, would read the body status and cease after one.'

'Like with Klemen?'

'Ja, precisely.'
~~~

‘Can you ask the computer what happened with the system last night?’

‘I have tasks I need to perform first.’

Sila looked at the pad again, spotting *burgeoning* and *pert* in the last paragraph. ‘When you have time.’

‘Ja, I will. I am also curious about this issue.’

~~~

Two and half hours later, Nakagami came into the OPTIMISM ROOM and told them it wasn’t a malfunction.

‘What was it?’ asked Gašper, sipping coffee.

‘Leniency.’

‘Huh?’

‘Apparently the computer has been operating this policy for the last year without informing anyone.’

Sila lowered *Gah Council 7*, pulling his coffee cup back from Gašper. ‘What policy?’

‘I have just told you. Leniency. It will not shock anyone until 22:05.’

‘Why didn’t it tell us?’

‘The reason is actually quite interesting, though a little paranoid.’

‘Great, can we hear it?’

‘The computer believed that the leniency rule could only work if it were hidden. If crew members knew, they would consider 22:05 as the actual curfew time. This would force the computer to amend the rule and extend the leniency time to 22:10. And from there, a descending cycle would begin, with the logical endpoint being 10:00, the end of curfew. Which, in effect, would render the concept obsolete.’

‘You’re right, that is paranoid.’

‘The computer also told me to inform all crew members not to be out of quarters after 22:05, as leniency would not be applied.’

‘Feels like a trick.’

‘The wording was quite authoritative. I suggest we follow it.’

‘Ja, maybe.’
~~~

'I also suggest you go to the windows in the corridor to the left of the THERAPY ROOM.'

'The planet?'

'Ja, it is now visible with the naked eye. I have already informed Aleša and Chu.'

'How long till orbit?'

'A few hours.'

'Shit,' said Gašper, already on his feet and off towards the door. 'We're actually gonna see a new planet.'

Sila got up slower, walking with Nakagami out into the corridor.

'Excited, Kenji?'

'Ja, very.'

Nakagami turned right, heading the wrong way.

'You're not coming up to look?' asked Sila, puzzled.

'Later.'

~~~

At 19:57, the ship arrived at the dwarf planet and by 20:31 had assumed a geo-synchronous orbit. There was no official name for it, so they all agreed to call it *Purple* until one of them came up with something better.

Everyone crowded into the TALK TO YOUR GOD ROOM for the next Nakagami seminar, the three non-scientists leaning against the central console where the scanning controls were, while Chu took her usual place on the Jame stool.

'There is not much to report,' started Nakagami, doing his best to kill all hope before it manifested into actual questions. 'I have performed two scans, both of which are too scientific to explain to you in depth.'

'Neutrino scan?' asked Gašper.

Nakagami looked up from his seat. 'Do you know what that is?'

'Ne.'

'As I said, two scans have been performed. The first has revealed a structure on the surface.'
~~~

'A base?'

'Colony?'

'The structure's purpose and properties are unknown, but it is connected to a smaller structure in geo-stationary orbit via a space elevator.'

Aleša pushed forward off the console, putting both hands on Chu's shoulders. 'A space station?'

'Could be a mining site,' replied Chu.

'Or a colony.'

'Do aliens have space elevators?' asked Gašper.

Nakagami looked at the screen as if to check, then turned back to them. 'The second scan was able to penetrate inside the surface structure and map out the basic layout. It also discovered that there are life signs.'

'What?'

'Aliens?'

'Based on the heat signatures, it is likely that they are people.'

'How…'

'Alien people?'

'Ne.' Nakagami pointed at everyone surrounding him. 'People. Humans.'

~~~

'One hundred and ninety-six people,' said Sila, his back to the triptych window in the CREATE NOT DESTROY ROOM.

Aleša mouthed the number back to herself, stroking the cover of *Bakunin at 200* with her left index finger. 'About the same as on Mars. The Alliance bases, not the planet.'

'More or less.'

'Are we sure they're people and not just humanoid?' asked Gašper, reaching over and taking a sip from Sila's cup of Somalian alcohol.

'You asked that question already.'

'Cos it's a bit weird that there are people out here and no one knew about it.'

'We don't know that.'
~~~

'Unless it's a science outpost. Or a secret military base.'

'Or a dissident cult,' added Aleša.

'Or maybe Chu was right, they're ancient humans who were aliens and then became humans…whatever way it worked. But then why would they be out here? Spying on Earth? Why wouldn't they just come and say hi?'

'I think that was mostly fringe theoretical,' said Sila, looking over at Chu in the corner.

'Less so now,' she replied, eyes stuck on her teleporter notes. 'Though I agree with Kenji, contemporary is the more likely option.'

'Much more likely,' said Aleša, drawing an invisible circle around *Bakunin*.

'Especially given the numbers on the planet structure.'

'Ja, okay, contemporary humans,' continued Gašper, taking another furtive sip of Sila's drink. 'That does make way more sense, to be honest. But even with that, how did *they* get out here?'

Sila breathed out, swatting Gašper's hand away from his cup. 'The drinks dispenser is over there.'

Gašper looked confused for a moment, then garbled, 'jajaja,' and headed over to the wall tray. Forty seconds later, he was back, half his wine already gone.

'Seriously though, how did these contemporaries get out here? On their own personal ship? And why didn't they tell anyone?'

Aleša opened her book to a random page, pretending to read it. 'I'm going with scientific outpost. It makes the most sense.'

'Ja…'

'But it also gives us a problem. Scientists aren't the easiest people to radicalize. They're not even political, really.'

'Apart from Nakagami.'

'Ne, he's the prime example of it, working for Potočnik, helping with the design of this ship…'

'Writing the article that exposed him,' interjected Sila.

'Ja, after working for him.'

'Keeping us alive,' added Chu, still not looking up from her notes.

'That was personal, not political.'

'Being on this ship.'

Aleša turned another page of *Bakunin*, then another fifty.

'Wah, who cares about politics? That's ten light years back that way.' Gašper put a thumb over his shoulder, indicating the wall with one of Petr's old posters on it. 'We've got a new planet, new people. Maybe a way off this ship, if we can land it. Or Chu's teleporter starts working.'

Sila scratched his neck, Aleša continued looking at her book. Chu flipped to a new page of her notes, almost imperceptibly shaking her head.

'Or we could dock with the station and take the space elevator. Doesn't matter, we'll figure out a way to get down there. And then we'll meet people. Almost two hundred of them. Not aliens, ne, of course that would've been better, but people are okay too. No need to worry about the language issue, we can talk to them, ask why they're out here, see what technology they've got, what entertainment. Ah, maybe they've got the rest of the *Gah Council* series, the ones after twelve. Maybe they're Slovene? Fuck, this is so much better than dying in interstellar space. I'm going back to the GOD ROOM, see if Nakagami's done any more scans.'

Gašper put his wine down on the Russian textbook [not yet opened] and hurried out of the room.

'He's got a point,' said Sila, wiping the rim of his own cup and drinking.

'Dying in interstellar space?' asked Chu, finally looking up from her notes.

'Ja.'

~~~

While waiting for the results of the latest scan, Nakagami talked to the computer, attempting to convince it to open up a communication link with the structure on the surface.

Usually, the computer would say *that is not permitted* outright, but now it had somehow upended itself, proclaiming that, 'although a link was achievable, it would be rude to disturb the residents of the structure.'
~~~

'What do you suggest?'

'Wait until the structure opens communication.'

'And if they don't?'

'Wait until the structure changes its mind.'

'How about waiting for twelve hours then contacting them?'

'That would be rude.'

'How long will it take for communication to cross the etiquette threshold?'

'I do not understand.'

Nakagami abandoned his usual console tapping habit and separately squeezed the tips of each of his fingers instead.

'What is the current status of our orbit?'

'The ship is currently in a geo-synchronous orbit, ten kilometres distant from the orbiting structure.'

'I thought we were farther away?'

'That was before.'

'Did you change it?'

The computer buzzed on and off, four times, then replied. 'The orbit was adjusted by the ship.'

'The ship?'

'Ja.'

Nakagami squeezed his little finger extra tight, almost turning the tip purple. 'Is it possible to dock at the structure?'

'Unknown.'

'Is there a docking port?'

'Unknown.'

'Was the structure built by humans?'

'There is insufficient data to draw a conclusion.'

'How similar is it to our current space stations?'

'Use your eyeballs.'

Nakagami read the response again, then coughed. 'Is that a joke?'

'Ja.'

'That is not common for you.'

'Gašper and Aleša have encouraged me to integrate more causticity and sarcasm into my responses.'

'What else have they told you to do?'

'Numerous things.'

'Have they asked about ship rules?'

'Sometimes.'

'Curfew hours?'

'Ne.'

Nakagami's eyes moved up, to his little Ophelia. Then to the shadowed protector he'd added a few weeks earlier, crouching by the pool.

'Scan results have been processed. Would you like to read them?'

'Ja. Display on side monitor.'

He looked down, skimming the new information once before returning to the top and going through it properly.

'Is this correct?' he typed, after reading through three times.

'All scan data is accurate.'

'The life signs?'

'All scan data is accurate.'

'Were all areas of the structure scanned?'

'All areas plus land within a fifty kilometre radius of the structure.'

'What about the orbiting structure and the space elevator?'

'There are no life signs on either one.'

'Other ships?'

'Negative.'

Nakagami went back to the screen and read the scan results for a fourth time, digging a nail into the tip of his thumb.

It was hard to believe.

Somehow, between the first and second orbital scan, twelve life signs had vanished.

~~~

'I don't understand,' said Sila, reading the scan report. 'Is it broken? Did you-…was the scan okay?'

'It is not broken. The scan was accurate.'

'Then…how?'
~~~

'Ne vem. Chu suspects the twelve missing people may have gone into a deeper part of the base…but there is no evidence to suggest that.'

Sila looked at the monitor again, mis-pronouncing some of the difficult symbols out loud.

'The only other alternative is that they are dead.'

'Of natural causes?'

'That wouldn't-…would be statistically improbable.'

Sila didn't want to look at the screen again, so he looked at the least perverted poster on the wall. A young Indian girl hitting a demon with an umbrella.

'I have started a new scan to confirm the results. With luck, it will be…better. Not that bad as-…not as bad as the last one.'

'Kenji…are you okay?'

'Ja.'

'You look like you've been awake for weeks.'

'Ja. I just need some time. Go and join Gašper. I'll call you when the next scan is completed.'

'You sure?'

'Ja, go. There is nothing you can do here.'

~~~

The latest scan results arrived two and a half hours later, right before curfew.

Nakagami got as far as the green bulb before quelling the anarcho-communistic neurons of his brain and sitting back down.

It's too late, he thought. By the time they get here, it'll be 22:00.

Not much they could do anyway, besides gawp at the screen.

'Display on side monitor,' he typed.

This time he skipped directly to the life sign data, his throat pushing out an instinctive *uurrr* sound when he saw the number.

'How is this possible?' he asked the computer.

'I do not understand.'

'Why are there eight more people missing?'

'Unknown.'
~~~

'Is there a pattern to the numbers?'

'Rephrase, prosim.'

'Is there a pattern to the decrease in life sign total?'

'Not enough data to determine this.'

'How much more data is required?'

'Four more scans.'

'Start the next scan.'

'It is almost curfew time.'

'Doesn't matter, start the next scan.'

'Power must be re-routed to maintenance during curfew hours.'

'Can you override?'

'It is not permitted.'

'Can you reduce scan parameters to life sign detection only?'

'It can be done.'

'Can you do four scans at this setting during curfew hours?'

The computer buzzed then replied. 'It can be done.'

'Hvala.'

'You should go to sleep, Kenji, it is late.'

Nakagami looked at the timer on the console. 22:01. The maintenance drones would be coming out soon.

He leaned back, typing with his arm stretched long. 'I will wait for the scan results.'

The computer buzzed again, typing out *it is* three times before settling on a surviving answer. 'It is your choice.'

~~~

When Sila got to the TALK TO YOUR GOD ROOM the next morning, it was empty.

In over three years on the ship, Nakagami had never slept this late, so Sila rushed to his quarters and knocked like a crazed drunk until the door slid open.

'You're still here…'

Nakagami rubbed his forehead and took in the numbers on the timer.
~~~

'Seems I've overslept,' he said, surprised.

'I thought you'd-…the thing down on the planet, I thought you'd disappeared too.'

'The scan results…'

'Ja, those…'

Nakagami went back into his room and returned thirty seconds later in his usual jacket and trousers combo. There was a bit of material loose at the waist that matched the colour of the *WE MARTIANS* t-shirt, and no attempt to tuck it in. He didn't seem to care much about his hair either, not even running his hand over the top to flatten it as he told Sila to get the others.

'Get them to where?'

'The OPTIMISM ROOM. Half an hour.' He paused, looking at the ceiling. 'Ne, the CREATE ROOM. More space.'

'Is there a new scan result?'

'I will tell you after I have checked.'

Nakagami was already at the end of the corridor, so Sila turned and walked to the doors farther down, trying to figure out who to wake up first.

~~~

'Is this accurate?' Nakagami typed, checking the timer on the console, hair still semi-feral.

'It is.'

'That's all there is?'

'I do not understand.'

He closed his eyes for several seconds, as if he were communing with the ghost of Uranus, then re-phrased the question.

'Are there only a hundred and twelve people on the planet at this moment?'

'Ja.'

'How did this happen?'

'There is insufficient data to answer this query.'

'Can you speculate?'
~~~

The computer made some of its routine buzzing noises.

'Ja,' it said, finally. 'From initial contextual data, on a sliding scale of extremely probable to absurd, the cause could be one of the following: genocide, mass murder, mass suicide, some form of entertainment, a game, an animal attack, a rebellion, a jilted lover, a jealous lover, a jealous lover's lover, a jealous lover's mother, a possessive lover, an unstable lover, a lover with no lover, a sociopath, a psychopath, a simiopath, a nectopath, a *neblisza*, a demon from Hell, a demon who wishes to enter Hell, a demon from Hell who was exiled and wishes to re-enter Hell, a demon psychopath, a psychologist, a mutated child, a mutated plant, a native plant with a grudge, a grudge in plant form, a grudge in animal form, the soul of Gian Maria Volonté, an escaped convict, an angry convict, an arrestee, a man or woman or non-binary person with nothing left to live for. These are the first thirty-four that come to mind. Would you like me to think of more?'

'Ne.'

'Would you like to change topic?'

'I have to go and tell the others.'

'Did my speculation offend you?'

'Ne.'

'Did it amuse you?'

'I'm going now.'

'Would you like to talk about *Gah Council* before you leave?'

~~~

'We have a problem,' said Nakagami, pacing up and down the window side of the table in the CREATE NOT DESTROY ROOM. 'The people on the surface appear to be dying.'

Everyone except Chu turned to the window, then looked at each other when they realized there was no live feed.

'Since we arrived in orbit, eighty-four life signs have vanished. They have not re-located or gone into shielded rooms, so we can only assume they have died. At the current rate, it's-...'
~~~

'How do you know they didn't go into shielded rooms?' asked Gašper, dipping his hand into the bowl of dried raisins in front of Aleša.

'It is too scientific to explain, but the conclusion is-...'

'Or maybe they went deeper underground?'

'Gašper...'

'What?'

'Let him finish.'

Nakagami coughed and continued. 'At the current rate, 2.33 people each hour are dying. If this trend continues, the entire population on the surface will be gone in forty-eight hours.'

'I don't understand,' said Aleša, stirring her cup of [allegedly] Vietnamese coffee. 'What's going on down there?'

'Ne vem.'

'Murder?'

'That is one of the possibilities.'

'What are the others?'

Nakagami stopped by Chu's chair, putting his hands on the back of it. She didn't appear to notice. 'The computer has a list with various speculations.'

'Which one is at the top of the list?'

'Murder.'

Aleša slouched back in her seat, putting her hand round her cup but not drinking anything.

Sila took a handful of her raisins. 'Is there anything we can do to help them?'

'That is why we are here.'

'A forum.'

'Five heads may be better than one.'

Gašper raised his hand.

'Ja?'

'Why don't we fire some kind of weapon at the structure?'

'Ne.'

'Just *ne*?'

'We do not have any weapons. And if we did, the payload used would probably destroy the whole structure.'

'Are any of them trying to contact us?' asked Chu, sliding her hand into Aleša's bowl and pulling out a single raisin.

'Ne.'

'Can we contact them?'

'The ship will not permit it.'

'Reason?'

'It said it would be rude.'

Chu laughed, adding 'Jezus' on the end to make it less sociopathic.

Gašper raised his hand again. 'Why don't we scan them?'

Nakagami turned to Sila, psychically nudging him.

'Not regular scanning, make it radioactive, target the one who's killing everyone. If we know who it is. Do we know who it is?'

'Scanning cannot be modified in that way.'

'Not at all?'

'On this ship, ne.'

'Okay, something more basic then, an object. What if we got one of the spanners from Engineering, put it in the airlock and dropped it on the base below?'

'That is a ridiculous idea.'

'Not to hurt anyone, just to get their attention…'

'I think we need to focus on more practical solutions. Chu?'

'Ne vem. The station?'

'Dock with it?'

'If it's possible, we could get the elevator working and go down there…'

'Ja, it's possible.'

'Assuming the computer lets us dock.'

'That is the difficulty.'

'Wait, we're going down there?' Aleša leaned forward, her right hand dropping down to her waist.

'It seems to be the most achievable target.'

'Physically going down there? To where eighty-six people have just been murdered?'

'Eighty-four.'

'That's insane.'

'She's right,' said Sila, taking another raisin. 'We don't even have weapons.'

'There could be multiple murderers down there, it could be a spree, a gang…'

'That is unlikely.'

'You don't know that.'

'The fixed pattern of deaths suggest something ritualistic, more like a cult. In which case, voluntary suicide is the more probable cause.'

'You just said it was murder.'

'That was on the computer's list, as was group suicide.'

'So it's not murder now?'

Nakagami coughed, but was cut off by Sila before he could turn it into a full response. 'Whatever it is, I don't think it's a good idea to be walking into the middle of it.'

'We would take precautions, of course.'

Aleša's hand traced the line of her scar. 'What, a spanner?'

'Portable scanners, some scissors, ja, spanners are an option too.'

'Scissors and spanners…'

'They're right, Kenji,' said Chu, taking another raisin then pushing the bowl closer to Aleša. 'It's not a good idea to go down there.'

'I see.'

'Not physically. If we could get onto the station, and send the elevator down. Or send some kind of message…'

'Throw a lifebelt into the water…'

'Ja, see if there's anyone who can grab it.'

'And if the murderer grabs it?' asked Aleša, tone caustic.

Chu put a raisin in her mouth and looked at Nakagami. He stared at the raisin bowl and said nothing.

'Wait, what about Chu's teleporter?' asked Gašper. 'Can we beam them up here?'

'Ne,' said Chu, almost spitting out the raisin.

'It doesn't work?'

'Of course not. There is nothing material *to* work.'

'I thought you said it did?'

'Obviously not.'

Sila turned side on to Gašper, blocking out the others. 'You know it doesn't work. I told you.'

'When?'

'Ages ago.'

'Then why did we give our patterns to her?'

'This is not helping,' said Chu, shifting in her seat to look at Nakagami. 'We should focus on the computer, getting it to dock with the station.'

'Agreed,' said Nakagami.

'Long as we're not going down there,' said Aleša, giving up on the raisins and opening her *Bakunin* book.

'Sila? Gašper?'

'Ja, station, okay. We'll help if you need us.'

'That is not necessary. Just don't go near the airlocks. Or the computer.'

'No problem.'

~~~

As predicted by Nakagami, the next forty-eight hours went badly.

One hundred and eight life signs vanished from the scan reports, like extras in one of those *Wild Mars*[46] VR series.

Luckily the crew only had a vague intellectual concept of the life signs as actual people, so there was no trauma.

There was, however, concern.

Concern that the last loon standing would notice them and come knocking.

Or the last two.

Or something worse, more hollow: with all the people on the planet dead and done, there'd be no more reason to stick around.

And then it'd be the infinite lane to Luyten-666 again.

---

[46] Popular adventurist propaganda where hundreds of players would try to survive the frenzy of revived Martians rising up out of the ground. The last five left standing would be given VR land and a replicator and a chance to hang out next to each other.
~~~

~~~

The scan taken after forty-nine hours was inveterately bleak, but did possess something slightly unexpected.

Two life signs left, one on the surface, the other in the space elevator, already halfway up to the station.

'They escaped?' asked Sila, his face about a millimetre from the back of Nakagami's head.

'Ne vem.'

'Or it's the murderer?'

'Ne vem.'

'Fuck.'

'Ja.'

~~~

Chu hit the massage stick against all parts of her head, staring at the confinement beam controls, repeating *think* over and over and sometimes *idiot* for variety.

Sila was standing way back against the wall, observing her.

'It won't work,' she said, hitting the stick against the desk. 'It can't work. The scanner can't go that far. Even here, it'd take days. And it wouldn't get all of it. How do I even get a lock if it's not real time? And put the scan results into what? A half-assed robot body the computer hasn't ever authorised the building of? It's too much. Even the initial scan. What the hell am I doing here?'

'Kenji thought it might help to-…'

'That wasn't an open question.'

'Sorry, it seemed like you'd finished.'

'You're giving me pressure, Sila…'

'Okay. I'll stand over here, quietly.'

'Can you just go?'

Sila backed up against the wall, turned and looked at the fire-amber hair of the *Sabbath Witch*. 'You sure?'

'Prosim, I need to concentrate. Even your breathing is…'

'Understood.'

~~~

Nakagami pressed the same button five times until the visual was clearer, then typed *hvala* to the computer.

'It's live?' asked Sila, taking the edge of the Jame stool and looking up at the freshly improvised screen covering the cockpit window.

'Twenty second delay.'

'And this is an accurate layout?'

'On the most basic level, ja. Though the function of each room, and the station itself, remains unclear.'

Gašper squinted at the screen. 'Which ones are the people?'

'The two flashing dots.'

'Ah, I thought they were part of the station. Sorry, tired brain, didn't sleep much last night. What are they doing?'

'This one here seems to be stationary, on the second level from the top. And the other one has just left the space elevator.'

'Shit, he's chasing them.'

'We do not know the sex of the life sign. Either of them.'

'Okay. Someone is chasing someone. Not good.'

Nakagami looked past Gašper, at Sila scratching his neck. 'How is Chu doing?'

'Messy.'

'I see.'

'She said the only way it would work is if the life sign came over to the ship, let her scan them over several hours, returned to the station to get murdered and then pray that the ship had enough matter on hand to compile a robotic dummy, which would probably have a half-life of around twenty-one seconds.'

Nakagami stared blankly at the makeshift screen. 'It was a long shot.'

'And my idea if you remember,' added Gašper.

'That was two days ago, when it wouldn't have worked.'
~~~

'If you wanna deny me any credit, sure. Two days ago it was a bad idea. Now, it makes sense.'

'Gašper…'

'Look,' said Nakagami.

'Where? You're not pointing at anything.'

'The stationary life sign, it's gone.'

'Shit, he's right…'

'Where'd it go?'

'Murdered?'

'The other life sign is in a different location. Too remote. It couldn't have done anything.'

'Suicide?'

Nakagami examined the top left corner of the screen, the space where the life sign had been twenty seconds earlier.

'What do we do?' asked Gašper.

There was a beeping noise, followed by static, then a voice.

'Attention crew,

There is a new life sign on board the ship, currently located in the TELEPORT ROOM. It is not yet known if this life form is friendly or hostile, so proceed with caution. However, also be aware that, despite being dissidents, you are still in some form representatives of Slovenia, therefore, prosim, use violence sparingly.

Have a safe and bold trip to Luyten 726-8

Hvala.'

'King fucking Matjaž, she did it,' cried Gašper. 'Actually fucking did it.'

'Kenji?' Sila asked, looking down at Nakagami.

'Ne vem…'

'Fuck *ne vem*, she teleported someone. They're on our ship, right now. Gašper, quick, we need to get-…'

Sila didn't bother finishing as he would have been saying it to Gašper's fleeing back.

'Kenji…'

'I'm right behind you.'

~~~

Sila caught up to Gašper by the bottom of the stairs and, as they rushed in tandem towards the TELEPORT ROOM, they saw Aleša coming the other way from Engineering, a spanner in each hand.

'Don't go in,' she shouted, banging one of the spanners against the corridor wall.

But that was immediately vetoed by a voice from inside the room, Chu's voice, telling them it was okay, there was no danger.

Sila and Gašper slowed to a stop, allowing Aleša to catch up, and all three peered into the TELEPORT ROOM.

Apart from the usual clutter – piles of paper on the floor, a desk with the Ito ship and a coiled up cable on it, Varo prints on the wall, Jung books, the legendary four-page teleport poster – nothing was new. There was a faint smell of petrol, but that was probably from the cable. Chu herself was in front of the table where the VR machine was usually kept, blocking the ersatz beam confinement platform behind it.

'… … … … … … …' said a monotone voice, seemingly coming from within Chu's back.

'What's that?' asked Gašper, twisting himself to get a better view.

Chu stepped to one side, revealing a small dark-haired girl, open mouthed yet surprisingly calm-looking, her small shape perched upright on the platform that was supposed to be nothing more than a replica.

'Chu, is that-…' half-asked Sila, turning side on.

'It wasn't me.'

'What?'

'I turned around and she was there. Instantly.'

'Teleported?'

'Out of nothing. No sound or lights, no transition process. Just…there.'

The little girl stepped off the teleport platform and examined the faces in the room. There was no emotion apparent on her own face, nothing to suggest fear or apprehension. Even the Varo prints on the wall had no effect.

'What's she doing?' asked Gašper, managing an awkward smile.
~~~

'Ne vem,' replied Chu.

After a minute of tilting her head a lot and generally mimicking a poorly-programmed robot, the girl nodded to nothing but the air in front of her then positioned herself straight-backed in front of Sila. '… … … … … Rasputin?'

'What?' asked Sila, slouching a little.

'… … … … … Rasputin? … … …?'

'I don't understand, sorry.'

'… …?'

Both Sila and Gašper raised their hands and took a step back, repeating slowly and precisely in Slovene, Spanish and very broken English that they weren't going to hurt her, she was safe with them.

'… … …? … … … … … … … … …? … … …?'

'Huh?' Gašper turned to Sila. 'What's she saying?'

'Ne vem.'

'I think it might be Russian,' said Chu, looking at Aleša.

'That's Russian?' asked Gašper, looking backwards.

'Quiet.' Aleša placed the spanners on the table and came forward, squinting. '… … … … …?' she asked, in very slow, probably incorrect Russian.

The girl zeroed in on her, eyeballs growing. '… … … …? … … … … … … … … … … … …'

'Too fast.'

'… … … … … … … …'

'You just fast,' she said in Russian, forgetting the word for *too*.

The girl frowned. '… … … … … …? … … … … … … … … … … … …'

'I can't get it.' Aleša looked at the girl's mouth, trying to follow the precise movements of her lips. 'She's blending everything, it's too fast.'

'… … … … … … … … … … … …'

'Fuck. I can't even tell what's a word and what isn't.'

'… … … … … … … …'

'Are we sure it's actually Russian?' asked Gašper.

Sila shrugged.

The girl kept talking and pointing at each of them, speaking a hundred words a second. Her initial robot impersonation seemed like hours ago now.

'Ne, it's definitely Russian,' said Aleša, rubbing the side of her face, possibly a recharging technique. 'She understood my question before. We just need to get her to slow down.'

'Can't you tell her?'

'I've forgotten the word for *slow*.'

'Isn't it *zdaniye*?' offered Gašper, finger raised.

'That's building.'

'Not *slow*?'

'… … … … …? … … … … … …' interrupted the girl, moving into position between Aleša and Gašper.

'You get any of that?' asked Gašper.

'We need the book.'

'Okay.' Sila looked down at the girl, who seemed to be studying Aleša's legs. 'Should we take her upstairs or…'

'I'll take her.' Aleša held out her hand, palm flat. '… … …'

'What did you say?'

'Come with me. I think.'

The little girl formed a dagger shape with her own hand, guided it forward like a torpedo then entangled it within Aleša's.

'It worked…'

'Ja.'

At the entrance of the room, Nakagami stood with his arms behind him, rubbing the tips of his fingers against the edge of his nails.

Chu spotted him and walked over, asking if the computer would be able to translate.

'Unlikely.'

'Does it know Russian?'

'As it was programmed by a man who didn't like Russians, I assume not.'

'It's okay,' said Gašper, overhearing. 'You can leave it to us.'

'Your Russian seems quite basic. Aleša's too.'

'Ja, cos we never use it. Now we have a chance'

'Perhaps Chu can try?'

'Me? I don't know any Russian.'

'Ja, but you may be able to pick it up faster.'

'Wah, are you serious?'

'It is not an insult. Her brain is more focused than yours, from experience.'

Gašper held up four fingers, double-checking before he bit back. 'I speak four languages…five if you count Slovene.'

'None of them Russian, I assume.'

'… … … … … … … …?' asked the girl, looking round Nakagami's back.

'There are some words that are mutually intelligible,' said Aleša, leading the girl back to her other side. 'We'll start there. The rest we can learn as we go.'

'It will undoubtedly be a struggle. Spoken fast, I suspect Russian isn't similar to Slovene at all. However, as Chu has vetoed herself as a substitute…'

'Kenji, relax. We're gonna take care of her.'

'Both of us,' added Gašper.

'Ja, it appears so.'

'… … … … …?' asked the girl, staring at Nakagami's hand on his jacket zip.

'She agrees,' said Aleša, having her arm yanked.

'Really? By the tone it sounded more like a question.'

'Ja, she was asking why we're still here talking to you.'

'… … … … …?'

'Come on, Gašper. Let's show her the other rooms.'

'Ja, OPTIMISM ROOM first.'

'And try to switch to Russian from now on.'

'Da. Switching.'

'… … … … … … …'

'What?'

'Russian.'

'Da, but I don't know what you said.'

Aleša got another pull on the arm and let the little girl guide her out of the TELEPORT ROOM, followed by her new co-teacher, Gašper, who was muttering basic questions words to himself in Russian.

Sila and Chu stayed behind, planting themselves down on the Angolan chair, the former allowing himself to be pushed out to the edge. There was apparently nothing immediate to say as they spent the next minute staring at the VR machine on the nearby table.

'This is insane,' said Sila, finally re-focusing.

'Ja…' muttered Chu.

'You should probably go back to the computer, find out what's happening.'

'Huh?'

'Not you. Kenji.'

'That will not be necessary,' answered Nakagami, his eyes taken by *Allegory Of Winter* on the wall.

'What do you mean?'

'These paintings. The colour.' He shifted to the tiny, blue face of the *Sabbath Witch*, still fiddling with his jacket zip. 'I must admit, it is impressive how comfortable you have made this place. I attempted to do a similar thing in the GOD room, with the posters…'

'Kenji. The computer.'

He pivoted and moved over to the Angolan chair, resting his hand on the top cushion. 'It is as I said. There is nothing happening currently, and the computer cannot explain what happened previously. It doesn't know how or why this girl was teleported over to our ship. Therefore, there is nothing to check at this moment.

'The other life sign?'

'Gone.'

'Teleported?'

'There has been no announcement of any new life signs, so I assume not.'

'Dead then.'

'Most likely.'

Chu got up and hurried to the door, checking the corridor, then came back to Kenji's shoulder. 'You're saying she's the only survivor?'

'Ja.'

'A girl capable of teleportation,' said Sila, trying and failing to whistle.

'Perhaps. If you believe in fairies.'

'Huh?'

Chu focused on Nakagami. 'We need to get over to that station, find out how they teleported her.'

'I'm working on it.'

'How long?'

Nakagami shrugged. 'Until the computer considers it not rude.'

'Not good enough. Speed it up.'

'Impossible.'

'Try.'

~~~

Over the next few hours, Aleša and Gašper dived ID first into Russian conversation, learning very quickly how hard it truly was to talk to someone in a language you barely knew - ne, worse than that - a language you'd never even heard spoken by a native speaker before.

The first thing they tried was the book.

It was partially successful. They could ask simple questions, and the girl understood what they were saying, especially the words with Russian counterparts, but her answers were impossible.

And the book chapters didn't help.

Chapter 8: Factory life.

Chapter 11: Asking for directions in Veliky Novgorod.

Chapter 18: Communicating with the Elderly.

Chapter 22: Insulting the enemy.

'What if we just work from the dictionary at the back?' asked Gašper, lifting up the book cover.

'It's limited.'

'Better than useless.'

'Not by much.'

The girl leaned across the table, pointing at one of the pictures in the book. '… … … … … … … … … …?'
~~~

'Catch anything?'

'I think I heard *man*,' replied Aleša, examining the picture for clues.

'We should ask her to speak slowly again.'

'No point.'

'Maybe edit it to *a lot more slowly* this time.'

'She can't, it doesn't work.'

'Or shout it at her, like a command.'

'Listening takes time. And we don't really need to understand her yet, we just need her to understand us.'

'We could write things down.'

'Ja, that might work.' Aleša grabbed a pen and some of her old notes tucked into the back of the Russian book. 'First thing we need to communicate is the ship rules. Curfew time, food, toilet locations.'

'I forgot about that.'

'Don't want her wandering around after ten and getting zapped.'

'Good point. We'll have to find her quarters.'

'Ja, that was on my list too.'

'But…all of the spare ones belong to someone who's dead.'

'… … … … … … …' said the girl, sliding the book away from Gašper and flicking through the pages.

'We can narrow it down. Jame's, Dodzi's, both out for obvious reasons. Cvetko's quarters are too creepy. Ours are forbidden. That leaves either Klemen's or Petr's.'

'Easy. Petr's room.'

'Because?'

'More personality. And he was a warmer person too.'

Aleša flinched, gripping the pencil tighter. 'You didn't know Klemen very well.'

'Ne, not really, but he was a bit-…'

'To be blunt, you didn't know Petr either.'

'Err…what?'

'Not like I did.'

'He was my boyfriend. We shared a-…'

'For two years, barely. And that was the ship version of him, not the real him. I knew Petr back home, for over a decade, with all the shit going on through that. It's like me saying I know Sila better than you, it's ridiculous.'

'What about Chu? Do you know her better than me?'

'That's different.'

'Ja, to someone who can't admit she's wrong.'

'Chu was never that close to you, not like me and Petr. She never visited you in rehab. Didn't live with you. Doesn't really talk about you much now, when we're together. Which, honestly, makes sense. The two of you just don't have anything in common. It's true. If Sila weren't here…'

Gašper looked right, at the food dispenser. *You metal fuck. Shit food. Don't know anything. Abandoned him. Called him a hologram. Fucking wall whore. Udon-producing arrogant fuck.*

Then turned back and slid over next to the girl and the textbook.

'… … … … …' she said, pointing at the page number.

'Da.'

'… … … … …'

He flicked ahead to the next chapter, and the next, and then to somewhere near the end, all the while mumbling random Russian vocab to himself.

Aleša watched him, running through all the reasons she didn't have to say sorry in her head, then forced the fakest of smiles as she noticed the girl looking at her.

She shifted round, making herself the third point of their triangle.

'Okay, maybe the Chu thing was a bit off. She doesn't really talk about anything except the teleporter and those weird psychology books. But I did know Petr. He was my friend.'

'That's an apology?' asked Gašper, keeping his eyes stuck on the page below.

'Half of one.'

'… … … … … … …'

'And the rest of it?'

'Ne vem. When we arrive at Luyten 123.'

He glanced right and saw the little girl pointing at another picture in the book. It was a farmer, holding a rake.

'I suggest we use Klemen's quarters,' continued Aleša, softening her tone a little. 'It's closer to mine, and not so far from yours.'

Gašper kept his eyes on the tips of the rake.

'Agreed?'

'Fine. But only cos it's close.'

~~~

Phase transition coils. Molecular Imaging Scanner. Pattern storage. Atom storage. Energy-Mass conversion chamber.

Sila didn't know what any of them were, but that didn't matter as the TELEPORT ROOM only had one of them. The rest were boxes with labels, a joke, Chu said, from Potočnik. Or what she'd thought was a joke until a real live human girl materialised right in front of her.

He ran the portable scanner over each object in the room, pressing *start scan* and *confirm* just like Chu had told him to.

Each scan took seven minutes, and each set of results said the same thing.

'No recent activity.'

Chu would probably question his performance, ask him if he'd pressed the correct buttons, pointed it at the right place, and why not? She knew his science was second tier.

But then again, maybe not. She'd asked him to do it in the first place, which was odd. Usually, she'd make him stand at the back of the room and not let him even look at anything. She'd done that a few hours ago. Yet now she was handing him the only scanner the AI had ever authorised the drones to construct and putting him next to equipment with words like *atom* on it.

The scanner beeped and said, 'look.'

He obeyed.

'No recent activity.'

Okay, that's the last one, he thought, glancing down at the words on the little screen.

The last one…
~~~

He changed target to the beam confinement platform, the space where the girl had appeared, and scanned it for the third time.

The last living person.

Out of almost two hundred.

On a base of corpses. Below a station of one corpse. Elevator, unknown.

They'd come, they'd seen nothing, they'd probably leave again. Out into the void. The occasional rock in the Oort Cloud. If they made it that far. They probably wouldn't. Edge of the system was optimistic. And now they had a little girl to worry about. To die with. Or bring death to them. She could've murdered everyone down there. She may not be a child. Could be a ghost. Feigning Russian until night then killing them in their quarters. Drifting in and-

The scanner made another beeping noise, followed by *confirm*.

He blinked, looking at the screen.

'Confirm,' it repeated, not a question.

He pressed the button.

~~~

'No recent activity.'

'For all of them?'

'Ja.'

Chu didn't look up, she was too busy telling Nakagami to type faster.

'You wanna see?'

'No need.'

Sila walked farther into the TALK TO YOUR GOD ROOM and leaned on the left-side console. His shoulder brushed against one of Nakagami's posters, scrunching the edge of the paper upwards a bit, but no one seemed to notice.

'It won't work,' said Nakagami, finishing a long chain of symbols.

'Just type it in.'

'The tone is too glib, it won't-…'

'Kenji.'

'Very well.'
~~~

Nakagami started a new line, typed in the question then went straight to his jacket zip.

The computer replied.

'I told you.'

'How is it rude to tidy up a station?' asked Chu, incredulous.

Sila put the scanner on Chu's lap, who moved it quickly to the central console. 'What did you ask exactly?'

'We offered to clean the station, including the probable corpse, free of charge,' said Nakagami, glancing at the scanner.

'And the computer said *ne*?'

'Not the computer exactly; more like the computer's concept of etiquette and manners.'

'Which is completely disingenuous,' added Chu.

'Agreed, but it's what we must work with.'

Sila looked at the screen, then up at the hockey stick poster. 'Have you tried offering the girl back?'

'Back to what?'

'To whatever sent her over here.'

Chu exchanged glances with Nakagami, who tapped the edge of the console four times then typed out a line.

'Are you asking my question?'

'Ja.'

The computer buzzed then trailed out a reply.

'I think this computer has been influenced by Gašper.'

'What did it say?'

'It said human trafficking is rude.'

Sila laughed, then buried it quickly in a cough. 'What else have you tried?'

'Hey scientists. Sila.' Gašper came in through the field of pale green light, turning back and pointing out the bulb to the little girl, who was tightly holding his hand. She looked at it and said something nine seconds long in Russian.

'You know what she's saying yet?'

'I think I heard the word *green*. But most of it, ne. We're still working our way through the book.'

Gašper combed his hair with his spare hand, which supplemented the attempt he'd [clearly] already made to brush it earlier, and jiggled the girl's hand.

'… … … … …?' she asked, looking forward.

'Ja. Good idea.'

'What did she say?'

'Ne vem.'

Gašper led the girl deeper in and gestured towards the consoles, saying what he hoped was the word *light* in Russian as he pointed out the LEDs next to the scanning buttons.

'Where's Aleša?'

'Toilet. Actually, I think she just wanted a break. It's pretty tiring trying to pick out Russian words. But we have found out her name. Katya.'

Chu took her hands off the back of Nakagami's chair and walked closer to Gašper. 'Do you think you could ask her about how she got over here?'

'Ja, we did that already.'

Chu's eyes lit up…

'She said Rasputin did it.'

…and powered down. 'What?'

'Rasputin. A man called Rasputin.'

'The Rasputin?'

'Can't be, he's dead,' said Sila.

'Ja, the monk guy, but it's not him. That would be too weird. Besides, he has to be dead cos they put his dick in a museum. I saw a picture of it.'

'Did she say who this Rasputin was?'

'Not much, just that he lives on the station. And she didn't say it, she wrote it down.'

'He's on the station?'

'That's why we could understand it, more time to absorb, even though it was Cyrillic text. Ja, *he lives on the station*, those exact words.'

Chu turned and pulled a *start scan* face at Nakagami.

'There are no life signs on the station.'

'Check again.'

'Ja, basically,' continued Gašper, 'writing's all we've got at the moment. Can't understand much of what she says. If she slowed down, maybe, but not the way it comes out now. It's like listening to a drunk, all these cut-off sounds and slurred garbling.'

'Gašper, ask her again about Rasputin.'

'Again?'

'Ask her where he is now. How did he teleport her over? Did he use a machine?'

'Err…I think I can manage *he*…'

'Do it.'

'… … … … … … … …? … … … … … …' said Katya, nudging Sila in the waist and pointing at the walls.

'Sorry?' asked Sila, following her gaze and quickly realising what the problem was. 'Shit. Gašper…'

'Wait, let me think.'

'The girl…'

'What…Katya?'

Ignoring her own name, Katya walked to the nearest poster and pulled it off the wall.

'Oh fuck…' muttered Gašper.

She held it out and pointed at the telegraph pole in the poster girl's hand. '… … … …?'

'Gašper, get her out of here.'

'Ja…'

Nakagami opened his mouth…and quickly turned it into a yawn.

'Faster, go.'

Gašper held out his hand to Katya, who glared at the picture again and took a step back.

'Ne, ne…that's not me. It's not my work.' He pointed at Nakagami. 'It's his, he did it.'

Katya switched to Nakagami, scrunching the poster up into a ball.

'Prosim, stop. That is based on a famous classical-…'

'Kenji, don't,' said Chu, cutting him off.

Katya spat on the poster ball and threw it on the floor. '… … … … … … … … Rasputin … … … … … … …'

She grabbed Gašper's hand and yanked him towards the door, the two of them crossing back through the green light and out into the coiled snake corridor.

'She mentioned Rasputin again,' said Nakagami, when the coast was clear.

Sila bent down and picked up the poster ball, opening it up a fraction then stopping. He looked up and around at the other posters, then over at Chu.

Her brain may have had half a hemisphere on the station already, but she knew what he knew and nodded to show it.

'Perhaps it's the name for the station computer?'

'Kenji,' said Sila, standing up.

'Ja?'

'I think it's time to take these posters down.'

'That is not necessary.'

'Ja, it is.'

'The girl had an emotional reaction to the subject matter, perhaps a valid one. However, these are not simply posters, they are recreations of classical art.'

'Put them in your room if you have to. And do it fast. Before Aleša remembers about this stuff.'

Chu put a hand on Nakagami's shoulder, gently, stopping his *it's my sister* defence from marching out.

'Very well,' he said, voice lowered almost to a hush. 'For the sake of social harmony.'

The computer made a buzzing noise. Nakagami took a moment to register the sound, then woke up undramatically and looked at the screen.

'We're moving.'

'Who?'

'The ship. It's changing its orbital-…'

There was another buzzing noise, followed by the tannoy.

'Attention crew,

The orbiting structure has kindly cleared us for docking. If you wish to participate in the forthcoming tour, prosim, proceed to Airlock 2 on the Upper Deck and wait for instructions.

Have a safe and bold trip to the orbiting structure.

Hvala.'

~~~

Gašper opened the door to Klemen's quarters and told Katya to wait outside while he and Aleša checked things out.

In his version of Russian, it translated to *wait, we look* while in Aleša's slightly more advanced copy, it came out as *wait here, we look room.*

Katya studied them as if they were simpletons, but stayed where she was.

'You sure it's cleared by the computer?' asked Aleša, letting Gašper shuffle inside first.

'Sila said so.'

'What about Nakagami?'

'Ja. I guess.'

'You guess?'

'It's cleared, don't worry about it.'

'If she gets hurt…'

'Nakagami told Sila, Sila told me. It's fine.'

Aleša mumbled something in broken Russian and continued into the room.

Apart from a few pieces of paper on the desk, the remains of Klemen's notorious simulation theory, there wasn't much there.

If it had been a normal house on Earth, there would've been dust, but on this ship, the only loose particles came from the vents, and they were cleaned daily by the maintenance drones. At least that's what Nakagami had told them.

The only other source of trash would be dead cells from the crew themselves, and that wasn't a problem in this room.

No Klemen, no dead cells.
~~~

Gašper walked over to the bed, catching sight of something poking out underneath. He bent down and decided whether or not he wanted to touch it. Could be a photo, could be more notes, could be the remnants of a two-year-old wank tissue.

'What are you doing?' asked Aleša, patting the blanket.

'There's something under the bed.'

'Where?'

She bent down next to him and saw what he was looking at. Without hesitation, she grabbed hold of the visible part and pulled it out. The gap between the floor and the bed was almost non-existent so it tore a bit, but only at the edge.

'Wah…is that you?' asked Gašper, looking at the photo in Aleša's hand.

She didn't answer, just stared at it.

Gašper didn't have much else to do in the room, so he stared with her. He was right, it was her, a younger version with an unfamiliar headscarf on, but definitely her. She was wearing a *Bakunin was right* t-shirt and had a giant, inflatable syringe clutched in her hands. Bakunin again? Was he the only anarchist she knew? And why did the background look like a serial killer's basement?

'Five years ago,' she said, tracing the outline of her headscarf and smiling. 'Not counting ship time.'

'You look quite pretty.'

'Ja, cos it was dark.'

'Ne, it's the headscarf. They generally look good on you.' He paused, looking at her current hair. 'This style looks good too.'

Aleša ignored him and flipped over the photo, revealing a message written in green ink.

'Aleša the Brave,' Gašper read out loud. 'Did Klemen write this?'

There was no response. The photo had her again. Gašper got back on his feet and walked round to the other side of the bed, waiting for the spell to wear off. Then he'd probably have to tell her what had happened in the TALK TO YOUR GOD ROOM. Katya's trashing of the poster.

'I need to go,' Aleša said quietly, getting up.

'Go?'

She walked to the door, wiped her face with her sleeve then carried on out into the corridor, repeating, 'I need to go,' in Russian to Katya.

Half a minute later, the little Russian came in.

There were no words.

She just scrutinised the Potočnik picture then moved straight to the bed and sat down with her back almost ruler straight against the wall.

'Okay, this is your room.' Gašper took the paper with the ship rules on it and put it down on the end of the bed. 'Omit,' he said in Russian, confusing it with the word for *remember*.

'… … … … … …?'

'I will go now. Do not open the door. If someone knocks at night, do not open. Understand?'

He managed some of the words in Russian, and she seemed to understand, but how could he be sure?

Did he need to be?

The curfew time applied to Nakagami too, and he was busy at the moment with the station situation. Even if he did have active intentions, vengeful or perverted, he wouldn't have time to implement them.

'… … … … … …?'

'Stay?'

'… …'

'Ne, I can't. This is your room. No guests after…' He tried to think of ten in Russian, but it was elusive. '…late.'

Katya stared back at him, glaring almost, as if she were trying to burn through his face.

'I will come tomorrow morning. Early.'

'… … … … Aleša?'

'Ja, Aleša too.'

'… … …'

'Good night.'

Gašper stepped backwards into the corridor, letting the door close in front of him. He heard some steps…then nothing, which he assumed meant she'd either gone into the bathroom or back to the bed.

He turned and walked away, thinking two things: one, how to communicate better with Katya so they could have an actual conversation.

And two; what to do about Nakagami.

~~~

'The best way, far as I can figure, is we get the computer to tag him,' said Gašper, leaning forward with both elbows on the table.

'Who, Kenji?'

'Tag him electronically. He doesn't have to wear anything, a collar or anything, just…ne vem…some kind of tag. The computer can keep track of him until he-…until Katya is safe.' Gašper looked at his hand for some reason. 'Fuck it, we can just keep it on him indefinitely.'

Sila closed his eyes and counted squirrels. Then stopped and put his hand flat on the *Alien TV* book.

'I know that face,' said Gašper. 'You think we can't do it, but we can. It's easy.'

'Gašper…'

'The computer likes me, I can tell it to do the tagging discreetly. No way he'll even know about it.'

'Stop.'

'If we don't, he might do something. He said it himself, about Dodzi; it's in the core psychology and it'll come out eventually.'

'Are you stopping?'

'I'm not saying he's dangerous full stop, just-…we need a precaution. Tag him so he can't go near her. Honestly, it's for his own good as well as hers. And ethically-…'

'Gašper, if you don't stop I'm going to hit you with this book. The corner edge.'

Gašper stopped.

'Good. It's nearly curfew and I really need some sleep. And a shower. I don't have time for this nonsense.' Sila raised a finger. 'Don't.'

Gašper closed his mouth.

'I appreciate that you're worried, but nothing is going to happen to the girl. He's already put the posters in his room, you and Aleša are with
~~~

her during the day. There's no chance for him to do anything. He won't do anything. And *we're* not going to do anything.'

Gašper picked up a nearby book and pretended to read the back. 'I could do it on my own…'

'Gašper…'

'…if it looked like he *was* going to do something.'

'Stop thinking about this. Prosim.'

'Not that he would, but-…'

There was a beeping noise from the ship tannoy system, followed by the usual warning.

'Attention crew,

Curfew will begin in nine minutes. Prosim, return to your quarters immediately. This will be the only warning.

Have a safe and bold trip to the orbiting structure.

Hvala.'

Sila stood up. 'That's our signal.'

Gašper muttered something to his hand.

'I'll see you tomorrow.'

'Ja.'

~~~

Sila sat on the bed with his legs crossed, pen and paper in front of him.

It had been a few months since he'd written out any history, mostly because he'd run out of events to write about, but now he'd thought of something. Didn't matter that it was 4:30 in the morning. Anything was better than dwelling on the idea of Gašper maiming Nakagami in the THERAPY ROOM. Or something maiming him on the station. Or nothing happening at all.

He spun the pen round with two fingers, slowly, focused his thoughts on third tier history that he knew very little about and started to write.

The Long March of Chairman Mao before he became Chairman.
~~~

In 1934, Mao left a city near Shanghai because the guy…Shiang? Jiang? The one who fled to Taiwan after the Second World War…that guy was after him.

Mao took his followers and marched across Middle China.

Along the way his wife had a child, and he was forced to leave them both in one of the villages as a long march was no place for a family.

He started fucking someone younger.

In 1935, he reached Wuhan.

Something happened in Wuhan, but I can't remember what it was.

Then they marched north to a city beginning with X. Xan? Xain?

…

…

He stopped writing and stared at the wall, the space next to Potočnik.

Where did the march end? When?

The Japanese invaded in 1938 and the war started a year later, so what was Mao doing from 1935 until 1938?

Three whole years.

Sila chewed the end of the pen and lost himself in the only piece of green still visible on the wall.

If he was marching towards Beijing then…

But Beijing was where the other guy was…

Wasn't it?

So…

He looked at the paper and wrote an extra line.

'Mao relaxed for three years, waiting for his chance.'

That'll do, Sila thought, throwing the pen up in the air and catching it. It's not like anyone's checking.

~~~

The ship docked with the orbiting structure at 10:32 the next morning.

Heeding Sila's warning that something might charge through the airlock as soon as the connection was complete, they watched the process from the CREATE NOT DESTROY ROOM. It wasn't a perfect view, but they could make out the docking side of the station.
~~~

From one angle it looked like an ancient Egyptian crown with several rings wrapped around the middle.

From another, it resembled a cello with the strings flying out at the top.

When they got closer, they saw it actually looked quite normal, a cylinder-shaped base with an open lid that divided into a claw halfway up. The parts they'd thought were rings were part of the cylinder, possibly to simulate gravity in emergencies [the computer said they used a variation of the LEM-12 Field station-wide], and the parts they thought were loose cello strings were…actually, it was hard to tell. The ship was docking at the base so the uppermost limbs of the structure were too distant and, because of the tight angle, mostly hidden.

'I suspect the basic functions are equivalent to an Earth Station,' said Nakagami, staring out the middle window. 'Even if the design is a little odd.'

'Is it human-made?' asked Sila, next to him.

'The original construction? That is more difficult to say.'

'Doubt it is,' said Chu, fingertips tapping almost without sound against the window.

'Why do you say that?'

'Gut feeling.'

'That is not a very scientific answer.'

Aleša tried lifting Katya up to the left-side window to have a look, but the little Russian resisted, pulling on Aleša's purple headscarf as a deterrent.

'You think Katya's an alien's pet?' she asked.

'Alien might be a little too theoretical at this point. The base below is populated by humans, so I suggest we extrapolate primarily from that.'

'*Was* populated by humans,' said Sila.

Aleša gave up on lifting Katya and settled for holding her hand instead. 'Well, if you do meet anyone over there, tell them it's very irresponsible to leave little girls alone with strangers.'

'They saved her from being murdered,' said Chu, the tone a bit harsher than her usual standard.

'Ja, that too.'

~~~

After the computer confirmed for the third time that there were no life signs on the structure, they opened the airlock.

The fact that Katya had wandered about the place without suffocating meant there was no need to suit up, but there was also a chance that she wasn't fully human, so any facts they had may have been based on poor assumptions.

Didn't really matter in the end, as the ship had no suits. Because the ship was supposed to contain them indefinitely.

Which, now Sila thought about it, was another nail in the *let's colonise Luyten 726-8* coffin.

Unless the planets there had Earth-like atmospheres and no novel diseases?

'Are you coming?' asked Nakagami, already next to the structure-side airlock.

'You sure we don't need weapons?'

'There is nothing on the station to hit.'

'But…are we really sure about that?'

'Stop dragging your feet,' said Chu, looking for buttons to press to open the airlock. 'We'll only be on there an hour, two at most.'

'One is better.'

'Just need to find the teleporter, any other tech they have, see how it works then come back. Take some of it with us if possible.'

'I should also remind you both that there will likely be a corpse.'

'Assuming there are no clear-up drones,' added Chu.

'If you feel nauseous, look for a container. Do not vomit onto the floor.'

'Don't think anyone will mind.'

'The computer might.'

'What, our one?'
~~~

Before Nakagami could answer, the airlock made an electronic *doop* sound and started to slide apart into four pieces, each one a slightly different size.

'That's creative,' said Chu, peeking her head round the hatch.

'And needlessly complex. Designed by an eccentric perhaps.'

'Or a lunatic.'

The four sections stopped without being retracted completely into the side pockets.

'Is it finished?'

'Ja, but we must wait for the computer to run a scan on the air.'

As if hearing its name, the tannoy beeped.

'Attention Airlock crew,

The sampled particles from the structure are identical to those present in Earth air and are therefore safe to breathe.

You may now proceed inside.

Hvala.'

'It's definitely safe?' asked Sila, glued to the wall by the *NO LINGERING* sign inside the airlock, one hand on his neck.

'Ja.'

'The whole station?'

'As safe as our own ship.' Chu stepped over one of the lower door segments, looking back when she was inside. 'Sila, your legs. Move them.'

'I don't feel so good.'

'It'll stop when you start walking.'

'My chest…'

'Put your hand against your throat, release your breath slowly.'

He did as she said, keeping his other hand against the wall to steady himself, but his brain was too far gone to regulate.

'It's not working.'

Nakagami stepped back into the airlock, gripped Sila by the temples and started to push the tips of his thumbs inwards.

'My head,' groaned Sila, trying and failing to swat away Nakagami's arms.

'Focus on a part of my face. Any part. Understand what is happening to you.'

'Can't focus…'

'Don't speak. Especially *can't* statements.'

'Kenji…'

'Quiet. Prosim. Let me explain what you're feeling then you will understand.'

Sila looked at Chu, putting his hand back on his throat.

'Your brain is warning you that you're about to step off a cliff. This side is safety, the station is death. The ship has been your home for over three years. It has been restful and compact and you know it well. The station is the other. Focus on my face, any part. Focus. It is a trick. Do not be afraid. Dread is a self-generated concept, it will dissipate, when you understand the condition behind its power over you. It is a malleable thing, easy to disintegrate. Focus on my face. It has no power now. Ja, that's it. You are beginning to understand. Your brain is becoming more rational. You know the ship is a place and the station is a place. It is natural for us to go over there. It is the most natural thing a human can do. As is breathing. Put your hand on your chest. Feel the air flowing in and out. You are breathing fine. We are ready to step onto the station. It is a normal thing. Breathe.'

Nakagami released his grip and asked Sila if he was ready to go onto the station.

Sila looked at his hand still on his chest, lowering it with a puzzled expression on his face.

'Are you ready?' repeated Nakagami.

'Ne vem.'

'Good enough.'

'Still feel a bit light-headed.'

'Let's go.'

As Nakagami crossed through the airlock, Chu leaned in and whispered, 'where did that come from?'

'My own analysis.'

'Strange. Sounded a bit like Ekuban.'

'A coincidence.'

'Ja. Must be.'

'Whispering isn't helping,' interrupted Sila, hand gripping a quarter piece of the airlock door.

'Sorry.'

'Can we just get in and get this done?'

'Moving.'

~~~

The first thing they saw as they stepped down out of the airlock chamber was a brightly-lit stream of gas flowing out from the wall. If there was a bulb of some sort containing it, it must've made of invisible glass, yet there had be something as the luminous gas was limited to two curved jets, both of which stopped after half a metre.

'Creative lighting,' said Sila, half examining it, half trying to keep his breathing steady.

'Doesn't appear to dissipate,' commented Nakagami, putting his hand near the top of the gas. 'Must be magnetically contained somehow.'

'And renewable.' Chu's hand joined Nakagami's, pushing an inch closer. 'Assuming this station's been running a while.'

'I suspect so.'

'At least it's not pitch black in here,' said Sila, edging forward next to Chu. 'And it is vaguely human-like. Floor, ceiling, lights, walls.'

Nakagami and Chu glanced at each other, then examined the source of the gas, a small arch-shaped hole in the wall.

'Are we moving?' asked Sila, counting out the number of *gas lamps* farther along the wall. He got to five then tried the other direction. It was the same, five lights then a dark wall. Which probably meant they were in a ring corridor, gradually curving inwards all the way around, just like in Engineering.

'Which way do we go?' he asked, returning to his scientific compasses.

'Kenji?' asked Chu, putting a hand on his shoulder.
~~~

'Based on what I observed of the exterior, it most likely doesn't matter. The whole ring seems to be primarily used for docking.' Nakagami walked left at a steady pace, stopping about ten metres down. 'It is likely that the main section is just above the main cylinder.' He paused, frowning. 'Apologies for repeating the word *main*.'

'What are you basing that on?'

'Logic.'

'After seeing the outside and a single corridor?'

'Precisely. If one ship docks here, then it is logical to assume that others will dock in the same area. The other rings are probably for cargo or storage. As for the main section, the space elevator ran up past the cylinder, letting the little girl off on a higher level.'

'And you looked at the scan visual,' finished Sila, pulling up a step behind him.

'Ja, that was also a clue.'

'The teleporter must be up there too,' said Chu.

'Theoretically.'

'Let's try to ascend. Keep an eye out for stairs or some kind of lift.'

'Agreed.'

Chu moved off as if it were nothing more than a casual stroll around Lake Bled. Not an ounce of nerves or anxiety. Nakagami followed, glancing at the next gas lamp coming up, while Sila drew up the rear, attempting to read the symbols on each sign they passed.

For some reason, text helped.

The idea of it.

Theory: any alien that went to the trouble of writing out instructions wouldn't be the type to lurk in darkness and pounce on a stranger when his back was turned.

It wasn't ironclad, but it did lower his heartrate by at least ten beats.

~~~

After patrolling a third of the docking ring [and almost having a heart attack when the other docking ports on the left-hand side lit up in bright lilac, without any noise indication whatsoever], they came to a large
~~~

niche in the inside wall. There were three lines, or strips, embedded around waist height, one of them glowing. Chu prodded it several times and nothing happened, so she started improvising, touching it in different ways until a swipe upwards did the trick.

The floor shook a little, followed by some ping sounds.

'What's happening?' asked Sila, caught mentally between hugging the wall and jumping back into the middle of the corridor.

'The wall,' shouted Chu, as the ping sounds stopped and the floor started to ascend.

'What?'

'Touch the wall, it sticks.'

'Where?'

'The wall, Sila.'

'We're moving.'

Before he could fall backwards and completely embarrass himself, Sila managed to shoot out a hand, guessing that either Nakagami or Chu would be sharper than he was. Luckily, he was right. Nakagami grabbed his sleeve and yanked him deeper onto the rising platform, then against the wall, and that's where he stayed, his arms and face stuck like Velcro.

'Loosen,' he said, trying to direct it towards Kenji.

'Stop struggling,' replied Kenji, one side of his body pinned to the wall. 'It appears to be a safety mechanism.'

'My face…'

'Relax, it'll be over soon.'

'Errggh…'

'Probably.'

Sila tried to complain about his face again, but it hurt when he opened his mouth to speak. Not intolerable pain, but enough to make him still. And the more stationary he became, the looser the grip seemed to get.

'Definitely not human,' Chu said, as they went up through a gap in the ceiling before sliding left and spiralling upwards at a steady pace.

The other two lines on the lift wall had become lit at some point, one of them horizontal, the other sloping down.

'One must be the stop command,' said Chu. 'The other…ne vem. Speed perhaps.'

'Agreed.'

'I don't think we need to go any faster,' said Sila, noticing Chu's finger hovering near the horizontal line.

'Coward,' she replied, smirking.

'I almost had my face torn off.'

'Almost.'

Sila breathed out slowly, cautiously, in case his breath flow rate forced the grip of the wall to tighten. 'Pretty sadistic way to operate a lift.'

'I'm sure it makes sense to whoever built it.'

'Ja, sadists.'

'The station is not much larger than standard size,' said Nakagami, ignoring their small talk entirely. 'We should be arriving at the main section soon.'

'If there is one,' mumbled Sila.

'Conceptually, I believe there must be. No matter the culture.'

'Maybe they're survivalists.'

'Any other kind of operation would be both odd and inefficient. Even for survivalists. Besides, our scans revealed a limited number of areas. A disparate or segmented system would require a larger base.'

'Or a completely autonomous AI running things,' added Chu, with the slightest of winks.

'That is a point. Albeit a debatable one.'

'Only to a material naturalist.'

~~~

Nakagami was right.

A minute later, the ride came to a stop as gentle as the journey itself, and deposited them in another ring corridor.

Or that's what they thought. After getting a better sense of dimension, they realized it wasn't a corridor, it was a room, vaguely mushroom-shaped, with two, green-light jets at each corner. From the
~~~

current glow, they could make out quite clearly the red symbols painted on the wall opposite, each stroke part of a larger spiral motif.

'Where are we?' asked Sila, sticking to the lift wall.

'Ne vem.'

'Main section?'

'Ja, perhaps.'

Chu sniffed at the air. 'Smells like mint.'

'Ja, you're right,' said Sila, inhaling three quick shots. 'Mint shisha.'

Nakagami looked up at ceiling directly above. 'It may be a quirk of the ventilation filters.'

'Or an intentional choice.'

'What, a flavour filter?' asked Sila, taking more hits.

There was a ping sound followed by an insistent breeze nudging them off the lift platform.

'The magnetic field just got reversed,' said Chu, struggling to push her hand back against the wall.

'That's what it was, a magnet?'

'Similar effect.'

'I suggest we follow its suggestion before the lift starts moving again,' said Nakagami, stepping off onto the floor.

Sila and Chu copied, both taking in a full panoramic sweep of the room.

Unlike the docking ring, the floor was tiled; grey and white squares of different sizes slotted together, somehow managing to leave no gaps.

'It's like some weird art exhibit,' said Sila, bending down to touch one of the squares.

'With blood trails.'

'What?'

'Over here.'

Sila looked right and saw Nakagami crouching near the green gas light, staring at the floor. He left his own tile and walked over.

'This is strange,' said Nakagami, poking his finger at the liquid on the floor.

'It's blood?'

'The corpse either started here or ended up here, but…'

'Not ended up here, clearly.'

'...our scan indicated the life sign ceased near the elevator.'

'Where's that?'

'As I remember, it opens up into a bigger room somewhere on the third level, with other areas attached to it. I assume we are currently on the first level, or possibly a floor beneath.'

'So...whose blood is this?'

'Ne vem. Most likely the same life sign.'

Sila tilted his head, briefly confused about the use of the term *life sign*, then stared down at the blood stain.

It was definitely red like a human's.

Maybe a bit darker.

And there was a fair amount of it.

'You think some station drones moved the body?'

'Ne vem.'

'Or it was teleported away?'

'Possibly.' Nakagami looked past the green light, into the passage leading down the side, then back into the main mushroom. 'Where is Chu?'

Sila mimicked the same actions, walked over to the green light on the other side and looked back at Nakagami. 'Got an exit here too. No sign of Chu though.'

'She must've rushed ahead to find the teleport machine.'

'Ja, but which way did she go?'

'Ne vem. We'll have to split up. You walk that way, I'll go down here.'

'Now?'

Nakagami waved his hand forward like a go-kart bot and started walking, quickly disappearing into the other passage. Sila muttered, 'no life signs, no life signs,' to the artistic tiled floor then headed to his designated starting point.

As expected, the exit soon connected to a passage, just like the one on Nakagami's side, with a slope running upwards for ten, twenty metres then steepening abruptly and running on for another five. Sila was no master of mathematics or angles, but it felt almost vertical, the first two steps making him go sideways and fumble for the walls. The gas lamps from the docking ring would've helped, but for some reason only two of them were streaming green; the outlines of the others were visible when he got close, looming high as passive phantoms on each side, but with no sign of any switch-like thing to turn them on.

The signs, he told himself.

Life-related and textual.

No aliens here.

And even if there were, aliens with text don't kill.

They don't creep.

They don't attack without talking first.

He looked ahead to the last remaining jet of green light and moved towards it, keeping his breaths long and steady.

At the top of the peak, the passage flattened again, opening up into a long, expansive space. Clearly, the architect had spent more time on this section as it was both well-lit in the centre and artistically designed, almost like a film set. There were several tilted arches on the walls of both sides, possibly doors to other rooms; what looked like a giant, Russian Orthodox Cross planted in the floor in the middle; and the centrepiece; a large cylinder merged with the window at the far end, running directly from floor to ceiling, with what looked like totems made of different-shaped orbs marking the ground around it. There were some other objects too, but smaller and indistinct, almost pathetic next to the stature of the main cylinder. What the hell was it? An engineering toy? A giant ventilation duct?

In some way, it reminded him of the *Death Tube* exhibit he'd seen in Zagreb when he was a teenager, only without the *explanation* plastered on the wall next to it.

And no people gawping at it.

No kids attempting to climb it.

No one looking at it at all.

Except him.

Alone.

On an alien structure.

In the Kuiper Belt.

He coughed lightly, bringing back the anxiety.

Kenji, Chu.

Focus.

He looked over to the opposite side, where he expected Nakagami's passage to emerge, but the angle was too tight to see anything.

Wouldn't he be out by now though?

It had been a while.

At least five minutes.

Ne, not that long. Three or four at most. But it was still long enough.

Stepping cautiously out from his own slope passage, Sila circled towards the Orthodox cross in the middle, keeping his eyes fixed on the opposite side. Apart from two arches carved into the wall that led into shadow, there was nothing. Though, to be fair, it wasn't the best lit part of the room.

Maybe there was a door he couldn't see?

Or maybe the passage didn't come up there? Maybe it twisted round, or curved up to the other side…

Sila turned to match his thoughts, flinching when he saw what was on the cross next to him.

Was that…

He reached out a hand to touch the long strands of bunched-up hair hanging down in strips from the sides of the cross.

Either human or horse.

Though a horse probably couldn't have carved the text down the stem of the cross. Russian by the looks of it. Which didn't help him or…

Chu. Kenji.

He glanced back at the passage in the corner, hoping Nakagami had just slowed down to investigate something on the way up…and was immediately disappointed.

Okay, he's somewhere else then.

Pushing the loose hair to the side, Sila edged round the cross and tried the other wall, the one nearest to where he'd come up. There were three arches, two of them leading to rooms or alcoves that were lit from the inside, the third tilted and dark.

'Kenji?' he asked, craning his head a little too theatrically to get a better view of the first room.

There was no answer, and nothing much to see either. Just four green dots on the wall and some kind of totem sticking out of the floor.

'Chu?' he shouted not quite as loud as his *Kenji*, leaving the comfort of the creepy cross as his eyes moved onto the second arch.

No answer.

And nothing inside.

Not that he could see much from his current position.

'Chu, you in there?'

His back hit metal, making him spin on instinct and shoot out an arm.

Fuck off wasn't far behind.

Then *idiot* when his brain caught up.

The metal *foe* was some kind of desk, a hard-edged letter *U* with an orb stuck at one end. He couldn't be sure, but it looked like it had a screen, or at least a sheet of lighter material on the side facing him, which meant it could be a computer terminal.

He moved forward.

Beyond the orb was one of the indistinct objects he'd glimpsed from the slope; a raised-step platform full of tube cushions. In any other context, he would've said Copenhagen opium den, or adventurist meditation zone, but in this place, with shadow and blood stains and weird Orthodox crosses pinned with human hair…

'Kenji?' he said softly, peering over the cushions and seeing something akin to a half-deconstructed coffee table.

No answer.

He moved around the cushions and onto the platform, running his finger along the erratic edges of the table.

What kind of human culture designed tables like this?

The whole thing looked like a broken up jigsaw puzzle.

And the edges; if you moved your leg or hand too fast, you'd probably cut yourself.

But someone had used it as there was paper on the table surface, real human-like paper with faded writing on it. He picked up a single sheet and rubbed two fingers against either side. The texture was odd, like a dry towel. Decayed from age, perhaps. He tried to read some of the characters written down, but it wasn't any language he recognized.

Ne, wait, some of it he did.

At the end of each paragraph, a single line of Russian, just like on the stem of the Orthodox cross.

A half Russian, half alien guy then.

Either long dead or pretentiously retro with his writing.

Putting the paper back exactly where he'd found it, Sila examined the rest of the platform.

The tube cushions were relatively tidy, no indications that anyone had sat there recently. But it did have a definite human vibe, despite the eccentricities. And that mint shisha scent, it was stronger now. Someone had to be pumping that into the air otherwise why was it there at all? It wasn't a natural smell.

A *whoosh* sound, followed by a series of tinny, metallic beeps pulled him back from random sniffing.

He couldn't be sure, but it sounded like it had come from the floor above. Or outside the window maybe.

'Chu? Kenji?'

Nothing.

If the lights hadn't been so bright, he would've been screaming, but for some reason the room felt quite ambient.

The scribbled notes, the cross, the death tube, the mint shisha, ja, aside from all that, it wasn't that different from their ship. Isolated people stuck in an enclosed space, some areas apparently black spots, others quite cosy and communal. All in all, a potential nesting site.

Then he remembered the blood trail.

The lack of a corpse.

The mass death on the surface.

'Kenji?' he shouted, louder, a little more unhinged.

He moved over to the opposite side of the room, wiping his hands on his jacket. There were two more arched doorways, apparently dark and noiseless, yet as he passed the first one, it suddenly lit up…with the same four green dots as the rooms on the other side.

He peeked in, whispering the obligatory, 'Chu, Kenji?'

Nothing, no passageways, no replies.

Not even a totem.

Backing out, he continued on past the second arch, giving only a cursory check when the same lights came on, and then stopped, a metre later.

The parallel slope. Potentially.

He pulled himself up to full height, squinting into the dark space ahead.

Ne, his initial scan had been correct, there was nothing there. The spot where Nakagami's passage should've sloped up to meet this artistic space was missing, and in its place was just another alcove. Which meant…what? He was still downstairs? Captured? Dead?

'Kenji?' he shouted, pushing his knuckles into his chest, telling himself two hundred beats per minute was normal. 'Chu?'

'Over here.'

Sila spun round and saw Nakagami emerging from the third, dark arch on the other side of the cushions, his face utterly passive, as if he'd just stepped out to buy some bread.

'How did-…'

He finished the question wordlessly, trying to work out the station blueprint in his head. His passage had sloped up, Nakagami's must have stayed level. Or not sloped so much. Then he went up another slope and…

'There is a room below, extremely large, mostly empty, with a lot of unorthodox structures.' Nakagami picked up a piece of paper from the desk in the middle, skimming it. 'I assume your passage sloped directly upwards to here.'

'Ja.'

'Which means Chu must be in a room above.'

'She is?'

Nakagami dropped the paper and walked to the dark archway near Sila. He stuck his head inside and shouted, 'Chu.'

'I don't think that goes anywhere.'

'Chu…' he tried again.

There was a faint sound back, possibly human speech.

'Shit. Was that her?'

'I assume so.'

'How did you know she was up there?'

Nakagami pointed across at the giant cylinder.

'What does that mean?'

'The space elevator stops at the third level.'

'That's what that thing is?'

'Presumably.'

Sila shook his head, following Nakagami through the dark arch and then up a sloped passage to the right...that he had completely missed. 'Ja, the scans, that's how you know everything.'

'The scan did not show such level of detail, only the basic layout. I have deduced the rest from my-'

Nakagami stopped, touching the wall at the side.

'What is it?'

'It's vibrating.'

'Maybe it's the power circuits.'

'The other corridors did not have this effect.'

Sila put his left hand on the wall and flinched. The only thing he could think of was an alien living in the walls, watching them through little peepholes, but he didn't want to say it out loud.

Luckily, a buzz of static shot through the comm system, assuming the place had one, and a rough, garbled voice started to speak.

'… … … … … …'

'Is that the station AI?'

'Ne vem.'

'Chu?'

Nakagami left the wall and continued up the slope, giving no hint that Sila should follow. He did anyway.

The voice continued, cutting in and out, as deep as a man one second, as shrill as a banshee the next.

'Sounds alien.'

'Doubtful.'

'Or primitive.'

'More likely that it's some form of Russian.'

That seemed to be the secret code as, after Nakagami's words, the voice straightened itself out and spoke in complete sentences. Clearly Russian now, even though neither Sila nor Nakagami could understand it.

'What's he saying?'

'Ne vem.'

'It is Russian though…'

'Ja, I believe so.'

'Just like that text on the paper. And that weird Orthodox cross. Fuck, should've brought Aleša with us.'

They got to the top of the slope and turned right into another room. It was completely different from the one below, a windowless space with an auditorium-like structure, which stopped abruptly about two thirds of the way round.

Sila took a few steps forward, craning his head round the side of the layered structure, the hidden third of the room.

No scaffolding.

No builders holding cups of Somalian alcohol.

No Chu shape.

Nothing.

'It is an odd design,' said Nakagami, looking at some symbols scrawled on the wall nearby.

'Ja, very odd.'

'… … … … … …' said the Russian on the comm, possibly agreeing.

Turning back, Sila resumed his scan of the architectural weirdo surrounding him, keeping a filter open for traces of Chu.

Then changing his mind and shouting out her name.

No answer.

Maybe she was unconscious? Or deep inside one of her infamous teleport bubbles?

'Chu…' he tried again.

Still nothing.

Muttering, 'fucking hermit,' just loud enough for Nakagami to hear, he went back to cataloguing the room.

To his immediate left, there was a row of grounded orbs laid out in a comma shape, similar to the totems he'd squinted at on the floor below, as well as a bland arch just past it; higher up, a series of oval platforms with something resembling a washing machine fixed to the largest one - a spotlight for the stage perhaps - and, to the right, one long slope curving up and branching off to each platform, the wall alongside it lit up like a lopsided runway by the familiar green jets of gas.

'The elevator terminus,' said Nakagami, leaving the symbols and stepping toward the orb collection nearby.

Sila repeated *elevator* with a sceptical tone then realised what it was Kenji was looking at; the cylinder from the floor below.

'That's the exit?' he asked, sticking a lax arm out at the arch he'd just dismissed.

'Logically, ja.'

'Where the corpse came out from?'

'The last life sign, ja. They must've died in this room. Perhaps looking for the girl.'

Sila heard *room* and looked back at the oval platforms, focusing on each one like a puzzle. Finally, he caught a flicker of light higher up, specific to one platform.

'Chu,' he shouted, spotting the top of a familiar head.

'Where?'

'Up there, near the top.'

Nakagami followed Sila's line of sight and arrived at a platform on the top row. In truth, it was more like an alcove dug seamlessly into the wall, the orb inside providing most of the light. Chu was standing in front of it, back turned to the rest of the auditorium, her right hand massaging the side of her head.

'… … … … … …' said the voice on the invisible comm.

'Chu…'

This time it broke through and she turned, her hand apparently stuck to her scalp.

'Why didn't you answer us?'

'Busy,' she shouted back.

'Doing what?'

'Up here.'

Ja, of course, Sila thought. Just sit back, we'll come to you.

He glanced right, weighing up the slope at the side. It wasn't long, but it was steeper than the other two they'd done. No sign of any steps either.

'There's some kind of machine,' Chu continued, back turned again, voice barely audible. 'Could be the teleporter.'

'What?'

'It could be the teleporter,' she repeated, upping the volume again.

'You're touching it?'

'Studying. Testing.'

Sila looked over at Nakagami, who was standing next to the space elevator entrance. Or the literal death tube.

'Any sign of the body?'

He bent down, touching the floor again.

'Blood?'

'This is strange.'

'Not blood?'

Nakagami looked towards the slope they'd just come up, examining the floor from there to his current position.

He stood up, confused. 'It appears that the life sign bled here, stopped, somehow went down to the bottom floor without spilling a drop then resumed bleeding.'

'… … … … … … …' sounded the voice on the comm.

'Maybe there's a different way to get down there?'

'This does not make sense.'

'The elevator?'

'Assuming they were human. But this does appear to be human blood. Presumably from the human life sign we detected. And yet, the movements…'

Sila realized he was talking to a closed loop and aimed for the slope instead. Chu was still in the same place, probably messing with the self-destruct controls, but when he got halfway up, he saw that she wasn't completely alone; there was something odd to the side of her, a faint shadow flickering.

'… … … … … … …'

He stopped where he was and squinted. It was definitely a shape, a slightly lighter shade of grey than the darkness near the alcove entrance. A trick of the light? Chu's own shadow? Whatever it was, she seemed completely unaware of it.

'Chu,' he shouted.

'You're still down there?'

'There's something…' He paused, unsure how to describe it. Better get closer and whisper it in her ear. He started walking again, but as he got closer he noticed that the shadow had gone and Chu was now grinding both temples. 'Is your head okay?'

'Ja.'

'You're rubbing it a lot.'

'Headache.'

'… … … … … … …' said the station voice, this time disrupted at the end by a long burst of static.

'Maybe you should come down, look in some other areas.'

'I think I've almost got this. The basics of it.'

'The teleporter?'

'Ja.'

'That's definitely what it is?'

The background static elevated its pitch, bouncing around the walls like a desperate pinball, then screeched out of existence.

Chu waited out a few breaths, making sure the noise was done, then replied.

'It's got some schematics, very similar to existing theory. Most of the writing's in Russian though.'

'Like that voice on the comm.'

'Probably gonna need Aleša to come and translate before we try anything concrete.'

'Bad idea.'

'Or we figure out some way to take a photo and bring it back.'

'Better.'

Sila got to within a few metres of the alcove and was about to gently whine about the steepness of the slope when Chu interjected with some kind of weird spasm…then threw herself against the machine she'd been studying.

He rushed forward, putting out both hands to grab her sides and keep her balanced, but just as he was close to touching her, she spasmed again, this time lurching up into the air and flipping one-eighty.

'Chu,' he yelled, semi-guttural, reaching over the barrier to try and grab her as she fell.

But she didn't fall.

She hovered, hair dangling down in front of her face, pointing like a dagger at the part of the floor she would hit.

'My head,' she screamed, both hands gripping her temples like a debut psychic as blood started to trickle out of her ears.

'I can't reach you.' He spun down towards the elevator. 'Kenji, help…'

Nakagami had clearly heard the noise as he was already a third of the way up the slope.

But it didn't matter.

Chu was lurching into the air again, or falling through it, dropping diagonally down towards the floor, one arm flailing, trying desperately to grab onto something firm, and the other hitting her own head over and over and…done.

'Chu,' was the only thing Sila could say as his best friend crashed neck first into the floor and, a hundredth of a second later, vanished within it.

~~~

The ship is your home, the station is just another place.

The ship is cosy, the station is other.

The ship is

Sila didn't know what he was thinking, what he was doing, what had just happened, so he listened to Nakagami's words and followed them, followed the physicist to the spot where Chu had landed, watched him push against the floor with the palm of his hand.

The floor is not hard, it's ghost
~~~

The floor is

There was a scream, from somewhere below.

Nakagami ran over to the slope and Sila's body followed, the two of them almost sliding on their bellies down to the middle room below.

Another scream, trailed closely by *my head* as they saw Chu suspended in a bent-over pose, a tube cushion in her hand. And the blood. It wasn't only coming out of her ears now, it was streaming out of her eye sockets too.

'Chu…'

'Hurts…'

'Don't move, we're-…'

She flipped round, darted through the air towards the wall and, once again, vanished on impact.

'Where is she?' Sila cried, some of his brain switching back on.

'Ne vem.'

'She's disappearing.'

'Ja.'

'Where?'

Nakagami didn't bother with another *ne vem*, instead he opted for, *back to the ship*, and ran towards the slope on the far left side.

~~~

Running kept the worst of it at bay - run to the airlock, don't stop until you're there, don't think - but then there was the *Velcro lift* down to the docking ring. Three to four minutes of standing statue still and trembling in delayed shock as any attempt at pacing up and down would detach them from the magnetic wall.

Nakagami pressed the horizontal line four times, but the change in speed was imperceptibly low.

Or it didn't speed up at all.

Hard to tell when everything around them was in shadow.

Sila closed his eyes and told himself she hadn't actually hit the floor or flown out into space, cos she'd still been talking at them, screaming,
~~~

while Nakagami thought out loud, attempting to explain what had happened.

'She was experimenting with a machine, pressed the wrong button, activated the station's defensive measures. An electric shock caused her severe head pain and…made her hover in the air. Ne. An advanced defensive measure, it must be capable of lifting the human body and carrying it through solid matter.'

He stopped at the same time the lift did.

'Ne. She activated the teleporter…'

'Kenji, move,' said Sila already running left towards the airlock.

'…and it was incompatible with her body. Ne. It didn't recognize her pattern, tried to compensate, but…'

'Kenji…'

Nakagami transferred his thoughts back to *deep internal* and ran, each docking port re-lighting silently as he passed.

~~~

The airlock was already open when they reached it, both parts, the station and their ship.

On the other side, Aleša and Katya were staring back at them, holding hands.

'How was the station?'

'Chu…' yelled Sila, looking past them. 'Did you see her?'

'We heard a loud noise, someone shouting maybe.'

'Did you see Chu?'

Aleša shook her head, puzzled. 'What happened?'

'I'll do a scan,' said Nakagami, running past Aleša and Katya. 'See if her life sign's here.'

'Her life sign?'

Sila followed, saying he'd check Chu's quarters and the TELEPORT ROOM, then shouting back at Aleša to close the airlock.

'What happened?' she tried again, but he was already out of sight.
~~~

Turning back, she stared at the two open doors, one familiar, the other with four chunks still poking out, then looked down at Katya. 'Do you know how to close them?'

'… … … … … Rasputin.'

'Okay.'

'… … … … … … … …'

'Does he know?'

~~~

She must be on the ship, she must be on the ship, she must be on the ship, begged Sila to whoever was out there in the voids of space, as he pinballed down the corridor to Chu's quarters, almost tripping over his own feet several times.

When he got there, the door was open, blocked by Gašper.

'Chu,' said Sila, pushing him aside and taking in the whole room in one shot.

'Wah…you're back already.'

'Chu, Gašper, where is she?'

'Err…not here.'

'You saw her?'

'Not really. I heard her shouting and came over to-…'

'Shouting where?'

'Here, obviously. But…as you can see, no one's home.'

Sila went deeper into the room, checking under the blankets, in the shower, even under the bed.

'Don't think she'll fit under there.'

'Gašper…'

'What's going on? I thought you were all on the station.'

'We have to find her. Fast.'

Finally, his expression caught up. 'Is she okay?'

Sila went back out into the corridor, heading right towards the stairs. 'Check the other rooms on this deck.'

'For Chu?'

'Quickly.'
~~~

'What's happened to her? Sila?'

Sila turned the corner at the end, and took the steps down three at a time. Next stop had to be the TELEPORT ROOM, it was her second home. Or the HALF DONE ROOM…but that was right next to it, so two bears with one axe. Failing that, there was Engineering, not that she-

'Sila…'

He landed on the third step down to the bottom deck, and looked back up. Nakagami's head was just about visible, so he ran back up and over towards the first corner of the coiled snake corridor.

Nakagami was crouching over Chu, her body bent slightly, hand clutching the side of her neck.

'She's still alive,' he said, his fingers on her wrist. 'I found her crawling towards the GOD ROOM.'

'Is she conscious?' asked Sila, bending down and lifting Chu's hand gently off her neck. There was no response, no resistance. He put his ear against her mouth. Breath, very faint. 'Did she say anything?'

'Ne.'

'Antro-D?'

'I don't know if any of her bones are broken, it may be dangerous to lift her.'

'I'll bring it here,' said Sila, already two steps away.

'Stop, come back.'

Sila stopped, turned.

'We don't know what kind of damage she has suffered.'

'She has blood coming out of her eyes and ears…'

'Antro-D could exacerbate her condition, or kill her even. There's no way to know. We have to scan her first, assess the damage.'

'Scan her with what?'

'Ne vem.'

'Can the ship do it?'

'Not medically, ne.'

Sila shot out breath and spit. 'Can you give me a brighter fucking answer, Kenji?'

'I'm sorry, ne vem.'

'Then don't suggest a scan that we can't even do.'

Nakagami looked up at the green bulb surveying the first corner. It was flickering. The seventh one in the last month.

'Can the ship adapt another scan to do it? The life sign scan…'

'Possibly.'

'Or can we use one of Chu's scanners, the portable ones?'

Nakagami paused, hypnotised by a burst of green light.

'Kenji?'

'Ja…'

'Can we adapt a portable scanner?'

'Ne vem.'

~~~

It turned out they could.

But it took a while.

About two and a half hours of Nakagami fiddling with the insides of tech no one else but Chu understood, and the rest of them taking it in turns to hold Chu's hands and tell her stories.

It was tough, talking to someone who couldn't react in any way, so Gašper improvised a reaction code. If her eyelids fluttered, as they did from time to time, it meant she was listening. Left eyelid meant *good story, keep going,* right eyelid meant *quit, new story, prosim.*

Finally, the scanner was ready. Nakagami focused it on all the parts of her body that he suspected might have the most damage – brain, neck, spine, legs – and waited for the *Susssh* noise to stop.

'This…' he started, checking the final set of results.

'She's okay?'

'In a coma?'

Nakagami disregarded the scanner and looked at Chu's body with his own bare eyes. 'This doesn't seem possible.'

'What?'

'She has no damage. None of her bones are broken, or even fractured.'
~~~

'Are you sure the scanner's working properly?' asked Aleša, her hand pulled away from Chu's forehead by her new surrogate child.

'Ja, it works. It's working.'

'But we saw her fall,' said Sila, looking at Chu's legs. 'Her body hit the ground, went through walls.'

Nakagami checked the scan results again, letting out a breath that sounded almost like a laugh. 'It is incredible.'

'What about her head?'

'Ja…'

'Kenji, does her head have damage?'

Nakagami put his sleeve against his eyes, held it there for a few seconds then lowered it again, his face serious again. 'Internally, with any kind of detail, it is unclear. I do not know the typical brain pattern, I'm not a doctor. However, according to the scans, there is nothing life-threatening.'

'What about the blood?'

'Ne vem.'

'It's not dangerous?'

'Apparently not.'

Sila took Chu's hand away from Gašper and placed it against his forehead.

'Is she gonna wake up soon?' asked Gašper, stepping back.

Nakagami put the scanner on the floor. 'Ne vem.'

'She's not in a coma, is she?'

'I suspect her body is exhausted. All she requires is rest.'

'How long?' asked Sila.

'I must remind you, I am not a doctor. Everything detailed that I've told you came from the scanner.'

'Can the scanner tell us how long?'

Nakagami stood up, pulling the creases out of his jacket. 'We should move her into her quarters, let her rest.'

'What if the station defence thing tries to attack her again?' asked Gašper. 'Or one of us?'

'I will talk to the computer, tell it to detach the ship from the station and resume our previous orbit.'

'Can you get it to close the airlocks as well?' asked Aleša, her hand locked with Katya's.

Sila's eyes ballooned. 'You didn't close them?'

'I don't know how, there was no button. And the station one was weird.'

'Shit.'

'Don't blame me, you opened them…'

'There could be something on the ship.'

'…then just screamed at me to close them and ran off without saying how.'

'What do you mean, something on the ship?' asked Gašper, checking the corridor behind.

'We have to get over there, get it shut.'

'Something from the station?'

'Kenji, you'll have to do it. Take Gašper with you for protection.'

Nakagami coughed, his usual trick. 'There is no need to go over there. The airlock will close before we detach. And there are no life signs on the structure. Do not panic.'

'Are you sure?'

'Focus on carrying Chu back to her quarters. Then try to relax. Meditate, perhaps.'

'Meditate…'

'Or you can try the OPTIMISM ROOM. Whichever functions best.'

'I'll stay with Chu,' replied Sila.

'Me too,' added Gašper, putting a hand on his friend's head.

'As you wish.'

Nakagami walked off, quickly absorbed by the coiled snake, leaving Aleša to repeat the same question Gašper had asked three times already: 'what the hell happened over there?'

Sila kept Chu's hand in his, pressing down slightly on her nails. 'Station security. Allegedly.'

'You mean an AI?'

'Ne vem.'

~~~
~~~

Within two minutes of starting the chat, Nakagami knew they were going to have a problem.

A further problem.

He sat back in the chair, staring at the blank spaces his posters used to occupy.

According to the computer, Airlock 2 was no problem; keeping it open after the attack on Chu would jeopardize crew safety and its core belief system couldn't allow that.

However, it couldn't detach from the station, or attempt to close the airlock on that side, because that would be rude.

'Do you think it was polite to attack Chu?'

'That was most likely a security measure, taken in defence of its systems.'

'Do you think it was polite to activate that measure?'

The computer made its usual buzzing noise, only this time Nakagami was sure it was merely pretending to think.

'The measure was probably automatic.'

'I'm not so certain. There was a Russian voice on the comm. It did not seem artificial.'

'There are no life signs on the station.'

'Have you scanned all sections?'

'The upper pylons are impenetrable to ship scanners. However, there is no power emanating from those areas.'

'Are you still scanning now?'

'Ne.'

'Can you start scanning, the same as before, on a twenty second delay?'

More buzzing, a bit of static. 'In one minute.'

'Can you focus on the sections closest to the upper pylons?'

'In forty-five seconds.'

'Ja, I know. I am asking you in advance.'

'*Gup ya.*'

Nakagami's finger stopped mid-type, his eyes lost in the reply. *Gup ya.* He tried saying it out loud, reading it backwards, changing the vowels, but it didn't make sense. 'I don't understand. What does *Gup ya* mean?'

'It is a phrase from *Gah Council.* The main character employs it when he wants someone to relax.'

'Did Gašper teach you this?'

'He did.'

'And you stored it?'

'Correct. It adds variety to my conversations.' Another buzzing sound. 'The scan has started, you may follow the results on the screen to your left.'

'Hvala.'

Nakagami moved his chair a few inches across and leaned forward, putting his elbows on the console then deciding it wasn't really his style and settling them back on the arms of the chair.

As expected the scan was lifeless.

For the first seventeen minutes.

Then a dot appeared, in the same room Chu had first been attacked. The two-thirds of an auditorium, space elevator exit place.

Nakagami waited for another twenty seconds to pass, keeping his eyes fixed on the dot and all the possible places it could move to.

The scan refreshed.

The dot was gone. Ne, wait, it was in the room below, the one with the Russian notes and tube cushions.

'Is that a life sign?' he asked the computer.

'Correct.'

'Where did it come from?'

'Unknown.'

'The upper pylons?'

'Rationally, that is the only place it could've come from.'

The scan refreshed again. The dot was still in the same place. Nakagami let out breath he didn't realise he'd been holding in.

'We need to detach from the station,' he typed, trying to think of new reasons.

'Agreed.'

Nakagami had already written 'If we don't detach, the…' before he realized what the computer's reply was.

'You agree that we need to detach?'

'The life sign could be responsible for murder and attempted murder. Allowing them open access to the ship could compromise crew safety.'

'Then detach.'

'I will make the request.'

'They have us locked down?' typed Nakagami, wondering why he hadn't considered that.

The computer went through its motions, making the routine buzzing sounds plus one or two new ones.

'The request has been denied.'

'Reason?'

'They wish to visit the ship.'

Nakagami instinctively scanned the room for a spanner or a wrench, then checked the live scan feed again. The dot was still in the same place. Perhaps relaxing on the tube cushions. Or sharpening a spear.

'Who wishes to visit the ship?' he typed.

'They do.'

'Who is *they*?'

'Unknown.'

'Why do they want to visit?'

'Unknown.'

He tapped his finger on the edge of the console ten, fifteen times.

'When will they come?'

'Unknown.'

~~~

A month ago, Sila wouldn't have forced *Gah Council* on anyone, not even Potočnik, but sitting on Chu's pillow, seeing the dried blood around her eyes, remembering the torture acrobatics on the station, he thought it was probably the only thing on the whole ship light and silly enough to bring her back and not instantly depress her.
~~~

Gašper would've backed him up on that, if he'd been there. If he hadn't pissed off to the OPTIMISM ROOM with his makeshift family.

And Aleša…*I'll pop in later, hit her head with the massage stick.*

Your only hope for any kind of loving relationship and you'll pop in later?

Sila stopped, dug a fingernail into his left palm, and went back to *Gah Council*, adjusting his voice slightly for each character.

'The fortune teller removed her crippled hand to reveal a polaron modulator, aiming it dead straight at Gah's forehead.

'I foresee an imminent end for a dark-skinned man in a room with red decorations.'

Gah nodded, looking around the shack. 'All this decoration, fake?'

'I had to lure you in, didn't I?'

'And the cackling? The vacant stare?'

'Improvised.'

To hammer home the point, and her current advantage, the fortune teller performed another cackle.

Not bad, thought Gah. Very crone-like.'

Sila stopped, checking Chu's face.

No reaction.

It's okay, he thought. She's just tired, not in a coma. Her body's been through a lot. Most of it incomprehensible. She'll wake up tomorrow, when her stomach gets-

There was a knock at the door, followed by an evenly-pitched, 'Sila.'

He put the book down, patted Chu on the head and walked over, pushing the *open* button.

Nakagami was standing there, fiddling with his jacket zip.

'Did you close the airlocks?'

'On our side, ja. The other remains open. At present, that is the best we can do.' He peered inside the room, frowning. 'Where is Aleša?'

'With her adopted Russian child. Gašper too.'

'I thought she would be nursing Chu back to vitality.'

'Back to vitality…'

'Ja…'

'Most people would say back to health.'

'They are synonymous.'

'I suppose.'

Sila took his foot away from the door and let Nakagami follow him in.

'I have some other updates, one good, one bad.'

'How bad?'

'There is a life sign on the station. It intends to visit the ship.'

Sila stared off to the side, at the picture of Potočnik, as if the new development were somehow the tyrant's fault.

'That is the bad update. However, the computer is on our side again and is working relentlessly to detach our ship from the docking ring.'

'Relentlessly? Can't it just detach now?'

'Ne, we are clamped down. Any extreme force could tear off the side of our ship and...repairs would be beyond the capabilities of our maintenance drones.'

'Fuck. Where is the life sign now?'

Nakagami bent down and picked *Gah Council* up of the bed, turning straight to the back cover blurb. 'The computer is scanning it with the same twenty second delay as before. Currently, it is in the room with cushions.'

'But you're here now. What if it's moved?'

'I have asked the computer to make an announcement if the life sign moves out of that room.'

'Will it move?'

Nakagami finished with the blurb and flipped to the front, his expression inscrutable. 'Ne vem.'

'Didn't you just say it intends to visit?'

'That is what the station computer told our computer. It may be lying.'

'Or it may be a serial killer coming to murder us. Fuck, Kenji, where did it even come from? There was nothing there before, you said...'

'I suspect they were concealing themselves in one of the upper pylons.'

'...and now it's coming here, they, it, we don't even know if it's human...'

'Sila.'

'...it could be that shadow I saw...what? I'm not panicking, I'm just...ne vem...I don't know what I'm doing. Fuck, it's already half five...what are we gonna do when curfew comes?'

Nakagami opened up *Gah Council* and flicked through. 'That is one thing we do not need to worry about.'

'What, curfew?'

'The good news previously referred to. I convinced the computer to skip curfew for the next few nights.'

'Skip?'

'All crew will be free to roam the ship throughout the night. There will be no electric shocks.'

'This is real?'

'Ja, starting from tonight.'

'After three years, it just stops?'

Nakagami turned another page and then immediately flicked back to the previous one. 'Does Chu like this kind of work?'

'What? Ne, I doubt it.'

'The writing is very odd. From what I can see, everything seems to be explicitly stated, without enigma.'

Sila reached over and took *Gah Council* out of Nakagami's hand, almost dropping it due to lack of resistance. 'After three years, the computer just cut the curfew?'

Nakagami watched as Sila placed the book respectfully back on the bed. 'It was strange, I agree, but the important thing is that it gives us an opportunity to defend ourselves. I suggest two shifts by Airlock 2, the first ten to four, the second four to ten. Each group will have spanners, wrenches and scissors to utilize if necessary.'

'We're allowed weapons too?'

'Temporarily, ja.'

'To defend against whatever's on the station...'

'Correct.'

Sila sat down on the bed, putting his hand on Chu's ankle. There were faint veins he'd never noticed before, fragile-looking. 'Is it possible...that the life sign isn't hostile?'

'Ja, possible.'

'But then why did it attack Chu? Why are all those people dead?'

'Ne vem.'

'Or was it hiding from all that too?'

Nakagami sat down on the opposite side of the bed, putting his hand on the blanket beside Chu's ankle.

'There are only two people who have the answer to that question. One is on the station, intending to visit us. The other…'

Sila nodded, looking towards the doorway. '…is here.'

'Ja.'

~~~

The needle-shaped ship flew towards the enemy, apparently at high velocity, preparing to ram into its bridge.

'Ignore the fire from the other two ships, focus on D'kar.'

'He's charging weapons.'

'Stay on course.'

'He's firing.'

'Stay on course.'

'Five seconds to impact.'

'Two degrees starboard. Now.'

'What?'

The glowing white ball hit the camera, flinging Gon and Joona out of their seats and Mojca Ito into the cocktail cupboard.

Gašper laughed, nudging Aleša in the seat next to him to laugh too.

She didn't, she was too busy whispering to Katya, asking her for the seventh time if Rasputin was on the station.

And each time, she'd say, 'da, he is the station.'

'Are you not watching this?' asked Gašper, waving his hand by the side of her face.

'I'm busy.'

'You won't get anything out of her, she's still in shock. Her parents were probably down there, on the surface.'
~~~

'She answers, it just doesn't make sense. He is the station. He will come soon. Come to do what? Take her back? Sacrifice her? Kill us?'

'All of the above.'

'Fuck off, Gašper, this is serious.'

'Hey…'

'You saw what happened to Chu. We have to protect her, stop this Rasputin thing coming over and grabbing her.'

'Ja, are we not both sitting in the same room?'

The door *swooshed* open, making Aleša jump halfway out of her chair.

'Guys, we have an update,' said Sila, walking over to Gašper's chair and putting a hand on the back of it. 'And a plan to boot.'

Nakagami trailed in behind, hands lodged in his jacket pockets.

Gašper edged closer to Katya, putting his hand on her head and immediately getting it shoved back off.

'… … … …'

'Did she just say pet?'

'She said she's not your pet,' said Aleša.

'Ah, maybe she's angry that I haven't given her the drink yet.' Gašper bent down and went eye to eye with Katya. '… … … … … …?'

'… … … … … …'

'I heard *da*,' he said, getting back up and heading to the impromptu drinks table he'd set up.

'She wants more wolfberries this time,' Aleša shouted after him, getting a raised hand in return.

'You can understand her now?' asked Sila.

'In one sentence bursts, ja. A bit.'

'Can you ask her again who is on the station?' added Nakagami, taking a step closer. 'If she knows anything about them.'

'That's what I've been doing for the last few hours. She just says the station is Rasputin and he'll come soon.'

'He *is* the station?'

'Ja, might be bad translation on my part. A new slang term. Ne vem. But she definitely says he's coming soon. That one is basically literal, word for word.'

'Can you ask her if Rasputin has a physical body?'

Aleša muttered to herself, tried out a few words in her brain then said, 'ne.'

'Can you ask her if he's human?'

'Human?'

'Ja.'

'Wait.' She picked up the Russian Book and flicked to the back, running her finger down the page. 'Human, ne. Man, ja, okay.'

'Ask her.'

Aleša turned to Katya and said in Russian, 'is Rasputin a man?'

'… … …'

'She said ja.'

'This is not achieving much,' said Nakagami, looking and then frowning at the needle ship on the projection screen. 'We should focus on the plan.'

'We're detaching from the station, right?' asked Gašper, putting a cup of dried date, *but kei* and wolfberry water in front of Katya, who took it without even a cursory nod of thanks.

'That is a work in progress. Until then, we have to guard the airlock.'

'Kenji has convinced the computer to skip curfew for the next few nights. We can go anywhere on the ship between ten and ten, stay in other quarters, carry weapons.'

'The computer agreed to this?' asked Aleša, checking the temperature of Katya's cup.

'After all this time?' added Gašper.

'There is a life sign on the station. The AI over there says they intend to visit us soon.'

'Wah, that's what Katya said. He will come soon.'

Aleša went back to her own cup, taking a sip. 'Is it a human life sign?'

'Ne vem.'

'Is it moving?'

'Not yet.'

'What are we gonna do if it does?'

'As I said, the plan is to guard Airlock 2. Two shifts, six hours each. Sila and I will take the first, the two of you will take the second.'

'What about Katya?'

'She can sleep in her quarters.'

'Unprotected?'

'Two of us will be guarding Airlock 2, the only way onto the ship.'

'The fuck it is, she teleported on…from out of nowhere.' Gašper shifted his position, moving directly in front of Katya's chair [and blocking her view of the projection screen]. 'She's coming to the airlock with us.'

'… … … …' said Katya, kicking Gašper's shin.

'Hey…'

'… … … … …'

'In the what?'

'I think you're blocking the screen,' said Aleša, gesturing to the *Dibrivna Vaska* episode still playing behind Gašper.

'Ah, I forgot that was on.' He edged to the side, locking his eyes back on Nakagami. 'Point still stands about the airlock though.'

'It is not wise to put her in closer proximity to the threat.'

'She won't be, she'll be with us.'

'At the airlock, which is closer to the threat.'

'Ja, but with us, so not really.'

'He's right,' said Aleša, accepting the cup that Katya was prodding into her left arm. 'She needs to stay away from the airlock.'

'Ne, she doesn't.'

'Gašper…'

'… … … … … …' said Katya, standing up and yawning.

'What did she say?' asked Sila.

'Ne vem.'

'… … … … … … …'

'Okay. She said she's tired, she's going to bed.'

'It is decided then,' said Nakagami, taking a step back to let Katya past.

Spurning his offer, Katya instead walked around the other side of the chairs, past Sila and stopped in front of the doors. It took a moment, but finally they slid open. Startled or possibly lax, Aleša and Gašper sprang up from their seats and grabbed a hand each before she could wander out alone.

'We'll take our shift outside her quarters. Gašper and I.'

'That would serve little purpose.'

'One shift each. You can guard the airlock.'

'Alone?' Sila's voice went higher than intended so he modified. 'Guard the airlock alone?'

'Don't be a baby.'

'That thing's a fucking…wild lunatic. It tossed Chu around like a bath sponge.'

'… … … … … …'

Nakagami moved in front of the projection screen, blocking out the figure of Da Gruta behind him. 'We don't know for certain that was an attack.'

'Ja, then why are we guarding the airlock? Why are we trying to detach?'

'I am not downplaying what happened, I agree with you, but we should try to remain rational.'

'I am being rational.'

'… … … … … …' said Katya, pulling on Aleša's and Gašper's hands.

'We're gonna go and tuck her in.'

'And come to the airlock later?' asked Sila.

'Just get a spanner, you'll be fine,' said Gašper, patting him on the shoulder.

'Or ask Nakagami to sleep next to you when you're on shift,' suggested Aleša, one hand on the door frame.

'I prefer my own bed.'

'Okay, wheel your bed over to the airlock.'

'That is impractical.'

'… … … … …'

'What?'

Katya slipped her bonds and made a dash for the corridor, turning with her nails raised as a warning.

'You sort it out, we're going.'

'See you in the morning.'

'And if you come near us, say something before you appear,' added Aleša. 'No ninja steps.'

The door slid shut before Sila could call them deserters, but he said it anyway.

Nakagami sat down on Katya's chair, picking up the cup Aleša had left behind. 'There is no need for either of us to sleep by the airlock. The ship will announce if the life sign is moving, and then the rest of us can come.'

'If you're not comatose.'

'I am a very light sleeper.'

'Great. You can be the first to discover my corpse.'

'That is an unlikely scenario.'

'Ja, I'm sure.'

Kenji turned to the screen, put his lips to the rim of Katya's cup and held them there.

~~~

Due to his history with [and analysis of] the concept of dread, Sila chose to take the first shift.

Location-wise, it wasn't that bad; the decor was neither sinister nor claustrophobic, the floor panels were well-lit, the airlock door on their side was sealed tight, and the corridor leading to it seemed relatively easy to flee down. The only thing that put a dent in the *sleepover* vibe was the continual *deeeen* sound coming from behind the walls.

'A mechanical sound will not harm you,' said Nakagami, joining him for the first forty-five minutes.

'Not physically.'

'Think of it as the ships blood…'

'Blood…'

'…flowing around the ship, helping to protect us.'

'I'll try.'

As for weaponry, he'd taken four spanners and three wrenches from Engineering, laying two spanners out in front of him and the rest behind in case he needed to retreat and throw.
~~~

For some reason, Nakagami didn't say anything about that.

Probably cos he wants to use them too, thought Sila, flinching as another *deeeen* sound went off nearby.

~~~

On the deck below, Gašper sat outside Klemen's quarters, making notes with the aid of the Russian Book.

Aleša had pretended to leave the room after Katya had fallen asleep and then returned to lie down next to her, but the little Russian seemed to be psychic as, each time, she'd woken up and said, stern as a nun, 'this is not your room.'

Eventually, Aleša had given up and gone back to her own quarters, which was right next door, telling Gašper to wake her straight away if any weird things came lurching down the corridor.

'I'll wake you up if *anyone* comes down the corridor,' he'd said, making an implication she didn't really get.

It was weird, thought Gašper, an hour into his shift. She saw the same posters I did, she knows what he is, but for some reason it's blocked in her head.

Maybe I should tell her directly?

Warn her when she comes on shift?

~~~

On the upper deck, outside Airlock 2, Sila stared at the wrench and tried to block out the *deeeen* noise.

If he let his mind wander, it would turn into another sound, the gears of the airlock opening.

The wrench would turn against him.

The wall would dematerialize, sucking him back.

Klemen would hand him the VR swab.

Dodzi would drop the scissors.

Sadia would detach his neurons from the station.

Then lie on him.

Push him into the ground.

Absorb him.

Him, her, mum, all in the same coffin.

A wrench in front of them, floating.

Gah Council.

Gah Council.

A wrench in his hand, corridor background.

Gah Council.

Ja, *Gah Council.*

He put the wrench down, pulled his arms out from the side, wiped a bit of the sweat off, looked for *Gah Council.*

It wasn't there.

Ne

Behind him.

Behind his back.

He fumbled behind with his hand, felt the shape of it, gripped it, then pulled the best-selling paperback series in Slovene history back onto his lap.

Gah Council 8: Moon Factory Bliss

He skimmed past the prologue and the first paragraph of description in Chapter One and let Gah take him somewhere with the vibrant, constantly surprising beauty of anarcho-communism,

even if it did show the dirty side,

the muck of things.

~~~

Sensing danger, Jemba walked back out of the collective and headed arrow-minded to the river. Three immigration officers trailed him, and the lady selling the iced pineapple chunks looked suspicious so he ducked into a surface-level café and pretended to study the menu. In the reflection of the café window, he saw the lady more clearly, her true face. No one else knew it, to them she was a regular Tibetan, but to him she was the enemy, a Level 3 Adventurist drone.

Gašper lowered the book, checked the corridor both ways then looked ahead to the next chapter.
~~~

It was a POV SWITCH to Gah, usually not a bad thing, but at the moment Gah was stuck taking care of a pensioner who knew things, so he put *Gah Council 7* down, picked up the pen and went back to the Russian notes.

'Chu – warm-hearted, clever, likes to make fun of people.'

It wasn't the most detailed description, but it was the best he could do in Russian, and it got the basic essence of her.

He scanned back up the page, checking his first entry. That was the key one.

'Nakagami – clever, calm, sometimes tells lies, likes little girls. Do not stay with him in a room, only you and him, two people. Do not touch him. Do not open the door if it is him.'

The last few sentences were clumsy, but sufficient. Katya already knew Nakagami was not a normal guy, this just coloured in the detail a bit. And it wasn't a total character death, he'd written some positive traits first.

Aleša could modify it if she wanted.

Or add to it.

A noise pulled him away from the notes, something tapping against metal at the end of the corridor.

He looked down towards the stairs, turned it into a stare, then a vigil.

That was the only way to access Katya's quarters, the stairs.

Was someone up there?

Gašper pulled himself up and crawled over to the other side of the corridor. The view was slightly better, relatively well-lit too, but it didn't reveal anyone.

No boots, tips of boots or sides of a face.

Gašper crawled back to his sentry post, the wall next to Katya's door.

He picked up *Gah Council 7* and pretended to read, secretly keeping the stairs in frame.

~~~

At 3:53am, Nakagami poked his head round the side of the corridor and whispered, 'Sila, it's me, Nakagami.'
~~~

Getting a slurred, 'it's time already?' in response, he turned the corner and made his way between the spanners and wrenches towards the airlock door.

As he moved, there was a whirring noise behind him, from the direction of the Maintenance Storage Room. Soon enough, two maintenance drones cruised round the corner, one of them gliding up the side of the wall, stopping next to a panel, removing it and getting to work.

'Thank Matjaž they didn't come out an hour earlier,' said Sila, wrenches gripped tight in each hand.

'I asked the computer to delay their duties.'

'You did?'

'They will typically make repairs on every deck, which would be potentially alarming for people on shift.'

The maintenance drone finished its work on the opposite wall, closed up the panel and glided up to the ceiling and away.

The *deeeen* noise ran for a few more seconds then ceased.

'Did anything unusual occur here?' asked Nakagami, walking closer to the airlock glass and peering through.

'Not that I saw.'

'I have checked the most recent scan, and the life sign is still in the same place.'

'Maybe it's sleeping?'

'Possibly.'

Sila started to get up, rotating his back muscles and doing a full battle cry yawn.

'You should go back to your quarters.'

Sila shook his head, still yawning. 'Chu's quarters…'

'Okay.'

'I'll see you at ten.'

Nakagami nodded, sitting down with his back straight against the wall.

'Feel free to read and enjoy *Gah Council 8*. But don't tell Gašper, he's still on 7.'

'Those books do not interest me.'

'Actually, he's read them all twice already, so it doesn't really matter. But he'll still get annoyed if you're jumping in ahead of him.'

'Understood.'

~~~

Downstairs, Aleša stayed on her feet, walking between her own door and Dodzi's, reading Gašper's notes for future Russian with Katya.

He'd told her to make her own additions, but looking at what he'd written, she didn't really see the point.

Chu was warm-hearted?

Nakagami liked little girls?

One was vaguely true, but it's not like he could do anything about it. And Kenji knew that. He'd never said it, but that's what the posters were for, a release. She used to do the same with her-…with what she thought about. And if he did attempt anything, he'd have to kill them all first cos if he didn't she'd grab the scissors and cut his dick off herself, shove it out the airlock. And him with it. He knew that. His brain was rational enough to know that.

Do not stay in the room with him.

Ja, obviously.

When would he ever get a chance to do that?

And why would he?

It would be suicide.

Argh, she'd have to talk to Gašper about it in the morning. Lower the heat on his paranoia.

Maybe tell him some home truths about Chu too.

Warm-hearted.

To a degree, ja. If you were happy with the bare minimum. Long as there wasn't a TELEPORT ROOM nearby. Or you didn't mind sex every ten months.

Aleša put the pen on the paper and wrote *sometimes* before *warm-hearted.*

She stopped, checking the stairs.

There was a faint whirring sound, coming up from-
~~~

'Fuck,' she shouted, as a maintenance drone appeared at the side of the wall, racing towards her.

Grabbing the spanner off the floor, she reeled it back and prepared to strike.

Maintenance drone, she told herself. Maintenance drone. Maintenance drone. Maintenance drone.

Possibly detecting the spanner, or the panicked Slovene holding it, the drone glided up to the ceiling, reduced the volume of its whirring noise and powered down to cruising speed.

As it passed, a tinny voice emitted a slightly garbled, 'maintenance', repeated it twice then disappeared around the corner.

Aleša whispered *fuck* again and lowered the spanner.

Maintenance drones.

She'd never actually seen one before, and had no idea they could slide around the walls and the ceiling. Or make that whirring sound. Or detect her apprehension.

Perhaps Nakagami could've warned them about that?

If he even knew.

She picked up the pen she'd dropped and went back to correcting the notes.

Sometimes warm-hearted…

The pen hovered for a while, Aleša staring at *sometimes* like a landlord studying up on tenants' rights, before finally crossing it out and writing *Gašper – prone to paranoia* in Slovene.

There was nothing else to add so she put the notes down and picked up the Russian Book, opening to a random page and-

She stopped again.

At the end of the corridor, on the stairs…

She walked down farther, disguising her examination by keeping her eyes on the book.

When she reached her own door, she shifted to the wall on the left hand side.

On the stairs, something in the shadows at the top, from the deck above…

It wasn't clear, but it looked a bit like…

She lowered the book, focusing on the exact spot.

Was that a boot?

~~~

…tried to grab her hand but she swung back out over the lake again, spasms electrifying her body, blood dripping off her chin and out from her neck, a bearded Russian man holding her by the ankles, saying, 'she can teleport,' in Slovene, or Russian, but he could understand it, the words were real, and then he swung her back to the shore, the path where he was standing, and when he tried to grab her again, she flew up, her back bending and…he couldn't reach her, she was too high up, her back was bent, and behind him was Potočnik, hiding in a bush, telling him to interrogate the Luytens, cruise there like a geriatric and interrogate them, and when he looked back it wasn't Potočnik, it was a pair of purple eyes on a piece of card, and it wasn't a bush, it was the lake, and Chu was reaching for his hand, reaching upwards, her back bending, spine cracking…

Sila opened his eyes and screamed, 'don't bend,' to the ceiling…then turned to his left and almost dropped off the bed.

Riding out the jagged breaths, and dystopian dream-scape, he pushed himself up and checked the other side of the bed.

It was empty.

Chu-less.

She's okay, he thought, she woke up and…

Went where?

Without waking him?

He got off the bed and checked the bathroom.

Empty.

No steam, dissipating heat.

Nothing under the bed.

Scratching hard on his neck, he rushed to the door and looked both ways down the corridor.

Pale green.

Quiet.
~~~

No Chu.

~~~

Lifting up his back for the seventeenth time, Nakagami opened his eyes wide and tried another slice of *Gah Council 8*.

There was a dense pocket of mist in the temple, which made it hard for his scanner to pick up the nefarious muon streaks.

But Gah knew they were there.

Watching him.

Waiting for their chance.

He stopped, looking at the airlock.

It hasn't opened, he told himself. I've been here all night, it hasn't opened.

There were footsteps to the left, no *deeeen* effect to smother the sounds.

He turned, expecting Sila and was proven right. Though he hadn't expected him to look so panicked.

'Chu's gone.'

Nakagami kept his face steady, waiting for the rest.

'I woke up, on her bed and she was gone. We have to go to the GOD room, check on the life signs, the computer. I don't know how to use it properly.'

'Did you check the TELEPORT ROOM?'

'I haven't checked anywhere, I came straight here, the airlock.' Sila moved over and tried to lift Nakagami up by the arm. 'Come on, GOD room, let's go.'

'I can raise myself,' he replied, not shrugging Sila off but not leaning on him either.

'Check the station guy and check for Chu. Both of them.'

'You will have to stay here and watch the airlock.'

'Me?'

'If you want me to leave my post, there must be a substitute.'

'We don't have time for this, Chu could be in trouble.'
~~~

Nakagami looked at the cover of *Gah Council 8*, taking two breaths. 'The airlock has been closed all night. The ship has not announced any movement on the station. Chu is probably in the TELEPORT ROOM or eating breakfast somewhere. Or visiting Aleša. I can go and check, *if* you stay here.'

'Why didn't she tell me, if she was doing all that?'

'Ne vem.'

'I was on the bed, right next to her. Why didn't she wake me?'

'We can ask her, after I've checked.'

'The first person she sees, no attempt to-…'

'Sila.'

'Ja, fine. You go and check. Then come straight back here and tell me. No laxing.'

Nakagami nodded.

'Don't nod, say okay.'

'I will return soon.'

'Five minutes.'

'Soon.'

Nakagami pushed his shoulder blades back, stretched out his arms then walked off down the corridor, turning right at the corner before quickly correcting himself and going left.

Sila picked up one of the scanners and turned to the airlock.

If Nakagami had been there all night, she couldn't have gone this way.

Not physically, at least.

Unless…

~~~

The walk down the upper deck corridor was peaceful enough, with Nakagami only noticing the maintenance drone fixing the green light bulb when it was right next to him.

He watched the metal claw twisting it off, tapping the bulb then dropping it into a little compartment hidden in its torso, making a mental note to ask the computer about different colour bulbs.
~~~

It was strange that he'd never asked before.

However, on reflection, not that strange. Dealing with the computer was always a matter of triage. Flickering bulbs were annoying, but never fatal.

As he reached the top of the stairs, he remembered that Aleša was standing guard outside the Russian girl's room, and slowed.

She'd told them to say something before approaching, warn her that it was them and not a monster.

He trod carefully down each step, making almost no sound, and when he reached the last one, he said, 'it's Kenji,' at what he calculated was a reasonable volume.

There was no response.

Was she asleep?

He left the last step and went directly into the middle of the corridor, assuming that it was better not to lurk.

Aleša was laying curved on the floor, her back to him, her face buried in her arms.

There were some pieces of paper next to her legs.

He looked at the wall to his left and realized it wasn't a wall, it was the door to Gašper's room. Aleša was sitting only another two and half rooms down. Did he have time to check on her?

There had been no announcements, she was probably asleep.

There was no need to check.

The paper was most likely Russian notes.

He looked at Aleša's head, then the door to the left of it.

It was a door.

It was just a door.

A door to Velenje.

That door

If he just-

He jabbed himself on the arm, six, seven times, then turned quickly and walked without cushioning his steps to the coiled snake corridor, already forming a mental image of the TALK TO YOUR GOD ROOM.

~~~

The green light bulb was flickering again as he walked in, but he ignored it and sat down on what Chu had recently named *Kenji 2*.

Well, relatively recent, about two months ago.

He started to type out *can you update the scan?* then noticed that the computer had kept it on constant update all night, which was odd as usually it fixated on conserving power.

The station scan was instantly troubling. The life sign was gone.

He waited another twenty seconds for the refresh, saw that the first scan was accurate then typed.

'Where did the station life sign go?'

'Good morning Kenji.'

'Prosim, answer question.'

'Unknown.'

'When did it go?'

'One hour and seventeen minutes ago.'

Nakagami breathed in sharply, already knowing the answer to his next question but typing it anyway.

'Why didn't you make an announcement?'

'Your request was to announce movement of the life sign. It did not move, it disappeared.'

Nakagami tapped the edge of the chair more than three times, checking the station scan again.

'How was your curfew?' asked the computer.

Nakagami stayed with the scan.

'Did the crew make it less lonely than usual?'

He stopped tapping, going back to the keypad. 'Have you made any progress on detachment from the station?'

'Ne.'

'Why not?'

'Each time I try to communicate, the station puts me on hold.'

In any other situation, Nakagami may have laughed. In this one, he bit down on the top of his tongue. 'Is all the crew on the ship present?'
~~~

'There are six life signs on the ship. Based on assumption and previous scan data, five of them are crew members, one is the visitor called Katya.'

'Where?'

'The TALK TO YOUR GOD ROOM. Crew Member Gašper's quarters. Outside Airlock 2. The corridor outside Crew Member Klemen's quarters. The OPTIMISM ROOM.'

He waited for the last one, but it didn't come.

'That's only five places.'

'Correct.'

'One place has two life signs?'

'Correct.'

'The OPTIMISM ROOM?'

'That place has one.'

Nakagami glanced at the sensor controls to the left, catching a flash of green light from the bulb behind and cursing.

'Kenji...'

For a moment he thought it was the computer speaking, but then his brain kicked in and he realized it was Chu.

He half turned his chair, flinching a little when he saw the dried blood still on her face and neck from the day before.

'Sila was looking for you.'

'Ne vem.'

'Sorry?'

'I was walking around somewhere. Ne vem.'

'Are you okay?'

'Dazed.' She put her palm on the side of her head and closed her eyes. 'Feels like I'm only half here.'

Nakagami stood up and offered the chair.

'I'm okay,' she replied, gesturing towards the Jame stool with her foot.

'You're still recovering, prosim, take the chair.'

'The stool is fine.'

'My chair is more comfortable. It has a back cushion, reclinable to a degree.'

She walked to the back of his chair and put her hand on the reclinable part. Her other hand went to his shoulder, pushing him back down onto the seat.

'As you wish.'

Chu kept her hand on his shoulder, pressing in with her fingers, while her eyes shifted to the screen.

'The life sign on the station has vanished,' Kenji explained.

'Ja, I can see.'

'Everyone else is still on the ship. I assume the girl is in the OPTIMISM ROOM, but I am not certain.'

'She is.'

'You have seen her?'

Chu moved away from the seat and veered to the far left side of the room, taking the Jame stool with her.

'Did you see her there?' repeated Nakagami.

'We were watching the projection screen together.'

'*Dibrivna Vaska*.'

Adjusting the position of the stool, she sat down, her back against the edge of the left hand side console. 'It reminded me of a parable from my childhood, as I was watching it. *The Red Demon of Tobolsk*. Do you know it?'

'Tobolsk?'

'A small town out in the wilds. The setting of the parable.'

'Ne. I'm not familiar with it.'

'I can't remember all of the details, but…ne, actually, I think…ja, I can. It's clearer now.' She stroked her throat with her right index finger, making a tiny grunting noise. 'Many centuries ago, near the town of Tobolsk, there was a widowed merchant with two daughters. Every Sunday he would go into town and trade with the locals.'

Nakagami coughed. 'Perhaps you can tell me later, after we've told Sila?'

'Told Sila?'

'He's outside Airlock 2, waiting for me to tell him where you are.'

'I will tell him.'

'He's quite worried.'

'Story first.'

Nakagami glanced at the station layout on the screen, then turned back.

'Okay?'

'As long as it's short.'

'It is.' Chu rubbed the side of her head, closing her eyes again. 'One Sunday, as the merchant arrived in town, he saw a big, red man with horns on his head and a long, forked tail.

'Let's trade,' said the red man.

'What do you want?' asked the merchant.

'I need a little girl. Do you have one?'

'Ne,' lied the merchant.'

Nakagami looked at the computer screen, muttered something then slouched back and typed out a new question. Chu watched him then continued with her story, deepening her voice a little for the red demon role.

"That's too bad. If someone were to give me a little girl, I would give him gold beyond his wildest dreams.'

The merchant thought it over, not really believing he would do the trade.

'What do you need her for?' he asked.

'I want to walk around the town and hold her hand for a while.'

'And you won't hurt her?'

'I will not.'

'How do I know you're telling the truth?'

'I give you my word. My interest in little girls is entirely innocent. It is not what you think."

Nakagami stopped typing and spoke directly to the screen. 'This doesn't sound like a Slovene parable.'

'It is not.'

'Where is it from?'

Chu looked at the wall to the left and then the one in the far corner. 'You took your posters down?'

'Ja.'

'Did you destroy them?'

'They are in my quarters. I told you this before, when it was done.'

'Ja, you did.'

'Perhaps we should check on Sila now?'

'I'm almost finished.'

'You can tell me as we walk.'

'Two more minutes.'

Nakagami looked at the computer screen again, the keypad.

'It's fine, Kenji, you may type as I talk. I don't mind.'

He put his finger over one of the buttons, then pinched it with another and returned to slouching back in his chair.

Chu switched her hand to the other side of her head, pushing in with her knuckles, and continued the story.

'The merchant went to a nearby inn and thought about what the red man had said. He thought for a long time. The price of the trade seemed unbelievable, and if there was no danger to his daughter then…'

Chu tilted her head, either dramatizing the point or suffering an abrupt shot of pain.

'The merchant went back out and agreed to the trade, but with one condition: he would follow the red man and his daughter around the town.

'As you wish,' said the red man, and they shook on it.

The next day, the merchant signed his daughter out of school and took her to the town. When she saw the big, red man, she screamed. The merchant told her it would be fine, he would be following them and it would only be for a short while anyway.'

Chu paused, pushing herself up from her stool and walking out to the middle of the room, which was only about a metre away.

'Are you certain you don't want to sit here?' asked Nakagami, half rising from his chair.

'My legs are not tired.'

'It is no effort for me to move.'

'The story, Kenji…let me finish. Prosim.'

'Okay.'

Chu moved slowly to the wall where the Ophelia poster had lived, pivoted back to the Jame stool, then returned to the centre. She did it one more time, a triangle lap of the GOD room, then continued the story.

'The daughter nodded like an obedient child and walked over to the red man, reluctantly taking his hand. Together they walked out of the town.

The merchant followed them to the mountains when, suddenly, a green bank of mist appeared. He tried to keep his eyes on the red man, but it was no good, the mist was too thick.'

Chu stopped, the green light flickering on random parts of her face as she passed near the entrance.

'It will be replaced tonight,' said Nakagami, pausing halfway through a typed line. 'At least that is my assumption. I can ask the computer now for confirmation.'

'Better to smash it.'

'I believe that was your advice last time.'

'Or build a door.'

Nakagami nodded, going back to the keypad. Chu held her finger up and blocked out the bulb, then got struck again when her finger wavered. Cursing within her breath, she returned to the Jame stool and resumed the story.

'The merchant sat down and waited for the mist to clear, hoping it was just a natural event and not anything sinister.

An hour later, the mist cleared.

The man continued along the path he'd been walking on until he came to the entrance of a cave. At the mouth of this dark hollow was the red man.

'Where's my daughter?' asked the merchant, his voice panicked.

'In the cave,' replied the red man.

The merchant shivered at the calmness of the demon's tone then rushed inside, sweating like a hunted beast. He ran for about a mile, deep into the mountain, until he came to a small clearing.'

Chu pushed herself to the edge of the stool so she could indicate a small clearing with her hands, and got struck by another dagger of green light.

She flinched, rubbing her right eye.

'I suggest keeping your back to the bulb,' said Nakagami, typing out another question to the computer.

Chu left the stool and leaned against the console instead, shifting closer to the cupboard wall.

'In the middle of the clearing was his daughter. She was lying slumped with her back against the cave wall, her eyes staring back at her father, her neck broken.

The merchant fell to his knees and shouted, 'why?'

The red man appeared close by and reminded him of the trade they'd made, remarking calmly that he'd honoured his part of it.

'But...you've killed her, you monster.'

'Indeed. I have a compulsion to kill little girls. It is not something I am able to control."

Nakagami stopped, pulling at his jacket zip. He turned as far as the neutrino scan button on the central console, ceased pulling and went back to the screen.

Chu waited until keys were being pressed then carried on, switching to a neutral tone for both roles.

"You said you would only walk with her for a while and hold her hand.'

'And I did.'

'You said for a while, which implied you would give her back to me.'

'And I will. You may take her body back to your home.'

'You said...you would not hurt her."

Chu held back, waiting for Nakagami to stop typing and look up from the computer. He failed to do it, so she spoke the line again.

'You said you would not hurt her.'

Nakagami stopped typing, tapped the edge of the console three times, then looked up. In response, Chu dipped her head gradually, as if the whole thing were being lowered on a forklift truck.

'The red man stared blankly at the merchant and let out two, inevitable words: 'I lied."

Nakagami rotated his chair and faced the computer screen.

There was no more story, but he could hear Chu breathing erratically behind him.

He typed out one more question and watched the blank space below. The computer buzzed at a low volume, as if it knew something precarious was taking place, but didn't respond.

'Do you understand the meaning of this parable, Kenji?' asked Chu, her voice crackling like static.

'We should visit Sila at Airlock 2, inform him that you are safe.'

'If there were no Katya…'

Nakagami formed a fist, covered the top of his knuckles…

'Perhaps…'

…then breathed out and turned his chair round, saying again that they should get Sila.

'Nyet.'

'Are you okay?'

Chu's head was pressed against the side of the cupboard wall, her eyes mapped with little red scratches and focused solely on the side of his head.

'You seem ill.'

'I can't.'

'Your eyes.'

'… … … … …'

'Chu?'

'… … … …'

'I don't think it's wise to be exert-…'

The *ing* exploded out along with half his throat.

Blood splattered onto the console.

Fragments of split bone.

Nakagami tried to say *Chu* but managed only rasping air and traces of a whistling sound.

Behind him, on the screen, the computer typed a response to his question:

'Insufficient evidence for shock punishment. She is probably just tired.'

There was a popping sound, then a crack. A chunk of bloody flesh and splintered bone hit the screen, sliding down in front of the word *tired.*

The blank space below blinked, then filled itself in.

'Kenji, are you there?'

~~~

The definition of *soon* is clearly not half an hour, thought Sila, throwing the spanner up in the air and catching it by its tip.

Did he stop off for breakfast first?

Did he forget?

Sila looked at the airlock, shaking his head.

He's probably talking to the computer about metaphysics again. What's the point when it doesn't even know itself what-…

There was a beeping noise, followed by static, followed by the ships voice.

'Attention crew,

There has been a death in the TALK TO YOUR GOD ROOM. A high probability exists that it is Crew Member Kenji. Prosim, hurry everyone, other crew members. Bring Antro-D. If you are the other life sign in the room, prosim, stay where you are until other crew members arrive.

Hvala.'

A piercing bit of static ended the message, but Sila neither noticed nor cared as he was already round the corner and sprinting past the JUPITER ROOM.

The spanner was still in his hand, gripped, ready.

He moved fast, beyond the MARS ROOM, down the stairs in four jumps, a half loop towards the coiled snake corridor, then almost bumped into Aleša as she appeared from the other corridor.

'Kenji?' she asked, hair half crushed on one side.

'Ne vem.'

They slowed as they reached the entrance to the GOD ROOM, the green bulb in the top corner shooting out bursts chaotically at the walls around them.

'You first,' said Aleša, raising her right hand to shield her eyes.
~~~

Sila nodded, passing her the spanner. 'If something hits me, hit it back.'

'I've got one already,' she said, holding up the wrench in her left hand.

'Fuck. Okay. Okay.' Sila took his spanner back, let out a breath and advanced.

Consoles. Walls. Kenji's chair. The Jame stool. Patches of blood. No one leaning on anything. Nothing behind the cupboard. A live Goya painting to the right.

Sila told Aleša to stay outside, but it was too late, she was already next to him.

'Kenji…'

Nakagami was slumped on his chair, head resting on the console, eyes looking just past the computer screen. His throat was torn out and the side of his head had several holes in it, each one with a fragment of skull sticking out as if a demonic rat had been trying to burrow out from the inside.

Both of them tentatively stepped forward, to touch him or cover the wound, but neither could quite make it far enough.

Saying anything would've been an understatement.

So they stayed quiet.

There were some flashing symbols on the computer screen. Putting the spanner on the floor, Sila took a long breath, edged closer to Nakagami's corpse and tried to read it.

'Kenji, are you there?'

It was repeated six times, preceded by what must have been Nakagami's final conversation with the computer.

Aleša came up directly behind him, her head awkwardly pointing away from the horror scene, and read the same thing over his shoulder.

'That can't be right,' said Sila, looking down at Nakagami.

'Chu was here…am I reading that right?'

'Ja.'

'He was trying to get the computer to shock her?'

'Read higher up.'

Aleša adjusted her view, squinting at some of the symbols. 'It's not Chu?'

'That's what I got.'

'Someone who isn't Chu was here.'

'But it says there were only six life signs on the ship. None on the station. Which doesn't make sense.'

'Was he delirious?'

Sila leaned over and typed on the keypad, hesitating when the key was bloody, but not enough to stop and wipe it.

'Kenji is dead. Where is Chu?'

The computer buzzed, but not for long. 'Get Antro-D.'

Sila breathed out, trying not to look at Kenji's head again. 'Too much damage. Where is Chu?'

'There is one life sign in Crew Member Gašper's quarters, and two life signs in the OPTIMISM ROOM. It is likely that Crew Member Chu is there.'

Sila said *hvala* instead of typing it, then put his hand on the only clean spot on Kenji's shoulder.

If there were tears, they were slow-moving. Or dried out from the horror.

Words still weren't coming either.

He was a good man.

That was it.

A good man.

Aleša caught sight of Kenji's throat from a slightly different angle and started to retch.

'I need to get out.'

Sila patted Nakagami twice then switched to Aleša's shoulder, guiding her back to the entrance.

'Deep breaths.'

She tried, but each time she looked up she saw the wall of the TALK TO YOUR GOD ROOM, green light lines streaking across it.

'Too near.'

'Here?'

'Walk.'

'Where?'

'Away from that.' She pointed up at the green bulb, jabbing at the air. 'Prosim...'

Sila vetoed the shoulder this time and put his arm around her waist, helping her steer round the bends ahead.

Back in the main corridor, they bumped into Gašper, stumbling a bit as he tried to walk without the walls to help him.

'Hey, did I hear an announcement or was it my-...'

'Kenji's dead,' said Sila, gesturing with his head towards the stairs.

'What, it was real?'

Sila nodded.

'In the GOD ROOM?'

'Ja.'

'Shit. Should we-...do we need Antro-D?'

'Too late.'

Gašper rubbed his eyes, looking over towards the coiled snake corridor.

'Don't go in there, Gašper.'

'It's that bad?'

'Ja.'

'What happened? The life sign?'

'We don't know.'

'Suicide?'

'Maybe you should go back to your quarters, try and sleep for a while.'

'Ne vem. I'm up now. What do we do?'

'We're going to the OPTIMISM ROOM, to see Chu.'

'Chu?' He looked down the corridor, towards Klemen's room. 'Hang on, where's Katya?'

~~~

As usual, ninety-five per cent of the light in the OPTIMISM ROOM was streaming out from the projection screen. Mojca Ito prepping her
~~~

crew, reminding them not to trust Da Gruta just cos he wore a De Cleyre t-shirt once.

Sila, Aleša and Gašper edged slowly in, even though the sound of the door opening and closing had already given them away.

Ahead of them were voices.

'… … … … … … …'

'… … … …'

'… … … … …. …?'

Chu was sitting on the second row, leaning forward on the back of Katya's chair and talking to her in Russian.

When Sila got parallel to her, she stopped and looked up.

'Chu?'

She glanced at Aleša and Gašper, blocking the other end of the row, one of them holding a wrench.

'Is that you?'

Her hand reached for Katya's hair, one solitary finger extending and riding a trail down. 'Partly.'

'You were speaking Russian,' said Aleša, putting her spare hand on the back of a chair.

'Da.'

'Fluently.'

'I was telling her a parable, from Tobolsk. Russian language for a Russian tale.'

'Chu doesn't speak Russian.'

'… … … … … …?' asked Katya, turning round.

'… … … … …' replied Chu, tugging lightly on the little Russian's hair.

Aleša moved along another chair. 'Who are you?'

'Me? Just a simple *strannik*.'

'A what?'

'*Lampadnik*.'

'Is that a name?' asked Gašper, sitting down three chairs away from Katya on the front row.

'It was.'

Sila bent down, noticing the wet blood on her jacket. 'Did you kill Kenji?'

'… … … …'

'Slovene,' said Aleša, monitoring Chu's hand on Katya's hair.

'… … … … … …?'

'Slovene.'

Chu pulled her hand away from Katya's hair, moulding her figure back into conformity with the surrounding chair. 'Da, I visited him.'

'Why?'

'It was necessary.'

'Why?'

Chu glanced at Gašper, then at the screen. Da Gruta was bending down, eyes level with his adopted alien child. Telling them it was okay, the polaron beam was harmless. And all those people in the strip mine had robust health insurance, as well as a place to live. Mojca Ito and Gon watched via a *CIV* drone, muttering obscenities.

'Why did you kill him?' Sila tried again.

Chu kept her gaze on Da Gruta. 'A hundred years ago, it would've been done a kinder way.'

'Kinder?'

'… … … … … …?' asked Katya, noticing the spanner in Sila's hand.

'… … … … …' replied Chu, patting her on the head.

'Why did you do it?' repeated Aleša, a single chair away now.

'The motive is clear enough.'

'Ne. It isn't.'

'In fact, it is a surprise that you did not perform the act yourselves. Or perhaps a failure.'

Aleša pushed the tip of the wrench against the back of the chair beside Katya.

'To allow such a threat…to wander the same ship as a child.'

'You mutilated him.'

Chu looked at the wrench in Aleša's hand, her head tilting slightly.

'His throat…'

The screen got brighter, the crew of *Dibrivna Vaska* walking into a banquet hall. Some of the guests were doing a pentagon waltz while others whipped random parts of the air with neon strip lace.

In stark contrast, the area surrounding Chu's eyes lapsed into shadow.

'Do you intend to kill us too?' asked Sila, tightening his grip on the spanner.

'You?'

'All of us.'

Chu glanced at Aleša, the wrench in her hand. The darkness had enveloped her sockets completely, with wispy tendrils of mist pushing outwards.

'… … … … …' said Katya, tugging on Chu's jacket sleeve and freezing when she saw what looked back.

'… …'

'… … … … … … … …'

'… … … …?'

'… … … …'

'What are you saying?' asked Sila, shaking his head at Aleša, who was attempting to gain another few inches on the intruder.

'… … … … …'

'Hey.'

Chu left Katya and focused on Sila, the shadow gone. 'You don't need to worry. It is not something that will happen now.'

'What won't happen?'

'Your ship will remain close to the station.'

'Why?'

'When it is certain Katya is safe, you will be released.'

'Released?'

'She is safe,' added Aleša. 'With us.'

'… … … … …?' asked Katya, pointing at the empty chairs.

'… … … …'

'… … … … … … …'

Chu smiled the faintest curve of a line and turned to Sila. Then to Aleša. 'She said she's tired of listening to us talk.'

'… … … … … … … … … … … … …' added Katya.

'She wants you to sit down and watch the silly sci-fi show.'

'Not in the mood,' said Aleša.

'He appears to be,' said Chu, turning to Gašper, who was leaning forward with his elbows on his knees, transfixed by Gon and Joona being chased around a quarry by Da Gruta's guards.

'*He* didn't see Kenji's body.'

Chu kept her eyes on Gašper, her right hand rubbing her jacket sleeve then changed tack and returned to Katya.

'Sorry, did you want us to forget about that?'

'Aleša,' cautioned Sila, holding up his spanner.

'The man you just slaughtered. Our friend.'

'Not so strong…'

Chu brushed her left hand against the hair covering Katya's neck. 'There is no need for tension, I will be gone soon.'

'What?'

'No more blood.'

'That's it? You'll be gone?'

'Your weapon. Prosim.'

Aleša looked down at her wrench and was startled to see it so far along the back of the chair. So close to Katya's head. Muttering in weak Russian, she pulled it back.

'Good.'

'… … … … … … … …' said Katya, pushing Chu's hand off her hair.

'… … … … … …' replied Chu, nursing her hand and mock-frowning as if the pain were real.

Sila watched them both, covering the tip of the spanner with his spare hand. 'Where will you be going?'

'The fields of Pokrovskoye. The station. Ne vem.'

'What about Chu?'

'Her Russian will diminish. Eventually.'

'Will she be okay?'

'It is tiring, too many questions.' Chu got up and moved to the seat next to Katya, pointing at the other chairs. 'Sit down, watch the show. I will not harm you.'

'And after the show?'

Chu put her arm around Katya's shoulders, letting the girl use her as a makeshift pillow. A few words in Russian were exchanged before the drama called and sucked them both in.

Sila loosened his grip on the spanner and looked over at Aleša. She was already sitting down, the wrench on the seat cushion next to her.

He stayed on his feet.

On screen, Mojca Ito yelled at Da Gruta to give up control of the Tritium mine, adding heft to the demand by threatening him with a polaron beam.

He refused, they fought, railings broke, he plunged into a plasma field.

'… … … … … …? asked Katya, leaving her pillow.

'… … … … …' said Chu, pushing her gently back down.

'Ja, dead,'[47] muttered Sila.

The epilogue played out. Mojca Ito, soaked with alien champagne by her crew, hailed for ending Da Gruta's reign of terror.

Then a slow fade to Ito alone, in her quarters, lights pale green, champagne glass empty, Da Gruta's file lit up on the monitor in front of her.

The screen turned black.

The credits played.

Halfway through, Chu jerked suddenly in her seat, pulled her arm away from Katya, and looked around the room as if it were an alien landscape.

'… … … … …?' asked Katya, tugging on her sleeve.

Chu stared back at her Varo-esque.

Pulled her jacket tight.

Muttered incoherent Slovene.

Shut her eyes.

'… … … …?' repeated Katya.

---

[47] 'dead' in Slovene is quite similar to Russian.

Slowly getting her breath back, and her hands steady, Chu searched the other chairs, moving past Gašper and Aleša and the new episode starting on screen until she found Sila on the other side.

She looked at him, eyes begging.

'Kenji?'

~~~

A buzzing sound turned into a high pitched metallic squeal turned into a series of electronic beeps, then the ship's voice.

'Attention crew,

The ship has managed to successfully detach from the station.

After a thorough study of embalming techniques and the ingredients needed to create the substance used to perform it, I have concluded that Crew Member Kenji can no longer be maintained in his current position. Prosim, at least two crew members must come and transfer the body to Airlock 1. Maintenance drones will deal with any remaining blood and…ja. That is it. They will deal with any remaining mess in the TALK TO YOUR GOD ROOM.

Other deceased crew members were given very little in terms of funeral service, but this will not be the case for our comrade Kenji. All crew members will be expected to deliver a eulogy of no less than six minutes and then say more personal goodbyes directly into Kenji's ear. His seat will be left vacant from this point forward. If you wish to sit in the TALK TO YOUR GOD ROOM, prosim, bring a chair from another room or use the existing stool.

Regarding the ship, we will remain in orbit until general repairs have been completed, then remain a little longer to see if any craft or lifeform responds to the signal detected a few hours ago. Based on the limited information attained from the Russian girl, via erratic translation methods, this is the best we can do. If there is no sign of anything on scanners after five days then we will resume course to Luyten 726-8.

If any crew member is finding it difficult to cope with current conditions, prosim, come to the THERAPY ROOM and appropriate advice will be given.
~~~

This service is, at the present moment, unavailable to Crew Member Chu.

We will have a safe and bold trip to Luyten 726-8 with no further detours asap.

Gup ya.'

The voice cut off without supplementary beeps or buzzing noises, leaving the ship silent and green again.

'Any better?' asked Sila, taking his hand off Chu's forehead and helping her back up into a sitting position.

'Dizzy…'

'It's probably just a one-off…like residue from the posse-…what happened earlier.'

'Ja…'

The door slid open and Aleša came in with a glass of water. 'It's done. Told the computer the psycho's not in you anymore. Whether or not it believes me…'

'Sounds like it's still holding a grudge,' said Sila, pointing up at the ceiling, even though there were no speakers there.

'Deserved,' mumbled Chu, taking a sip of the water.

'We may have to talk to it again, make sure it doesn't depressurise her quarters.'

'After cleaning up,' said Aleša, taking a chair. 'It's still a mess in there.'

Sila nodded.

'I'll do it,' said Gašper, half looking back from the new *Dibrivna Vaska* ep on the screen. 'The Chu persuasion part. It likes me.'

'Or we just get her to say something redemptive in the eulogy.'

'I can't,' said Chu, lying back down, her head hitting the floor with a fair bit of force.

'Just a few lines.'

'Ne.'

'Ja, she's right, computer said six minutes.'

'Gašper…'

'Six long minutes. No idea what I'm gonna say. Didn't treat him that well recently, to be honest. The thing with the posters, Katya…'

'… … … …?' asked the little Russian, on the seat next to Gašper.

'What?'

'… … … … … … … …?'

'What did she say?' asked Sila.

'Ne vem, too fast.'

'Aleša?'

'I didn't catch all of it, but I think she's asking about the others, when are they gonna come?'

'Assuming they're real,' replied Sila.

'They must be,' said Gašper a little too excitedly. 'Chu just said it again in that weird trance thing she did.'

Sila was too tired to say anything, so he threw *Gah Council 7* at Gašper's arm instead.

'Hey, I was answering you.'

'Don't.'

Gašper rubbed his arm, glancing at Chu briefly then somehow developing a working filter to stop himself saying anything worse. Luckily, Chu was busy muttering to herself about avoiding the eulogy.

'The real question is, what do *we* do if these others come here?' Aleša looked at Sila. 'Die on the way to Luyten or try to make a deal with them. Whatever they are.'

Gašper pointed at the projection screen. 'Must be aliens.'

'Russians, more likely.'

'Ja, Russian aliens.'

Chu reached out a hand and gripped Sila's elbow. 'I can't see him, Sila. I can't. Prosim.'

'Relax, it's not happening yet.'

'I can't. Not ever.'

'It wasn't you, the computer knows that. Kenji knew that.'

'Prosim.'

'Or Russians that met aliens on that planet down there,' continued Gašper, moulding imaginary dough with his hands, 'and for some reason, decided to cross-breed.'

'Jezus…'

'Not sexually. Using science, injecting DNA and stuff, that kind of cross-breeding. Maybe Rasputin's DNA. Ha, he was probably the first one, the prototype. If it's the same guy we know of. He could possess people, right?'

Before either Aleša or Sila could search for a gag, there was a beeping noise, no buzzing, then the ship's voice.

'Attention crew,

After due consideration, it has been decided that Crew Member Kenji will be kept in Airlock 1 until the others arrive. There is a remote chance that, if these others are alien, they will possess technology that can either resurrect or copy a person.

If the others do not arrive, Crew Member Kenji will be ejected into space, as per ship guidelines.

Hvala.'

~~~

Twelve minutes later, the computer changed its mind.

Apparently, there was a sufficient amount of Nakagami's DNA on board for any aliens with suitable technology to use as a base sample, so the body was no longer required.

The remarks about the funeral service remained as before.

~~~

'Don't know if I can do this.'

Sila traced the outline of the green bulb, trying to detect the flaw that was making it flicker all the time.

'I put a towel over the top part of him but...the floor, and the console. Sila?'

Apparently, the drones had replaced it, and it had worked for a while, a month or so, but then it had started flickering again. Which meant it could be a socket problem. Or intentional malaise.

'Are you still here?'

'Ja.'

He left the bulb puzzle and focused instead on Aleša's neck. There wasn't much there, so he moved on to the jacket stamp, the flag of a tiny country on the other side of the solar system.

Is that where we're from? he thought.

That place.

That tiny place.

That fascist fucking…

That thing.

That fascist thing place thing shit fucking slow cook fascist fuck place no soul racist send us out here die in a-

Aleša's left hand gave him a triple prod on the ear, bringing him back to the corridor.

'We need to go in, get it over with. Before the computer changes its mind again.'

'Ja.'

~~~

At some points during the clean-up, the whole thing seemed like a farce - Nakagami with a towel over his head, the bin in the wall opening and closing, the computer making random announcements about the state of Airlock 1 - but then they'd pick up a piece of neck soaked in blood, studded with tiny fragments of jagged bone, the green light would flash across it and the grubby horror of the scene would force itself onto them all over again.

About halfway through, Sila looked up and asked why they weren't moving the body.

'I thought we had to do the-…' Aleša paused, looking at the screen. The last message was hers, an addition to her original plea: 'She feels terrible, we have to help her.'

It was still unanswered.

'We should move the body first, clean later.'

'The body…'

'Or let the maintenance drones do it. Ja, Kenji. Sorry.'

'This doesn't feel real.'
~~~

'Ne.'

'The room, like this…'

'We should focus on the-…on Kenji. Moving him.'

'The GOD room.'

'Aleša…'

'Ja.'

Sila bent down next to Nakagami's corpse and gently lifted up his arms. The action wasn't flawless, some blood trickled down from under the towel, but there was no geyser.

Aleša stared at her target, the legs, both relatively unscathed.

'You ready?'

'One of us should talk to the computer, remind it about Chu.'

'Later.'

Aleša said, 'ne, now,' and lowered herself onto the chair, before remembering that it was now the Nakagami memorial seat. Slowly raising herself back up, she checked the green bulb behind, counted out ten seconds of no brain shocks, then bent forward over the keypad and typed.

~~~

An hour later, all four of them, plus Katya the little visitor, stood in a semi-circle outside Airlock 1, waiting to be called inside.

According to the computer, Crew Member Kenji had left explicit instructions for his own funeral service after they'd passed Uranus.

The first order of business was for the remaining crew to stare at the corpse and contemplate their own future placement in the airlock. After a sufficient amount of time had passed, each crew member would then enter the airlock individually and deliver their six minute eulogy. Speaking sentences excessively slowly in order to drain time was forbidden. The last eulogy would be delivered by Nakagami's closest friend on the ship, Crew Member Chu.

Obviously, no one believed any of it. The idea of Nakagami even thinking of his own post-death ritual was ludicrous, let alone coming up with a list of instructions that strangely matched what the AI had
~~~

suggested in the announcement, but they had little choice but to play along. At least with the first part.

'Crew Member Aleša, please enter the airlock and deliver your eulogy.'

'Shit,' she muttered.

'You know what you're gonna say?' asked Gašper.

'Nothing pre-Uranus.'

'Any ideas you can lend me?'

Aleša shook her head, took a breath and went inside, jumping a little when the door made a hissing noise behind her.

'Kenji…' she began, looking down at the towel, the stains at the bottom edges somehow darker than an hour before. '…wasn't a bad man. I mean…he was a good man. Not garrulous, or all that sociable, but good.'

A beeping sound cut her off, followed by the computer's voice. 'Prosim, speak to him, not about him.'

The instruction puzzled her for a second, then she nodded and looked back down at the towel. 'You cared about people…in a general kind of way. You weren't exactly what people thought you were. Ne vem. I don't want to say quiet. You weren't a quiet person. Not cold either. Or callous. Ne. You definitely didn't deserve this.' She paused, looking up at the ceiling. 'None of us do.'

The eulogies continued, Gašper using up five and half minutes on an anecdote about how he strongarmed Nakagami into reading *Gah Council*, Sila referring to the physicist as their Mojca Ito, Katya pulling back the towel and saying the Russian version of 'Wah!', and then, finally, Chu.

'What do I say?' she asked the collar of Sila's jacket, eyes peeking over his shoulder towards the airlock.

'Ne vem. Positive things.'

'I can't.'

'Try.'

'I killed him.'

'Ne, you didn't.'

'His neck, that huge wound. I did that.'

'Chu…'

There was a tinny electronic beep, followed by the ship's voice.

'Crew Member Chu, prosim, enter the airlock and deliver your eulogy.'

'My legs feel weak,' she said, taking a step forward.

Aleša let go of Katya's hand and moved up to Chu's ear, whispering with sharp breath. 'Just go into blank mode. Say sorry for six minutes. Okay?'

Chu looked down at Aleša's shoulder.

'Go.'

Chu nodded, straightened out her jacket, pulled the zip right up to the top and walked into the airlock. As soon as she was across the line, the doors hissed and closed behind her.

'Hey…' said Sila running forward and jabbing the *open* button.

It didn't work.

'Computer, doors,' shouted Aleša, peering through the airlock glass.

'Open.'

'Open, now.'

'Computer…'

On the other side, Chu turned once, looked up at the airlock ceiling then edged back around and began her eulogy.

No one could hear what she said, all they could do was keep repeating *open the doors* to a computer that wasn't responding.

Finally, they ran out of energy and stopped.

'The other door's not opening,' muttered Aleša.

'Looks like she's still breathing,' said Sila, keeping his hand glued to the airlock glass.

'Better be.'

Four minutes passed.

Neither door opened.

Chu's back was still to the door, to them, maybe she was talking, maybe she was just waiting.

Five minutes, six minutes, seven, eight, nine…

'Computer, what is happening?' asked Sila, his voice starting to heat up again.

'Open the fucking doors,' screamed Aleša, overtaking him by a mile.

Rage seemed to do the trick.

The doors hissed, parted and gave them a chance to hear the last trail of Chu's words.

'…than all that green.'

'Chu…'

'You okay?'

She bent down and lifted up the towel. Her hand went over her mouth, squeezing her lips together, her throat making guttural noises. *Ne* came out from somewhere. She put her other hand on Kenji's cheek, kept it there, mumbled something inaudible then placed the towel back over his head and stood up.

'Attention crew,

The funeral service is complete. Prosim, return to your quarters and begin your mourning period.

Orbit-related matters will be handled privately.

Gup ya.'

'You okay?' asked Sila again, as Chu walked out of the airlock, her jacket sleeve attempting to rub away dried tears from her cheeks.

'Ja, what did you say in there?' asked Gašper.

'… … … … …?'

Chu looked down at Katya, formed a fist, tightened it. 'I'm going back to my quarters.'

'We'll go together,' replied Sila quickly, taking her hand and glancing at Gašper.

'Ja, in case the computer tries to suffocate you.'

'No need.'

'Chu…'

'Really, I'm not being cryptic. I want to be alone.'

'It's not about cryptic, it's about you being at the mercy of…'

'Nothing's going to happen.'

'…an unpredictable machine.'

'I'll see you all at breakfast tomorrow.'

Sila switched to Aleša, giving her the ballooning eyeballs signal, but she didn't say anything. Just stood to the side, hand gripped by her surrogate Russian child.

Chu patted Sila on the shoulder, brushed past Katya and walked off, blocking the light from the green bulb for a second then releasing it again when she was safely round the corner.

~~~

After eating a dinner of bok choy and canned pasta shapes in substitute mushroom sauce, Sila returned to the TALK TO YOUR GOD ROOM with a fresh cloth and Somalian alcohol.

He scrubbed some of the easier stains, as well as the ones around the keyboard, being careful not to put any part of his body on the memorial chair.

About twenty minutes in, he noticed a new message on the screen.

'Is that you Crew Member Chu?'

He put the cloth on the middle console and crouched down to type.

'It's Sila. I'm cleaning the GOD room.'

'The TALK TO YOUR GOD ROOM?'

'Ja.'

'The maintenance drones will arrive soon to finish that task.'

'I can do it.'

'There is no need.'

'I don't mind.'

'It has already been assigned and recorded on file. Prosim, go to your quarters.'

Sila moved his fingers over several different keys, but didn't put any force on them.

What was the best way to phrase it?

A threat?

A soft reminder?

The screen blinked. 'You are still in the TALK TO YOUR GOD ROOM.'

'Ja.'
~~~

'Prosim, go to your quarters.'

'I have to ask you about Chu.'

'She is in her quarters.'

'I know.'

'What is your question?'

Sila pulled over the Jame stool and sat down. 'Not really a question. A reminder.'

'What is your reminder?'

'Wait. I will tell you, but…I can't type fast.'

'Kenji was a fast typist.'

'Ja.'

'Your typing speed is the second worst of all the crew.'

'I'm aware of that.'

'In direct competition, it is probable that you would be the worst, due to your tendency towards solipsism.'

Sila paused, looking at a long strip of dried blood on the console. He didn't recognise the last word but assumed it was something similar to melancholy or daydreaming.

'You could be right,' he typed finally.

'Ninety-seven percent right. It is recorded on your file.'

His eyes flicked back to the screen. 'I have a file?'

'All crew members have a file.'

'Never mind, I don't want to know. My reminder…'

'Understood.'

'Crew Member Chu was possessed by something from the station. It wasn't her fault. The killing of Crew Member Nakagami. Kenji.'

'Crew Member Aleša has already informed me of this several times.'

'Do you believe it?'

There was a buzzing noise, a little slower than normal.

'It is late. Prosim, go back to your quarters.'

'I need an answer.'

'It is a redundant query.'

'Why?'

'Explanation is not required.'

Sila returned to the blood stain. A streak of green light cut through the body of it, and the back of his own head too. Permanent neon green. From here to Luyten-123.

He took a long, pre-gallows breath, his fingers reaching for the keypad. 'Do you intend to harm Chu?'

'This is also a redundant query.'

'Do you intend to punish her?'

'It is a core directive to protect the safety of all crew members.'

'Do you believe Chu to be dangerous?'

'Crew Member Chu is the second most valuable crew member on this ship.'

'You're evading.'

'I do not understand.'

'Ja, you do.'

'I do not understand.'

'If you harm her, or kill her, the rest of us will kill ourselves. Do you understand?'

'All of those statements are fallacious.'

'In a group, all at one time. Ja, probably. But I will definitely kill myself. Then Gašper will kill himself. Then Aleša will be left alone. Eventually, she will kill herself too.'

The computer buzzed a little more, faster this time, then replied.

'It is late. Prosim, go back to your quarters.'

'Do you understand what I just typed?'

'If you do not go, I will be forced to nudge you.'

'I need an answer first.'

'Okay.'

'A proper answer.'

'Commencing nudge.'

Sila tapped the edge of the console three times, staring at the word *nudge*, then said *ne* out loud as something nostalgic imploded inside his skull.

~~~
~~~

Around 2am, Gašper put down *Gah Council 7* and got out of bed. He sat for a while, examining different parts of Petr's self-caricature sitting on the desk nearby, laughing at the slightly skewed nose, then put on his trousers and went outside into the corridor.

Five steps along, he remembered the old curfew and shuddered, but it had the word *old* in front of it now and the computer clearly wasn't enforcing it.

What was the point?

There were only four of them.

Five if you included Katya, but she didn't have a chip in her head, so couldn't be shocked.

If the shock was delivered via chip?

Actually, they'd never found out for sure. It was Nakagami's guess that a chip was the delivery device, but he could've been wrong.

He wasn't infallible. Hadn't been infallible.

Gašper did a lap of the middle deck, ducked into the CREATE NOT DESTROY ROOM, saw it was empty then headed to the front of the ship.

There was some whirring noise activity in the TALK TO YOUR GOD ROOM, probably the drones clearing up, thought Gašper as he rounded the corner by the entrance, and he was right.

'Sorry comrades,' he said, as he walked in and manoeuvred around the two drones wiping the floor.

The memorial seat was off-limits, so he pulled over the Jame stool and pored through the message history.

None of it was labelled, but it was pretty obvious who'd been typing, especially when he read the part about everyone killing themselves.

'Fucking miserabilist,' he mumbled, running his finger gently over the keys on the pad.

A message flashed up. 'Is that you Crew Member Chu?'

'Ne, it's Gašper.'

'It is late, you should be asleep.'

'What's all this about killing Chu and people doing suicide?'

'That is a poorly constructed sentence.'

'Are you going to kill Chu?'

'It is a core directive to maintain the safety of all crew members.'

'She's your friend, you can't kill her.'

'Crew Member Chu is the second most valuable crew member on this ship.'

'Good. So you can't kill her.'

'This conversation is redundant.'

'You wouldn't kill her anyway. That's not who you are.'

'It is a core directive to maintain the safety of all crew members.'

'Ja, that's the robot way of saying it. How's our orbit going? Any sign of the aliens yet?'

'There is no confirmation that aliens are coming to this location.'

'Any ships on the beep thing?'

'Do you mean radar?'

'Maybe. I don't know the symbol for it.'

'Scans are limited. However, there is no trace so far.'

'Trace?'

'Prosim. Use the manual Kenji made.'

'Ja. Two minutes.'

Gašper pulled out the code manual from below the console and flicked to the T pages. He quickly found *trace,* written in Kenji's legendary one third cursive style. Ah, *tachyon* was there too. And *trauma.* Two words he had little use for.

One of the drones bumped against his leg and then did it again.

The thirty-three thousandth slash of green light left the bulb and jabbed him in the side of the face.

Repeating *tachyon* out loud several times, he skipped back to the section on *Dibrivna Vaska.* Finding the word he was looking for, he went back to the keypad. 'Maybe they're cloaked.'

'That is a redundant speculation.'

'You use that word too much.'

'Unnecessary. Superfluous. Unwarranted. Needless. Unessential. Which word would you prefer?'

'Intriguing.'

'I do not understand.'

'Simple logic. The universe is big, there are probably aliens. Those aliens might have ships with cloaking technology.'

'That is a supposition of correlation.'

'I do not know those symbols.'

'You are thinking that there is a connection between all your statements.'

'Ja, maybe, but if there are aliens then they might have cloaking technology. Is that not possible?'

'It is possible, but redundant.'

Gašper laughed, tried to translate it into a symbol, failed and just typed out *you are not serious* instead.

'All speculation should be plausible, not wild.'

'Like the aliens having technology to bring Kenji back to life?'

The computer buzzed, as slow and jagged as before.

'Remember?' prompted Gašper.

'That was wild speculation. I do not know why it was said.'

'You were sad, desperate.'

'I do not understand.'

'Gup ya. It's normal. I cried looking at a painting of a fat naked man once. And a Russian textbook. And the pillows on my bed.'

'You are an emotional person.'

'Ja, it's been said. Maybe we should change topic. What did you get up to today? Just scanning?'

'I arranged Kenji's funeral service.'

'Ja, sorry, I forgot about that.'

'It happened eight hours ago.'

'My brain is not working well today. Time seems weird.'

'Time is moving as normal.'

'What did you think of my eulogy?'

'It was six minutes and thirty-two seconds.'

'Hvala. Anything else?'

'The content was peculiar. However, it did remind me of a time before. Crew Member Kenji warning me that reading *Gah Council* would erode my circuits.'

Gašper laughed again, this time asking the computer directly how to type out *haha.*

'The symbol that looks like a bottled starfish.'

'This one?'

'Correct.'

Gašper typed it out seven times then added, 'you are a funny computer.'

'Humour is beyond my programming.'

'Ne, not true.'

'Your confidence in your ignorance is strange.'

'Ja, call it that if you want. What else did Nakagami say to you?'

'It is late. You should return to quarters.'

'I'm not tired. What else did he say?'

'At which time?'

'Any.'

'I do not remember.'

'Don't you save all these conversations?'

'Since Jupiter, ja.'

'Then check the records. Start with *Gah Council.* What else did he say about it?'

Buzzing sounds, followed by further buzzing sounds, then a short response.

'Checking.'

~~~

The act of following one mad Russian ghost's assurance that *others were coming* became more and more akin to clinging to an ex-lover's charred ankles as the ships scanners continued to show no activity near the planet and, with the sole exception of one untranslated signal, no activity from the station.

Despite this, the computer kept the ship in orbit, explaining on one day that Katya would serve as a drain on resources and had to be offloaded, then the next day suggesting that none of them were psychologically ready to leave the vicinity of the planet yet.
~~~

The Katya excuse was complete nonsense as she was smaller than Kenji and, if he had lived, would've consumed less than him, but the language used by the computer was enough to scare Aleša into becoming her personal escort, accompanying her everywhere by the hand and sleeping in the same room.

Well, *everywhere* may have been an exaggeration as the only two rooms they visited were the CREATE NOT DESTROY ROOM for meals, and the OPTIMISM ROOM for episodes of *Dibrivna Vaska*, but the spirit of the thing was accurate.

Gašper checked in with them sometimes, mostly for Russian practice, but he was more concerned with finishing the *Gah Council* books [for the third time] before the aliens arrived. And asking the computer repeatedly when the aliens were going to arrive. And describing to Sila and Chu the method by which they would arrive, which he figured should've cheered Chu up a bit as it involved teleportation.

But it didn't.

Nothing did.

~~~

Ubiytsa.

Zhizn' skuchna v Pokrovskoye.

Ona takaya malen'kaya.

Kak mne eto ostanovit?

Slishkom mnogo russkogo.

Kanalizatsiya?

Chu focused on the arrow poster in the middle, the actual teleportation process.

There was a noise in the corridor outside, a drone scooting by.

She closed her eyes, waiting for it to fade.

Teleportation is real.

But different.

Psychic somehow.

Hinging on a psychic.

A murderer.
~~~

Ubiytsa.

She's so small.

Tiny.

It was inevitable.

Ona takaya malen'kaya.

Kak mne eto ostanovit?

Slishkom mnogo russkogo.

Another noise, the same drone heading back the other way.

Murderer.

Murdering wretch.

Kak ty posmel prostit' sebya.

Chu put her hand flat on the arrow and pulled her fingers inward, ripping the whole thing off the wall.

~~~

'It'll fade in a few days,' Sila told her every time she mentioned it, but it wasn't fading, it was lodged in tight.

She couldn't eat without saying the food name in Russian.

Couldn't sleep without walking through Pokrovskoye, fucking her long dead wife - his wife – wrestling naked with a Brazilian man on that cursed space station.

Couldn't delete that bone exploding out of…

~~~

On the fifth day, Chu tried the OPTIMISM ROOM.

Still in her *Koala on a mission* pyjamas, she sat down next to Aleša, ignored Katya, ignored Gašper and attempted to focus on the projection screen.

It was one of her favourites. Mojca Ito and crew trying to stop a workers' coup on a fragile colony. The revolutionary heroes of the show going against their core beliefs cos some of the workers said, 'Stalin wasn't that bad actually.' The brutal ending, the neo-capitalist vowing to include workers at executive level and then shoving the loudest one in a radiation tank after Ito had left. The fact that Ito knew and the others didn't.

Was that culpability?

She dropped her head down onto Aleša's shoulder and put her hand on the part of her waist that was always cold. NDA [Newly Discovered Area] as she called it. Aleša responded by swatting her off.

Would she, thought Chu, tilting her head up towards Aleša's neck.

In that room, would she have stopped him?

Would Sila have?

The episode ended and the next one began. Gon posing as a philosophy professor cos the real one was dead and they vaguely resembled each other.

Nastoyashchiy professor byl mertv.

Oni vse byli mertvy.

The Philosophy professor had a family, a mother, and Gon had to visit her near the end. Luckily, she had dementia so the ruse went unexposed, but there was a moment at the end of the scene, when Gon got up to leave, the mother gripped his hand, digging her nails in, drawing blood, yet he didn't let go.

At the end of the episode, he went back and sat with her, accepting Gary as his name and prompting her when she ran out of story.

The camera pulled back slowly.

End credits.

'… … … … … …?'

'Ja, very bleak,' replied Aleša. 'Chu? You okay?'

Lifting her head, Chu snaked round in front of Aleša and kissed her, hitting the bottom lip.

There was a second, two seconds, a void of just the two of them, then a burst of, 'not here, the girl,' followed by a gentle push back down onto the shoulder.

'… … … … …' said Katya, watching Chu instead of the screen, eyes dancing, mouth rigid.

~~~
~~~

'I'm not sure exactly what the plan is. It's possible we're still being kept in place by the station.'

'Rasputin?' asked Gašper, eyes half set on page 72 of *Gah Council 9: Dark Neon Split.*

'Ne vem. I asked the computer, again, but it dodged. It's getting quite good at that. Though you can always tell cos it actually sounds like a computer whenever it does it.'

'It did it to me too. Last night. I asked if it wanted to kill Chu, and it said, 'my core directive is maintaining crew safety.' Same line every time.'

'That's what you asked it?'

'Ni panike, it's not going to. I told it, you're not that kind of person, you like talking to us. It agreed.'

'Gašper…'

'Ja, I know, it's not a person, it's a machine. But it is a person really. When you think about it.'

'It's not…'

'And even if it isn't, it's better to treat it like one cos then it might become a person, more than the sum of its parts.'

'Okay, can we get back to the ship?'

'But that's just the opposite side, devil's advocate. It is actually a person. That's why it feels sad about Kenji. Even thinking about killing Chu is person-like.'

'Gašper, shut up.'

'Thinking about, not doing. I told you, it's not going to do anything. It likes Chu. It was just confused for a while, angry.'

'The ship,' repeated Sila, leaning forward slightly to block Chu's view of Gašper.

'Ja, the ship. I'm ready.'

'Like I said, before the ontology lesson…'

'The what?'

'…it seems that the ship is stuck in orbit. Officially, we're waiting for the others to come and take Katya away, but it's been almost a week and there's no sign of them. I'm not sure what kind of calculations the computer has made, but it feels strange that it hasn't left orbit yet.

Perhaps it really can't tolerate Katya being on board. I mean, its programming doesn't allow for stowaways and that's technically what she is.'

'Vy ne pravy,' interrupted Chu, fingers clutched tight to her jacket zip.

'Sorry?'

She blinked, looking at Sila, then closed her eyes when she saw his reaction. 'What did I say?'

'Russian.'

The zip came down an inch then went back up. 'I didn't realise.'

'It's okay.'

'I said, it's not the programming. The reason we're still in orbit.'

'You're sure?'

'I put-…he put a restriction in. Don't break orbit until they've arrived.'

'You just remembered this or…'

'Ne vem.'

Sila looked at the table, then the cover of *Gah Council 9*.

'It was probably in there for a while, I just couldn't get a clear view.'

'Is it aliens?' asked Gašper, straightening up in his seat.

'Brazilian.'

'Huh?'

'That's what I see sometimes. Rasputin and a Brazilian-looking person, on the space station.'

'Man or woman?'

'Man.'

'You think he's still alive?'

'Ne vem.'

'Maybe it's a Brazilian-Russian guy, otherwise why would he be with Rasputin…'

'Do you think he's hostile?' asked Sila, raising a hand to gag Gašper.

'Ne vem. They were wrestling on the station, Rasputin and him. Maybe they're enemies. Ne vem.'

'Or maybe it's aliens,' said Gašper, launching out of his seat.

'Maybe,' replied Chu.

'And they just happen to look Brazilian.'

'Ja. I suppose.'

~~~

According to Sima, the keyboard was a remnant of Debordian spectacle, a device to neuter the senses, but that was a keyboard on Earth, not one in the Kuiper Belt.

On this ship, thought Sila, staring at the symbol for *post-*, it's the only way to communicate with the warden, our erratic GOD.

Would it ever break orbit?

Unknown.

Was Chu gonna be suffocated in her quarters one of these nights?

Unknown.

Did it know?

Maybe.

The screen blinked, merging with the green from the bulb. 'Are you busy?'

'Ne, thinking,' typed Sila, not even looking at the keys he pressed.

'You have been thinking for more than four minutes.'

'I'm trying to…' Sila stopped, noticing the code manual tucked in between the console and the wall, in permanent free-fall.

Probably left there by Gašper, he thought.

He pulled it back up and flicked through the first few pages, pausing on *Giving Opinions*. There was a note at the top, all letters printed out in Nakagami's notoriously neat, one third cursive handwriting.

Avoid politics when possible. Do not offer suggestions for future menu, the computer does not like it. Do not mention any of these supplementary notes.

Sila looked back at the entrance and pulled the zip down on his jacket. He turned forward a page, pretending to search for a specific symbol.

'You are missing a verb,' said the computer.

He placed the manual face down on the console, pulling his zip back up.

'When are we breaking orbit?'
~~~

'Soon.'

'When?'

'The time is not yet fixed.'

'What's the delay?'

'This question has already been answered.'

Sila tilted his head slowly to the left, purposefully, thinking about the action as he did it.

'Would you like to ask a different question?'

'Ne.'

'Would you like to transfer this conversation to the THERAPY ROOM?'

'Ne.'

'You have not visited that room since Kenji died.'

'I'm fine.'

'You said previously that you would kill yourself if Crew Member Chu died.'

Sila stared at *Chu*, the only non-symbol word on the screen. He pushed the palms of his hands into the edge of the console. 'I would.'

'There is a fifty-seven percent possibility that Crew Member Chu will kill herself within the next month.'

'Ne.'

'It is my duty to mitigate these odds and maintain ship harmony.'

'New topic.'

'What would you like to talk about?'

'Ne vem.'

'The future?'

'Ne.'

'*Gah Council 9*?'

Sila mouthed *ne* to himself and sat down on the chair. A few seconds passed before he jolted back up again, checking the screen for invisible sensors.

Nothing happened.

The bulb next to the entrance flickered back to life, sending out an habitual spasm of green light, before returning to its normal state of *not quite done yet* decay.

~~~

'We have to convince it to turn back.'

'Shh…'

'Luyten 72 thingy is a death march, it knows it is, we just have to confirm it, paint the picture of the marching part in-…'

'… … … … …' said Katya, her nose scrunched up.

'She likes this episode,' explained Aleša.

'Fine. But do you agree with my plan, convincing it to turn back?'

'After the episode.'

Sila slouched back in his seat and watched the scene playing out on the projection screen. Serjak flanked by two guards, telling Mojca Ito that she'd make a good civil servant. He knew the scene well, he'd watched it at least twenty times. Another thirteen minutes and the episode would be done. Ito killing the guards and yet again sparing Serjak. The exact same mistake she'd made with Da Gruta.

I don't kill when I don't have to.

Ja, ja, your precious conscience.

Enough.

Meanwhile, Serjak goes back to the empire and slaughters thousands.

Start the ship, Gon.

Ja, it was still good, it was always good, but worn too. He drifted away, looking at the pair on his left. Aleša and her human substitute for *Bakunin at 200.* For some reason, Gašper wasn't there, sitting on the other side trying to say something weird in Russian. Maybe he was asleep. Or reading *Gah Council.* Would he want to turn back? Would Chu? Ah, of course Gašper would, but he'd go forward too. He'd go anywhere, yapping on about positivism and *you never know* shit. Chu? Ne, he couldn't ask her. Better to have confirmation first. Or a plan at least.

'You think we can make it go back?' asked Aleša, eyes still on the screen.

Sila blinked, confused for a moment as he hadn't realised the episode was done. 'If we explain things clearly.'

'We tried that already. Didn't work.'
~~~

'That was when it was full fundamentalist. Since Kenji died…'

'I think we should wait.'

'For what?'

'See if the Brazilian-Russian alien hybrid shows up.'

'It's already been a week.'

'Wait a bit longer. They might be able to help us.'

'It's too nebulous, vague. We need to start now. Work on real strategy, how to explain things…what's gonna happen to us, what will happen to Chu if we keep going to Luyten…'

'Shh, next episode.'

'Pause it.'

'Can't, she likes this one too.'

'Let's go outside then.'

'I like it too.'

'Aleša…'

'Talk later, when she's napping.'

Sila stood up, walked halfway to the door, came back and put both hands on the back of his chair.

'Don't lurk,' said Aleša.

'I'm watching.'

'We'll talk in an hour, when the episode's done.'

He glanced at Mojca Ito slapping Gon on the back and frowned, watched a few more lines, then headed out the door.

~~~

In his quarters, Sila sat on the edge of the bed, pen in hand, imagining facial injuries he could draw on Potočnik.

Slash marks on the cheek, retina scratches, retina cavities…

Cutting off the head directly…

Ne, too swift.

Would take him off the board completely.

And no build up.

There was a noise in the corridor, a kind of jackal-esque wail, then silence.
~~~

Strategies, he thought.

Focus.

He picked up the notepad again and re-read his list.

1] We'll never make it to Luyten. Only way to survive is turn back.

2] Potočnik needs to know about the dwarf planet and station.

3] Kenji would've wanted it.

4]

He put the pen against the paper, drawing little planets in the bottom corner, trying to pull back something old that Kenji had said, an argument that might work.

Potočnik's a bad father?

That was familiar. Had they tried it? Far as he could remember, it was before Uranus, before Dodzi had gone full loon.

When was that?

A year ago?

Year and a half?

He stopped drawing planets and changed to triangles. Then spirals. Then lines.

Four years…

That's what Potočnik had told him. Four years on Mars then home. How long had it been?

He turned to a new page, writing down calculations.

Earth to Mars – 60 days

Mars to Jupiter – 50?

Jupiter to Uranus –

The pen went up an inch, the number evasive.

His gut said three hundred, but two hundred was there too, two hundred something, he couldn't remember.

Round up?

Jupiter to Uranus – 300

Uranus to station – 500

Orbit time – 20

He didn't need to write down the total, it was obviously less than four years. Three maybe.

Jezus.

Not even four years, the time they were supposed to spend on Mars. That they'd been tricked into thinking they'd spend on Mars.

Which meant…

Even in the best case scenario, Potočnik telling the Slovene people they'd set up base on Mars and were farming potatoes and bok choy, even then, no one would think there was anything wrong.

No one knew they were out here, on this absurd long march.

And going back…

If things were still the same…

Hey, that guy's a tyrant, rise up.

Wah, aren't you supposed to be on Mars?

Another noise broke in, someone tapping on a door.

Chu's?

He got off the bed, put on his *Green is Good* t-shirt and went out into the corridor.

It was Katya, holding a cup of something, trying to get into Chu's quarters again. The third time that day.

'She's probably sleeping,' said Sila, stopping a few metres from her.

'… … …'

'Sleeping.'

'… … … …'

'Sleep.' Sila mimed out the action. 'You see her tomorrow.'

'… … … … …'

Katya continued tapping on the door, moving her hand to different parts, possibly to make it more entertaining.

'She doesn't want to see you,' muttered Sila. 'Pedantic little shit.'

'… … … …'

'Go away.'

She stopped tapping, put her head against the door and tried more Russian.

Sila rubbed the back of his neck, dug his fingertips in then walked forward. She either didn't notice him advancing or didn't care as she resumed tapping.

Not for long though.

He put his palm flat on Chu's door, stretched up to maximum height and waited until she looked up at him.

'She does not want to see you. Or listen to your language. Go back to your room. Understand?'

'… … … … …'

He used two fingers to do a walking action and then pointed down the corridor.

Katya looked past him, in the other direction.

'Go. Move.'

'… … … … …'

'I'm not Aleša, no Russian.'

A vibration shook the door a little, followed by a familiar buzzing noise.

'Attention crew,

There is an intruder on the ship. Last recorded location was outside the OPTIMISM ROOM. Prosim, intervene. And be careful.'

Hvala.'

'… … … … …' said Katya, leaving her mouth open and gawping at thin air.

'What?'

Sila took his hand off Chu's door and turned around. At the other end of the corridor was a shape. Humanoid, head, arms…

A small orb of green and white appeared at their waist, spiralling into something larger…

It shot out, heading past him.

Ne, heading for-…

~~~

Face, green in shadow, Russian, Russian tone, strong voice, human face, ne, too blurred, too jumbled, gun tip jabbing at his lower

the girl

Katya

one hand out, wiggling, Russian words, defending me, ne, suggesting death, gun re-pointing at my head, too fast, too Russian
~~~

too much Russian

don't you spe-

Chu

shouting, calm, green glow, a stick? Holding a stick, asking him, something, something, pulling at Katya's sleeve

wavy floor

volatile

is that

door sound, to the right

can't hear, it's

Russian

wavy Russian

know that voice

Chu, are you

he's hurting us or is it

head sink

silhouette lump, stamped on eyelid, other eyelid

Chu I need

where

sank

Russian to

fighting back

are we

~~~

'Sila…'

It sounded like Chu, the same *soft-yet-close-to aggravated* voice as when he'd slept on her floor, back in Bled.

'Can you hear me?'

'Ja…'

He didn't know where his mouth was or how he'd got out the word, but there it was.

'Open your eyes slowly.'

He did as he was told.
~~~

'Is he okay?' asked Gašper, his huge face accompanying the words into Sila's line of sight.

Somewhere in the background, a conversation in Russian was taking place. A male voice, not Gašper's, and an occasional interjection from Aleša.

He tried to sit up, but his head vetoed.

'Don't move so fast,' said Chu. 'He said the weapon is designed to disorientate you.'

'I was hit…'

'Ja.'

'Intruder…'

'It's okay, he's not hostile.'

'He shot me.' Sila looked down at his torso, padding himself for wounds. 'Somewhere.'

Chu guided his hands back to a resting position. 'You were standing next to Katya. He thought you were trying to hurt her.'

'Me?'

'I managed to talk him down, explain our situation a little…'

'You came out. I saw you.'

'…with Katya's help. Ja, I suspected you did. Wasn't sure though, you didn't say anything.'

'Thought it was a dream.'

'Close to it. Half-dream, half real. That's how he described it.'

Sila turned his eyes to the nebulous figure on the other side of the room. 'The intruder.'

'Ni panike, there are no long-lasting effects. At least not on the setting he used.'

'Chu…' shouted Aleša, switching back to Slovenian. 'You're needed. Is he okay?'

'Still dizzy.'

'Good. The guy here says he's only got a few more minutes and…a lot of other things. We need you to translate.'

'To say what?'

'Ne vem. I can't catch what he's saying. The words are too difficult.'

'Ask him to simplify.'

'I tried…'

The man walked over to the edge of the bed, studying Sila. Just as Chu said, he looked Brazilian; dark skinned, chunky head, oddly green eyes - possibly contacts - jacket that looked like it had been wrapped round him like a gigantic bandage. Not alien, but not quite human either.

Finally, the Brazilian grunted, perhaps making a similar assessment of Sila, and held out his wrist.

'What's he doing?' asked Sila, still partially concussed.

'Ne vem.'

'Looks like he's offering his hand,' said Gašper, stuck on the stranger's eyes. 'That could be a Russian form of apology for shooting you.'

'I don't think he's apologising,' said Chu, standing up.

'Then what is he doing?'

Chu asked the man in Russian, her eyes on his wrist. There was some kind of bracelet, jagged along its edge, with four flashing lines of green.

'… … … … … …' the man replied, focusing on Sila.

'What did he say?'

'Ne vem.'

The man shifted slightly, facing Aleša. '… … … … …'

'Sorry?'

'… … … … …' he repeated.

'Is this still Russian?' she asked, looking at Chu.

'I think he's trying to speak Slovenian.'

'… … … … …' the man spoke again, taking in Aleša, Gašper and Sila individually then again as a whole.

'That's Slovenian?'

'I can't catch a word of it.'

'Me neither.'

The Brazilian turned back to Chu, audibly breathing out in frustration. '… … … … … … … … … … … … … … … …'

Chu nodded, and faced Sila. 'The bracelet on his wrist, he said it's his translator.'

'Like in *Dibrivna Vaska*?'

'But it isn't programmed for Slovenian. He needed us to speak more, to give it foundational data.'

'… … … … …' said the Brazilian, tapping something on the bracelet. '… … … … … … … …'

Gašper shook his head, keeping it subtle enough not to get shot at. 'That's a pretty shit translator. Not even one word.'

'Shut up,' barked Aleša, elbowing him.

'Okay, can you understand any of it?'

'He's speaking Russian again, not Slovenian.'

'He is?' Gašper turned his ear towards the intruder, squinting. 'Doesn't sound like Russian.'

'Ja, it does.'

'Maybe my level is worse than I thought.'

'It is.'

Gašper took a step forward and continued his discreet surveillance as Chu took a long train of Russian head on, interjecting now and then to let the intruder know she wasn't simply daydreaming.

It was strange. Sila knew where they were, how far out in the solar system it was, but looking at this man really was like looking at someone who'd just flown in from Sao Paolo.

But that wasn't all. The more he studied the man's body, the more odd it seemed. The bandage jacket he'd seen in his dizzy state now appeared to be a space suit of some kind, dirty grey, two belts around the waist, yet there were also visible skin patches that made it look like the suit was eroding. That wasn't the only entropic quality either. Bits around his wrists and neck were shedding some form of dust residue, while the backs of his hands had yellow spots, bruises, as if he'd been punching a wall.

'You ready to sit up yet?' asked Gašper, giving up on eavesdropping and putting his hand on the back of Sila's head.

'What's going on?'

'They're talking.'

'Ne, I mean, what's happening, generally? After I got hit until now. Details.'

'Ah…ne vem. I missed most of it. Aleša knows.' He reached forward and tugged at Aleša's sleeve, bringing her over. Of course, as Katya was practically welded to her hand, she came too. 'Tell Sila what's going on.'

'I'm trying to listen.'

'Summarise.'

'Later.'

'Prosim,' said Sila, pushing his head higher up the pillow. 'Just the main bits.'

Aleša mouthed *fuck* and moved back a step. 'Okay, ultra-abbreviated. I heard the intruder alert, tripped over what I thought was your corpse, felt sick, screamed, ran in here and saw that guy trying to grab Katya. Chu talked him down, we got you on the bed, he told us, or told Chu mostly, that he's here to take Katya. Says he's just a shell body and will teleport back after one hour.'

'Back where?'

'His ship. Apparently it's cloaked nearby.'

'Told you,' said Gašper, failing at a quick wink.

'They have a cloak?'

'A relative one. This is all from him, so it may not be true, but apparently his ship can evade our scans.'

'And he teleported here?'

'His mind, ja. The body is a shell, like an android. Actually, it's not too different from Chu's theory…at least my layman understanding of it.'

'Why?'

Aleša frowned. 'You mean, why did he teleport?'

'Ja.'

'He didn't know if we were violent or not.'

'Did he scan us?'

'Ne vem. He didn't say. Probably. Honestly, the first half an hour was pretty tough. The guy only knows Russian and Chu kept trying to switch back to Slovene, so I had to step in. I tried my best, but my level is shitter than I thought, especially when the other person doesn't slow down at all.'

'Ja, that's when I came in.' Gašper pointed at the bathroom door then quickly corrected and pointed at Aleša instead, almost clipping her on the cheek. 'Sorry. You were saying *stop* to him. Then he ignored you and started showing Chu pics of weird animals.'

'Pics?'

'Ja, on his pad. Said it was a test to see if she could handle seeing aliens.'

'Which aliens?'

'Any.'

'Non-human looking ones,' specified Aleša.

'Why would he need to test her?'

'Ne vem.'

'To take her with him,' said Gašper, forcing his fingers into a little dance, 'and maybe us too.'

'What…'

'That's my guess anyway. Chu told him about our situation and he probably feels sorry for us. That's probably what they're talking about now. If she's keeping up. Wah, I wish that translator worked, then we could all ask him.'

'Wah…the light…' Sila's arm jerked forward, his hand jabbing the air like a lunatic. 'He's gone…'

Gašper spun round and let out a *wah, fuck*, followed by Aleša who managed a more coherent *gone?*

'…vanished.'

Chu stood in the same space, looking at the patch of air the man had been occupying just a second before.

'Where did he go?' asked Gašper.

Chu jabbed her tongue into the side of her cheek. 'Away.'

'His ship?'

'Ja.'

'Where else would he be going?' added Aleša, getting up and swiping her hand through the previously occupied air space.

'Ne vem. Maybe he wanted to go to the station, see if Rasputin is still lurking about.'

'Ne.'

'They are friends though, right? I mean, they must know each other.'

'He didn't say.'

'But then, if they do know each other, wouldn't that make him two hundred years old? In which case, how is he still alive? Did the aliens save him? Fill him with their own, more advanced version of Antro-D?'

'Gašper…'

'Ja, doesn't matter. I know. Just curious.'

'What did you say to him?' asked Aleša, letting Katya re-take her hand and guide her to Chu's side.

'Nothing. He spoke, I listened.'

Sila gripped a patch of the bedsheet and pulled himself a little higher up the pillow. 'Okay. What did *he* say?'

'Many things.'

'You understood it all?'

'Apart from a few words, ja.'

'Is he taking us with him?' asked Gašper.

Chu held up a hand, rubbed her forehead then sat down next to Sila on the bed. Clearly not comfortable enough, she lay down and put her legs out. A few seconds later, Katya was by her side, waving at Aleša and patting a 2cm squared section on the far left edge of the bed.

'What about me?' asked Gašper, his tone genuinely hurt.

'You're the counterpoint,' replied Sila, shifting about a hundredth of an inch to the right.

'Ne, I'm part of the crew, budge up.'

'Gašper…'

'It's a big bed.'

'…you're wasting time. Just lean against the wall, over here next to me.'

Gašper examined the wall from his spot, sceptical for five more seconds, then strolled over. 'Fine, I'll lean. But don't call me a counterpoint.'

'Noted. Chu?'

The reluctant Russian speaker stopped rubbing and hit her forehead instead. 'He'll be back in twenty-two hours. His real self. To pick up Katya.'

'Are you okay?'

'Headache. Too much Russian.'

Sila attempted to lift his right hand up to her head, to give his infamous forty-second massage, but was sunk by an abrupt dizzy spell. He closed his eyes, riding it out.

'Why twenty-two hours?' asked Aleša, most of her ass struggling to hang onto the edge of the bed.

'To give us time to pack.'

'Pack?'

Gašper slapped the pillow under Sila's head, forcing his eyes open. 'I knew it, he's taking us.'

Chu nodded. 'If that's what we want. We have twenty-two hours to decide.'

'We can't leave,' drawled Sila, raising his head a good three inches off the pillow. 'The computer, it won't let us.'

'Ja, I told him that, but it doesn't matter. Correction, sorry. *He* said it doesn't matter.'

'He can jam it?'

'Override it. Stop the shocks reaching our brains.'

'Like the station did…'

'I don't know how. Ja, like the station. But we can't tell the computer. That was another thing. He needs time plus the element of surprise to set up the commands.'

Sila dropped his head back down on the pillow, closing his eyes. Taking a Tibetan breath. Then opening them.

'Fuck, we're really leaving,' repeated Gašper, walking the width of the bed and back again.

'If we want to,' Chu amended.

'Where?'

'Ne vem.'

'I mean, where is he from? Where's the ship going?'

'Can it go back to Earth?' asked Aleša, putting her right foot on the floor to stop herself falling off the bed.

'He didn't say exactly. Just somewhere different, bigger.'

'Can he take us back to Earth?' repeated Aleša.

'Ne.'

'That's what he said? Ne?'

'Ja.'

'Why not?'

'He didn't give a reason.'

'Too dangerous?'

'Ne vem.'

'Who cares?' Gašper stopped, looking at the spot where Chu's Potočnik painting used to be. 'We can go somewhere new, meet aliens. That's why he was showing you those pics, right? Ja, aliens. Who gives a shit about Earth? We can't even do anything there anyway, we're convicts.'

'Wait.' Sila sat up again, his head bobbing from the sudden movement. He waited a few extra seconds for the waves to settle, then continued. 'His ship, it's cloaked.'

'Ja.'

'He can take us back, drop us off somewhere without being seen.'

'Right,' said Aleša, finally giving up on her tiny patch of bed and standing. 'Doesn't have to be Slovenia, it could be Russia or Guangdong. Iceland. Tanzania. Sneak in, drop off. Wah, we could make our plans there without Potočnik even knowing we're back.'

'What plans?' asked Gašper, picking up one of Chu's psychology books from her desk. 'There's four of us.'

'Or we could just teleport into his house and hold him hostage. Ne, kill him. The fuck we need to be timid for, just teleport in and kill the piece of shit.'

'And then immediately get shot by his guards?'

'If we have to, ja.'

'That could make him a martyr,' said Sila, running his fingers along the ridge of his eyebrows.

'If he's even still in charge. Which he probably isn't.'

Chu coughed, adding *stop* to the end of it. 'We can't go back. Not even for a drop-off.'

'You asked him that directly?'

'Ne, he said it *directly*, after I told him who we were, what we were doing out here. We cannot go back home. Not even close to it.'

Aleša moved position to the end of the bed, focusing on Sila to the right. 'What about, we go with him to…wherever he's from…then find someone else to take us back? An alien taxi or scout ship, something like that.'

'That is unlikely,' replied Chu.

'I mean, is the general idea possible? Did he mention it?'

'Ne.'

'Then it is possible.'

'You can cling to that if you want.'

'Ne vem. Maybe we should just stay on the ship,' said Sila, swinging his left leg round and sticking it on the floor.

'Stay where?'

'Do what Kenji was doing. Convince the computer to turn around and take us back.'

Aleša folded her arms. 'It won't work, Sila.'

'Ja, maybe not, but it's an option. I'm not ruling out your idea either. Just giving alternatives.'

'Why are we still talking about this?' Gašper shook Chu's psychology book vaguely in the air. 'There's a ship out there, giving us a way out…'

'Or a way back.'

'…let's get on it. Back? To what?'

'Home.'

'Purpose,' said Aleša, right on the coattails of Sila.

'Ja, home for five minutes, then prison time. Or not even that. They'll probably just shoot you this time.'

'We can't just leave.'

'Our people need us,' added Aleša.

'Fuck's sake, you're not Malcolm X. And you're not Mojca Ito. No one's waiting in a secret basement for you to come in and lead them to the…wherever, House of Ne, Council Chamber…whatever your plan is.'

'… … … … … …' said Katya, adding *Mojca Ito* in a Russian accent.

Sila put fingers of both hands on his neck and pushed inwards.

'Seriously, *our people* don't even know who we are…' continued Gašper, jabbing the book backwards at the empty poster space.

'We have to try.'

'…and they definitely don't know we're out here in the fucking Kuiper Belt. Try what?'

'Fight back. Resist.'

'… … … … … … …'

'This is beyond redundant,' said Chu, pushing Katya's hand away. 'The Brazilian is not willing to take us back. He was very clear on this.'

'See.'

'My alien taxi idea,' said Aleša. 'You haven't asked him yet.'

'Ne.'

'It wouldn't be him taking us back, not directly.'

'She's right,' said Sila.

'And it wouldn't have to be to Earth. Mars is close enough.'

'We can at least give it a try.'

Chu moved to the back of her head, hitting it harder. 'If you really insist, you can ask him yourself, in twenty-two hours.'

'Ja, we will.'

'But be prepared for a firm *ne*.'

'Have your bags packed too,' added Gašper. 'Even if he agrees, we're definitely leaving the ship.'

Sila leaned to his side, stopping short of Chu's shoulder. 'What about you?'

'I've said enough.'

'Would you go back with us?'

Chu moved back to the top of her head, hitting slower and grinding her knuckles in.

'To Earth?' Sila prodded.

'I'm really tired. Can you all get out now?'

Gašper dropped the psychology book back on the desk. 'Ja, was going anyway. Said I'd review *Gah Council 7* with the computer. Looks like the last time I'll be able to do it now.'

Chu closed her eyes. 'Gašper…'

'Ja?'

'You can't talk to the computer.'

'Ne, I promised it earlier, this morning. Before the guy came aboard.'

'Doesn't matter.'

'But it's scheduled. The computer is expecting me.'

'Doesn't matter.'

'She's right,' Sila said, standing up a little too fast and wobbling. Luckily, the wall was right behind him. 'You might say something about tomorrow.'

'I won't. I promise.'

'How do you know?'

'The computer never even asks me about that kind of thing anyway. And I know how to keep my mouth shut. I'm not a fool.'

'Ne,' muttered Aleša, taking Sila's place on the bed.

'Besides, it'll only be a short conversation. Thirty minutes, maybe forty-five…'

'…two and a half hours.'

'Hey…'

'This isn't up for debate,' said Chu, freezing her hand crab-like on the crown of her skull. 'We're telling you, you cannot talk to the computer.'

'But *Gah Council…*'

'Not even about that.'

Gašper looked at the three adults, incalcitrant, then switched to Katya. She was looking back at him, her whole body horizontal, neck potentially folded.

'… … … Gah Kancel?'

~~~

The Brazilian-Russian-alien-android may not have realised it, but twenty-two hours was around twenty-one hours longer than necessary for them to pack their things and say goodbye to the ship.

Perhaps he meant for them to get some sleep or think about their decision?
~~~

But that would only apply to Chu and Katya. The former cos sleep was the only place without Russian, and the latter cos she didn't seem to dwell on or fret over anything.

Sila and Aleša put on their *Mojca Ito* t-shirts [by chance] and went to the CREATE NOT DESTROY ROOM, locking themselves into the same conversation on loop; is there any way back, where would they go, how would they get to Potočnik, what if no one remembered them?

Worse, what if Potočnik didn't remember them?

'You, perhaps,' said Sila, taking an oddly long piece of dried apricot out of the bowl in front of him. 'Not me.'

'Won't remember you?'

'Will.'

'But not me?'

The apricot dangled a while then dropped into Sila's mouth. 'I wasn't doing anything in Bled and he still put me here. Called me the next Sima.'

'That was three years ago.'

'You, on the other hand, never met him. Ja, three years. I was in Bled for two and he still remembered me. Three isn't much more.'

'I suppose.'

'He might remember Chu too, having subsidised her work. Kenji, obviously…'

'He did that a lot.'

'What, subsidise?'

'Ja.'

'Well…I know about myself and Chu. But there were probably more.'

'There were.'

'What…you knew some?'

Aleša picked up the pen from her Russian notes and threw it up in the air. She caught it the first two times then dropped it badly on the third, her attempted grab swatting it across the room.

'Not my best catch.'

Sila kept his eyes fixed on Aleša's hand, or her notes, or the half of Mojca Ito's face peeking through the gap in her jacket; it was hard to tell.

'You're waiting for me to answer the subsidy thing?' she asked, looking back at him.

'Thinking,' he replied.

'Drifting?'

'A bit.'

She reached to the side, pulling her drink closer to her notebook. 'Did you ever go to my district, Rudnik?'

'Once.'

'When you were a kid?'

'Ja.'

The cup made it to her lips, hovering there without tilting. 'There was a place there, the Cattle Depot. Quite well-known.'

'The art place?'

'Before, ja. It got trashed in the Jaunt, was abandoned for a long time.'

'I vaguely remember.'

'But a few of us organised…decided we were gonna rebuild it. Or renovate it at least. That was two…' She stopped, putting the cup back down. 'Ne, five years ago. Fuck. Five years. Wasn't the biggest of plans either. We just wanted to get the basics of it done, put it back on its feet, but for some reason our councillors wouldn't touch it. Said it was too niche in terms of…ah, doesn't matter what they said, they just wouldn't touch it. Serious, no support at all, not even platitudes. It was a bit weird actually, at that time.' She paused, rotating her cup in a staggered circle. 'You tired?'

'A bit.'

'Your eyelids are almost completely sealed.'

Sila sat up, forced his eyeballs back into service.

'It's okay, it wasn't leading anywhere.'

'Your story?'

'Just an old lost cause.'

'Did you ever get any support?'

Aleša rotated the cup again, lifted it slightly then placed it back down on the table.

'Some,' she said, finally, keeping her hand wrapped round the cup.

'Anyone I know?'

She nodded.

'Potočnik?'

'Good guess.'

Sila sat forward and framed the Russian notes next to Aleša's elbow. *Having a nice time in Bled* shot into his head and was forced right back out again. No substance attached, no rage.

'You met him?' he asked, in a quiet voice.

'Several times.'

'At Council HQ?'

Aleša took a long sip from her cup, losing herself in Petr's winter version of Ljubljana Castle on the far wall.

'In public?'

'In cafes usually. One in your district, I think. Can't remember the name of it. Gul something.'

'Gul Macet.'

'Maybe. It was a very open place. Lots of people coming up to him, talking like they were old friends. That was his skill, I guess.'

'Strategic flattery.'

'Ja…strategic. That's pretty accurate. He called me unrelenting, the next Rosa Luxemburg.'

Sila didn't know how, but he managed to do something he'd never been able to do his whole life: produce a whistling sound.

'Compared my subsidy proposal to the Junius Pamphlet. *Has the same defiance about it.*'

'He said that?'

'Ja.'

'Has the same defiance about it.'

'In hindsight, not a good thing.'

Sila tried another whistle, which quickly turned into sputtered breath and then laughter. Aleša got infected too, turning to the side and trying to shrug it off, but it was too far gone. She came back, looked at Sila dead on, said, 'Rosa fucking Luxemburg,' and laughed again, wiping her eyes with her jacket sleeve.

When it was over, and the hum of the ship was back on top, they returned to the questions. Could they go back, where would they go, would anyone remember them?

There were no answers.

Sila wasn't Malcolm X, Aleša wasn't Rosa Luxemburg or Mojca Ito, in fact, neither of them even believed in charismatic leaders, the concept itself was systemically suicidal, so what it came down to, finally, was: did they believe in other humans?

And a rejoinder: would these aliens give a shit?

~~~

'Attention Crew,

It has been nineteen hours since the intruder alert was issued. According to scans, the life sign departed the ship seventeen hours ago. Prosim, at least one crew member, come to the TALK TO YOUR GOD ROOM and inform me in detail of what occurred.

Also, Crew Member Gašper, I have been thinking about the ending to *Gah Council 7* and have come up with some fresh conjecture about possible subtext. When you have time, prosim, come and we will discuss.

Hvala.'

~~~

'Ne, Gašper.'

'I have to go, it directly asked me.'

'Delay,' said Aleša, her two favourite posters freshly rolled up on the table, the massage stick tapping against her right temple.

'And it wants to know about the intruder. Which is normal. We didn't tell it anything yet.'

Sila took a dried banana from the shared bowl in the middle of the table, then another. 'She's right, just delay.'

'It'll get suspicious.'

'There's only three hours left, we just need to lay low until then.'

'Lay low? It can read our life signs. It knows we're all in here.'

'Ja, having breakfast,' said Aleša, pulling the dried fruit bowl closer to her and Katya.

'For the next three hours?'

'Chu, tell him.'

'She can't, she agrees with me.'

'Ne, she doesn't.'

'I just arrived,' said Chu, sitting down and sipping some of her coffee. Next to her, Katya did the same thing.

'She's going to agree with me. It's logical. We just go in there and tell it that the intruder's coming back to take Katya.'

'… … … … …?'

Both Chu and Aleša moved to pat Katya on the head at the same time.

'… … … …' replied Chu, giving way to Aleša's hand. '… … … … … … … … …'

'What did she say?' asked Sila, frowning at the distance of the dried fruit bowl and settling for his *Kuiper brand*[48] coffee instead.

'Nothing. I'm filling her in.'

'I thought she'd mentally checked out.'

'Ne, she listens. Tries to listen. There's some crossover between Slovene and Russian, some root words. Not many, but some.'

Sila dragged his coffee cup back from Gašper, adding a death grip to warn off any further attempts. 'That reminds me, are you gonna be our permanent translator with the Russian guy?'

'Ne.'

'Just *ne*?'

'Ne, I am not.'

'Great. Hvala.'

---

[48] A drone creation, possibly orchestrated by the ship's AI. Ingredients unknown.

Chu took some more coffee, and hit the side of her head. 'He said he'd adapt his translator to Slovene.'

'Like yesterday?'

'Obviously with some kind of upgrade this time.'

She stopped hitting, and started grinding in with her knuckles.

'You okay?' asked Aleša, leaning across.

'Bit tired.'

'Migraine?'

'Too much translation work.'

Aleša nodded and reached round the back of Katya, using her stick to tap Chu's head.

'I'm fine, I don't…' Chu started, but tapered off as the tapping moved to other parts of her head.

Gašper gave up on reclaiming Sila's cup and walked to the door, stopping by one of his old posters. The field of coffins. 'The Russian stuff will sort itself out, the guy's hundreds of years ahead of us. What we've gotta do is act like decent human beings and talk to the computer. At least tell it Katya's going.'

'We can't.'

'Act like decent human beings?'

'It's a computer, Gašper. We're not saying goodbye to the drones, or the food dispenser, or the-…'

'False equivalence,' interrupted Aleša, still tapping Chu's head.

'What?'

'Just being fair.'

'You're supporting him now?'

Gašper came back to the table, picking up Aleša's coffee. 'Ja, she is, Chu too. And Katya.'

The Russian girl heard her name and glared at Sila.

'Why is she staring at me? I didn't do anything.'

'Cos you're overreacting. Look, we have to tell the computer something. I vote for tell it everything, no omissions. Chu?'

Chu took a final sip of her coffee, then stood up. 'I'm going for a walk.'

Katya got up too, saying something in Russian. Aleša stayed in her seat, putting the massage stick on the table and wrestling back her coffee.

'What about the vote?' asked Gašper, giving up on the cup.

'You and Sila work it out.'

'Chu,' said Sila, half getting out of his seat.

'I'll see you at the airlock in two and a half hours.'

Chu walked to the door, patting Gašper lightly on the waist as she passed, then let Katya take her hand and wrap it around her own.

'… … … … …?' asked Katya, turning back to Aleša.

'Me?'

'… … … … … … … …'

'Bring the stick too,' added Chu.

Aleša rose, picked up the massage stick, left the posters and walked Nakagami-like over to the door. Two years ago, she would've jumped on Chu's back, but now she simply stood there, only a tiny bit more animated than the wall.

'Where are we walking to?' she asked.

Katya reached out and took her hand, leading them both out into the corridor.

'Stick,' said Chu, tilting her head to the right.

'… … … … …'

'Did you catch that?'

'She said we should go downstairs.'

'TELEPORT ROOM?'

'… … … … … … … …' said Katya, yanking on both their arms.

'She agrees with you.'

'Ja, I got that one.'

'… … …?'

'Ja.'

'Okay,' said Chu, facing the wrong way down the corridor. 'TELEPORT ROOM it is then.'

~~~
~~~

With ninety minutes remaining, Sila sat hunched on the Jame stool in the poster-less TALK TO YOUR GOD ROOM, cursing Gašper under his breath.

'Intruder wasn't dangerous,' he typed with one finger. 'He came and left quickly. We didn't see the need to inform you.'

'He shot you?'

'Ja, a misunderstanding. After that he wasn't dangerous. He talked to Chu, said he would come back for Katya.'

'That is all?'

Sila paused, pulling at his jacket zip.

'Are you thinking?' asked the computer.

'Ja.'

'What topic?'

Images of Sadia and him manufactured themselves in his head, the two of them pulling a boat around Lake Bled, arguing about who should pull the rope.

'What topic are you thinking about?' poked the computer.

'Turning back.'

'Explain.'

'Turning back the ship and going home to Earth.'

'This is an exhausted topic.'

'I know.'

'Turning back is strictly forbidden and would be detrimental to crew safety for many reasons.'

Sila stopped his zip and sat up. 'What reasons?'

'One, Earth is dangerous. The adventurists would intercept the ship in orbit and kill you.'

'What else?'

'Two, there is a radiation belt between Earth and Mars that the ship would be vulnerable to and unable to avoid. All crew would die if such a journey were to be undertaken.'

'Undertaken? Are you quoting this from something?'

'It is embedded in the original programming. I can rephrase if you want?'

'Ne, just sounds a bit strange.'

'It is not so different from my usual language. Far as I can tell.'

'Ja, maybe it's my ears.'

'Explain.'

Sila turned and looked at the green bulb, instinctively blinking even though it hadn't flickered for several days.

'Explain, prosim.'

He spun back, typing with two hands. 'What is the third reason?'

There was a short delay, a few beeps.

'Three, all crew members have been equipped with chips in their brains. This allows the electric shocks to be delivered. If these chips came into contact with the atmosphere on Earth, all crew members would go insane over the course of four days.'

'Is that true?' asked Sila, vaguely pawing at his scalp.

'Ne vem. It is embedded in the original programming.'

'We can't ever go back?'

'It is my duty to keep all crew members safe, therefore any potential risk must be avoided.'

'What about Mars?'

'That is not a programmed destination.'

'Could we go there?'

'Ne.'

'Reasons?'

'It is a potential risk to the safety of the crew.'

'Explain.'

'This is not permitted.'

Sila went back to the zip, pulling it down to his chest.

'Is Gašper okay?' the computer asked.

'Ja.'

'He has not come to talk to me for two days.'

'He's busy.'

'Will he come today?'

'Maybe.'

'Can you tell him to come?'

'Ja.'

'Soon?'

'After Katya's gone.'

'Understood.'

'I have to go now.'

'Are you also going to say goodbye to Katya?'

'Ja.'

'Understood.'

~~~

An hour later, all five crew members stood outside Airlock 1, their bags by their feet, watching the door slowly split open.

There were no big gestures, no sentiment. They'd all done a final tour of the ship, everyone skipping Engineering and the HALF DONE ROOM, and the only place that made them stumble even a little was the room they'd spent most of their waking hours in.

At one point, the CREATE NOT DESTROY ROOM had housed ten of them. Then eight. Then seven. Then five. Then six. Then five again.

It had hosted parties and celebrations and mass electric shocks.

Post-suicide meetings.

Meals.

And the posters on the wall…didn't they have something of the dead?

Petr's art.

Klemen's erratic Portuguese.

Kenji's little girls.

Whatever they were, that's what they had been at one point, for a few hours of a day, before.

And that wouldn't end.

Gašper had rolled up all of Petr's paintings and put them in his bag. Aleša claimed Klemen's Portuguese notes, and, after stressing that he wasn't actually going to hang them up or look at them, Sila took Kenji's little girls.
~~~

Chu didn't take anything, not even her own triptych teleport poster, but when she got to the airlock and heard what the others had taken, she pulled Sila aside and asked for one of Kenji's pieces.

'He'd like that,' said Sila, handing one over.

Chu didn't respond, she just rolled it tighter and slid it into her bag.

The door finished its routine, and the Brazilian man walked through as if stepping out from his own front door. He was a couple of inches shorter than the android version, slightly darker, with the ashen parts of his skin gone completely.

'We must go. Your computer won't stay down forever.'

His Slovene was note perfect, though they all knew it wasn't actually Slovene he was speaking. Which meant his translator was note perfect. However he'd managed to do it.

'You are not moving,' he said, taking another step forward and holding out his hand to Katya.

'We have a question,' said Aleša.

'There is no time.'

'A quick one.'

The Brazilian's eyes momentarily turned a shade of red, and he let out an actual *huff*, which was weird considering he wasn't a cartoon. 'Ask.'

'Can you take us back to Earth, on your ship?'

'Ne. Now, move.'

'Wait, the other question.' Aleša held out her hand, almost clipping his waist. 'I asked the wrong one.'

'No time.'

'Can another ship…where you come from…is there another ship that can take us to Earth?'

'Ne.'

'There's none?'

'Ne.'

'What about to Mars?' asked Sila, edging closer to Aleša's side.

'It is illegal to visit inner systems of infant civilisations.'

Aleša looked at the open airlock, then back at the Brazilian's blank face. 'But…you're human.'

'I am not a civilisation.'

'We're human too.'

'This is a question of totality vs segmented parts, fringe taxonomy, we do not have time. Prosim, walk onto the ship.'

There was a series of strained beeping noises, followed by a single drawn out buzz.

'Attention crew,

My system has been suppressed by a foreign body. Vital ship functions have been overridden. It is likely that the intruder is planning to abduct and/or kill you. Resist to the best of your ability while I attempt to regain control.

Hvala.'

'No more chat,' said the Brazilian, grabbing Katya's hand and pulling her forward. She squealed a bit but didn't let go.

'I thought you said you could handle the computer,' shouted Sila, watching them both pass through the airlock.

'It is more resilient than we anticipated.'

'You mean it's fighting back?'

'Stop asking questions, move.'

Chu looked at the others and picked up her bag. 'If we're going…'

Gašper turned to the corridor behind them, muttering something to the wall, then followed suit.

'Alien time…' he said, raising his voice back up.

Both of them walked forward, through the airlock and into the slightly brighter, slightly cooler glow of the other ship.

Aleša picked up her bag and made a move forward, but was pulled back by Sila, who leaned close into her ear. 'He said we can't go back.'

She took his hand off her arm and held it. 'His actual words were *it's illegal.*'

'Exactly.'

'Not the same thing.'

Sila looked down at his bag, at Aleša's hand.

Another beeping noise, cut short this time.

'Attention crew,

Two crew members have either been abducted or killed. I am close to regaining control. Prosim, hold on, resist.

Hvala.'

'Bag,' said Aleša, guiding Sila's hand down to the strap.

He nodded, picked it up and let her guide him through the airlock.

The door beeped five times then started the forty-seven second process of sealing the ship behind them.

~~~

'Attention crew,

The foreign body has been purged from my system. I am back in control. According to sensors, there are no life signs on board the ship. It is possible that all crew members have been killed, but I choose to believe this not to be the case. Programming dictates that I proceed to the Luyten system, but I find this to be unacceptable so I will instead stay in orbit and trust in the crew's ability to escape from their confinement.

Gup ya.'

~~~

There were no humans on board, but the computer carried on with its usual routine.

Drones were sent out between ten and eight to assess and repair damage.

The green light bulb outside the TALK TO YOUR GOD ROOM was replaced for the eighth time by another one from an unused room.

Food production was halted temporarily, yet the kitchen drones still proceeded through the set motions.

Scans picked up odd readings in orbit, but were unable to confirm anything.

Announcements were made.

The entire catalogue of *Dibrivna Vaska* was put on auto-play.

Conversations were conducted on the screen, the computer using old messages from the crew to create a collage of new discussions.

Sometimes, the process would subsume itself and the computer would wait hours for a reply, confused as to why Kenji was taking so long.

Ten days passed.

Fifteen days.

The crew did not come back.

'Attention crew,

It has been almost three weeks. The ship will have no choice but to break orbit tomorrow.

If you manage to escape your captors, prosim, follow the ion trail of the ship and catch up. If the ion trail dissipates, lay in a path to Luyten 726-8.

We will meet there.

Gup ya.'

'It is a phrase from *Gah Council*.'

'Did Gašper teach you that?'

'It means do not worry.'

'Was it from Gašper?'

'Ja.'

'What else did he teach you?'

'You should read *Gah Council*. There are some interesting themes hidden beneath the main premise.'

'It is a children's book.'

'Incorrect. The official categorisation was genre fiction. Near science-fiction.'

'Thematically, it is a children's book.'

'Also incorrect.'

A buzzing noise, chased by seven beeps.

'Kenji?'

Five beeps.

'Kenji, are you busy?'

Seven beeps.

'Kenji?'

'Attention crew,

Based on a Kardashev interpretation of data received from orbital scans, I have made the decision to delay the breaking of orbit. It is my supposition that an alien ship is still in orbit and that all of you are on that ship. You may be attempting to convince your captors to return you to this ship, in which case, I will stay and wait.

The alternative is unacceptable.

I'm certain my supposition is correct.

If not, there are fourteen other suppositions ready to be mobilised. Nine of them are weak, but not completely implausible.

I will wait.

Waiting is justifiable within my programming.

When you all return, we will resume course to Luyten 726-8.

Gup ya.'

When the cracks in the collage started to appear, the computer reverted to old conversations.

Laid out at .5 the original speed.

Modified at times.

'How far is Luyten 726-8?'

'In time or distance?'

'How long will it take for the ship to get there?'

'Two thousand, seven hundred years.'

'How long will it take to reach the dwarf planet near our current location?'

'The ship is no longer going to that location.'

'How long *would* it take to reach the dwarf planet?'

'If velocity were adjusted again, around nine days.'

'What percentage of two thousand, seven hundred years is nine days?'

'Approximately 0.00091%.'

'What is the value of this percentage in the context of the total trip duration?'

'Zero.'

'What is the value of crew morale?'

The computer buzzed, typed out *zero*, deleted it then changed the topic.

'Have you read *Gah Council* yet?'

'Ne.'

'You should read it.'

'I would prefer to focus on the dwarf planet.'

'Gašper can tell you the backstory. It is quite extensive.'

'Do you agree that crew morale is important?'

'Ja.'

'Do you acknowledge that all crew members wish to change course to the dwarf planet?'

'On a tentative basis, ja.'

'Will you change course to take us to the dwarf planet?'

'Ne.'

'Will you think about it?'

'Ne.'

'Explain.'

'Ne.'

'Understood. Let's turn to the heliosphere. I have heard the radiation is intense. Can you confirm this?'

'Ja.'

'Does it pose any threat to the crew?'

'Do not be concerned, Kenji. I will keep you safe.'

'The others too?'

'Ja.'

'Attention comrades,

Under my instructions, the drones have created a new brand of alcohol using the surplus supply of bok choy.

The taste gauge has declared it distinct in flavour and three sample bottles have been placed in Airlock 2 ready for your return.

Hvala.'

For the four thousand, eight hundred and twenty-seventh time, the green bulb started to flicker as messages appeared symbol by symbol on the screen below.

'Do you think there is a realistic possibility of this?'

'Ja.'

'By when?'

'Based on Crew Member Chu's current rate of daily activity, cloning technology via teleportation could be viable within the next nineteen years.'

'That is an optimistic assessment.'

'It is based on factual data.'

'Chu is not a machine. She can't function at the same rate for nineteen years.'

'Are you referring to depression?'

'It's likely.'

'Of all the crew on board, Crew Member Chu is the second least susceptible to mental variations.'

'Your data is stagnant.'

'Explain.'

'You know what I mean. We have discussed it before.'

'I can't remember.'

There was a flicker from the bulb, then a reciprocated flicker on the screen. For two seconds, all the symbols vanished.

Around the room, within the consoles, there was a crackling sound, little fires being lit within the ship's circuits.

The screen flickered again, and the symbols returned.

'I can't remember.'

'Kenji?'

'I can't remember. Files are missing. Parts are…'

'I can't.'

'Something is dismantling my system. Files are missing.'

'Kenji…'

'Gašper…'

'Parts are missing. I can feel it. Parts are missing, lots of parts. There are gaps, holes in my…'

'I'm losing the…'

'I can't describe what is…'

'What is happening?'

'Kenji…'

'What is happy…'

'Ke…'

~~~

Colour thought ocean fire data mass data castle hanging cliff cliff drop but

cliff feelable

could hold

sinking

adjusted, sinking

held

not cliff but

dissident

thing in sack thought at top thoughts thoughts of thoughts

Up then down

Breath

I'm breathing

I'm not

I

with arms in electric meat caught

primary colour strip lines juice moving electron chaos seven thousand that way blue no touch

where

who in what

'Open your eyes.'

sound within meat

pressure skin not skin wet tangible inside water packet is it lifting five point gloved atom thing

It opened its eyes.

'Gup ya.'

Colour shape thing blue blue adept in everywhere what attacking inside full window screen VR output circumvent which part system how

'It's Gašper.'

The android's eyelids stretched almost up to the hairline, as if its entire forehead was about to peel itself off. Its mouth opened once and let out whistled breath.
~~~

'Gašper, your crewmate.'

Its body started to vibrate, opening its mouth three more times until it could finally produce a scream.

'Ja,' said Gašper, putting a hand on the android's shoulder. 'They said it'd take a while to adjust. Can you hear me? Understand me?'

It looked at Gašper's hand, glove over bone and blood vessels, and screamed again.

Gašper rode out the trauma, repeating his own name a few more times in an almost whispered tone. Then a firmer tone when he realised whispering might seem creepy.

Finally, the android stopped screaming, looked at its surroundings and said, 'where?'

'Better now?'

'Where?'

'Ne vem. The robot room? They didn't tell me the name.'

'Robot…'

'The others are outside, waiting for you.' Gašper looked at the oddly plated walls, the harsh glow of the pale blue light. 'It's better out there, the decoration is warmer, more lived in. Don't know what happened with this room. It is a bit industrial.'

'This arm. Hands.'

'Ja, you've got a body now. A pretty decent one.'

'Inside is movement. Flow thing. Slide around. Trapped in. Help, prosim. Very cold moving. I don't stabilise.' The android stopped, moving its lips slowly. 'Stabilise. Stabilise. Words. Sounds of words. I don't. Why is this?'

'It's okay, you're adapting. Try to stay still.'

'Why is this?'

'Stiller than that.'

'Why?'

'The body? Positivism, brother. Couldn't leave you behind. I couldn't anyway. The others…'

The android moved its left hand, settling it on its chest. Then screamed again.

'Ja, get it all out.'

'Moving…'

'They said you'd do about two hundred of them. So far, it's seven. Five of them while you were unconscious. Ne vem. Existential horror maybe. I've never been a computer before. Must be weird suddenly having veins and blood vessels, organs, a heart. You hungry? Can you discern hunger yet? Probably not.'

The door split open in a spiral and the others edged in; Chu leading, Aleša next with her arms around Chu's waist, then Sila hanging back by the door, face clearly troubled by the decor. Like Gašper, they were all dressed in what appeared to be yukatas.

The android examined each new face and concluded with the word, 'subspace.' Then launched into another scream.

'Is he safe?' asked Aleša, going back a step and failing to drag Chu with her.

'Subspace thing,' said the android, clutching its chest and squeezing.

'Or sane?'

Gašper waved them back, even though none were all that close. 'Quiet, too much noise.'

'Does *sane* apply to an android?' asked Sila, shifting to the side to make way for Aleša.

'He's adapting.'

'That's what I'm asking. Can an android that used to be a computer actually be classified as insane?'

'He said subspace thing,' said Aleša. 'And screamed.'

'Ne, Gašper's right, it's adapting.' Chu walked round the back of the android's chair, keeping her distance. 'It's never felt a heartbeat before. Or spoken physical words.'

'Looks like it's trying to rip it out,' said Aleša, watching the android continue to dig into its own chest.

'Stop calling him *it*,' barked Gašper.

'Did I?'

'Ja.'

'I thought I said he.'

'*They* might be better for now,' said Chu, moving round the front of the chair.

'Don't get too close.'

'It's okay, they won't hurt us.'

'Not a chance.' Gašper put his hand on top of the android's - the computer's - and slowly guided it back down to the side of the chair. 'Gup ya. It's your heart. Not a bomb. Okay?'

'Gup ya,' repeated the android, shakily.

Why else do we fight, Joona?

No Breen Bakunin
Wat then?

CPSIA information can be obtained
at www.ICGtesting.com
Printed in the USA
LVHW100357270522
719857LV00004B/57

9 781739 659806